James Blish was born in East Orange, New Jersey, in 1921. He attended Rutgers University and then served in the U.S. Army as a medical worker. He had taken his degree in biology, but had already begun selling science fiction stories in 1941, and felt that he was more interested in writing than in a laboratory career – although he always retained his disciplined attitude toward the sciences. It was Blish who first bestowed the term 'gas giant' on the Jupiter-type planet, now the accepted astronomical phrase, and who predicted the Martian craters before they were discovered. By the time of his death he had produced over 500 titles including short stories, articles, TV and motion picture scripts, novels and poetry, many of which works have been translated into over 20 languages. Short stories have appeared, sometimes repeatedly, in more than 80 anthologies and collections.

After his release from the Army he married Virginia Kidd, and they had two children. They separated after twenty years, and in 1964 he married Judith Ann Lawrence. At that time he was recovering from his first bout with the cancer that eventually caught up with him.

His output includes six collections and more than 25 novels, almost all of which are science fiction. He was one of the world's best-known s-f writers and an acknowledged authority in the field. He was Guest of Honour at the 18th World Science Fiction Convention (Pittsburgh, 1960) and at the 21st British Science Fiction Convention in 1970. He served two terms as vice president of the Science Fiction Writers of America, on whose behalf he testified before the U.S. Congress. Articles about Blish and his work have appeared in England, France, Italy and even the U.S.S.R., as well as in many American journals.

Before his move to England in 1969 (when he saw a bumper sticker saying 'A Knighthood for Benjamin Britten', there was no turning back) he wrote most of his stories in 'spare time' from his full-time job as public relations counsel. The last few years of his life were spent in the countryside near Henley-on-Thames – between the British Museum and the Bodleian Library at Oxford.

He was devoted – and expert – in classical music, and at the time of his death was about to undertake a novelistic biography of Richard Strauss. He also loved cats and English beer.

Among his published works are two tetralogies: The *Cities in Flight* series – *They Shall Have Stars (Year 2018!)*, *A Life for the Stars*, *Earthman Come Home*, and *A Clash of Cymbals (The Triumph of Time)*; and the group collectively called *After Such Knowledge*, taken from the line of T. S. Eliot, 'After such knowledge, what forgiveness?'. This group comprises an historical novel, *Doctor Mirabilis*, a pair of novels of modern black magic, *Black Easter* and *The Day After Judgement*, and a s-f novel, *A Case of Conscience* (winner of the Hugo Award as best science fiction novel of 1958). Blish felt that however disparate the treatment of his theme, each of these works was concerned with a single problem – the moral dilemma of knowledge.

Other well-known works include *The Seedling Stars*, *Jack of Eagles*, *Midsummer Century*, *The Night Shapes*, *The Quincunx of Time*; and his two books of criticism, *The Issue at Hand* and *More Issues at Hand* were among the very first serious works in that area. The *Cities in Flight* series and a novel for young people, *Welcome to Mars*, have been adapted for film production. And of course, his adaptations from the TV series *Star Trek*, which he regarded as a project that was introducing a whole new audience to the delights of science fiction, are probably known by anyone with a TV set.

James Blish died in July 1975, and is buried in Oxford in the shade of Magdelene College in the University that he loved and honoured. His library and papers are in the custody of the Bodleian Library.

AFTER SUCH KNOWLEDGE

ALSO IN LEGEND BY JAMES BLISH

Cities in Flight

JAMES BLISH

After Such Knowledge

Arrow Books Limited
20 Vauxhall Bridge Road, London SW1V 2SA

An imprint of the Random Century Group

London Melbourne Sydney Auckland Johannesburg
and agencies throughout the world

A CASE OF CONSCIENCE
First published in Great Britain
by Faber & Faber 1959
Arrow edition 1972
Reprinted 1975, 1979 and 1984

DOCTOR MIRABILIS
First published by Faber & Faber 1964
Arrow edition 1964

BLACK EASTER
First published by Faber & Faber 1968
Arrow edition 1981

THE DAY AFTER JUDGEMENT
First published by Faber & Faber 1972
Arrow edition 1981

AFTER SUCH KNOWLEDGE
Legend edition 1991

Printed and bound in Great Britain by
Cox & Wyman Ltd, Reading

ISBN 0 09 983100 7

CONTENTS

DOCTOR MIRABILIS

For Virginia

Truth is the daughter of time

ROGER BACON

And now through every window came a light into the chamber as of skies paling to the dawn. Yet not wholly so; for never yet came dawn at midnight, nor from all four quarters of the sky at once, nor with such swift strides of increasing light so ghastly... The King cried terribly, 'The hour approacheth!'

E. R. EDDISON: *The Worm Ouroboros*

We are as dwarfs mounted on the shoulders of giants, so that we can see more and farther than they; yet not by virtue of the keenness of our eyesight, nor through the tallness of our stature, but because we are raised and borne aloft upon that giant mass.

BERNARD OF CHARTRES

There are no dead

MAURICE MAETERLINCK

CONTENTS

DRAMATIS PERSONAE

in order of their appearance

ROGER BACON of Ilchester, clerk.
ADAM MARSH (or, de Marisco) of Wearmouth, Franciscan, lecturer in theology at Oxford until 1250, confessor of Eleanor of Pembroke and later of her husband.
ROBERT GROSSETESTE, Bishop of Lincoln.
WILLIAM BUSSHE of Dorset, Merchant of the Staple.
WULF, a serf of the Bacon estate.
TIBB, a thief.
SIMON DE MONTFORT, Earl of Leicester.
ELEANOR OF PEMBROKE, sister of the King, widow of the Earl of Pembroke, wife to Simon de Montfort.
HENRY III of WINCHESTER, King of England, son of King John.
PETER DES ROCHES, tutor to the King, Bishop of Winchester.
EDMUND RICH of Abingdon, Archbishop of Canterbury (later canonized).
GUY DE FOULQUES, papal legate in England and Cardinal-Bishop of Sabina; from 1265, Pope Clement IV.
PETER DE RIVAULX (or, des Rievaux), nephew to Peter des Roches.
JOHANN BUDRYS of Livonia, clerk.
ALBERTUS called MAGNUS, Dominican, regent master at Paris, sometime Bishop of Ratisbon (later canonized).
RAIMUNDO DEL REY, clerk.
PIERRE DE MARICOURT (Petrus Peregrinus), a noble of Picardy.
JULIAN DE RANDA, clerk.
MATTHEW PARIS, Benedictine, historian to Henry III.
LUCA DI COSMATI, artist.
LORENZA ARNOLFO PICCOLOMINI, Marquis of Modena, and patron of Luca.
OLIVIA PICCOLOMINI, daughter to the Marquis of Modena.

THOMAS BUNGAY, provincial minister to the Franciscans in England 1271–75.

RICHARD RUFUS of Cornwall, regent master in theology at Paris and Oxford.

JOANNES, a clerk, apprenticed to Roger Bacon.

RAYMOND OF LAON, clerk to Guy de Foulques.

SIR WILLIAM BONECOR, emissary of the King to Clement IV.

JEROME DI ASCOLI, minister-general to the Franciscans 1274–89; thereafter Pope Nicholas IV.

OTTO, a gaoler.

ADRIAN, a voice.

RAYMOND DE GAUFREDI, minister-general to the Franciscans from 1289.

Time: 1231–94 A.D.
Place: England, France, Italy

FOREWORD

Though Roger Bacon is generally acknowledged to be one of the great figures in medieval history, and in particular, one of the forerunners of modern science, astonishingly few facts about his life are known. There is a sizable Bacon legend, but of this the historical Bacon was only temporary custodian: the famous story of the brass head, for instance, is an ancient Arabic legend, which first appeared in Europe in the tenth century as a tale about the mighty Gerbert (later Pope Sylvester II) from the potent hand of William of Malmesbury. In Roger Bacon's own time, it was being told about Albertus Magnus. It became attached to Bacon only late in the sixteenth century, via a play called *Friar Bacon and Friar Bungay* by Shakespeare's forgotten rival Robert Greene. (The play itself has been called an attempt to imitate Marlowe's *Doctor Faustus*, but there seems to be good evidence that Greene's work was first; in any event, it is still worth reading.) Since 1589, the brazen head has lived an underground life as the golem, Frankenstein's monster, Karel Capek's robots and their innumerable spawn, and today, perhaps, as Dr. Claude Shannon's mechanical player (after Poe) of indifferent chess. Tomorrow, Dr. Norbert Weiner warns us, it may be outthinking us all – and Dr. Isaac Asimov thinks that will probably be a good thing.

The appearance of Roger Bacon as the hero of the Greene play, however, is no accident of legend. The historical Doctor Faustus – a dim figure indeed – became in the same way a vehicle for timeless preoccupations of the human mind, which tell us a great deal about ourselves but almost nothing about Faustus himself. The Bacon legend, which is *not* the subject of this novel, haunted Europe in the same way until the end of the seventeenth century.

What remains behind as reasonably certain knowledge about Roger Bacon's life would hardly fill a small pamphlet;

and the more intensively the man is pursued, the more what was once thought certain about him tends to melt into doubt. What little we know about him personally comes entirely from his own testimony, particularly in the *Opus Tertium*, the *Compendium studii theologiae* and an untitled work, evidently intended as a covering letter for the works for the Pope, which is usually called 'the Gasquet fragment'. The *Compendium*, as my last chapter indicates, shows clear signs that his memory is failing; and as for the other two, they were intended to impress his patron and hence are not wholly reliable as autobiography, as well as being riddled with contradictions.

Except for an anonymous writer who saw Bacon at a gathering like the one described in Chapter VII, not a single soul in his own lifetime ever managed to mention him by name in a writing which has survived, not even people he obviously knew intimately; and we have the text of only one letter *to* him, that being the mandate of 1266 from Clement IV. A Roger Bacon does appear in one of the footnotes to Matthew Paris' *Chronica majora*, but few modern scholars believe that this anecdote can refer to *the* Roger Bacon. (I disagree, as Chapter III shows, but there is simply no present way to settle this question except by intuition.)

An unknown amount of Bacon's own work is missing, in addition to the fact that not all that is known has yet been published. He mentions two treatises, *De generatione* and *De radii*, which have not yet been found, and the many unpublished unattributed manuscripts of the period in European libraries may include many more. There are no Bacon *incunabula*; the Voynich manuscript, in which W. R. Newbold claimed to have found an elaborate cypher concealing a knowledge of human anatomy which would have been staggering even for Bacon, was once thought to be in his own hand, but modern scholarship has discredited hand and authorship alike (and cyphers, as we have learned painfully from Ignatius Donnelly and his followers, are not reliable clues to the authorship of anything). The only authenticated sample of Bacon's handwriting is that of the corrections – not the text – of the piece of the *Opus Majus* in the Vatican Library.

Finally, just the published body of Bacon's work is so vast – some twenty-two thick volumes, plus smaller pieces – that no one has ever attempted a definitive Collected Works, and the existing partial collections, those of Steele and Brewer, are arranged in no rational order. Furthermore, for the reader who would rather not cope with medieval Latin, only the *Opus Majus* and a few much smaller works have ever been translated, and the translations are long out of print. It is easier to deal with a mountebank like Giambattista della Porta, whose *Natural Magick* can be bought today in a facsimile of the handsome 1658 English printing, boxed; but a universal genius is born mutinous and disorderly, and remains so seven hundred years later.

This is a wholly inviting situation for a novelist, providing only that he has the brass head to believe that he can turn a universal genius into a believable character; but he must not pretend that the book he writes from it is a fictionalized biography. Under the circumstances it would be impossible to write any such work about Roger Bacon. What follows is a fiction. It is as true to Bacon's age as I have been able to make it; there is, at least, no shortage of data about the thirteenth century – the problem is to mine it selectively. Roger Bacon himself, however, is unrecoverable by scholarship alone. The rest is – or should be – a vision.

A word about language:

The reader may wonder why I have resorted here and there to direct quotations in Latin, especially since the characters are speaking Latin a large part of the time and I have been content to give what they say in English. The reason is that these exceptions, these ideas and opinions written down seven centuries ago, might otherwise have been suspected of being a twentieth-century author's interpolations. There is always an English paraphrase close by; but the direct quotations are intended to demonstrate that I have not modernized my central figure, and did not need to do so.

I must, however, admit to one modernization, this being the translation from *De multiplicatione specierum* in Chapter XII. Here it seemed to me that the Aristotelian terminology Bacon uses would be worse than impenetrable to most modern readers. Hence I have followed Sarton and others in converting what Bacon calls 'the multiplication of species' (which today suggests that he must have been talking about biology) into 'the propagation of action', which shows that his subject is physics. Several other Aristotelian terms, such as 'agent' and 'patient' have suffered a similar conversion at my hands.

As for the English, I have followed two rules. (1) Where the characters are speaking Middle English, I have used a synthetic speech which roughly preserves Middle English syntax, one of its several glories, but makes little attempt to follow its metrics or its vocabulary (and certainly not its spelling, which was catch-as-catch-can). (2) Where they are speaking French or Latin, which is most of the time, I have used modern English, except to indicate whether the familiar or the polite form of 'you' is being employed, a distinction which should cause no one any trouble.

I am greatly indebted to W. O. Hassall of the Bodleian Library, Oxford, for help in locating pertinent manuscripts; to L. Sprague de Camp, whose vast knowledge of the history of technology I mined mercilessly; to Ann Corlett, Algis Budrys, L. D. Cole, Virginia Kidd, Willy Ley and Henry E. Sostman for invaluable criticism and suggestions; and to Kenneth S. White for pushing me into the project in the first place.

JAMES BLISH

Arrowhead,
Milford, Pennsylvania

Implicit prima pars:

FORTHE, PYLGRYME, FORTHE!

I: FOLLY BRIDGE

It was called the fever, or the plague, or the blue-lips, or the cough, but most often simply the death. It had come north across Folly Bridge into Oxford with the first snow, and at first had shown a godly grim decorum, spreading mainly inside the enclave of the Jewerye, so that the mayor and the burgesses of Oxford decided that there was nothing to fear from it.

The astrologers agreed. There was every heavenly sign that the city would be at peace throughout the whole of A.D. 1231. Certainly there would not be another pestilence; and certainly not in October, when Jupiter, Venus and the moon would be in trine before All Hallows' Eve.

Besides, the Jews had excellent physicians, even one or two from Bologna. There was nothing to fear.

Now it is too late to be afraid, Roger thought. The words came to him not as his own thought, however, but like an aphorism which he had only remembered; it was the way he had learned to distinguish the prompting of his self from the general tumult of notions which stormed tormentingly out of his soul the instant he started awake. He stood motionless in the pitch-black, freezing stone corridor, hands folded tensely into each other under the coarse hempen robe he had thrown over his clothing when Adam Marsh had brought the word and called him out, listening; but the self had nothing further to say.

It had said all that was needful. It was too late to fear the death now. Neither the Bolognese Jews nor anyone else had been able to prevent the death. If it was not yet a plague, it had not much further to spread to become one. Half the burgesses were stricken of it already, and the school was dissolved into a shivering huddle of coughing shadows. No classes had met for over a week; no convocations had been called since the death had taken the prior of Carfax; the halls were silent; the students huddled on their pallets, too sick to care for themselves, or providentially too well to risk breathing the prevalent miasma outside the dormitories. Here, at the Franciscan school, the gloom was absolute, for the death was visiting the lector.

Roger's heart filled; he could feel his knuckles crackling under the robe. Since he could see nothing at all in the damp-ticking black passageway, he could not prevent himself from standing suddenly, also in his shivering shift, by the bedside of his father in the blocky fieldstone house outside Ilchester now abruptly gone, as his father was gone eleven years. *Domine, Domine!* Until that moment he had not loved his father. How little he had been able to anticipate even in his new rough boyhood, five years old and already master of the wide-nostrilled sweaty horses trembling with day-end exhaustion in their stalls, that Christopher Bacon's rude remote justice would some day be replaced by the trade-swine arrogance of Robert Bacon, hardly eight years Roger's senior!

And now Robert Grosseteste was dying, too, only a door away in the timeless darkness. *Justice is Love*, the self whispered suddenly. And he had no answer. The vision of his father's death vanished as suddenly, leaving him empty in snow-covered Oxford, a black mark on a black ground inside a black box. If Robert Grosseteste died, where could Roger go then; what would he do; what would he think? Adam Marsh was well enough, but no man can have three fathers; besides, the gentle Adam lacked both the strength and the desire; he was a brother and would never be more – not a brother such as Robert Bacon, but a brother in love. As a father, he had no vocation.

Adam was with the lector now; had been with him a long time. In a while, perhaps, he would emerge and say: 'It is over.' There had been no assurance that the lector would be able to see Roger at all; it had been with a shock of guilty delight that Roger had heard that he even wanted to see Roger, but even of that there was no proof. It might only have been an idea of Adam's; he might have been summoned only on a chance.

On the thought, the door opened a little, letting a wedge of smoky orange light into the corridor. That was all. There were no voices, no footsteps. A draught began to move gently past Roger's face, seeking the smokehole of the lector's fireplace and discovering to Roger that he was sweating under his cassock even in this black realm of liquid ice. The light wavered and lost some of its yellowness, as though a few tapers were nodding and blowing inside the room. Then a long-fingered hand, deeply chiselled on the back with shadows between the tendons, took the door by the latch and pulled it soundlessly to again. Perhaps it had been only a wind that had opened it to begin with.

But Roger knew the hand. He stood in the blackness and struggled with a jealousy only a little away from love. Never mind that Adam Marsh of Wearmouth had come to him the moment it appeared that the lector might die; he was only trying to prove to his student how high he stood in Robert's esteem. Never mind that Adam had recognized the quick wit of the seventeen-year-old who sat under him in theology and had won him a place at Robert's lectures to the Franciscans; Roger could have done the same for himself. Never mind that Adam did seem to stand high in the esteem of the lector, and in the general esteem of the Order; he was only thirty-one years old and had become a Franciscan only last year. One Robert Bacon was enough; *Domine, Domine!*

But it was not true. *Justice is Love.*

The words drove the jealousy from him, though he fought sullenly to hold it. There was something about the self that hated emotion, and particularly the red emotions, the ones that fogged the eye, inside or out. Why should Grosseteste have called Roger at all? Roger and the lector had never even spoken, except once or twice in passing. Grosseteste had his own favourite students – Adam, obviously, and a frighteningly brilliant lecturer in his mid-twenties named John of Bandoun – and could hardly be aware of the deep, irrational awe he had inspired in some anonymous franklin's son from Ilchester.

Justice is Love, the self said again in its sweet bodiless voice, and the fury was gone. Suddenly, he was only a man in a corridor in a hall in a town in a snowfall, his eyes as empty as embrasures, his head capped like a merlon in winter with coldness. For an instant he did not even know his own name; he stood as alone as a planet in the general dark.

It had been a long day, like all days: the bell in the night, calling him out of bed to church for matins and the lauds, the seven psalms of praise; the Divine Office at prime, six o'clock in the morning, still full darkness and the cold at its bitterest, seven psalms, the litany and the mass with freezing toes; midday mass and then the meal, roots and eggs and water, and the sleep of afternoon – but no sleep for Roger, because of the letter; then the bell again to sing nones at three o'clock; and studies, but again no studies for Roger, because Robert Grosseteste was sick and Adam beside him, and one of the Bolognese, too, especially dispensed to minister to an archdeacon thrice over; then supper, wastel-bread, butter and beans, with a little ale (the letter had made him cautious of spending any money on wine, for the first time in his life; besides, it was written in Aelfric, 'Wine is not a drink for children or foolish people, but for the old and wise'); then the bell, and compline.

And then the summons from Adam.

He lifted one hand under the robe to finger the bulge of the letter, like a man cautiously investigating a fresh wound. It was a dirty scrap of old vellum, grey with erasures; under its present burden could still be seen the shadows of minuscules which had been the previous writing. These were almost clear at the bottom of the letter and Roger had been able to work out a little of it: '. . . e ministr e omnib fidelib suis Francis e . . .' – possibly a piece of some charter. But this game had run out quickly, and the faint remains of what the palimpsest had carried before it had been pumiced for the charter proved even duller: pieces of a crabbed hymn by some barely literate canon. There was no way to put off thinking about the message on top in new ink.

It was brief and disastrous enough. A villein whom Roger did not even remember had thought well enough of him to dictate it to Ilchester's recorder, and had it sent to him by the most reliable means available to a man with neither purse nor freedom: a beggar. It said:

> þis daye d Burh hiȝ Menne haþ despiled
> Franklin Bacon & putte alle in fleyht to
> ferne Strondeȝ Ihab aseyden for Mr
> Roher ac hem schal cleym it Aske of þe
> Franklin hiȝ serf Wulf at þe Oxen
> Ad majorem gloriae

This, in an oval-rubbed spot in the centre, surrounded by a haze of extinguished knowledge, or what passed for it. There was, unhappily, nothing in the least cryptic about the message. It meant that Roger's home was gone and his money with it. Somehow the soldiers of the King's justiciar, scouring the country for remaining pockets of baronial resistance, had happened into Ilchester, and had seen in the substantial heirs of Christopher Bacon, freeman landholder, some taint of sympathy with the partisans of the rebel barons, or some stronghold for the mercenaries who had infected the whole east of England, since the evacuation of the French in 1217. The rest had followed inevitably. No matter that Ilchester had always been an uneventful town, notable for nothing but its Wednesday market and its authorized fair every twenty-ninth of August; Hubert de Burgh stood accused of the failure of last year's expedition to the west of France (regardless of the fact, or, as Adam Marsh had remarked sadly, perhaps because of the fact that the justiciar had advised King Henry most strongly against any such hunting party); he was out to prove that French sedition was still eating away at the body politick, even in a place as unlikely as Ilchester, and that the King's justiciar was swift and terrible in hawking it. And so, farewell, suddenly, to the ancient yeoman house of Bacon, though it had yet to see partisan, baron, Frenchman or mercenary; the serfs would thieve away the harvest, and leave the family only exile and poverty. The reference to 'ferne Strondeȝ' could only mean exile for Harold, Christopher's brother; he was the last of authority in the family to remain in Ilchester; not even Hubert de Burgh could touch Robert Bacon in his factor's fastness in London.

Very well; and so, good-bye as well to new copies of old books, to virgin parchment, to clean quills and fresh ink, to meat and to wine, to warm wool and pliant leather, to a new growth in wisdom under Oxford's once *magister scholarum* Robert Grosseteste, to a doctorate in theology, to becoming (*Thou art addled in thy wits!* the self cried in its sweet voice) the world's wonder in moral philosophy. From now on, he would be poor. Robert Bacon would not help him, that was certain; Robert had been scathing, indeed flyting, of Roger's scholiast bent and his penchant for the Latin language of the papal parasites, and of the money spent to support it – a scorn which had not been much tempered by the fact that Robert had twice been captured by the soldiers of Prince Louis' invading army shortly after the thirteen-year-old Roger had entered Oxford, and had had to ransom himself. By now, Robert thought of Roger as a renegade from the family – and never mind that the still younger Eugene, now fifteen and at the new University of Toulouse, had shown the same scholar's bent without being flyted for it; nor that now in London Robert was farther away from the family than Roger and had even less of the grain on his tongue; still the indictment stuck.

As well it might, the self whispered in the darkness. *Distresseth thou thyself, an thy people be dispersed? Justice is Love.*

And it was true. He was more distressed by the loss of his money and his problematical fame than by the loss of his kin and seat, and more urgent to reclaim whatever effects the unknown Wulf had hidden for him than to succour his sisters, let alone the serfs. Perhaps there was even some money left; Christopher had always been careful to conceal caches of several scores of pounds at a time about the acres during the invasion against just such a catastrophe as this, and did not dream even on the day of his death that his sullen second-born son had found the records of those oubliettes and broken the cypher which told where all but two were buried. Roger had never touched but one, and that one of the two not mentioned in the cypher at all, but deducible by simple geometrical reasoning from the positions of the others; he had lifted a heavy stone and there it was, and he had taken from it one pound, no more, as an honorarium to the power of his boy's reasoning, watched only by three snotty-nosed yearling calves – all of whom had died not long after of the trough fever. It did not seem likely that either a serf or a pack of de Burgh's mailed looters could have had the wit to uncover even the encyphered hideyholes, let alone Roger's deposit-lighter-by-one pound; and at the worst, there was still the undiscovered, unrecorded burial, which, by evidence of its highest secrecy, might well be the richest of all – and a problem worthy of a subtle intellectual soul as much for its difficulty as for its treasure-trove.

And after that discovery, there were certain burials and other concealments that he had made – nothing that this Wulf could have known about, but as close to wealth as mark or pound might be in these times. There was, for instance, a flat glass that he had made from a broken wind-eye in the buttery, with a thin poured lead back in the centre of which he had dug out a peephole; through that chipped spot one might look in a dark room into a cat's eye, reflecting a candle flame into the cat's eye from the glass side – particularly into the eye of massive old Petronius, the black arbiter of the barn rats – and see deep in the lambent slitgated sphere a marvellous golden sparkle, overlaid with dusky red vessels. What might you see inside a man's head with such a tool? He had tried it with the infant Beth, but there had been no light in her eyes that he could see, and besides, his mother had cut the experiment short with a withing. In another pocket in the house he had hidden a small clump of nitre crystals which he had culled with reeking labour from the dungheap; he did not in the least know what they were good for, but anything so precisely formed had to be good for something, like the cylindrical bits of beryl which he had split from a prismatic rock, which laid on a page fattened the strokes and made even dirty minuscules easier to read. Every man has sisters; but how many men have such tools, and such mysteries?

Suddenly he realized that he was trembling. He let go of the letter and clasped his hands back together violently. If there is one thing in the world I will do, he told himself in the tear-freezing darkness. . . . No, if there is one thing in the world I will not do, *Domine, dominus noster*, I will not let go. I will not let go. Thou hast taken away mine house; so be it. But Thou shalt not take away from me what Thou hast given me, which is the lust to know Thy nature.

I shall never let go.

The wind made a sudden sucking sound somewhere in the convent and poured itself up the throat of a chimney with a low brief moan. The corridor lightened slightly, flickeringly. The time had come; Robert Grosseteste's door was open. Adam Marsh was standing in the muddy, wavering light, one long hand crooked, one deep shadow laid along his narrow pointed nose.

'Roger,' he said softly. 'Roger? Art still there? Ah, I see thee now. Come in most quietly, he is asleep, or so I think. But would talk with thee.'

Roger stirred, painfully; his bones were almost frozen. He cleared his throat, but his whisper was still harsh when it came forth:

'Adam, if he is so ill—'

'Certes he is ill, but would see thee all the same. He asked for thee, Roger. Come in quickly, this plaudering lets the chill in, too, and he needs warmth.'

Roger moved quickly then, fighting the stiffness, and Adam shut the door behind him with a miraculous soundlessness. If the room had been chilled during their brief exchange, Roger could not detect it; the air seemed almost hot to him, and the heat from the ardent coals in the fireplace beat against his cheeks and made his eyes tighten. Though there were two candles on a lectern against the wall to the left, and two more on an age-blackened, book-heaped table butting a wardrobe just to the right of the door, the room was quite dark all along its peripheries; the light and heat made an island in the centre, between the door and the hearth, where the low narrow bed was drawn up, parallel with the low stone mantel. The bed was deep in disordered robes and blankets.

The matter of the letter and his patrimony fled tracelessly from his mind the moment he saw the massive head of the lector upon the bolster, its bushy grey monk's tonsure in a tangle under a blue woollen skullcap, the veined eyelids closed in deep-shadowed sockets, the skin of the face as tight and semi-transparent as parchment over the magnificent leonine cheekbones. Bending over Robert Grosseteste and listening with cat-still intentness to his breathing was a fierce-looking swarthy man in mouse-coloured breeches and a saffron tunic; the ear that was tipped down to the lector was bare, but from the other a gold earring lay along the cord of his neck. As Roger made an involuntary half-step forward, the swarthy man held up one palm with all the command of a lord.

'Very well,' the swarthy man said. 'A will stay on live, an his stars permit it. But these are mischancy times. Give him of the electuary when a wakens.'

'What is it he hath with him?' Adam said with an equal intensity.

'Not the consumption,' the Jew said. 'Beyond that I am as ignorant as any man. If there's a crisis, call me no more; I have done what I could.'

'And for that all thanks,' Adam said, 'and my purse. Would God might send thee His grace as well as His wisdom.'

The physician straightened, his eyes burning sombrely. 'Keep thy purse,' he said between startlingly white teeth. The purse struck the stone floor almost at Roger's feet and burst, scattering coins among the rushes and the alder leaves spread to trap fleas. 'Thou payest me ill enough already with thy blessing. I spit on thee.'

For a moment it seemed to Roger that he might actually do just that, but instead, he strode past them both with an odd, stoop-shouldered, loping gait and was gone. Adam stared after him; he seemed stunned.

'What did I say?' the Franciscan murmured.

'What matter?' Roger said in a hoarse whisper. He was having difficulty in keeping himself from tallying the spatter of coins in the rushes; he felt as though the parchment in his pocket had suddenly been set afire. ' 'Tis but a Jew.'

'As were three of the nine worthies of the world,' Adam said gently, 'and among Christians there were eke but three, as among the paynims. Since Our Lord was a Jew as well, that giveth the Jews somewhat the advantage.'

Roger shrugged convulsively. This was an ill time, it seemed to him, to be resurrecting the Nine Worthies.

'Thou'dst talk nonsense on the day of wrath could it be mathematical nonsense, Master Marsh,' he said edgily. The words, as they came out, appalled him; suddenly, it seemed as though he were giving voice to the self for the first time in all his guarded life – here in the presence of an undoubted elected saint, and of the angel of death. But it could hardly be unsaid. 'Forgive me; Christ is as Christian a worthy as He was a Jew, it seemeth me. And meseemeth the *Capito* yonder as worthy a Christian as Godfrey of Bouillon, and leader of as worthy a crusade. I count ignorance as deadly as the paynim.'

Adams stared at Roger a little while as though he had seen the youngster for almost the first time. After a few moments, Roger was forced to drop his eyes, but that was no better, for that brought him back into encounter with the money on the floor.

'A dangerous notion, and a bad piece of logic,' Adam said at last in a strange voice. 'Thou art an ill-tempered youngster, Roger. Nevertheless, thou remindest me that our matter here is with the lector, not disputation; which is a point which pierceth, be it never so poorly thrust. Let neither of us raise our voices again here.'

'So be it,' Roger muttered. There was a long and smothering silence, during which Roger began to hear the slightly ragged, slightly too rapid breathing of Robert Grosseteste, as though his lungs were being squeezed by a marching piper of the Scots to keep him harrowing the air. As time stretched out under Adam's level eyes, the pace of the breathing increased; and then, with a start, the lector coughed rackingly and jerked his great head up.

'That shall I do,' he said in a thick, strangled voice. His head moved uncertainly and for a moment his eyes rested on Roger without seeming to see him. Adam stepped forward and Grosseteste's head turned once more, but his eyes were still glazed; two hectic fever-spots began to burn on his cheeks, as though they had been rubbed with snow. Seeing the great head lolling thus frighteningly brought home to Roger as nothing else had done the precariousness of the lector's future from moment to moment; he was, after all, fifty-seven years old and the uprightness of his life had not prevented it from being most active and taxing. He had been the chancellor of the University until 1229, when he had resigned the post to give the lectures to the Franciscans, and in the short course of Roger's own lifetime he had been archdeacon of Chester, Northampton and Leicester, one after the other. No man in orders had ever been more attentive to the needs of his parishes; no member of the Faculty of Theology more assiduous of the needs of the whole University and all three thousand of its students; no scholar more careful to build the massive learning which alone justifies a master to lecture before the young. Were God to terminate his life in the next instant, no man could call it anything but long, full and rich in works – and the death had been laying an especial hand on the old.

Adam Marsh, murmuring something indistinguishable, was kneeling beside the bed, holding an enamelled Syran wine glass to Grosseteste's lips. The lector drank with difficulty, made a fearful face and then lay back among the blankets with a shuddering sigh. The quiet seeped back into the room, which was becoming hotter and stuffier with every instant; nevertheless, the lector's breathing was becoming a little easier, and he seemed now to be relaxed without either trembling from weakness or looking flaccid with morbidity. The honey vehicle of the Jew's electuary obviously had not much sweetened the dose, but the active principle of the slow-flowing mass was quick to take effect. Mandragora? No, that would have put the lector back to sleep, whereas he was obviously not under any narcotic, but simply more composed, less desperately distracted by the failure of his flesh. He lay staring at the dark flickering ceiling for a long time.

'Adam,' he said at last. 'I have been charged.'

'Rest thee and let it wait,' Adam Marsh said softly.

'Nay, the time is too short. I have been given a charge and will keep it, an I live. It came to me while I slept, and from God as I no doubt. And it concerneth thee, Adam.'

The Franciscan gathered his cassock up and sat down cross-legged amidst the rushes and alder leaves. 'Say on,' he said resignedly. Roger was startled at the overtone of sadness in his voice.

Grosseteste heard it too. Still looking up into the shadows, he said quietly: 'Thou may'st not refuse preferment all thy life, Adam. Offices are repugnant to thee, as I know well. But should God take me, thou shouldst become first in the Order in the realm; dost think Hubert de Burgh's countess ward hath sought thy counsel to no holy purpose?'

Roger looked up sharply, but at once he realized that Grosseteste had intended no reference to his own cloudy troubles in Ilchester. There was as yet no indication that the lector even recognized his presence. Hubert de Burgh was the King's justiciar, a public figure – it were folly to suppose that any reference to him was *ipso facto* a reference to a student at Oxford only two years come of age, even were that student Roger Bacon his unique and universe-pivot self.

'God will leave thee with us,' Adam Marsh said. 'Thou'lt not die. This I know.'

'But there's no escape there for thee,' Grosseteste said,

with the faintest of ironies in his voice. 'I have been charged, as I rede thee. And I live, I must resign my benefices and preferments, and devote myself to piety and contemplation, as befitteth one brought to the very verge of judgment. I shall keep only the prebend in Lincoln; that, will suffice. Therefore, live or die Robert Grosseteste, thou must take responsibilities, Adam, and offices eke if it thee requireth. There can be no more exits for thee from these matters.'

'As God willeth,' Adam said.

'As God would have me bequeath it thee, Adam,' Grosseteste said in an iron voice. 'Shirk not, nor say me nay what I have charged thee.' His head turned on the bolster and Roger flinched from those driving grey eyes, though they were not bent on him at all. In his heart a certainty that he should be present at this recondite death-bed quarrel not at all fought breast to breast with a self-urged demand to speak and settle it, and with the simple alarm of the vegetative soul at being in the presence of death at all, and with the immortal soul's urgency to bear witness in the presence of God, and with the intellectual soul's pride of proof of what the *anima* was well content to believe and demand that all else be taken on faith as well – faith being at the heart of things.

It seemed unjust that all the natures of man should already be at war within him, but it was not a surprise to him any more to find himself the ground of such a battle – nor to find the hailing arrows of the self penetrating every link and joint of the other armies to slaughters, routs and senseless strewn bleeding heaps of mail which had once been proud-mounted and pennon-bearing arguments. The self was Frankish; the last arrow always was his, and like the shaft which had ended Harold at Hastings, it went to the brain. Roger said:

'Master Grosseteste. . . .'

The lector did not reply, but after a while, he shifted his glance. Instantly, Roger was ashamed to have spoken at all; but the self was not abashed.

'Thou shouldst redeem thy chancellorship here in Oxford,' Roger heard himself saying. 'Piety without contemplation is but an exercise, and contemplation without learning is an empty jug. Thou art the only master who ever lectured on perspective here; yet, surely there is more to know in that subject alone. And we are much in need of masters in Aristotle here, the more so that his books of nature and the *Metaphysics* are banned in Paris.'

'Banned in Paris?' Adam said. 'That's but a farthing of the whole. The University itself is closed entire these two years past. Perhaps half our scholars are come from there, on the King's direct promise of their safety.'

'I wis, I wis,' Grosseteste said. ' 'Tis common knowledge.'

'But not the whole,' Roger said with helpless boldness. 'I've myself seen a letter from Toulouse – I've a brother there – 'ticing scholars to lectures on the *libri naturales* because of the ban on them in Paris. Doubt not that we have many such scholars here to hear such lectures, on the same account. And we be poor in them lately.'

This, as Roger knew well enough, was inarguable, though that alone was a poor reason for his breaching the decorum of a sick-room with disputation. It had been Edmund Rich of Abingdon who had been the first to lecture at Oxford on the *Elenchi*, but he had said his last word on the subject of Aristotelian logic when Roger had been six years old; today, the saintly old man lectured only in courses of theology far too advanced for Roger to attend. Master Hugo still continued to drone on about the *Posteriores*, his own pioneer subject from Aristotle, but nobody would learn much logic from him any more – he had gone frozen in his brain, as often seemed to happen even to doctors when very old (*It need never happen*, the self whispered with sudden, distracting irrelevance). As for John Blund, who taught the books of nature, he appeared to think of nature only as a source of examples for sermons, bestiaries and cautionary tales. Beyond these three, the only Aristotelians at Oxford today were Robert Grosseteste, Adam Marsh . . . and Roger Bacon, at least in one pair of eyes.

Whether or not that seed had been planted in Grosseteste's mind could not yet be riddled. The sick man continued to look at Roger with that upsettingly penetrating speculative gaze.

'Paris will be opened again ere long,' he said at last. 'His Eminence hath been bending many efforts to that issue, and indeed, can hardly fail, unless the struggle with the Emperor hath sapped his ancient strength entire. Yet, meseemeth that we still have here some advantage. Aristotle on dreams is galling hard for a schoolman with's eyes closed to experience and nature; should see dogs dream of rabbits and think thrice, but dogs are naught to bishops; would only ban nuns from keeping them, which is impossible; women are women, *quod erat demonstrandum est.*'

He sighed and looked back at the vault. For a moment, Roger was sure that he was asleep. Then he sighed again and said:

'I am astray. Nay, I see the road again. There'll be no lectures from Aristotle at Paris, not in my lifetime. Dogs are ne to the purpose; I was wandering. But on th' eternalie of the world, there shalt crack their brains for years to come. And eke on motion – there's a potent farrower of heresies undreamed. And light – there's heresy upon heresy in the *Perspectiva,* given a sciolast to seek them instead of using his eyes, and the Arabs to confound dogma at every stand. Boy, how old art thou?'

Roger came back to consciousness with a terrible start. The vitiated air and the lector's wandering had conspired to throw him into a standing slumber full of weary portents, all charged with dread, all fled of meaning now. He said:

'Seventeen.'

'Thou hast two years before thee to become a Bachelor in thy faculty, and then two more years to thy Master's degree. Thou'rt to undertake explication of the texts thou invokest, and in disputation thou'rt a child, as is plain to hear. And yet, wouldst teach Aristotle at Oxford?'

To begin with, the self said. No response could have been further from Roger's desire; he was in full confusion and retreat; the lector had found out not only his ambition, but the mean and inept method he had come here to use, the practice of trickery at the deathbed of a holy man. Yet, somehow he must have said it aloud, word for word at the prompting of the self, without even hearing it. He did not know he had said anything until he heard Adam Marsh laugh.

'To begin with?' the Franciscan said. 'Thou'rt frantic, Roger. Seek ye the doctorate in the sacred college? Dost know that will take thee sixteen full years after thou hast thy secular mastership? Canst thou do all that from the Frideswyde chest? And from such poor beginnings in humility?'

'What's this?' Grosseteste said. He pushed himself painfully back on to his elbow and stared at Adam. 'Hath the boy need of the chest? An 'tis so, thou dost ill to mock it. Tell me the truth of this matter, Adam. If 'tis true, wast ill concealed; much rides on this, as thou shouldst know all too well.'

Adam looked down at the floor in his turn. Roger was as much astonished at his abasement and at the unforgiving condemnation in Grosseteste's tone as he was at the revelation that Adam knew about the letter.

'His family is suddenly afflicted,' Adam said in a low voice. 'He hath had a patrimony, but witteth not whether he hath it still. Whether or ne he needeth the chest I cannot say; ne no more can he.'

And to be sure he could not. The chest in the priory church at St. Frideswyde, in whose dissolved nunnery and in that of Oseney Abbey Oxford had been founded more than a century ago, was a benefaction long established to help poor students; but was he *that* poor already? It was hardly likely; in extremis, he could always sell part of his library; but no, in the ensuing eighteen years with which Adam had mocked him, he would have to add to his manuscripts, and most expensively; he could not take from Peter to pay Paul. But did that bring him to the Frideswyde chest? It was impossible to know. It depended, he realized suddenly, on the peasant Wulf – and on the astuteness of the justiciar's raiders. And to go all that long distance home to find out –

seventy-five miles as the crow flies, and not by crow either, but on the back of the best horse he could hire, and that probably no courser's prancing jack – he would need now to know just how much pocket money he had left, a thing he had never counted before in his life.

'How knewest thou this, Adam?' Grosseteste said. Roger looked gratefully toward him. It had been the very question he had wanted to ask, but could not.

' 'Tis common fame in the Faculty of Arts,' Adam said. 'The word was brought by a beggar who knew a little his alphabetum – enough, certes, to riddle out the pith of it. I have told thee before that Roger's not held high among his peers; hath a high opinion of himself, and no will to conceal it. There are those who have hoped him some such misprision, and be not slow to spread the tidings.'

'For which act their souls will suffer grievously, an they bring it not to their next confessions,' Grosseteste said heavily. He was interrupted by a seizure of hacking, raw-edged coughs. Adam bent over him but was waved off. After a while, the lector seemed to have recovered, though his breathing was still alarmingly dry and rapid. Again, looking at the ceiling, he said:

'The common rout customarily hateth and distrusteth the superior soul; 'tis a sign to watch for. Boy, thou shalt have thy wish, an thou performst all thy tasks as faithfully as thou shouldst; and eke much more that thou dreamest not of now – though I see that no man may hazard a tithe of thy dreaming. First, thou must go home and find all the truth of this beggar's message, and succour thy family an thou canst. The Frideswyde chest shall be opened for thee, I shall see on't. Leave thy books in Oxford and all else but very necessaries; and when thy business in the south is done, return here incontinently and take thy degree. I shall promise thee no more but this: make Oxford and Aristotle thy washing-pot, and thou shalt cast thy shoe over many a farther league ere this night's intelligence hath its full issue, an it be the will of God.'

His voice died away in a whisper, and his eyes closed. For

a long passage of sand in the glass, neither Adam nor Roger moved or spoke; but at last it became evident that the lector was asleep. Adam took Roger by the elbow and led him, tiptoeing, to the door.

'Thou'rt fortunate,' Adam murmured in his ear. 'Visit me tomorrow after sext, when we'll conspire how to see't brought about. Now thou must go.'

'I am most deeply—'

'Hush, no more. It is he, not I, who hath done it – and more than thou wittest, as he said. Bear in mind that he may yet die; I would not have had thee here so early, but that he would have it so. Go, thou, speedily.'

Bowing his head, Roger went out. The door closed behind him with that same magical soundlessness. The coldness in the black corridor cut like knives, but he hardly marked it for the brand that was burning within his breast.

II: NORTHOVER

It was more than hard for Roger to leave behind him, over Folly Bridge, those grammars of Priscian and Donatus, together with the *Barbarismus* of Donatus and Boethius' *Topics*, which were his texts in rhetoric; and the *Isagoge* of Porphyry, that great hymn and harmony of logic – all the beloved books of his trivium years, all so essential, all so expensive of copyists and of virgin parchment. It was even a worse wrench to have to leave in Adam Marsh's care his precious works of Aristotle: the *Logica antiqua* in the eloquent translation of Boethius, the *Logica nova* in the new, zigzag, fantastical translations from Avicenna with the Arab's heretical commentaries, the *libri naturales* from the hand of Oxford's own John Blund, who taught them (as befitted such an idiot as Blund) as a dialectical adjunct to the trivium, rather than as a part of metaphysics in the quadrivium where they plainly belonged. (But that was hardly unusual, Roger reflected on the back of his placid horse. Had he his own way, the whole subject of rhetoric would be subsumed under logic.) But there was no help for it: the books had to be left behind, and that was that.

Nevertheless, he had his copy of the *Metaphysics* in his saddlebag as he left Oxford. Nothing in the world could persuade him to leave it behind. It had been the key which had let him into his still unfinished quadrivium years with an understanding of the four subjects – arithmetic, geometry, astronomy, music – so much in advance of his masters as to excite his vocal and injudicious contempt (injudicious only because vocal, for Roger knew not a single student who was being taught as much Aristotle as he wanted; the masters were far behind the scholars there, and getting farther every day). Of course Aristotle was of no special value on music – Boethius was still the best authority there, once he left off reprising his descants on the consolations of philosophy, a subject upon which he apparently had taken pains to become the dullest man in the world – but as a systematic summary of the world of experience in every other category, the *Metaphysics* was unique. Roger had copied it himself to be sure of having every word right; it was worth more than diamonds, which would have taken up far less space in the saddlebag, but which dissolve in goat's blood. Nothing would ever dissolve the *Metaphysics* but a human mind, and that not soon.

The horse was as cautious an idiot as John Blund, but in two or three days, it got him from inn to inn on to the marches of Salisbury Plain, stopping at every roadside ditch to crop the watercress. It had seemed the strongest and healthiest animal the courser had had for the money – six whole pounds – but it had never entered Roger's mind to suspect that it might have been *overfed*; yet, it put its nose into the sweet herbs like serfs putting their elbows on table, full and waxing lazy as freemen, and as disputatious. At the last inn before Salisbury, he saved the price of the beast's hay; the next morning it suddenly discovered that it knew how to trot.

This far from satisfied Roger's passionate urgency, for he had been unable to get away from the Great Hall for nearly a month, what with duties, observances and arrangements; but he had a three days' journey ahead of him, and he knew better than to force the animal. He had had a fair dawn to start in, warm for November, so that the snow was going, and the road was soon to be a motionless river of mud; but this early in the day the earth was still frozen, and the high sky was an intense, almost Venetian blue without a finger of cloud. Before him stretched the reddish, chalky-loamed downs in a broad undulating sweep, littered by the thousands with those huge blocks called sarsen stones or grey wethers (and to be sure they did look a little like a motionless flock of sheep from a distance) which had been used by the unknown builders of the enigmatic and faintly sinister structures at Stonehenge and Avebury. Had Merlin truly been their architect, as one of the *romans* would have it – and by what magic had he moved such enormous stones, some of them as long as twenty feet and as big around as forty feet? There was another *roman* which called the great circle at Avebury a monument to the last of the twelve Arthurian battles, in which case Merlin could hardly have been involved, having been by that time himself ensorcelled by Vivien – had there ever been any such magician, a question which, like that about the stones, did not strike Roger as very profitable. Still, the stones *had* been moved, some of them over long distances, so it was plain to see that there must be at least *a* method – whether it had been Merlin's or not – and that was discoverable.

The horse tired and began to amble again, so that before noon by Roger's stomach – which reminded his brain that today was the eleventh of November, and the eleventh of November was Martinmas, and Martinmas was the time to hang up salt meat for the winter, and there was salt meat in his saddlebag, and he was hungry – he was beginning to fear that he would have to spend the night out alone on the Plain. There was a good deal of danger in that, for the Plain was bloody ground, a favourite spot for pitched battles and for thieves alike.

Nevertheless, Roger had to face the prospect. From this point in the road – little more than a track, meandering around the hills, following the contours of the land – there was no inn or habitation in sight, and none, very likely, this far out. It was, of course, perfectly possible that he had got lost.

Abruptly, his eye was distracted by a flurry of movement ahead: straight out from behind the next wave of low hills something small, dark and compact went hurtling into the blue sky like an arrow. It was a hawk. Roger watched it soar with astonishment and increased disquiet, for he could not but regard it as ominous. No such bird would be hunting in the middle of the Plain at this time of year – it would be an unusual sight at any season – and why would a human hunter be hawking in such cheerless, unfruitful country?

But hunter it was, human or devil; he topped the rise now

on his horse, a tall burly figure, bearded and cloaked, and pulled to a stop while he was joined by two more riders. The hawk wheeled high above them, screaming disconsolately. The three, plainly regarding Roger where he had halted on the ancient, pre-Roman trackway, talked among themselves, leaning in their gear. After a while, the tallest of them raised his left hand as if in salute; cautiously – it could not but pay to offer friendship, or at least neutrality, especially as he was outnumbered – Roger saluted back, and immediately felt like a fool, for beyond him the hawk screamed again, stooped and came down, sculling to a perch on the gauntleted wrist with a noble display of wingspread.

Roger lowered his arm and loosened his sword. Though, as a clerk, he was under the protection of the Church, he was not naïve enough to expect this to be respected by a pack of highwaymen. Furthermore, as a clerk he had a right to the blade, and as a scholar, he was as expert with it as the next; the students were a squalling, brawling lot, very likely to summarize disputations with blood, and when one was not defending one's self against some such 'argument', there were the burghers of Oxford to be on guard against – there had been four outright riots between the scholars and the townsmen in Roger's time, in two of which he had had to slash his way out without wasting an instant on ethical or moral niceties.

It certainly would not do to get killed now, with such great prospects a-dangle in the near future like the grapes of Tantalus, though rather more indefinite. Miraculously, Robert Grosseteste had cleaved to his life – or had been so cleaving still when Roger had left the Great Hall. He was still gravely ill, to be sure, and unable to see anyone except his physicians, and Adam Marsh his confessor, but the crisis seemed to be over, and Adam had estimated cautiously that three months of pottages, gruels and broths would restore him to something like his old strength. The death seemed to be generally on the wane; lectures had been resumed at the University, and trade in town was almost back to normal. The burghers buried their dead and agreed solemnly that it had not been a pestilence after all, but only a narrow escape from one.

The party to the south was moving down the hill toward Roger now, and with every moment seemed to be growing larger; following the three leading horses came a train of pack-animals, heavily laden, two by two over the brow of the hill. Suddenly Roger realized what it was that he was seeing, and with a sigh of relief allowed his sword to settle again.

The big man was obviously a wool merchant, his two companions prentices, chivvying a purchase of fells and hides over the downs. And in fact Roger knew the man; had he not been now close enough to recognize, the hawk should have given him the clue, for there was only one such merchant customarily buying in Dorset and Somersetshire who went about with a peregrine falcon on his wrist: William Busshe. The falcon's name was Madge, and Roger even knew that the horse was called Bucephalus after the legendary animal of Alexander the Great, but was always addressed as 'Bayard'; for he had watched this same man bargaining for the spring clip and the fall hides for ten years before leaving Oxford, haggling solemnly with his father until Christopher's death, and thereafter, first with Robert and then with Harold.

Busshe recognized Roger simultaneously and pulled to a second time, his shaggy eyebrows rising almost into his Flemish-style beaver hat. Wearing that expression, he looked almost like a sheep himself, despite his forked brown beard and the fact that his face was, of course, not black. His vair-collared cloak spread like Madge's wings as he put his hands on his hips. Feeling the reins on his neck, the big bay promptly began to graze, and Roger had to hold John Blund's head up sharply to keep him from following Bayard's example.

'How now, young Roger,' Busshe said in his heavy, deliberate voice. 'Little I expected to encounter thee on this dreary moor, and in sooth, I wis not whether't be well met or ill with us.'

'No more wis I,' Roger said, with some return of his

uneasiness. 'Meseemeth 'tis early for thee to be faring north with sealed bales, this being but Martinmas. Someone hath slaughtered early, and I greatly fear that 'tis Yeo Manse hath done it.'

'Thou wert ever a gimlet-eyed youngster,' Busshe said. 'Thou hast seen to the heart of the matter. There's a knight of the justiciar sitteth as lord in thy cot, hath ordered the slaughter a week ere we had arrived, would sell me the fells at half the prices I'd contracted for with Franklin Harold these eighteen months gone. And so much and no more did I pay him, seeing that the slaughtering had been hastily done to fill's purse quickly, and the wool thus not of the first quality.'

Roger felt a brief flash of anger, but after a moment, he realized that it should not be Busshe at whom it was directed. He was doubtless telling the exact truth – after all, he had no part in this quarrel – nor could it matter in the least which price he had paid, since none of it could go to the family under the circumstances. If Busshe had cheated the justiciar's equerry out of his very shirt (though nothing could be more unlike Busshe), Roger ought indeed to be pleased. But it was hard to think of a year's flock spoiled and knocked down for the enrichment of some marauding noble in de Burgh's service without feeling a general anger at everyone concerned, even the silent prentices who were watching him with evident sympathy.

'Then are we much despoiled?' Roger said after a while.

'Nay, this knight, a highteth Will of Howlake, hath far too stern a hand; a hath kept the serfs hard at it and much increased the rents and the boon work. All thy kin are gone, but for thy sisters, no man knoweth where. How farest thou?'

'To the manse, to retrieve what I may,' Roger said, preoccupied. 'And my sisters?'

'In the women's houses, where, by order of Franklin Harold's steward, they be so craftily clothed, this Will of Howlake knoweth them not from villeins' women.'

'I thank God for't.' Indeed, the whole situation as Busshe

outlined it seemed far from the worst that Roger had imagined. Though he had had no experience of such an occupation as Yeo Manse was undergoing now, the pattern had been familiar for centuries, and Will of Howlake's behaviour did not sound like that of a man who expected to remain lord of the property for long. He was wringing the good out of it with the stringency of a man who expects recall, and so was adding to his personal store, as well as to that of Hubert de Burgh, by as many marks a day as the manse could possibly be made to yield. A brief cruel plundering of that kind had proven the ruination of many a holding – lords who expected to be awarded the property were kinder to it – but the orchards and fields and gardens of Yeo Manse were extensive, and Roger did not doubt that they would survive such treatment, were it only not much prolonged. It meant that the serfs and even the stewards would be despitefully used while it lasted – but their days were miserable enough even in normal times – their reward only in heaven, never in this world.

'Thou'rt ill advised to go hither,' Busshe said in a troubled voice. 'Howlake is wroth at having missed taking every man in the family; an thou becomest known to him, wilt go ill with thee. And thy fat gelding there wheezeth like a monk with the asthmaticks – 'tis plain to see a's all out of the habit of work.'

Madge stirred her wings under the cloak, and Busshe lifted his left arm to the sky again. Reluctantly the red peregrine climbed on the air; being recently fed from Busshe's own hand, she wanted only to sleep, or at least to perch quietly and pursue some single savage thought, but hawks had to be exercised or they would not hunt – indeed, would forget even how to come home. Busshe put his hand back on his hip again, and Madge began to circle at her pitch, crying Kyaa! Kyaa!

'Come thou with us till yon Howlake's outworn his commission,' Busshe said. 'We're to Northleach to cast a sort of fell and fifty tods of Cotswold wool, dear though it be at eleven shillings; thence to our offices in London for th' assizes at the Leadenhall, and to pack sarplers for shipboard. Our quarters be in the Mart Lane, not over-far from where thy brother Robert doth deal in Egypt's cotton and I wis not what else. An 'tis money thou seekest, belike a will succour thee. Mene-whyles we'll put thee on a proper horse, and give yon hay-bottle bales to carry; and thou'lt add thy blade to ours 'gainst thieves or Lombards, as is equitable.'

It was a generous offer, and for a moment Roger was tempted to accept it; he did not underestimate the risks he was taking. But it was not, after all, money that he was primarily hoping to recover, and he knew besides how little likely he was to be given any money to go back to Oxford from Robert Bacon's hands; then he would be stranded in London, with no possible course but to ship with Busshe's wool to Flanders and try his luck in Paris at the dormant University. That was out of the question; he was not ready for that by years.

'Nay, I cannot,' he said. 'God's blessing on thee, William Busshe, but I'm bidden to Ilchester, and thence to Oxford, and will abide the course. I'll recall thy kindness in my prayers.'

'As it pleaseth thee,' Busshe said. 'Fare thee well, then.' He called Madge home and hooded and jessed her; and in a while, the last of the procession had vanished to the north.

Gloomily, Roger got John Blund into motion, more than half convinced that his refusal had been the worst kind of folly. He was not even much cheered by the sight of a distant inn from the top of the next rise, nor finding, as he drew closer, that the 'bush' or sign was up on the ale-stake, meaning 'open for business'. Good wine needs no bush, but he was in no position to pay for good wine, nor bad, either. And there could hardly be any money for him at Yeo Manse; he was making this wittold's pilgrimage for the sake of nothing but a few childish trinkets....

A few toys, and an *ignis fatuus*, a will-o'-the-wisp drifting far in the future, conjured into being by a Greek dead fourteen weary centuries already.

*

Yeo Manse was not, properly speaking, in Ilchester; legally, it was in the parish of Northover, on the other side of the river, connected with Ilchester by a low stone bridge. Northover was, however, nothing notable as a town, while Ilchester stood athwart Fosse Way, a major road through the district ever since the Romans had built it, and the Bacons had seen the advantages which would accrue from identifying with Ilchester quite early on – long before most of the other local franklins had, in fact. The parish church of St. Mary had been established by Christopher Bacon's grandfather as a chantry where masses were to be sung for his soul by a single priest; later, Christopher's father and two other freeman landholders had contributed the silver and the boon work which had raised the squat octagonal tower, so oddly pagan and brooding for a Christian temple, and since that time, all the Bacons who had died at home had been buried there.

How the town had prospered since was clearly visible to Roger from where he had paused in the early morning light just over the rim of the valley. The chessboard of orchards and pastures was sere and without motion in the cold of Autumn-Month, but from the clustered houses and shops south of the Yeo, there rose many slow-writhing lines of hazy white wood-smoke; and the bare trees of the churchyard could not conceal the elegance of St. Mary, with its new (no older than Roger!) horizontal building abutting the octagonal tower, which had piers formed of mouldings in stone at doors, windows and arcades. Ilchester was a borough of substance now: it even had bailiffs, though only as of last year.

What of substance now remained for Roger of Yeo Manse was the question. Ilchester itself did not, from this distance, look at all disturbed by the incursion of the King's justiciar, but that meant only that de Burgh's knights had not burned anything down – for which, of course, one should thank God, but not too hastily, for there were worse depredations possible which would still leave behind just so superficially peaceful a scene as this. The problem now was to skirt Yeo

Manse closely enough to assess how it had fared, and thence into Northover to find that inn called the Oxen by the serf Wulf (there were four or five inns by that name in Ilchester, at least two in Northover to Roger's knowledge) without being recognized for what he was by some soldier of Will of Howlake. To do so without being seen by some such man was out of the question, but Roger was reasonably sure he could pass any casual inspection – after all, his breeches and coarse surcoat were just like those of a thousand other young men from the anonymous poor, except that they were slightly less threadbare. Unless he was incautious in his curiosity about the manse, he would probably not be picked up at all; and even if he were seized and searched thoroughly enough to turn up the manuscript in his gear, he could feign to be a goliard – one of the many raggle-taggle vagabond scholars who, eager enough for learning but utterly impatient of university routines, wandered from teacher to teacher and monastery to monastery, themselves teaching or writing anew the text of one or another of the Miracle plays in return for their instruction and keep. He would get by with such a deception if he had to practise it. The danger did not lie there. It lay in the good possibility that someone in Northover, someone who belonged there, would recognize him under the eye of someone of Howlake or de Burgh, and speak too soon and too loudly.

He dug one heel into John Blund; the horse moved reluctantly, and just as reluctantly Roger gave it its head, for the side here, though only half as steep as a roof, offered no road – he had quitted that before topping the crest out of elementary caution – but instead slippery out-croppings of rock and moss, giving way farther down to a tumble of rubble, like a talus-slope at the foot of a cliff, full of incipient shifts and slides and glistening menacingly with frost. No man could presume to guide a horse over such ground, but instead, must let him put each of his four feet where he chose and as delicately as he could manage, until he showed himself willing to resume his gait.

And, in fact, to Roger's faint surprise, John Blund

managed the sliding course without even a serious stumble, though there was one rock-tumble moment when he seemed certain to break a foreleg, and probably to pash his own and Roger's brains out as well. It was over in half the time it would have taken to say a pater noster, however (and in actuality, it had doubtless taken no more than ten pulse-beats); and then the horse was clump-clumping across rimed brown grass in a complacent trot he had decided to undertake all on his own. Roger found himself grinning. A lifetime of intimacy with horses had convinced him that nothing else on four legs can be so stupid, but so frequently and humanly overwhelmed by its own good opinion of itself.

He had, as well, good reason to be pleased with himself, for as he resumed the reins, he found himself and John Blund crossing a frozen ditch into a broad ploughland which he recognized at once as bordering on the west vineyard of Yeo Manse. He could hardly have arrived at a safer quarter of the estate, this time of year, for, to begin with, it had always been the poorest cot in its *fisc*, secondly, the most remote from the seigniorial manse and hence from Will of Howlake, thirdly, the cot (if Roger's memory, dim here, could be trusted) of the serf Wulf (who could be presumed to be haunting some tavern in Northover to the detriment of his week work), and finally (though this, at least, could be laid to no foreplanning on Roger's part) today was obviously a boon-work day: for on the other side of the vineyards, where the little group of sod houses belonging to this and three other cots were huddled, Roger could see a group of small hunched figures assembling, most of them carrying axes, mattocks and adzes – a wood-cutting gang – and hear the shouts of a dean, one of Tom the steward's overseers, distant but clear. Shortly they would be moving off to give their one day's work out of the week at the big house; in fact, they were moving away from him already. Thinly over the motionless fields a hoarse baritone voice began bawling:

Bytuene Mershe and Averil
When spray biginneth to springe,

The lutel foul hath hire wyl
On hyre lud to synge. . . .

but the lyric, so plainly of spring and the gentry, came stiffly from amidst the rime-caked villein's beard on to the November air and began to fade:

Ich libbe in love-longinge
For semlokest of alle thynge,
He may me blisse bringe,
Icham in hire baundoun. . . .

and yet, just as the hewing party was almost gone entirely to Roger's sight, other voices, equally unmusical, began to float back the round:

An Hendy hap ichabbe yhent,
Ichot from hevene it is me sent,
From alle wymmen mi love is lent
Ant lyht on Alysoun! . . .
lyht on Alysoun! . . .
on Alysoun! . . .

Alysoun, said the Yeo Valley. *Alysoun . . . soun . . . soun. . . .*

Heaving his huge keg of a chest up and down, the horse blew solemnly between his thick mobile lips, and Roger, too, resumed breathing with a subdued start. What was left behind of the world was essence, without sound, motion or life, keeping its slight claim to be real in the rank order of the generation of forms only because it was – least close of all secondary qualities to the primary and real – still bitterly cold. In contemplation of these things as they always had been, it was impossible to believe that Yeo Manse had changed or could change in th'eternalie of the world. Though Heraclitus had never been able to put his foot twice into the same river, he had never been in any doubt about which was river and which was foot (one was cold, one got cold; but how in memory could he trust the order of these events, one being – secondary – used to judge the primary other?); everything changed, but only to remain more and more perfectly the same, like the River Meander which cut new banks and channels every year to maintain that clear, fixed, Platonic word of which the river in flux could never be more than a shadow.

But the shadowy solid horse beneath him, still sweaty after its delicate slide into the valley, trembled and reminded him that this was no ultimate Horse he was riding, he himself no Idea of Man, and Yeo Manse no shadow of some ultimate Estate; they all had names, and things with names pass away. He would have to give this horse-with-a-name (though it be John Blund, or just 'yon hay-bottle') a rub before very long or it would come down with the glanders – and though there might be some ultimate Glanders in Plato's cave, when one hitched it to a horse with a name, one had a sick horse, which was a good deal more serious in this world than any coupling of Sickness with Horseness; and the Heraclitean river – not the Yeo, but a much more drastic Meander – flowed in an underground torrent beneath Yeo Manse, too, as under all things else.

As that river flowed on inexorably, the morning grew older . . . it must be well after eight already . . . but for a while Roger found himself unable to move on, urgent though his errand was, and more urgent though the danger grew with each increment of delay. These ditch-guarded pasturelands deep in long brown grass, the vineyard surrounded with its fence woven on close-set stakes, the ploughlands lying humped and frozen in the heatless sunlight, the owl-haunted timber stands, the willow plantation where withies and barrel-hoops were cut, the palisaded orchards where every tree was a boy's lesson in climbing for the daylight and a well of sharp cider and perry for the evening meal; the voices of the serfs, the shapes of the hills, the blue bend of the sky over the wrinkling Yeo . . . these were all his home, now most strangely and heart-breakingly hostile in its absolute, changeless stillness. It had been with bitterness and defiance toward Robert, and an unbrookable, long-swelling passion to be free of Yeo Manse once and for all, that he had left this place to become a clerk, but never with any thought that it would itself reject him in its turn. No, Yeo Manse had borne the Bacons on its breast for centuries, and would always lie awaiting his return, should he deign to make it. . . .

His shadow, wedded to that of John Blund, slowly lost stature on the earth beneath him. His breast hollow with sullen, helpless loneliness, he turned the horse's head northward. There was nothing more to be learned here; it was all exactly as it had always been . . . except that it was suddenly an alien land.

We shall not all die, the self murmured; *but we shall all be changed.*

'Us be an old man, Meister,' Wulf said. 'Old and cleft a bit, as it mote be said, and most deaf and blind eke, as mote be said, and good for naught. But us remembered thee.'

Old the man was, without doubt nearly eighty, his hairs white, his teeth gone but for a few brown tusks, his skin the texture and colour of bad leather. Even across the splintery trestle table in the Oxen, he stank most markedly, a mixture of sod, sweat and a sour and precarious digestion; yet, curiously, his homespun was sturdy and almost clean, and his filthy ankles rose out of crude but strongly stitched slippers of hide so well and recently cured that the pointed toes still protruded straight ahead – in proud contrast to the points of Roger's own shoes, which tended to fold under the balls of his feet every third or fourth step.

'How didst thou know me?' Roger said, shifting his stone mug on the planking. 'And how canst thou lurk here away from the manse, morning as well as night? Inns are not for serfs, even such a one as this.'

The old man smiled dimly, as though recalling some exercise of craft half a century bygonnen. 'Us knew thee, Meister,' he said. The gnarled hand closed about a leather tankard but did not lift it. 'Us saw thee and followed thee when thou wert but a new lamb. Nay, a badger, thou wert, with a girt chest and shoulders, and always at digging and burying. Wold Wulf was proper crofter then with's boy to lead the oxen, twice as old as thou art and with boys of his own now, Meister; and us good for naught in these years, as mote be said, but for to hold the cot till us be called. Us be'ent missed now that oor son's a man grown and ploughs and has childer. Nay, wold Wulf may go where us will, as mote be said, and there's an end to it, Meister.'

Roger frowned, unable to press the question further, but remaining as puzzled as before. Of course the grandfather of a serf's family would not be missed from the work – he had understood that much of the mystery of the unremembered Wulf the moment he had been confronted by this snaggly sour-breathed ruin; but when his query to the suspicious host had flushed Wulf at last, the old man had been brought from the back of the inn, still wearing a nightcap in the midst of the day, so that it had been made most clear that he was living at the Oxen, which was impossible for a serf, though he be the grandsire of all the serfs that ever were.

The old man seemed to have forgotten that that question, too, had been asked him. He stared with his white-filmed blue eyes at the fire, over which a soup of some kind – from which a faint additional odour of hot mutton fat attested to the early kill at Yeo Manse, for under normal circumstances, no mutton could yet have reached so mean an inn as this – was seething in a huge black kettle hanging from an iron chain.

'Us were a sheep herd, then,' he said abruptly. 'Us took they sheep to the uplands for pasture, with Hob that was wold Wulf's dog that died afore thee'd remember him, Meister, and wold Wulf's boy that keeps the cot now to carry the hurdles. And Tom the steward, that was no older than Wulf's boy, he told us to mind thee when thee wandered, Meister, as wander thee did till us was blue out of breath. A-diggin' up and a-buryin' thee was, and in and out of rafters and trees—'

'Go thou to the point, old man,' Roger said, gripping the edge of the table fiercely with both hands. Yet he was sure that he already knew what the answer was to be. 'Why didst thou write to me? What hast thou for me?'

'Us shall show thee, Meister,' Wulf said with a secret smile. 'Us can't show thee here, but us has it all, fear thee not. Us took it all, and more. Us made proper fools of they King's men. Us took away thy diggings, and put thy buryings in they ilke holes.'

'*What dost thou mean?*'

'Nay, Meister, glare not so at wold Wulf,' the serf said, beginning to snivel. 'They was but bits of trash, as mote be said, like boys ud bury—'

Roger fought back his temper, as best he could. There would be no point in so alarming the old man that he became incoherent.

'Tell me what thou hast done,' he said, with a gentleness he was still far from feeling. 'And hew to it quickly and directly.'

'Aye, that be what us was doing, Meister, an thee'll let us. Meister Christopher that was thy father was a gentry-man, could read and cypher, and yonder King's men be gentry, too, as mote be said. Wold Wulf ud not want his hands snipped off for thieving – or drawn and quartered like a common traitor, they being King's men. Us thought better to leave summat in they holes, an they King's men find some writing of Meister Christopher to riddle where they holes be duggen. So us put matter into 'em from thy boy's holes, that thee made when thee was a-writing precious little, Meister Roger. All the rest us has here.'

The old man looked filmily at him with a mixture of hope and senile cunning, slightly tinged with reproach.

'All?' Roger said.

'Nay, not all, Meister,' Wulf said. 'Thee knows a poor serf's let into no inn free, nay, nor wears new shoes neither – us be not so blind us can still see thee a-looking at oor poor feet. But us be eating of naught but millet porridge and a mite of dredge-corn; thilke ale thee did buy us, and the first wold Wulf's tasted since us runned away. But all the rest, us has, Meister.'

'I thank God thou didst not run clean away,' Roger said grudgingly.

'Where ud us rinnen, Meister? Us be full of pain in the bones and good for naught, as mote be said. Here's a safe enough cozy for wold Wulf that's as near to his Maker as may be, and knew thee'd nowt but leave us silver penny to buy a herring with till us be called.'

'Show me what thou hast.'

'This way.' The old man got up stiffly and led the way toward the kitchen. On the other side, he admitted Roger into a narrow room so hot, airless and foul even in this weather that Roger could hardly drive himself further once the door was opened. The door itself was fastened with nothing but a staple.

'Thine host hath doubtless stolen it all in thine absence,' he muttered, trying to hold his breath and breathe at the same time.

'Nay, Meister,' Wulf said absently. 'He's wold Wulf's nephew-in-law – no slyer ever put green vitriol in vinegar, but won't steal from us till us be dead. Here, now—'

He rummaged in a heap of filthy straw while Roger accustomed his eyesight to the dimness. There was literally nothing else in the room but a low, broad three-legged stool and an anonymous heap of rags.

Then, grunting, the old man had hauled from the straw a purse of rawhide almost twice as big as his head. 'Here it be,' he said, setting it on the stool. 'Us saved it all for thee, Meister Roger.'

Roger pulled open the mouth of the bag and plunged a hand in, his fingers closing convulsively in the cold, liquid mass of coins. He carried the handful to the door, which he opened slightly to let in a little more light.

The coins were in little the hoard of well more than a lifetime. Anyone looking at them could have told at once that the Bacons were wool-sellers, for nearly every coin of commerce rested in Roger's fist: English pennies and ryalls, new and old shields of France (the old worth something in exchange if they were real, the new clipped even if genuine), the golden Lewe of France, the Hettinus groat of Westphalia (debased), the Limburg groat (debased), the Milan groat (debased), the Nimueguen groat (debased), the gulden of Gueldres (much debased), the postlates, davids, florins and falewes of the bishoprics of half of latin Christendom (debased beyond all reason). Obviously Wulf's host (and nephew) had much depleted the real value of the hoard by taking from the serf nothing but English money, but this handful of dubious riches could not be blamed on Wulf and the innkeeper alone: Christopher Bacon should have had better sense than to bury foreign coins, or for that matter, to have taken them in payment from William Busshe or anyone else. Probably he had never had any reason to suspect even the existence of the intricacies of foreign exchange, being naught but a farmer all his life long; to him these clipped and adulterated coins with their exotic designs and legends must have seemed mysteriously more valuable than the mere pennies paid him year after year by his tenants – why else would he have gone to the trouble of burying them?

Yet Roger was little inclined to absolve his father for that, let alone Wulf and his nephew. What he held in his hand was all that remained of his patrimony – that and the rest of the trash in the purse – and though it would be impossible to judge what it all amounted to until he had a chance to count it through somewhere in safety, it was clearly far from any sum sufficient for his needs. And for this, this ignorant, smelly old man had buried Roger's rhombs and his glass and his time-costly measuring tools for the discovery of a pack of raiders!

He swung away from the door in a fury of frustration and hurled the coins at the wall. Wulf dodged clumsily away from the sudden motion, but in a moment he was standing again as straight as his old man's back could stiffen.

'Thee must be more quiet, Meister,' he said. 'Else thee will properly lose all.'

'Thinkest thou I have aught to lose, old man?' Roger said between his teeth. He strode to the stool and jerked the drawstring of the purse tight savagely. 'Nevertheless, I thank thee for thy cunning, stupid drudge though thou be'st. Dost think Will of Howlake will never hear of thee, dwelling here like a freeman after eight decades as a serf? Thinkest thou he'll not dispatch his men to seek thee out, and ask thee whence thy sudden riches came? Thou shouldst have run till thy bones broke with thy weight, wold Wulf; for traitor they will adjudge thee, and draw out thy bowels, and pull the rest of thy corse asunder 'twixt four horses!'

'Aye, us thought it mote be so,' Wulf said, 'And thee wilt leave us nothing, Meister, but they orts there that thee flung away?'

Roger opened the door and turned back to stare at the serf for the last time. 'Certes, I'll leave thee more,' he said savagely. 'Dig thou for that boy's trash that thou stol'st, and give that to thy nephew-in-law for thy meat!'

But the old man no longer seemed to be listening, as though he had known what the answer must be. He was on his knees, patiently picking over the filthy straw for the discarded, debased, fugitively glittering coins.

It had been no part of Roger's intention to strike out for Oxford again without so much as a night's rest, nor with the same horse, either, but the dead weight of the knobby purse impelled him to triple caution; now, surely he dared not risk search, let alone recognition. He risked only a long meal for himself and John Blund and then struck out during the afternoon sleep, not daring to hurry while he was still anywhere in the valley, but thereafter driving the horse at a merciless gallop until it began to sob and heave.

In a small, forest-bordered meadow, which did not look tended enough to belong to any farm, he dismounted and tethered the horse after watering it from a tiny stream, little more than a runnel. Here he risked a fitful nap, standing with his back against a tree and with his hand on his sword. He had intended no more than an hour, but somehow he fell asleep even in this position and dreamed that a ring of bowmen with the heads of foxes had tied him there and were stuffing eleven pounds three and a half shillings Fleming into his mouth one red-hot penny at a time.

He awoke with a start which nearly toppled him – for his knees, which had bent somewhat, ached horribly, and he was stiff throughout his body with cold – to find the sun almost touching the hills to the south-west, and someone on horseback sitting above him hardly more than ten paces away.

He had the sword only half out, with a creakingly ugly motion which would not have been fast enough to discourage a boy with a quarter-staff, when the fox-head dissolved back into the nullity of dream and he saw that, in fact, the rider was a girl. Furthermore she was smirking at him with an infuriating disrespect.

'Well then,' she said, 'tha be well overtook, by Goddes bones. Art going to run a poor maid clean through the butter-milk? Tha'll first needs be friendlier with thy girt feet, boy.'

Roger ground his teeth in exasperation and forced his aching muscles to pull him into a more human stance. He looked about for John Blund and found him, munching brittle grass with his eyes half closed, which made him look at once maidenly and vacuous – an expression which, for some reason, infuriated Roger all the more.

'And who beest thou, lip-kin?' he said, glaring up at the girl. She was, he saw now, probably about fifteen: a good, bouncing year for a peasant girl, though she did not talk quite like a serf's daughter, despite her West Midlands dialect. The horse, a small sturdy cob, was not any serf's draft animal either. Her hair was cut short – which was good sense for peasant girls looking to provide as few handholds for rapists as possible – but the stray curls of it that came out from under her black woollen wimple were little flames of dull gold. He felt his glare dimming a little, entirely against his intention.

'Tha can call me Tibb, an I let thee,' she said. 'Tha'lt better clamber on thy bulgy-eyed dray there, afore some coney kicks tha in thy ribs. An tha'rt faring somewheres, at least I know the roads.'

This sounded like the best advice, unpalatably though

the spoon was being proffered. He picked his way cautiously to John Blund and untied him from his stump.

'Whither farest thou, then?'

'Nowheres that tha'd know, by the looks of tha,' she said, swinging her own horse around. 'I'm to my uncle's inn, with whey and buttermilk – didst think I was jesting? Well, certes I was then – from Northover parish. An tha hast money, tha canst find lodging there; otherwise, tha'lt find it a cold night outside our very door.'

'Thou dost not sound so cold in the heart,' Roger said.

'Softly there, boy. I've a needle in my girdle, shouldst tha need stitching.' She looked back at him, still smiling. 'Tha canst not draw before me; that tha's shown every owlet in Rowan Wood already.'

'I molest no one,' Roger said stiffly, 'ne childer nor animals.'

'There's a light oath,' Tibb said. 'Naytheless, ride closer then, and work the cement out of thy sword-elbow. I was fond to stop for thee, this is a bad hour; canst tha strike if we be beset?'

'Fast enough,' Roger said. 'No man becomes a master by his wits alone.'

This outrageous lie passed between his teeth before he was quite aware of it; yet he was disinclined to correct it. The day, in particular, and the journey, in general, had cast a false air around everything, and around his own bitterness, a tatterdemalion motley.

'I guessed tha clad too fair to be but clerk,' Tibb said. They were riding abreast now. 'Art tha a Grey Friar?'

'Nay, that's to come, an God willeth.' Was that the indirigible self again? He had never thought of such a thing before. But what else could have spoken this? It was hardly possible that any mood inspired by a dirty blonde peasant girl should suggest his becoming a mendicant.

'What dost tha teach?'

The lie was becoming exceedingly complicated, but it was too old now to bury. 'Logic,' he said. 'Have we a long ride further?'

'Nay, not in full day. But these shadows are mischancy; 'ware sink-holes.' Almost on the word, the cob stumbled and righted itself with a muted nicker of alarm, and Roger grasped the girl's hand.

''Twas nothing,' Tibb said; but she made no move to free herself. They rode side by side for a silent while. The sun was almost gone, though the sky was still half bright.

'Tha'rt a strange twosome, as crossed as herring-bones,' Tibb said. 'A ninny scholar, a sleepy swordsman, a well-clad clerk. And a boy man.'

'I am indebted to thee,' Roger said shortly. 'Mock on.'

'I may, an it pleaseth me. Ah, go up!'

The sharp change in her voice made Roger sit bolt upright in the saddle.

'Here – what's amiss?'

'I shan't tell tha. Yes, I shall, it'll give tha thy turn for mockery. My garter's fallen untied, ne more, and I'll lose it ere we see home.'

Roger looked away at the deepening twilight until he got his breath back. 'Small ills, small remedies,' he said. 'I'll take it up for thee.'

'Not here,' Tibb said tranquilly. 'The Plain's just ahead. I'd not see myself surprised out of these gullies – there are knives abroad here. Tha shouldst know that much.'

She was not content until they were on the flat top of a rise some five minutes' ride on to the Plain, and it was almost dark. Then, without a word, she slid rather ungracefully off the cob and sat down on the hard earth.

She was most matter of fact in allowing her garter to be tied; and in allowing him to find deeper in her skirt a fold which needed some stitching beyond the repair of any needle she might have had with her (nor did he detect any such bodkin as she had threatened him with; only a button which gave but would never fasten). By the time all the repairs were made – it was far from the first time she had employed such a tailor, that was plain – the night was pitch black and Roger was as sweating cold as he had ever been in his life.

Tibb tucked one leg under the other and stood up, helping

him to his feet. 'Tha'rt a wolf cub,' she said. 'A fierce beginner. Tha hadst best kiss me afore I kick thee.'

He took her around the waist, which was surprisingly small for so broad a belly and bosom, and kissed her, but this only made her laugh. 'I thank thee,' she said. 'Let's mount; there's still another ride to take.'

He groped his way on to John Blund and followed the sound of the cob's hooves, not sure whether to be alarmed or assuaged, and too sleepy to be sure he should care.

'Thou'rt no beginner, Tibb,' he said. 'Thou'st churned thy buttermilk to whey before this nightfall.'

'Tha'rt being over-nice for a lover,' Tibb's voice drifted back to him. 'Tha meanest maidenhead, tha shouldst say so. 'Twas only a trouble to me in the bed; waxed cold, waxed hot; and in smalwe stead it stood me. That which will away is very hard to hold.'

And then, eerily in the cold night, she began to sing in a piping, clear, sweetly tuneful voice:

> '*Ye mayds, ye wyfs and witwes*
> *That doe now her my Songe*
> *Doth younge man put kyndnesse*
> *Pray tak it short ne lange*
> *Fer theyr be nat sich comfortal*
> *Lyk lainnage wyth a Man*
> *To cum Downe a downe,*
> *To cum Downe,*
> *Down a down a.*'

The plaintive song died echolessly; and after a while, a tiny spark of light rose from behind an invisible hill some inch or miles ahead.

'There, 'tis home. Ready thy purse, sweet goliard.'

He heeled the exhausted horse forward and caught her about the waist.

'Sweet Tibb, I was too soon for thee—'

'Nay, boy. Go up. Get thyself a bed. Mayhap I'll come to thee. Go now.'

'Thine oath, Tibb?'

'No oath from me – ne to no man without bed to raise horn in. Go up, and then I'll think more on it.'

'Thou art an ungrateful whore.'

'Tha'rt a foraging pinchpenny. And I love thee. Let me, now. Go put thy bone to bed and mayhap I'll cast thy dice for thee once more – ne more will I promise. Be off, coney-snare.'

Grumbling, he helped her to dismount, and took both horses around to the back, where a mute and scrofulous dwarf, apparently recognizing Tibb's cob, took them both without demur and began to unload the cob of its leather bottles. The inn struck him no less grimly than the mute; mostly without light and full of sprawling men who watched Roger, scratching in their patches, from under brows as dense as thorn-bushes, while Tibb's uncle bit with an appalling yellow canine into the Philippe d'or Roger proffered for his pallet.

Tibb came back to him some time before dawn, but she had company. No sooner had she thrown her leg over him and welcomed him home than the room was full of creeping bravoes. She fought hard to hold him down when he snatched up his sword, but evidently she had under-valued his devotion to the purse: he shucked her with one great seizure of his back-muscles; and when she sprang to block the door while they slashed at the rest of the blackness toward him, he spilled her decoy's ouns into her polluted shift with a single cut and escaped into the morning over her, the purse slung over his shoulder and pounding against his spine, as he ran for the stables and John Blund.

III: BEAUMONT

It fell by the stars that, early in 1233, the Henry called Winchester who was Henry the Third, eldest son by Isabella of Angoulême of that murderous, incompetent and yet princely-hearted usurper King John, moved his royal person and his court into his father's birthplace, for the hunting; which was published abroad. This place was Beaumont Palace, without the earthenworks and timber of the north wall of Oxford town, overlooking Osney and Port Meadow. There were boars and stags in the King's woods there, but more was intended than hunting. Beaumont was but four years seized back by Hubert de Burgh from a traitor to the French – one whose large bones had been burned, and his knuckles, spine, fingers and toes scattered like dice, every last die unshriven for the Resurrection.

It was by this proximity to Oxford that Adam Marsh – in default of Robert Grosseteste, who was in retirement in service of his God and naught else – was found at Beaumont with many others of church, university and town on the night of the King's third coming of age, that being the feast of St. John; and having the skill to speak Romance of both the Norman and the Iberian kind, was taken up into a history totally undesired by him; as follows:

That Henry III was of age could hardly be doubted, he being now twenty-nine years old and having been declared of age twice before: first by Pope Honorius III in 1223, at the instigation of Hubert de Burgh, to justify the resumption of all the castles, sheriffdoms and demesnes granted since Henry's accession; and again in 1227, when Hubert himself declared the King of age – as by then he had become enpowered to do, having gradually married his way, one marriage after another to the number of four, to the tacit mastery of the regency left vacant by the death of William Earl-Marshal of Pembroke in 1219. That everyone sufficiently understood the lesson had been well enough attested by the sudden self-exile of Peter des Roches, the Poitevin Bishop of Winchester, Henry's tutor and Hubert's most bitter enemy. Should anyone be so blind as to miss the import, however, Henry was pleased to allow Hubert his homage for the title of Earl of Kent.

Ask for this hero now and find him justiciar of Ireland, the meanest royal grant in all Christendom; for tonight Henry, pale as whey and speaking out of the side of his narrow mouth so quietly as to terrify the most loyal and most noble subject of the crown, was celebrating with wine and flesh his third coming of age, the repudiation of Hubert de Burgh. The great soldier who had refused King John the blinding of the captive Arthur of Brittany, and yet had stood fast by John when some other hand of John threw that young owner of John's crown into the Seine; who had adhered to John even after the barons had enforced on the King the Great Charter; the admiral who had sunk Eustace the Monk and all his pirates' fleet in the straits and thus cut off Dauphin Louis' last hope of holding any part of England; and scourge of all earls who would take from the King's hand what was divinely and rightfully the King's – that great soldier and administrator was tonight to be cast down.

Nothing of this was apparent to Roger, who was too surprised to find himself Adam's familiar (chosen, Roger supposed shrewdly, to express Adam's forbidden rebellion against so worldly a commission – and because Roger could not only speak fair French, but also, being recently come into more than two thousand pounds, could clothe himself for such a function) and too confused by the rebounding noise, the flare and smoke of the torches, and the press and stink of so many elegants and their scarcely less elegant cup-bearers in Beaumont's great hall. Even the dogs, of which there were a great many, seemed surer of foot and favour in this roaring cave than Roger was; he recognized no one but the King himself, and the King only by his expression – that half-lidded, pale, incontinent cast of the young man to whom alone is given the power to slay any person on whom he looks, and needs only to be jostled in the press to put that power to the proof.

Adam, however, was not so easily confused. 'Stay close,' he said at once to Roger in his smooth Frankish. 'Here's a fine display of Latins; there's des Roches back – and there's his nephew, Peter des Rievaux; and there's Simon IV's son of Montfort. . . . There's Poitevins wherever you look; a fair *auto da fe* on Hubert! Would God we'd kept home.'

He darted suddenly sidewise into the milling army of courtiers and servants; Roger, concerned to begin the evening, at the very least, with obedience to Adam's command to 'stay close', was nearly brained by a boar's head on a vast dish of pewter which came sculling between himself and the Franciscan as he tried to follow. When he caught up with Adam again, he was earnestly in conversation with that hawk-beautiful young Frenchman he had just previously identified as Simon de Montfort.

'I think my suit goes well enough, I thank God,' Simon was saying. 'It's no easy matter to find one's self an alien in a land one has always thought of as one's own; but this is a time of overturns. In the meantime, four hundred marks a year is what the King hath settled on me, and four hundred marks is perforce what I must suffer.'

'No news of Amaury?'

'Ah, there's the heart of it,' Simon said ruefully. 'He's constable of France now; why should he want an earldom, too? Yet, well I know that it is not Leicester itself he covets, but only for that brotherly rivalry we bore each other from the cradle – there's the scar for it, and he hath a like. Were Amaury to give place, I'm the next surviving, and should do homage for the honour of my father's shire instant upon the news.' He smiled suddenly. 'And, certes, also upon the look in the King's eye, to manœuvre for the weather-gage.'

He turned his head suddenly toward Roger, his smile still present but no longer ironic, like a man who hopes for but knows better than to expect a pleasure. 'And who's this, Adam? I've not seen him before, I know.'

'True,' Adam said. 'He's called Roger Bacon, of a franklin's family in Ilchester; a scholar with us. The Bacons suffered somewhat at Hubert's hands, yet not so much as they might have, it appears.'

'Grow thou in learning,' Simon said in English, searching Roger's face with alarmingly penetrating eyes. Then, in French again: 'Yes – what think you of these proceedings, most Christian Adam? I doubt not that our Hubert's been extortionate, else how would any armed man hold troops together? Territory's to be lived on, and to be just with later, if time permit; and Hubert's an old soldier, thereby rich, in the natural order of things. Is the Crown so poor it must bite coins out of its own swords?' He gestured at the pack around them. 'It has not that appearance – though I speak from four hundred marks' pension, as I grant.'

'And from overlong from these shores as well, I fear me,' Adam said. 'The docket is far more grave than that, and far graver the exactions for it. Last year, a huge pack of robbers took from the granaries the harvested corn of the Roman clergy, throughout most of England. The corn was sold and the money vanished – much, it appears, as largesse to the poor. It's said this was more of Robin of Sherwood's doings; the harpers will not let that poor highwayman rest at his crossroads. But your friend Bishop Peter of Winchester—'

'Not so,' Simon said, in a voice so quiet that only Adam and Roger could have heard his words. 'Pray exercise better taste in friends in my behalf, Adam.'

'I'm glad to hear you say so. Nevertheless, Peter des Roches alleged to have captured certain of the robbers, and made them to confess that they had warrants from Hubert, and from the King, too, given them from Hubert's own hand. Witnesses there were none, but at the end of July, Henry dismissed Hubert in favour of Stephen de Segrave – and then came this enormous letter in charges and demands: that Hubert account for the estates of Pembroke and Strigul—'

'Then the second earl is now dead as well?'

'Yes, two years ago; there's another Marshal, Richard,

but not of age yet. Also, Hubert was to account for all liberties, losses, taxes of the fifteenth and sixteenth part, castles and preserves withheld and restored – I cannot begin to summarize it. Following these, charges of treason, of conspiring the people to riot against the Latin emissaries of His Holiness, of seeking to become such a hero in the sight of the mob as Robin Wood was against King John, and more, and still more; so that Hubert fled his kinsmen in Ireland and took refuge in sanctuary at Bury St. Edmunds. Whence, however, the King had him dragged, naked.'

'Ah no. Can there be more? This to Hubert? Would God allow?'

'God thinks continually on all our sins, and waits,' Adam said sombrely. 'And there's little more. They essayed to fetter him, but some common smith refused, saying he would put no irons on the man who restored England to the English – with your pardon, Simon. Hence, they closed Hubert in the Tower, till Bishop Robin of London heard how sanctuary had been breached, and as good as ordered the King to return him to Bury St. Edmunds. Where he is now; and that is all.'

'I'd credit it from none but you,' Simon said. 'Had he no defences?'

'One bad, one worse. He would have it that a charter from King John exempted him in perpetuity from any examination of his accounts – which means only that he was guilty of embezzlement, the privilege all soldiers claim, my lord, as I have just heard it from your lips. Upon this, Peter des Roches, of course, ruled that the charter died with King John – and then, by ill luck, Henry asked Hubert to produce revenues from a place called Yeo Manse, that was this my familiar's property till Hubert took it; and there were none at all – not a groat, nor a broken brass penny for the Crown; a singular accident, but had it not come thus about, the King would have found something as suitable; Henry means to crush Hubert entire.'

'I heard,' Simon said thoughtfully, 'that the King near stabbed him at Portsmouth four years ago – solely for want of ships to send against the French provinces.'

'That is true,' Adam said. 'I was there. Henry was mad as wolves.'

'Well,' Simon said. 'I must think on this. Pray for me, most Christian Adam, for I need this King.'

'Certes, and he needs you. Only keep my counsel—'

'That I'll not swear, for you know I shall.' Simon bowed briefly to the stunned Roger and vanished into the crowd with a grace not even Adam could have equalled.

'Is it true—' Roger began, inadvertently in English.

' 'Tis true entire – and forget thou every word. Thy bag of coins is Henry's, should he or any of his o'erhear thee. And speak no more English, or thou'lt be taken as a spy of Hubert's, aye, and so shall I.'

'But this de Montfort—'

'Trust him; and hush, thou'rt being far too far a plauderer for the role I cast thee in. I brought thee here to listen; listen thou!'

'Yes,' Roger said, 'but, Adam—'

Adam ducked his head in a brief nod of satisfaction and began to worm his way through the gathering once more. He had only just disappeared again, however, when a blast of sackbuts and clarions froze the whole small cave world upon the instant. King Henry, having finished with feasting, was ready to begin those ceremonies by which, could he but keep his head sufficiently cool, he would complete the severance of his right arm.

Knowing well enough what course the King's evenings of state took by ordinary, and how to clock them by the clepsydra of the wine in Henry's glass, Adam Marsh escaped by first intention the theatre of this proposed amputation before the heralds of it had properly tautened their lips against their instruments. This he did with some misgivings, especially on behalf of Roger Bacon left behind in the flickering underwater darkness of the feast-hall among many fish all strange to him, and not a few dangerous, too; but Adam was impelled, for he had already spied escaping before him with her ladies the King's sister, Eleanor of Pembroke, whose confessor he was, and whom he followed forthwith in the utmost disquiet.

He knew well enough where to find the Lady Eleanor where else she might have gone in drafty Beaumont; but once out of the hall he did not hurry, walking instead as gravely as he might in his youth through the barrel-vaulted corridors with their smoke-blackened hangings, appearing not to notice the gleam of the occasional torches against the chain-mail of the King's sentries standing in their niches like statues of saints militant. It was his duty not to alarm his penitent – she who had so much to alarm her already, though but barely turned twenty-four: not only sister of this royally incontinent King, but widow scarce two years of the son of William earl-Marshal of the realm, once holder of those Pembroke estates (which she could never convey) for the stewardship of which Hubert de Burgh had failed to account. Small marvel that she had found herself unable to stand placidly at her brother's side while he trumpeted wrath on the beloved stern guardian of her bridal fief, the green pleasaunces of which – now nothing to Henry but money, and the heady possibility of blood – encompassed as well all the garden-ensorcelled girlhood she would ever be able to remember.

Adam was not challenged as he crossed into Eleanor's apartments in the left wing of the castle, but he was recognized quickly and embarrassingly by her tiring-maid, a fresh girl of eighteen attached to Eleanor's service as a courtesy by the Bigods, her dead husband's claiming relatives; a girl all too plainly bemused enough by Adam to see in him her Peter Abelard, and herself an Héloïse; but Eleanor was not there. She would, therefore, be in the chapel which her brother had made for her, which was at some distance from the apartments; but there was a passage that Adam knew of, which perhaps King John had known but Henry did not, which led quite directly to the priest's hole in the chapel from nearby, through the walls. It had been Eleanor who had shown it to him, for it debouched into her most private chamber, disguised as the monstrous black oak door of a wardrobe; and he took the route at once, shutting his Héloïse manquée out first (and not without a shudder) with, 'I will wait here.'

She was waiting for him as he settled into the stone-cold niche. Though the chapel was dark except for two tapers burning before the altar, that was enough to figure for him the marvellous bent head in profile through the confessional window – once, no doubt, a full door to be used in passage to whispers and confessions in composition, not absolution, of sin. *Dona nobis pacem*, Héloïse-and-Abelard. . . .

'Father . . . I was waiting. You said . . . ?'

'I was catching my breath, my lady. It's a long clamber here. And we'll needs be quick; I've a scholar above, promising, but too green in the vintage to leave abroad among so many Latins; and thy brother will call on me ere this work of his be done. And very ill it is, too.'

'Certes, but rest thee a moment, Father, all the same,' she said in a low voice – hardly more than a whisper but for the music in it. 'Please, my need is greater. I'm afraid, I am most afraid.'

He saw her head turn toward him with this, and even in the two-starred darkness, he was momentarily riven of all his good advice by such fairness, less than half seen though it was. Judging both by images and by such members of the line as Adam had seen, the Plantagenets had always been notable for personal beauty – at least from Cœur-de-lion on – but Eleanor, of the high brow and wide green eyes, was to Adam that trial of his vocation which is greater than all the trials to which the princes of the world are subject, since to them it need be no trial at all.

'You have more reason to fear in this cubby than you would in the hall,' he said. 'In seclusion, you appear most pointedly to be taking Hubert's part. Your brother will be all the less likely to privilege you at Pembroke if you so humiliate him – as all will see it, not just the King.'

'Then, shall I stay and weep in their very faces, while they cast my uncle down? I have infuriated Henry with far smaller shows.'

'But that's a woman's role,' Adam said patiently. 'To weep shows the kindness in your heart, even toward a miscreant. But to be absent – that might mean complicity. Besides, my lady, Henry's mind will dwell not long on Hubert now, for he'll find matters far more quick to spark his tinder than your uncle is, before this feast is over. Therefore, I pray you, be present at the Hubert part, so's not to be marked partisan while that runs its course; and should you weep, it will yet be forgotten when Henry weeps, as he's sure to do, aye, and gnash teeth, too.'

'You choose odd words to calm me, Father,' she said; but there was a slight trace of amusement in her voice. 'Must you be so ominous?'

'By no means, my lady. That was not my purport. I mean only that the defiance of the barons is a greater thing to the King than his sudden hatred of Hubert, and will so seem to him when he thinks on it a little further. And if you follow me, my lady, your brother's every outcry against these rebel earls may yet be a golden note in the ladders of your ears, and of your fortunes, too; for there's one with us in Beaumont tonight who cannot but rise in the pan as the barons go down – and would, I doubt not, count it his deepest desire to bear you with him.'

She laughed suddenly in the dark chapel, setting echoes afire. 'Father, how secular the errands that you scurry on! Has this unknown sent you with this Cupid's message? Or hope you to be my brother's Vulcan, to catch the unknown and Eleanor in the same net?'

'Neither, my lady,' Adam said, his throat a little thickened. 'I come on my own recognisance; and depart the same as I came in.'

'Swef, swef, douce Pere. I was mocking. I know not how I'd have lived without you since my noble lord went thither. I will go now, borne on as much as bearing your advice. Bless me.'

He did so; and with a rustle, she was gone, leaving him

staring at the two far-away candles, now guttering so low that the images in the chapel no longer seemed to have any heads, and nothing was left of the Christ above the altar but two feet and a nail. Still he waited, until she should have time to pass around her apartment by the long route and resume her place near her brother's chair. As he waited, he slowly turned cold again, and one of the tapers burned blue and went out.

Thanks to this necessary wait, even the short route back through the walls and the wardrobe did not bring him back to the hall until much of the fury there had worn itself thin. He arrived only just in time to hear, but too late to prevent, Roger Bacon giving advice to the King.

Which had been no intention of Roger's, ne as he would have seen it earlier even the part of sanity; nor could he have said afterwards which of many small steps might have taken him otherwhere than to that brink, however he might have turned (but did not turn) each one. The hubbub after the sennets died soon under the King's ophidian eyes. In the smoky silence the white-faced Henry curled his hands around the lion-paws of his chair and said:

'Sound again for my servant Hubert de Burgh.'

The heralds lifted their pennoned instruments and sounded, the hoarse Plantagenet battle-view halloo which, the singers said, had been Blondel's first notes to Cœur-de-Lion imprisoned: but nothing happened. The dark hall became deathly quiet. A white-lipped look from Henry set the heralds to sounding once more, and then again, but no one appeared, no one even stirred. At long last, Peter des Roches leaned in his rich bishop's brocade to the King's ear, his ringed fingers shielding his mouth. Henry, very pale, listened without expression, and finally nodded once, sitting back in his chair.

'I have treason all about me, gentleman and ladies,' the King said quietly. 'My justiciar that was answers me not, and no one stands forth in his stead. My barons and my earls that I called to this feast are not here. They say they fear treachery, that sit in their fastnesses and treason plot against their King.'

He snatched up his goblet suddenly and drank with a kind of desperate greediness quite unrelated to thirst. Then the goblet hit the table with a noise like the fall of a hammer, and Henry's eyes were roving over his audience like the eyes of an executioner.

'Where are my earls, where are the barons of England?' he said hoarsely. 'Let us have passed here a decree which will tell them who is their King. Here we have a sufficient gathering of nobles, as the Great Charter insists. Give me that order – an order to compel, by England and St. George.'

He swung on the Bishop.

'Be better advised, an it please you, my lord King,' Peter des Roches said softly, folding his plump white hands together. 'These barons have defied you already, and by special messengers. No new demand will win aught more for the Crown. Seek to summon them instead; sound for them, as you sounded for Hubert de Burgh, and prove will they respond.'

'There's none of them here to hear,' Henry said. 'Why sound sennets to absent ears? They fear me, and that's the end of it. I want an instrument that brings obedience, not a noise that won't be heard outside Beaumont.'

His eyes lit on Simon de Montfort. 'Montfort, what say you? Is the throne of England to woo those rebels back with music? Or shall we have our decree as we have demanded it? Advise me; I am weary of these counsels of caution from all these mitred heads.'

'Sound, my lord King,' Simon said. 'Indeed, sound thrice, for the hearing of these the barons' messengers. And let them bear back your summons. If your nobles fail to answer your triple summons, they will be as little likely to honour a decree passed for you by the Frenchmen they hate and mistrust.'

'Guard thy tongue, Montfort. Thou'rt in my court by sufferance. If your next word is in praise of Hubert—'

'And so it would have been, my lord King,' Simon said

steadily from his place below the Bishop. 'The barons trust Hubert; they do not trust me. They do not know even who I am. Nor do they trust any Poitevin.'

'You bewray your suit for Leicester, Montfort—'

'You asked me to speak, my lord King,' Simon said. 'Had I told you only what you wished to hear, I'd better been silent. If that only's what you will from me, then away Leicester; I'll not so traduce my Crown to win a fief, nay, not now nor ever; my head's thy forfeit for it, my lord King – today, tomorrow, forever.'

'Stop, that's more promise than I've asked thee for,' the King said. 'Press me not so closely, Montfort; when I want your head, I'll ask it. Why can nobody advise me without throwing his life at me? When did I ever ask that for the price of oats? Witness all here that I am not, not, not my bloody father!'

No one answered. Henry calmed himself with a deep draught of the green wine. Then he began looking through the press again, his shoulders hunched; but was distracted by the return to his table of the lady who had been pointed out to Roger as the King's sister, with several of her household. The King stared at her, frowning, and looking for a moment a little confused, and then back at the lower tables.

'Is there no one here to profess the word of God?' the King said, beginning suddenly to smile. 'Who reads for England at the King's feast? Where is the Church in this my hour of extremity? A word, a word! Where are my Oxford scholars? Where's the great Grosseteste? Where is my sister's confessor; where's that subtle boy Adam de Marisco?' He was standing now, his hand rolling back and forth on its knuckles on the table before him, like a battering-ball encrusted with jewels.

And then he saw Roger. 'Now there's one,' he said. 'Rise, scholar of Oxenford, and profess the word of God. Read to your King, as you were summoned to do. Your head is safe; I swear, I am not blood-thirsty. Rise, and rede me.'

Everyone turned to look. There was no way out. Roger

rose, his shanks as shaky as reeds.

'Good, he rises,' the King said. 'Now speak. What says my English church? Has it anything to say to me? Speak.'

'My lord King,' Roger said.

'I hear you, friar. Say on.'

'My lord King . . . I am not in orders. I am only a poor student.'

'Speak,' Henry said. 'Advise me.'

'My lord King. . . . Then I will ask you: What is most dangerous to sailors? What fear they most?'

'A riddle?' Henry the Sailor said, smiling. 'Very well. I know not. Those whose business is on the wide waters know best, not I. What's the answer, sweet scholar?'

'My lord King, I will tell thee,' Roger said. 'The answer is: Stones and rocks.'

The King frowned. 'Oh? Dost thou make game of thy King, friar? Or. . . . Aha *Petrae et rupes!* Your Grace, he means you; what think you of that? Shall I then be quit of you again?'

It was plain that Henry was joking, after his fashion, but Peter des Roches, who obviously had read Roger's meaning instantly and had been staring at the tonsured clerk like a man attempting to memorize a text, could manage only a rather grim smile. The moment the Bishop's gaze turned, Roger sat down.

'Henry is King,' the Bishop said, 'and will do what he will do. Meanwhiles, my lord, I judge Montfort's words not ill advice.'

'What Satan's imp made thee say that?' Adam Marsh's voice hissed suddenly in Roger's ear, making him jump in his chair. 'Dost not know Henry's calling "the Sailor" only on de Burgh's account, since the sinking of Eustace in the straits?'

'He called on me,' Roger said sullenly. 'He called you first, and you not here to hear it.'

'Couldst not praise piety, or say aught else equally harmless? The giving of advice to this King is a career likely to end suddenly.'

'Then example me, Adam,' Roger said, a little grimly. 'He's looking at thee now.'

'What say you, Marisco?' Henry said. 'Reserve not thy wisdom for women and clerks. Shall we follow Montfort in this?'

'My lord King,' Adam said steadily, 'I was not here when Montfort spoke, and know not the import of his proposal. But well I know him to be wiser for his years than was even his father; I can say no more to the point.'

'And enough!' Henry said. 'Conspiracies within conspiracies! Nevertheless, we will be governed once more, and only once more. Segrave, your Grace, Montfort, Rievaux, let it be heard that we summon the barons of England thrice, to see whether they will come or no. They are called to attend us at Westminister – we will set them July eleventh, that no man may say he has failed to receive our letters. There we will fairly hear their suits, and fairly consult with them on their problems. What think ye, my lords?'

'That is kingly done,' Peter des Roches said; but he seemed a little uneasy, and Roger, regarding him covertly, was reminded that John Blund – the man, not the horse – had been raised this year and cast down as Archbishop of Canterbury in a single six-month.

But that was no concern of his.

IV: WESTMINSTER

How to live to very old, Roger wrote scratchily with the goose quill, *and enjoy it.* At this point a lump in the ink blocked the quill and he had to stop to clear it; but that done, he was able to sand his title and regard it critically.

He did not like it. It promised too much, especially from the pen of a man in his early twenties; and never mind that that was at Providence's gate, whence had come the commission. Better to say: how to postpone the accidents of age, and preserve the senses. No, still better to omit 'how'; say, *Liber de retardatione accidentium senectutis, et de sensibus conservandis.* That needed nothing more than a dedication; he dipped the quill and added, *ad suasionem duorum sapientum, scilicet Johannis Castellionati et Phillipi cancellarii Parisiensis.*

Nobody would be likely to question that since it was perfectly true – and yet, he was as instantly stabbed by the conviction that it was not true in the eyes of Veritie. Philip the Chancellor had invited somebody of Oxford to write a work on the postponing of old age, and with the suggestion that, were it to prove worthy, it might be sent to the Pope; but 'somebody' was not the same as 'Roger Bacon'. The assignment of the task to Roger had been wholly the doing of Grosseteste.

The pinprick of this thought brought with it again the desolate realization of how much had changed in Roger's world, as it had in the world at large, since that moment of incredulous triumph five years ago when he had counted over the gold and the trash in Wulf's bag in this very room, laboriously allowed for the rates of exchange on every piece and found himself the possessor of close to two thousand pounds; and the realization, too, that the decision the changes were forcing on him could not be delayed much longer.

He had told no one of the sum he had recovered, not even Adam; word of that kind travelled too swiftly, and he had been grimly determined to hold every coin until the moment when circumstances absolutely forced it out of his grasp. Adam, to be sure, knew the general outcome, but he did not press Roger for details once he had satisfied himself that Roger was no longer in any danger and could, when Adam needed him, make himself presentable at court. What Grosseteste knew or thought about the matter was unknown to Roger, and now doubtless would always remain so. The rest of Oxford saw only that Roger continued to live frugally, or perhaps even a little more frugally than he had immediately after learning of the disaster at Yeo Manse, and that he had become almost completely solitary; any rumours that might have circulated of his recovery of funds – and there were, of course, bound to be many of these – died quietly away in the face of these obvious misleading facts.

What the situation was now at Yeo Manse he did not know and was afraid to inquire. Will of Howlake was, of course, long gone, withdrawn to serve the more immediate needs of his desperately besieged lord; but if Harold had returned to the manse – or if he had, whether he knew anything of the depredation of his brother's buried hoard – Roger had heard no word of it. A letter from Toulouse a year ago had shown Eugene equally ignorant, as was expectable; even had Harold repossessed the property, he was an indifferent correspondent. With this blank spot in his mind where Ilchester should be, Roger was uneasily content; the last word he wanted to hear was some news which would force him – or even make him feel that he ought – to return any part of the money.

He laid down the quill on the lectern and stared blindly out of the single small window, now blazoned with yellow fire from the westering July sun. Near by was the stack of new parchment awaiting his fair copy of the book, not a sheet of it more than close calculation had shown him he would need, but still representing an expenditure which would have startled any of his fellow-clerks out of their illusions about 'poor Roger Bacon'; next to it, the heap of tattered and smudgy palimpsests which was his draft, his maiden experience as a writer, more than fifteen thousand words put down with pain less than a thousand at a time, with every day's end a new problem in resisting the temptation to write 'finis' during the first half of the task – and then, suddenly, the luminous moment when task transforms itself into mystical experience, whereafter the temptation is to turn the illumination to an orgy and never stop at all.

But he was unable to go back to his fair copy now, inviting though all that virgin parchment was, and imperative though it was to have the work ready to be sent to Paris before this month was over. Instead, he moved suddenly to sponge off the face of the sheet which had carried his outline for the work; and on this, while Oxford slept the midday sleep outside his hot, still cell, he began slowly to write down a letter to himself, beginning.

i: Robt Grosseteste has left Oxenford.

He had only slowly become aware of what it was Grosseteste had been about during his long meditative convalescence, and had been even slower to connect it with those few words of mysterious promise spoken to him by the lector during the winter of the death. Doubtless Adam had known all about it, but he had said nothing; in the meantime, Roger had been left tacitly to understand that his new privilege as a teacher of Aristotle – now much threatened by the arrival of Richard Fishacre, a frighteningly learned master who had brought with him a new translation by Michael Scot, with commentaries by Averroes – was the whole sense to be read in that sickbed adumbration. It had certainly seemed sufficient at the time; to Roger's elation, he had become the first man ever to teach at Oxford before entering upon his secular mastership in the Faculty of Arts; and he had made much of the opportunity, so that after the passage of less than two years the students crowded into his classes (some of them, no doubt, there simply to hear him say something outrageous, as under the prompting of the self he occasionally, helplessly did, but most to hear the new knowledge discoursed by the only regent master in Oxford who had it at his fingertips.)

All of which had been so enormously satisfying that he had neglected to think, until last year, of where he might hope to go next, even putting off as of no special urgency the question of whether or not to read for the Faculty of Theology. Certainly it had never entered his head that the now inaccessible Grosseteste might have been engaged in politicking, even of a peculiar and limited kind; Adam Marsh, yes – though Adam appeared to hate any involvement with the powerful, there was something in his nature which drew the powerful to him with almost the force of love – but certainly never the lector. Besides, Roger had been too busy; preparing his lectures, gratifying though it was, multiplied the difficulty of becoming Master of Arts, which, in these last two years, involved the explication of exceedingly difficult texts and rigorous practical training in disputation; and his unwelcome, unavoidable involvement in Adam's outside affairs had further deprived him of contemplation when – as he now saw, but perhaps too late – he had stood most in need of it.

And then, after a lapse of years, Grosseteste again called Roger and Adam Marsh to his study and unleashed his levin.

'Roger, I've seen too little of thee,' he said without preamble, 'but thou wilt understand when I tell thee that I mean now to assume the bishopric of Lincoln which Adam and the King alike have been urging on me. Hence, I must leave Oxford; the next lector to the Franciscans will be magister Hugo, as Adam knows; thou wilt approve, Roger, I ne mislike.'

'Yes,' Roger said faintly, stunned.

'Good. Now I must tell thee what work I've been about since Adam first brought thee to me as a stripling. I've said naught of it before, it being mischancy and far too far in the balance; but the finger of God hath been on me since mine illness, o happy accident! and now it must all be broached, and brought into flower. I've been conspiring all these years with Philip the Chancellor to bring about the restoration of the University of Paris, and in particular, to see that blind prohibition of Aristotle rescinded there. In large, we've succeeded; but who'll teach Aristotle in Paris now? There they've no students grown in him, let alone a master. Yet we have such a master to send them, Roger. Wilt thou go?'

Roger could say nothing at all; he felt as taken up out of his waters as a little fish in a net; yet, at the same time, the brand was alight again in his breast as burningly as ever in his life, and more, more.

'That's early asked, Capito,' Adam said, eyeing Roger with what seemed to be amusement. 'Let be a while; I ken our Roger better thilke days, and the dose is heavy.'

'I wis it well,' Grosseteste said, nodding gravely. 'Say on, then; wilt have it so, Roger?'

'Please,' Roger said. 'I'm lost as lost may be.'

'Spoken like a Platonist,' Adam said, still with that slight gleam of amusement. 'Knowest thou then, Roger: Philip the Chancellor would have us provide him a book from Aristotle, new-written, which he might send the Pope as evidence of the uses of learning; the subject to be the postponement of old age. We've promised him just such a work, but are in some straits as to who shall have the writing of it. We are too busy both to compose any such book in a useful period of time, nor are we as perfect Aristotelians as we'd like. John Blund is gone from us, poor wight, and our saintly Edmund Rich is Archbishop of Canterbury in his stead. There's to come to us next year a great master named Richard Fishacre, but alack, that's next year and not now. Whom have we but thee?'

Whom indeed? – Roger's own silent argument at the sickbed now turned upon him.

'Which should be naught but to thy liking, Roger, an I read thee right,' Grosseteste added. 'There's scholarship in thy blood, as is plain to see, not only in thee, but eke in our Dominican frater Robert.'

'The eminent Robert's no kin of mine,' Roger said, for

sheer want of knowing what else to say; he a little welcomed the diversion. 'The name is very common, Master. I've a brother Robert, 'tis true, but he's no scholar; my younger brother Eugene may become a scholar in time, by God's will.'

'Well enough; but not to the point,' Adam said. 'Wilt thou undertake the book? Thou canst make free of my library, and Master Grosseteste's, where there's sure to be much thou might simply copy for better speed; yet, harm there'd be none were it to be a work of some substance in the art of medicine, for Gregory's much enfeebled as thou knowst, and the next Pope may be hardly so great a friend of universities.'

'That being so,' Roger said, 'why not thy Dominican physician, Master Grosseteste? I know naught of medicine—'

'And John de St. Giles knows naught of Aristotle,' Grosseteste said, 'and being rusty in disputation, writes but slowly and that with a club foot. Nay, Roger, Adam is right; thou canst consult with John to thy profit, I ne doubt, but thou art the man an thou'lt grasp the nettle. The burden's great, I grant thee, but why else did the lord God give shoulders to His children?'

'I know not,' Roger said. 'But thus I'll answer you, my Masters: certes, I'll write you your book, but Paris is a second question which I must abide. In all this time I've thought myself to be reading, when the time came, for a doctorate in theology, as is small secret anywhere in Oxford. Moreover, I've much in mind to study in the natural sciences, and where in Paris would I find. . . .'

Here he faltered and found himself unable to continue. Grosseteste would soon leave Oxford to be charged with the largest diocese in England, reaching from the Humber to the Thames. Where in the world would Roger find another master in those sciences, even at Oxford? It was not a subject that interested Adam greatly, despite the younger man's mathematical bent.

'But to what purpose, Roger?' Grosseteste said. ' 'Tis

always and only the end in view which doth condemn or purify. True that the arts help purge us of error and guide to perfection *mentis aspectus et affectus*; yet belike are they that well of water dug by Isaac called *Esdon*, signifying contention. But the *scientiae lucrativae*, as medicine, the two laws, alchemy – they signify enmity, *puteus, qui vocatur Satan, quod est nomen diaboli*.'

'From thee this is a hard saying,' Roger said, 'that art first in all the world in the *libri naturales*.'

'But the purpose, Roger! Dost thou wish to preach, then the sciences be well enough, after thou art become a theologian; but thou knowest well that many learned men wis not how to preach ne wish to; they whore after such sciences as will add to their riches or repute; one studying medicine to cure the sick and be made wealthy, or raise the dead and be called a magician; another alchemy, to make heavenly what's naturally impure, yet without a dram of piety; another music, to cast out demons; another wonders, such as stars, winds, lightning, beasts, stones, trees, and all else that appeareth wonderful to men's gaze. Yet, theology is first among all studies, through which a man might know all such marvels better and more notably – not for vain glory and worldly wealth, but for the salvation of souls.'

'Master Grosseteste, well I ween all knowledge to be theology's handmaiden,' Roger said haltingly. 'Nor do I run after knowledge for greed or pomposity, but out of the lust to know, which I count holy. Even in the Proverbs be we commanded to love wisdom for its own sake; for whatever is natural to man, whatever becoming, whatever useful, whatever magnificent, including the knowledge of God, is altogether worthy to be known, *integritas eorum quae ad sapientiam completam requiruntur*. No more can I answer thee.'

For a moment, Grosseteste seemed taken aback; then he smiled gently. 'Which will suffice for the present,' he said. 'We'll not compel thee to Paris, Roger, an it be not thy will and desire. Only be not hasty-firm in thy choice, which thou mayst repent no matter how it goeth. Enough for now that thou'lt give us a book for Philip de Greve—'

'How long a book?' Roger said with new, sudden misgiving.

'How long is a book?' Adam asked reasonably. 'No longer than the subject; that's all that's proper. Put down what's known of the postponement of old age – which is next to nothing, surely – and such conjectures as thou thinkest worthy so to dignify. A fair summary of Aristotle on thilke subject will be thy meat, and all else be subject to thy discretion.'

'There be books of Scripture a copyist with a fine hand might encompass with a single sheet,' Grosseteste said. 'Should what thou'lt add to Aristotle be no more than that, none could think ill of thee on that acount; though I hope that thine ambition will let itself be bolder.'

And deep in Roger's heart came again the voiceless whisper of the self: *Thou kennst me over-well, Seynt Robert.*

And there it was, awaiting the copyist whiling his day's pittance of working time on a letter to himself: Greece, Rome, Chaldea, Arabia, Zion; fire, air, earth, water; Aristotle, Galen, Avicenna, Rhazes, Haly Regalis, Isaac, Ahmed, Haly super Tegni, Damascenius; cold, heat, moisture, dryness; aloes, balsam of Gilead and Engedi, basil, wild cabbage, calamint, camomile, wild carrot, cassia, the greater celandine, cinnamon, saffron, dittany, elder, fennel, fumitory, hellebore, hound's tongue, mace, marjoram, myrobalan, olea, penny-royal, pomegranate, radish, rhubarb; blood, phlegm, yellow bile, black bile; the seven *occulta*, ambergris of the whale, the pearls of Paracelsus, the skin of vipers, the long-lived anthros or rosemary, Galen's body heat of the healthy animal (whether child or fat puppy), the bone which forms in the stag's heart, the fat underflesh of dragons; and the precious incorruptible underground sunlight of gold, that *aurum potabile* which being itself perfect induceth perfection in the living frame....

The copyist looked away; the quill scratched; the letters flowed slowly and formed in small clots:

ii: Marisco will have us alle politick'g, scilicet the Capito & that Roher call'd Bachon, inside a xii-month.

This was not a new thought, for he had scarcely escaped from within the breastwork and bastion of Westminster Hall that furious April of 1235, more than a year ago, before the self was whispering it; yet, he was no more comfortable with it now than he had ever been.

At first he had thought he had been reprieved. He had expected to be haled by Adam *ex studio* to the King's proclaimed parliament with his surly barons; and though he had never before been to London, the prospect did not gratify him – one exchange with Henry had been more than enough for Roger. But for reasons unknown, Adam went alone to the 1234 meeting, which apparently had proven as unproductive of earls and barons as had the Oxford conclave.

Not long after that began the rebellion of Richard earl-Marshal. There was hardly a sign of it in Oxford, where nothing of moment was going on but the establishment by the King of a hospital for pilgrims and the sick, near the bridge; but the roads became less safe than ever, and in the north and in Ireland the whole countryside was said to be smoking with pillage and slaughter. At the beginning of November the whole of England was assaulted by thunderstorms more clamorous and violent than any man could remember, so that the serfs began again to mutter that old saw, 'Weep not for death of husband or childer, but rather for the thunder'; and on St. Catherine's Day, November twenty-fifth, the King's forces met Richard's before Monmouth in a battle that left the earth deep in slaughtered foreigners, yet gained the earl-Marshal nothing except to preserve him a while. There was another such blood-letting on Christmas Day, equally indecisive; and the word from elsewhere in the kingdom was that the holdings and estates of the rebels were being vengefully put to the torch and their people cut down, freemen and serfs alike, by French-speaking bands with letters from Henry, It was not a good season for pilgrimages.

Yet, by March, Adam had brought Roger warning to prepare to attend at Westminster, where the King on the ninth of April would at long last have the assemblage of his full court, saving only those who still cleaved to the earl-Marshal and to de Burgh. The meeting had evidently been arranged by Edmund Rich, perhaps the only man in England still fully trusted by both sides. Roger was not overjoyed, nor did the possibility of seeing his London brother after the meeting was over tempt him even slightly; but Grosseteste would be there, since he was soon to be elevated to the bishopric, vacated by Edmund a year before; and Adam would have no other familiar with him but Roger, which ended any argument Roger was empowered to offer to the contrary.

The trip to London was long, and Adam had seemed both elated and secretive about some matter which, since he could not penetrate it, soon had Roger miserable with mixed curiosity and boredom; attempts to produce conversation on any other subject ran up against the blank wall of Adam's preoccupation:

'Adam, what thinkest thou of the *intellectus agens*? Of the nature of it?'

'Hmmm? Why, 'tis the raven of Elias.'

'But the raven was not *of* Elias himself. What is the signification? That the active intellect is more of God than of man?'

'No, not exactly.' And that was all. Or:

'Whom shall we see at Westminster? Hath thy friend de Montfort been confirmed in the earldom of Leicester?'

'Yes, two years ago. Nay, not properly confirmed, but the land and appurtenances of his father were conveyed to him.'

'Then we shall see him?'

'Nay, an God willeth. He's abroad, I trust, or else will need to be.'

Obviously nothing was to be learned from such scraps of enigmas, and Roger had retreated, at first sullenly, then with an increasing preoccupation of his own, into the interior composition of the *Liber de retardatione*, about the possibility of which he was then only beginning to become aroused; and so they jogged the rest of the way in a mutual silence, broken only by the commonplaces of journeying, of which Adam seemed wholly unaware and to which Roger eventually became quite accustomed.

London itself had proven to be overwhelmingly like a gigantic Ilchester in the midst of a perpetual market day, a seemingly endless labyrinth of narrow streets and alleys choked with stinking ordure and with stinking people. The rain, which fell every day and night that Roger was in London, did not the slightest good, for it was accompanied by no slightest breath of April breeze; the stench simply rose a little distance and then hung in the fog, refusing to disperse, while below on the cobbles, the sludge thrown down from the second-storey windows was spattered impartially upon walls and pedestrians alike by every passing horseman. Like sin, such filth was the common situation of humanity, but Roger had never before encountered either in so sensible a concentration.

It was better as they approached the Hall, which stood directly along the Thames; for though the river itself sublimed into the air the miasma of the grandest Cloaca Maxima of them all, here at least the air could distinctly be felt to be in motion. Nevertheless, by the time he and Adam were left alone in their separate cells in the palace, Roger was more than ready for the spring bath with which he had already planned to conclude the long trip.

What he had expected to follow upon their arrival he could not have said, but in fact, there was nothing of any moment. They had reached the Hall early in the afternoon, and Roger spent the rest of daylight prowling his cell. Occasionally, a distant sennet announced the arrival of one of the barons and his suite; on each such occasion, Roger halted his pacing and looked out his one window, but for the most part there was nothing to see but fog; when, once or twice, the fog lifted slightly, nothing but the river. The day, a dim and depressing one even at high noon, died early, obviously of suffocation. A man came with a lit rush and touched it to two tapers beside Roger's low wooden bed – even inside the cell the air was so moist that both flames showed haloes only five paces away – and then there was another long wait. Part of this he was able to fill as a matter of course with the prayers appropriate for the hours; but he was able to go no further with the book on old age without writing materials, and perhaps could have accomplished as little with them, for he discovered that away from his references he could not call a single quotation to mind with surety – either something had abruptly gone wrong with his memory or (the self suggested with its usual exacerbating abruptness) his memory had never had the true scholar's infinite retentiveness for the letter of the text. The simple attempt to choose the least unattractive of these two new appearances made him feel slightly motion-sick, like a child taken trotting for the first time; and as the hours lengthened, the giddiness seeped down into his knees and began to transform itself implacably into panic.

Someone knocked. After his first start, Roger jerked open the door with a great surge of relief travelling through his muscles. Anything that would serve to take him out of this prison-yard circling had to be welcome.

It was Adam. 'Eheu,' he said, twitching his long nose. '*Stercor stercoraris!* I was about to ask thee if thou'd supped, but that could no man in this chamber-pot. Ho, Roger, ware the candles—'

Roger missed the candles, but he did not miss the bed, though he tried. He gasped and glared at Adam.

'God pardon me, and do thou, too,' Adam said, instantly repentant. 'Here, let's sponge thee off and get fresh linen – hold off, thou'rt but making it more hopeless – and then we'll have thee changed to higher quarters. Stay'st thou here and thou'lt suffocate; look how blue yonder candles burn; 'tis like the vault of a sewer.'

He helped Roger to strip, steadying him, and bathed him again.

'Full many a rogue's died from taking such a refuge,' he

said, wrapping the still-damp surplice over the warm dry shift he had removed from his own back. 'There's a foulness collects over still sewage that kills even rats. I myself have seen spectral fires burning over cesspool-heads, in the midst of nights; demons, belike, come to breathe what's closest on earth to their air in hell.'

'How can a demon leave hell by first intention?' Roger asked, staring with fascination at the nearest candle-flame. It was undeniably mantled with blue, but not the blue of incipient guttering-out; the flame itself was as tall as ever.

'Ah, Roger, as to that, no demon's ever left hell, nor ever can; yet, they appear. Don thy shoes, Roger. Did not the prophet Elijah appear before all during Passover to tell of the coming of our Lord? Yet left not that place where he abode? These things lie in Nature, or in Miracle; as to the latter, the Angel of Death is everywhere, and yet always in heaven; as to the former, the sun is in heaven, but his light is ubiquitous and all-pervasive – thus speaks one who comments on the Haggadah, with wisdom as I ne doubt. What doest thou? Save the linens, the King's household will wash them!'

Roger carefully finished stuffing the window with the sticky bedding and clothing, adding straw judiciously here and there. 'Peace, Adam, I mean not to throw them to the Thames. Mayhap I'll trap a rat, should thilke chamber be such a death-cell as thou foresee'st.'

'But to what purpose?'

'None. To see an it will happen. Now I am ready. Whither away?'

Adam shook his head. 'Thou'rt mad as Henry. Well then, away; I have in mind that we should while away our time with certain persons close to the King; whereby all may gain, be we politick enough. There, close thy door and let thy miasma collect, if that's to be the boy's bird's egg, and take a breath. Now forward, for we're already much delayed.'

The air in the corridor was to be sure so much better than anything Roger had breathed in the last few hours that it made him dizzy all over again; he had to steady himself against the wall for a moment. While he waited, another notion came into his floating, nearly detached head.

'How didst thou read in this infidel text, Adam? Have you Hebrew?'

But it was too late; the preoccupied, eager, secretive Adam of the transit to London was back with Roger now. 'But little,' the Franciscan said. 'Come now, for tomorrow is Henry's day; tonight we must put his house in order, though he wis it never. . . . But first to sup in my chambers, where thou'lt learn ease a while; for truly I ne'er before saw clerk nor Emperor with so wild an eye. When thou opened to me first tonight, thy left eye was stuck shut, and thou didst know it not, nor when it opened; as a two-eyed Polyphemus I can conduct thee nowhere.'

'I'll see, an there be light. Go on.'

But, in fact, he saw little; or rather, saw as much as usual, some of it doubtless of pith and moment, but without understanding. To begin with, he remained more light-headed from the miasma than he realized until too late. The meal with Adam gave him little to occupy his intellect, Adam waxing more secretive and preoccupied by the moment; and the meal being accompanied through some whim of the King's with an excellent Spanish sack, and Roger having scarcely tasted wine of any quality since that crucial Fall of 1231, he left Adam's table in a mixture of befuddlements.

Then, Roger was reasonably sure, they had gone to the apartments of someone who could only be the King's sister Eleanor, where Adam had disappeared for what seemed in retrospect like a long time, but might have been shorter than a low mass, considering all the poisons – material and spiritual – adrift in Roger's brain. There was perhaps nothing very unusual about this, since everyone knew that Adam was Eleanor's confessor – and yet, Adam beforehand had been so full of conspirator's airs about it that even a clear head might not have known what to think. The apartments themselves were sumptuous, far more so than any possible apartments at Beaumont, which, after all, was closer to being a castle than a palace, but Roger was in no position to enjoy their richness even had he had a taste for such things; for it shortly became plain to him that his role, as Adam had intended it, was to be a lure for a brash tiring-wench named Judy who otherwise would have been an inconvenience to the Lady Eleanor and the Franciscan.

Thus the visit to Eleanor's rooms was long, uncomfortable and mysterious, and if the King's household was in any way set more in order thereby, Roger did not come within bow-shot of knowing how or why that night. Adam looked stern when he emerged at long last, and he left behind him the sound of suppressed weeping – but perhaps tears were the customary cost of settling a Crown more firmly. If so, Roger was grimly happy to remain a perpetual antechamberer in such matters.

Yet, he was at the same time in a fury with Adam, and promptly turned on him a denunciation so stammering and disconnected that he scarce understood two words of it himself.

'Eh?' Adam said. 'Master thyself, Roger, I pray thee. What's this? There's no harm in Judy for thee, be thou only on thy guard as becomes a churchman—'

'That – that's naught to the purpose. Deny thou if thou canst that thou intendedst naught else but to throw us together, for thine own easement? I'd have thee know that I'm no brawling clerk. I'll have no more to do with women, ne ladies nor tiring-maids nor whores, attendest thou me? How dost thy conscience rest to have led thy fellow in Christ into such a test?'

'Swef, swef,' Adam said. ' 'Twas not meant to be a test, Roger, only a diversion; whyfor so savage? A peasant girl is not a pestilence.'

'Devils live in them,' Roger said, the sullen fumes in his head seeming to issue forth in wreaths with the words. 'They are all thieves and whores, to the Last Judgment.'

'No Christian may declare another eternally damned except on pain of sin,' Adam said. 'How wilt thou preach, and yet have naught to do with women? They are the half of mankind.'

'Nor will I preach, be that the price of it, whatsoe'er the *Capito* would have me do. Better to teach than to go down among these placket-pickers.'

'A grave matter to be making puns upon,' Adam said, looking at him speculatively. 'Then thou hast decided for Paris, Roger?'

'Mayhap,' Roger said. 'Another trap, Adam? Is this then the corner that thou meanest to drive me into? Take care, I may bite thee!'

'Thou'rt ill,' Adam said. 'I was mistaken to take thee at all. Thou'rt so disputatious at thy worst, Roger, I'm forever mistaking it for thy best. Go thou to bed; I'll manage without thee; there's still more to undertake, but needs a brow as cool as stone, else better not to undertake it at all. Dost remember the way?'

'Better than thou. Go to; I've had enough.'

Adam nodded curtly and turned off through a door which Roger had not even noticed, leaving him alone and suddenly much more befuddled and afloat than he had realized. He had, he understood with the awful clarity of the drunken man, just created a disaster for himself, though how it had come to this end he could not riddle. Nay, he had not created it entire by himself; Adam had been as much to blame as he. And now the Franciscan was gone, with a brusque order to Roger to return to his room, his promise to find Roger something better than that sink-hole quite forgotten in his passion to play with the lives of more important people.

So mote it be, the self whispered icily inside Roger's swimming head. *Time will discover who these self-same worthies are*. Snatching a torch from a bracket, Roger blazed his uneven way back to his room, at the head of a comet of smoke and sparks. He butted the door open blindly and thrust the torch inside.

The whole room turned into a solid block of blinding yellow flame. The door slammed against his forehead. The slam was like a summary of all the thunderclaps since creation. The floor shuddered with it, the very palace seemed to rock.

He did not know that he had fallen until the back of his head struck the stone. The shock was stunning. When he was able to see and think again, he was as sober as though all the wine had been bled out of him by some miraculous barber. He was slumped against the opposite wall, every bone aching. In the distance, he could hear shouts and the sound of running.

It was impossible to imagine entering that room again, much less striking a light there. A demon had come to breathe the poisoned air in very truth. But the sound of running was coming nearer – and tomorrow was the day of all days for King Henry; he would be sure to take such a blast as the worst kind of an omen. Suppose he were to discover that it had taken place in the room of that same man who had flung 'stones and rocks' in his face at Oxford? Men had been burned as sorcerers for less.

Someone in mail ran by him in the blackness, clinking and wheezing, and trod without noticing it on Roger's out-turned ankle. Biting his tongue to keep silence, Roger wormed his way up against the wall to a sitting position, drew his knees into his chest, and drove himself to his feet. The runner went on. Calling upon God in his heart, Roger crossed to the door and pushed it. It opened at once.

The air in the room smelt burnt, but no longer foul; perhaps the demon had gone. Holding that thought high, Roger groped across the room to where he had last seen his box. It was there, and in it the two flints, a bit of tinder, the stub of a candle. It was hard to strike a light with hands that shook so, but he got one after only five tries.

In the weak light, the room seemed utterly undisturbed. No: the plug of wet bedding at the window was gone, doubtless destroyed by the flight of the demon. The tapers that had been brought earlier had been blown out, but not toppled, and he lit them from his stub.

The air was flocculent with fine fingerlings of falling soot.

When his hand came trembling away from his cold wet brow, it was smeared greasily with the stuff, as though it had been settling on him for hours. Also, there were splinters in his face – a sizeable number. He closed one eye, then the other; no, they had missed his eyes; but they were beginning to hurt. And he did not dare call for a surgeon, nor take a needle to them himself – such wounds would be marked at tomorrow's convocation; better to appear tomorrow with a puffy face and let it be ascribed to excess. Adam himself might be the first to so interpret it, if perhaps not the first to speak it out. The soot could be wiped off somehow.

The hubbub was farther away now, and sounded as baffled as it was angry. The immediate danger seemed to have passed. As for tomorrow that would take care of itself.

But how under God had it happened? Surely demons did not come to live in poor students' rooms simply because they liked the air there; after tomorrow, someone else might sleep here, and become slowly surrounded by the same miasma, and become as sick. And suffer the same lightning? Perhaps, if he sealed the room . . . and thrust a torch in it after. . . . Clearly there was some connection, but Roger could not grasp it. Abruptly he was felled by exhaustion as though by a hammer. He barely had time to shed himself of his coat before sleep claimed him on his straw, leaving all the candles still burning.

That Henry had been shaken in his Hall was at once to be seen in the High Chamber that merciless April morning, for he came before his earls and his barons, his Poitevins and their relatives in search of preferment, and before Edmund Rich and his bishops with the face of a man who has slept not at all, but wrestled the whole night long with terror and a bad conscience. He seated himself without a word and regarded all before him with alarmingly bloodshot eyes.

Roger, less than nothing among all these high counsels, was not noticed at all, except by Adam, who shot him one startled glance and a half-smile of commiseration, and as promptly seemed to forget that he existed. With Edmund was Grosseteste, magnificent and strange, not yet consecrated but full of works, and often consulted by the bishops around Edmund; and at Grosseteste's elbow was Adam. Among the barons Roger recognized Simon de Montfort, somehow no longer beautiful but as sternly handsome as a shaft of granite, yet oddly ill at ease, as though he found himself torn between the earls and the Frenchmen who were his countrymen. If de Montfort looked ill at ease, however, Peter des Roches looked positively ill; his plump face was like whey.

The King continued to say nothing at all. At last, however, a herald ventured to offer him the mace. He took it without seeming to notice what it was; his eyes shot open in alarm when he heard the trumpets.

'Eh?' he said hoarsely. 'Well then. Speak, someone.'

'I will speak, my lord King,' Edmund Rich said. His voice was quiet, but it filled the Chamber. 'We are here that thy kingdom be no more dismembered. These thine earls and barons have gathered with us under the protection of Christ the Almighty King and His vicar on earth, under whose sign and seal thine earthly kingship has its patent, and under none other.'

'Go on,' Henry said.

'Aye, that we will. My lord King, didst hear the earthquake eat at thy kingship only last night? What dost thou say to this? Shall these ancient stones quiver, and thine heart be unmoved?'

'We called you, as we called you all oft before, to seek composition,' Henry said with a whisper of the old arrogance. 'We have never sought else. Therefore, say forth, and affright us not with thunders.'

The words were brave, but the tune was almost humble. Here is a king, Roger thought, with a heart of wax.

'There is no way but this,' Edmund said. 'Thou shalt repair thine errors, my lord King, or thou shalt be excommunicated. The church hath protected thee long and long, since thou wert in swaddling clothes. It will withdraw that protection momently. Act now. Begin with these Poitevins, who have leeched at thee and thy kingship long enough.'

The King turned suddenly to look at Grosseteste. Adam whispered into Grosseteste's ear; the great head nodded slowly. The King clenched his hands and looked away again, and his eyes lighted on Peter des Roches. For a long moment these two stared at each other in a passage at arms which was as silent and furious as an embrace.

'Thou,' Henry said, 'thou adder in our ear.'

'My lord King, consider—'

'Speak no more, thou compromiseth thine holy mission,' Henry said, his voice beginning to rise. 'We command thee. Obey.'

Des Roches looked at the flagstones.

'Go thou back to thy bishopric and attend to the cure of souls, as God permits thee. And thenceforth, on no account, meddle with the affairs of this our kingdom.'

Henry's head jerked sidewise. 'Peter de Rivaulx.'

'My lord King.'

'We command thee without fail to give up our royal castles to us, to render us an account of our royal monies, and immediately to leave our court.'

'My lord King, it shall be so. Only a few days for the accounting—'

'Leave our court!' Henry said, lurching to his feet. 'By Goddes bones, wert thou not beneficed and admitted to the rights of the clergy, we should order thine eyen twie enriven from thy skull, thou that stolst from us the loyalties of our earls, and whispered blood, blood, blood in our ear all the nights and days! Out, out!'

Rivaulx knew his king; he picked up his skirts and ran. Peter des Roches hung back, ashen but clinging to some last unimaginable shred of dignity, but most of the Poitevins were swirling after Rivaulx, trying to sneer into the blackly triumphant faces of the barons.

'Go not without our charge, pack-rats,' Henry shouted after them, brandishing the mace. 'You are expelled one and all, from our court and from our country and from the charge of our estates. Go you away to your own burrows, and never show your faces before us again, else we shall use your skulls as bowls.'

The last pair of Poitevin heels scuttered out of sight like magic. Roger had to press his hand over his splinter-stitched lips until the pain came to keep from bursting into laughter. The King, his chest heaving, looked over the rest of the Chamber and saw nothing but solemn approval. After a while, he sat down, and settled his trembling body forward in an attitude of command.

'First things first,' he said, in a voice that shook only a little. 'And now, Archbishop Rich, let us compose our kingdom as well as may be. Wilt thou to Wales? We'd have Richard earl-Marshal back, an it could be brought about; let us all make peace, by Goddes bones.'

Edmund Rich bore toward Henry the look of an eternal judge. 'How can that be, my lord King?' he said, in a voice as unforgiving as riven stone. 'Dost thou believe I can undo all thy treacheries with Richard Marshal?'

'Then take with thee whomsoe'er thou willst. Whoso'er is highest in probity in thine eyes, and in Marshal's. We see with thee the Bishop of Chester, and eke the Bishop of Rochester. That should be a deputation worthy of trust. What think my barons of this?'

There was a short consultation. Then de Montfort stepped forward.

'Thou, Simon? Art so quickly leading earl of the realm? We like this not.'

'Nay, my lord King. I am the least, and therefore can speak for all, rather than for myself alone. And this is our rede: An thou become reconciled with Richard, we shall be reconciled with thee.'

'We have made you concessions enough,' Henry said, rolling the rings of his knuckles back and forth along the arm of his throne. 'But we shall abide you. Richard Marshal shall live and live in our honour, will he desire it. Enough. We are ill. We thank you for your graciousness. This convocation is ended.'

He relinquished the mace and stepped unsteadily down.

The sackbuts sounded while he walked behind the throne and went out through the same small door he had come in. Under the vair of his cloak, Roger saw, the shanks of the beautiful Plantagenet legs were as thin as rushes.

What remained of the convocation began to move and break into groups, with a general murmur of bemused and cautious self-congratulation. The Bishops of Chester and Rochester edged through the muggy press toward Edmund Rich – obviously the Welsh adventure was going to require planning of the most mischancy kind – but Rich was already deeply in converse with the Oxford group, in which Roger found himself included without protest, and the two appointed bishops hung back deferentially until this conference should be through. No such considerations restrained Simon de Montfort, who found his way directly to Adam.

'What news?' he said, drawing the Franciscan a little aside. 'No, no, Roger, ye needn't withdraw, I remember thee well; "stones and rocks"; the best advice our Henry ever had. Well, dear Adam?'

'She is willing,' Adam said, with a glance over his shoulder at Grosseteste. The master appeared to be out of earshot. 'I had no easy road in my suasions, but she sees that 'tis the only way out of her present dilemma. She's affrighted of thee a little, which I assured her was unfounded quite. The rest, Simon, thou must do thyself; this present marriage of thine is without my demesne.'

'Well I ken it,' Montfort said. 'I have work in progress to dissolve it. It may be that I shall have to go to the Holy See; if so, very well, I shall. What thinkest thou of today's bit of business?'

'I mislike it. Doubtless the earl-Marshal will trust the Archbishop; but can he trust the King?'

'I greatly fear that he may,' Montfort said grimly. 'Though certes Henry means what he says, he has the Plantagenet bias for tortuous dealings. Roger, we are well met today; there is one here, Guy de Foulques, the papal legate, who hath heard of our Oxford scholars' studies in the natural sciences; and I have told him of the book thou art writing, as Adam told it me. Thou shouldst talk with him a while, an Adam can let thee; for if thy book be well received de Foulques may ask thee for more at some later date.'

'My lord,' Roger said. 'Gladly. Though I am exceeding poor in knowledge of the sciences as yet. I am astonished that thou know'st my passion so well, when as yet it be no more than that.'

'Simon never forgets a face or a fact,' Adam said with a half smile. 'He is my perpetual despair. By all means, take him with thee, Simon, for there are still some favours to be curried ere the other matter is made certain.'

'Come then, Roger.'

How much had been done and undone since then! There had been as much promise, precisely, in the meeting with Guy de Foulques as Montfort had foreshadowed, but that promise depended upon the completion of the present book, which lay neglected still. That the marriage of the King's sister to Simon de Montfort would be celebrated was now certain – for that had been the meaning behind Adam's high manœuvring, that, and that Adam would become spiritual adviser to both the earl and his countess thereafter; which meant that both Adam and Grosseteste would inevitably become court personages, and Roger, too, if he remained, if only through Adam's inexplicable delight in involving Roger in these matters, and the earl's incredible desire to do everyone he knew a service (which, thanks to the earl's miraculous memory, seemed to include everyone he had ever met). As for Henry, his court remained the same as it had always been, an incredibly complex little society in which affairs managed to go backwards and forwards at the same time: Richard earl-Marshal had sensibly refused the King's peace offer even when it had been delivered by three bishops, but had later been taken prisoner by a set of treacheries so involved that even Henry's worst enemies suspected that he could have had no hand in some of them, and had died of his wounds on Palm Sunday; yet Hubert de

Burgh and the nobles had, nevertheless, become reconciled with Henry the day before the Sunday preceding the Ascension, though there was not a baron to be found who did not believe the earl-Marshal a martyr – all in all, no court to leave a sane man time or sanity for any study of the sciences. Oxford would be no better now, not with Adam utterly taken up in de Montfort's affairs, Grosseteste consecrated by Edmund Rich at Reading the next June, and now Richard Fishacre steadily cutting into Roger's ephemeral reputation as resident master in Aristotle.

The sun was almost down, and the treatise on old age still resting unfinished. The letter to himself was unfinished as well; it would never be done; it was slowly winding itself into a Gordian knot which would make a decision impossible, rather than offering him through the sternest of logic any decision upon which he could depend. Nothing remained now but what he wanted to do, for the letter to himself made nothing clear about the logic of events, except that there was no logic to them except in the mind of God.

Well, then, Paris.

That road, too, had seemed impossible, without spending almost the whole of his hoard. He had driven himself to see his brother Robert before leaving London, but that had been as profitless a meeting as he had known it would be *ab initio*: where Robert had been without sympathy for Roger's clerkship at Oxford, and contemptuous of Eugene's at Toulouse, the idea of expending good pounds to send Roger from Oxford to Paris had provoked him to gross and intolerable laughter. They had parted in a blizzard of enmity; Robert's last words were a flat order to return to Ilchester to put the estate in order, or be disowned the moment that Robert could legally consider Harold Bacon dead. Roger could only turn his back and exclude Robert forever from his memory; *and from rumour*, the self told him with icy satisfaction, *to the end of time*.

Nevertheless, it could be done, and without too much diminishing the bag of money. It was only July; by swinking, he could complete his secular mastership by the end of summer. Between then and Martinmas would leave him enough time to complete the book for Philip the Chancellor, and give him in addition a little time to work on something to satisfy Guy de Foulques; perhaps something on light, a subject about which Grosseteste had written extensively already, so that Roger would again have a library upon which to base his first draft.

And Martinmas was slaughtering time. Soon thereafter, in the winter storms, William Busshe would be leaving one or another of the Cinque Ports with his sarplers and fells for Wissant. With him would be one Roger Bacon, lately of Oxenford, master in Aristotle to come to the hundred colleges of the University of Paris, under the aegis of Robert Grosseteste, scholar to all the world.

He sponged out the letter to himself in the last light of the day. Tomorrow he would write again, but to another self: Magister Roger, whose works were writ for popes.

Explicit prima pars.

Sequitur pars secunda:

TO FERNE HALWES

V: STRAW STREET

There might have been a time, in Roger's mind belonging so safely to history that it might have happened on the moon, when William Busshe had been young. Busshe himself remembered it well: then he had sailed out of Maidstone and across the Channel in a barge – of necessity, to begin with, since she had been his first vessel, and secondly because nothing larger could have passed under Aylesford Bridge. She had displaced twenty-two tons, and had cost him exactly three pounds; not quite a fair price, but a good enough transaction for a youngster, especially one who meant to do his own sailing, as well as his own trading in the Staple.

The barge had been called the Maudelayne Busshe, after his mother, but now was the *Maudelayne* only, as a more considerable enterprise better meriting the protection of heaven. She was five times the displacement of her original; about four times the price, neither a bargain nor an extortion; sailing out of Hull with a crew of nine (not counting her master, still Busshe himself, and the boatswain and cook); loaded with packs of fells (four hundred to the pack, eighteen packs in all, some forward of the mast under hatches, some in the stern sheets, the summer fells marked X and the winter fells O in red chalk – but not all Busshe's wool, for he knew better than to ship his whole consignment in one bottom, his though she be; and besides, on the wide waters he was a master, not a merchant, and there was a profit to be taken in shipping the sarplers of other traders); loaded also with bows and quarrels for every man, boarding hooks, pikes, pitch and a barrel of darts, in case of Scotsmen, Lombards or other pirates; with salt fish, onions, bread and beer in case of being blown far off course; and, this time out of the glowing, wrinkling bay, in honour of a promise, with Roger Bacon.

Of that choppy black howling crossing Busshe was to say thereafter that even the rats were sick, and his sailormen that none but a saint, a devil or William Busshe could have forborne to cast his wool overboard for the saving of his life. This, however, was the turn of the dice that a man chanced when he shipped with Busshe, for it was known that no storm had ever wrested a single sack from him since the day he had burned his whole cargo under the hatches rather than let it go to two close-pressing Lombard corsairs (the stench had been ferocious, and the Lombards, quite without Busshe's anticipating any such outcome, had lost him in the huge pall of greasy black smoke which had lain in the wake of the *Maudelayne*); most of his crew, all the same, had been with him for fifteen years.

As for the supercargo, it took Roger three days, in the house of Busshe's host in Wissant, to stop the earth from swinging under him and to look without horror at his own face on the surface of a broth. It was only then that he discovered he was in Busshe's customary bed, wide and deep, with a fine mattress and two linens and the richest of coverings.

'Never mind. I've slept in that bed these dozen years, I've naught to suffer for a night out of it. Eat.'

'Yes. But William . . . was I . . . meseemeth I was dying, or so praydeth I. But do storms . . . doth the sea always. . . . I would say, did I commend me to God for a trifle?'

'Nay. 'Tis not always thus. But it's never a trifle. To say sooth, young Roger, we 'scaped narwe. But rest thee, and sup, for that's a voyage past.'

Roger shuddered and tried the broth. His shame was promptly overcome by the marvellous discovery that he was hungry. Only toward the last swallows did he remember what he ought to have been thinking of from the first.

'William – my chest? My books?'

'Yonder. Dost think, young Roger, that William Busshe would save a fell and drown a book? Merchant I be, but nat so ill a man as that.'

'God's blessing on thee,' Roger said with a great puff of a sigh. 'And on thine hosts, now that I reflect on't. I'm a trial to all, I fear me.'

Busshe smiled. ' 'Tis an old song in Wissant. Half the populace is just in from the keys, and the half of that abed with the sea-sickness, at least as the winter draws in. I am just up of it myself. Nay, I meant not to 'stonish thee; I'm oft fearful seasick; so be we all from time to time. 'Tis the Channel – no lilypond when the wind's from the north.'

'God preserve me from it till I die. Why persisteth thou, William? Dost *like* being seasick?'

'Nay, there's a fool's question. 'Tis what I do, ne more, and it bringeth me money, on which I am most fond. Were I not William Busshe, by God's hand, might I be fond on something quite other; but there, I'm not; and thilke other'd be the selfsame drink, half honey, half aloes. It is so decreed, and therefore are we bidden to use one another kindly, lest the bitter half make us doubt even the love of God.'

'Nay, never! Forgive me, but thou art wrong entire. There cannot be a dewdrop of that doubt in a Christian heart – least of all thine.'

'Wait,' William Busshe said heavily. 'It will assault thee, in due course, thouten thou beest heavy with sainthood, young Roger. Then wilt thou need the love of man. If thou canst find none better, pray for me then; or for some beggar; only thus is the cup passed. But enough, enough. How wilt thou go to Paris?'

'Oh,' Roger said, 'somehow.' He was not ready to think of travelling again yet; instead, there hovered in his memory, from Hroswitha's *Abraham* – how oddly Terence-like a comedy to come from the pen of a nun in the convent of Grandesheim! – the speech of the anchorite to his more-than-Alexandrian sinner: *Who despairs of God sins mortally.* Busshe did not have the look of a man in pain of mortal sin; yet he had not only accepted the error but was counselling it, which made him at the least an abettor of heresy.

If William Busshe were an evil man, how then could a

good man be known? For a moment Roger felt as though the seasickness were returning, but it passed; it passed. The question, unanswered, remained.

By the river on the left bank the water in the evening whistled like sleepy blackbirds: *Vidi . . . viridi . . . Phyllidem sub tilia . . .*; or with a brief flourish of breeze would start up a lisping distant nightingale, *Veni . . . veni . . . venias . . . ne me more facias. . . . Hyrca, hyrca, nazaza, trillirivos! . . .* Across the Seine, the Ile de la Cité gradually lost reality, and Notre-Dame with it, almost as though one could see the cathedral schools falling silent with the night; the stews about the cathedral would be noisy till dawn, but they were too tangled to allow much light to escape across the river. Candles still burned visibly in rooms here and there on the Petit-Pont, little stars votive to the philosophers who lived there, the rising Parvipontani; on the water, Roger thought, they looked like real stars, except for their yellowness. Would they seed jewels into the mud of the river, as the real stars gave birth to jewels in the hot press of the deep earth? Probably not. It was by no means certain that real stars were so potent, though the best authorities maintained it to be true. How, after all, would one test such a notion, the deep earth being so furiously hot and so close to hell, as one could see readily in the volcanoes of Greece and Italy, the *mofettes* of Eifel, the hot springs of Baden? And of what use would the answer be, except to defraud further such princes as were already fond on alchemy? None, almost surely – unless one appeal to Cato, who said that to know anything is praiseworthy.

But Cato was only another authority. Suppose him to have been wrong; how would one test that?

Roger sighed and got up. His walk had been a failure: none of these questions would be of any use to him in Paris, even should he by some miracle be given the answers to all of them. Besides, the plain fact was that he was hungry, which made coherent argument hard come by, even with himself.

Behind him he could hear the early-evening noise of the Latin's quarter, not very Latin now since the English nation had moved its drinking headquarters to the Two Swords in the rue S.-Jacques. The move seemed more than likely to lead to trouble, though of trouble of that kind there was already more than enough.

Roger picked his way carefully. There was still some warm light, but it was deceptive, and the pavements of Paris had been very little repaired since the Romans first built them; in fact there was a doggerel verse going around among the students which derived Lutetia, the Latin name for Paris, from *lutum* – mud. Latrines generally gave into the sewers, which were not sewers at all in the Roman sense, but only open channels in the middle of the street; and though carts were not allowed in town – because their nail-studded wheels further pulverized the Roman paving-stones, and made new ruts in the mud to divert the sewage – horses were, which piled up more soil than an army of the blessed scavengers, the belled pigs of St. Anthony, could cope with were every day a night and every night an eternity. Even during the day one could not walk in Paris at all without high, heavy, thickly-soled shoes, intolerably expensive though they were for students. To walk at night one had to be rich, for though there was some light from the windows of houses, the streets themselves were not lit, so that one could not take three steps in the dark without turning into a dung-beetle unless one could afford a linkboy.

The English were hard at it as he passed the Two Swords; evidently they had taken in fees from new members or new officers, and were now engaged in drinking up the surplus. At the moment the singing was being done by the Germans, in their own language, but obviously in honour of their English co-Nationals, since the song was about the 'Chünegin von Engellant' – not Henry's new queen, probably, but instead Eleanor of Aquitaine the long-mourned.

Later in the evening this wine-warmed fellowship would begin to evaporate into slandering all the other nations, beginning, in the natural order of things, with the French –

who were puffed with pride, everybody knew that, and dressed themselves like women – and their substituent countries: the vulgar, stupid Burgundians; the fickle Bretons who had killed the Great King, Arthur; the grasping, vicious and cowardly Lombards; the Romans with their noisy slander and their silent seditions; the cruel and harsh Sicilians. Since there was a grain of truth – or at least a grape – in all this, the game once started quickly became a contest in the kind of student malice they had all learned from Buoncompagno. The Normans, a whole nation in themselves, generally were dismissed as being no more vain than the French, but much more boastful. The Picards, too, usually won free with no more than a few elaborate but barbless quills; but their substituent Flemish were proclaimed to be fickle, gluttonous, lazy, and so soft they would dent like butter; while the Brabantians were at the least rapists, robbers, pirates and murderers who could not even compose a neck-verse for the saving of their lives.

At the best, by morning the Germans would be accusing their friends the English of being drunkards, and challenging them to heist their cloaks and show their tails; the English would countercharge gluttony, obscenity and berserker fury; pots would be thrown, and all would retire to nurse their noddles and wish they had studied canon law, the lectures on which did not begin until mid-morning – every other course in Paris began at six. At worst, someone would suggest that the insults be taken down the street and shouted in the windows at the Sign of Our Lady where the French Nation met, or perhaps the French would conceive this notion first; in which instance there would be before morning several clerks who would copy out no more letters home begging for money or a new shirt, and several masters who would dispute no more – and never mind that Paris sternly forbade the carrying of arms by scholars.

As Roger passed by, however, the Two Swords fell unwontedly quiet. After a moment he could hear a single counter-tenor voice, as pure as any he had ever heard in this life:

'Ich sih die liehte heide
in gruner varwe stan.
Dar suln wir alle gehen,
die sumerzit enphahen. . . .'

and to his own astonishment felt the tears start into his eyes, little though he knew the language. Alarmed, he walked faster.

Elsewhere the street was in its more usual state of evening irreverence. Overheard in one of the hostels, a poor thing which could have held no more than ten fellows and a master as poor as they, the dice were already rattling, for there were three baskets of waffles or rissoles hanging out the window, and some lucky *socium* of the college had also thrown himself a sausage: there it dangled, with two cats hopelessly a-siege of it in the street, their spines stretched like mandolins, their fretted noses bumping speculatively against the empty burdened air. Roger's belly twinged in sympathy, and he bought from the next *pâtissier* he saw in the street an eel pie which filled all the rest of his walk with a marvellous vapour of garlic and pepper; and then, belatedly remembering patient John his companion in the room on the rue de Fouarre, from another pastryman a tart filled with cheese and eggs. Since he was already carrying another heavy bundle, he had to juggle them all before he could resume walking; and then, the two cats who had before been observing the Constellation of the Sausage (or two exactly like them) were following him instead. Behind him the sounds of the English Nation died away, but there was no less music for that; it was everywhere in the transparent Paris evening, now and forevermore, world without end.

It had been a cold rancid meat indeed to devour that he had been forced, that first spring in 1237, to matriculate at Paris as no more than a mere yellowbeak, despite Grosseteste's cachet and the existing invitation; but the charter of 1231 was explicit about the matter: there were three years of additional studies which Roger must undertake before he could be allowed to lecture on Aristotle or even any lesser subject. And worse: by the time he arrived in Paris, Philip the Chancellor had died, breaking the link which might have brought Roger's book on old age to the attention of the Pope. Three years the book had rested in Roger's box, and three years had he ground away at the corn of knowledge as it was milled in Paris, until the hull of his ambition was almost worn away into dust. But it had not been all chaff: as a non-regent master he was neither expected to join a Nation nor maintain rooms for teaching; the former had spared him the ritual dehorning, confession and degrading penitence the Germans invariably imposed upon new English Nationals, while the latter had spared him his purse. In nights as white as Virgil ever knew, he had ground his teeth to be no more than another master of arts in young and strenuous Paris, a valley seething with the ferments of Franciscans versus Dominicans, Alexander of Hales versus Thomas Aquinas, Nominalists versus Realists, while Roger Bacon swinked away unknown, his lectureship still to come. But his examination before the new chancellor was fixed, at last, for the day after tomorrow; and he was prepared, aye, prepared with a thoroughness he had earlier never even imagined that he would need – prepared to take examination in full university if the chancellor so ruled, and the hot cheeks thereafter would not be Roger Bacon's!

It was a long climb to his room – four flights of black and ancient stairs. They invariably left him a puffing and helpless target for the sallies of his room-mate, unable to give back in kind for minutes at a time. The tow-headed Livonian youngster – unlike Roger, a true yellowbeaked freshman without a degree to scribble after his name – seemed to be in an unusually pensive mood tonight, however, for all he said was:

'How was the walk?'

'Well enough,' Roger said, putting his bundles down on his bed.

'Is the Seine full of philosophy tonight?'

'Alas, no. Only water.'

'A pity.' Then they were both silent. They had spoken as always in Latin – not only because it was the rule, with informers or 'wolves' everywhere to turn one in to the university if one didn't, for a portion of the fine; but because Roger did not understand a word of John's language, nor did John any other that Roger knew. John, who was standing at the desk, had already looked back down at his book, as if his mind had never really been drawn away from it. In the light of the single candle his face seemed oddly old; but after a moment his nostrils began to twitch.

'Aha,' he said with satisfaction. 'The magician has waved his wand again. What have we here?'

'An eel pie—'

'Fie, Roger!'

'—and a cheese omelette pastry. Judging from the pepper, they may both be a little fleshy.'

'That's what pepper is for; who sees fresh meat in the city? Ah, this is good, very good. The song's right:

Bad people, good town
Where a ha'penny buys a bun.'

Non vix a triginta ha'pennies had gone into those pastries, but Roger as usual said nothing. In these years a peculiar horror of being thought generous had begun to colour his already well-set secrecy about his money; he could not afford to seem to eat or live better than John, yet he was constantly being tempted into such extravagances as this. The deceits he had worked out to justify them would have done credit to a poet.

'There's else for you in the other bundle,' Roger said. 'I found you your *Ars dictaminis*, though why you need it I can't think. You write as well as any student I ever knew.'

'Thank you,' John said, lifting the book with gentle hands. 'The very book, and not much scuffed, either. How did you do it?'

He had done it simply by going to the bookstalls of the Little Notre-Dame, but he said: 'The man who had it owed me a favour. I'll not be able to do it twice. Better not put it up to Decius again.'

'Aha, you remind me, I have somewhat for you, too,' John said triumphantly. 'Look: a quart of wine.'

'Now you are the magician. Where'd you get it?'

'Well,' John said, 'you see, dice aren't as bad as you paint them. Yesterday while you were in class four of us were playing and I lost. (This is a complicated story, Roger, I warn you.) I hated to drop out, because I was playing with those three from across the street, the Picards who live in the garret and have one gown for the three of them to go to lectures in. Then in came the cat from the same place, the one that belongs to the landlord, so I said, "Look, here's a fellow that eats regularly and never pays a penny; let's make him play." '

'Where on earth do you find these wild notions?'

'They come to me,' John said modestly. 'Well, so I folded the cat around the dice, as it were – you understand, with all four paws over them. I shook him a bit – the fat thing didn't even meow – and threw, and he lost.'

'*He* lost?'

'He threw the dice, didn't he? So I wrote a little note to the landlord, explaining that the cat had lost a quart of wine and hadn't paid up, and if he didn't pay up in due course we'd have to collect his pelt instead. (Cats make good gloves, did you know that, Roger?) I tied the note around his neck. Well, the Picards went home and I didn't think any more about it until this afternoon when the cat came back; and he had the money around his neck.'

Roger stared.

'He did, Roger, I swear. And there was a letter from the landlord, asking us please not to make the cat play any more, because he's so old that his eyesight is poor, so he can't count his throw. And here it is.'

'The note?' Roger said. 'Or the cat?'

'No,' John said innocently, 'the wine. I seem to have mislaid the note.'

'You have swept the field,' Roger said, laughing in spite of himself. 'If there were a doctorate of lies, I'd vest you in it and then disband the faculty. Well, then, let's have a toast to Decius.'

'With a whole quart of wine we could have a mass to Decius – but then we'd have to have those thirsty Picards in for servers,' John said. 'Well, then, away with it: To the dice! Ah. Roger, Albertus Magnus is your first master, isn't he?'

'Yes,' Roger said shortly. He had not been getting along well with Albert of late. Perhaps he had been winning too many arguments.

'Are you ready for examination?'

'I'm sure of it,' Roger said. 'I selected the *De plantis* as a text. I know it by rote.'

'Dangerous; Albert knows his vegetables even better than Aristotle. Speaking of which, how about the dinner?'

'What dinner?'

'Dear God, Roger, three years in Paris and you don't know how these things are won? You don't consort enough with students, like me. Well, Albert will set what other masters will attend, of course. How many would that be?'

'John, please begin again. What are we talking about?'

'We are talking,' John said sternly, 'about your pre-examination dinner, which you will pay for. A few florins go a long way in these matters. If you can afford it, buy them all a free bath beforehand, too. Nay, look not anxiously at your box, Roger. I know you have money, you have only been pretending to be as poor as I. You've been buying me books and wine and food, and I am not a stupid man; I've known it the better part of two years. I've given back as good as I could, and now let me advise you, take some money out and spend it openly on a banquet. The masters expect it. And I beg you, count your money ere we part, so you'll know I've touched not a coin, nay, never even looked into your chest.'

Roger swallowed. 'Are we parting? I'd hoped not. But I'm the stupid one, it appears.'

'Who knows?' John said. For a moment he wore the same

abstracted look Roger had surprised on his face earlier in the evening. 'In this world everything happens suddenly. But will you take my advice?'

'I'll think about it,' Roger said. 'But I'm not much moved to do it. I know my book, and can dispute. That ought to be sufficient.'

'Ought to be is not is. Well, never mind. You'll dispute with Albert? There's pride for you!'

'Nay, he surely won't examine me. I am not his favourite student; I argue more than he likes, I think. I expect the Chancellor.'

'Why, in heaven's name? He *never* comes to examinations any more. Or do you mean Gautier de Chateau-Thierry? He never comes to examinations either – you know as well as I do that he's hardly a year into his duties, he pays as little attention as possible to the university. Or are you the son of some great lord?'

'No,' Roger said, and hesitated; and at this moment the self cried soundlessly to him, *Speak!* so that he nearly started. 'The university invited me. I am supposed to teach here, after my inception. I don't think I can banquet my way into such a post. They will ask me hard questions and insist that I be letter-perfect in them. Nothing else would be fair.'

'Aha. Yes, fair. Well . . . perhaps so. Too bad; some of those fellows haven't had a bath since Gerbert rode the eagle. When I study under you, Roger, I will buy *you* a bath and a banquet, if I have to borrow the money from my sister. By that time you may be as dirty as Thomas Aquinas himself – layers and layers of accumulated dignity.'

'And when did you last bathe, Daun Buranus?'

'Students aren't allowed to frequent public baths,' John said, regarding his bowl of wine critically. 'So you must not tempt me, Roger. So you're to be a regent master. And all the time I thought you were just a harmless black magician, too backward on his grimoires to be admitted to a coven. Think how my soul's been in peril.'

'The more so if you wait long enough to study under me. By then you'll be far away, and holy.'

'Perhaps,' John said. 'But perhaps not. I've no great stomach for a mission in pagan Livonia. I was thinking before you came in tonight, I might make a good graduate beggar. I know all the degrees of staleness that bread can go through and still be bread, and every tune that King Borborygmi sings. And the truth is, I'd rather study than preach.'

And I, the self said piercingly.

'Well then. It's not so difficult to become a *vagus* without losing one's tonsure, bulls or no bulls, if one does it in the name of learning. I've near completed the trivium, and shall have my secular mastership; and thence I might go to Montpellier, if you like, and become a physician; and still my bolt's not shot, I could spend seven whole years more at Bologna and become a doctor of law. And it might take me two or three years just to get from one school to another, if I sang well along the roads.'

'Doctor of civil law?'

'To be sure; canon law's not for the roads. As is only just: if your clerk's to claim the privileges of the altar, then he should stay close to it. But who knows? To become a doctor of *both* laws might keep me another seven years *in studio*; that would put another face on it.'

'You have more faces than Janus, but still. . . . It's not an ill way to learn. I've hardly decided myself what I'll do. I've no gift for the road, that much I know.'

'It's probably more curse than gift,' John said. 'But both are callings – if I have the word right. In my country we have only one word for all three, and you use it on pigs. A sad condition for a language to be in. And look you, alas! The wine's gone.'

That was just in time, for the taper was almost gone,too. The murmurous night world around them had suddenly become very fuzzy in all its categories. They shook their heads over the empty quart, frugally blew out the candle-stump, and let time swallow the dregs of the day.

In the early morning, John was gone, his few possessions with him; nothing remained but a small book bound in black, placed on the lectern where Roger would see it. No other trace of the life they had led together, as warmly uncommunicative as cat and puppy, existed now in the room but a memory of the plans John had hinted at while the candle flickered; and these rang hollow at dawn. Had the Livonian youngster really stolen away, even before his inception, to join the *Ordo Vagorum*? Nothing was left to say aye or nay.

On the morning of his examination, Roger looked down at the empty pallet for a long time, as a man looks who would part with his first friend, and cannot; while the light grew pitilessly, and the time drew nigh.

And then, as always, someone was singing, and the song came floating through the window like eiderdown:

> '*Li tens s'en veit,*
> *Et je ei riens fait;*
> *Li tens revient,*
> *Et je ne fais riens. . . .*'

Enough; that was how it was. He looked at the book on the lectern, but he did not need the self to tell him that he did not dare open it now. After the song had come cockcrow; and after cockcrow, bells. He donned his gown and left.

'*Sit thema,*' Albertus Magnus said, but he was drowned out. The hall had been filling for nearly an hour, as the word got around that Albert was examining a student, and that the student had answered eight questions out of eight on his book. But the noise and the movement in the hall failed to divert Albert's hooded eyes. He stood before the leaves of his manuscript, as blocky and immovable as a sarsen stone in his stiff black master's robes, and watched Roger where he stood sweating ice in the dock. It was intensely hot.

'*Sit thema,*' Albert said again with his glacial patience: '*Queritur quomodo materia est una, an numero vel genere vel specie.*'

It was a little quieter now, and Roger needed the quiet. There was something like Nemesis in Albert's heavy-lidded regard; nothing, that look seemed to say, could come from this disputation to Roger but disgrace. Had his contentiousness really inflamed the German that far? Never mind, it was too late; the question, the question!

It was frightening enough. The doctrine with which Albert had presented him was the first of the questions which had led the teaching of Aristotle to be forbidden until now. It was the essence of the heresy of David of Dinant, unless it could be answered; matter cannot be one in number and the same throughout the Creation, else there is no need even for God. But did Albert want him to argue it from Aristotle, *per se et per accidens*, and thus show himself to be too good an Aristotelian to be immune to the heresy? Or did he mean to force Roger into making a ruling of his own, independent of authority, and thus diminish his standing as a lecturer-to-come on Aristotle? It was not a question of knowing what *the* answer was; to any Aristotelian that was perfectly clear: matter, being imperfect, incomplete and ignoble, cannot be one; but instead, a question of knowing the dangers inherent in the problem. There was no doubt that Aristotle sometimes gave the wrong answers, but he never failed to ask the right questions, and this one was fearsome; did Albert really want to hear Roger argue it?

'The universal forms are not one in number,' Roger said at last, in a dead silence. 'They are multiplied as particular forms are received. Even were primal matter one in number, it cannot remain so: *sic non est una numero, tamen est numerositate essentie.*'

The whole hall was holding its breath. Albert's expression did not change; he simply turned a page; but that was enough. Someone in the corner of Roger's eye rose and pushed excitedly out into the streets.

'*Sit thema,*' Albert said: '*Queritur diversas substantias et animam in corpore hominis esse, qui adducantes Aristoteles viditur dicere in sexto-decimo librorum suorum de animalibus.*'

The eyes looked at Roger as though seeing inside his flesh

to the very selfsame self; and thilke self set up such a sweet silent storm of rage that Roger shrank away from it, dazed and shocked. He had never doubted until now that the thing with the bodiless voice belonged to him in some way, even spoke for desires he was not yet ready to acknowledge, perhaps in the long run to his greater good; but this dizzying fury! – the voice might have been a demon's. He felt himself turning pale, and closed his eyes for a moment. When he was able to open them again, a small group of medical students in the forefront of his vision was whispering together interestedly.

He set his teeth and said to the self, *Silentium!* The storm in his blood did not stop, but it abated a little; enough for Roger to reset his jaw into the substance of Albert's question. There was now no doubt in his mind but that Albert meant to take him step by step through every opinion of Aristotle which had once been, and again might be, a breeder of heresy. Now in particular he was demanding knowledge of the selves and the souls that Aristotle had detected deep inside every man: the active intellect which reasons; the non-reasoning intellect which bears like scars the wounds of experience, and which can prevent the *intellectus agens* from talking or even thinking about a painful subject; the entelechy or vegetative self, which does not think at all, but can compel a man to breathe even when he is determined to yield up all that, and to digest even an eel pie, or heal over a hopelessly running sore; and all those others – the ones that think; the ones that perceive; the ones that desire. Were all these one soul, or was a separate soul required for each?

Aristotle himself was of no help here, as was the case with all the great potential heresies. He had simply looked into the mind of man and reported it a single substance multiplied by secondary virtues, some more perfect than others, as Averroes agreed; but he had never ruled on the question of separate substantial forms. Yet for one entrusted with the care and cure of souls, everything depended upon whether the sinner were single and indivisible, or in himself a little Hell and Heaven of warring factions, all originally from God, all at odds now.

As thou knowest, the self said in a tiny whisper in one ear, indefeasible and terrifying. In this extremity, Roger remembered the teachings of Richard Fishacre, of whom he had been so jealous just before leaving Oxford, and put out his hand to them as a man drowning to a battered log.

'A Christian may hold three views on this matter,' Roger said, and then had to clear his throat. '*Estimant enim aliqui, quod vegetabilis et sensibilis et rationalis sunt una et eadem forma, et variantur tantum secundum operationem.*'

'*Et?*' Albertus Magnus said.

'*Alii posuerunt quod in homine est anima unica forma numero.*'

'*Et?*'

'*Tertii ponunt quod sunt tres formae et tria haec aliquid in hominibus a quibus sunt istae tres operationes—*'

'– *cui plena contradicit Magister Augustinus*,' Albert said, in a voice as quiet as rats scampering up a hawser. Roger could hear the intake of breath all over the hall. '*Et?*'

'*Diffinere non audeo*,' Roger said stonily.

For a moment Albert stared at him in stunned disbelief.

'Thou art not permitted to entertain no opinion of thine own on such high matters, youngling,' he said at last. His voice was still very quiet, but it was as wounding as sleet. 'Answer thou me, or stand down.'

'Corruption shall put on incorruption,' Roger said. 'As it is given. Thus is the soul of man a composite substance, composed of a sensitive soul and a vegetative soul, alike corruptible, and the intellectual soul which is incorruptible; yet from each of these is made by God one soul *secundum subjectum*, summarized in perfection as Aristotle teaches; one, composite and perfect; diverse and simple; matter and form, natural and derived from nature, but perfect in its unity before God, whence it came.'

'Ah,' the hall said, generally. Albert flicked the massed benches a glance of subdued scorn, but there was obviously no more to be pursued down this road. The self – whatever it was in the eyes of God – had built around Roger such fortifications as would not be breached in an afternoon, nor in a year. For the first time in all Roger's experience, it seemed to be singing; and to his horror, it could not carry any tune, but whined away like a wheel of wet slate cutting a green log. Its ordeal over, it had abandoned Roger's body, which promptly began to tremble like an aspen leaf; yet his ordeal was still young.

The ordeal was, however, curiously slow to resume. Albert turned a page, and then another, and then seemed to become preoccupied with his clothing: first adjusting his bishop's mitre forward until it made five distinct furrows in his rather sloping brow; then folding his robe carefully over his left arm before leaning upon that forearm on the open book. Suddenly he looked up again at Roger, but only to ask him a wholly simple double question as to whether or not all motion was animal motion, and if so whether or not the heaven had life. The very simplicity of the query baffled Roger, the more especially since it was fully dealt with in the *De plantis*, and the examination on that book was over; had Albert reverted to it to gain thinking time? If so, best not to give him the satisfaction or the opportunity. Roger disposed of the double question with two quick denials. 'In addition', he said, 'the text makes it clear that Aristotle is here citing other writers' arguments; hence it would be wrong to maintain that his statements on this subject are authoritative.'

But Roger had underestimated his opponent; rapid as Roger's answer had been, the next question followed even faster, and the next, and the next. Was substantial form arisen out of nature *per generationem*, or induced by special creation? How shall we interpret Aristotle's position that dreams are never sent from God and cannot be interpreted? Are the movers of the inferior orbs continuous with the First Cause, and if so were they needed to implement Creation, to produce their own inferiors, or to operate these inferiors after the Creation?

They were not, it was true, particularly hard questions, and Roger was slow to realize why Albert was requiring that they be answered under so much pressure. When in the middle of his argument on medium and motion the self suddenly presented him with the key to the riddle, he was furious all over again. Every hailstone in this storm of questions was derived directly from the thousand-and-one objections to Aristotle's teachings embodied in the writings of William of Auvergne, Bishop of Paris, upon whose review of the written record of this examination Roger's appointment would finally depend. Albert was rushing him in hope of provoking a slip or a potential heresy, since he could hardly have supposed that Roger would have come to the examination unaware of the Bishop's mountain of quibbles. Evidently the book before Albert was a compendium, including at the very least the *De universo*, the *De legibus* and the *De anima*.

The hall – now so packed that you could not have thrown a melon without striking a student or a master – was utterly silent, and the massed faces turned from one man to the other as though following a tossed ball. Probably not one man in ten was able to follow the argument, since it was being conducted in a subject that had not been taught at the university since before Roger's birth; but plainly the crowd had caught its import long before Roger had. As he reached his peroration, Roger faltered, trying to recall what he had said in his helplessly quick answers which might make grisly interesting reading for Bishop William, but it was all gone clean out of his head; it was all he could do to conclude the period he had going.

'*Sit thema,*' Albert said instantly, and in the same grindingly monotonous voice: 'Whether the world existed from all eternity, as Aristotle says; or whether it was created by God.'

As Roger opened his mouth to answer, there was a roar from the hall; and that noise of amazement and delight saved him. Albert had almost achieved his effect: lulled by the long series of petty points as well known to him as breathing, Roger had been about to render a quick opinion on the most terrifying problem in the whole of Aristotle. But the mob had sensed the trap, and its baying cry of appreciation had sprung it prematurely.

Now the ordeal was at last begun again.

'The world,' he said slowly, 'was created by God, nor does the letter of Aristotle's argument deny this; it is Averroes who imposes this interpretation upon the text. *Non tamen recipitur, si factus est, in vacuum nec in plenum sed in nihil, et ideo mundus non est eternus secundum Aristotelem et veritatem.*'

'If God created the world, He had a sufficient reason, otherwise this detracts from His omnipotence.'

'This I concede, Magister Albert.'

'Therefore did not this reason exist before the world existed? Did it not in fact exist *ab eterno*?'

'I believe it did, and that this is the sense in which Aristotle must be read.'

'Then,' Albert said, 'was not the Creation in fact *per accidens*?'

'No; because to deny God the power to create the world at some single time also detracts from His omnipotence.'

'Oho,' said somebody in the front rows. He was hissed at.

'Yet if sufficient reason for the world existed *ab eterno*, the Creation implies a failure on God's part to observe His own holy law.'

'Not so,' Roger said. 'That law applies only in nature; *non valet in voluntariis, nec est querenda cause sue voluntatis.*'

Albert shuttered his eyes against a gentle murmur of laughter from the part of the hall where the faculty of theology had gathered. It could not have been pleasant for him to be reminded before an audience that even in the course of a formal heresy-hunt he must not question the causes of God's will.

'The moment of Creation,' he said ponderously, 'divided existence from nothingness, the one after the other, implying the existence of time *ab eterno*. Motion is the measure of time; therefore motion existed *ab eterno*; therefore the thing moved; therefore the world.'

This fiendish argument left Roger floundering; though he

thought at once of the 'eternal now' of Paramedes, he could hardly be sure that it was relevant, let alone admissible. The hall held its breath in sympathy.

'Motion and nature are inseparable,' he said at last. 'Thus what came into being at the Creation were those things, which were to be measured, not measure itself. Time is of God, and eternal, but motion is of the world, and temporal.'

'Then it follows that time will last to eternity, beyond the world and motion. If for this there is sufficient cause, why not also for the world?'

'Sufficient cause exists, but not sufficient virtue,' Roger said. 'Infinite virtue exists in the First Cause, which if He filled the world with virtue, could make it last forever; but He chooses to give the world finite virtue only, so that it may last a long time, but not forever, as He will last. Equally, He could end the world now, but has promised us He will not, till the number of the elect be made up.'

'It is not reasonable to suppose that Aristotle knew the number of the elect,' Albert said harshly.

'This I concede. Nevertheless he was divinely inspired and does not deny the faith. He says that without time there is no motion, implying that motion did not begin in time, which we have shown to be true; and in the *Metaphysics* he says that there are always first things, otherwise there would be no later things; hence even in Aristotle the world has a beginning, as all else.'

'He says it will have no end; no time nor motion.'

'Which any philosopher may say, Magister Albert; this lies not in the realm of the provable, since it lies in the future which is not knowable by argument; nor does a beginning assume an end. In the future all that is knowable is by revelation.'

'I concede this,' Albert said with a sour grin.

'Then it may be shown that this revelation was vouchsafed,' Roger said evenly, 'and that Aristotle knew that motion would end, though time might not. He has it in the *Ethics* that if man is to have happiness, it can only be after death. How can this be? Only after the resurrection of the body; and this will never happen until the number of the elect is filled, in Aristotle exactly as it is in *Revelation vii.*'

People were standing up now all over the hall, and there was a growing shuffle and drumming of feet. The students were beginning to demand that Albert concede; already the examination had set records for severity and for patience, and the long low sunbeams slanting over the benches from the mullioned windows were an unnecessary reminder that even the second meal of the day would be missed should Albert persist still longer. The German set his lips and glowered at his book.

'If the world is not *ab eterno*—' he said, and the hall shook with howls of protest. He straightened his back and stared over all their heads, waiting. It took a long time.

'If the world, nor motion, nor even time,' he said, and though his face would never show itself shaken, the zigzag grammar betrayed him into Roger's hand as surely as a written surrender, 'and the Word of God tells us that these three things are true, is it nevertheless *possible* that the world was and is eternal?'

'No, it is not,' Roger said. 'Since everything that is comes from something, all causes must regress indefinitely to that one thing which comes from nothing and was caused by nothing. That, being prime and perfect, can be God and none other; wherein lies the eternity of which Aristotle speaks, and not elsewhere.'

The hall hung on the breathless verge of riot. Albert lowered his head, but he was still looking at Roger. In that look Roger knew that they were to be enemies forever, and was content.

'*Quod concedendum est,*' Albert said, and closed his book.

VI: THE CHARNWOOD HILLS

To Adam Marsh the abrupt disappearance from Oxford of Roger Bacon, that winter of 1237, without word or screed, was puzzling; surely the boy could not have imagined that Adam would hold against him a quarrel born from the twin agents of miasma and wine? Yet was it so Roger-like as to raise no eyebrow even among the boy's few acquaintances who soon forgot; but it remained on Adam's mind until word came that Roger was indeed in Paris. Then Adam's mind was freed for higher matters.

The world was moving, and be Adam never so agile, its heavy footfalls were thudding in his spoor. Frederick II had taken an Empress less than seven weeks after Grosseteste's consecration as Bishop of Lincoln. This Empress Isabel had seemed, at first, of little moment to him, especially compared to the letters that Pope Gregory had sent throughout Christendom on September fourth preaching a new crusade; but both meant heavier papal levies upon England, a matter about which Grosseteste was already incensed and which hence could not but be of moment to Adam whether he willed it or no. In his natural mind, nothing would have moved him so much that same year as the death of Michael Scot: for of kings and princes there were, the groaning world well knew, far too many, but of great scholars never more than a famine; but now it was these very kings and princes who were to be Adam's familiars, and this, mathinketh it hem with whatever saving irony he might, by his own devious intercession – there being no pebble too small to lame the cloven hoof of the world, and set it to limping ponderously at one's back thenceforward.

Nevertheless it had somewhile seemed to him that his cross might be lifted from him – grief though that lightening might be – and thus fit him to bear more gladly such lesser burdens as kings and princes and offices. And in truth the world seemed docile enough to his management at first. In the stifling, unpromising calm of 1236 King Henry had allowed Simon de Montfort sufficiently to shake off the royal displeasure to attend, as lord high steward, his marriage to another Eleanor, daughter of Ramon Berenger, count of Provence; and therefore to attend with gradually increasing frequency such meetings of the royal council as Henry could be persuaded to call. As spiritual adviser to the new queen, as well as to de Montfort, and as lawyer and theologian to Boniface of Savoy, the queen's uncle, Adam's excuses for avoiding the confessional of Eleanor of Pembroke became more and more many-coloured and plausible (though not without night-thoughts of the state of sin in which he stood even now, through having heard her past confessions with emotions he himself dared to confess to no one, at least not yet). Furthermore, he was all the better placed to advance the one cause which would divide him from Eleanor as cleanly and finally as the knife-stroke which split Hermaphrodite and Salmacis into the two sexes in the Greek story: the marriage of Eleanor to Simon.

Confession, he thought hurriedly – yet again and again – could follow. As deliberately he shied away from imagining what Grosseteste would say when he heard it. Grosseteste had himself urged Adam not to shun offices: whence all else.

The marriage first, confession after, and abide the outcome. It was, he well knew, a poor formula for salvation; but damnation spread its cold green talons wherever else he might turn.

It was far from easy to predict with any confidence what the king would make of such a marriage, but Adam hazarded that he would endorse it. It had been Henry who had effectively delivered Leicester into Simon's hands, by forcing Amaury de Montfort either to concede to his brother or become an Englishman; the loss of Normandy had taught Henry, it seemed, the dangers of a divided allegiance. Was not the next step obviously that of allying Leicester with the

Crown, as the other earldoms had already fallen? So Adam conceived it.

And so indeed it fell out, with in fact more royal favour than Adam had dared to pray for, with a ceremonial marriage at Westminster in 1238 on the day after Epiphany; the king himself gave his sister away. The ceremony was secret, on Henry's insistence; and as secretly Adam Marsh crept away to savour in his wound the salt of his self-congratulation, and repair if he could his soul for confession.

Into which vigil without any pause came the grinning mask of his folly, to remind him that even now, like that hero of Horace, he trod on smothered fires, scarce extinct – and that like any silly scholar he had trusted the ambition of a king to be somewhit less fond than the follies of churchmen and lovers.

For of course the secret could not be kept: Henry's very reasons for holding the wedding privately were warrants of publication and torches to the faggots. Henry could hardly have cared that the marriage of his sister to a foreigner would be gravel in the craw of the common mob, ne more did this occur to Adam, so new was he to these high concerns, until far too late; but the outcry of the barons, Adam knew equally belatedly, could have been no surprise to Henry. After all, the queen was still barren; were that curse to persist Eleanor of Pembroke's child might one day inherit the throne, and this a child by a man still no more than an alien – no matter when, if ever, Henry chose to confer Leicester formally upon Simon.

The uproar was terrifying even to Adam, and he could imagine with anguish what ill it was working in his spiritual charge, who had trusted him utterly in the engineering of this very disaster. And between the mob and the barons the tinder of another rebellion seemed to await no more than the first spark.

'Which I would abide,' Simon told him quietly, 'did I think aught to be gained. But the barons are children to be rattling their swords against Henry over such a trifle, and did I let it proceed so far, I'd find myself on the wrong side to the offending of mine entire good sense. I'll not divide England for a marriage, even to Eleanor.'

To this Adam for a while had no reply; but remained at gaze through a long low window, wherein was framed beyond a deep, gloomy sea of still forest, part of a low but rugged range: the Charnwood Hills, hazy in a pelting cold rain. It was here in the hunting lodge of Simon Iv. de Montfort, the dead earl Simon's father, some nine miles from Leicester near Hugglescote, that Simon had been accustomed these six years past to entertain Adam, and Adam's increasingly weed-choked rivulet of advice; but lately the Franciscan had become more and more a stranger in the lodge.

'And then?' Adam said at last, in a voice which sounded to himself as louring as the brow of Bardon Hill to the north. 'Would you dissolve the marriage, then? The succession—'

'Nay, that I'll not – did I say that? The succession's a bauble against such a diamond as my lady, most gentle Adam; for that, as for much else, I'm in thine eternal debt. But who's to have it? Not Salisbury surely, and there's no earl of Chester now. Best to defer to Cornwall, as is meet for a brother-in-law.'

'But how? Richard too is childless.'

'Ah,' Simon said, smiling, 'there's an art to deference, most gentle Adam; I've explored the matter. Richard's the brand ready to be cast, that much is plain. Yet consider: Should he set England aflame like the earl-Marshal before him, it must be against the King his brother; and will some child of Richard's be king of England thereafter, canst thou conceive? Nay, not from this present quarrel, unless I'm fond altogether; the barons need the mob, and the mob's not so easily to be embroiled in more wars of succession, not so soon after King John, howsoe'er it mutter and mowe.'

'I defer to thee,' Adam said. 'Lately I am affrighted by the ignorance from which I meddled. But doth Cornwall see tomorrow as thou dost?'

'I'm prepared to prove that question,' Simon said, not smiling now. 'I've sent him a letter, saying I will retire from the royal council. This will suffice, I am sure.'

'But shall hardly morsel the King, Simon; it is as good as admission of wrong on his part, to have sponsored the marriage.'

Simon shrugged. 'I'll please the King again in some other season, so only it shall go on raining rain in this one, and not blood. Let's put it to the test, and make of Henry a second question, once he sees his realm subside. He'll love me less shall I pit him against his barons with his own brother bearing their pennons.'

He paused and lowered his head until his long, hatchet-like face seemed about to split Adam's skull with the intensity of its closeness.

'My countess asks for thee, most Christian Adam,' he said. 'And thou hast absented thyself from me as well no little while. Bethink thee, while I repair my temporal faults, of those absolutions I'll have need of ere all this be ended; for I'll best be my own governor forenenst Richard Cornwall, but thou'rt my minister afore God to reckon it all up; otherwise I am done. With thine help I shall be God's instrument, Adam. I trust thee for this, wherein I am all otherways helpless; be not removed, I beg of thee.'

Thus capped and shod with lead, Adam Marsh stumbled like an old man back to Oxford, and prematurely to his confession before Robert Grosseteste, Bishop of Lincoln; and got therefrom his early reward.

'These are sins grievous and multiple, yet am I confounded to condemn thee,' Grosseteste said in a heavy voice. 'I foresee many such I shall commit, and wonder what penances to give for sins I know to be grave, yet might enlist the princes of the earth in the army of God. These are the sins of prelates who serve princes, as thou and I must do, Adam; let us not be bewildered, but act as we are counselled to do in 1st Corinthians: *Let no temptation take hold on you, but such as is human.*'

'A text without a gloss,' Adam whispered. 'Art not all human – or all demoniacal?'

'Adam,' Grosseteste said, 'despair thou not of God, which is verily a demoniacal temptation; or thou shall tempt me too, and I am as vulnerable as thou. We know well enough what "human temptation" is. It is when one sees no escape from danger by man's help, and so suffers it humbly for God's sake, confiding in His help. Only thus could we trust ourselves to serve the princes of this world – even such as Henry, or Simon.'

'Then is Simon so great a sinner? His heart is large, Capito, if I am any judge of men, and certes he means to serve God in every way a prince can. Nor loves England any the less, ne more than do thou and I. How shall I absolve him of sins lesser than mine – or thine, as thou wouldst have it?'

There was no answer for a long time. Grosseteste leaned his head into his hand, so that his eyes were covered; but Adam could see the corners of his mouth turning down and his lips firming, gently, but implacably. At last the bishop said:

'Simon's marriage is an abomination to the Church as well, Adam. I though thou knew'st this, else why didst seek absolution for thyself, not first for him? Because in the matter of his wife, thine eye offended thee? In plucking out thine eye, thou hast fostered mortal sin among thy parishioners; it is not thus that we are instructed to cure souls.'

Stunned, Adam shook his head. His hope of being unburdened in this confession had never been great enough to help him toward it, but this blow was from the only quarter whence succor might have come. 'Dear Christ forgive me; I did not know. Tell me, where doth the fault lie?'

'In thee, Adam; it was to this that I thought thee confessing, until now. Thou shouldst ken full as well as I that Eleanor vowed a chaste widowhood on the death of William Marshal—'

'Capito, Capito, dost think so little of thy student?' Adam cried in anguish. 'That's a very commonplace;

couldst believe I'd ignore it? Eleanor herself hath assured me that there was no such vow, long ere I broached to her the first whisper of my brokerage.'

'Women see the truth in strange lights when marriage is in question,' Grosseteste said with a heavy frown, 'and stranger still if the marriage be of great advantage. Hast no better warrant that no vow exists?'

'Nay, and ne more requireth I,' Adam retorted. 'The lady hath been my penitent these many years, and I say she hath it not in her to speak untruth to very strangers, namoe to kinrede.'

'Let be; thy lauds become thee, Adam, but suffice not for the hour nor th'offence. Well, I must ponder this; let's to lighter business for the nonce. It was misfortunate that I could ne attend the ceremonies of thy brother's degree, most gentle Adam; but ordain him priest was I able, and have done, as thou asked me; I see he's told thee that. For now, I propose him to be of my *familias* under canon Robert of Cadney, who hath resigned his deaconry at Kelstern in suit for the rectory of Heckington, to which he'll sure be instituted be he not superseded. Be this stile o'er-passed, I've in mind to make Cadney precentor of Lincoln in due course; doth this make a suitable tutor for thy brother, think you?'

'That is most generously done,' Adam said. 'As always, thou givest with both hands, Capito. I am more than abashed, and pray thee use my brother henceforth on his merits, not as my kinsman.'

'Assure thyself, ne more have I done algates. Now, as for Simon: Meseemeth this a matter for Rome, he being beyond my dispensation as the husband of a sister of the King; nought can serve here but papal absolution, and sanction of the marriage.'

'Which he will but purchase, as thou knowest,' Adam said hoarsely, breathing again the fumes of the pit reopening at his feet, 'and it be worthless thereafter at Rome's whim.'

'Nothing is more likely,' Grosseteste agreed, but his voice was gentle, almost serene. 'Yet there is but one Holy Father, most gentle Adam, and he is Gregory until God wills it otherwise. The corruption of the Lateran is a stench even in our northern nostrils; yet it is from thence that Simon's absolution must come. Naught else is possible, but that we must eat of the dish that is set before us, or starve. And this be thy special penance, Adam: That thou shalt bear this rede to Simon thyself, in thy proper person.'

Adam swallowed. It was an irregular penance, reflecting Grosseteste's odd notion that atonements for sins ought also to do, when possible, some positive good; the bishop was famous for them. For an instant Adam was moved to protest that such an errand was in itself an occasion for sin in the present matter, but the words stuck in his throat, for-why he had failed even now to confess the root sin; that word he had been unable to utter even to himself, as though the very sound in the inner ear would crack all dams. Nothing would do now but that he help himself, wearing such armour as he could scavenge from the waste countryside of his own soul.

'That me regards,' he said. 'But I will bear it.'

Though it was not the errand itself that Adam feared, but rather its certain consequences; which indeed followed with the implacable logic of evil, whose arrangement of events is without those catastrophic breaks with the past which, because they are unpredictable, men called Providence. In brief, Simon acquiesced to the pilgrimage on which he was bidden, as aforetime in draughty Beaumont he had indeed said he would do at the first necessity. He was embarked for Rome within the fortnight.

Thus when Adam found himself for the third time that year riding under Bardon Hill, it was with Eleanor and her retinue – and Simon in Italy. It had been from the need of any further such encounter that Adam had been seeking all along to withdraw, a fact which, he suspected with wretchedness, she had smelled out at long last. In consequence their conversation was very strange.

Simon characteristically had left almost all his knights at home, and they saw no reason to let autumn wither in neglect of the hunting; the undulating tablelands of the

Montfort holdings were particularly rich at this season in stag and other game. Priests and women being wholly unwelcome even as spectators at such work, Eleanor and Adam were left to ride the more open aisles of Charnwood forest near the lodge, with no company but that of her ladies.

She rode looking straight forward, her eyes calm and contemplative, her profile in an exquisite balance of awareness and repose upon which Adam could hardly bear to look. Off, there were sometimes the calls and cracklings of the hunting, but they were muffled and carried no meaning here. The day, too, was curiously muffled; for though the sun was brilliant, in the tall Charnwood aisles there was a diurnal dusk, paved with flickering many-pointed little suns like a spatter of golden tears.

Their confession was already over. It had been brief, for Adam had aforetime given Eleanor his last word of secular counsel in the confessional – and this impasse was what it had come to. As for Eleanor, such sins as she had to offer were never very deadly, beyond perhaps a touch of pride too pathetically close to trust in the goodness of others to be censurable by anyone. He had tried to fatten somewhat the unusual brevity of this confession with a special pleading, secular enough in intent to be sure, but bearing closely enough upon the cure of souls to pass over the sharpening edge of his scruples; but to this Eleanor had responded so little that he found himself unable to press it further.

And now there was the rest of the day to pass, for Adam could not leave for Oxford until the next noon, when some of the knights would again be available to convey him, as Simon had ordered. He would have been glad enough to leave all by himself, but Simon would hear of it and Simon's household would suffer; in such matters the new earl, like the old, was cold to anything but instant literal obedience.

'Tell me of thy brother, Father Marsh,' Eleanor said after a while. 'Is he as gentle as thou art?'

'That I hardly know how to answer, my lady. I'll bring him thee, an thou'lt have it so, and thou canst examine him at pleasure. Is a scholar of parts, so I think, and firm in piety.

Yet 'tis but a young man; I'll not abuse thee with o'ermuch praise of what's unproven.'

'Doth he favour thee?'

'Why, perhaps. None could deny us our father. Otherways the resemblance is not strong, I am persuaded – though the Bishop doth insist it is uncommon close for brothers with so many years between 'em. Again, be thou the judge; for I'm of such a mind as fails to recognize its very image, more than not.'

'So do I mine,' Eleanor said. 'I'd not have it that there could be another such as I, nay not even in a glass. I think verily I'd not seek God Himself, did I believe his to be mine own image and likenesse, as is written; but I am wicked, I think that impossible entire, and that is my small salvation.'

'Certes – He is not the image; we are. That "wickedness" is but the glass between, which shows the left hand where the right should be—'

'I know these significations,' Eleanor said. 'Give me leave, Father, to be weary of them today. 'Twas I spoke of them first, but I was ambling. Thou shalt instruct me in them later, let me pray thee.'

Adam bowed his head. 'Command me.'

'Tell me then of Robert of Cadney.'

Now he could see where she was going: she had reversed him, and brought his last plea out of the confessional into the dappled secular day.

'Forgive me, my lady, but I do not know that priest. I've told thee all I know, which I have from the Bishop; all else is hearesay.'

As she made to speak, there was a faraway shouting, and then just ahead something started up of a sudden, thrashing in the underbrush. Their horses balked, almost together, and peered about with bulging eyes, tossing their heads as if hoping to feel the reins go lax enough for a bolt. Adam pulled to, sharing their caution; were it a boar, there might be danger.

But it was only a sheep – a squat, short-legged ram of that immemorial race peculiar to dark Charnwood forest, which had probably stared up at the first Roman invaders of its aisles with this same expression of idiocy, blank, furious and sinister. For a moment it stood with its legs spread out, like a mis-made four-legged stool; then it spun, with astonishing swiftness for so clumsy-looking a beast, and disappeared with a scrambling bound.

'Belike he thought us alnagers, come to collect the wool-tax,' Eleanor said.

'Smalwe thought in that skull, I ween,' Adam said. Something in the animal's face had shaken him, though he could not say what it was: as though all his life he had been reading in a *roman*, and closing the book, had looked up into the eyes of a headsman. 'Yet I'm persuaded we should turn back, my lady.' Tis clear we're verging on the marches of the hunt, and our next visitant may be not so benign – or so timid.'

'An thou wouldst, Father,' she said quietly.

As they turned about, Adam saw to his greater disquiet that they had somehow outstripped Eleanor's entourage, or lost it. He cast about distractedly, but nothing he saw reassured him; and now the forest sighed and the aisle ahead was suddenly a-twist with falling leaves: the winds of dusk were beginning to rise.

Yet instead of pressing forward, they seemed to move very slowly, and even slowlier; and at last their horses were standing stock still, side by side; and they two, the riders, stirrup to stirrup. Just as abruptly, the wind died, and the leaves came rocking silently down the still air, or spinning like children's boats in a whirlpool.

'Then I shall say what I have in me to say,' Eleanor said quietly, as if there had been no interval at all, 'which is for no other ears but thine; for soon there'll be overhearers aplenty. And bitterly it mathinketh me to say it . . . yet thou dost not know the despair thou'st cast me in with thy today's redes and purposals, nay not a tithe of it. And I know thou art not cruel.'

'My lady—'

'Please . . . this our time is brief enough. And well I wis

that any holy father in the Bishop's *familias* must be good and noble, and befitten for the cure of worthier souls than mine. Yet that's no balm to me that am nigh without a friend . . . my first lord dead; the justiciar my guardian still with charges of treason hanging o'er's head; my brother the King mad, as I can say, deny it who will; my lord that is may not be my lord tomorrow, maugre any pieces of silver he can offer the Vicar of Christ. And now, now thou wilt give me over to some good and noble priest whose very face I know not! Gentle Adam, I beg thee – if by the will of God I am to be tried again, I will have courage – yet must I go without friend either spiritual or temporal in such an hour? Doth God intend? Adam, hear thou me, desert me not for the love thou bearest me, that moved thee to bring me to my lord . . . that moved thee to offer for my soul thine own brother. I beg thee, let this cup pass from me.'

Her voice failed, and there was silence, except for the wind; and then, an agitated feminine murmuring in the middle distance ahead. The horses' gait quickened a little; they knew the way now; and Adam could well imagine with what relief the ladies would welcome back their princess. He took a breath and brushed the leaves off his thighs.

There was now no time left for him to give Eleanor any reply, except cryptically; but no more was needed to convey his refusal, the only reply he could utter. The word had been spoken, that very word which he had prevented himself even from thinking for these many years, and it was a word of power.

No matter that on Eleanor's lips it might intend no more – as he would pray, if he could – than its Biblical meaning; for there it is also written that love suffereth long and is kind; and the species of love is not qualified.

And still he dared to hope for a respite, if not for a pardon. Simon returned in October. By his mien of cheerful cynicism, his ordinary humour in prosperous times, it was widely read that the papal Rota had not found his arguments unattractive; nor had Richard of Cornwall, which seemed to satisfy the King, at least outwardly. Perhaps, against all normal expectation, the matter of the marriage was now settled.

But Adam was not sanguine. And in fact on November first, All Saints Day, there was a new star born *in caudam Draconis*; and by the feast of St. Edmund it stood forth blazoned, baleful and anarchic across half the night sky, the greatest comet since Hastings.

Adam had no superstitious horror of comets; unlike the mob, he knew what they were, and their place in the scheme of things. They were simply bodies of earthly fire which, because of an affinity for one of the fixed stars, had been sublimated and drawn into the sublunar heavens, there to share the motion of the star that had called them up. But it followed from this that on the earth there would be an infirmity or corruption in the men, plants and animals over which that star principally ruled.

And the stars in the tail of the Dragon ruled those who ordered their lives by princes.

VII: THE CAMP OF PALLAS

Without any warning, there came swimming into Roger's head a memory of the green comet of 1238 so vivid that the low stone building above him almost dissolved, and with it all his new friends. Streaming with pale cold colours for which there were no names, the comet rode before his eyes in the darkness of Peter the Peregrine's most secret workshop, breathing its fumes and adding to them.

Surely it had a meaning; but what? That comet was three years gone and all its panics with it, yet there it was, flowing motionlessly through the black sky of Roger's bemused mind, like a reminder of worlds transmundane not vouched for nor even allowed in experience, in history, or in the Scriptures: an arch of light as demanding as a word from the mouth of a demon.

In the furnace-cluttered cellar the great smear of starlight, like an infernal rainbow, soaked gradually into the nitred vaulting. After a while it had vanished, merging into its own phantom in the light-generating eye, and thence back into the ghosts of memory. For a moment he was inclined to ascribe it to the caprices of whatever mephitic vapour Raimundo del Rey was elaborating, but a closer look showed that the young Spaniard was not yet through with his third distillation; the elaborate still, with its many-beaked 'pelican' alembic, water bath and furnace (it was the athanor that he was using, despite Peter's protest that it was too hot for the work, because it also heated the damp cellar better) required constant tending. There was to be sure an alchemical smell in the air, but Roger, who had had a little prior experience with Raymond's concoctions, thought he recognized it; which meant that it could not be the totally new principle Raymond had promised.

'Now,' Raymond said regretfully, 'we'll need to put out the furnace. The distillate burns readily, and what I'm about to show you is even more inflammable. I'm drained; will anyone volunteer?'

After a moment's hesitation, young Julian de Randa arose from the opposite side of the circle and solemnly doused the coals by the usual method of urinating on to them. There was still some fire when he was finished, but shutting off the draught would smother that quickly enough. Up to this point Peter had simply watched and listened gravely, as was his custom, but now he interrupted.

'Raymond, we have one new *socium* tonight; it would be better were you to explain *ab initio.*'

'Certainly,' Raymond said, with a wide gesture. 'What I began with was ordinary aqua fortis; the kind brewed from corn is better than brandy for this purpose – the smell doesn't let the outside world know what you're doing so quickly, and it leaves less gummy residue in the alembic. This, one distills three times with quicklime, as I've just completed doing here.' He lifted a shallow dish a third full of clear, colourless liquid, cautiously, using a rag to protect his hand from the residual heat, and showed it around. 'The distillate is completely pure potable spirits, fire without water – or almost, for of course without a little water it would be flame. It burns on a surface without burning what's under it. Two or three swallows of this and Bacchus will envy you; four or five, and it will knock you down.'

He grinned cheerfully at Roger. Their relationship was a peculiar one, very unlike the usual commerce of master and student. In fact, these roles were reversed, for in all things that mattered, Raymond was now the master.

This had happened most suddenly, and over a single word in the *De plantis* over which Roger had stumbled in class: *belenum.* The stumble had been followed by a roar of laughter from his Spanish students which had first baffled and then infuriated him; for it had turned out that the man who had put the Arabic version of the *De plantis* into Latin had simply left standing any Arabic word he did not know. Translations were full of strange words from the same source: alkali, zircon, sherbet, camphor, borax, elixir, talc, nadir, zenith, azure, zero, cipher, algebra, lute, artichoke, rebeck, jasmine, saffron.

This was no trouble to the Spaniards, who through long forced intimacy with the Moors knew from infancy that *belenum* was only *jusquiamus*, the common henbane; but their laughter had cut Roger to the liver. He had lost no time seeking among them for one to tutor him in Arabic, and Raymond had expressed the most quickly of all his interest in the small fees involved. Even more important, it had been Raymond who had introduced Roger into the clandestine circle of Peter the Peregrine.

'This much I have demonstrated before,' Raymond was saying. 'But this is not the end. Here in this flask I have vitriol. Now if one takes up the vitriol in a glass straw as you see me doing here, and adds it to the spirits drop by drop . . . you must be very careful, it may plash or sputter, not good for the eyes. . . . Now perhaps you will begin to smell it. This I call sweet vitriol and I warn you . . . it dizzies the mind as no wine could ever do. Also, it is highly volatile . . . in a little while it will be gone into the air. . . .'

'A very fearful apothecary you're likely to prove, Raimundo,' de Randa said. 'Each new principle's more potent than the last; and far more likely to bowl the patient over than to cure him.'

Now Roger could in fact begin to smell it: an odour sweet indeed, and heavy, yet which penetrated into the brain with the directness of a driven spike. There was no odour in his experience with which he could compare it; it was closest, perhaps, to that of a corpse which has lain in the sun several days, and yet not like that at all. After a while, Roger tentatively decided that it was rather pleasant.

'I believe I've died already,' someone else added.

Underneath the general laughter, however, there was a thorough-bass of grudging respect, which Roger could not help but share. Ungrounded though he was as yet in any but the very simplest elements of the arts alchemical and medical, he felt vaguely that any substance which affected the animal body, and indeed even the vegetative soul, as readily as did Raymond's essences must have some implications for physic, whatever its apparent inutility in the raw state; and utility, after all, was the test of knowledge. It required little imagination, for example, to conceive that in a case of brain fever, an electuary made with Raymond's sweet vitriol might go to the seat of the illness like dew rising to the sun.

Raymond, however, did not respond to these sallies. He was concentrating upon his drop-by-drop transfer of the vitriol to the spirits, his small lower lip caught between his teeth. The smell grew sweeter, and heavier.

'Roger,' Peter said. 'What have you this time to add to our knowledge? Rumour has it that you prosecute certain investigations on your own.'

'Several such, though only the most minor,' Roger said slowly. 'I am only a beginner, Peter, as you well know; and began small, as is suitable, with certain superstitions.'

'As?'

'As, it is generally believed that hot water freezes more quickly than cold water in vessels. The argument in support of this is advanced that contrary is excited by contrary, like enemies meeting each other. This I have tested, and it is not so. People attribute this to Aristotle in the second book of the Meteorologics; but in fact he says no such thing, but only something like it that's been read carelessly – or worse, translated carelessly: that if cold water and hot water are poured on a cold place, as upon ice, the hot water freezes more quickly; and this is true, as experiment shows.'

'Good; I wonder why?' Peter said. 'Now there's a thing. But it's autumn now, and winter a long time gone when that test was made, surely. Have you aught else?'

'Mmmm . . . somewhat. This belief that diamonds cannot be broken except by goat's blood, which I believed since my childhood myself: it's false, whatever you may read to the contrary.'

There was a snort from the other side of the circle. 'Whoever read that and believed it,' a voice demanded, 'except our Roger?' In the gloom, Roger could not decide who was speaking.

'Unfair,' Peter said instantly. 'A test is a test, whether the answer be No or Yes. What grounds of your own do you have, goat of Picardy, for believing that they *don't* dissolve?'

'I knew you'd say that. Very well. But what grounds, then, do we have for believing that the test has been made? To make such a test one must have (a), a goat, and (b), a diamond. I see nobody in our college who could pay the price of (a).'

And there was the money again, daily adding to an already intolerable burden of evasions, disguises, lies, betrayals. He was beginning to hate it, and hate most of all his inability to let go of it. But here, at least, he had been no more than foolish, in choosing unthinkingly so expensive an experiment.

'I had a little money,' he said. 'I have it no more. Now I have the diamond, and I was cheated, it's but a chip hardly big enough to see. If anyone would care to buy it from me . . .? Or a goat with a rag tied around one foreleg? He has a kindly heart, but stinks, and munches the straw from my bed directly beside my ear while I'm trying to sleep.'

There were no takers, at which he was just as well pleased; for the goat was in fact a nanny, which he was economically milking – with an occasional squirt from the teat for John of Livonia's friend, the dice-playing cat. He was not over-fond of goat's milk, but lately he had become used to the cat, which reminded him a little of that old Petronius of his Ilchester youth, and belike also of John himself. Yet that *vagus* had left behind in the room on Straw Street a memento of power which had changed Roger's life; he was in no danger of being forgotten for neglect of his cat. All the same, the cat was a companion in Roger's bosom, where John had gone away entire.

The fumes were now very thick, and Roger wondered that he had at first thought them pleasant. Now indeed they were reminding him of something, but groping through them for the memory proved almost impossible . . . nevertheless, he captured it at last. It was the thudding flocculent memory of the explosion at Westminster.

'It might be well,' he said hesitantly, 'to snuff the candles as well. There's enough light from the window.'

'Why?' Peter said.

'Well, the fumes. . . . Substances as volatile and mephitic as this have an affinity for fire; Raymond so testified.'

'Oh, it only burns if you touch flame to it,' Raymond said. 'Then it goes up all in a puff, and ware eyebrows! But there's no danger from the candles.'

He straightened uncertainly; and somehow dropped his pipette on his foot. It shattered promptly, but luckily there was no acid left in it.

'Tcha,' he said. 'Well, now I believe we are finished. If anyone would like to come up and inhale the vapour, let him come. But I will warn him, breathe shallow; this sweet vitriol of mine puts chickens to sleep for half a day.'

As he spoke, he moved away from the beaker with caution; and Roger, observing more meaning in the movement than in the words, decided at once to remain where he was. Julian de Randa, however, came forward with customary brashness, and lowering his face over the quiet white liquid, sniffed sceptically.

He straightened as suddenly as if he had been kicked; but he did not quite stand erect, but rather at a slant, as though the whole room suddenly had been tilted by some silent earthquake. His hand groped for support, and came to rest flat on the top of the athanor, which had hardly cooled at all in this short time. Roger winced in anticipation of the inevitable scream.

It did not come. Julian walked crabwise back toward his seat in the circle. Before he got there, he had collided heavily with the sharp corner of a table; but this, too, he did not seem to feel. With the utmost care, as though climbing down the face of a precipice, he lowered himself into a sitting position; smiled a magnificently silly smile; and fell straight back, his head hitting the sod floor with a soft thump.

'Mother of God!' Peter cried.

'Never fear,' Raymond said, in a slightly thickened voice. 'I warned him, anyhow, didn't I? He'll sleep a while, and wake up none the worse.'

'But his hand! It's seared, you can smell it, even through

your devil's vapour. There's lard in the kitchen, someone fetch it – or no, I've sesame oil right here. And lint, there in the cupboard with the funnels. Quick!'

He knelt beside de Randa, who was breathing most gently, his mouth wide open.

'That's a frightful burn,' Peter whispered. 'And look you, he's sleeping – nor felt a pang when he leaned against the furnace! Help me, del Rey; this is your fault, your experiment is a very qualified success at best. You *must* learn to think twice. If he complains against us to the colleges, or dies, our circle is foredone.'

The whole cellar was in an uproar now, but much of the scurrying was not notably purposeful. Throughout it all, Raymond's saucer of sweet vitriol sat neglected, continuing to sublime into the close air, to the subtle but marked confusion of everyone in the room. It was now so strong that it was making Roger sick. He arose quietly – and slowly, after what he had seen – and took up the beaker.

This close, the odour was unbearable. Holding the beaker at arm's length, he went up the stairs and out the door, into a blast of sunlight which was stunningly unexpected: he had forgotten that the gathering had commenced before noon, for it was always the next thing to night in Peter's cellar. After a moment's fuzzy thought, he set the beaker down against the wall of the building, in the direct sunlight.

A wandering, cruel-ribbed dog saw him put the dish down and came trotting over, a little sidewise . . . and then, as suddenly, it cringed away and ran upwind. A more sensible nose than any down below stairs, obviously. Roger moved upwind himself, and sat down on a sill to clear his lungs; and instantly, like a stone dropping into a well, he fell asleep.

He awoke in cool moonlight, still and stiff, and not yet quite clear-headed. His first thought was of the comet; and then, like the prompting of the self, but without its gnomic directness, came another vision; that one needed no intoxication of any sort for hints of worlds transmundane . . . for there was the spectre of the moon, riding overhead at any hour of any season, blotch-faced, corpse-like, keeping its own calendar, neither here nor there nor in Paradise.

He stirred tentatively, and found that his joints ached even more than he had thought; and further, he was feeling sick, as though he had eaten bad food; which disturbed him, for though his frame had always been gaunt, he had never been ill except transiently. It would be best, he thought, to sit still a while, and stretch out the stiffness gently. It was perhaps dangerous to sit on a sill by one's self at night in Paris, but the narrow alley here was deserted, and Peter's laboratory was in a part of the city so appallingly poor that footpads would not be likely to think it profitable browsing ground.

And all as well indeed, this obscurity, as it was deliberate and necessary; Roger himself would never have heard of Peter, being a faculty member at Paris, except by thilke design and plan – plus certain dissatisfactions which the Englishman Roger's self had poured out to Hispanic Raymond during an Arabic lesson. Not that heroes were hard to find; everyone in Paris worshipped them, as a matter of course, if only because there were so many. Each order had its own: the Franciscans' was Alexander of Hales, the author of the stupefying *Summa Theologica*; the Dominicans boasted first of all of their angelic doctor, Thomas Aquinas – a huge lard-tun of a man who was not above calling himself 'the swine of Sicily', and wrote to Roger's furious annoyance in a script so tiny that even copyists could not read it exactly – and secondly, Albertus Magnus.

It had been toward Master Albert that Raymond, as an apprentice apothecary, was most naturally drawn. Just so had it been with Roger; and to see this history unfolding once more under his nose in the person of Raymond was more than he could bear, not only in the light of his own disastrous victory – as a result of which neither Albert nor any master beholden to him would now acknowledge Roger's mere existence, even to the extent of giving way to him in the street – but because of discoveries he had made since which had cast over the whole of his Parisian venture the shadow of grievous fraud. In particular, Albert claimed not to have entered into the Dominican order until the age of 28, yet it was inarguable that he had actually done so at a very early age; which he could hardly have done had his birth date not been falsified for the purpose; though Roger had been unable to find certain confirmation of this, he was here willing to trust a deduction which could lead no other where. It was certain enough, forsooth, that Albert had slipped, as handlessly as an eel, by the many years of philosophical disciplines which were invariably enforced upon the minnows like Roger Bacon . . . and most certain of all, because made certain by Roger's direct experience, that Albert today multiplied his learning – as when, belike, had he not? – by the mechanical grinding of the thumbscrews upon the advanced university students whose teacher he purported to be. Who could not wax fat, had he blood to drink?

Certes, Albert was brilliant. He worked diligently; he had read and observed much; he wrote fluently; he summarized wittily; he talked unceasingly; possibly, with God's help, he dreamed fruitfully. But all this was magpie labour without some organon of knowledge to which the nuggets and the digging could relate; and of this Albert was almost wholly innocent; he traded instead upon a mixed coinage of dogmatism and intuition. And this, in God's name, was a fraud; this, in the holy name of God, was sinful beyond all sins, though there was no name in the Scriptures which such a sin might wear with certainty as yet. In the meantime, *item*: Albert knew nothing but the rudiments of the *perspectiva*: yet he presumed to write of optics *de naturabilis*, almost as though a deaf man should lecture on music. *Item:* Albert was ignorant of speculative alchemy, which treats of the origin and generation of things. *Item:* languages – he was unable even to use a simple Greek word without defining it in a fashion which threw sense out of the window.

Currently it was being said in Paris that Albert was a magician; and that in fact he had built himself by arts magical a head made of brass, which could answer any questions proposed by man. Of course, the head was said to exist no longer; Thomas Aquinas had happened upon it, and finding himself unable to cope with its powers of reasoning, had broken it into a thousand pieces with his staff. It was a pretty fable, but for Roger it stood for everything that seemed to him to be urgently wrong with the University. That Albert could have built no such head was beyond dispute, for of the arts magical he was ignorant beyond all his other ignorances; and as for Thomas, a blow from a staff was an argument without standing in logic. Were heroes made of such clay? Or of such clay as Alexander of Hales was made, for that matter? Yet Albert, through a reputation as a teacher made elsewhere than Paris, was applauded by the whole city as the equal of Aristotle, Avicenna, Averroes – and as a scientist could have been put into Master Grosseteste's pocket without disturbing a fold of the Capito's gown. Was it for this that Roger had given up Grosseteste, and Oxford as well?

Raymond had listened to this jeremiad to the end with an expression peculiarly undisturbed. When it was over, he had said only:

'Master, I know nothing of all this against Albert, and in truth I'm sorry to hear of it. Yet it's all of a piece with Paris, that I'll agree; the natural sciences here are in so sorry a state that I'm afraid to tell my father how I'm wasting his money. But there is a remedy. Can I trust you?'

'Trust me?' The question was so unexpected that Roger did not have time to take offence at it. 'In what?'

'In a secret, *idem est*, there are real scientists in Paris; but they are not at the University. I can introduce you to a whole circle of such, wherein you will learn more in a day than most masters have to teach in a lifetime. But this is no light matter, I'll need have oaths from you ere we seek it out; and should you refuse me such, our studies together must end, lest some lapse betray it to you.'

'No, no, Raymond, I'll give you my word. But wherein lies the need for such ceremonies?'

'In more dangers than you know. It's true that Paris is full of little circles of students and masters where one might discuss a subject in an informal manner, without *Queritur* and *Quod sic videtur* and *Sed contra.* But the University frowns on them, as being "colleges" unauthorized by the charter, and not under the control of the Chancellor. Ours is one such, and its purpose is the study of the natural sciences, and hence of Aristotle too where he applies. You can see how quickly the suspicion of magic, or heresy, or both, could become affixed to such a "college"; wherefore I ask first your most holy and hermatic oaths of secrecy.'

'Done! Let's go at once.'

Thus, not at once, but not long thereafter, did Roger make the acquaintance of Pierre de Maricourt, that extraordinary son of minor Provençal nobility who called himself Peter the Peregrine because he had been to Palestine on Gregory's crusade. Tall, grave, reserved, judicious, and yet almost shaking just beneath his skin with the violence of his love for raw experience, Peter dominated his 'college' like a bonfire inside a ring of candles, though every man in the circle was intellectually freakish and unique, a *lusus naturae*, a lapse of nature's attention to the forming of men's minds. By bent, in so far as he could be categorized at all, Peter was a mathematician; but even beyond figures, and relationships, and mensuration, he loved data – drawn nets flashing full of them, traps a-team with them, compost heaps a-squirm with them, skies a-boiling. At first, it appeared, he had been content with many small nets of his own devising: he walked in the fields, he collected specimens, he questioned travellers, he devoured the narratives and the opinions of laymen, old women, country bumpkins; he wanted to know about metals, mining, arms and armoury, surveying, the chase, earthworks, the devices of magicians, the tricks of jugglers – anything at all that an omnivorous soul could call knowledge. Where he could not go himself to find the facts, he sent emissaries, trading first of all upon a small inheritance, and secondly upon his nobility, which he had used as a defence against becoming a religious of any sort, ne monk, friar nor clerk. How he had come to think at length of the still greater net of the 'college' he had never said; but they were all his emissaries now.

Until now, in fact, there had been only three great sciences; but Peter, Roger thought, might be said to have found a fourth. It lacked only a name by which to hail it. The science of tests? No, that was too mean, it suggested uroscopy, or auspices. It was a science of the whole of experience, as distinguished from theory alone, theory superior, autonomous, empty: it was a *scientia experimentalis*, serving all other sciences and arts, yet somehow superior to all, out of which might come either confirmations of systems, or things as yet beyond systems. The notion was strange in his grasp; it conformed to nothing that he knew, and already was sliding evasively away in the deceptive colourless moonlight.

As he fought to hold it, someone directly beside him groaned most piteously. He straightened with a start and an almost universal twinge and cast about, one hand clapping his side for the sword of which stringent Paris had deprived him; but there was nobody in sight, not even at his elbow where the sound had seemed to well up.

Then there was a rustle and a grunt, and out of a thick black pool of shadow there rose into the moonlight the head of Raimundo del Rey, almost like the head of John the Baptist except that it was blinking rheumily. He looked at Roger for a moment without recognition, and Roger could smell traces of his sweet vitriol still freighting his breath. He licked his lips two or three times, rubbed his eyes, and looked about.

'Ah,' he said at last. 'So you're awake. That was a very shambles; I little suspected how far the fumes would penetrate in that stable of a cellar. And then, finding you here, Master, I feared I'd done you some ill too, and I sat me down to watch—'

'Nay, I was only asleep.' Roger smiled into the darkness, visualizing Raymond himself nodding while on sick watch; he still had far to go to make an apothecary. Yet he forbore to loose the shaft, ready though it was at his lips. It had occurred to him lately that he had lost John of Livonia in part through some fault in himself, in that he had always been too little giving of himself no matter how innocently John might invite such confidence; so that with Raymond, he was resolved to be less cautious, wherever it might lead. But there was caution and caution; to allow his tongue to vent its mockery too readily would not be a valued gift for a poor young student.

'A strange business,' Raymond said, getting up and looking about once more. 'And do you know, Master, the very dish sublimed into the air after the sweet vitriol in it – a thing I never saw before. There was no man with us with the wit to steal it, that I'll certify.'

'Oho, Raymond, there give I you the lie. I had, and I did. I set it here – no, a little to the left. . . .'

But of course it was gone, taken while Roger slept, nor could anyone honestly call the taker a thief. There it had sat on the open street, a perfectly useful dish of glazed clay with a fine pouring lip and not a crack in it, and how could the sleeping clerk six feet upwind of it be its owner?

'Nor were you,' Raymond said ruefully. 'Well reasoned all around; I'll just bake me another. And therefore, let's be off. By the look of the stars, real thieves aplenty are abroad by now, and I'm not steady enough for any sort of fight.'

'Certes; lead on, for I've clean forgot the way back.'

They moved slowly, feeling for the stepping-stones; this had been a Roman trackway with ruts for the wheels of carts cut into the roadbed. Several times in the cool moonlight Roger could see the forking of the ruts which indicated the start of a siding, where one cart might wait while another passed on the main track; but of course the sidings had long since been built over.

'And how like you our circle of real experimenters, Magister Roger?'

'More than well, Peter in particular.'

'Peter of Picardy is the noblest intelligence of these degenerate times,' Raymond said forcibly. After a moment's silence, he produced an apologetic cough. 'Your pardon, Magister Roger, but when I think of all those tonsured donkeys sitting on their gilded chamber-pots at the University, while a mind like Peter's cannot draw a class except by some mean device as these our arcane trappings and oaths, I lose all my patience. You'll be well astonished when I tell you what he's launched on now—'

'I'm certain of it, Raymond, but say on more softly, else some cutthroat will be stalking us.'

'Yes, certainly,' Raymond said, in a voice perhaps a tithe softer. 'He's preparing a treatise on the lodestone, and on all the species of magnetism. He does strange things with corks and bowls of water, and says that they *prove* that the world is a sphere. Not a new idea, certes; but to claim proof, that's a long bold leap upward from a floating cork.'

'It's plain you're not from a seafaring people,' Roger said, 'for there's proof aplenty of that in ordinary experience; otherwise how could a man on top of a mast see a port in the distance before his mates on deck can descry it? Were the world flat, those on deck would be closer to the port than the man on the mast is, and should see it better, not worse.'

'How so?' Raymond said, scratching his head.

'Why, in accordance with the Elements – eighteenth and nineteenth propositions in Book One. The line from deck to port is one leg of a right triangle, while the line from mast to port is its hypotenuse, which is necessarily longer. But now our score is even, for no more can I see what lodestones have to do with the matter than you can.'

'Hm. It's not the geometry that confuses me, but the instance. I don't think of the propagation of sight as Euclidean.'

'It is totally Euclidean; I can show this; in fact I'm thinking of writing a book about it.'

Raymond stopped so suddenly that Roger bumped into him.

'Another book? Master – again I ask your pardon, but I ask my question from love, and hence for forgiveness on that account. How long can you keep your health, working day and night in this kind? Small wonder that you fell asleep in the street – you the least affected of all the company by my sweet vitriol, as your light-fingered exit showed forth. But well I know that you are already working on some commentary, for I've seen the pages lying here and there when I've visited your room; and you've your classes; and the study of Arabic with me, a bad teacher in a difficult language; and your experiments, as with the goat, and the rates of freezing of ice; and then these night-wanderings to Peter's house, and perhaps to more such colleges unknown to me.'

He turned left and a strange dim light fell across his face; then he vanished. Turning the corner after him, Roger saw that they had debouched into Straw Street. It was only slightly brighter than the rest of that part of Paris through which they had walked, but their eyes had become so used to the darkness that the difference was immediate. The noise, too, was much as usual; some part of the student nations was always awake.

'Fear not for me,' Roger said gently. 'I'm a wobbly spring lamb no more, nor yet the dotard of the flock; I know what I do. And do you persist, I'll put you that same question: for where I teach, there do you study; where I study, you teach; and prosecute experiments more dangerous than mine, by the look of that we've just but barely escaped; and sit at Peter's feet of nights, longer than I. All that needs be added is a book in the writing, and I'll give you a florin if you'll deny it exists.'

Raymond stared at Roger for an instant, and then began to laugh helplessly. 'Magister Roger, I fear me you are a magician before me, I that burn to master the art so that I can hardly sleep in the few hours I'm abed. Indeed there's to be a book, though as yet it's scarce more than a title, since I'm still striving to learn what it shall contain. And so I lose a florin. When I bring you your lesson tomorrow, I beg you let me bite it, for I think I've never seen a real one before.'

It was only by biting his own cheek that Roger was able to prevent himself from offering the florin anyhow, and that only out of bitter memory of how divisive the money had already proven. The self, ordinarily so fuming with heady, notions and the startling bubble-bursts of aphorisms unwritten, slept as quietly as a coiled snake at moments like this; though he was certain that, like the snake, its eyes were open, it remained as silent as it must have been at the dawn of the world, when then as now it saw everything, but then did not know what to think of it. Roger was by now quite certain that the thing was ignorant of morals, and therefore lived in some intermediary region between his highest faculties and his vegetative soul; yet all his other attempts to assign it a sphere of action had failed – perhaps because it knew that when he found it, he would extirpate it, if he could.

'Certes I will, and my thanks, Raymond,' he said before the door of his house. They shook hands, a little solemnly, for the custom was still new to Raymond; and then, with a more practised bow, the student-master was gone toward his own poor room.

Upstairs, the goat, on a short tether, was nevertheless chewing upon a book. She sprang sidewise with fear at Roger's sudden snatching of the manuscript, and hit the end of the tether so hard that she fell down all of a scramble. No real harm had been done, however; the book was only a copy of the simplistic *Sentences* of Peter Lombard, which Roger knew now by heart and despised with equal thoroughness. With a grimace, he threw the goat the rest of the despoiled pages and knelt to check the wound under the old rag knotted around her left forearm, just below the elbow next to her chest.

The wound was healing without incident. While he examined it, the goat butted at his neck and shoulder with such gentle solemn affection that he kissed the end of her nose before going back to his lectern. That version of the *Sentences* had been a fair copy, made at a cost of nearly three pounds from the original Lombard manuscript on the University shelves, and might have been sold – or better still, traded for a book of Seneca or something else worth reading; but never mind; it had found its ideal audience.

Waiting for him on the lectern was his own manuscript, a commentary, as Raymond had guessed easily enough – for almost all the new books produced in at least the past two centuries had been commentaries on older authors. But as Roger stood to it in the flickering light of the single candle at the head of the board, he found that his head was still too adrift with sweet vitriol, even after so long a walk, to permit him to write. Instead, he drew to him his older author: that book that John of Livonia had left behind as a gift, now for Roger Bacon the book of all books beyond every other in the world, save only the Word of God.

For on the morning after Roger had bested Albertus Magnus in full University, he had found that book to be *The Secret of Secrets* – a letter to Alexander the Great from his teacher, Aristotle.

Roger had never seen it before; he doubted that anyone else in Paris had; the very existence of such a document semed to be unknown. Yet no man who knew the style of the Stagarite could read this infinitely precious document and think it anything but authentic. Where John had come by it was a mystery, but that he had known or guessed at its value was suspect in the manner of its arrival: a gift to Roger, in return for Roger's gifts to John of books that John loved or might find useful. Or perhaps John had not guessed, but had only recognized as any literate man would the name of Aristotle, and had bought the book in the hope that his difficult Aristotelian room-mate might be pleased.

Justice is Love, the self sang, and Roger nearly upset his high stool in the violence of his urge to kick out at that interior prompter. That the voice spoke the truth was undeniable, as any man could read in the Book of Job; but it was a less than welcome truth at this moment.

All the same, here was the great letter with its incalculable riches, the *Secretum secretorum* itself: wherein the secrets of the sciences were written, but not as on the skins of goats or sheep so that they might be discovered by the multitude, to the breaking of the celestial seal; from a hand that would rather love truth than be the friend of Plato. Here it was said that God revealed all wisdom to his holy patriarchs and prophets from the beginning of the world, and to just men and to certain others whom He chose beforehand, and endowed them with dowries of science; and this was the beginning and origin of philosophy, because in the writings of these men nothing false was to be found, nothing rejected by wise men, but only that which is approved. And yet on account of men's sins the study of philosophy vanished by degrees until Thales of Miletus took it up again, and Aristotle completed it, in so far as was possible for a man in a pre-Christian time.

Pope Gregory was dead, otherwise only a single section of the *Secretum secretorum* would force the complete revision of Roger's book on old age; this being a chapter called the Regimen of Life, wherein it appeareth that the inestimable glory of medicine, as being more necessary to men than many other sciences, was discovered to the sons of Adam and Noah, they being permitted to live so long for the sake of completing its study. Nor was the shortening of life from that time on due to the decay of the stars from their most favourable position at the moment of creation, as was commonly taught; but in part to the accumulated sins of men, which be remediable under Christ, and in part to accident, which is remediable by medicine; so that it is not in the stars that a man must pass a weakened constitution and a shorter lifespan to his sons, but a better pathway there be if he but know how to take it; for God the most high and glorious had prepared a means and a remedy for tempering the humours and preserving health, and for acquiring many things with which to combat the ills of old age and to retard them, and to mitigate such evils; and there is a medicine called the ineffable glory and treasure of philosophers, which completely rectifies the whole human body.

Of medicines for the spirit there was also God's plenty: 'Avoid the inclinations to bestial pleasures, for the carnal appetites incline the mind to the corruptible pleasure of the bestial soul if no discretion be used. Therefore the corruptible body will rejoice, and the corruptible intellect be saddened.

The inclination to carnal pleasure therefore generates carnal love. But carnal love generates avarice; avarice generates the desire of riches; the desire of riches generates shamelessness; shamelessness generates presumption, and presumption generates infidelity . . .' a strange catalogue of deadly sins to a Christian eye, both in selection and in order, yet incredibly appropriate admonitions for an Alexander; nor did Aristotle neglect medicines for the body politic of his prince: 'Take such a stone, and every army will flee from you. . . . Give a hot drink from the seed of a plant to whomsoever you wish, and he will obey you for the rest of your life. . . . If you can alter the air of those nations, permit them to live; if you cannot, then kill them. . . .'

Yet these matters and the most secret of secrets of this kind had always hidden from the rank and file of philosophers, and particularly so after men began to abuse science, turning to evil what God granted in full measure for the safety and advantage of man; until he should strive that the wonderful and ineffable utility and splendour of experimental science may appear, and the pathway to a *scientia universalis* be again opened.

And that by thee.

'Stand forth!' Roger shouted hoarsely. The goat leaped to her feet and was again thrown by the tether. Roger swallowed and resumed his perch.

'What art thou?' he said quietly. 'I demand thou answer, in the name of Jesus Christ our Lord.'

For a while there was no answer; and Roger noted that in the darkness beyond the candle flame there were strange amorphous patches of colour, pulsing and elusive. Moreover, his giddiness was worse; was that still the sweet vitriol, or was he in truth working too long, as Raymond—

I am the raven of Elias.

'That is blasphemous and untrue. I charge thee, tell me who thou art!'

I am the man.

'What man is this? Tell me thy signification, else I'll exorcize thee straight!'

Thou art the man.

'Speak on.'

Thou art the man, shalt bring back into the world the scientia universalis. *Thou shalt make of it an edifice, unto the glory of thy Lord. All help I shall give thee, that thou requireth.*

'How?'

As food brought unto Elias in the desert. Thine edifice shall touch Heaven, and on its brow be written, Knowledge is power.

These cadences were putting him to sleep. Almost he failed to see the trap, that self-same trap into which the builders of Babel had fallen.

Nay. Moral philosophy is the pinnacle, otherways nothing can touch Heaven.

'How dost thou know?' Roger whispered.

Forbye the light of knowledge the Church of God is governed; the commonwealth of the faithful is regulated; the conversion of unbelievers is secured; and those who persist in their malice can be held in check by the excellence of knowledge, so that they may be driven off from the borders of the Church in a better way than by the shedding of Christian blood.

'And – this is the meaning of that saying, Knowledge is power?

All matters requiring the guidance of knowledge are reduced to these four heads, and no more, the self sang sweetly. It was strange and horrifying to hear it discourse of these matters weighty and unusual in that same remote, bodiless, tuneless whine, as though it sang only to amuse itself.

The pages of the *Secret of Secrets* wavered and blurred before him, and he closed the book. He could think of nothing else to ask; he was suspended in an ecstasy of disbelief. In that emptiness, the self sang suddenly:

Time is.

'Yes,' Roger said, wonderingly. 'It is the subject of motion. But I don't—'

Time was, sang the self. *Time was.* Behind the voiceless music, Roger seemed to hear an endless mirroring of echoes.

'Is this the bread thou bring'st me, raven?' he said sternly, though the words came forth more than a little slurred. 'Well I know that time is single and linear, and giveth up one age belonging to all ages. This is a necessary conclusion, and doubted by no one skilled in philosophy. Nor is it opposed to the sacred writers and principal doctors, but is in agreement with their view. Why triest thou this axiom with me?'

Fool!

The moment hung. The point of the candle-flame bobbed up and down, like a fisherman's float moored above ripples. When the self spoke again, its distant soundless voice was as terrible as the strokes of a gong of brass.

Time is past!

The candle went out.

Whence from the darkness there rose rank upon rank of armed men with Saracen faces, and the faces of sheep, and the faces of demons, too bright in their chains to look upon massed under the invisible sun, passing in their thousands as men who march to the last great engagement; and with them thousands on horseback, and more on animals not yet seen in the world; and many bearing strange engines; and at their head was Antichrist. Yet in a twinkling, all this terrible host shrank, so that each man was no bigger than a grain of millet; and then even this emmet army was turned out of sight, as an image vanishes when the glass is turned; and naught left behind but the whitecaps of some torrent, stretching to the far horizon, as if one looked in vain across a strait for the coming invader. Things moved, like Leviathan, beneath these waters, but they were engines, and there were men in them; and there were dragons in the air like the dragons of the Aethiopians, yet there were men in them; and there were moles under the earth, and men rode them, all in mail, and with terrible countenances. And one wearing a cowl came and stood upon the headlands above the wide waters, and held up such glasses and mirrors as were necessary to show forth these things. And the mirrors turned, and there across the wide waters was the self-same army brought close again, yet now every man was as great as a giant across that distance, so that every link of the mail could be counted. And the mirrors moved, and the head of him in the cowl appeared in the air above the army, greater than any of them, and burning as it were of brass in a furnace, yet was not there; and many of those giants threw down their engines of war and fled; yet the host came on. And he made in the air certain compositions, which a man might know only by smelling them, or not at all, but which were certainly fell, for the ranks toppled in windrows; yet on came that inexhaustible host, and at their head was Antichrist. And he in the cowl held out his hand over the wide waters, and in the palm of it were certain crystals like saltpetre from a dungheap; and he wrapped the crystals in a scrap of parchment without any writing on it, and cast it into the wind, crying,

LUPU LURU VOPO VIR CAN UTRIET VOARCHADUMIA TRIPSARECOPSEM

whereat all that army was seen to fall in a single flash of lightning, and with a roar of such sharp thunder that the cowl flew from the skull of him that had cried out; and he fell dwindling away to nothing, like an ever-burning lamp cast into the sea.

After that for a long time there was darkness and silence. It was not the nothingness of sleep, in which the consciousness of time itself is obliterated, so that in an instant the night is gone that wakeful men could vouch for. Time passed, but what events marked it in that sable silence could not be known, nor words spoken reach the ears, nor any touch penetrate.

Then he moaned, and heard, and confused light passed before his closed lids. In a while it was gone. In the new darkness he almost awoke, drawing a breath only to discover that he could hardly breathe, and that he was soaked in sweat. Someone murmured near him, and there was an answer; he understood neither. Now, however, he could fall into true sleep.

In the early morning the world crept back into his room,

grey and cautious as an old man. He turned his head exhaustedly. Raymond was lying in the straw beside his pallet, supine, his mouth open, snoring softly. The man at the lectern had his head buried in his arms, but while Roger watched with detached wonderment, he lifted heavy eyes and stared upward at the weak light coming in the window, as a man seeing somewhat unwelcome but beyond his powers to undo. It was Peter the Peregrine, his profile so gaunt and hungry that he looked like a beggared Simon de Montfort.

Then he was aloft, tottering toward the pallet on spider's feet.

'Roger! You're awake? Shh, don't speak, rest.' He stirred Raymond with a toe; the boy only groaned. Peter nudged him harder.

'Be quiet, Roger; you're a sick man. Raymond, thou Spanish cow, get up and act the apothecary, in God's name! Julian, light the lamp and heat me some of that goat's milk; he's come around. Gloria! But let's look lively.'

Perhaps it was still only Tuesday, and time now for the Arabic lesson? But why were Peter and Julian here . . . and where were all those mailed glittering men? Then he remembered, seeing the cowl fly back from the skull in the instant of that enormous noise, and fainted.

Nearly the whole college was there, bustling and anxious, when he opened his eyes again. Hands lifted his head gently; other hands gave him something warm and sweet to drink; there was a cold wet cloth on his brow. Peter hovered over him like a man on stilts.

He felt weak, but curiously tranquil, as though he had just accomplished some great work. There were now so many things that he understood that it seemed to him that he had for the first time left his long childhood.

'How do you feel, Roger?' Peter said.

'Content. God bless you all.'

'You were very ill. We did our poor best, but in sooth there was little enough to do but pray.'

'I had the death,' Roger said tranquilly. 'I recognize it

now. Perhaps it's been pursuing me all this time; but now I've slipped away.'

Peter's face grew more worried; Roger shook his head.

'Nay, Peter, I'm not raving, only thinking back. I didn't mean to speak in riddles.'

'I *told* you you were working too hard,' Raymond said, appearing next to Peter. 'Will you heed me now?'

'It's true you ought to rest,' Peter said, 'if you can, Roger. Is there no place you could go – perhaps to visit relatives in England, or in the mountains? Some place in the south would be the best of all, if that's even barely possible.'

It was, of course, wholly possible; for now that he had decided, with an inspiration which had sprouted fantastically from the very heart of his delirium, what was to become of him, the problem of the money had solved itself; and a trip to the south would consume a substantial sum. It seemed so easy now that he knew, beyond all doubt, that he was to make of himself a scientist *instead of* a theologian; he had simply never thought of it in those terms before.

A rest in the sun . . . and leisure to read as much as he wished in the Vatican Library, greater even than the University's. And why not? The time had come to repudiate Paris in any event, it had given him all that it had for him, and were he to stay on much longer he too would harden into the same mould as those tonsured donkeys he and Raymond had been flyting just before the death had seized him in its fowl's claw. Toulouse did not attract him either; the last letter from Eugene had reported that the university there had restricted the teaching of the *libri naturales* for the first time in its history – a long step backward into the darkness. The rest of the Latins would soon follow; for the first act of Innocent IV after his coronation (his first, that is, after his wild flight from the Emperor who had sponsored him) was to rescind Gregory's acts of absolution of the Paris masters who lectured on the books of nature. The fever was already festering in Paris itself: the Dominicans had promptly forbidden all members of their order the study of medicine and natural philosophy, Aristotelian or otherwise. The handwriting for Latin Christendom was on the wall; the darkness was coming back.

Yet it might not reach England, where Roger's friends were in the ascendancy in court and church alike, and where independence of the Pope would continue a long time after it had been snuffed out on the continent, despite Henry's proclaimed vassallage to Rome. Later, the continent might change again, for letters from Adam Marsh intimated that Guy de Foulques, the papal legate whom Roger had met briefly at Westminster, might find himself in the apostolic succession – and Innocent, in revolting so instantly against Frederick II of Hohenstaufen, had not laid the best foundation for a long pontificate.

Oxford, then, was the place; Oxford, by way of Rome.

Someone coughed lightly. 'Shh, he's asleep,' Peter's voice said, in a whisper so intense that it was almost savage.

Roger opened his eyes at once. 'Nay, I was but thinking of what I should do; and have concluded, I must leave off work and rest; wherefore I'll go to the Holy City for a time – perhaps as long as a year.'

'Gloria!' Raymond crowed excitedly; and immediately his face turned sober. Roger wondered if he had suddenly thought of the loss of his Arabic tutoring fees; but never mind, all that would be well shortly.

'Most excellent wise,' Peter said. 'And now, we'll let you rest; and come bid you farewell when you're ready.'

'No, Petrus Peregrinus, there's one more favour I've to ask of you. Help me up.'

'You're mad,' Peter said, horrified. 'You must rest absolutely; though you know it not, a full week has passed while we watched you, and the better part of another. You are not ready for any sort of venture, but must rest, and eat.'

'A brief venture only – nor will I be dissuaded, gentle Peter. First someone must open my chest and take out my money; someone strong in the thews, for there's a lot of it, and much adulterated with base metals. Raymond, do so. There's the chest, lift the lid, and there you see the bag; set it out.'

The rest of the college gathered around curiously, except for Peter, who remained by the pallet, disapproving yet obviously without enough foreknowledge to raise any objection he could think reasonable.

'Now, Raymond: select what coins be most useful in Paris this year and count out five pounds all around, except to Peter – which I charge you all, use either in learning, or in such charity as your dear souls showed me in my illness. As for you, gentle Peter, well I know you're not without resources, but that's not the issue. You should be wealthy, too, but that's not within my power; I will you out of my little death fifty pounds, for your college and its master.'

The bag slumped open on top of the chest. Peter might have been about to protest, but if so, the sudden small flood of coins out of the bag's mouth paralysed him with astonishment. Roger was filled with glee; how much more joyful a thing it was to spend money than to hide it! The coins chinked musically as Raymond, biting his lip and sweating, poured share after share into the hands of the fellows of Peter's college. Then he stood aside, and Peter approached the bag hesitantly. He looked down at it for a long time without moving; without, it seemed, even blinking.

'Peter, I beg you,' Roger said. 'Fifty pounds is but a fraction of the whole, your own eyes so testify. Take it; for there's much else yet to be done.'

Peter nodded blindly, and reached into the bag. When he was finished counting, he discovered that he had no place about his person to put fifty pounds; one of the fellows tied it up for him.

'So. Now I require you all, help me up, as first I asked. Julian can carry the rest of the money; I once ran with it, when there was more, and he's far larger a carl than I.'

'But Roger,' Peter said. 'This wealth – what mean you to do now? Think me not ungrateful, but is not this wholesale generosity a little fond? Bear in mind, you're not wholly in your right humour, and. . . .'

'. . . And was always a little strange,' Roger said. 'Never fear, Peter, these since yesterday are different times, and better. I'll not scatter the rest of my patrimony in the streets of Paris; I mean to keep it, until I may use it again in the study of the sciences. And this day or die I shall join the Franciscans who are rich in learned men, for only strict sanctity of life can foster true philosophy; thenceforward shall I be poor in Christ. Who will help me? Peter, Raymond, Julian, lift me up!'

And silently: Lift me; I must be in orders, before another voice say again to me: *Time is past*. I have seen the powers of the Antichrist.

They would have improvised a litter, but he would not have it; so they bore him downstairs in the cradle of their interlocking hands, and set him on his feet in the blinding sunlight; Raymond on one side, Peter on the other, and the rest of the college knotted around Julian and the bag, glowering at passersby. While they stood waiting for Roger's nausea to pass – for he was really as weak as death, and knew well that he was wood to insist upon today for so solemn a step, and so taxing – a voice came calling against them in the middle distance.

No one seemed to notice; they shifted Roger's weight, and the weight of the bag, preparing their first steps. After a while, a man in tatters came in sight at the intersection and began to cross it slowly, limping painfully and indistinguishable with dirt. That way led toward the English Nation, and he was crying in English as he stumped the street:

'An alms for John. . . . Only a penny to touch the bowl of Belisarius. . . . Only a sterling for John the Pilgrim. . . . An alms for John, who hath the very relict of Belisarius the Anointed. . . . Only a penny. . . .'

Then he stopped, and caught sight of the unusual still group in Straw Street. He swivelled around and came toward them, his gimpy leg making poor weather of the broken paving, holding out a wooden bowl with carven writing around its edge. He needed a crutch, that was plain, but he had none.

The fellows around Julian closed ranks and jostled forward, but the beggar went by without paying them any heed.

His filthy hand, missing its middle finger, thrust the bowl toward Roger.

'An alms, clerkly sir, to thy better health. Only a penny.'

For a moment the two haggard men looked each into the eyes of the other. Why Roger was so moved he did not know, but leaning for the moment more heavily upon Raymond, he stretched his hand out to the bag and by the feel of the metal fumbled out a penny. No more, no less; this was what had been asked; he reached it out to touch that most famous of all begging bowls, which had been freighted once with tears from the blinded eyes of the last general to defend Rome from the infidels. Surely he who carried that bowl in the streets of modern Paris must be a holy man.

'God bless thee, Daun Buranus, holy friar,' the beggar said. 'I'll will thee my relict, an thou livest.' He tasted the penny, and put it away in his rags. 'God bless thee, students. Alms, alms for John! Only a penny for John the Pilgrim! . . . Only a sterling to touch the bowl of Belisarius. . . . An alms for John. . . . Alms, an alms for John. . . .'

Sweetly the cry died . . . *hyrca* . . . *hyrca* . . . *nazaza* . . . *trillirivos* . . . and with a heart waiting to be filled, Roger Bacon turned his burning face toward Rome.

VIII: KIRKBY-MUXLOE

The announcement of the King being even more wearisomely held back than was usual at a commanded secret audience, Adam March cleaved, perforce, to his room; where, even after many prayers, he found ample time remaining in which to think of what he might say to Henry, and Henry to him; and each of these imagined interviews was more disquieting than the last.

The very walls and village were disturbing, not only because Adam had never been there before, but also that the King himself was strange to them, as belike all of his line had been. The castle at Kirkby-Muxloe, a property of Simon de Montfort's, was beyond being merely ancient. Regarding it, one could hardly bring one's self to guess at who had built it, maugre what might have happened in its narrow precincts since. In so rude and disproportioned a keep might the Grendel-worm have been slain, that the most brutish of the serfs used under their breaths to frighten their children. The outer works might have been more recent, but looked much older by fault of neglect; for a work of Norman design cannot simply be maintained, it must be constantly under construction, otherwise it falls down almost at once.

Without a past, it frowned emptily upon the town from its tonsured hill. Someone had been there, once, for torches had smudged the ceilings inside; but who? No one could say. This room and a few others had been hastily furnished, but only because Henry had demanded of Simon a place of meeting secret and unlikely enough to permit him to pursue one single matter of state without interruption until the King should in his own time have done with it. Hence they were in Kirkby-Muxloe now, but neither wind nor wall would grant that they occupied it. Here they were less even than ghosts, for that nothing that had ever happened to their ancestors was more than a rumour of a rumour. It was not only for warmth and for the modesty of his Order that Adam kept his hands inside his sleeves, and not only from diligence that his thoughts pursued imaginary audiences with Henry which gave him no satisfaction nor comfort.

About the Inquisition itself, he believed, he might with confidence offer certain reassurances. The King necessarily still had vividly in his mind that series of Lateran edicts against heresy by which the Emperor had bought the favour of Honorius III for his coronation, and later, the favour of the Church as a whole despite his break with that Pope. In these Henry, a pious king, could hardly have seen any real access of devotion on the part of the Emperor; it was very plain that Frederick was no friend of the Church, nor in fact of any religion, true or heretical. No, the real motives had to lie elsewhere, and where but in the greater aggrandizement of the imperial power, over even such lands as England? And if so, what could be more alarming to a devout king with a heart of wax, than the joy with which the Church itself had adopted these edicts as its own?

This, Adam was almost convinced, was needless alarm. It had to be granted that Gregory IX seemed also to have embraced the edicts; but Adam was wholly familiar with *Ille humani generis* and *Licet ad capiendos*, the two papal bulls involved, and it was quite clear from their texts that Gregory's intentions had been to limit the Emperor's statutes, not to extend them. The bulls did no more than invest all preachers of the Dominican Order with legantine authority to condemn heretics without appeal; and even this power he had at once further limited by placing the selection of the Preachers Inquisitors in the hands of the provincial prior involved. That so heavily qualified and cumbersome a procedure might represent any threat to Henry's throne or realm – that Frederick might reach through it and grasp the King – this was only a fancy.

But intentions are not the only forces that rule popes; and the first bull in question had been promulgated in 1233 on April 20, which was not a saint's day; the second on May 20, 1236, which was not a saint's day either; two days later in the one case, only a day later in the other, the Pope might have been vouchsafed better guidance. The fact, in any event, remained, that the Inquisition was *already* reaching into England – and not by the agency of the Friars Preachers either, but in the hands of a Franciscan: Robert Grosseteste.

In the face of this, how could Adam rationally assure the King of anything? It was even possible that the Capito had been prompted to this surprising new outburst of zeal by the urgings of some within his and Adam's own Order, discontent that only the black-robed Dominicans should be deemed worthy of the pursuit and punishment of heresy. Nor could it be said with any assurance that the English nation lacked the inquisitorial temperament – not here in Kirkby-Muxloe, inherited from the man who had extinguished the Albigensian heresy in the field in a torrent of blood.

And hindsight made it equally clear that what Grosseteste was doing was wholly consistent with his nature, his conscience and his history. The regularity and severity of his visitations to the deaneries, chapters and monasteries of Lincoln were already famous; he had long fought for the resumption of this right, which had fallen into disuse even in his own cathedral chapter, and had been confirmed in it by the new Pope, Innocent IV, only last year. He had proceeded to apply it with such vigour that the religious houses were already wondering that they had ever called his predecessor *omnium religiosorum malleus*, 'the Monastery-Hammer'.

In this light, it might even be accounted remarkable that Grosseteste had allowed nine years of his episcopate to elapse – ten since Gregory had issued *Ille humani generis* – before proclaiming throughout his diocese a synodal witnessing. Yet this too was hindsight; for the *teste synodale* was hardly comparable to the ordinary visitation, even of Grosseteste's drastic kind. In these the people were only involved peripherally, being assembled to hear the word of

God, and bringing their children to be confirmed; inquiries into parish administration and correction of abuses came later, after the bishop had preached, not to the people, but to the clergy.

The net of the *teste synodale* was drawn much wider. As the bishop reached each parish, the whole body of the people was assembled in a local synod, from which Grosseteste selected seven men of mature age and proven integrity. These were sworn upon relics – of which there was never any scarcity, though no doubt some were spurious – to reveal without fear or favour whatever they might know or hear, then or subsequently, of any offence against Christian morals. The accused – noble or commoner, priest or parishioner – were summoned before his archdeacons and deans, and examined under oath.

Most of the abuses which came to light during a visitation were, alas, wholly ordinary: the holding of markets in sacred places, which had been expressly forbidden by Gregory ten years ago; the *scotales* or drinking bouts; the open celebration of the pagan Feast of Fools, on the same day as the Feast of the Circumcision, also proscribed for a decade; the gaming in churchyards; the clandestine marriages in inns of youths no older than fifteen, valid to be sure in canon law by vows *per os* alone, yet sinful without the Church; the paying of milk-tithes not as cheese, but as a pailful spilled on the floor before the altar; Sunday work; the overlaying of children; the squabbles over precedence in the Pentecostal processions to the cathedral . . . all familiar, all unlikely to be stamped out, few so horrible as to justify the application of the law, and none, surely, heretical. For the people it were better to be fatherly, and seek to be loved, rather than merely to be obeyed. Nor did the visitations find much to write against the clergy: some slackness, some simony, some embezzlement, some collecting of moneys at Easter from those who came asking the sacrament, some exacting of corpse-presents from the dying, but again no sensible trace of heresy; nothing, indeed, but cupidity, for which preaching and correction might not suffice, but all the same would have to do. And nothing anywhere in all this could have reached the ears of Henry the King by ordinary, nor interested him if it had – forbye at his most watery, he knew well what ought and ought not to engage a king – had it not been for the *teste synodale* still blowing like a gale through the diocese of Lincoln.

With a start, Adam became aware that he had been staring for some moments at a small painted figure, at first seemingly on some flat surface near at hand, then suddenly far away at the base of what Robert Bacon – no, it had of course been Roger, not the stable, wise Dominican – had called 'the cone of vision', and now plainly in motion toward him, its footsteps beginning to tick like dripping water in his ears. He stood up, feeling cold rills of sweat running down his ribs, trying to retake possession of the laws of perspective which the Capito had taught him, yet unable to focus his eyes beyond the walls of the cell in which he had been praying and hoping for all the seven hours of the ecclesiastical day; it was as though the distant marcher had indeed stepped down from the nearest wall, still clad in the indigo and madder and mosaic gold of a fresco, leaving behind a wall of Kirkby-Muxloe as dreadfully bare of any human touch as it had always been.

Yet the ticking went on; and in an instant the cell turned inside out to his eyes, and the reaches before him with it. At once he saw what he should at once have seen; and could not forbear to laugh. There were no doors in Kirkby-Muxloe, only low stone entrances which probably never had been curtained, and surely never had been closed. He had been sitting all this time looking down a passageway, down which the revenant was coming; had he not been pondering so earnestly what he could say to Henry, he might have been spared these tapestried illusions, and apprehended instead only what there was to be seen and naught more: a familiar of Edmund Rich, his name unknown but his face comfortable to Adam, a mere piece of ecclesiastical furniture – not a ghost, but only a lawyer.

'Friar Marsh: I am bidden to summon you, and bring you to the Archbishop. And he bids me say: The King is with us.'

Adam took a deep breath and covered his forehead with his wimple. 'Bless you,' he said, 'and lead me; for the love of Christ our Lord.'

'We thank you; enough,' Henry said, resettling the silver clasp of his robes on his right shoulder with slender fingers. 'We forgive you these ceremonies; there is work to be done, and quickly. Take your places.'

Adam studied him as they all moved to the table. In this vein the King was sometimes at his most dangerous, because least like himself. His white hands were bare, and so were his robes; in fact he wore no ornament to body forth what he was except the workaday fleur-de-lis coronet. Beneath that circlet his handsome, long-nosed countenance with its delicious red mouth was both framed and softened by the curls of his hair, almost like those of a page, and of his short silky beard. By the many furrows between his brows, and the set of his lips, it might have been thought that the King was only troubled, or perhaps even sorrowful, but no more than that. His voice was even and reasonable.

It was when Adam looked into Henry's eyes that he knew he had reason to be frightened. He wondered, a little, why he was not.

'My lord King, an it please you,' Edmund Rich said, and bowed his head. The iron fleur-de-lis tilted almost imperceptibly, as if in the gentlest of hot breezes, while the Archbishop made some brief benediction too much under his breath for Adam to catch. Possibly Henry could not hear much of it either, though Edmund stood immediately on his right hand. Then they were all seated around the table and Adam had a moment to tell over the beads of these his confreres in this hermetic conference.

To Henry's left, Simon de Montfort, in half mail. To Edmund's right, a thin sallow grey-haired man with a pointed nose, wearing a spotted pallium, with inkpot and quills before him; Adam remembered him without quite being able to name him. To Simon's left, Adam himself. Between Adam and the man in the pallium, a baron Adam had never seen before, and knew better than to heed; an abject thing created by Henry to honour the letter of the barons' demand that one of them be always in attendance in matters of state; if he held any castle, it was probably something like Pontrhydfendigaid or Biddenden the Less. He was magnificently attired, but might equally well have come in cap and bells.

A small company, in a small bare ancient hall; and the air as taut and full of incipient thunder as a drying drum-hide.

'We are not again to be menaced and forestalled by the Bishop of Lincoln,' Henry said pleasantly. 'We have called you here for your advice as to the means, but the end is already fixed in our heart. To wit, this *teste synodale* is pernicious, and must be ended.'

'How, my lord King?' Edmund Rich said. 'It is dangerous, yes; pernicious, perhaps; but eke an established and ordered procedure of the Church. How prevent an ordained bishop from it?'

'This we have summoned you to ask,' Henry said. 'We are not ignorant in these matters. The great Grosseteste may use this procedure, or not use, according to his best judgment for the cure of souls. We do not hold his judgment in the highest regard today. We still bear in mind the congratulations he sent to us in Wales.'

This reference baffled Adam entirely, as by their expressions it did also Simon and the counterfeit baron. Edmund only shrugged.

'You cannot choose not to understand us,' Henry said, his eyes narrowing. 'Matthew, enlighten them.'

The narrow man in the pallium, whose pen had been squeaking and sticking away over a new parchment at almost miraculous speed, dropped his quill on to the table, where it made a shiny irregular black clot. He bent out of sight, and materialized from between his feet a thick roll of manuscript. This, when he began to read from it, turned out to be part of a mensual of Henry's reign – an account so detailed and full of gossip that Adam was amazed to find the King even tolerating it, let alone sponsoring it.

Now he knew the man in the pallium: this was the clerk Matthew Paris, appointed by Henry to continue the history of the Plantagenet kingships begun by Roger of Wendover, and whom Adam had first seen at Beaumont, avidly recording Henry's strafing of Hubert de Burgh. Incredible! Henry was a notable patron of the secular arts, that was well known; but how could he stomach a historian so contemptuous, and not only between the lines, even of his good gifts? Like much else about the King, it passed understanding, or even the hope of understanding this side Jordan.

'Also in this month of 1236 was issued by the King to the Abbott of Ramsey a mandate requiring that he act as an itinerant judge in the counties of Buckingham and Bedford,' Paris read in a sort of scornful gabble. 'To this Grosseteste Bishop of Lincoln raised strong protests and asked recall of the mandate, declaring to all who would heed that canon law forbade all clerks below the rank of sub-deacon to become justiciars under princes; to which purpose he cited 2 Tim. ii. 4, *nemo militans Deo implicat se negotiis saecularibus*, and many other authorities both sacred and secular; among these being his contention that such a king treads on the verge of the sin of Uzzah, who usurped unto himself the office of priest—'

'My lord King, have we not laid this ghost these ten years bygonnen?' Edmund Rich broke in. 'I see that this ill-favoured scribe hath been a-reading at my letters, and indeed intercepting them unless I doubt mine ears. Thereby he knows, and my lord should know, that neither I nor any other prelate of substance supported the Bishop of Lincoln's position on this question to such an extreme; finding which, he fell silent.'

'We assure you that he was still sending us archdeacons to the very field of battle, a good four years later, to accuse us of violation of the liberties of the Church,' Henry said. 'This is the Welsh affair of which we spoke; had the preferment at issue not been resigned by him whom we had named, the Bishop'd be gnawing at our laces still.'

'Sure not, my lord,' Edmund Rich said, forcibly calm. 'I deem we'll hear no more of it henceforth.'

'Will we not?' the King said. 'Matthew, read on.'

Matthew Paris peeled off a great limp sheaf of pages, tucked the roll of them under the rungs of his stool, and resumed reading at once, as though he had targeted this next passage like a lancer aiming his point at his challenger's visor.

'And in this month of 1245—'

Adam stiffened; suddenly this was no longer a history. Whatever Paris was about to read had happened only last year.

'... King Henry was much vexed to be told by the Bishop of Lincoln that he would not yield the church of St. Peter in Northampton to one Ralph Passelew, a forest judge deserving in the sight of the King. And to the King's vexation the Bishop replied, first, that he sought not to give offence but only to make composition of the difference, out of concern for the souls of the said parish, and out of zeal for the King's honour; second, that he begged the King's clemency for opposing him; third, that he hoped for an audience; and fourth, that he hoped that the King shared with the Bishop the desire that all things be directed to the glory of God, the salvation of souls, and the liberty of the Church. And fifth, that the Bishop was right, and the King wrong.'

'But this should indeed all have been settled, my lord King!' Edmund Rich protested, his face white. 'I wis nat how it came into your majesty's hands at all. Ralph Passelew himself never took it to the secular arm. He sued Archbishop Boniface under canon law for a mandate of institution in eight days, and won it; but I was forced to tell the most holy Boniface that such an appointment would bring scandal upon the Church, and also assuredly upon himself—'

' "... since thou wilt be acting not out of zeal to do what is right, but only out of fear of the King," ' Matthew Paris added from text, his forefinger following the contracted, unforgiving minuscules of the code on the page before him.

Edmund stared at the historian, and after a moment's thought, crossed himself. Adam did likewise, but only abstractedly, as a man who would do himself no harm but did not seek to ward off any positive ill. He had found himself wondering why Matthew Paris should have written of these matters with such malice, and why he was now contributing his most carefully selected arrows to the King's bow. It was plain that Paris did not love the King; nor could he have borne any grudge against the Capito for past visitations, for his own monastery at St. Albans was exempt and always had been. Could it be that he was a man compelled by his single gift of history to take no man's part but his own, or that of his words? If so, never mind that to declare any man surely damned was a sin; Matthew Paris was as damned as any living soul could conceivably be, and the *Logos* itself would forbear to pity him.

'And?' the King said.

'You have exhausted my knowledge of the matter, my lord King,' Edmund Rich said. 'But I had thought it composed; and well it should have been, long ere now.'

Adam raised his hand. The circlet inclined toward him, and the eyes looked at him.

'Most Christian Adam: proceed.'

'My lord King, I know of this tangle, and the ways of it, all too well. Ralph Passelew is an outworn story to me, and to all of us in the parish; was once much loved and honoured, and deservedly so by your majesty, as any wise and just master hunter should be honoured. But in his dotage he hath presumed upon the Crown to aspire to a prebend, that should have rested in gratitude in your majesty's bounties. Robert Grosseteste had warned him, long before his dotard's greed reached your majesty's ears, not to hope to exercise such an office, which if won would lead to imprisonment for all involved, clergy and laity alike. So the law runs; but he was senile, and would not listen.

'Only then was the Capito forced to appeal to Boniface,

begging him not to allow this most dearly beloved old man to sue for any post in the Church. I myself helped to compose that letter, in which we said that such an installation would be to the detriment of Boniface his suffragens, whom it was his duty to protect. Boniface was ne more pleased by this our intercession than is your majesty, but he was forced to allow us our argument, seeing in the light of reason that it could hardly be gainsaid. Hence he proposed to us that he should instead institute in Northampton in due course a Master John Houten, then currently archdeacon of the church; to which we of course consented, since pastoral care was our only object . . . not, not certainly, to thwart our King.'

'Your King named Ralph Passelew,' Henry said.

'He was very old, my lord King,' Adam said steadily, 'and though every man loved him, he was not even a clerk, let alone a prelate.'

'Where is he now?'

'He died, my lord King, on the feast of St. Blase. That this petty broil still diverts the most high King of England from his affairs of state is not by the intention of Robert Grosseteste, Bishop of Lincoln. God and the King I beg give me leave to say that someone else is inflaming your majesty's good sense.'

'Beware,' Henry said, almost sleepily. Matthew Paris' quill squeaked and sputtered. Adam bent his head and fell silent. So did they all.

'But where are we now?' Simon de Montfort said at last. 'We've argued ourselves into an ingle, and yet it has nothing to do with why we're here.'

'Nothing, Simon?' Henry said.

'Very little, my lord King. We have been talking all along about his complaints against the Crown; but let us look for a moment at what the Capito doth to the realm now, and will do henceforth if we cannot say him, Stop! all in one voice. For look you, I am but a plain soldier as God knoweth, yet it seemeth me that after contumacy the gravest of crimes for any monk is to publish the secrets of hall or chapter to the laity, whereby he becometh a fautor of popular scandal and bringeth holy Church herself into scorn and disrepute; which rule of sense hath mostly prevailed in the practice of visitation, to the protection of rude and ignorant men such as I am, in constant peril from the meanest of temptations. This rule the noble Robert of Lincoln hath now put into desuetude – in quest of perfection of spirit among his flock as I ne doubt, but to visible confusion and despair.'

'We dare not hope,' Edmund Rich said heavily, 'that corruption shall put on incorruption in this life.'

Adam was uncertain whether this was intended to be taken as agreement with Simon's proposition, which had stricken Adam with certain doubts as to the purity of his own attitudes which he had never entertained before. Simon, however, seemed to adopt the Archbishop's words as though they had been his own.

'I thank you, my lord. Yet this is not yet all. These massive public examinations of the conscience of a whole cure bring eke *in communis fama* the sins and purported crimes of everyone drawn into the net, noble and commoner alike – and so in the end, when the noble Robert hath withdrawn to his next county, wife will ne longer bow the neck to her goodman, burgess hath no obedience from his citizens, no landholder buys and sells from any other, sheriffs are scorned, serf thinketh his lord ne better nor worse than himself, allegiances fall all awry, charters are turned into scraps; fealty itself becometh naught but a word, and may yet sink to less than a word, even to you, my lord King: to the yelp of a kicked cur who kens the foot in his ribs and licks it, sithen it belongeth to the only hand that will feed him.'

The counterfeit baron looked as though he were about to cheer, but somebody must have trodden on his toe; he looked glumly down again. The King, who had been drumming his fingers upon the table-top, gradually brought his tattoo to a stop. It had been slowing noticeably during Simon's peroration.

'Both halves of this judgment be but simple sooth,' he said. 'And so we will speak plainly. We doubt not any fraction of the fealty of Robert of Lincoln; but 'tis mortal clear what dangers he is courting. The bondsmen hate the clergy, we need not Grosseteste to be warranted of that – out of that passion sprang the last insurrection, which our barons were not loath to channel under the pillars of our throne. We do not wish these nobles afforded another such pretext: wherefrom, this meeting.'

'The danger is clear,' Edmund Rich admitted. 'Though, my lord King, when it hath passed away, I will remind your majesty again that in the matter of the prerogatives of the Church against the Crown I will be as strong a champion of Bishop Robert's views as ever I was before. But let us put that to one side for this day. Frater Marsh, thou art not without influence in the Bishop's household. Canst not prevail upon him to be less drastic? This is our quarrel too; and our just grievance with Rome will hardly be mitigated if the Bishop himself, our strongest spokesman, knows not that he promulgates in England the newest and most perilous of Papal oppressions.'

'I sorely misdoubt me that the Capito can be influenced of anyone in this,' Adam said heavily. 'His righteous wrath is at its hottest, as indeed how could it not be, considering the magnitude of these evils he upturneth daily at the synods? Nor would the rede of Earl Simon be calculated to moderate his holy fury. This is a saintly man, as your lordship knows well, and as we all seek to be. He's nat to be wooed by arguments from expediency; is from the outset far too great a logician, maugre the affront to the moral laws he'd smell like brimstone smoking up from the very first such word.'

Henry was drumming on the table again.

'Thou wilt try this course, most Christian Adam,' he said.

'Certes, my lord King, I will. Lack of zeal be'eth not my cross this day, but only misfaith in the efficacy of what's commanded. Can all these wise heads here think of *nothing* better?'

Henry's fingertips beat a soft rataplan. 'We will sit here,' he said, licking his moustache, 'until they do.'

This had been announced as a relatively ordinary midday meal, but nothing could be entirely ordinary in which the King was involved. True, the gathering at the dais was not large, consisting only of Henry, flanked by two knights; Simon and a trusted captain of his father, his devotion formed during the Albigensian campaign; the counterfeit baron, uncompanioned; Matthew Paris; Edmund Rich and his lawyer-clerk; Eleanor of Leicester and her handmaiden, and Adam Marsh. Only a dozen in all; but this was reckoning without the entourages of the King, Simon, the Archbishop and the baron all assembled at the lower tables, their usual tumult of banging tankards and bragging not greatly subdued by the royal presence. Add to these, too, the bread-cutters and the water-carriers, the squire at the hall dresser who poured the wine and gave out the cups and spoons, the usher at the door, the waiter and two servitors at the high table, and even a clerk to count Simon's silverware on and off. It was not such a crush as Adam had survived at Beaumont, but in his present liverish spirits it was sufficient to threaten him with a headache.

And the food came on without let or respite: black puddings, roasts of venison, herrings in wine, trout with almonds, spiced pottages, ducklings in verjuice, vegetables in vinegar and fruits in wine sauces, turnip jam and pumpkin jam, sweetmeats, pastries, wafers and entremets, all sifted over with ginger, cinnamon, cloves, cardamom, pepper, galingale or sugar, even the meats; and more wine than Adam would otherwise consume or see consumed in a six-month.

Nor was this all of his trouble; for this was for Simon an occasion of state, and where by ordinary his lady would have sat by her lord, today he had found it more fitting that she should be attended by their joint confessor, at the other end of the table. It was of course unthinkable that Adam should not discourse with her at all; though this was his inclination now, neither the amenities nor his duty to her soul permitted that. Nevertheless, he was at a loss for words, and filled with a sudden, ill-defined resentment toward Robert Grosseteste.

She did not allow this long. Reaching out a narrow white hand, she plucked a sweetmeat from his neglected dish and nibbled it judiciously.

'The Father is contemplative today,' she said without looking at him, licking her fingers daintily. 'Whence this wintriness, most Christian Adam?'

Adam shrugged. 'In sooth, I know not,' he said uneasily. And in fact, he realized, though he was not without some skill and craft as a diplomat, he fathomed himself not half so well as he often understood others. He knew well, for instance, that Roger Bacon and many older men often had found him somewhat of an enigma; that was easy to read in their faces. He wondered if they would be amused to know that his soul baffled himself as much as it did them. 'Belike 'tis this confrontation with thy royal brother.'

'I sensed it was going ill, and much regret to have it so.'

'There may be more. He is being white-faced and scrupulously polite.'

Eleanor crossed herself. 'Yet that's nat the all of it, I wis,' she said. ' 'Tis plain, that's but the rope that turns the windlass, by which we ken there's water in the bucket though it be never so far down in the well.'

Adam was forced to smile by the outrageous trope; like many another noblewoman, Eleanor evidently could listen to minstrels more often than was good for her.

'Bail away, my lady,' he said, 'though I'll warrant thee, there's naught below but mud.'

'Gems are born in that,' she said, with some determination. 'Well, then, I'll confess thee, good Father! Examine thy soul, and speak it.'

This was probably safe ground. At the least, they were exchanging words, no matter how like they were to gibberish, which would look more in keeping to Simon than his former sullenness.

'I was thinking when first thou spakest, my lady, of the Bishop of Lincoln,' he answered dutifully. 'In this there's naught surprising, sithin we've talked with the King about naught else all day.'

'True,' she said. 'And the noble Robert is thine oldest friend, thy teacher, thy spiritual father. How now this coldness?'

'Coldness?' Adam said, astonished.

'Certes; an thou hearest it not in thine own voice, remarkest thou on how thou spakest not of a man, but only of an office.'

'Thine ears be sharp indeed, my lady. 'Tis true I feel a certain distance, though I wis nat why or wherefore. Again, belike 'tis only this foredoomed occasion; for he hath all unwittingly caused me to appear before the King to answer to him, and utterly without those recourses which the King ne'ertheless demands of me. But stop, these are the reasonings of a child, to hold the Bishop responsible for my small embarrassment, that he wots nat of, and never meant to cause. 'Tis all this wine that hath me by the wits.'

'Fear not, I'll shrive thee for thy gluttony,' she said, and lifted a goblet to her own lips with a smile. 'I'll press thee more yet, Father, for now at least thou'rt plaudering with me. Art thou alone in this?'

'I fail to understand.'

'What Henry wants, he would from thee alone?'

'Nay,' he said slowly, 'nay, nat so. He would have it from any man here, could any bring it him. But none can.'

'Then still thy coolness is unplumbed, most Christian Adam, for e'en unwittingly the good Robert hath not singled thee out; yet speakest thou as if he had. Why is this so?'

These questions were verging upon impudence from a penitent; yet she was in her own house, as he was not. He must abide the course; indeed had consented to it. Perhaps it was indeed the wine, but for whatever reason he felt impelled to give her a little of the answer – not all, not all – as it began to appear to him. Though such a course was as hazardous as rope-dancing, that too seemed to urge him forward.

'No man can wholly love justice,' he said slowly, 'e'en

from the mouth of his confessor and brother in Christ. I did confess to our saintly Robert; and until this day, I deemed I had done my penance in sufficiency. Mayhap my heart seeks now a drop of mercy, and findeth it not, and so blames Grosseteste.'

'Now I'll not ask thee what that sin was, Father, for a game is but a game,' she said, her face instantly grave. Surely she had no notion that it was in this cast of mind and countenance that she most wrung him. 'I perceive I played at *bric* with fate-straws, and will cease; forgive me.'

'Nay, I thank thee for thy goodness,' Adam said. 'Thine innocence is proof against offence; and truly, what transpireth here hath no connection with this expiation, a burden I wrought solely for myself. I told thee, there was naught down there but mud.'

But at the same moment, the rope broke under his weight and, falling, he saw. With it his voice broke too, beyond all hazard of his mastering it, as he tried to cross over the last five words.

She turned her head and gazed at him, her delicate brows lifting slightly. He tried to look away, but could not. When at long last she spoke, it was in a whisper, so that he could not hear her over the noise in the hall; but he could read the movements of her lips.

'I know it,' she said. 'I know it. Otherwise how could it matter here? It is I. I am the occasion of this sin. *It is I.*'

No power on Earth or under it could have prevailed upon him to peril her by the faintest sign of assent; but there came to him no Power from Heaven by which he might have summoned the strength to deny it. For a few falls of grains through the neck of the glass, there were no powers, and they two were the only living things in Kirkby-Muxloe, or in all the world.

Henry would have left by nightfall, but that no course forenenst Grosseteste had emerged which was agreeable to all; so that now he would have to stay another night in Kirkby-Muxloe.

'Very well,' he said, arising at last from the table. 'We will make our own composition of this matter, as time and again we are driven to do. We will have the sheriff of Lincoln serve a writ upon Grosseteste, requiring this Bishop to show forth upon what grounds lay persons of his diocese are forced to take oaths against their wills. And if that serveth not, we will direct our sheriffs in general to allow no layman to appear before this Bishop to answer any inquiries under oath – nay, even to give statements on other matters, maugre marriages and wills, against the customs of the realm and to the prejudice of the crown. That, we hazard, will put this *teste synodale* to the halt; think you not, gentlemen?'

He did not wait upon an answer.

After some while, there was the five-fold sound of breathing being resumed. At the sound they smiled at each other, tentatively, ruefully.

'Ne doubt it will,' Simon said.

'Ne doubt it will,' Edmund Rich agreed sadly. 'And equally surely, will inflame anew the quarrel between Grosseteste and the King.'

'Canst thou not forewarn him, holy Edmund?'

'Impossible. He's still afield with Roger de Raveningham and five other clerks, turning up fresh scandals. Nor could that help us now. These acts the King proposeth, he'll see as fresh interference with the rights and liberties of the Church, to the detriment of her disciplines. And he'll be right.'

'Ne doubt the good Grosseteste hath justice on his side,' Simon said gloomily. 'Yet his case would be the more defensible, had he himself been less careless of the rights of his majesty. Witness the dischurching of the sheriff of Rutland.'

'I am unfamiliar with the instance, my lord earl.'

'I wis it well,' Adam said. 'A clerk, his name unknown to me, was deprived of his benefice for incontinence, during a visitation; but refused to surrender it, whereupon the Bishop excommunicated him, and ordered the sheriff to imprison him. But this sheriff of Rutland was a friend of the contumacious clerk and refused to act; whereat, Grosseteste excommunicated the sheriff as well. An arbitrary act, I thought then, and I think now; yet what else could the Bishop have done?'

'Why, simply what precedent would dictate,' Simon said. 'That is, a letter to the King, asking for royal assistance, and setting forth the cause. Henry then orders the chancery to issue a writ *de excommunicato capiendo*, ordering the sheriff to seize the clerk—'

'Would he in sooth have done so?' Adam asked.

'Henry? Why should he not? He would under those circumstances have had no cause for anger. You see him misfortunately, when he's most crossed, and then he's wood, I'll nat deny what's writ on cedar; but grant him what's a king's, he can be reasonable then. And here, look you, the king's bailiff cannot be summoned before an ecclesiastical court in a secular matter, as in fact Innocent IV had to remind the Bishop in this very affair. And hear me, my lords, though canon law's a mystery to me, I ken the civil as well as I can find my own bum in the dark, and this testifying under oath we've been debating all day so fruitlessly is just as clearly illegal.'

'My lord earl hath read this law aright,' Matthew Paris said quietly.

'Be still, gossip; and leave us.' Paris smiled and gathered up his quills and biblions. When he had gone, Adam said:

'And what of the King's appointing abbots as itinerant judges, withdrawing them from the cure of souls to collect money for the King's ever-empty purse? That in the long run is what led to that Passelew affair, as your grace doubtless knoweth.'

Edmund nodded heavily. Simon sighed and said,

'We need better scholars on both sides, meseemeth; though none like that I put out the door, I'd trust him nat to sell me a dead horse. And I myself lack time to be a lawyer, and bear sword besides. Tell me, most Christian Adam: what hath been the fate of thine aforetime familiar, that Roger Bacon who put the tinder to the Poitevins? There perhaps was the ilk of sightly and forward student that we most lack for now; and 'twas not long years past I heard the papal legate say the same, that is a friend to all of us, no man may grant less.'

'Forward and sightly and scholarly, that I ne gainsay,' Adam said; but by now of this day his heart in his breast was hot and black as a lump of peat-coke. 'And hath joined the Franciscans, as he writeth me, as a lay brother. Yet never have I seen any novice more unpromising for these our purposes, or e'en for those of Holy Church alone. If the King fears the Inquisition rightly, Roger's very presence would be a danger; he is arrogant, disputatious, impatient, cold of mien, condemnatory. . . . Not my first election for a man of God.'

'Oh? Art aware, most Christian Adam, that thou art describing someone an enemy would say much favours thee?'

The peat-coke turned dull red and began to smoulder.

'Nay, my lord, I was not. But I'll abide it, and we shall shortly see. Roger returneth to Oxford as regent master in Aristotle, to second the learned Richard Cornwall, this next year.'

'Surprising, in view of what you say. By whose appointment?'

'By whose . . .?' Adam said, himself surprised. 'Why, mine, of course.'

Explicit secunda pars.

Sequitur pars tertia:

OF HEM THAT YAF HYM WHERWITH TO SCOLEYE

IX: VILLA PICCOLOMINI

And now, was it all over – or all but over? Strange it seemed to Roger, as he rode north with the post through Italy, toward the cold green sea and home, that an interlude which had begun so greyly could have ended in such a burst of colour; strangest of all, perhaps, that the beginning had seemed anything but grey, even in the midst of his illness.

In Rome the Franciscans had housed him, simply but comfortably, in a monastery in the Travestere, the arrowhead-shaped part of the city on the other side of the Tiber. From the campanile of the monastery, he could see the ruins of the Circus Maximus, if he cared to climb the tower. He often did, after his strength returned a little – not only to look at the Circus, but also to marvel at the sky, which was of an intense cobalt such as he had never imagined could have existed. If from that side he turned his back on Rome, he could see the hills of the Janiculum, thatched with the flat green domes of pines.

Below there was little to see but tenements, but it was simple enough to cross the Pons Aemilius – called by the unclassical citizens the Ponte Rotto – into the rest of the city. He did some sightseeing, helped more or less by an exceedingly worn copy of *Mirabilia urbis Romae*, a compilation lent him by the brothers; but he was bitterly disappointed to find that most of the ancient structures were little more than heaps of rubble, some of them so dispersed that it was impossible to visualize their original plans even with the help of the guide-book.

What was happening to the old monuments was painfully visible to him whenever he approached the bridge in the morning, where he passed a house of some size which seemed to be made entirely of marble fragments from the pillars of history. An inscription over the door said that the house belonged to Crescentius, son of Nikolaus, but there had been no Crescentius in it for over fifty years; otherwise Roger might well have gone on inside and kicked him.

For the most part, however, he simply wandered, looking for nothing in particular, ready to be astonished at whatever the next turn of the narrow, crooked streets might bring. Though modern Rome was far from being as populous as it had been during its great age – the brothers guessed that it might contain thirty thousand people, most of whom lived huddled together about the strongholds of the barons – it was always busy; and the yellow brick with which it seemed everywhere to be faced contrasted sharply with Roger's memory of Paris, giving the Eternal City an oddly incongruous air of gaiety. If Paris had been music, Roger thought, then Rome was light.

It was none the less somehow saddening to hear with his own ears that the language of the Romans was not Latin, though he had known in advance that it was not.

One major surprise was the discovery of the bookshops of the Via Lata, in the very shadow of the arch of Claudius – not just stalls, but full-fledged bookstores. The booksellers assured him that Rome had had bookstores even under the Republic, and moreover, each man insisted that his store had in fact been in its present location since before the birth of Augustus. To prove it, they offered to sell Roger original incunabula from such hands as Cleopatra's, forehandedly penned by that queen in a number of modern languages.

Such dubious wonders aside, however, the stocks of the stores did not prove to be nearly as various as those of the pedlars of Paris. On reflection, Roger decided that this was only to have been expected, since Rome had not the good fortune to be the home of a great university.

Nevertheless, he found enough of interest to lure him gradually back into the habit of study, and thence almost insensibly out of the Roman sun, back toward that darkness from which had issued,

LUPU LURU VOPO VIR CAN UTRIET VOARCHADUMIA
TRIPSARECOPSEM

Of these words there could be no doubt whatsoever, nor

had there been any when Roger had heard them uttered at the climax of his struggle with the death. He had seen them also; or, perhaps, he had only seen them and not heard them at all, for he could not remember the timbre of the voice he knew had spoken them. On the other side, he could ne more recall the size of the letters nor the hand they were written in, though his memory for such things was nigh on perfect; yet at the same time he knew that none of the message had been in minuscule, but rather throughout in Roman capitals like those he had seen only yesterday graven over the Forum.

Well, not all dreams are from God, just as Aristotle said, no matter what the nit-pickers of Paris made of the doctrine; and if some are from demons or the self or one of the souls, should any man be astonished that they were sometimes hard to riddle? What remained was what remained: here, that the spelling of these hard words in an unknown language was perfect, maugre the ambiguity of the senses by which they had reached him in the dream.

Nay, not an unknown language entirely, for it was this that had given him his first key. VIR was a Latin word, UTRIET favoured a Latin word in despite of the fact that it was free of sense, LUPU was Latin but for one missing character – which if supplied, however, would make VIR incorrect, or else *lupus* was, since both were grammatically uninflected. It was clear that the frightful meaningless pronouncement had to be an anagram, not a language, but the parent language had to be Latin.

At first there had seemed to be no way to establish this with certainty. The resemblances could be artificial, or indeed provoked, by some artificial breakage of the line which did not follow the real pauses between words at all. But the slippery certainties of the dream allowed him to think that the spacings were not wholly without meaning. Almost beyond doubt, neither VIR nor *lupus* were the words meant, but their separation into words that favoured Latin could not be an accident; there was Latin in it, that much the separations clearly intended to convey.

Was there also Greek? The fragment ARCH in VOARCHADUMIA suggested it. In a message containing fifty characters – or fifty-seven, if he were intended to count the breaks between the words – how likely was it that the four-letter form ARCH, almost diagnostic of Greek, could occur even once? Roger did not know, and nothing in his mathematics suggested to him any way of finding out. There were so many Greek words almost unchanged in Latin, for that matter, that there might well be no Greek to be deduced from this single grouping, but instead further confirmation that the whole would be Latin when he had it in his hand.

Thus slowly, slowly, and without real awareness of the road, he began again to resume his night-time existence. No one at the monastery took real heed of him or ever had, even as a novelty, for pilgrims were common enough at all seasons. As a visitor he was not so closely bound to the regimen as were the brothers, and when he first failed to appear from his cell for the better part of three days – he was in fact asleep, utterly exhausted – it was assumed simply that he was in retreat. Thereafter he rose famished, foraged briefly to break his fast, and then was back at the task, filled with solemn high excitement verging once more on delirium, hard put to it not to begrudge it even his devotions. The friars, their just sleep warded by the mercy of thick walls, neither saw his candle-flame nor heard him coughing in the black chill of midnight.

Yet for all his labours the riddle remained as unbreakable as an Etruscan inscription. Increasingly he was driven back out into the day, in a grim canvas of the bookstores for anything that might help him, did it have to be Cleopatra her spurious self. The booksellers took to greeting him with less and less eagerness or even patience, for by now they knew that they had not what he asked for and were without hope of finding it; which in turn only increased Roger's desperation. Forgetting to eat, marching around and around the centre of the city in broken sandals, back and forth under the arch with its garret inscription DE BRITANIS, he at last heard one of the shopmen say,

'Him? That's the English ghost. They say he's come to haunt Claudius for killing the Druids.'

Roger turned. For a moment he was blinded by the sunlight, for in the past few weeks his eyes had begun to hurt and water constantly. After a few moments of blinking, however, he saw that he was being regarded steadily, and had the instant impression that he too was being haunted.

The bookseller was leaning out of the wide window of his shop, which like them all had a wooden front set in a grooved travertine sill. In the narrow doorway stood a layman whom Roger had seen often before, though he had not realized it until now: a thin swarthy man in good cloth, perhaps a form of livery – though expensively cut, it was not otherwise ostentatious, and bore no devices. On the instant of recognition, Roger knew that he had been being followed.

As their eyes met, the man stepped at once into the street and came toward him. Roger almost moved away, but something held him: neither hope nor fear, but some fascination which was neither, and perhaps no more than hunger and weakness.

'Most Christian friar,' the man said, in excellent Latin. 'I beg your blessing and indulgence. May I speak with you?'

'Certes,' Roger said. Then, in confusion: 'Why have you been trailing me?'

'Ah, you noticed! In truth, I didn't set out to do so, not at first. Let me first name myself: Luca di Cosmati, secretary-in-chief to Milord Lorenza Arnolfo Piccolomini, marquis of Modena and senator of Rome under the Emperor and Jesus Christ our Lord. And you, clerkly sir?'

'Roger Bacon, Franciscan and doctor of arts.'

Luca smiled. It was a thin smile, but not unpleasant. 'A scholar, I knew it well! I said so myself! Your patience for an explanation. It's one of my duties to seek books for the marquis' library, the most notable in Rome; and well you know, I observe, how many rounds of the stores must be made on such an errand, and how barren they be by ordinary. Lately I was charged to find a book of Seneca—'

'Yes, Seneca! Have you seen any—'

'Nay, alas. But there you have it. Wherever I went, there were you, seeking the same author, and often others whom the marquis has, or would have if he could. An unusual circumstance, eminent doctor, for Rome is not these days a bookish town; my lord is not its only bibliophile, but the rest are possessors only, not students, and buy any trash or forgery offered them.'

Roger found himself returning the smile. 'A man may buy whatever he can pay for, but that kind of buying is hard on poor scholars.'

'And on wealthy ones, books of all kinds being rarer than riches. And so, good sir, I took to following you, to make certain I was right in taking you for a scholar; and when I was certain, I so reported you.'

A chill struck in the small of Roger's back. The phrase was not a happy one. He made an abortive move of his hand toward his sword, but he had given it up over a year ago, on the day he had taken orders.

'Nay, be not alarmed, most Christian friar. Milord Modena welcomes scholars, whom he loves dearly. I am sent to beg you to be his guest at dinner.'

Thus began Roger's association with the Piccolomini family, and the belated dawn of his Roman years.

The family was large in estates, but startlingly small in number. The marquis' villa at Tivoli, not far from the enormous reaches of the Emperor Hadrian's, had few but servants to walk its mosaic floors and silent gardens; the line was dying out. That first dinner was attended only by Piccolomini himself, a stringy man of fifty with the long nose, lean face and sparse hair of a Caesar off some worn silver coin; his daughter Olivia, a withdrawn, austerely beautiful woman, but taller than Roger and far into her twenties; and Luca, the secretary-in-chief who had recruited Roger, who was treated by the marquis, who was his patron, as a brother and confidant. It would have been an easy position to abuse, but Roger never saw Luca abuse it; in fact, he seemed to cherish it.

After only a few hours of Piccolomini's company, Roger could begin to see the sources of Luca's loyalty and affection. The marquis was the gentlest of men, but that was not all. Like Luca himself, he loved learning and beauty with a great and almost exclusive intensity.

'I am only officially a senator, you must understand,' he told Roger. 'Roman politics sicken me; I withdrew years ago. These barons! They may be noble in the sight of God, but I hope He does not need my help to love them, or I shall be damned. What think you, friar Bacon? Am I so obliged?'

'The Scriptures seem to say so,' Roger said thoughtfully. 'But the translations are so corrupt that it is often hard to choose between the Word and conscience.'

'That would not be surprising after all these centuries,' the marquis said. 'But it might be difficult to prove. Is there then much textual criticism afoot in Paris these days?'

'Hardly any,' Roger admitted. 'The idea, such as it is, seems to be my own. I have been trying to learn some of the languages needed: Arabic in particular, but I mean to go on to Hebrew and Chaldean if I can find teachers—'

'Then you must of course use my library while you are here,' Piccolomini said earnestly. 'There must certainly be some works in it which are to the purpose. I no longer recall everything I have, the shelves have become so crowded in recent years, but Luca here can help you; he keeps the catalogue.'

'There is, I believe, a Hebrew grammar,' the secretary said. 'I fear I can't vouch for its merits, if any. But it might serve as a beginning.'

'There, you see?' the marquis said, his enthusiasm visibly mounting. 'And of course you have other studies that you might be able to prosecute here.'

'You would be doing Milord a favour,' Livia said with a half smile. Her Latin was perfect to the point of elegance, a circumstance so incredible in a woman that Roger thus far had been unable to answer her directly except in monosyllables. 'He seldom has anyone to talk to but Luca and me.'

'Which is usually more than sufficient,' the marquis retorted. 'You will find Luca a man of parts, I assure you, friar Bacon. In fact the Cosmati are a gifted family, all artists of stature for three generations. Luca's brother Jacopo is even better than he is.'

The secretary smiled without malice. Evidently he was used to this gibe. 'Which is why you are my patron instead of his.'

'Wait until the Church is through with him and then see how long you'll last! But no, he doesn't know where the books are. And, friar Bacon, you already know that the city is a desert where books are concerned. It's the greedy collectors who make it so, including of course myself. Our imperial ancestors invented few new vices, but private art collecting seems to have been their own authentic discovery. It would hardly have been possible to the Greeks.'

'How so?' Roger said.

'Why, it was the old Romans who wrote into law the principle that the man who owned a painting, for example, was the man who owned the board it was painted on, not the artist; and the same with manuscripts. Private collecting really began with that, because it made it possible for a man to become wealthy without having done any of the work involved, simply by saving the board until the painting on it became valuable. And so you can't find a book today in Rome that isn't nailed down, and with a hugely unjust price on it. There are no libraries but private ones, and all of us scheming to unearth a new treasure and snatch it to our bosoms before somebody else happens upon it.'

Roger laughed. 'But this would seem to mean that there must be *some* men in Rome to whom you could talk of learning, Milord.'

Piccolomini only shrugged; it was the girl who answered. 'Father may be the only collector in the city who *reads* books.'

Once more, Roger was shocked into silence. Though Luca had used almost the same words on the Via Lata, they had then seemed only banter.

'Then the matter is concluded,' the marquis said. 'You will live with us. I am sure nothing but good can come of it. As a beginning, let me show you the library now.'

The library was in fact a marvel, second only to the University's own at Paris, and far superior to any Roger had seen at Oxford, even Grosseteste's. But it was only one marvel of many.

The beauty of the villa itself was of a nature wholly new to Roger. The omnipresent thatch-roofed pines under their multiple spindly trunks were no novelty, but he had never seen cypresses before; here they were everywhere, marching in straight lines right across the landscape to the horizon. Under his window, and in almost every other sheltered spot, grew low bushes with shiny dark green leaves which bore oranges – small ones, but to Roger marvellous enough, for until now the fruit had been only a name to him. Piccolomini's vineyards were familiar enough in principle, for Roger had seen grapes aplenty around Paris and even at home; but his father had told him often enough that the vineyards of Ilchester were the outcome of an unprecedented century of fair weather, and that the time would surely come again when there would be no such tipple as British wine.

At Tivoli all this abundant natural beauty had been subdued into a kind of order, made to grow against and soften a backdrop of marble arches and pillars, or taught to sweep into exfoliative Euclidean curves and aisles. The Piccolomini gardens were not large by comparison with those of many of the marquis' neighbours, but they had been laid out by Lorenzo di Cosmati, grandfather of Luca, before Roger had been born, and were such a work of art as Hadrian's villa itself could not boast: a serene and ravishing island in which to walk in the morning, amid a purity of doves. And over it all was the Tyrrhenian sky, even more intensely blue than it had seemed over the city proper, out of which poured sunlight in overwhelming profligacy.

And the food! Roger had never before dreamed that there

could be so many different kinds of things to eat. Northern food repeated itself endlessly, disguised only by its many sauces and spices. Here he seldom recognized what was in his bowl, and on some occasions was sorry to have asked; he was, *exempli gratia*, more than fortunate to discover that squid was delicious before learning what he was eating. But this passed quickly; there was too much of moment on his mind to allow him a pause in which to become also the inventor of squeamishness.

The standards of cleanliness were equally new to him, and had to be taught him, none too gently, by the attendant assigned to him: a stout old housekeeper, once Livia's nurse, who overcame with granite obduracy his initial scandal at being tended by a woman, and saw to it that his linens were fresh, his sandals mended, and his feet clean. Piccolomini's estate made its own soap, a substance rarer than diamonds; here it was largely *lapis Albanis*, a mixture of lava and ashes, which eventually wore down to a central sliver abrasive enough to point nails, but the old matron saw to it that he learned its use. He found himself taking more baths in a month than he had formerly taken in a year.

The housekeeper herself was harder to become accommodated to. *Pro forma* monasticism in this warm radiant air did not put up a serious battle, but his old bitter distrust yielded less easily. It was several months before he could bring himself to accept that her warm and rather quarrelsome concern with him was totally without predatory intent, and ran much deeper than he could in any justice have expected or asked. She had of course been assigned to him by the marquis; Roger was her task, like any other task; but beyond that, she worried actively and constantly about the pale English friar, often to a knife-edge beyond which he did not know whether he would shout with exasperation or burst into helpless laughter. She was the first woman of this kind that he had ever encountered; and he awoke one dew-cold morning to her morning scolding, after nearly half a year had gone by, with the realization that he liked it.

Livia was the second. It was through her that Roger first

came to understand the essence of her father's loneliness, his generosity to a stranger, the curious tone of wistfulness that perpetually underlay even his most abstract and scholarly conversations. Most of the Piccolomini fortune was founded in lead mines – half the plumbing in modern Rome had come out of them – and no subject interested the marquis less than public works, except perhaps lead itself, or politics. Of his surviving children there were only two, and the other was the son of whom his wife had died in childbirth: Enea Silvio, who had fled the marquis' bewildered hostility the moment he had come into a marriage portion, and lived now in Siena, incommunicado and – Roger deduced – disinherited. No one was left the marquis but Livia, whom he had given at his own hands the broad humanistic education that Enea Silvio had sullenly refused to suffer, let alone absorb.

('That explains much,' Roger said in the library, when they were alone together. 'I have never heard a woman speaking Latin before. It surprised me.'

('It explains more than I find comfortable,' the marquis said. 'That precisely is why Latin is only spuriously a universal language, friar Bacon. It is never spoken to women any more. Women are confined to the vernacular, whatever that may be. On this account alone, Latin is dying.'

('Surely not! It is the language of scholars, everywhere; and the only written language of note. Under those circumstances, surely it can hardly matter whether or not it is spoken to women.'

(Piccolomini had given him a long, slow look, and at last seemed to be about to comment; but instead, again, he only shrugged.)

Nevertheless, it was not too hard to see that Livia's learning had unfitted her as a woman, as witness her spinsterhood still persistent in her third decade, in despite of both her father's wealth and her dark personal beauty. Young Roman princes bored her, and she alarmed them; and now there was added the simple problem of age, itself a proof that there was something amiss with the girl, a proof that grew more convincing simply by itself growing older.

None of this could matter to Roger, who found himself able after only a few months to accept her presence in the library, and her knowledge of subjects in the scholarly province. To him, everything at Tivoli was strange and hence might well be usual; he had no touchstones. She was inarguably well read – no match for Luca, who seemed to have vast stretches of the library by rote, but on the other hand more than simply a reflection of her father. She not only knew the texts, but often saw into them in a way entirely her own. After a while, Roger was taking so little notice of her sex that he talked to her in much the same style he might have adopted with any fellow scholar, maugre the parcel of respect he owed his noble host, and was occasionally surprised to find that he had been assuming knowledge on her part that in fact she lacked. By ordinary, this amused her, though he could not imagine why.

She was also far more sympathetic to Roger's interest in engineering than was her father, who was actively depressed by the practicality of his imperial ancestors; the marquis was not precisely pleased that the Goths had cut the aqueducts nine centuries bygonnen, but there was something in the manner in which he had referred to the incident which suggested that he thought it had served the Romans right for being so in love with piling one stone on top of another. About this difference Roger and his host drew nigh to real disputatiousness until Livia stepped in, diverting Roger into daytime tours of the Roman public works and so freeing his mind for nocturnal conversations more to the Piccolomini taste. When the marquis was ill with the Roman fever, as he was with increasing frequency as the second summer wore on, Roger and Livia walked in the garden and talked – of the lost secret of mortar, of active geometry, of what the buried floor of the Forum might have looked like, of the crime of quarrying ancient monuments, and other suitable subjects, while the housekeeper, Roger's servant, kept to her marble bench and looked up at the stars, sighing resignedly.

But there was nothing to sigh about. Roger had never

before felt so well, so young, so totally alive. The climate, the sunlight, the food, the beauty, the feast of reason, the antiquities, the friendships, the solicitude, all seemed conspiring to make him positively sleek. Sometimes in the fluttering evening in the Piccolomini gardens, listening to Livia's grave melodious voice and breathing draughts of citron and other perfumes, he would hear also through the doves' wings a long, long story being told by a nightingale; and with it came down around him such an imminence of the glory of God that he could not even give thanks silently, but only hold Livia's hand until some cough or stir from the marble bench brought back the lateness of the hour. Then they would part; there was always tomorrow; and besides, Roger was now required to wash his feet.

Above all there was the library, and the marquis of Modena himself. It was surprising how infrequently Roger could bring himself to think of the cipher, for all the wealth of help he now had; but somehow it never seemed to be a suitable subject for conversation. Piccolomini's enthusiasms lay elsewhere; he was a humanist, not a digger. Yet he would talk gladly of the sciences, so long as Roger cleaved to Nature as a source of correction for corrupt texts, and stayed clear of aqueducts and other plumbing. Moreover, they had early found in their joint admiration for Seneca – of whose works the marquis owned the most extensive collation Roger had ever seen, including portions of books previously quite unknown to him – a common ground in moral philosophy which widened and deepened with every evening's conversation, until Roger had to invoke a fortnight's retreat to assimilate all this magnificence, and make it his own.

It was difficult, in part because he had written nothing in nearly two years. It was, furthermore, not a formal book that was wanted here, but a schema, a hierarchy, which should of course be logical, but must in a sense be architectural as well, related in all its parts like the stones of an arch. He found himself spending almost as much time drawing diagrams as in penning argument. The struggle was protracted, for there were at least three grand elements struggling for mastery in his mind, each of which had somehow to be reconciled to the others: First, the vision of a universal science which had begun to haunt him ever since he had first read the *Secret of Secrets*; next, the domain of experiment versus revealed knowledge; and finally, the domain of the moral law, which could be allowed supremacy over the other two, but only in so far as it could be shown to derive from them.

At the end he was still unsatisfied, and gave over reworking the manuscript only out of regard for his host's patience. He did not read it that night, however, but instead used it only as in the past he had used lecture notes. The marquis listened attentively to the solemn friar who might have been his son; but he did not stint to ask questions.

'First of all, we have all the several separate sciences as they have come down to us, that is, imperfectly,' Roger began. 'I mean to include mathematics, and then medicine, alchemy, perspective, agriculture, all the sciences of natural philosophy. It is clear enough that they are all connected together and depend upon each other, as you can see most clearly in a science like medicine where the physician who knows neither alchemy nor astrology cannot be a scientist at all. He must know equally well the connections between these other sciences, as well as their relationships to his own.'

'In what way? It seems a lot to ask. I can see that some knowledge of the patient's auspices might be useful, and that a knowledge of drugs is essential. But otherwise the connections are superficial, are they not?'

'By no means,' Roger said warmly. 'For example, what might suffice against a disease of the kidneys, which are ruled by Venus? It would not be enough to know in what house Venus stood when the patient was born, which is astrology; or in what house she stands now, which is astronomy; or in what houses she will stand for the rest of the course of treatment, which is mathematics. There are likewise herbs that are governed by Venus, which is agriculture; and so is the element copper, which is alchemy. And the worst pitfall here is that the traditional medical texts say almost nothing of all this. I would rather not go into it now, but I have counted no fewer than thirty-six such grave defects in the classical teachings; I mean to write a book about it some time soon.'

'Do so, I pray,' the marquis said, blinking. 'I did not mean to tempt you into a divagation.'

'Then I mean to ask, How do we know what we know? These imperfections are rampant. They are even in Aristotle, partly because of the abominable translations we use, and partly because he concealed some knowledge for good reasons, as you can see in his book of secrets. Here we see the defect of revealed knowledge and belief, that again there is no certitude in it.'

'Is this not a dangerous doctrine?'

'No. St. Augustine himself counsels us against making fools of ourselves by quoting the Word of God to deny some plain fact of nature, because when such an apparent conflict exists, it must mean that we have misunderstood the Word. People are constantly misunderstanding the Word – otherwise we should not be plagued by heretics. Now this brings me to my experimental science, which is not a part of the sciences of natural philosophy or mathematics, not a "true" science in that sense, but nevertheless is superior to them all. It unites natural philosophy with revealed knowledge because it gives them both certitude; and imparts to each and all three dignities, which are its three prerogatives. I have written them down, thus:

'First, verification. Until you have this in your hand, anything you "know" about natural philosophy, from revelation and authority, is simple credulity, which is only the first stage of knowledge.'

'Even from Aristotle?' the marquis said. 'Even from this mysterious book of secrets?'

'O, that is only the other side of the same coin. I will believe anything, no matter how apparently incredible, if it comes to me from a sufficient authority; but that means I must have faith that he has performed the experiments he says he has performed, and observed what he says he has observed. Aristotle passes this test – I have actually repeated some of his observations myself, and they were correct. And this is a necessary proviso, for no man can live long enough to repeat every experiment in history; perfect scepticism. Josephus says that the ancients lived long lives simply out of the necessity to *understand* what they had learned.'

'I am answered. What is the second dignity?'

'The second is the one that we have already exposed, the drawing together of the separate sciences so as to see their relationships to each other, *quod in terminus aliarum explicat veritates quas tamen nulla earum potest intelligere nec investigare*. Again to cite an example, who has not seen sick dogs eat grass? Might not a man study the behaviour of animals to see how they prolong their lives, and thus recover knowledge of some healing herb long lost? Here would be a plain case of two sciences contributing to each other in a way that the man working only in one science could never hope to see. And here, most plainly, experiment is not a separate science in the usual sense, but a leaven of power at work throughout natural philosophy. And this represents the second stage of knowledge, which is simply experience.

'Now at last we come to the third dignity, again emerging from experiment: The use to which all this knowledge is to be put, for the protection of Christianity, the greater glory of God, and the greater welfare of man. And precisely here lie the greatest difficulties, because this is the domain of the third stage of knowledge, that is, reason, which must also decide to what uses knowledge *ought not* to be put. The man who sees the possibilities of the several sciences, and uses them as Archimedes did to make engines to defend Syracuse, is a man of power – of awful power if the book of secrets is correct, and I myself have had certain revelations . . . but of these I am still too uncertain to speak.

'Still it is clear, Milord, that the pinnacle of this schema must be an ethics. Moral philosophy is its outcome and its king. And it is here that I have made no progress at all. There is of course the ethics of Aristotle, but that emerges from natural philosophy, revelation and authority *as he knew them.* His knowledge is better than ours on most counts, but poorer on some crucial matters – most obviously, that he could not be a Christian, but there are others as well. And this is why our converse over Seneca impelled me to the impoliteness of all this scribbling.'

'The study of nature is not my study,' the marquis said gravely, 'and on the whole I do not regret my incomprehension. But I have believed since the death of my wife that God meant my house to be the womb of something greater than the continuance of my line. And, praise Him, I have been allowed a glimpse of it. I might have been vouchsafed more had I not been jealous of it, for which I beg your forgiveness.'

'Mine? Milord Modena, your kindnesses will be remembered in my prayers all my life long.'

'Perhaps not,' the marquis said. 'You see, while you were in retreat, Luca brought me a letter for you. I kept it, not wanting to abort the work for which I might some day be remembered, if only in God's eye. I failed to think until too late of the injury I might be doing you, were it a letter of moment. With shame, I give it to you now.'

He handed the packet across the table, and Roger broke the seal without haste; he had already recognized the hand, that of one of Adam Marsh's familiars. The message was brief – a mercy, since the candles were now burning very low.

'You have done me no harm at all, Milord. I am simply called home, and given new tasks I fear I ill deserve. It is good news, and in no wise urgent.'

'I thank God,' the marquis said. 'Of course I knew it was to bring our visits to an end; that was fore-ordained and I must abide it. But I am emboldened to ask a favour.'

'Anything in my power, Milord.'

'Then . . . would you leave me the book you read from tonight?'

'Why, certainly. But Milord, it is incomplete.'

'I know,' the marquis said, very quietly. 'It is a child of this house. But I would have it if you could yield it up.'

Silently, Roger laid the manuscript upon the table. Then he drew back the top leaf, and picking up a dripping quill, wrote across the top of it: *Communia naturalium – I.*

The marquis received it in a like silence, and held out his hand. As their fingers touched, a candle crackled and went out.

The housekeeper prophesied disasters as she packed him up, but he was used to that now. Why she should seem to be pitying him at the same time was impossible to guess; for he had never been happier in his life than in these two years.

He found the courage to tell Livia so when they parted . . . but that too ended in mystery, for as Luca and he rode companionably from the gate, he saw that she was silently weeping.

Going north, he had nothing left to think about but the cipher, which belatedly had almost solved itself, while he had been thinking about the recension of the *Communia* he had given to Piccolomini. In the midst of these labours he had been vouchsafed a revelation of a kind, though a difficult one and without any promise that he could trust. It had been simply a prompting from the long-silent self; and it said nothing but, *Count.*

After pondering this word long and long, in some bafflement as to whether or not it was itself another word of the cipher, he had used his last days in the marquis' library to ferret out three long books to study – books on subjects of so little interest to him that they threatened to put him to sleep after the first chapter. (That in itself had proven unexpectedly hard; there was virtually nothing at all in this vast ranking of manuscripts which was not wholly fascinating, regardless of subject.) He counted every character in all three, and made up a table of how many times each letter occurred. He had intended to go on to make more tables, the next to tabulate how many times pairs of letters occurred, next triplets, the next fours, but he had utterly failed to anticipate how stupefying just the first task would be, and how long it would take him; and his time was running out. He would have liked, also, to make up a congruent table for three Greek books of similar length, and make allowances for the differences arising out of the relative shortness of the Greek alphabet, and the fact that one letter in Greek might often stand for groups of two or even three in the Latin; but there was no time.

But the Greek tables did not turn out to be pertinent. With incredible swiftness the unbreakable pronouncement began to rank itself into meaning, so fast indeed that he did not pause to consider it for sense until well past noon; it was enough to see the words surfacing, one by one, like a procession of dolphins each bulging at the forehead with patent wisdom yet seeming to the sailor on such seas as alike as pea-beans.

Then, famished once more without being aware of it, and almost mortally exhausted as well, he stopped and looked. He had supplied the wolf his serpentine tail or yard, and on that model given another to LURU as a word plainly encoded on the same model; but as he had expected, that wolf had vanished now. The man in the middle, the still unbroken VIR, now stood in the heart of an explosion, with saltpetre on the one shore and sulphur on the other. He had now: *Sed tam sa petr . . . e sulphur*, separated still by VOPO VIR VOARCUMIA RICO, but he was in no doubt that something enormous had already happened. Standing himself in the middle, Roger remembered the sharp crepitating crackle of the saltpetre crystals, salvaged from his father's dungheap, under the blow of a rock in a boy's hand when he tried to shape them into larger rhombs through which to look into the eyes of Beth or old Petronius or at blades of grass, and had got nothing but that noise and a puff of pepper-smelling air for his pains; and on the other bank, there thudded in his memory the exit of the demon from the window of his noisome room at Westminster. In the middle with him was the dream, in which these huge ciphered words had become an explosion like nothing so much as the earthquake which shall exhume the dead for the Last Judgment.

He began to tremble. These words were words of power. Even in the terror of the vision he had not dreamt of how much power there was in them, nor could he yet fathom why it was being put into his hands; for he knew well enough what it was. This was the *ignis volans*, the flying fire of the Hellenes which had been lost for all these many centuries; and Roger Bacon had been told in one single struggle with the death how it was to be made . . . and of what horrors would follow. How could that be? In Simon de Montfort's grave words, would God allow? Yet He had allowed it to the Hellenes; and now in this age it was almost, almost come down to a simple piece of alchemy, about to flow from the quivering tip of the quill in Roger's hand.

Yet not quite. The rest of the anagram, it seemed, would not be broken. Again and again Roger rearranged the remaining characters, but nothing emerged but a Satanic gabble, more impenetrable than the four remaining blocs themselves. Yet it was as sure as death and resurrection that this was alchemy entire, and nothing more. What could be missing? Saltpetre and sulphur and . . . what?

Roger went back to the tables of numbers, though they were now hard to read in the light of his candle. Wiping his eyes and forehead, he tried again, counting, half asleep, gradually losing once more his awareness of the meanings of words, only seeking to see in the numbers some relationship which. . . .

And then, in a moment of whirling delirium, he had the dream back, and with it the answer. That answer was numbers. Why had he not seen before that all those U's could not be told from V's in Roman capitals? There it all was, the great fish at the bottom of a pellucid pool:

SED TAM SA PETR RC VII PART V CAROUM PV NOV
CORULI V E SULPHUR

It was painfully crabbed Latin, but certainly correct, for it was in the style of his demon self, which spoke nothing well but English and that not often; and its meaning was totally beyond argument. With the elisions expanded, the pronouncement said: *Sed tamen salis petre recipe vii partes, v carbonum pulvere novelle coruli, v et sulphuris.*

FOR THIS TAKE SEVEN PARTS OF SALTPETRE, FIVE PARTS OF POWDERED CHARCOAL FROM YOUNG HAZELWOOD, AND FIVE OF SULPHUR

He was versed enough in alchemy to know that nothing useful could be expected unless one began with pure substances, he had absorbed that in Peter the Peregrine's college; but he knew well enough how to proceed. Alongside his Arabic lessons he had learned the test for pure flowers of sulphur, which should crackle faintly when rubbed between finger and thumb; he had known from boyhood how to dig a pit in which fine charcoal is burned; and from boyhood too he remembered without irony that the most refined of all saltpetre is to be found in a dungheap. Nothing remained but to go forth and procure these things.

And this white flash of knowledge took him no longer to encompass than would have sufficed him to write down the shortest verse in Scripture; which reads, *Jesus wept.*

X: ST. EDMUND HALL

Much had changed at Oxford, as was only to have been expected; and yet in that special world which was called into being by its very name, the University had not changed at all; it was almost deceptively peaceful: the same streets, the same customs, and above all the same faces, unchanged after so much had changed him. To be sure, Adam Marsh had gone quite grey about the temples, but it did not make him seem old. Grosseteste was only just as grave and venerable as he had always been, no more; the Bishop was properly beyond age, as though he had been canonized at birth. If the King's aborting of his *teste synodale* – a confusing story, of which Roger heard so many conflicting versions that he gave it up as little better than a myth – disturbed him, he did not show it, nor did he speak of it. Roger saw him but seldom, as before; and Adam, more than ever preoccupied with the affairs of state which he loathed and loved, was at court or at Leicester for much of the year.

After the pleasures and explorations of reunions were past, Roger rather welcomed the relative solitude of the new life. He had much to do, beginning, appropriately, in the a's, with alchemy. His lectures were time-consuming, for he had discovered in himself a real passion to teach – had, indeed, discovered it in Paris; but herein lay the principal change since he was last at Oxford, in that he was now a master, weighty with respect, and could to some extent allot his own hours. He was somewhat at a loss to account for the obvious tentativeness with which the other masters treated him, however, until he discovered that Richard of Cornwall had bruited it about the University that this Roger Bacon was a dangerous sciolist: at Paris he had attended other men's lectures and confounded them before their students with questions they could not answer.

Well, Roger had done that now and again, in particular to

a booby-headed master in Euclid's *Elements* who had not actually known enough geometry to calculate the volume of a mousehole; and then there had been that lector on the law of Moses, four out of five of whose statements about the chirogrillus Roger had pointed out to be wrong; that one could count himself fortunate, since the fifth statement had been as wrong as the others. But it was a custom in Paris; Albertus Magnus had done it to Roger once, after his débâcle at Roger's examination, though happily Albert had come out again the loser and had immediately – and balefully – given up the sport as unprofitable.

As for Richard Rufus of Cornwall, rumour had it that he would not be making mischief for long, for he had received a permission – in essence, an order – from John of Parma, Minister General of the Franciscans, to return to Paris to lecture on Lombard's *Sentences*. From what Roger knew of the man, it seemed a wholly appropriate assignment.

In the meantime, Roger contentedly made many bad smells and burned himself repeatedly, to considerable profit. Within a span of two years he had mastered most of the appalling jargon of alchemy, designed not to communicate but to conceal, and was able to record with satisfaction the discovery of methods for refining three metals to the pure state. One of these – he had no names for them, and the books did not know them – seemed to be a genuine element, which when blended with iron made a mixture of phenomenal hardness perhaps promising for arms and armour. Each of the other two exploded when dropped into water, an observation which nearly cost him his eyesight, and gave him a festering sore on one shoulder which took three weeks to heal. Since nothing so fickle could be of any practical use, he dropped the matter there; if he needed a loud noise, he had the secret of the cipher – the first alchemical formula he had tried. It had worked awesomely well, particularly when, as in the vision, it was packed tightly into a parchment roll and lit with a spill at one end.

With the aid of the Arabs, whose language he now knew well enough to be able to distinguish a stylist from a plodder, he began himself to write on alchemy: in particular a new translation of excerpts from Avicenna, centred upon such passages as he had himself been able to test, or to enlarge upon. It did not greatly surprise him to find that knowing how the experiments went in practice was almost as corrective of bad translation as was a knowledge of Arabic grammar; the world, it was perfectly clear, was only the other form of the Word, and often much easier of access to its meaning. This work with the text of the great Islamic physician sent his pen scratching into several side excursions, wholly natural to his way of thinking now, into medicine. Among these was a revision of his first attempt at a book, made long ago at Oxford: *Liber de retardatione accidentium senectutis et de sensibus conservandis*, the book on old age, undertaken this time at the request of Piccolomini, marquis of Modena, brought to Roger in a letter from Tivoli as equally far away and long ago. It was a hair-raisingly bad book and probably could not be much improved, but this recension, at least, would have the benefit not only of Avicenna but of the book of secrets.

Richard Cornwall stubbornly refused to disappear. His health was uncertain, and the Paris appointment had not been to his taste. Misfortunately, Adam Marsh took his part. He wrote to the provincial minister, begging him to allow Cornwall to stay; Oxford, he said, would be delighted to keep him. Cornwall was now spreading the word that this Roger Bacon was obviously also a magician, in which he was aided more than a little by the notorious stinks, noises and oddly-coloured lights which emanated of nights from Roger's cell in St. Edmund Hall.

These sinister mutterings reached the students, as they were bound to do. The young men looked to Roger now not only for outrageous propositions – which taste was inevitably gratified, for Roger generated outrageous propositions these days as naturally as other men breathed, and with almost as little awareness of it – but also for miracles. He was tempted, and after a while he fell: with the help of alchemy, small 'miracles' were not hard to produce, and

Roger quickly discovered that they were dramatically useful as teaching aids.

Cornwall's sickly malice puzzled Adam sufficiently to move him to question Roger about it, but Roger's theory – that it derived from Albertus Magnus, whose familiar Cornwall had been for a time in Paris – would not have sat well with the lector, and so instead he professed ignorance. In the end, Adam contrived to set it down to academic jealousy over the popularity of Roger's lectures on the *libri naturales*; and these indeed were now more of a success than ever, since Cornwall had indirectly led Roger to exhibit experiments in the hall.

Nor were these the only good to emerge from that malice: for the provincial minister sent his clerk, one Thos. Bungay, to Oxford in response to Adam's letter, to investigate the merits of the case. Though he decided in Cornwall's favour, that is, that he need not go to Paris, the incessant chatter he had to endure about that sciolist and magician Roger Bacon aroused his deepest curiosity.

Within half a day Bungay and Roger were fast friends. Thomas was an astronomer, which happened to be the next item but one in the a's, just after astrology. Within six months he had applied for leave to study at Oxford; within another month, they had together leased the massive eight-sided gatehouse across St. Aldate's Street in the walls. This blocky structure, which was eighty-four feet high, served them as observatory. In addition, Thomas lived there; Roger, for the time at least, kept to his quarters at St. Edmund to be near his classes, but it was already evident that he and the University would probably benefit alike were he to take his stenches elsewhere – regardless of the fact that he was already better than half done with alchemy.

They were, they discovered, remarkably alike in some ways. Thomas Bungay was plump and affable, but he was in his heart a solitary man – and like all such, as ready to cleave to another of his rare kind as one lorn Assyrian to another. He had the love of knowledge, though with him it looked mostly toward the stars (still, he had recently been reader in theology at the nascent University in the distant marsh town of Cambridge). And despite his higher rank in the Order, he plainly regarded Roger as his teacher, deferentially playful though their manner was toward each other. He had caught the vision, at least in part.

Also they quarrelled constantly; and drank more than was good for them; and stayed up all night, studying the stars; and planned to live forever. They were alike ridiculous in their tonsures, tunics and talk, middle-aged and laden with learning, and all unaware in love; two men in a desert.

'Tonight we shall have Venus and Jupiter in conjunction in Aquarius.'

'Good for us. Where's the wine?'

Nothing disturbed them, though 1250 was a year of overturns. The Emperor Frederick died; they said, *Requiescat in pace*, and watched the occultation of Vega by the moon. To find a book for Thomas, Roger went briefly to Paris, where with his own eyes he saw in the streets the leader of the Pastoureaux rebels; the sight interested him mildly, but he was in a hurry to return home. This year, too, Adam Marsh left Oxford for good, forced to give up his lectorship to the Franciscans by the pressure of his political duties. Roger and Bungay attended his last lecture, where he created a sensation by conferring upon a youngster named Thomas Docking – no older than Roger had been when Grosseteste had plotted to send him to Paris – the unprecedented honour of succeeding to the readership (though not, since the rules forbade it, to the title itself; this and its prerogatives would be held in abeyance until a formally qualified master could be chosen; Docking's was an interim appointment, and even this did not wholly please the University).

The departure of Adam cost Roger a pang, but its sting too was solved by the new friendship with Bungay. Besides, the vision was growing clearer every year; he was now occupied, as a work of preparation, with the writing of a gloss for the *Secret of Secrets*, of which he had found at Oxford four mutilated copies. Fortunately, the MS given him in Paris by John Budrys of Livonia appeared to be perfect – fortunately, because his money was now sensibly diminished. One of the pre-conditions of the *scientia experimentalis*, it was beginning to appear, was a bottomless purse.

He was still incubating, too, that same treatise on the causes of the rainbow which he had conceived as a member of the Peregrine College; but no question of perspective he had ever encountered was so difficult as this. He could advance no farther than a plateau of theoretical nihilism, represented in manuscript by nearly a score of leaves demonstrating that all the existing explanations – even Grosseteste's, even Aristotle's – were inadequate. The road to a valid theory, however, remained invisible.

Cornwall was now lecturing on the *Sentences* in Oxford, instead of at Paris, and in his success seemed to tap a fresh well of slander. The new campaign finally succeeded in annoying, not Roger, who was too preoccupied to do more than take perfunctory notice, but Bungay.

'Thou should'st take steps against that man, Roger.'

'O, I may at some time, meseemeth. But truly he's so stupid that I'd have scant use for his good opinion anyhow. In the meantime he is doing no particular harm.'

'There thou'rt mistaken, I avow,' Bungay said earnestly. 'Thou hast not been in orders as long as I. He may well be damaging seriously thine hopes for advancement. He stands higher than thou dost, and ne matter how stupid he appeareth to thee, he hath a reputation for wisdom among the vulgar. Let me assure thee, politics among the Franciscans is quite as complex as it is at Westminster – though eke a measure quieter.'

'Hmm.' This put a somewhat new light on the matter. Roger could hardly afford not to think about his hopes for advancement in the Order, to which were tied his hopes of continuing his work; there was now no question but that the money would not last many more years. 'What wouldst thou recommend me? The civil law? He doubtless knoweth far more about that than I – most of his ilk seem to think about very little else.'

'I couldn't advise thee there myself; like thee, I would tend to avoid it. Nay, I was hoping thou might'st think of some way of pulling his teeth – perhaps by depriving his accusations of some of their force. . . . ?'

'Nay, I'll not do that,' Roger said firmly. 'These little shows of experiments are valuable to the students, and on the other side I'll not alter my teachings to what that ass thinketh the truth, for accommodation's sake or any other. But thou hast given me another notion.'

'Good. What is it? Or canst thou say?'

'I think so. I am going to show him that in one respect, at the least, what he is saying about me is true and correct.'

Bungay looked alarmed; but having started the juggernaut rolling, he knew better than to stand in its way.

Roger much begrudged the time he had to devote to thinking the idea through, but after a while he began to see a certain beauty in it. It emerged, first of all, from Richard's widely known and constantly reiterated views on the question of the plurality of forms: the same subject over which Roger had disputed with Albertus Magnus; and secondly from Richard's own peculiar method of disputation. He appeared to think that his position on the matter was substantially that of Albert, but in fact he had grossly oversimplified Albert's stand, if indeed he had ever understood it at all; the plurality of forms, Richard maintained, was contrary to the teachings of the saints. This was his way with the philosophers he expounded: mostly he simply denounced them, and when he did bother to explain their views, he did so in a form not likely to be recognized by the authors. All this had been true of him in Paris, and he had not changed.

On the doctrinal question, Richard's trimming of it to fit into the Procrustean bed of his understanding had led him straight into the theological position that Christ had become a man during the three days between His death and the resurrection. This view was no novelty – nothing new interested Cornwall – and hence failed to cause any real stir at the University, but it was ideal for Roger's purposes because it was logically absurd. In fact, it was incipiently heretical; a sound logician would need only a motive to transform it from a blunder into a scandal. Albert would never have fallen into such a trap – and Roger, having debated the plurality of forms with Albert to a standstill, did not anticipate that so weak a logician as Cornwall would be a serious adversary.

He was, in short, readying himself to demonstrate to Cornwall, on Cornwall's person, that this Roger Bacon was indeed and in fact a dangerous casuist.

Then Grosseteste died between the Feast of the Holy Guardian Angels and the *Translatio Edwardi Confessoris*; and for three days the bells boomed forth their grief from every tower in Oxford, aye, and in England. He was interred in an altar tomb of blue marble, with a border of foliage around the table, which was supported at the corners by four pillars, in the south aisle of the church of Lincoln; and with him his ring and staff. There were reports of miracles and nocturnal wonders, doubly marvellous in a man once but a word away from imprisonment by papal order; and yet one manifested to no less a person than the King, to whom in a vision a voice whispered, *Dilexit Dominus Edmundum in odorem benignitatis, et dilexit Dominus Robertum in odorem fidelitatis.*

In the solemnity of this event, which drew together Church and Court, Order and University in a common pageant of mourning, and in the intensity – as always unrealized until now – of his own loss, Roger almost forgot that mannequin figure Richard Rufus of Cornwall; and when he saw the man in the procession at Lincoln, again through an air shivering with the mortuary words of the bells, it was only with shame for the meanness of his own scheming. This was the second death high in University councils within a year, for the regent master, John of Garland, had preceded the Bishop of Lincoln into the shadow. There was time to think, too, of what consequences the removal of Grosseteste's counsels might have on the King; a matter necessarily of the most significance to Adam Marsh, but Roger had seen quite enough of Henry to bring him to speculating uneasily. The Bishop had been almost the only strong palisade between the English Church and the Crown – as well as between the English Church and the Apostolic Camera; and, moreover, one of the principal buttresses of Simon de Montfort's party.

But much though the death of Grosseteste signified to Roger, it was apparently not enough to distract Cornwall for long. The return of the faculty from Lincoln had not been a week old when the campaign was resumed. Bungay did not have to warn Roger a second time, for now he was indeed in a white fury, less in his own behalf than for what he took to be, for reasons obscure even to himself, a disrespect to the dead.

He promptly set his arrow and let fly. It was ridiculously easy, like shooting a popinjay from three feet away. It was also wondrous noisy: Roger's very appearance at Cornwall's lecture set the students to chattering so that the lecturer could scarce be heard. The argument with the master himself went so exactly as Roger had imagined it would that the older man might well have been reading lines from a written-out miracle-play. Some of the students, of course, took his part, and the result was something as much like a small riot as may be.

Bungay was appalled. 'The University will send thee down,' he said shakily. 'If they do so, I will go too; I provoked thee.'

'There's naught to fear, Thomas. A few cuffs given and taken in a lecture hall are commonplace. The University never pays the slightest attention.'

'Oh, so?' Bungay said doubtfully. 'Well, thou know'st them far better than I. But whatever they may do, I question that thou hast accomplished anything of value. At the very least, Cornwall will surely retaliate.'

'Certes,' Roger said. 'Nothing is surer. Therefore the problem is, how to tempt him to retaliate in some way further disadvantageous to him. There too, meseemeth I have the answer.'

'Roger, it seemeth *me* that thou shouldst give over. It

mathinketh me that I ever tempted thee in the matter. This time it is certain to be still worse – thy methods are so drastic, Roger.'

Roger smiled, a little grimly. 'This will simply be the same allegory, played backwards, as it were. Dear friend, I will tell thee, I am going to announce a lecture on magic.'

'O, suicide! Roger, Richard fancieth himself a student of that art, as am I a little, and I credit him. Thou wilt gain nothing of it – and Holy Church forbids it. Well it feared me thou wert setting thyself something foolish.'

'All this is to the good,' Roger said. 'Each of these aspects will appear unto Richard – and he will appear unto me. The day will be Wednesday next. Bruit it about, Thomas; bruit it about.'

The hall was of course more than packed, and there were many there who looked with curiosity at the apparatus on Roger's table – devices without which, by now, he would have looked near naked to his usual students. These last looked with indifference even at the caprice of a candle burning in the middle of the afternoon, knowing well that something would be done with it in due course.

Cornwall was there, with his faction of loyal students. Thus far, however, he had said almost nothing, for Roger had carefully left him few opportunities to object. Though Roger had published abroad the title, *On the nullity of magic and the usefulness of nature*, a paradox designed to start many an amateur metaphysician from his chair, in the main body of his exposition he had steered a middle course: explaining the major assumptions of magic briefly, and without details that a real student of the subject could find in fault; and showing that these were contrary to the teachings of the Church, a proposition to which no one would dare to dissent regardless of what he believed. The Cornwallians were having rather a dull time of it, and so, for that matter, were the students.

Never mind, affairs would become livelier in a moment; for Roger was about to expound the substance of his dream.

He said:

'Thus we dismiss speculative alchemy, since we see that metals cannot be transmuted *per speciem.* Aristotle in the *Meteors* means that only nature can transmute species. Art cannot *secundum speciem, et non negat quod non possit per naturam. In essentia et differentia specifica non potest transmutare*, as Aristotle says in the *De metallis.*

'But there is another alchemy, operative and practical, which teaches how to make the noble metals and colours and many other things better and more abundantly by art than they are made in nature. And science of this kind is greater than all those preceding because it produces greater utilities – not only wealth and many other things for the public welfare, but the discovery of methods for prolonging human life.'

Cornwall coughed and subsided. Roger challenged him with a look, and the man bristled. He said:

'Certes a preachment of magic.'

'Not so!' This was the beginning. '*Narrabo igitur nunc primo opera artis et naturae miranda, ut postea causas et modum assignem* – in which there is nothing magical, *ut videatur quod omnis magica potestas sit inferior his operibus et indigna.*'

There was a stir as he paused again, and his students grinned at each other: Roger was about to be outrageous again. Cornwall was smiling too, now crouched smugly beside his mousehole.

'Item,' Roger said, '*nam instrumenta navigandi possunt fieri ut naves maximae ferantur uno solo homine regente, majori velocitate quam si plenae essent hominibus.*'

He paused yet again, but expected no objection, and got none; there were seafarers in the room who had talked of such things themselves, or dreamed of them; and surely there was nobody present who did not already know something of the lodestone.

'Item: *Currus possunt fieri ut sine animale moveantur cum impetu inestimabili.*'

'A wise man,' Cornwall broke in with a snort, 'would call

such *auto-mobile* nothing but dreams.'

'Except, perhaps, for the scythe-bearing chariots with which the men of old fought? But perhaps you are right, magister Cornwall. I proceed: Item, *possunt fieri instrumenta volandi ut homo sedeat in medio* – revolving some engine, necessarily, magister Cornwall – *alae artificialiter factae aera verberent modo avis volantis.*'

Cornwall seemed stunned. It was one of Roger's own students who said incredulously, '*Flying* machines, magister Bacon?'

'Flying machines,' Roger said. 'Item, *possunt fieri instrumentum, parva magnitudine, ad elevanda et deprimenda pondera paene infinita*—'

'O, certes,' Cornwall said. 'You could move the world with such a lever.'

'No, it would not be long enough, magister Cornwall, as is plainly written in Archimedes. But nothing could be more useful in emergencies. By a machine three fingers high and wide, and of less size, a man could free himself of all dangers of prison, for instance. And his friends, if he had any.'

There was some laughter, but it was uneasy. Even Roger's own students, it seemed, did not entirely welcome the admixture of flyting with true disputation; perhaps they thought he did not need it. He went on: '*Potest etiam facile fieri instrumentum quo unus traheret ad se mille homines contra eorum voluntatem*——'

'I find it', Cornwall said, 'rather crowded in this hall already.'

Another ripple of laughter. Flushing helplessly, Roger ploughed ahead: ' – and attract other things in like matter; for instance, thunderbolts.'

Now the laughter was at full roar, and plainly at Roger's expense. Even his own partisans could see that he had lost his temper.

'I will go on. *Possunt etiam instrumenta fieri ambulandi in mari vel fluminibus sine periculo* – even to the bottom without danger, even as Alexander the Great explored the secrets of the sea.'

'According to what authority?'

'Ethicus the astronomer, as is well known,' Roger said with concentrated scorn. '*Haec autem facta sunt antiquitus et nostris temporibus facta sunt, ut certum est*; the same is true of the flying machine, though I have not seen one and know of no man who has—'

'Nor has anyone else.'

'—but I know an expert who has thought out the way to make one.'

'Ah, excellent,' Cornwall said. 'Let him then bring home the bacon.'

The hall skirled with a glee of catcalls. Roger said, through his teeth: '*Et infinita quasi talia fieri possunt . . . ut pontes super flumina sine columna . . . et machinationes et ingenia inaudita*—'

'Belike,' Cornwall said. 'I hear nothing myself.'

'Then I need a louder voice, magister Cornwall,' Roger said harshly. 'Let me introduce you to a childhood friend of mine, Sir Salis Petre. He has a small voice by usual; but *per igneam coruscationem et combustionem ac per sonorem horrorem possunt mira fieri, et in distantia qua volumus ut homo mortalis sibi cavere non posset nec se sustinere*.'

Cornwall laughed, '*Quomodo?*' he demanded.

Roger picked up the tight roll of parchment and touched it to the flame of the candle. As soon as it was smouldering well, he threw it to the floor before the table. The nearest students drew back uneasily, but Cornwall only shrugged his shoulders.

'*Quomodo? Ecce!*'

The scroll exploded like two dozen thunderclaps, blowing out the candle and filling the hall with pungent grey smoke. With howls of panic, the students broke blindly for the door, striking out first with fists, and then with knives, to be first out. Cornwall, however, was closest and was first out by several rods – most fortunately for him, or they would have trampled him. Down the corridors they poured, cloaks flying, their cries echoing:

'Beware of the magician! Beware! Beware! Beware of the

magician! Beware!... Beware....'

Then Roger was alone, except for a few groaning wounded. Blind with triumph in the black powder-reeking air, he clung to the lectern with both hands, and shouted after them all at the top of his voice,

'TRIPSARECOPSEM!'

No plot in history, it seemed, had ever succeeded so well. From that day forward Oxford was unbearable for Cornwall; in his humiliation, he appealed to Adam Marsh to reverse himself on the matter of the Parisian post. With a sigh – for though he would still have preferred Cornwall to remain at Oxford, he was in truth becoming a little weary of the man – Adam again wrote the provincial minister, and shortly thereafter, Richard Rufus of Cornwall was no more to be seen. Roger and Bungay drank a toast to his departure, and went back to their more serious matters.

That would be, however, the last favour Adam would be able to do for anyone at Oxford, master or student, for his influence had evaporated. Earlier on, he had appointed Thomas of York as regent master, to fill the vacancy left by the death of John of Garland; and Thomas, wholly against the customs, was a man without a degree from the Faculty of Arts. It was recalled that Adam had done something like this before, in the case of Thomas Docking, but this instance was far more serious. The outcome was a disastrous quarrel with the University.

Effectively, however, he had left Oxford three years before; to Roger the whole dispute, though it was common gossip, seemed remote and unreal. He was now embarked upon the composition of a *Metaphysica*, a heavy task to which he had cheerfully allotted himself five years, allowing for other work to go on at the same time. There was God's plenty of that, for about the University he was now famous – or, he thought, perhaps infamous would be a better word. Though cries of 'Beware of the magician!' still sounded in the halls, they became more and more feeble with the exile of Cornwall, and even while they were at their loudest he had more students than he could comfortably handle. He was required by the Order, however, to try.

Some of this weight was lifted within a year, fortunately, by a sudden increase in the popularity of theology as a subject; for toward the end of 1254 there arrived at Oxford the first copy of the *Introduction to the Eternal Gospel* of the Franciscan Gerard of San Borgo. Its reputation had preceded it by months, for in fact the book was creating a furor throughout Christendom – a fact Roger could well understand after reading it himself.

The Eternal Gospel of the title was the work of one Joachim of Flora, a Calabrian visionary who had predicted that an Age of the Holy Spirit would begin in 1260, ushered in by a new Order of monks headed by Merlin, and heralded by the dissolution of all disciplinary institutions. It was Gerard's contention that the Franciscans might become this new Order, provided that they return to the rule of absolute poverty laid down by their founder.

Roger and Bungay discussed the work through many a night, as did half of Oxford. To Roger, at least, there seemed to be reason and justice in much of Gerard's contentions.

'Including the prophecies, Roger?'

'They will have to wait upon events, of course. Yet the imminent coming of the Antichrist hath also often been prophesied; it seemeth me only reasonable that some great spiritual leader might arise at the same time to combat him. But thou kenst well that it is not the prophecies that are creating all this dissension, but the doctrine of renunciation of worldly possessions.'

'It hath put weapons into the hands of our enemies, that much is evident,' Bungay said thoughtfully. 'William of St. Amour in particular, an implacable man. He holds it as evidence against us from our own mouths.'

'He will use it eke against the Dominicans if he can,' Roger predicted. 'Yet still I hold that Gerard's argument hath reason behind it. Consider, I urge thee, how St. Francis himself may look from Heaven upon the vast holdings of property we have accumulated in his name. Indeed, we should thank God that he was excepting Christ the mildest of men, or else we might find ourselves all barefoot in the road at this very moment.'

'Many are saying what you say, Roger, yet withal I'd not proclaim it quite so loud. Joachimism is perilous close to becoming proclaimed a heresy; Innocent hath already called a special Council in Anagni to condemn the book – Gerard's, I mean, not the Eternal Gospel itself.'

'And Gerard?' Roger said.

'Is in the hands of the Inquisition.'

That ended the conversation for that evening. Yet for some months it appeared that Bungay's forebodings had not been fated to be borne out, for in Anagni matters had gone somewhat askew. The proximate cause, apparently, had been that same William of St. Amour, who had rushed to Rome to denounce the orders root and branch, and found a sympathetic ear – or a malleable mind – in Innocent IV. The result, whatever the cause, was a bull, *Etsi animarum*, seriously curtailing the privileges of the orders; not a victory for the Joachimites, but not a rebuff either.

The next act of Innocent IV was to die, to be succeeded by Alexander IV, who promptly repudiated *Etsi animarum*, fanning the flames higher once more. William of St. Amour, frustrated and furious, left Rome as hurriedly as he had entered it – he was a man who did everything in great haste, including thinking – and dispatched over Europe a polemic, *De periculis novissimorum temporum*, in which the orders were depicted as themselves inviting the advent of Antichrist. Gerard of San Borgo remained in his dungeon, the first to reap his own whirlwind.

(*Milord Modena: I send herewith for your kind attention the book* De erroribus medicorum *which I promised you in Tivoli. Ad majorem gloria Dei, R. Bacon.*)

There was a diversion: the killing in Lincoln of a boy named Hugh, widely described as a ritual murder by Jews – a story which grew as it travelled until the poets took it up, after which all possibility of learning the truth disappeared forever. There were miracles, and proposals of canonization, and Hugh was buried next to Grosseteste in the hope of speeding the lad's Elevation; but the campaign to canonize the Capito had itself bogged down. In the meantime, Hugh's enthusiasts pressed his cause with Heaven by putting to the torch such houses in various Jeweryes as seemed worth looting.

The Joachimite furor went on, until it had forced out of office the very general of the Franciscans himself, John of Parma, for pronounced Joachimite leanings. His successor was Bonaventura, a dour and energetic theologian whose closest friend was the Dominican Albertus Magnus: a friendship bodying forth the inexorable enmity felt by both men toward anything which stirred up trouble between the orders, in especial Joachimism with its grandiose claims for the Franciscans as the coming Order of Merlin.

'I told thee, Roger, politics is no whit less complicated here than at the Court!'

'Brother, I believed thee then.'

But Roger had almost given up following these coils; two years of them had exhausted his attention for such theological hair-splitting; though he was still troubled by a suspicion that Gerard had been right, and that the mounting troubles between the orders might well presage the coming of the Antichrist, voicing this opinion won him nothing but dark intimations that he must be a heretic and a disciple of the Antichrist himself. Bungay had called that tune rightly enough. Besides, the *Metaphysica* was still far from finished, and now there was a-borning a work on weights and measures, the *Reprobationes*. Politicking could go on without him.

'An alms, an alms for John! An alms for John, who hath the very begging bowl of Belisarius! Only a penny to touch the bowl of Belisarius!'

'Hark. What's that? Listen!'

'To what? What is it, Roger?'

'Below – that cry in the street. Listen.'

'An alms for John! Only a penny! An alms, an alms for John. . . .'

'. . . I hear nothing, Roger. Art well?'

Politicking went on without him, and reached to him. In 1256 Bonaventura voided the appointment of Thomas Docking, despite his new degree, and named a new lector to the Franciscans at Oxford, and regent master to boot. The successor to Adam Marsh's chair, and Grosseteste's before him, was Richard Rufus of Cornwall.

One month later, Bonaventura interdicted Roger's lectures at Oxford for suspected irregularities, namely, Joachimism and magic, and recalled him to Paris.

Cornwall had paid his debt, however belatedly.

Parting once more from Oxford, and now also from Bungay, was bitter; but the sharpest pang, which did not strike until Roger was better than half across the Dover Strait, was also the least expected: to realize only now that in all this time, he had never once visited Ilchester, nor even thought to do so.

The cold winds blew him on regardless.

XI: ST. CATHERINE'S CHAPEL

On the road to London yet another time, yet another wearisome time, Adam Marsh took thought most conscientiously of those high matters which awaited him at the end; but only, as it were, within his intellectual soul, that raven of Elias. If long practice in manœuvres he abhorred had given him nothing else, it had trained him to reflect simultaneously upon two wholly different sets of circumstances, with the set he loved less relegated to the outermost regions of his mind, where it ticked away like a water-clock without the necessity of paying it much heed: *will, guilt, will, guilt.* ...

Today, in his sensitive soul, that ticking went endlessly toward reminding him that he was fifty-seven years old. No! Yet it was most certainly correct; his age was always one year less than the last two digits of the year; and this was certainly 1258, and the dregs of it at that. It had been almost two years since Roger Bacon had ruined himself at Oxford with his arrogance, as Adam long ago at Kirkby-Maxloe had greatly feared that he would, and been recalled to Paris . . . and it had been almost ten years, nay eleven, since he had seen Eleanor of Leicester.

For that punishment – for he could not but regard it as such – high matters were at least in part responsible, and could not be kept as far from his heart as his will would bid them stay. It had been eleven years ago that Henry, no doubt with a view to removing from England a continuing wellspring of defiance, had named Simon de Montfort his *locum-tenens* or Seneschal in Gascony, and had kept him there for six years; would indeed have kept him there forever had it not been for the stupid zeal of Henry's friends, who stirred the Gascons to so many complaints of cruelty and injustice – plausible enough, if one recalled the Albigensians – that the earl was provoked to come home and demand trial. He had been acquitted, but was still affronted and had demanded reparations, thus leading to still another quarrel with his liege which could surely have been avoided had Simon's enemies simply left well enough alone.

Henry knew this; last year he had sent Simon abroad again as one of his ambassadors to France. Beyond doubt there had been other reasons as well, for the reparations had not been the only cause of the broil in 1255. That had also been the year when the King, at the behest of the Pope, had allowed his second son Edmund of Lancaster to claim the Crown of Sicily, with the clear expectation that the realm was to pay for a war of succession on Edmund's behalf over that much-disputed Kingdom; and Simon was scarce in France again before Henry's brother Richard earl of Cornwall – that same earl to whom the King had earlier mortgaged sole right to extort money from the Jews – sued for the Imperial throne, his election bribery again to be paid from English taxes.

Remote, remote – yet painfully close to the heart. Surely it was but natural in the earl of Leicester to take his lady wife with him to his estates in Gascony, no man could dispute that. He was not even depriving her of a confessor, for she still had Adam's brother Robert, now Dean of Lincoln and a strong clerical partisan of Simon's cause against the King. Yet that argument cut two ways: for by the same reasoning could it be called natural to leave her there for three years more, while he fought at home with the King? Certes, for all of England was a-shimmer with rebellion, and a man with a Gascon sanctuary for his lady could not but count himself fortunate. The fact that, once more back in England, he was still without Eleanor was amenable to the same explanation.

There was without doubt a curse upon the land, and that not only the burden of Henry's and Rome's rapacious greed; for the harvests this year had been the worst in memory, and famine was everywhere. Thousands had starved to death in London alone. No one who loved her could wish Eleanor anywhere but where she was.

Yet the thorns of guilt steadily poisoned Adam's blood, and in his soul there whispered constantly another explanation. That voiceless whisper was abetted by additional circumstances: for though the insurgent barons claimed St. Robert of Lincoln as their chiefest patron (notwithstanding that the Capito had yet to be canonized), Simon himself no longer spoke more than perfunctorily to Grosseteste's only spiritual heir, regardless of opportunity.

Did the earl know? But what was there to know? There had been no sin committed, nay nor ever would be. But to this objection there was an inexorable reply in Scripture. Eleanor was surely guiltless; but this could not be said of Adam, in his heart nor in Heaven.

He had been tempted eke to think that Heaven had a little conspired to help him in these outward events, keeping Eleanor in Gascony the while his old age crept toward him. Too, his services as mediator were still in demand at court, maugre Simon's absences and his coldness, for the primate, Boniface of Savoy, made no secret of his admiration for Adam as an expert lawyer and theologian; and the primate was also a member of Simon's party. Two years ago Boniface had even tried to win Adam the see of Ely, an attempt abetted by the King, who perhaps saw in this a way to placate two clerical opponents at once. Doubtless Henry was unaware of the gulf that Adam sensed between himself and Simon; yet even if he had, Henry knew also that Adam confessed his Queen. The see, however, was refused, for the Lateran still remembered Grosseteste with little love, and would not advance his most favoured familiar even at the petition of Rome's most obedient secular prince.

Heaven's help or no, Adam's essay to pluck out his offending eye also had failed.

Simon's return had been stormy beyond all imagining, and though the King had prepared for it, he had not thought far enough ahead. At the April parliament in the Great Hall at Westminster, the barons, at Simon's advice, had arrived in complete armour. They stood as silent as statues while the King's half-brother, William de Valence, denounced the earls of Gloucester and Leicester as the sources of every evil under which England was suffering. Even de Valence's rather shaky denunciation of Simon as 'an old traitor and a liar' went by in a silence so complete that Adam had been able to hear clearly the scratch and sputter of old Matthew Paris' goose-quill.

Evidently de Valence had misinterpreted that silence, for his next words to fall upon Adam's incredulous ears had been a demand for more money. After a moment, Simon had wordlessly deferred to Gloucester.

'Nay,' earl Bigod said. 'More money paid to the Pope, on behalf of the King's son and his Sicilian Crown? Not a mark!'

'It lieth nat with thee to refuse us, my lord Gloucester. An ye be mutinous, we shall send thee reapers and reap thy fields for thee.'

'And I will send ye back the heads of your reapers,' Bigod said evenly.

The King had entered as he was speaking, and for the first time there was movement: there swept through the statues a threatening clatter of swords. Whatever Henry had anticipated, it had not been this, but he was far quicker to see what was under his nose than his half-brother had been. He said at last:

'Am I then a prisoner?'

'Nay, sire,' earl Bigod said, but his voice had been most grim. 'But we must have reform.'

'Reform, Gloucester?'

'Yes, sire. Know ye that all here are sworn to die, rather than that England be ruined by the Romans.'

There had seemed to be no immediate danger of death to the full-armed barons, but the King had been reduced rapidly to a stuttering transport of terror. It had not proven an onerous task to extort from him the appointment of a Council of twenty-four lordships, to meet at Oxford in October and draw up a table of reforms.

That meeting Henry's partisans had promptly dubbed the Mad Parliament, but none there took heed of that to their hurt. One of its earliest acts was to invest Simon, first, with the post of military commander-in-chief for the seigniorial forces, and second, with the custody of the castle of Winchester – whence, to guard against any surprise, the Mad Parliament at once removed itself before completing its table of wrongs to be righted. The table itself was nevertheless titled the Provisions of Oxford, to ensure the preservation of the letters patent under which the twenty-four had begun their labours.

Ere that work was through, Henry's power – or at the very least, his power to make mischief – had been wrenched from his hands; the Mad Parliament had given over the taxing of the realm, and much else, to three committees of its own. Little could have galled Henry more than to assent to such Provisions, but assent he must, albeit they were capped by the boldest insult offered to the Angevin crown since 1215: the demand that he reaffirm, on holy ground, the Great Charter which his father had so unwillingly signed that June 15th at Runnymede.

It was to this high and ominous ceremony that Adam was riding now, in the greyness of his old age and the shadow of his guilt.

It had pleased the Mad Parliament to give Henry his choice of holy ground, and he had chosen a ruin: the Westminster Abbey of Edward the Confessor, which that saint had spent most of his life a-building, and which Henry himself had pulled down in order to erect something even greater to the Confessor's memory. Nothing of the original was left now but Edward's high-raised shrine, and the new minster, though it had already cost a vast sum, was still radically incomplete.

Nevertheless Adam could bring himself to admire it; the King as a patron of the arts was not an inconsiderable man, whatever his other weaknesses, and it was already plain to see that this church – of which Henry was in part also the architect – would be nobly beautiful, could it be finished before the money ran out. In the meantime, the conclave forgathered in St. Catherine's Chapel, one of the few chambers which was whole.

No arms nor armour now, but instead crimson, gold and vair, all new, without so much as a grease-spot: all the chief lords of England, each with a lighted taper in his hand; Henry the King, his face white as milk, the shadows on it deeply cut by the upcasting light of the candle in his own hand, slightly a-tremble; the princes, Edward wearing the dark brow of suppressed mutiny; the bishops, the primate, even the papal legate, Guy de Foulques, Archbishop of Sabina himself; and from somewhere in the darkness the cat-purr of the aged Matthew Paris, *scribble . . . scribble. . . .*

They had already begun when Adam entered, and he was far from the centre of the conclave. Much indeed had changed since he had stood at Grosseteste's elbow in the Great Hall and heard not only the public words but the private consultations. Yet from scraps of murmurs Adam quickly divined where they were at: earl Bigod was reading, in a monotonous, rapid drone-bass, the articles of the Great Charter, and had already reached the twelfth.

'No scutage or aid shall be imposed on our kingdom, unless by the Common Council of the realm . . . and in like manner it shall be done concerning aids from the City of London. . . . The King binds himself to summon the Common Council of the realm respecting the assessing of an aid (except as provided in XII) or a scutage. . . .'

And to each of these Henry the King said, through nearly motionless lips, 'We so swear,' and signed himself.

'. . . to be proportionate to the offence, and imposed according to the oath of honest men in the neighbourhood. No amercement to touch the necessary means of subsistence of a free man, the merchandise of a merchant, or the farming tools of a villein . . . earls and barons to be amerced by their equals. . . .'

'We so swear. . . . We so swear. . . .'

'. . . nothing shall be taken or given, for the future, for the Writ of Inquisition of life or limb, but it shall be freely granted, and not denied. . . . No freeman shall be taken or imprisoned or disseised or exiled or in any way destroyed, nor will we go upon him nor will we send upon him except by the lawful judgment of his peers and/or the law of the land. . . . We will sell to no man, we will not deny to any man, either justice or right. . . .'

'We so swear. . . . We so swear. . . .'

'. . . reaffirm Article I that the Church of England shall be free, and have her whole rights, and her liberties inviolable. . . .'

The tapers burned lower; the chapel was reeking of sweat and tallow; but at last the earl put aside his parchments.

'We so swear.'

The King let the words fall almost in a whisper, and then stood frozen for what seemed a long fall of sand. Then he dashed his taper to the stones, and cried out thinly:

'So go out with smoke and stench the accursed souls of those who break or pervert this Charter!'

By the breathless pause which followed, Adam knew that this oath had not been prescribed by the bishops for this occasion. Then Simon de Montfort's own taper struck the pavement, and the chapel rang with his voice, repeating the words.

The barons followed his lead, in a ragged chorus. Within no longer than it took to say a Paternoster, the chapel was plunged into blackness, choking with wick-fumes . . . and then, it was a-shuffle with men edging cautiously, blindly toward the doorway each remembered as being the nearest.

Adam pressed stumblingly through the slow-milling shapes, making haste slowly lest he jostle someone with hand on dagger, toward where he had last seen earl Simon, guiding himself by the one remaining, distant star of Matthew Paris' candle-flame. It was slow work, against the main current; and by the time he had reached his goal, the smoky chapel was empty of all but himself and the nodding, grinning historian.

Thus, Simon de Montfort's farewell to his confessor; for he was at once to go on an embassy to Scotland. There was naught left Adam Marsh now, *nec spe nec metu*, but his judgment, which was not to be found in this world. In greyness and in shadow, he rode without haste toward Oxford to await it.

XII: THE CONVENT

And this, then, was the first year of the Age of the Holy Spirit! Small cause 1260 had given Roger Bacon for joy; and though what he had been able to learn about the world outside the convent walls was little, he saw small hope for that world either, except it rejoice in the imminence of Antichrist.

Within the convent, each day of this putatively great year dripped away exactly as had each day of the preceding three, worn down under the corrosion of his 'corrective discipline' – changing straw; sweeping out cells; carrying slops and night-soil; teaching a few young apprentices to the Order; copying Psalms; dipping candles; washing bottles; mending sandals; and praying for deliverance. He could look forward now to naught else.

In the dragging-past of these lifetimes of days, but little study was possible, and less work; yet for a while he had refused to be defeated. The *Reprobationes* was finished; and an introduction to a new subject, *De laudibus mathematicae*, and even the work itself, a *Communia mathematica*, although only in first recension. But nothing was so time-consuming as computation; and in especial one needed tables, which he had neither the leisure to search out nor the money to buy.

The money was gone, all gone, leaving behind only a sort of lightness in the head, as that of a man but recently delivered of a fever; or, more to the purpose, of a man in the aftermath of far too much wine, miserable in the knowledge that the only cure is more, and that not to be had.

Nor was there any help for him from his brothers and superiors. In Oxford he had been at the least a resident master; here, he was nothing. Early on, he had proposed to them that for the fame of the convent, in Paris where scholarship was everything, he should write for them a summary of everything that he had read or found in the natural sciences from the beginning, a *Communia naturalium*, to be published on to the shelves of the University; surely a better use for a scholar than setting him to changing beds. He had shown them the preface for such a work; they had laughed at it. He did not speak to them now unless spoken to, and that was seldom.

A few threads to the outside still were allowed him. Eugene wrote to him: outraged at still another prohibition of Aristotle at Toulouse, the younger brother had at last come home to Ilchester and taken up the galling burden of the damaged estate – a victory for Robert which Roger seldom cared to think about. Belatedly, because he had been so long out of England, Eugene had discovered the greatness of Grosseteste, and was buying copies of his works as he could. Unable to share in the problems of the estate, Roger could at least feel with Eugene the poignancy of the murder of the younger man's studies, and wrote for him a summary of the Capito's teachings on time and motion, with a commentary; Eugene drank it down like water in a desert and prayed urgently for more, but from the fastness of the convent there was little more to give.

Too, there were letters from Bungay, who had left Oxford in disgust at Roger's exile and returned to his post as the vicar of the provincial minister. But they were seldom heartening:

I must tell thee that the turmoil is in no wise lessened and that most of what was gained in St. Catherine's chapel hath since been lost, an I understand it aright. No sooner did earl Simon return from his embassy to Scotland than the King charged him with fixing the particulars of the peace with France, a matter which kept him away most of this year; and in the meantime the 'bachelors', as they now call those knights and gentry created out of incomes of fifteen pounds a year, those that were formerly contented to be no more than coroners and jurymen, have had a Mad Parliament of their own. Now they demand that the barons concede to them as vassals and tenants those same privileges wrung by the baronage from the supreme landlord the King, and being rebuffed, do repair increasingly to the royal above the seigniorial justice. In this matter earl Bigod appeareth helpless, referring to it as a disturbance in the commonalty, which is in no wise the case, but serveth all the same to drive many a weaker baron to the King also, in hope of better arms against this mythical insurgency. This division Prince Edward hath been quick to exploit, and it feareth me that earl Simon's return from France hath not been speedy enough to compose it. Thou wilt recall how at the birth of Edward our Henry was so eager to receive gifts of congratulation that it was said at the Court, *Heaven gives us this child, but the King sells him to us*: I fear that we shall suffer much more at the hands of this prince before we suffer less. Remind thyself however how much of what I say needs must be rumour; for that chatterer Matthew Paris the King's historian is dead, and his thousands of leaves of gossip are shut up by the monks of St. Alban's; and this year hath died also the most Christian and most noble Adam Marsh, the last of our Order who might have known the truth. – *Thos.*

Here indeed was cause for sorrow, and for despair. Who now was left to him but Eugene, and Bungay? There still existed the small circle of the Peregrine College, but he had been able to visit that only the once since his exile, and had found all there strangers to him but Peter de Maricourt himself. Moreover, it was dangerous to keep such arcane company, never for Roger more so than now.

He moved about through his galling chores in a mist of lassitude and weariness. The days went by. Were it not for the frequent Holy Days, he would have lost all track of them. Listlessly, he recast his notes from his lecture-battle with Richard of Cornwall into a small volume, but even the panoplies of that demonic vision had lost all power to move him now; the words came as slowly from the clotting quill-tip as those of a neophyte, and the temptation to write 'Finis' at the bottom of each new page was almost irresistible. In the end, he dispatched it as a letter to Eugene, who was baffled by it, particularly by the passage on black-powder, which Roger in a moment of prudence had partially re-encyphered.

It was well that he had not published it. But a month after, there was read forth to the brothers of the convent at early Mass, by order of Bonaventura, the new Constitutions of the Chapter of Narbonne:

'Let no one glory in the possession of virtue in his heart if he puts no guard on his conversation. If anyone thinks that he is religious and does not curb his tongue, but only allows his heart to lead him astray, then his religion is vain. It is therefore necessary that an honourable fence should surround the mouth and other senses and acts, deeds and morals, that the statutes of the regulars may not be destroyed by perfect men, but kept intact, lest they should be bitten by a snake when they let down the barrier....

'Let the brothers carry nothing in words or in writing which could conduce to the scandal of anyone....

'Let no brother go to the court of the Lord Pope, or send a brother, without the permission of the Minister-General. Let them, if they have gone otherwise, be at once expelled from the Curia by the procurators of the Order. And let no one apply to the Minister-General for permission unless serious cause or urgent necessity demand it.

'We prohibit any new writing from being published outside the Order, unless it shall first have been examined carefully by the Minister-General or Provincial, and the visitants in the provincial chapter.... Anyone who contravenes this shall be kept at least three days on bread and water, and lose his writing....

'Let no brother write books, or cause them to be written for sale, and let the Provincial Minister not dare to have or keep any books without the licence of the Minister-General, or let any brothers have or keep them without the permission of the provincial ministers....

'We lay under a perpetual curse anyone who presumes either by word or by deed in any way to work for the division of our Order. If anyone contravenes this prohibition, he shall be considered as an excommunicate and schismatic and destroyer of our Order . . . brothers incorrigible in this shall be imprisoned or expelled from the Order. . . .

'If anyone think that the penalty for the breach of statutes of this kind is severe, let him reflect that, according to the Apostle, all discipline in the present life is not a matter for rejoicing, but for sorrow; yet through it, it will bear for the future the most peaceful fruit of justice for those who have endured it.'

It was an immense document, the proclamation of which consumed most of the morning, but the sense of these rubrics was all too clear: for the defence of the orders against the seculars, and the defence of the Order against itself, the Minister-General had instituted a censorship.

His friends dead, or beyond his reach; himself forbidden to publish; the vision a vapour. Wherein lay the usefulness of labour, if nothing was to come of it? Wherein the beauty, where there were none to see it? Why write at all, if there were to be none to read? He prayed for guidance; but the silence flowed on, unresponsive.

Another year. Silence, and apathy.

And then, abruptly, he was awake; it was as though he had been plunged into icy water. The convent had a visitor – not in itself unusual, nor that Roger should know the man, albeit but slightly. His name was Raymond of Laon, but it was what he was that mattered: he was a clerk in the suite of Guy de Foulques.

A friend alive – never mind how remote a friend – and a Cardinal! There was help here, could he but engineer it; why had he not thought of this expedient before?

Moreover, it required scarcely any engineering, for Raymond himself asked to see Roger, and permission was granted.

'The Cardinal charged me to make certain of your whereabouts, Master Roger,' Raymond said nervously. Obviously he had been warned that the case confronting him now had been one of peculiar fractiousness, and still full of potentialities for schism.

'Make him aware, I beg of you, Raymond. There was a time when he spoke with interest of my studies in the sciences, and asked for writings. Tell him I would make him a book of these, were it not for the decrees of Narbonne.'

'He has no power to exempt anyone from those,' Raymond objected. 'True that he's a Cardinal, but also a secular; durst not interfere with the rules of the Orders.'

'Of course; but surely he might relieve me of my burdens in some way? As matters stand today, I am forbidden to keep books, let alone write them – I have preserved all my manuscripts only by keeping them circulating among certain friends here in Paris, and even this may be "publication" within the meaning of the sixth rubric of the Narbonne Constitutions.'

Raymond was thoughtful. 'I will tell him what you say,' he declared at last. 'I know of no prohibition against it, though belike he may. And the very worst he can say in reply, to me or thee, is, No.'

'God bless you, Raymond. I shall pray for you all my days.'

The dirt flew under Roger's besom that afternoon, albeit he was otherwise careful to show the brothers no elation after the interview; neither, however, did he satisfy their curiosity – seen solely in their glances, for they would have scorned to speak it – as to the business of a Cardinal's household with an inconsequential friar under corrective discipline. Nor did he reveal the secret elsewhere as yet, so that Eugene must have been baffled all over again to receive of a sudden this from his exiled brother:

Man, in so far as he is man, has two things, bodily strength and virtues, and in these he can be forced in many things; but he has also strength and virtues of soul, that is, of the intellectual soul. In these he can be neither led nor forced, but only hindered. And so, if a thousand times he is cast into prison, never can he go against his will unless the will succumbs.

But there was much preparation to be done while Guy's reply was awaited; and this Roger prosecuted with a cunning which surprised even himself. It could not be concealed that he was suddenly and furiously writing again – in fact his best pupil Joannes, a brilliant thirteen-year-old who worshipped his Master, was under orders to report such an event at once – but to the expected prompt question Roger was able to proffer nothing more incendiary than a set of fearsomely complex tables of numbers.

'To what purpose?'

'These are notes toward a better calendar, Father. Doth it not seem ridiculous that with the one we have, we cannot even say with certainty what is the veritable date of Easter? That can hardly be pleasing to Our Lord, that we must celebrate His resurrection on the wrong day, more often than not.'

This was unexceptionable; in due course the censors, though uncertain whether to be suspicious or to rejoice in the reclamation of an erring brother, even allowed *De termine Paschali* to be copied and published. By that time, Roger was deep into the composition of a *Computus*, which on early inspection by the brothers proved to be even more technical – so much so, as Roger had foreseen, that nobody else in the convent but young Joannes could have even a hope of understanding it.

Thereafter, when they saw him drawing geometrical diagrams, the brothers avoided asking questions which might prove embarrassing to themselves. Thus they also successfully avoided discovering that these were not part of the incomplete *Computus* at all, but instead were the visible signs of a process destined to reduce the very Ark of the Covenant to naught more than the passage of sunlight through raindrops.

In all this, young Joannes was a willing conspirator. He was a black-haired, hollow-eyed youngster, painfully thin and awkward, of no known family – a charge of the Church. He was eager and quick, despite his talent for knocking things over when he was excited, and was filled with delight at being made privy to the secret. He was even more delighted to realize that he and he alone, of all the learned minds in the convent, was capable of following the racing of his Master's thought; and in sober truth, at Roger's hands he already knew more of the laws of optics than had the great Grosseteste himself, as Grosseteste had known more than Alhazen.

Even Joannes, however, despite the most careful and elaborate instruction, was left gasping at the next leap, which went soaring directly from the propagation of vision into the propagation of force:

Every efficient cause acts by its own force which it produces on the matter subject to it, as the light of the sun produces its own action in the air, and this action is light diffused through the whole world from the solar light. This force is called likeness, image, species and by many other names, and it is produced by substance as well as accident and by spiritual substance as well as corporeal. Substance is more productive of it than accident, and spiritual substance than corporeal. This force produces every action in this world, for it acts on sense, intellect and all the matter in the world for the production of things, because one and the same thing is done by a natural agent on whatsoever it acts, because it has no freedom of choice; and therefore it performs the same act on whatever it meets. . . . Forces of this kind, belonging to agents, produce every action in this world. But there are two things now to be noted respecting these forces; one is the propagation itself of the action and of force from the place of its production; and the other is the varied action in this world due to the production and destruction of things. The second cannot be known without the first. Therefore it is necessary that the propagation itself be first described.

. . . But when they say that force has a spiritual existence in the medium, this use of the word 'spiritual' is not in accordance with its proper and primary meaning, from 'spirit' as we say that God and angel and soul are spiritual things; because it is plain that the forces of corporeal things are not thus spiritual. Therefore of necessity they will have a corporeal existence, because body and soul are opposed without an intermediate. And if they have a corporeal existence, they also have a material one, and therefore they must obey the laws of material and corporeal things, and therefore they must mix when they are contrary, and become one when they are of the same category of forces. And this is again apparent, since force is the product of a corporeal thing, and not of a spiritual; therefore it will have a corporeal existence. Likewise it is in a corporeal and material medium, and everything that is received in another is modified by the condition of the recipient. . . . When, therefore, Aristotle and Averroes say that force has a spiritual existence in the medium and in the senses, it is evident that 'spiritual' is not taken from 'spirit' nor is the word used in its proper sense. Therefore it is used equivocally and improperly, for it is taken in the sense of 'inperceptible'; since everything really spiritual . . . is imperceptible and does not affect the senses, we therefore convert the terms and call that which is imperceptible spiritual. But this is homonymous and outside the true and proper meaning of a spiritual thing. . . . Moreover, it produces a corporeal result, as, for example, the action of heat warms bodies and dries them out, and causes them to putrefy, and the same is true of other forces. Therefore, since this produces heat, properly speaking, and through the medium of heat produces other results, force must be a corporeal thing, because a spiritual thing does not cause a corporeal action. And in particular there is the additional reason that the force is of the same essence as the complete effect of the producer, and it becomes that when the producer affects strongly the thing acted upon.

. . . Since, therefore, the action of a corporeal thing has a really corporeal existence in a medium, and is a real corporeal thing, as was previously shown, it must of necessity be dimensional, and therefore fitted to the dimensions of the medium. . . . If, therefore, the propagation of light is instantaneous, and not in time, there will be an instant without time; because time does not exist without motion. But it is impossible that there should be an instant without time, just as there cannot be a point without a line. It remains, then, that light is propagated in time, and likewise all forces of a visible thing and of vision. . . .

The poor youngster was not to be censured for his incomprehension; for Roger, as he himself well knew, was reinventing physics, an endeavour in which he had had no predecessors since Aristotle himself. The existence of this seminal document, like that of the *Perspectiva*, was hidden with Joannes' aid as runner by putting it into circulation in the Peregrine College, which now as before did not care to reveal its own existence, let alone what it was reading. Peter, Joannes reported, said of it only:

'Were this from any other hand, I would have called it gibberish.'

No matter; as an experimenter first and foremost, Peter could not be expected to have much knowledge of or patience with the ancient problem of the multiplication of species – as Aristotle and the Arabs had called the propagation of action; and besides, the work would in the end be only a part of that *Communia naturalium* the proposal of which the convent brothers had so scorned. Its comprehension could likewise wait; for the ignorance of the times there were sufficient causes – not alone the coming of Antichrist foreshadowed in the strife of which Bungay wrote anxiously:

Civil war hath broken out anew, and no man may say from one day to the next how he views his expectations. Henry the King hath repudiated the Provisions of Oxford, and the barons, led by earl Simon, have taken to the field. Of late they have made several victories in the West and South, and have taken London with the greatest fanfare of welcome from the stinking populace. Yet methinks our Henry is but temporarily cowed, for it is most clear that

Leicester's support is still much divided. Give thanks to God that thou art where thou art.

– but, also, as Roger saw upon one false dawn among many, the whole failure of any scholar in history to divine how knowledge (it mattered not what knowledge) might be made trustworthy.

Since the days of revelation, in fact, the same four corrupting errors had been made over and over again: submission to faulty and unworthy authority; submission to what it was customary to believe; submission to the prejudices of the mob; and worst of all, concealment of ignorance by a false show of unheld knowledge, for no better reason than pride.

'I had better get this out of the house right away,' Joannes said, when he had caught his breath.

'Memorize it first, while the ink dries. If the College loses it, we will need to write it again.'

'I don't even want to think of it again, Master. Uhm . . . it lacks a title.'

'So it does,' Roger said. 'Very well. Write at the top, *De signis et causis ignorantiae modernae*. . . . It is dry? Then, run.'

Joannes ran like a deer; but no industry of his could take that explosive doctrine away. Within a week, Roger was writing it again: the *scientia experimentalis*, that knowledge from experience of which even Ptolemy had spoken and henceforth had ignored, had found its method and its sieve, by the mercy of God, the negative fervour of Socrates, and the voiceless, pervasive whisper of Roger Bacon's imprisoned demon Self.

Thereafter, he was ready to go back to the *Computus*; but he was interrupted by Joannes, in a transport of excitement. After two whole years and more, the letter from Guy de Foulques had arrived.

It was on first reading all that Roger could possibly have wished it to be: a mandate from Guy de Foulques, Cardinal-Bishop of Sabina and papal legate in England, to send him forthwith, and notwithstanding any prohibitions to the contrary of Roger's Order, the *scriptum principale* which Roger had offered on the natural sciences. But Roger's elation was short-lived; for on the very next reading of the letter, it became apparent that something had gone seriously awry.

Only to begin with, this prince required that there be sent to him forthwith the long-promised synthesis of knowledge, of the completion of which, after so many years, he was delighted to hear – but there was no such book, nor indeed more than the shadow of one. How had this happened? Roger could but speculate; yet it seemed to him that the fault must lie with Raymond of Laon, or in the caution which had led Roger to send Guy only a verbal entreaty. Perhaps Raymond had taken Roger's reference to those manuscripts in the hands of the Peregrine circle to be chapters of some large work and had so informed the Cardinal; whereas they were of course only isolated *opusculi*, now on this science and now on that, and some not formal works at all, but only letters. Of those two major works with which Roger had meant all along to crown his life, the *Communia naturalium* and a *Summa salvationis per scientiam*, only the first existed, as a few scraps; the second he had not even begun to think about.

Moreover, the charge that Roger was to send this work notwithstanding any prohibitions of his order to the contrary was followed by the stunning words, 'in secret'. Guy's letter provided no way around even the most minor of the prohibitions of Narbonne; nor even any direction to Roger's superiors at the convent for the easement of his menial duties; on the contrary, Roger was specifically forbidden to speak at all to the brothers of the very existence of the mandate.

Furthermore, the Cardinal-Bishop of Sabina and papal legate in England had sent no money. Perhaps, out of older memories of England, he had thought that a scholar-son of Christopher Bacon of Yeo Manse would hardly be in need of it.

Yet withal, this was the mandate that Roger had sought; and, being a mandate, that he must obey.

The absolute overriding need was money – first of all for books, particularly the *De ira* and *Ad Helviam* of Seneca which Piccolomini had shown him at Tivoli, and Cicero's *De republica*. Also he was still lacking essential astronomical and mathematical tables. All these he could probably set one or another of the students in the Peregrine circle to searching out, but he would have to stand ready to pay for them. It would be useful to have an astrolabe, too, and a new set of magnifying glasses – most of his present ones were badly chipped.

And the greatest expenditure inevitably would be for the writing of the book itself. His usual failure to be satisfied with any manuscript until he had revised it four or five times consumed huge amounts of parchment, but there was no help for that; indeed for this labour he must be more scrupulous than ever before. The MS. completed, there would then be the copyists to pay, since the injunction to secrecy and the censorship alike would make it impossible to have the work copied inside the convent.

There was no one to turn to but Eugene, harassed though the boy already was. The only deference Roger could show toward his younger brother's burden was to ask for the smallest possible sum compatible with the work to be done; after some calculation, Roger fixed that, not without misgivings, at one hundred pounds. He took no pleasure in the writing of that letter.

That much passed over, the next question was, what kind of a work should it be? There was only one possible answer, grim though it was: nothing less would be suitable for Guy than the *Communia naturalium* itself. Finishing that under the restrictions and distractions of this confinement, he realized glumly, would probably take five years.

The sooner begun, the sooner ended; and there were, he realized, certain expedients that might shorten the labour. As a second move, he dispatched Joannes to recover everything that was in the keeping of the Peregrine College. Much of it, he hoped, might go almost verbatim into the final document, thus sparing him the recomposition of many whole chapters.

While he waited, he proceeded with the *Computus*, conspicuously strewing its pages about his cell. Its value as a mask was now even greater; and besides, it too could go into the final document when it was completed – which, in view of its complexity, might take almost as long as the *Communia* itself. Well, durability is a virtue in a mask.

Slowly, the scattered manuscripts came back. He was astonished at their bulk; this was the first time he had seen them *en masse*; there were no less than eight books here, all but two begun since his exile, all but one completed since then. That one, the *Metaphysica*, was not suitable for the major task; in fact, reading it now, ten years after its inception, he was strongly tempted to destroy it; but the others would almost surely fall into place as he proceeded.

Only then did he become aware that, despite the impressive mass of leaves now stored in his chest, there were at least four smaller works missing. The *De secretis operibus naturae* and the letter on time and motion could doubtless be recovered from Eugene, but that still left the alchemical summary, which had cost him so much in apparatus in noble metals and in rare drugs, and the book on astronomy. Repeated inquiries by Joannes produced no results; somehow, the College had indeed lost them.

That had, certes, always been a part of the risk; and since the *Summa alchemica* had been published, it might be possible to have it copied from the shelves at Oxford; but for the astronomical work there was no recourse but to write it all over again when the appropriate point in the *Communia* was reached. Now unquestionably he would have to have that astrolabe, and an armillary sphere, and star-charts . . . more expenditures to contemplate.

'How long is it since you've been outside of nights, Master?'

'Eh? Truly, I don't know. Perhaps months. Two months, at the least, I believe.'

'Then you haven't see the comet. It's a monster – covers

almost half the sky. You've never seen anything like it.'

'*You* have never seen anything like it.' Roger corrected him, remembering with a chill the cold glare in the Dragon of his first Paris days, an incredible twenty years ago. Naytheless, he took himself outside to look at it, and found that Joannes had been right: this one was much greater. Such an apparition could not have been vouchsafed for any mean mischance, but Roger could not spare the hours needed to riddle out its astrological import; if the thing had, as it appeared, been generated under the influence of Mars, its portent was bloody; but he contented himself with thinking, uneasily, that a disaster requiring so terrific a prognostick would be unlikely to have much bearing on his personal problems.

And perhaps it did not; for what astrologer could say with confidence that the ill foretold might not be some plague or war far in the East, of which the Latins would never hear? Yet for Roger the word he heard was disastrous enough. Bungay wrote:

Earl Simon hath been excommunicated by the papal Curia, but it doth not appear to have depressed his secular fortunes overmuch. He hath behind him the reformers among the barons; many of the knights and gentry; all of Oxford, eke including the students; and much of the commonalty, to which the Dominicans are appealing on behalf of the poor, with the preachment that Pope and King is an unnatural marriage. There hath been a pitched battle on the heights above Lewes in Sussex – scarce twenty miles west of where Hastings was fought under another such comet – and with an equally strange outcome. Earl Simon's forces appeared on the field at the head of some fifteen thousands of citizens of London, marching to the tune,

Nam rex omnis regitur legibus quas legit
Rex Saul repellatur, quia leges fregit.

On May fourteenth they joined, and Prince Edward was lured into breaking and chasing the rabble, while earl Simon and the barons devoted themselves to smashing the main body of the King's army like a nut beneath a hammer. Both Henry and Edward are prisoners, and Simon hath gone to London, where on St. John's Day he summoned a parliament and proclaimed his purpose to draw a new constitution. I know no more this day, dear brother, and for fear of interception offer thee no comment, but only this story as I have it, I think, reliably. – *Thos.*

And on the same ship, apparently, had travelled the reply from Ilchester:

Alas Roger I can be of no help to thee and may never see so much money as 100 pounds again. This our South is overrun with rebels and Yeo Manse having once been held by de Burgh was ruled to be King's land and taken from us; with what little I myself was allowed to keep have had to ransom myself, and may yet be in such a toil again. Our brother Robert is reported slain, having taken the field with the Londoners at Lewes all unaware that his own side was doing this ill work at home; and so are the fortunes of the Bacon name and family at an end. Pray for me, as I for thee. – *E.*

All this news was nearly a year old, but it was final enough; it contained no cause for hope that any later word would be better. For this conclusion came verification at first hand from Sir William Bonecor, a knightly neighbour and friend of Christopher Bacon.

'Eugene hath told me how to find thee,' he said in English, a language Roger had not heard spoken in a decade; 'and as I am carrying letters from Henry to the new Pope, I paused to see thee. But 'tis true, what thy brother writ thee: the Manse is bankrupt. Of Robert there is no certain word, but belike he's dead; Edward's slaughter of the Londoners was fearsome, and many died of panic.'

'God rest Robert, alive or dead,' Roger said dully. 'But Sir William, what's this of the King? Wast not taken prisoner last May?'

'Aye, but not for long. It happened early this year, after earl Simon's second parliament – a vast muddle of boots and bare feet, including not only the barons, but two citizens from each city, two townsmen from each borough, two knights from each county, and two witches from each coven for all I ken. But it was scarce concluded ere Prince Edward escaped and put himself at the head of a royalist army; and King's man though I be myself, little to the credit of the barons is it that so many then defected from Leicester, who had given them naught but devotion. He was returning from the field in the west, marching to join his son at Kenilworth and thence home, when he was surprised two days after Lammas by Edward at Evesham; and comported himself most knightly, as the tale runs; sent his barber to the top of a church tower to read the 'scutcheons as they forgathered below, and noted down his rude descriptions of these blazons and assigned them names, till 'twas plain that even Gloucester and Roger Mortimer had gone over to the King; whereupon went out among his army and quoth, "Commend your souls to God, my beloved; for our bodies are the foe's." For nigh half the afternoon the battle was in doubt, but in the end 'twas the King's, and earl Simon slain.'

And yet another death of the most beautiful and noble. It no longer bore thinking about.

'God grant that will be the end of all this strife. Tell me, an thou canst, what manner of man is this Clement the Fourth? Here we've heard naught but the bare word of his election.'

'Why, Roger, thou know'st him as well as I, it seemeth me. Clement is he that was our jolly-solemn legate, Guy de Foulques – or Foulquois, as the Frenchmen call him.'

Roger could not find a word to say. The white-haired knight nodded sympathetically.

'Strange, is it not? Never did I dream he had the makings of a Pope; indeed I thought his Cardinal's hat sat ne so up-and-down as was seemly. But 'tis His will.'

'Sir William,' Roger said with all the intensity he could muster; 'wilt thou do the Bacons, who owe thee so much already, one last service?'

'Why, certes, am I able. How wild thine aspect, Roger!'

'Your pardon, but it means much to me, much perhaps to us all. I must write a letter to this Pope, at once. Wilt carry it for me?'

'An it's nat too wearisome long in the writing. I must leave within the week.'

'I'll give it thee tomorrow, promptly after lauds. And charge thee too with a verbal message, an I may; that will be brief.'

The old man smiled. 'Lay on, boy, and I'll be thy post.'

XIII: THE BOWL OF BELISARIUS

Never was there a more delicate task of composition than the making of that letter. What was to be gained was enormous: freedom from the censorship; freedom from his chores; freedom from money; perhaps even freedom itself, pure, unqualified and complete. Yet there stood in the way his failure to reply to the first mandate, now a good two years old; this would have to be explained, yet not at such length as to appear that he was seeking redress of a grievance. It would be best simply to touch upon the difficulties of writing anything at all inside the convent; to suggest that there existed remedies for the evils – all the evils – besetting the Latin Church; and to leave the matter of money for Sir William to broach *viva voce*, should the Pope show interest in these propositions.

After the letter, he was left with naught to do but to continue with the *Communia*: but this went badly. In part, he was beginning to realize reluctantly, the difficulty lay in his own limitations, in that he was now attempting to deal with a science of which he had had no personal experience. The attempt to apply the sieve of the causes of error to the writings of other men sometimes left him with no statement that he trusted, and at others with an account of the subject so confused as to be unworthy of its valuable parchment.

In addition, the daily difficulties were mounting once more. No matter that he stood under no accusation, and that the work he was doing was officially understood to be blameless; the disguise was wearing thin; these comings and goings of minor eminences inevitably aroused the suspicions of the brothers once more, and coupled with Roger's visible industry, convinced them that something was afoot. They did not need to know what it was to conclude that Roger had best be hindered in its prosecution.

Nothing, overtly, was changed, but his chores were enforced with great strictness, and Joannes was expressly forbidden to go outside the convent walls without permission from above – a permission Roger knew better than to ask. In the *longueurs* of scrubbing and sweeping, and in the hours of despair over the blotted, scratched-out, interlined and cut-apart leaves of the *Communia*, there was ample time to reflect upon the temerity of what he had done, and on the magnificent unlikelihood of its coming to any good end, or indeed to any outcome at all.

This cloud grew month by month – irrationally, for well Roger knew that two years might pass before a busy Pope might reply to a letter of no official urgency – no matter how urgently the writer had put his case – and the reply could find its way from Rome to Paris. By spring he had convinced himself that Clement, had he read the letter at all, had called to mind Roger's failure to respond to his first mandate – which, after all, had also been solicited – and had dismissed the matter out of hand.

And indeed the reply was very late; it arrived on the Feast of St Ursula and Her Companions, and was dated June; had at the best spent a long summer among the avalanches:

Dilecto filio, Fratri Rogerio dicto Bacon, Ordinis Fratrum Minorum.

Tuae devotionis litteras gratantes recepimus: sed at verba notarimus diligenter quae ad explanationem earum dilectus filius G. dictus Bonecor, Miles, viva voce nobis proposuit, tam fideliter quam prudenter.

Sane et medius nobis liqueat quid intendas, volumus, et tibi per Apostolica scripta praecipiendo mandamus, quatenus, non obstante praecepto praelati cujuscunque contrario, vel tui Ordinis constitutione quacunque, opus illud, quod te dilecto filio Raymundo de Laonuno communicare rogarimus in minore officio constituti, scriptum de bona littera nobis mittere quam citissime poteris quae tibi videntur adhibenda remedia circa illa, quae nuper occasione tanti discriminis intimasti: et hoc quanto secretius poteris facias indilate.

Datum Viterbii, x. Cal. Julii, anno II.

CLEMENT IV.

DEO GRATIAS. AMEN. AMEN. AMEN.

Oh, Deo gratias, amen! His day was come: Friar Bacon, the obscure, the rebellious, the exiled, the scorned and despised, had indeed become that Magister Roger of whom he had dreamed before he had ever left home: Magister Roger, whose works were writ for Popes!

He studied the miraculous document long and long, not only for the fiercely solemn delight with which it filled him, but also because he was determined, equally fiercely, that it should be put to the best possible use. It was enough like the first mandate – indeed, some of their phrases were identical – to contain many of the same traps. Clement had not only remembered the first mandate, as was clear, but had come very close to repeating it. There was the same requirement that Roger's writings be sent to him 'in good letters', which of course meant that copyists would be required; the same requirement that the work be sent regardless of any provisons to the contrary in the constitutions of the Order; the same corollary failure to include any instructions to the brothers for the mitigation of Roger's menial duties; and above all, the same injunction that all this be done in secret. Furthermore, there was again no money – either Sir William Bonecor had failed to carry that part of the message, or he had not put the case strongly enough.

What, then, was he to do? On the face of it, a mandate from the spiritual emperor of all Christendom should be the most powerful of instruments; yet in point of fact, it seemed to leave him very much where he had been before. He could still proceed no further without making a thorough, indeed a drastic attempt to raise money; for this he needed time, and the whole purpose of corrective discipline, no matter who was corrected, was to fill up time which might otherwise be used for thinking or some other mischief.

Roger sloshed his mop thoughtfully into a corner. It had not occurred to him until now, but under circumstances of this kind the injunction to secrecy would be impossible to fulfil, no matter how faithfully he himself obeyed it. The use of outside copyists would defeat it. If they did not pirate the work itself as it passed through their hands – the usual practice in a university town if the work in question appeared to be of some substance, likely sooner or later to be saleable to students – one or another of the scribes, sooner or later, would be sure to whisper to Roger's superiors the word which would undo his triumph, branch and root. Then he would have no choice but to show the brothers his letter from the Pope, and secrecy of any sort would be at an end.

But there were, to be sure, different kinds and degrees of secrecy; and it might be possible, by forfeiting the lesser, to preserve the greater. The question was: since secrecy *in toto* was impossible, what aspect of it would be the greater in Clement's eyes? To answer that, one would have to know why Guy had enjoined it in the first place, and not even a hint of such a reason appeared in either this or the earlier mandate. It would have to be a reason which would be as compelling to Pope Clement IV as it had been to the Cardinal-Bishop of Sabina, a reason which did not change and might indeed loom even larger with the donning of the Tiara.

One such which might have bulked large to a Cardinal, a reluctance to interfere with the internal discipline of the Orders, could hardly crouch so obstinately in the way of a Pope, on whose sufferance both Orders – both founded within the lifetimes of living men – depended for their existence. Yet young though they were, and corrupt though they were even in their youth, the Orders had proven their value to Christendom, and no Pope could now want to see them disrupted, let alone dissolved; so it might well be assumed that Clement, like his predecessors, would wish to avoid any move which might promote dissension between them – such as permitting an errant Franciscan to publish in despite of the direct prohibition of his Minister General; and publish, furthermore, an extensive work in the natural sciences which the Dominicans were forbidden to study at all.

In so far as Roger could determine, the reasoning was sound, but the conjecture upon which it ultimately stood was a shaky one indeed upon which to build in addition a course of action. Nevertheless, he had no better foundation; and its consequences were that, first, what Clement would most desire would be the concealment of the nature and content of the work, not only from the world, but from the Franciscans themselves; and, second, that in defence of this the larger secrecy, the smaller secret of the existence of the mandate might in middling-good conscience be sacrificed. Were the conjecture to be true, then it would follow that while the first mandate – from the Cardinal – might or might not specifically identify the work to be prepared as dealing with the natural sciences (as in fact, of course, it did), the second – from the Pope – would not; and this indeed was one of the major differences between these otherwise so similar documents. The logician in Roger shuddered at the prospect of launching into these unknowable seas aboard the keelless, sailless, rudderless fallacy of affirming the consequent; but the self whispered, *What choice?* And answered, *None, none.*

He sought out the Father Superior, and showed him the letter. The consternation it produced was gratifying, but dangerous as well; to the demand that Roger surrender it for an examination in council and by the provincial minister, Roger refused on the grounds that it was addressed to him and was his property, which was inarguable except on the rarefied theological ground that as a Franciscan he had no property – an argument too tainted with Joachism to be usable here. After three days the provincial minister was called in, to see whether by the plea to the Pope on Roger's part of which Clement's letter plainly gave evidence, Roger had transgressed the fifth rubric of the Constitutions of Narbonne, which forbade any Franciscan to approach the Pontiff without many specific permissions; but the mandate, whose authenticity could hardly be doubted, was a white-hot iron to be thrust into the placid, indeed stagnant waters of a Parisian convent of no other account, and the charge was dismissed on the technicality that the text of Clement betrayed no intention on Roger's part to pass over his superiors to the Holy Father simply to prosecute a grievance, the main act the fifth rubric had been inscribed to prevent. In this much, *Deo gratias*, the discretion he had exercised in casting the plea had been paid back.

Suspicion, jealousy, envy, all these remained; to which was added even a certain savagery in the enforcement of his daily tasks; but the words and the signature of the Pope could in no wise be contraverted, nor could the brothers deny him time to go forth into the city to raise money for copyists – they being no better able than he had been to interpret otherwise Clement's command to secrecy.

For the rest of their malice, he had a sufficient remedy, in his heart. He wrote to Eugene, without exposing the subject: 'It is the vice by which man loses himself, his neighbour, and God, which forces him to break peace with all, even with his dearest friends. He disparages everyone with insults, and assails everyone with injuries; he does not omit to expose himself to all perils, and is not afraid to blaspheme God.'

He had none to say to him, 'Art aware, most Christian Roger, that thou art describing someone an enemy would say much favours thee?' That man was dead.

Thus armed, he went forth into the city, which he had not seen since before Rome. By the river there was a ruin which he studied silently for a long time before his memories of both towns combined to give him understanding of what had happened: the Parisians had clumsily piled a third course atop the aqueduct, and the whole long structure had come pouring down in a rain of ill-cut stones, leaving behind naught but a few arches and a parade of jagged stumps, like a burlesque of cypresses. There was a monument to ignorance that would stub toes and bark shins for centuries to come; but he had no time now to brood over it any further, let alone teach simple Roman engineering to the rough-dressed heads of Paris. His present errand was to Louis IX, King of France.

There was no one to tell him that this were madness, since he had broached it to no one but himself. It seemed to him to be a simple and sensible project: it was the best visible use to which one could put a letter from the curator-princeps of the next world to a prince of this, and Louis was the best kind to read the message, as Henry III would doubtless have been the worst. Louis loved knowledge, and had been for a long time the patron of Vincent of Beauvais, a Dominican who had written in the domain of theology just such a work as Roger was now asked to write in the sciences; had in fact not only made Vincent his librarian, as Luca di Cosmati had been made the librarian of Piccolomini, Marquis of Modena, but had made him teacher and guide to his royal children.

The letter, indeed, did bring him to the king; but it also struck him dumb. Louis was remotely kind, as well as amused, but would know what business it was of the Pope's that demanded so much money; and seeing from the letter that this could not be told, and from the shabbiness of the emissary, of whom he had never heard, that it could hardly be a matter of state, dismissed Roger with such a purse as he might give to any other medicant and turned his mind to the next petitioner.

The purse was full of clipped trash, worth perhaps two pounds after the counterfeits were shaken out: a magnificent gift for a beggar, but a day wasted for Roger; he retreated at dusk to the convent, gloomily biting the ragged coins and spitting them out on to the cobbles.

It seemed reasonable, nay inevitable, that the response of any other high personage who did not know Roger would be the same, or perhaps much less gracious than that of the Saint-King had been. Such remaining quality as did know who Roger was, was in England, effectively beyond his reach for the indefinite future; and, of course, in Rome, which was no aid either. But wait: there was the Marquis of Modena.

But the more he considered the matter, the more reluctant he was to ask the grave scholar of Tivoli for money. Roger had not written to Piccolomini in a dozen years; and though there were assuredly many good and sufficient reasons for this, to break such a silence with a series of excuses directly followed by an appeal for funds would hardly sit well with the Roman aristocrat. Yet Roger was on the Pope's business, and durst not let any field lie fallow that he knew might bear.

In the end, he wrote to Livia instead, explaining the circumstances frankly in so far as the mandate permitted him to do under his interpretation of it. Then he promptly forgot about this essay, for nothing was surer than that any response would be much delayed. If any money did indeed arrive from that source, it would not do so until he was in the concluding days of the work; and that would be just as well, for it would be then that the copyists' bills would be falling due one after the other.

His next port of call was the laboratory of Peter the Peregrine.

'Roger, you know well that I am cut off from my family as of old,' the experimenter said when he was finished. 'Yet you gave me money when you had it, and I'd not be such a poor Christian as to refuse you now. What to do? Well, here's two pounds, as a beginning – a most poor beginning, but I am a poor man.'

'Believe me, Peter, I take it as gratefully as if it were riches; as from you it is. Could you, perhaps, suggest where else I might go? I have already tried the King.'

'You have? Well, you were always bold. Belike I'd have gone to him myself, had I a mandate from the Pope in my scrip . . . but I doubt it. Now let's see. . . . It would be easier, had we still the same circle of students as in the old days, to whom you gave your money; then we could simply pass a bowl around. Well, I can do that anyhow; I'll tell those present that it's a special assessment, and either they pay up or school's out. But it'll not produce so much as it would have did they know you and I could explain.'

'Would it do any good, do you think,' Roger suggested tentatively, 'to explain it all the same, and tell them that I am the author of all those inflammatory books they've been reading?'

'No, probably not,' Peter said, frowning. 'They're an anti-clerical lot; what care they for the Pope's business, especially since I cannot say to them what precisely it is? Yet it might be as well to tell them that I am collecting the money for you. After all, they did lose four or five of your books, the young noodles; had those parchments belonged to the University library, the fines would have stings in them for fair; I'll sting 'em too.'

'I am more grateful to you than I can say, Peter.'

'I have my reasons,' Peter said, smiling. 'Say me neither yea nor nay, but you prosecuting a business of the Pope's must concern some work of knowledge, and you being who you are, it is bound to be knowledge in the natural sciences. I can think of nothing more worthy to be pressed upon a Pope; I have given my own life to them – what's a few pounds?'

That interview cheered Roger for the remainder of the week; and at the outcome, he had six pounds, counting the two from the King. Yet there was no objective reason for cheerfulness – six pounds was almost as little use as no money at all; and he had exhausted his roster of noblemen, major and minor alike. Well then, merchants.

Here again, he knew of none but William Busshe, an Englishman; but that limitation was not without hope. It was true that the rebels had controlled the Cinque Ports – it was at Dover that they had met Guy de Foulques on his landing as mediator from the then Pope, and had torn the proposals he carried into a thousand bits and cast them into the sea – but they might not control them now, after Evesham; and in any event they had wanted the ports for the revenues, to help keep their armies in the field, and so would have had their own interest in the maintenance of shipping. What cost Roger more worry than this theory of strategy was winning from his superiors permission to make the long trip to Wissant; he won it at last not by an exercise of subtlety, but by flourishing the papal mandate at them like a bludgeon.

He had no hope of finding Bushe himself, for this was not the season for it, nor had he learned to know the family of Busshe's hosts, during the three days that he had convalesced in their house, well enough to ask money of them. But he had with great care prepared a letter to William to be placed in their hands against the time when the *Maudelayne* should again be in port with its packs of fells. He knew the host at least well enough, he believed, to charge him most urgently with its cherishing, and most prompt delivery.

But Busshe was there. After some hesitation, and much whispering up and down stairs, the eldest daughter of his Flemish partner brought Roger to him, with her finger laid to her lips.

Busshe lay in that same great bed in which Roger had once recovered from his sea-sickness. His hands, that had hauled cordage in Channel storms, were crossed impotently in his lap, and beneath the linens lay the shadow of a torso as narrow and as lax as a length of tarred rope. His hair, totally white, was spread out on the bolster; and in all of him there was no colour, save for a bright-busked patch of red on each cheekbone, and the blue shadows under the closed eyes.

Below, there continued the muffled sounds of comings and goings: the host's family, physicians, solicitors, agents, creditors, even sailors; Roger had seen, however, no ecclesiastics as yet. After a while, without opening his eyes, Busshe whispered:

'The plate . . . the plate. . . .'

Roger understood very well; there had been just such a vigil of kites at his father's last illness, and Robert, who had scattered it with brutal efficacy, had not then been too self-removed from his next-youngest brother to explain it. Roger bent and touched Busshe's hand gently with two fingers.

'Dear friend,' he said, and then was forced to swallow. 'They cannot seize thy plate for thy debts. Thou'rt not at home.'

The dying man's eyes opened at the touch, looking steadfastly at the ceiling. Nevertheless, he said:

''Tis Roger of Ilchester. Hast come to pray for William Busshe? I am thy debtor.'

There was no answer to be given; the question was as good as an indictment. The feathery voice said on:

'I have many such. The horsemen . . . at Dover . . . took away my sarplers. Bare 'scaped I with my ship. . . .'

'Rest, William, I entreat thee.'

The hands stirred, fruitlessly. 'Nay, no need. Well wis I . . . I be not long on live. . . . Thou'rt older too, Roger.'

'Rest thee, in God's name. How may I help thee?'

At that, William Busshe's head turned on the bolster. His eyes glittered, but did not seem to see; it was the look of a limed bird. 'Pray,' he whispered; 'pray. We will foredo them, thou and I, Roger. Ever scrupulously fair and honest was I with them; and now . . . they're below dividing me, like . . . the cloak of . . . many colours. Seek in my chest, Roger.'

Roger looked about. 'Good William, for what?'

'The *Maudelayne*. The title's there. Nay, first the key . . . 'tis under this pillow.'

Gently, Roger extracted it, and opened the chest. In it there seemed to be nothing but a jumble of clothing.

'The jerkin . . . 'tis sewn flat into the right-hand corner. Thou art tonsured; say that I gave it thee to be shriven.' He gasped, and his eyes closed.

Roger hastened to him. The sweat-beads on the white forehead were cold under his palm. But once more, Busshe's lips moved.

'Now . . . do I thank God . . . that one came to see me . . . in mine extremity. . . . Roger . . . what dost do?'

Through his tears, Roger croaked forth the best half-truth of his life.

'I am an adviser to the Pope.'

'Ahhhh. . . .'

The wrinkled mouth failed to close. Roger knelt; and remained kneeling for a long time.

When he was able, he closed the blind eyes with two groats, and locked the chest; and then folded the papery hands about the key. Then he signed himself; and laying the leather jerkin over his left forearm, quitted the cold room.

The kestrels were gathered just outside, and all up and down the staircase. Roger closed the door softly, and turned upon them a stare all the more terrible for its blindness. He said: 'It is ended.'

There was a ragged susurrus of breath. 'Good friar, we thank thee,' a heavy male voice said unctuously. 'Wilt come below, we'll sign the book; and raise a goblet for the soul of the departed; and give thee somewhat for thine office, and thine holy Order.'

'I have this for charity, and require naught else,' Roger said harshly, showing the jerkin, all Channel-weathered as it was. 'Show me thy document, and I'll leave thee straight to thy mourning.'

Forever after, he would remember Wissant not for the rumble of its trade or the slapping of its waves, but as the dry sound of hands being rubbed together.

Out of this revulsion and guilt he lost much, forbye he could not bring himself to pause in Wissant to sell the title of the *Maudelayne*, nor even to engage an agent, but waited for this until he was back in Paris; and so for the beaten ship realized but six pounds – three times what Busshe had paid for her in his unrecoverable youth, but that had been before the wars, when the pound had been the hardest coin in all of Christendom; and the journey to and from the *Maudelayne*'s master had itself cost Roger nearly a pound. The net was ten pounds.

Tragic though it had been – and selling the *Maudelayne* had been more than a little like selling one of his sisters – the success of the trip, thus qualified, led him to thinking farther afield. Not to Rome, naturally, and certainly not to England; but since the brothers had let him go as far as Wissant, then most of the Gallic nations should be open to him. For example (though it was the only example that occurred to him): it had been Simon de Montfort who had brought Roger to the attention of Guy de Foulques, thus in a sense beginning all this; or it had begun even before, when, as

Eleanor's Confessor, Adam Marsh had arranged that marriage. And Simon's widow was now in exile in Gascony. Why not?

The brothers produced reasons like virtuosi; Roger demolished them. The demolition would have accomplished nothing had it not been for the precedent of the journey to Wissant, which had weakened their logic as the mandate of Clement had weakened their authority. Roger handed his mop to Joannes, who flourished it like a banner, and set forth.

The castle in Labourd was not yet ruinous, but it had not far to go; and it was almost empty; if the man-at-arms who took Roger to Eleanor was not the same, without his mail, who later served as her footman, they were at the very least fraternal twins. The footman had first to drag off an enormous slavering mastiff which snarled and roared at Roger till the bare hall rang shatteringly; the footman would have taken the beast entirely away, but at a motion from Eleanor, he instead chained it to a ring in the near wall, where it stood straining, its snarls as steady and unsettling as the noise of an anchor-hawser running out.

Though the clamour distracted him, Roger somewhat welcomed it too; for many years had passed since he had seen Eleanor last – never, he recalled slowly, since Beaumont, for despite their propinquity at Westminster their paths had not crossed there. And he had never noticed then that she was beautiful; he saw it now for the first time, as, *But she is still beautiful.*

He could hardly interpret what he meant by this, except that he knew vaguely that she was older, somewhat, than he was; which meant that she was more than fifty *ae*. How much more mattered not in the least, for to Roger's eyes she had not changed: tall and slender she stood as before, eyes the colour of sheet lightning under the broad brow, hands white, tapered and smooth as an eidolon of Mercy, issuing from the sorrowing sleeves. Looking at her, Roger's demon self said to him, also for – alas! – the first time: *Livia too was beautiful.*

'My Lady,' he said above the growls of the animal. 'I . . . presume upon your mourning, and ask your pardon. I am about a business for his highness the Lord Pope, otherwise—'

'Most Christian Roger, thou'rt welcome.' Roger took a step forward; the dog leapt against the chain, shouting. Like a girl, Eleanor clapped her hands to her ears. 'Oh, we shall never hear each other! Hanno, I'll switch thee!'

She smote her hands together, once. 'Bring him his bed – else will I never hear the friar's holy rede!'

The footman silently brought a circular rag carpet of no particular colour and far gone in dog hairs, and threw it cautiously against the wall under the ring. Hanno stepped on to it one vast pad at a time, and then turned on it as if making up his nest, until he had created a grey lump of cloth far too small to sleep a puppy upon. On this he sat, regarding his mistress with patient reproach, and growled thereafter only faintly, deep in his chest, when Roger raised a hand, or breathed.

With one eye nevertheless upon Hanno, Roger tumbled forth his errand. As Eleanor listened, her eyes closed slowly, until at the end her spare strange beauty was not that of a woman, nor even of a statue, but that of the Platonic absolute of which all beauty is but a shadow in a cave, cast by the Fire beyond fire. Hanno grumbled and lay down; Roger faltered; beyond the embrasures, the sweet birds of Gascony faltered too.

Then her lids flew open. 'Oh,' she said, putting her hands to her throat; 'oh. Sweet Roger Bacon, I am old. Oh, an I could give thee what thou need'st! But I am not what I was – and though so praydeth I to the Virgin, nay never could I give, but only take. I think I must be damned.'

'Good my lady! . . . None can know that to be true. Thou art noble surely, and wise; why dost despair of God? Hast not courage? I know thou hast.'

'But have not love?' Eleanor said. 'Not that? I prayed for it when I was married to Pembroke, as a little girl; prayed to give it, that I might be worthy of receiving. And oh in what perfect measure my lords gave it me, and so also my sons – and they are gone, all gone from me who failed them. I loved them. I loved them, oh Mother and Bride; but it was not enough. They were all taken away.'

'My lady. . . . We shall all be taken away.'

But she was already kneeling, her tears coursing over the backs of her hands. The monster coughed, but made no objection when he knelt with her, though its eyes were smoky as obsidian.

After a while, she stood, and it was almost as though they had only just met.

'Forgive me, Friar Bacon. I am not myself today. Now let us see what I can do for mine enemy the Pope.'

With a subdued shock, Roger realized what she meant, and raised a hand to halt her, but she would not be halted.

'Once had I hope of those high designs of my lord of Leicester, those Mad Parliaments and new charters, those forays of peoples against princes,' she said somnolently. 'I little thought the King my brother capable of withstanding Simon, strange though the Earl's purposes oft struck me. But the King's course was also the Pope's, and mayhap God's – I took that too little into mine accountings, and so am bereft, as now you see me; that course prospers, while my lord's is dead with him; as you here and now remind me in heaven's own good time.'

'Not I!' Roger cried. 'I am on no business of King Henry, good my lady.' But the words sounded thin in his own ears. The Pope had been, and was still, Henry the King's ally . . . and for her, the civil war had been, literally, husband against brother.

'Nay, nor did I mean my words to be taken so. In thee, I see only the prospering of God's business in Rome, through its best English instrument; we French are near outworn. So taught me my lord to think of thee, Friar Bacon, when I knew thee not; my lord, and eke one other.'

'One other? Forgive me, my lady – I ask it not in vanity, but for the judgment of mine own soul in hope of heaven: who was that one?'

Her eyes closed again for a moment. 'I cannot speak for him.'

'Well wis I. Yet was it – was that one Friar Marsh?'

There was no answer. After a while, she clasped her hands and walked slowly to a near window.

'Let us speak no more of all those that are dead . . . no more of these, but only on thine errand. How may I help? The way is far from clear. I am in perpetual exile, a widow, and without arms. Were this fief threatened, I could not protect it; were the castle besieged, I could not hold it; nor have I men to collect my taxes, so that I cannot even keep my fortifications in repair. Of late, some worthy franklins have remembered who was my lord, and his strange doctrines; and thus emboldened, have banded together, against some future war, to buy the castle from me, with myself as . . . caretaker. Though I have refused, I shall not be able to refuse a second time, and will instead betake myself to Montargis; but I have not these monies yet.'

'Good my Lady. I should have anticipated of this some substantial part. Give me but a shilling for mine Order, and I shall not trouble thee more.'

She swung quickly upon him. 'This to me, Roger Bacon? I am Eleanor of Pembroke and Leicester, and sister to a king! Shall it be said that she gave the Vicar of God a shilling? Wait.'

She left the hall, supple as an elm, and seemingly as tall. Roger was left alone with Hanno, who had risen, and blinked at him with slow implacability. A sweet smell of apple-blossoms drifted in through the window she had quitted. Suddenly, as though he had come to some dim conclusion, the huge dog lay down once more and put his head on his paws.

When Eleanor returned, she bore in her hands a small casket of boxwood, with iron clasps: a mean thing, and crudely carved, yet she held it before her as though it were more costly and more fragile than a crystal egg.

'When I was but a princess five years old,' she said quietly, 'Hubert de Burgh that was my guardian gave this to me. I wore it round my wimple, and feigned to be a queen; and, as so feigned I, so was I. I kept 't for mine own daughter; but now I shall have none. See.'

She lifted the lid and held out the rude jewel-box. Within, upon a fold of worn damask, lay a child-size coronet of gold filigree, set with pearls and fronted by a cool amethyst about the size of a millet. The woven gold was much dulled by time, but glowed slowly with a reddish light, as if in the sleep of Charlemagne. Roger lifted his eyes and tried to see her as a child with this above her brows, and for an instant did so; then the pain in the present eyes, womanly beyond all compare since the orange gardens of Tivoli, sponged away the vision and left him empty.

'My Lady . . . it may be that I do not understand. Is this—? I dare not think it.'

Her eyes shuttered. 'Were you to refuse me, I would take it ill. Here, please, Friar Bacon. Take it. I have held it far too long; that child is dead.'

Numbly, Roger took the boxwood chest. How had he come to this? Surely he had never been formed to be a beggar; for the wounds were dreadful.

The coronet did not prove to be as valuable as he had hoped, but nevertheless it brought him by far the largest fruit of his beggary yet: thirty-five pounds, bringing his total to forty-four. And unexpectedly, while he was in Gascony, there had arrived for him a letter from Rome.

It was very brief:

My daughter Olivia whom you address is gone into a convent. I send you herewith ten ducats. Had you written to me I would have sent more.

MODENA

And so, another friendship spoiled by his gracelessness; it was easy to see, now that it was too late, wherein the affront had lain. And the price of his friendship was ten ducats, or approximately three pounds.

His time was virtually run out. The new year was upon

him, and the brothers were demanding that he return to his duties. There was nothing left to do but go to the usurers; a step that was anathema to him, but all other possibilities were exhausted. He was forced to visit three of them, for no one would give him any substantial sum, because of his visible lack of good security; it was only upon his promise to send an expense account to the Pope that they would give him anything at all.

Even this petty scrabbling was brought to an abrupt end upon the arrival of four more pounds from Peter Peregrine – not by the sum itself, but by Roger's discovery that Peter, having gotten wind of Roger's dealings with the usurers, had mortgaged his house for the money. This was truly the final humiliation; the firm sign to stand fast with what he had.

As early as Epiphany it became clear to him that the *Communia naturalium* would have to be abandoned. It could no doubt be finished at a later date, when he had had more time for study and for consultation with other experimenters and philosophers, but he could not encompass all of the natural sciences for the Pope in his present state of ignorance and confinement. There could be no *scriptum principale*; the best he could hope to achieve would be a *persuasio* of some length, an attempt to convince the Pontiff of the value of natural knowledge, and the importance of supporting its investigation.

Nevertheless even this would have to be most carefully planned. After a week, he had an outline which seemed satisfactory as a start. The letter would be divided into seven parts: The first would expose and analyse the four causes of human error, and here he could use a great part of the *De erroribus* verbatim; next would come the relationship between natural philosophy and theology, with special attention to the problem posed by the knowledge of the pagan philosophers and poets, and its solution as revealed in the *Secret of Secrets*; third, the beauty and utility of the study of tongues, with brief discussions of Hebrew, Chaldean and Greek, and a commentary on the evils of faulty translation; fourth, a demonstration that mathematics is the key to all other sciences, beginning with *De laudibus mathematicae*, and drawing examples from astrology, astronomy, calendar reform, chronology, geography and optics; fifth would follow the *Perspectiva*, covering the general principles of vision, direct vision, reflection and refraction, with an analysis of the anatomy of the animal eye, and in addition enough of *De multiplicatione specierum* as was needful to show that the propagation of light was only a special case of a universal property of space and time; sixth, an exposition of the virtues and methods of experimental science, with a demonstration of its powers provided by the treatise on the rainbow; and finally, moral philosophy, the crown and seal of the whole, the science of the salvation of man. It would be no small task in itself; but unlike the *Communia*, at least it looked practicable.

And thus it began:

A thorough consideration of knowledge consists of two things, perception of what is necessary to obtain it, and then of the method of applying it to all matters that they may be directed by its means in the proper way. For by the light of knowledge the Church of God is governed, the commonwealth of the faithful is regulated, the conversion of unbelievers is secured, and those who persist in their malice can be held in check by the excellence of knowledge, so that they may be driven off from the borders of the Church in a better way than by the shedding of Christian blood. Now all matters requiring the guidance of knowledge are reduced to these four heads and no more. Therefore, I shall now try to present to your Holiness the subject of the attainment of this knowledge, not only relatively but absolutely, according to the tenor of my former letter, as best I can at the present time, in the form of a plea that will win your support until my fuller and more definite statement is completed. Since, moreover, the subjects in question are weighty and unusual, they stand in need of the grace and favour accorded to human frailty....

Now there are four chief obstacles in grasping truth, which

hinder every man, however learned, and scarcely allow anyone to win a clear title to learning, namely, submission to faulty and unworthy authority, influence of custom, popular prejudice, and concealment of our own ignorance accompanied by an ostentatious display of our knowledge. Every man is entangled in these difficulties, every rank is beset, for people without distinction draw the same conclusion from three arguments, than which none could be worse, namely, for this the authority of our predecessors is adduced, this is the custom, this is the common belief; hence correct. An opposite conclusion and a far better one should be drawn from the premisses, as I shall abundantly show by authority, experience and reason. Should, however, these three errors be refuted by the convincing force of reason, the fourth is always ready and on everyone's lips for the excuse of his own ignorance, and although he has no knowledge worthy of the name, he may yet shamelessly magnify it, so that at least to the wretched satisfaction of his own folly he suppresses and evades the truth. Moreover, from these deadly banes come all the evils of the human race; for the most useful, the greatest, and most beautiful lessons of knowledge, as well as the secrets of all science and art, are unknown. But, still worse, men blinded in the fog of these four errors do not perceive their own ignorance, but with ever precaution cloak and defend it so as not to find a remedy; and worst of all, although they are in the densest shadows of error, they think they are in the full light of truth. For these reasons they reckon that truths most firmly established are at the extreme limits of falsehood, that our greatest blessings are of no moment, and our chief interests possess neither weight nor value. On the contrary, they proclaim what is most false, praise what is worst, extol what is most vile, blind to every gleam of wisdom and scorning what they can obtain with great ease. In the excess of their folly they expend their utmost efforts, consume much time, pour out large expenditures on matters of little or no use and of no merit in the judgment of a wise man. Hence it is necessary that the violence and banefulness of these four causes of all evils should be recognized in the beginning and rebuked and banished from the consideration of science. For where these bear sway, no reason influences, no right decides, no law binds, religion has no domain, nature's mandate fails, the complexion of things is changed, their order is confounded, vice prevails, virtue is extinguished, falsehood reigns, truth is hissed off the scene.

And with this, he was launched upon such a fury of composition as he had never known before in his life; nor, in fact, had ever been known in the history of the phenomenal world.

The letter grew and grew, and the months went by: the Purification of the Virgin, St. David, St. Richard, Inventio Sanctae Crucis, St. Barnabas. By June, a year after Clement had sat down to write to Roger, he had gotten only as far as the analysis of the rainbow, and here he was forced to stop by the discovery that, of the nineteen experiments by which he proposed to demonstrate the nature of the bow, he himself had not performed three, and that they did indeed require an astrolabe; and in addition, he needed to observe a lunar rainbow, which stubbornly failed to appear for nearly a month. Only then could the writing be resumed.

The feasts marched by: Visitatio Mariae, Lammas, St. Giles, the Holy Guardian Angels. At last he was launched into the section on moral philosphy; he knew as he worked that the pressure of time was coming between him and the subject, but for time there was no remedy but eternity.

The letter was finished on All Saints' Day, almost precisely ten months after he had begun it. It would take more months to copy, for its length was almost half a million words.

While he waited on the copyists, he began the composition of an introductory letter for this huge mass of leaves. He was by no means through; for as he worked, he was dogged both day and night, labouring and resting, by the whispering of his demon self, tormenting him constantly with the thought that the large work might well be lost amidst the perils of the road, and never reach Clement at all. At the very least, the introductory letter should contain a summary of the plan of the work, and of its major conclusions; this would be useful as well, were the Pope to be too busy to read the large work, as was also wholly possible.

But the self did not let him rest even there. There were sections of the large work that were inexcusably badly argued, particularly the discussion of the seven sins of theology; the analysis of astrology was scrappy and inconclusive; and although Roger had discussed medicine at some length, he had said almost nothing about alchemy, that most useful of the ancillary sciences, and the one in which – though for the wrong reasons – any prince would be most likely to be interested.

All these matters went in, and more besides, until what had been meant to be but an introductory letter had become a treatise in itself; by no means so formidable as the first, but still a good thirty thousand words long. More expenditures! But there was no question but that it, too, would have to go to the Pope; he dispatched it to the copyists, and began all all over again to write an introductory letter, this time for both works.

Though he had not spoken of it as yet in the convent, Roger had already conceived the scheme of sending his *persuasio* across the Alps in the hands of Joannes. There was probably no wise man in Paris who would be as able as the boy to explain to Clement the difficult passages in the work, should the Pope require it; and for Joannes, the opportunity to exhibit his understanding before the Supreme Pontiff was such a one as no apprentice would dare aspire to in his usual life, nay not even in his dreams. Roger had allotted the boy some mention in the large work, but a more elaborate introduction might not be amiss – especially in view of the possibility that Clement might not read the large work at all.

Then the large work came back from the copyists. Roger was appalled. It was an even poorer performance than he had realized; it would have to be extensively revised, especially the first three parts. As for the seventh part, it was hopeless; no amount of revision would rescue it in the time he had available.

While he wrote, the small work also came back; and with it, the bills. They took the remainder of the sixty pounds cleanly away, leaving behind only the small sum Roger had set aside for Joannes for the journey to Rome. Yet the large work was now so heavily marked that much of it would have to be copied over again.

From this dilemma there was only one way out, regardless of the Pope's command: he would have to show the large work – but certainly not the small, for that contained a passage on the spectacular stupidities of Alexander of Hales which might well be judged to be in violation of the provisions of Narbonne, as tending toward the division of the Order – to his superiors, and appeal to have it copied in the convent. It was risky; and Clement could not be told of it; but all the money was gone, and so naught else would serve.

In the meantime, he still needed to write an introductory letter to both works, for he had cannibalized the second such for the revision of the large work so heavily that hardly anything was left of it. Best to abandon that for the time being, and make still a third introduction – this time strictly confined to its purpose; if the second introduction were on the verge of becoming another volume of Roger Bacon his universal encyclopedia of all that was known or knowable in the world, it would not suffer for being held back a while; nor would Clement suffer the lack of it, or know that he so suffered until he saw it; after which, if God allowed him wisdom, he could not but forgive, and learn; or else, what was knowledge for?

The response of the Father Superior to the large work was unexpected, and more than welcome: he not only found it unobjectionable – though there were some harsh words in the first section, they were not applied to anyone by name – but admirable. Though he did not say so outright, the notion seemed to have occurred to him that perhaps there was after all some fame to come to his convent through the activities of this obscure but obviously learned friar – exactly as the exasperating man had claimed all along.

Regardless of what he thought, what he did was gratifying. Not only did he authorize the copying of the large work inside the convent, but also relieved Roger of his corrective discipline until the labour for the Pope should be completed. In casting his ruling in this form, he inadvertently put himself into Roger's hands; for both the third work – as Roger was now coming to think of it – and the *Communia naturalium* were for the Pope, as he could abundantly prove, and not even he could say how long it would take to complete them both. It would be a matter of years, without doubt.

The brothers, by dividing the task among themselves, speedily finished the copying of the revised large work; and the almost intolerably excited Joannes, with many protestations of his undying love and gratitude, and attended by many prayers for his safety, was sent forth into the city to seek out and join a party ready to journey over the Alps.

With a sigh, and an additional prayer for the safety of his fifteen months of unremitting labour, Roger returned to his writing. To be able to study and compose once more without distraction or impediment was a blessing; he felt, indeed, like Cicero recalled from exile. And there was still much to be done: in addition to writing a discussion of the nature of a vacuum, and many other matters not covered in either of the two departed works, he had now to consider what his course was to be were the response of the Pope to be favourable.

For this he had already developed a plan, which he had outlined briefly in the final introductory letter; namely, that the Pope – and other princes too, if necessary – sponsor a true compendium of all knowledge of the natural sciences, for the edification of laymen, each section on a special science to be written by a man learned in it. It was now time to develop the proposition and think it through.

Obviously the book must be true throughout, and its truth proven as far as possible by trustworthy experience. The contents would have to be chosen carefully and in a systematic way, so as to avoid the manifold confusions between metaphysics and the natural sciences which were the bane of the universities. Brevity too would be a virtue in a work for laymen, and this might well be difficult to achieve, not only on account of the well-known tendency of even the best scholars to be as pompous as possible, but in addition because there would surely be areas of study where brevity would prove to be incompatible with clarity. The work would need as its director something more than a mere commentator and guide: he would have to be someone skilled in a special science, as yet uninvented, which would examine the findings of each of the other sciences as given, and draw them together into a meaningful whole.

Roger set himself now to the creation of that new science, so that if word should reach him that the Pope looked upon the initial effort with approval, he should not be found unready, as he had been found before. And then, too, would be the time to present to the Pope his tally of the expenses he had incurred on behalf of the Curia.

He worked with great care now, since the need for haste had disappeared, making every argument as closely reasoned and perfect as was in his power. That some of these were consequently extremely difficult and dense of texture he was well aware, but after all, Joannes would still be in Rome to explain the hard parts if Clement required it.

He had begun in mid-April; by August he had a work of some sixty thousand words, with which he was thus far reasonably well pleased; and he paused to consider what should be done with it. Though it was unfinished, it might be as well to offer what he had to the brothers, for copying while he worked on the remainder; this would save much time when the next papal mandate arrived. But after long thought, Roger reluctantly decided against it. The difficulty lay in the fact that the new work opened with a long account of the difficulties he had undergone in writing the first two; and though it was all only too true, assuredly the brothers would take it ill. He was equally determined not to remove the passage, for it was the very heart of his case to Clement that his expenses should be repaid. He would have to copy it himself; and that being the case, it were sensible to finish it first.

But he had gone little farther ere he was called before the Father Superior.

'Friar Bacon, it is ordered that thou art released from all discipline, and permission is granted thee to return to thy parent house of our Order at Oxford.'

Roger's heart nearly stopped. Surely, surely this was a sign of favour from on high!

'For what reason, Father, I beg thee? And who hath so ordered?'

'No reason is given. The order cometh from the provincial minister; and could not have been issued, of course, without the knowledge and consent of the Minister-General. Beyond that, we know nothing.'

'But my works for Pope Clement! Is there no word from His Holiness at all?'

'No word,' the Father Superior said, signing himself. 'His Holiness is dead.'

XIV: THE MINISTRY

Too numb to feel despair, Roger returned to his old eyrie in the gatehouse. He had not even Bungay to share it with him now, for Thomas was still the vicar of the provincial minister of the Franciscan order in England. He was quite alone; and the great work of his life was gone as well, dropped into a vacuum; *nihil ex nihil fit*.

He never found out why it was that he had been sent home, nor whether Clement had read any part of his letters, or ever had received them. He wrote to the papal secretary and got no answer, which did not surprise him; that beleaguered man had matters of more moment to think about. The death of Clement had thrown all of Christendom into confusion. The disorders between the regulars and the seculars had broken out anew, and with more virulence; and so had the rivalries between the two Orders, thereby further worsening the situation. Polemics accusing the Orders of dreadful sins and excesses, very reminiscent of William of St. Amour – who had himself indeed returned to the offensive – again abounded, and both Bonaventura and Thomas Aquinas found themselves occupied almost full time in composing answers to them.

The centre of the storm was in Paris, where the polemics flew like snowflakes; but no centre of learning and piety was immune. Roger arrived back in Oxford, in 1269, just in time to be a witness to a scarifying dispute between the Dominicans and the Franciscans, on the virtues of poverty versus the Franciscans' practice of it, held in public before the entire Faculty of the University. The throne of the emperor, too, was vacant and in dispute, and in the Italian peninsula, now almost wholly in the hands of Charles of Anjou, there was civil war. Even after five years, the bale and woe distilled by the great comet through the ambient air was implacably at work.

Roger was not greatly surprised. He had told the Lord Pope himself that the Joachite prophecies, and those that warned of the imminence of Antichrist, were worthy of being credited, though with due caution as to the date they gave; these disorders were but further evidence to the same effect; but Clement had been taken, and there was now no Pope to hear such counsel, let alone heed it. Nor was Roger disposed to give it; caution was not in him, but his taste for Church politics of this kind had never been great, and the long grinding of the years of corrective discipline in the convent had worn even that little down to nothing, as, he realized dully, it had from the outset been intended to do.

He had before him, too, another example, should he thus far have failed to draw the moral. There was now being circulated among the Faculty of Arts – and throughout Europe, apparently – a letter on the theory and the uses of magnetism, from the hand of Peter the Peregrine. The circumstances of its writing were curious: somehow, as a Picard, or perhaps even by choice, Peter had been caught up in the army of Charles of Anjou, and on the eighth of August, while sitting out the siege of Lucera, he had decided to summarize his twenty years of study of the problem, and put it into the hands of a countryman, lest the knowledge die with him. He began:

You must realize, dearest friend, that the investigator in this subject must know the nature of things, and not be ignorant of the celestial motions; and he must also make ready use of his own hands, so that through the operation of this stone he may show remarkable effects. For by his carefulness he will then in a short time be able to correct an error which by means of natural philosophy and mathematics alone he would never do in eternity, if he did not carefully use his hands. For in hidden operations we greatly need manual industry, without which we can usually accomplish nothing perfectly. Yet there are many things subject to the rule of reason which cannot be completely investigated by the hands.

It was all reasoned with the most admirable rigour, and buttressed everywhere with experiments with lodestones of all kinds, including spherical ones, and with both pivoted and floating needles, the latter collimated against a reference scale divided in the Babylonian manner into 360 degrees.

It was a monument to what could be accomplished by a carefully planned programme of study, from which, until this mysterious adventure with the army of Anjou, Peter had not deviated in all those twenty years; and thus the virtue of silence and study, as opposed to the search for fame and position. For those same twenty years what had Roger to show, but two inordinately swollen manuscripts which now were lost, and an incomplete third impotently addressed to a prelate already dead? Nay, his rule would be silence and study from this day hence; naught but silence and study.

Nor did it fail to occur to Roger that between Peter's presence outside the walls of a town in southern Italy, and the mortgaging of his house to raise money for Roger, there might be some causal connection. Toward the usurers which Roger had visited, he felt neither obligation nor compassion; usury was a sin, for which they would yet pay more dearly than by the loss of the paltry sums they had lent him; and besides, they were of course only Jews, since no Christian could engage in such commerce. But Peter, should he survive, must have back every penny.

The most obvious route to this goal was to write and publish books, from the sale of which the Order would profit, and would allow him a tithe. Though the censorship of Narbonne was still fully in effect, he was now more sophisticated in the various ways of coping with it, and he had several new advantages. Chief among these was the presence of Thomas Bungay in the office of the provincial minister, from whence permission to publish a work by Roger Bacon might be much more easily won than had ever been possible in Paris. Furthermore, there was no real impediment to the publication of works which obviously could add no faggots to the fires of controversy now raging within the bosom of the Church.

Roger tested this hypothesis with a Greek grammar. It was published without question, and widely copied; in the first year of its existence, it brought in as his share almost a pound. For a subsequent Hebrew grammar there proved to be much less demand, as he had anticipated, but again its publication had been brought about as easily as though there had been no censorship at all. Encouraged, he set himself next to finishing the *Communia mathematica*.

In the meantime, necessarily, he had also resumed lecturing. It swiftly developed that he was widely remembered at Oxford, and though he was now less bold than he had been with his physical demonstrations, he still found a lively audience. He initiated a class in astronomy; and because this had to meet at night, discovered also that his reputation as a magician had not only survived, but grown, fed apparently by his Parisian incarceration, for which no reason had ever been made public at Oxford. In default of such a reason, there was a saying about – 'There is no smoke without fire' – which he admired almost as much for its elegance as he despised it for its injustice. Against these rumours, in any event, there was no remedy but circumspection, an art he set himself to practising with all the fervent clumsiness of any neophyte with neither experience nor talent.

The *Communia mathematica*, finished at long last, was published without incident; it proved popular; the account for Peter was growing, minutely but perceptibly. Now seemed to be the logical time to finish the *Communia naturalium*; though it was not without elements of controversy, it was probably not too highly spiced a dish to be inedible by Bungay, who had now succeeded to the provincial ministership itself; and so sizeable a viand would surely fatten the Peregrine fund considerably.

Silence and study; and let the world wag. It was managing that task, on the whole, little more badly than usual. The papal interregnum had ended, after three years, with the election of Gregory X; the event undammed a tremendous outpouring of prophecy, most especially from the Joachites, who saw in Gregory the Ultimate Pope predicted aforetime in the *Introduction to the Eternal Gospel*. Roger was hopeful, but reserved judgment. Richard of St. Amour was no longer alive to dispute it; and the death of Gerard of San Borgo, in the eighteenth year of his imprisonment, raised his partisans to new frenzies.

These half-thought-through prophecies and polemics filled Roger now with nothing but cold disgust, but he was most highly resolved to stay aloof. Still he could hardly argue, even with himself, that these coils and toils could not have been avoided years ago by application of but a little knowledge; and he permitted himself the most oblique of public comments, by making his perfect copy of the *Secret of Secrets* available to the University, and with it an introduction explaining its significance. Both Bungay and Oxford were stunned and delighted, and the work did not go back on the shelves for more than a day before it was out to be copied again; but the time for it was past – or perhaps not now to come for a century. Aristotle's advice to the god-king Alexander served, in the meantime, to swell the Peregrine account.

Yet it did appear that Gregory X was not entirely comfortable at finding himself depicted by the Merlins and others as a fractional messiah, or anti-Antichrist. In the second year of his episcopate, he called a Council at Lyons, to discuss all the troubles of Christendom, spurious and real; but he had no proper appreciation of which was which, and the Council's decisions could not have made matters worse had they been deliberately calculated to do so. At the death, before the Council had even met, of Bonaventura, it was nothing short of inevitable that the new Franciscan Minister-General should be the dour Jerome di Ascoli, the bitterest enemy the Joachites had in all the Latin world. Nor did Jerome lack for new reasons. He was barely installed before being called back from a mission to the Greek emperor by the first real outbreak of Joachite violence, in a small central Italian seaport called Ancona; the brothers had taken a decree of the Council to be an endorsement, and rebelled when their Order failed to take the same view. Jerome retaliated by casting all the dissidents into prison for life, and on the spot.

Deeper and deeper all these holy men went into the mire; it was as though the guidance of God had been withdrawn from the world until the end should come. How to keep silent now, on the very verge of Armageddon? Knowledge should be useful! and for the lack of it these devout knaves were stumbling to and fro as blindly as sheep in a burning fold. *Speak*, the self insisted, almost as though it were pleading with him. *Speak!*

But speak in what voice? None listened to Roger now, beyond the confines of his special competencies. Daring to attack these follies he had, and bitterness enough as well; but he had no audience that might effect the changes that were most needed in the world. Suppose that he were to undertake at last that compendium of philosophy which he had so often projected, and from which he had so often been turned away – how would he finish it in time to reach those who would need to read it, and how shoulder aside all obstructions vehemently enough to cast sulphur into the eyes of the Antichrist before it was too late?

These questions allowed him no recourse. He must try to write that work, though he had never been less ready. And it must begin with a frontal attack, for the time for prudence was run out.

As he wrote, the memory of his slights began to rise and rise in him, until in his throat he could taste nothing but bile all the day long, and all the night too; until the very ink that dripped from his quill was greenish with it, until his every word was engorged with it. Now was the time, not only to name errors, but to name names:

For nearly forty years the University of Paris has been dominated by some who have made themselves into masters and teachers of the subject of philosophy, though they have never learned anything of it worth while, and either will not or cannot, being utterly without training. These are brothers who entered the two Orders as boys, such as Albert and Thomas and others who in so many cases enter the Orders when they are twenty years of age or less. They are not proficient because they are not instructed in philosophy by others after they enter, because within their Order they have presumed to investigate philosophy without a teacher. So they become masters in philosophy before they are disciples, and so infinite error reigns, and the study of theology is brought to ruination, and with it the conduct of the Church.

The work went quickly; though long, it took him less than a year; but after he sent it to Bungay, the silence was protracted, while the world decayed apace. He sent a query, but no answer came back; and then, much later, a brief word that the provincial minister was John Peckham, Friar Bungay having been called to other tasks, and could Friar Bacon somewhat better describe the MS. in question, of which there seemed to be no record?

The first inkling of the truth reached him when the lector to the Oxford house, the Dominican Robert Kilwardby, called together all members of the Order in the city to hear the condemnation, by Bishop Tempier of Paris, of no fewer than two hundred and nineteen 'erroneous theories' now rife in Christendom, and in Paris in particular; to which Kilwardby added some of his own. Roger had been present at such a reading before, when the constitutions of Narbonne had been proclaimed, but that had been a short proclamation and a mild one compared to this. Bungay had yielded up his ministership to suppress the *Compendium studii philosophiae*, and indeed seemed to have run away with the MS. for none knew now where he was, solely to protect his friend of old – thus perilling, for love, his immortal soul.

That mortal kindness, however, did not avail; Thomas had thought only of what might happen in England, but it was the responsibility of the Minister-General's office to think of all Christendom. Within the month, that office had called in all suspect members of the Order, to present themselves in Paris, and give an account of their teachings and writings on these errors. At the head of those called from Oxford, despite all Bungay's good and desperate offices, was the name of Roger Bacon.

The office of Jerome di Ascoli at the Ministry was windowless, and bare but for a long massive table. Behind this sat Jerome himself, flanked by two brothers who seemed to be lawyers; with him too were the Parisian provincial minister and a secretary. Before the table stood Roger; but it was not he whom Jerome first addressed.

'I am no little irritated,' he said slowly, but in rather a pleasant tenor voice, 'that this case should have come before me. These extremists are constantly distracting me from the serious business of the Church. Why could not it have been dealt with locally, as I have frequently ruled?'

One of the lawyers stirred uneasily. 'It was called to Your Eminence's attention *de multorum fratrum concilio*.'

'Because of the negligence and sloth of the provincial minister in England. I will write to Friar Peckham of this. It is my main duty to prevent schism in the Order, not to question brothers on such petty offences as I see here written down. Astrology! Magic!'

'The man is also charged as a schismatic, Your Eminence.'

Jerome looked down the parchment before him, and then nodded curtly. 'I see. Then I am forced to conclude that neither of you yet knows how to draw up an indictment. You civil lawyers will be the bane of the Church. Let us dispose of these pins and needles.' He turned to Roger a face like a rusty hatchet. 'Prisoner, do you practise the art of astrology?

The word of address shocked him, though he had expected naught else; but Roger was not afraid of the question. 'No, Your Eminence; but I am a student of it.'

'Precisely,' said Jerome, looking back at the lawyers; 'and so are Thomas Aquinas, and the Bishop of Ratisbon, and half of the scholars in Christendom.'

'But, Your Eminence, the astrological doctrines of Albertus Magnus have been specifically condemned by Bishop Tempier!'

'Since this man has not taught them at Paris, that is quite beside the point, and ought not to be in the indictment at all.'

'Nor would I ever have been guilty of such, Your Eminence,' Roger said. 'I do not subscribe to the doctrines of the *Speculum Astronomiae*.'

'There, you see?' Jerome waved the subject away. 'Now, magic. Let me see – night walking; a brass head; raising demons; what alewives' tales! As a student of astrology, naturally the man must look at the stars, now and again. But here's somewhat of substance: a defence, in writing, of the books of magic condemned at Paris. Prisoner, do you acknowledge this?'

'Yes, Your Eminence. But I am and have been all my life an opponent of magic, and have written a book to prove its nullity.'

'Then what's this document?' Jerome demanded.

'Your Eminence, the books are largely nonsense, but they contain nothing that is contrary to the Christian religion. It seemed to me to be unjust that they should be condemned by men who had not even read them. So said I in that writing.'

Jerome looked at him narrowly. 'That was contumacious. And this on raising fiends – it is sworn to by a number, including our learned brother Richard of Cornwall.'

'Your Eminence, I but demonstrated in a lecture how one can make a loud noise with a composition of saltpetre. Richard Rufus was – disconcerted.'

Jerome suppressed a slight smile. 'Can you show it me?'

'Certes, Your Eminence, with proper materials, as many times as you wish. You could do it yourself.'

'Nay, I dislike noise as much as Cornwall. Let us press on. You are alleged to hold to Averroeist beliefs on the unity of the *intellectus agens*.'

'Your Eminence, if your clerk will bring you the record of my reading for my secular mastership, which I took here in Paris, you will find that I specifically and successfully argued against that view with Albertus Magnus himself.'

Jerome swung on the lawyers once more. 'But this is the document adduced in evidence! What does this mean?'

'Your Eminence – we took the argument to tend the other way.'

'Then why would the prisoner adduce it himself? Let me see it.'

The fascicle of the transcript was handed to the Minister-General in silence. He studied it, frowning. Roger found that he was beginning to become tired with standing; it occurred to him, with some surprise, that he was sixty-three years old. But he knew that he would remain standing for a long time yet.

'You gentle scholars,' di Ascoli said finally, 'cannot read, either. This is admirable disputation, and to the complete refutation of Averroes on this subject. Your incompetence leaves me no choice: all these charges are dismissed, categorically and completely.'

'Your Eminence,' Roger said huskily. 'You are as just as you are merciful.'

'Rejoice not yet, Friar Bacon. The remaining charges are of the utmost gravity. For the safety of your body, and the salvation of your soul, I bid you answer me thoughtfully. You are accused of having published forth, not once but many times, a belief in the prophecies of Joachim of Calabria; of Merlin; of the Sybil; of Sesto; and of others whose names are unknown. Do you deny any part of this?'

'I do not believe that they can all have been wrong.' Roger said steadily. 'The ultimate source of all knowledge is revelation, which is given, according to Scripture, to those who lead perfect lives. Can there have been none such in our time?'

'That is not for me to say, nor for any man. I speak now only of Joachim, putting these others aside. You are aware that the doctrine of the Eternal Gospel is adjudged schismatic?

'Yes, Your Eminence. But it is not yet proclaimed a heresy.'

'True,' Jerome said grimly, 'else would you be in the hands of the Inquisition, and not here. You have written that this doctrine in particular is worthy to be believed. Do you cling to this rede? Beware what you say!'

'I believe it to be true,' Roger said. 'I writ His Holiness Clement IV, of glorious memory, that I so believed. Shall I deny it to any other?'

'Then we are done,' Jerome said heavily. 'What matters the rest of this tally? Impudence to superiors; public attacks on eminent Dominicans, leading to strife among the regulars; infractions of the discipline of the Order, such as publishing letters to the Pope; provocation of dissension – all beside the point. Yet stay, these are also heavy charges. For the record, Friar Bacon, do you deny them?'

Roger stood silent.

'Shall it be said that you offered no defence? The Lord God seeth into thine heart, Roger. Testify, I beg thee.'

'I do not deny these last,' Roger said, wringing his hands, 'They are true. I have been frail and contumacious indeed, and ask your mercy; and the mercy of Jesus Christ our Lord. In His name I ask it.'

'In His name thou shalt be given it, in every possible measure,' Jerome said, holding out his hands across the table. 'These other charges are but internal matters of the Order, for which punishments are prescribed; for example, for publishing without permission letters to the Pope, three days of bread and water, and the loss of the writing. But Roger, for the schismatic, repentance is not enough; thou must recant, else thou are still lost. What thinkest thou, in this thine extremity, of the doctrines of the Eternal Gospel?'

Roger said stonily: 'Your Eminence, I believe what I have thought for twenty years. I believe them to be true.'

Jerome sank back in his chair. The lawyers were congratulating each other with their eyes; but the provincial minister said:

'Your Eminence – on this matter of publishing to the Pope: The record will show, and I so testify, that I gave the learned friar the necessary permission.'

Jerome looked at him for the first time. 'Yes. I will deal with you later.'

'But I submit, most humbly, to Your Eminence that these letters were commanded by the Holy Pope himself.'

'It shall be so regarded; but what does that matter now? There is only one charge of substance here, and of this, the prisoner is guilty. He has spoken, published and acted in support of a doctrine leading toward the division of our holy Order; in plain controversion to many prohibitions thereof; and in the confessed knowledge that this was being furthered by his every word and deed.'

The Minister-General stood up, resting his fingertips upon the table. His eyes were hooded and dark.

'Friar Roger Bacon is remanded to the company of his fellow schismatics, in the March of Ancona, there to be kept in hobble-gyves, with none to speak to him, for all the rest of his natural life; and on his deathbed, he shall be deprived of the sacraments of holy Church, and buried in a common grave; and his writings are forbidden all men from this time forth.

'This inquiry is now declared closed. Martin, have chains brought.'

Explicit tertia pars.

Sequitur pars quarta:

HOW THAT WE BAREN US THAT ILKE NYGHT

XV: THE MARCH OF ANCONA

In the wall opposite the black iron door there was a curious niche or alcove, whose original function was wholly puzzling. Two stone steps led into it, and within there was a single block of granite so placed that a man might sit there, sidewise; but to what purpose was impossible to fathom. Overhead in this alcove was a breach in the wall which went to the outside, but it was so high that, even standing on the block, Roger could barely touch it – nor could he have seen through it had it been placed lower, for his fingers told him that it slanted downward from the inside; so that it could not have been placed there for an archer's convenience. By the rime of seepage around the sides of the cell, it was plain that a third of the chamber was below the water line; so that the exit of that small rectangular hole, no bigger than the end of a book, could not be more than four feet above the ground; perhaps less.

Each day, from that slanting, recondite embrasure, a beam of dim yellow light made a blurred patch on the ceiling of the cell, coming gradually into being long after dawn; it was brightest and had the sharpest edges at noon, and then faded again. Otherwise it did not change; certainly it never moved.

But it was the only source of light that he had. Early and late in the day there was a little glow in the alcove from the downslanting hole, but only when the sun was directly on the ground on which it looked, would it make that blurred rectangle on the ceiling. On rainy days, there was no light at all, and the floor of the cell became an even sea of thick mud, through which his hobble-chain dragged the decaying strips of old rushes, and his privy-hole filled to the brim. On such days he sat on the stone block in the niche, huddled away from the dripping walls, and listened to the endless hollow sighing of the Adriatic; that sea was, he knew, very near, though he had not been permitted to observe just where in Ancona his prison was.

On bright days he tended his calendar, though after only a few months he no longer had any confidence in it; nor had he from the beginning any belief that it was going anywhere but toward his death; it had simply been something to do. He made it by lifting the centre link of his chain, which would reach about a foot up the wall from the dirt, and making a scratch with it in the nitre. The early scratches, however, already were tending to fill with a stiff gluey stuff, vaguely blue-green when the light was brightest, though they were almost surely not much more than a year old. By summer, they would be unreadable, indeed obliterated.

Once a day, also, he took up his vigil by the slit in the iron door, ready to thrust out his bowl as soon as the hinges at the end of the corridor screamed and the horses began to trample and snort expectantly. After the horses were fed, Otto would dump into Roger's bowl, as into everyone's as long as it lasted, some of the gelid, mouldy mash from yesterday's trough. On holy days, if Otto was not too drunk, there was also a sprouted onion, often less than half soft. You withdrew the bowl quickly, because Otto would knock it out of your hand if you appeared to him to be begging for more, and might not give it back to you for days; and you ate quickly, so as to hold the bowl out again for water. Occasionally, for a joke, you got horse-piss; but usually it was water.

During these transactions, Otto could often be heard swearing at the horses, especially when he was leading them in or out, or when one of them trod on his foot; but he never spoke to a prisoner. That was forbidden. Nor did they talk to each other any more; that had been difficult from the outset because the cells were so far apart, and there were many echoes; but also it disturbed the horses, and betrayed the attempt to the gaoler. Now no one spoke, except those who were too sick or daft to know that they were speaking, and none answered them. Occasionally, on the hottest days when the ground was almost dry, there came the brief musical rustle of a chain, and then another; that was their conversation.

Some sounds besides those of the sea came into Roger's cell from outside. There was obviously a road not far away – close enough to allow him to hear, now and then, the bray of a donkey, a clanking of pots, the bell and cry of a leper, or even indistinct human voices, sometimes of children – and, daily, Otto hitching two of his animals to the wagon, to go buy in the market for the brothers far above. To hearken to these, Roger came more and more to spend even fair days in the alcove, where, furthermore, he now and again was vouchsafed a vagrant current of sweet air. But this was impossible to do in the winter; though there was no part of the cell that was not cold then, the niche seared the skin even through the rags, and the wind made a prolonged dismal fluting over the lip of the mysterious embrasure, as it did also during storms.

Then, too, there were the animals. Nothing could be done with the rats; sporadically, Otto tried to trap them, and in consequence they were unapproachable. But Roger found that mice made pleasant companions. They were exceeding shy; yet by long patience he trained several to trust him, and one would even sit on his palm, grooming its fur like a cat but with much quicker strokes – there was something almost bird-like in the movement. He had little to give them for a reward, but that little seemed to be more than they were accustomed to. For some reason, it never occurred to him to give them names.

The cockroaches, like the rats, were invincibly self-centred and vicious, and horribly stupid, too; Roger learned to loathe them. But he also learned to his astonishment that spiders, for all their cruelty, love music. There was one near the door which would invariably let itself down on its cable if he whistled. It did not seem to be able to hear the voice, which was fortunate; for the second time Roger tried it with a fragment of plainsong, several other prisoners took up the tune, the horses panicked and kicked each other, and then there was no food for three days. In Roger's nightmares, all the fiends had horses' heads.

And for more than a year – or was it two? – he tried to compose in his mind the *Summa salvatione per scientiam*; not that there was any hope of committing it to writing, but only to see how it would go; and perhaps to memorize it then, to have it in his soul for the Judgment. Thinking without parchment and quill was not so impossible as he had always before supposed, and for a while he fancied that he was making a little progress; until he realized that for the want of authorities to quote, he had been for months inventing them; one, a St. Robert of Lincoln, had even somehow in his mind acquired a life history, although he knew well enough that there was no such saint.

Hunger impeded him as well, and cold; even the stench, though he was no longer more than intermittently conscious of that; and the constant galling of the gyves; and the swollen bleeding gums of the scurvy; and then, the gradual, inexorable dementia of pellagra, until he sometimes could not tell the imaginary vermin which gnawed him from the real. Now when he sat all day in the niche, he thought more and more of less and less: over and over again, one sun-ripe day in the gardens at Tivoli would pass through his memory, and then again, and again, like the combers of the unseen Adriatic; or he would dwell helplessly upon some line of Boethius, whom as a boy he had so meanly despised . . . the little lambs, frisking their tails in spring . . . the little lambs.

One year as he sat, it seemed to him that he heard someone breathing. He made nothing of it, for he often heard such things; they were only sent to torment him; often he had been promised even death and it had been snatched away. Yet the sound was very loud, and ragged, and after a while began to turn into sobbing. It was the voice of a child; and real or unreal, Roger was of a sudden distressed with God for the sorrows of His children.

He tried to speak, but could not; it had been too long. The second time, some words emerged, though in no voice he recognized as human:

Demon, do not weep.

The sound choked off abruptly; and then there was the faint drumming of running footsteps; and that was all. Yet some days later, Roger again heard the sound of breathing – now rapid, but somehow no longer sorrowful.

'Who is there?' he whispered.

The breathing quickened further, but there was no other reply. Perhaps it was an Italian demon, and did not understand good Latin. He had a little Roman, remembered from – he did not know when; he tried that.

'Who is there?'

'Are you real?' a child's voice came back to him, tremulous, in that language. It came, like the sun, through the brick-shaped hole. He had not expected so hard a question, and tried to think of an answer; and when he had given it up, the light was gone and so was the voice.

Nevertheless it was back the next day. 'Who are you in the hole?' it said directly.

That was easier. 'I am called Roger Bacon, the schismatic.'

'Are you in prison?'

'Yes . . . yes, I am.'

'Everyone says the March is a prison. But the friars say it is only an old monastery. Were you a grave sinner?'

'Very grave. . . .'

'Then I shouldn't talk to you.'

'That is also true.'

'How did it happen? Was it *very* grave?'

'I do not know any longer how it happened. Why were you weeping, when I first heard you?'

'Was I? I don't remember. I sit here all the time, in this little niche in the wall, when I'm thinking. Maybe they'd punished me. But it never spoke to me before. Can you see through that black place?'

'No.'

'Can you see my hand?' There was a faint sound of scrabbling, very like a rat's, and then the tips of four small fingers wove like seaweed over Roger's head.

'Yes. I could even touch it.'

The fingers were snatched back. For a while there was silence. Then:

'Do you know any stories?' Far off, in Ancona, a bell began to toll. 'O, I have to go. Will you be here tomorrow?'

There was a long hiatus, until Roger became sure that it had been only another hallucination. But finally the voice came back, again demanding a story, and during their exchange, Roger learned that he was talking to a boy of six *ae*, the youngest son of an olive merchant. Roger told him the story of Thomas Aquinas' encounter with the brazen head of Albertus Magnus, but he did not much care for it; the story of how the mighty Gerbert rode the eagle was better received.

Each day, Roger ransacked his memory for legends; and in the meantime, he was gradually building up a picture of how they sat together. It seemed evident that this twin alcove had originally been nothing but a priest's hole, which meant that his wall had once not been on the outside of the fortress; the structure must have been centuries old to have required such thick inner walls.

There came a day when the boy came into earshot already babbling excitedly, of what, Roger could not tell; and then, there was the slow, also indecipherable rumbling of an adult male voice. Then, came the usual gambit: 'Here I am today, Roger. Tell me another story.'

Roger was ready, for having run out of folk-tales, he had been for some weeks steadily working his way through the *Aeneid*; though puzzled, he proceeded as well as he was able. The preceding night had been unusually wretched, and his voice often broke, but he managed to finish without other incident.

The boy's voice said clearly: 'See? What did I tell you!' And then again there was the slow rumble of the adult voice. Now it was all over, and Roger would have to go back into the silence; obviously the boy had told his father or some elder brother of the delightful mystery of the talking wall, and he would be forbidden to come again; no one of mature years in Ancona could fail to know what the March was.

The deep voice stopped. The boy said, all in a rush: 'My father says you are a learned man and very kind and is there anything you need?'

He seemed thoroughly delighted with himself. But how to answer the question? There was nothing that Roger did not need. After a while, he said, slowly, 'I thank your knightly father. What I most need is better food. But I fear me it will never pass through that stone rat-hole.'

The boy reported this. Then he said, 'My father says if you had a bit of money could you put it to any use?'

'I do not know. I would have to try.'

Now there came the scrabbling sound of the boy's hand, and then the pursed fingers were above him, like a closed anemone, precariously pinching a coin. As Roger took it, the hand was hastily withdrawn, as though the flesh behind the voice were still more than the boy could bear. Roger stood shakily on the stone block and looked at the chip of metal in the scant light. As nearly as he could tell, it was a ducat, not much clipped.

'God bless you both. I would my blessings were of some avail. I . . . can say naught else.'

A silence. The sea moaned.

'My father says that Virgil is said to be a waste of time except in Latin. Can you teach me that?'

Roger put out a hand for support against the wet stone. 'I can teach you better Latin in a week than any other master could teach you in a year.'

'He says I will be back tomorrow. O Roger, I wish I hadn't. Now it will be more like school.'

'Oh no. You will see. We will go right on telling stories.'

On the next morning, Roger left his bowl on the stone seat, and instead held out into the corridor his open palm with the ducat in it. Such was the gloom out there that Otto, seeing nothing but the hand, passed by with a snort; but at the end of his rounds he was back again, peering more closely first at the outstretched palm, and then bending to glare through the slit. Finally, he took the money. Roger left his hand where it was.

'Where'd you get that?' Otto growled. Though it was difficult for him, he was obviously trying to be as quiet as possible. It was the first time he had spoken to a prisoner since Roger had come to the March – somewhere between four and six years. Roger remained motionless, and said nothing.

'Somebody's talking to you through some hole, eh? I can seal that up in a hurry.'

Roger withdrew his hand. 'They give me money every day,' he said.

'Much good it'll do you.' But Otto did not go away. Finally he said: 'What do you want?'

'Some fruit. A bit of fish. Even a little meat. Clean water.'

Otto laughed. 'How about a stoup of wine, Your Lordship? Go back and rot.'

The next morning, there was nothing put into Roger's bowl. Otto came to him after the rounds and said, deep in his throat: 'Where is it? Hand it out.'

'I have nothing yet.'

'So you get nothing. Hand out the ducat.'

'No.'

Otto went away. After three days, Roger had two coins to chink together in his cupped palms as Otto went by; and on the fourth morning, his bowl held not only the usual mash, but also a decayed orange and the head of a herring. He gave back one ducat; and after thinking the matter over for a short while, Otto silently took it.

The feast was more than Roger's body could bear: he lost it all into the privy-hole. The next, however, he kept down; and although there were other bad days, he began gradually to feel stronger. Having someone to talk to was almost more healing than the food.

In this most curious of all schools the boy, whose name was Adrian, learned in fair weather his Latin and his Greek and his logic, and even other subjects that could not ordinarily be taught through a hole, such as the Elements of Euclid and descriptive astronomy. Roger saved his ducats as he was able, and in turn learned the unspoken art of mutual blackmail, at which, though the advantage lay sometimes on this side and sometimes on that, he found himself to be a better practitioner than Otto; for in the majority of their conflicts, Otto was faced with the ultimate resource of the condemned man, *nec spe nec metu* – no hope can have no fear. Nor had the gaoler any real cause for complaint, for even the most that he gave for the money would buy a score of times as much in the outside world where he moved free.

On one fine spring morning Roger was ready for the most bold of all his undertakings. Though he had been unable to win himself new rags or new rushes, because Otto would not enter the cell for any amount of money, so that no betterment could be gained that would not pass through the slit in the iron door, he felt well and cheerful; and he had hidden in the privy-hole – for there was no other place to hide it – no less a sum than twenty-seven ducats, hoarded over three years. For this wealth he meant to demand nothing smaller than the removal of the horses from the corridor. He did not think that Otto would try to take it away from him, not after having been three years sole owner of the golden goose.

But Adrian did not come that morning; nor ever came again. While Roger waited in the alcove, the ducats in the privy were given out one by one, for nothing but food; and the moment Roger began to try to conserve them, Otto sensed that there were soon to be no more. For the last few he gave back nothing but the old slops from the horse-trough, and for the last one, he gave nothing at all, but simply starved it out of Roger's hands.

A fuzzy square of light on the ceiling, motionless. No, it was raining. A wailing in the night; someone was dying. A wrinkled scum of ice over the privy. Blood in his mouth, and livid spots under his filth. Horses with rats' heads. Rain. An incessant hammering. The little lambs in spring. The structure of the eye. As I shall prove to Your Holiness by many examples. Look in the mirror, Beth, just for a moment. Would God allow? If you have no time to examine these difficulties, Joannes is more capable than anyone. I gave him thirty pieces of silver. I have these smaller manuscripts, *aliqua capitula*. Here, Petronius, here, puss. Why don't they stop that hammering? Virtue, therefore, clarifies the mind so that a man may comprehend more easily not only moral but scientific truths. Is it today that He gives us the onion? *Forsan et haec olim meminisse juvabit*. Tonight we shall see Mars and Jupiter in trine. Sit here, Livia. Is that rain again? I will explain everything. Silence and study. If I were not so cold, I could explain it all. Mother of God, sit here. I can explain it all.

One morning there was a commotion in the corridor after the horses were taken out, an angry shouting, and the flaring of torches. It went on all day, and in the evening the horses were not brought back. When the noise resumed the next morning, he crawled to the slit to watch.

The trough too had been removed. Otto was directing some three or four men with spades; they seemed to be attempting to clear the corridor out, a truly Augean task. From this activity as much as from their talk, which Roger could hardly understand, he deduced painfully that some important personage was coming, to see that the remnants of the schismatics were still properly imprisoned.

This could be of no moment to him. None the less he watched; for any change, however trifling, in the routines of the March helped to pass the iron days. The shovelling and cursing went on all week, and now that the horses were gone there was also a change in the food – lumps of bread instead of congealed mash. At the end of the week, it might have been said that the corridor was a little cleaner.

On Sunday morning – easily identifiable by its bells – the visitor came. Roger could not see him, but he heard the door open, and then a strange voice:

'Are these the spirituals, the disciples of Joachim?'

Its tone seemed angry, perhaps even incredulous. Otto's

reply was in so unusually low a voice that Roger could not make it out.

'Would that all of us and the whole Order were guilty of such a charge as this! Gaoler, release them.'

'Release them? But Your Eminence, my most clear instructions from Your Eminence's predecessor—'

'He is no longer responsible for the Order. I am. Let them out, I say!'

One by one, the black doors were opened, protesting blindly for that they had not been stirred in more than a decade. Several of them required the combined strengths of Otto and all his crew. At each cell, the ritual was the same:

'I am Raymond de Gaufredi, Minister-General to the Franciscans. Who art thou, holy friar?'

'I am called Angelo of Clareno, Your Eminence.'

'Go thou with God, where thou willst. Strike off his chains.' And then there was the sound of a hammer.

But not after all at every cell, for there were several of those wretches who could neither reply nor come forth, but needed to be led out, or in one instance, carried; and there were some doors which no longer needed to be opened. Roger watched and listened with only the barest comprehension of what was happening, and that little not to be believed, until the slit that fed him was jerked away from his face with a mighty squeal.

'Who art thou, holy friar?'

'I . . . am called Roger Bacon, Your Eminence.'

'Go thou with God, where thou willst.' At Roger's feet, Otto knelt with the hammer.

'Your Eminence . . . your pardon, if I . . . would you tell me . . . what year is this?'

'The one thousand two hundred and ninetieth of Christ our Lord.'

The hammer fell, and thus he was answered. It had been thirteen years.

XVI: FOLLY BRIDGE

Blind as moles they blundered about in the even lemon glare of the sunlight, all those that survived, as confused and full of wonder as men just expelled from a garden. For the serious business of convalescing, Raymond di Gaufredi gave them three whole months, and they all went about it with the high seriousness of scholars; though there were some hurts no herbs nor unguent nor hour could heal, especially in that fortress in whose dungeons they had so long groaned and heard no other voice.

For Roger, it was overwhelming. He could assimilate it only a little at a time, beginning with such small matters as he had become accustomed to seeing at the boundaries of the universe: cracks in the wall, the taste of salt, the touch of water, the shape of his shadow; and then, gradually, the sound of voices; and then, the movement of their sense.

While he was working at it, one came to visit him, from the village – not Adrian, but some merchant, of whom he had never heard, and whom he had sent away. He was not ready for worldly converse yet; he had talked too long to himself. And he was only confirmed in this when they told him – everyone was still 'they'; he was not yet able to tell one face from another – that the visitor had left him a purse. With horror, he sent it to di Gaufredi, without stopping even to look at it.

Gradually, too, and then voraciously, he won back the knack of reading, though it gave him blinding headaches; and through this began once more to grant the world a population, with names and actions to which the minuscules testified. The written words could not give him back his thirteen years, but they could in part give them back to the world, prove that it had had a history even when he had not been watching. Through the words of the play, he was able to see the possibility of actors.

Among these he was at first more interested in the dead, as least likely to have changed; but even this was not always true. While Roger Bacon, living, had gone down into his long defeat, the dead Simon de Montfort had clothed his memory in triumph. Edward the King – who had in fact been wholly in control of England ever since Evesham, though he had not been crowned until late in 1274 – had had the excellent good sense to adopt the parliamentary revolutions of his slain antagonist, and in addition, to act at once to restrain the exactions of Rome – a victory for another corpse militant, Robert Grosseteste.These moves won back Edward Longshanks both barons and rabble, as well as ample time for hunting and jousting, and the wresting of North Wales from the hands of Llewellyn (although there were said to be some signs that that conquest was in danger of slipping away).

As for the living, Jerome di Ascoli had become Pope Nicholas IV; and he had small reason to be pleased with the new English King. Moreover, he had neither anticipated nor desired that his vacated office over the Fransiscan Order would be filled by Raymond de Gaufredi; for Raymond, though wholly free of any actionable taint of Joachism himself, could never believe that there was any heresy in its doctrines nor any evil in its adherents. What Raymond had done in the March of Ancona would be even less to the new Pope's liking, yet Raymond was far from finished. He now proposed to send all those he had delivered, when their health permitted it, as missionaries to Armenia.

This mission, Roger was permitted to decline – not only by virtue of his age, which was now seventy-six, but also because upon examination it appeared that he had never been a missionary Joachite, and that the reasons for his punishment had been much more complex than were those that had been applied to Angelo and his brothers in the March. There was still extant a prohibition, obtained by Jerome from the then Pope by special letter, ruling that the dangerous doctrines of Roger Bacon be totally suppressed. Without knowing or wishing to know what these dangerous doctrines might be, Raymond nevertheless had no desire to turn them loose among the schismatic Armenians. It were more prudent to let Roger go back to Oxford, where among the sophistications of a great University his mysterious teachings might not lack for refutation.

In addition, this disposed of the purse, the mere existence of which troubled Raymond sorely, and which Roger could no more explain than he: the money could be used to cherish the frail scholar on the long journey, surely a small enough gesture from the Order at whose hands he had undergone so much that was evil.

And thus did Roger Bacon return at last to that gatehouse above Folly Bridge, in which he and Thomas Bungay had once studied the stars.

Here, all alone, he began once more to write, slowly, painfully, but with an iron determination, that great work with which he had wrestled so vainly in his first years in the pit in Ancona: the final statement of the case for salvation through science, to be awakened gently from slumber under a title that suggested nothing so explosive: *Compendium studii theologiae*. While he could hold a pen, the living might yet outrun the dead; Simon de Montfort might rule a nation – though hardly more than one, for only the English were so phlegmatic of humour as to make practicable the admission of so many plebeian voices into the high art of government – but what if Roger Bacon established domain in the minds of men?

The dream kept him alive, and kept him company. None asked him to lecture now, nor required aught of him at the house of the Franciscans. He was forgotten: a ghost, scribbling away in a tower, sometimes wondered at by late-walking students when they looked up and saw his flickering window.

So, after a year, did Bungay find him, when after this kind old man heard in his hermitage that among those released from the March of Ancona had been one man called Bacon. He brought back with him that manuscript of the *Compendium studii philosophiae* for which he had imposed his own exile, and they kissed each other. Roger forbore to ask what pain Thomas had suffered in his behalf, and Thomas forbore to say, for they understood one another, and that were pain enough.

Now it was almost as it had been of old. They talked far into the nights, though their voices were very reedy; Thomas did what little housework there was to do; and Roger wrote. Late in autumn, there came to the gatehouse an absurdly young olive-skinned yellowbeak, already slightly a-shiver with the first intimations of the English weather, who gave his name as Adrian something and desired to study with Magister Bacon, but Thomas turned him gently away. The time for that had passed; now all possible protections must be raised about the book.

Word by word, leaf by leaf, the great work evolved, and Bungay read it as it came from Roger's squeaking pen, as it could have from no other. It began quietly enough, with a note that until now, Roger had been prevented from writing certain useful things, but had made all haste to remedy the matter. There followed the outline of the four causes of error; the indictment, though a most gentle one it was in the eyes of the man who had lived in hiding for fourteen years with the *Compendium studii philosophiae* for a pillow, of the errors of men considered wise by the world; the statement of how the argument to follow would be conducted....

All the purest Roger Bacon; and yet Bungay. as page followed page, refrained from weeping only by a pure and agonizing act of will.

Roger's memory had failed. Not his memory of his reading or of his past, nay, that was there written down in vivid detail, but his memory of what he was doing from minute to minute. There were four causes of error, he wrote; but on the next page were given only three; he had forgotten not only the nature of the fourth, but that he had promised four at all.

And yet neither elegance nor eloquence had failed him. The reasoning was superbly close; the writing sometimes crisply brilliant, sometimes wryly humorous, sometimes filled with visionary beauty. But no mercy could blind Bungay to the central chasm: Roger was arguing now only with the shadows of his old subjects. The great work had all the apparatus of mastery, but it was not about anything. It had nothing at all to say.

Spring came; the leaves emerged, one after another, covered with delicate writing, dedicate with traceries to the sweet glory and love of God, words and works at once. On the last day of May, Roger cried out, and made a great blot; and had Bungay not been by chance at his elbow, would have toppled to the rushes.

Thereafter he did not speak or move, though his eyes were open. Bungay composed him tenderly, and then could naught but wait, and pray. He prayed for eleven days; and on the Feast of St. Barnabas, he heard below a cry on the bridge, most dim and distant, but approaching.

'An alms for John! An alms, an alms for John! Only a sterling to touch the bowl of Belisarius! Only a penny for John!'

Rising stiffly, Bungay went to the broad window, in his mind some vague memory of a street-cry that only Roger had then heard; vague, but as disquieting as a badly remembered oracle. The limping beggar crossing Folly Bridge was old, as old as Bungay himself, and as weathered as a seaman; but he looked up into Thomas's face with eyes of brilliant blue, and in that moment did not seem to be old at all. Taken aback, Thomas quit the window, but an almost inaudible bubble of breath behind him made him ashamed, and he returned. He called down:

'Boy, is that – is that indeed that ancient relic?'

'Indeed, lofty friar. Only a penny.'

'Wilt swear to it, on peril of thy soul?'

'I durst not, Franciscan father. Well know you how many frauds be sold to such as I. Yet long hath it kept me on live, in all the countries of the world; and thus hath performed at least one miracle.'

'Much need have I here of another. I pray thee, bring it up.'

The beggar bent his head, and disappeared; but was heard almost at once upon the stairs. When he entered the tower room, he offered the bowl, but Bungay shook his head, and pointed silently.

Roger had not moved; he lay with his ankles crossed, like the effigy of one who had been to Palestine. His nose was transparent and fleshless, and his temples drawn into his skull, as were his ears, so that the ear-lobes stood out. Above black sockets his taut forehead was rough and parched; and his face was the colour of lead.

'Dear Christ!' the beggar said; and his craggy cheerful face coursed suddenly with a torrent of tears. 'Friar or fiend, is this my last trap in the world? Oh, shame, oh shame, I never did any man harm – Lord God, why this to me?'

'What?' Bungay said, alarmed. 'Peace, man, or thou'lt do him injury. Art so compassionate toward every stranger? If so, God bless thee; but it were better to be quiet; else take thy relic to some lesser pallet. Heed me, beggar; and mine every word; and hush!'

'No stranger to me,' the beggar said, choking. 'This is my *doctor mirabilis* that was; my master in Paris. Oh Christ, his ankles, his eyes – they have tortured him!'

'Nay; he was but imprisoned. Didst truly know him?'

The beggar stood to the pallet, and gently set the bowl against the sunken cheek. 'Certes. 'Tis Roger Bacon.'

Bungay signed himself; for this were a palpable miracle in its very flesh. 'Now surely thou wert sent. What is thy name?'

'I was Johann Budrys, of Livonia; which means, John the Free. But long and long have I been only, John the Beggar.'

'Beg thou with me.'

They knelt together. Neither could think of anything to say. Heaven heard them, belike; but there was silence after.

'This was a holy man,' Bungay whispered at last. 'None credited him his piety and kindness, for that he was so perverse . . . forever at hares and hounds after matters men are forbidden to know.'

John the Free looked up.

'Pious?' he said slowly; 'yes, he was often pious. And kind, too, when it occurred to him; but that was not often. But there can be nothing that is forbidden man to know since we ate of that Apple; for it states in the Proverbs that knowledge is good and beautiful for its own sake. Nay – they that did this know he was a wiser man than any of his persecutors.'

'The Order and the Church', Bungay said indignantly, 'would never persecute—'

'Hist! Listen, holy friar!'

Roger's breathing had changed. His eyes moved.

'Roger . . . rest thee easy. Friends are nigh.'

Roger sighed. They bent closer.

'Thomas?' The word barely stirred his lips.

'Yes. Rest, Roger.'

'I . . . shall rest . . . after a while. It is time.'

He stirred again; and then, was almost up on both elbows. He said clearly:

'Bitterly it mathinketh me, that I spent mine wholle lyf in the lists against the ignorant. Enough! Lord Christ, enough!'

'Roger! Roger—'

But now at long last he saw, for a moment; and cried out again for love of vision, its usefulness and beauty; and for the loss of it; and reached for his pen; and went whirling down into silence and study; silence, silence and study.

Explicit Liber Fratris Rogeri Baconis.

DOMINUS ILLUMINATIO MEA

NOTES

Almost everyone mentioned in this book was a real person. The invented characters, such as Tibb, are usually obviously that, but there are some borderline cases. One of these is Raimundo del Rey, who appears both as one of the Spanish students who laughed at Roger's ignorance of Arabic (we know none of their names, but the incident is frequently mentioned in Roger's writings) and for that unknown alchemist to whose works the name of Ramon Lull was later signed (we do not know his name either, but we can be quite sure that the author in question was not the historical Ramon Lull, who was an unusually wild breed of mystic innocent of any interest in the sciences). About Roger's apprentice in Paris we know only what Roger tells the Pope, which is obviously exaggerated, and what the legend says, which is pure fantasy. The members of Roger's family, similarly, are either real or unreal according to your preference; in my account they conform to what little he tells us of them, but he gives no names and in other respects as well I was free to exercise considerable invention. (On this part of the subject invention is rife even among historians; for instance, the flat untruth that the Dominican Robert Bacon was the scholar-brother of whom Roger speaks has been demolished again and again, yet it crops up once more in Sir Winston Churchill.) The Marquis of Modena and his daughter sprang into being out of the opening line of the autobiography of Pope Pius II, a Piccolomini, in which he states that his family came from Rome – a statement most scholars consider doubtful; but the Marquis's runaway son was certainly real, and I presume I do not need to vouch for Luca di Cosmati. William Busshe is, of course, a pure invention, as are Wulf, Otto and Johann Budrys of Livonia; but Raymond of Laon and Sir William Bonecor were real, spear-carriers though they are in this text. As for Friar Bungay, his association with Roger is wholly legendary, but since virtually nothing is known about him except that he existed, I felt free to accept it.

One example will suffice to show what use I made of the Bacon legend. The incident in which Roger dispenses learning through a hole in his prison wall is as completely mythical as the brazen head; we know nothing at all about those silent thirteen years. It is a charming story, however, and I adopted it because it seemed to me that if Roger were imprisoned incommunicado, as the other Joachites were, it offers an explanation of how this compulsive teacher and propagandist was able to retain his sanity as well as he did. The reader ought to be told, however, that some Bacon scholars think he was never imprisoned at all. This notion I judged to be nonsense – or at the best, Church apologetics, in which this subject abounds. All the pertinent documents say that he was; the best the apologists have been able to do is to point out that the documents, all dated after his death, are not entirely reliable; but of what medieval document might this *not* be said?

One of the most curious quirks in the history of science is the relative weighting of two Englishmen whose names, entirely by accident, are easily confused: Roger Bacon, and Sir Francis Bacon. Both wrote enormous studies of the sciences of their times; both advocated experiment about theory; and both were masters of language, which guaranteed that they would be widely read. It is Sir Francis who is generally credited with being the philosopher who acted as midwife to the birth of modern science, particularly because he wrote and published in the seventeenth century when modern science was visibly a-stir; Roger's efforts, on the other hand, were ignored in his own time and for centuries thereafter, and lately historians of science (a relatively new discipline) have tended to dismiss him as a mere encyclopedist who contributed nothing new.

It is a pity that no major theoretical physicist or mathematician of our time has read either man. My own firm opinion is that Sir Francis Bacon's scheme for the elaboration of the sciences is purely the work of a literary genius, marvellously gratifying to read, but without the slightest demonstrable influence upon the history of science; in fact, had the scheme ever been realized, it would almost surely have set the sciences back a century or more, for Sir Francis, though surrounded by scientists of the first order, never had the slightest insight into how a scientist must necessarily think if his work is to come to any fruit whatsoever. The test of this judgment is that it is impossible to show *any* line of scientific thought after Sir Francis that is indebted to the *Novum Organum.*

Roger Bacon, though in his maturity an elegant stylist, was never even at his best an artist; but he was a scientist in the primary sense of that word – he thought like one, and indeed defined this kind of thinking as we now understand it. It is of no importance that the long list of 'inventions' attributed to him by the legend – spectacles, the telescope, the diving bell, and half a hundred others – cannot be supported; this part of the legend, which is quite recent, evolves out of the notion that Roger could be made to seem more wonderful if he could be shown to be a thirteenth-century Edison or Luther Burbank, holding a flask up to the light and crying, 'Eureka!' This is precisely what he was not. Though he performed thousands of experiments, most of which he describes in detail, hardly any of them were original, and so far as we know he never invented a single gadget; his experiments were tests of principles, and as such were almost maddeningly repetitious, as significant experiments remain to this day – a fact always glossed over by popularizations of scientific method, in which the experiments, miraculously, always work the first time, and the importance of negative results is never even mentioned. There is, alas, nothing dramatic about patience, but it was Roger, not Sir Francis, who erected it into a principle: 'Neither the voice of authority, nor the weight of reason and argument are as significant as experiment, for thence comes quiet to the mind.' (*De erroribus medicorum.*)

It would be hard to find any branch of modern science which was *not* influenced by Roger's theoretical scheme; yet by the same token this leaven was so slow-working that I could do little justice to it in the course of a novel. Where I could legitimately do so, I have offered hints; but I could not, for instance, say anywhere but here that:

– a passage printed from Bacon provided Columbus with one of his chiefest theoretical props in presenting his case to the Spanish court;

– Peter the Peregrine's MS. *De magnete* greatly influenced the epoch-making treatise of Sir Francis Bacon's contemporary William Gilbert on the same subject, because Gilbert – as he says in explanation in his first chapter – attributed Peter's conclusions to Roger Bacon:

– the whole tissue of the space–time continuum of general relativity is a direct descendant of Roger's assumption, in *De multiplicatione specierum* and elsewhere, that the universe has a metrical frame, and that mathematics thus is in some important sense real, and not just a useful exercise.[1]

In some small instances, the work of lesser men did not prove to be easy to explain in fiction, either; for example, that the curious 'sweet vitriol' discovered by the alchemist I have dubbed Raimundo del Rey was what we now know

[1] I have quoted part of Roger's reasoning on this point in Chapter XII, but there is really no way short of another book to convey the flamboyancy of this logical jump, which spans seven centuries without the faintest sign of effort. The most astonishing thing about it, perhaps, is its casualness; what Roger begins to talk about is the continuum of action, an Aristotelian commonplace in his own time, but within a few sentences he has invented – purely for the sake of argument – the luminiferous ether which so embroiled the physics of the nineteenth century, and only a moment later throws the notion out in favour of the Einsteinean metrical frame, having in the process completely skipped over Galilean relativity and the inertial frames of Newton. Nothing in the tone of the discussion entitles the reader to imagine that Roger was here aware that he was making a revolution – or in fact creating a series of them; the whole performance is even-handed and sober, just one more logical outcome of the way he customarily thought. It was that way of thinking, not any specific theory, that he invented; the theory of theories as tools.

as ether (the anaesthetic, not the substrate). For this dilemma of historical fiction about science, I have found no workable solution but this long apology.

Roger's argument from Josephus in Chapter IX is a misquotation. What Josephus actually said was that the ancients were given long lives because they could not otherwise have made accurate astronomical observations. This may seem even more preposterous than what Roger makes Josephus say, but at least it is Josephus's own opinion, whereas the other is only Roger's. He often misquoted his authorities, even his revered Seneca, whom he misquoted at great length. It is of course entirely possible (especially when he is quoting Seneca on ethics) that he had hold of an edition now lost, which might or might not have been closer to the original than the ones now extant; and quite often the variations must have been simply copyists' errors and/or mistranslations, against both of which Roger rails in work after work.[1] On the other hand, he may have introduced at least some of these distortions himself, for forensic effect, which would have been entirely in character. Since we are dealing here with an age prior to the invention of printing, the more charitable interpretations cannot, at the very least, be disproven.

Money in the thirteenth century was scarce and its value in modern terms is difficult to estimate, since so many payments – especially to the Church – were made in kind, and because there were then so few things to buy. It is probably conservative to reckon the English pound of the period – which was then a real pound of English pennies, the most stable coin of commerce throughout the century – at about forty-five 1960 U.S. dollars. Since the income of the average parishioner was about ten pounds a year, it can be seen that Christopher Bacon, who was able to bury two thousand pounds without

[1] Roger's own scribes for the *Op. Tert.*, which includes a diatribe against the dog-orthography of his times, delivered the text back to him faithfully corrected into the *mumpsimus* it denounced.

even knowing (because of his ignorance of foreign exchange) the exact worth of the hoard, must have been a wealthy man indeed.

The best scholarly study of this subject known to me is Stewart C. Easton's *Roger Bacon and his search for a universal science* (Columbia, 1952), a warm, witty and elegant book. I am enormously indebted to it, particularly to its critical bibliography, which is a guide to everything about Roger Bacon which pretends to be factual, even encyclopedia articles and the scrappiest of pamphlets. Where my interpretations differ from Easton's, he is more likely to be right than I. The *Britannica* article's bibliography, however, also refers the reader to the Bacon legend; Easton studiously ignores this, but it is one of the reasons why Bacon is still a seminal figure in the Western world.

BLACK EASTER

(or *Faust Aleph-Null*)

Why, this is Hell; nor am I out of it.
CHRISTOPHER MARLOWE

In memoriam C. S. Lewis

CONTENTS

Author's Note

There have been many novels, poems and plays about magic and witchcraft. All of them that I have read – which I think includes the vast majority – classify without exception as either romantic or playful, Thomas Mann's included. I have never seen one which dealt with what real sorcery actually had to be like if it existed, although all the grimoires are explicit about the matter. Whatever other merits this book may have, it neither romanticizes magic nor treats it as a game.

Technically, its background is based as closely as possible upon the writings and actual working manuals of practising magicians working in the Christian tradition from the thirteenth to the eighteenth centuries, from the *Ars Magna* of Ramon Lull, through the various *Keys* of pseudo-Solomon, pseudo-Agrippa, pseudo-Honorius and so on, to the grimoires themselves. All of the books mentioned in the text actually exist; there are no 'Necronomicons' or other such invented works, and the quotations and symbols are equally authentic. (Though of course it should be added that the attributions of these works are seldom to be trusted; as C. A. E. Waite has noted, the besetting *bibliographic* sins of magic are imputed authorship, false places of publication and back-dating.)

For most readers this will be warning enough. The experimentally minded, however, should be further warned that, although the quotations, diagrams and rituals in the novel are authentic, they are in no case complete. The book, is not, and was not intended to be, either synoptic or encyclopedic. It is not a *vade mecum*, but a *cursus infamam*.

Alexandria (Va.)
1968

JAMES BLISH

Preparation of the Operator

> It is not reasonable to suppose that Aristotle knew the number of the Elect.
> ALBERTUS MAGNUS

The room stank of demons.

And it was not just the room – which would have been unusual, but not unprecedented. Demons were not welcome visitors on Monte Albano, where the magic practised was mostly of the kind called Transcendental, aimed at pursuit of a more perfect mystical union with God and His two revelations, the Scriptures and the World. But occasionally, Ceremonial magic – an applied rather than a pure art, seeking certain immediate advantages – was practised also, and in the course of that the White Monks sometimes called down a demiurge, and, even more rarely, raised up one of the Fallen.

That had not happened in a long time, however; of that, Father F. X. Domenico Bruno Garelli was now positive. No, the stench was something in the general air. It was, in fact, something that was abroad in the world . . . the secular world, God's world, the world at large.

And it would have to be something extraordinarily powerful, extraordinarily malign, for Father Domenico to have detected it without prayer, without ritual, without divination, without instruments or instrumentalities of any kind. Though Father Domenico – ostensibly an ordinary Italian monk of about forty *ae*, with the stolid face of his peasant family and calluses on his feet – was in fact an adept of the highest class, the class called Karcists, he was not a Sensitive.

There were no true Sensitives at all on the mountain, for they did not thrive even in the relative isolation of a monastery; they could not function except as eremites (which explained why there were so few of them anywhere in the world, these days).

Father Domenico closed the huge Book of Hours with a creak of leather and parchment, and rolled up the palimpsest upon which he had been calculating. There was no doubt about it: none of the White Monks had invoked any infernal power, not even a minor seneschal, for more than a twelve-month past. He had suspected as much - how, after all, could he have gone unaware of such an event? – but the records, which kept themselves without possibility of human intervention, confirmed it. That exhalation from Hell-mouth was drifting up from the world below.

Deeply disturbed, Father Domenico rested his elbows upon the closed record book and propped his chin in his hands. The question was, what should he do now? Tell Father Umberto? No, he really had too little solid information yet to convey to anyone else, let alone disturbing the Director-General with his suspicions and groundless certainties.

How, then, to find out more? He looked ruefully to his right, at his crystal. He had never been able to make it work – probably because he knew all too well that what Roger Bacon had really been describing in *The Nullity of Magic* had been nothing more than a forerunner of the telescope – though others on the mountain, unencumbered by such historical scepticism, practised crystallomancy with considerable success. To his left, next to the book, a small brass telescope was held aloft in a regrettably phallic position by a beautiful gold statuette of Pan that had a golden globe for a pediment, but which was only a trophy of an old triumph over a minor Piedmontese black magician and had no astronomical usefulness; should Father Domenico want to know the precise positions of the lesser Jovian satellites (the Galilean ones were of course listed in the US Naval Observatory ephemeris), or anything else necessary to the casting of an absolute horoscope, he would call upon the twelve-inch telescope and the image-orthicon on the roof of the monastery and have the images (should he need them as well as the data) transmitted by closed-circuit television directly to his room. At the moment, unhappily, he had no event to cast a horoscope either from or toward – only a pervasive, immensurable fog of rising evil.

At Father Domenico's back, he knew without looking, coloured spots and lozenges of light from his high, narrow, stained-glass window were being cast at this hour across the face of his computer, mocking the little coloured points of its safe-lights. He was in charge of this machine, which the other Brothers regarded with an awe he privately thought perilously close to being superstitious; he himself knew the computer to be nothing but a moron – an idiot-savant with a gift for fast addition. But he had no data to feed the machine, either.

Call for a Power and ask for help? No, not yet. The occasion might be trivial, or at least seem so in the spheres they moved, and where they moved. Father Domenico gravely doubted that it was, but he had been rebuked before for unnecessarily troubling those movers and governors, and it was not a kind of displeasure a sensible white magician could afford, however in contempt he might hold the indiscriminate hatred of demons.

No; there was no present solution but to write to Father Uccello, who would listen hungrily, if nothing else. He was a Sensitive; he, too, would know that something ugly was being born – and would doubtless know more about it than that. He would have data.

Father Domenico realized promptly that he had been almost unconsciously trying to avoid this decision almost from the start. The reason was obvious, now that he looked squarely at it; for of all the possibilities, this one would be the most time-consuming. But it also seemed to be unavoidable.

Resignedly, he got out his Biro fountain pen and a sheet of foolscap and began. What few facts he had could be briefly set down, but there was a certain amount of ceremony that had to be observed: salutations in Christ, inquiries about health, prayers and so on, and of course the news; Sensitives were always as lonely as old women, and as interested in gossip about sin, sickness and death. One had to placate them; edifying them – let alone curing them – was impossible.

While he was still at it, the door swung inward to admit an acolyte: the one Father Domenico, in a rare burst of sportiveness, had nicknamed Joannes, after Bacon's famous disappearing apprentice. Looking up at him bemusedly, Father Domenico said:

'I'm not through yet.'

'I beg your pardon?'

'Sorry . . . I was thinking about something else. I'll have a letter for you to send down the mountain in a while. In the meantime, what did you want?'

'Myself, nothing,' Joannes said. 'But the Director asks me to tell you that he wishes your presence, in the office, right after sext. There's to be a meeting with a client.'

'Oh. Very well. What sort of client?'

'I don't know, Father. It's a new one. He's being hauled up the mountain now. I hear he's a rich American, but then, a lot of them are, aren't they?'

'You do seem to know *something*,' Father Domenico said drily, but his mind was not on the words. The reek of evil had suddenly become much more pronounced; it was astonishing that the boy couldn't smell it too. He put the letter aside. By tonight there would be more news to add – and, perhaps, data.

'Tell the Director I'll be along promptly.'

'First I have to go and tell Father Amparo,' Joannes said. 'He's supposed to meet the client too.'

Father Domenico nodded. At the door, the acolyte turned, with a mysterious sort of slyness, and added:

'His name is Baines.'

The door shut. Well, there was a fact, such as it was – and obviously Joannes had thought it full of significance. But to Father Domenico it meant nothing at all.

Nothing, nothing at all.

The First Commission

[In] the legendary wonder-world of Theurgy . . . all paradoxes seem to obtain actually, contradictions coexist logically, the effect is greater than the cause and the shadow more than the substance. Therein the visible melts into the unseen, the invisible is manifested openly, motion from place to place is accomplished without traversing the intervening distance, matter passes through matter. . . . There life is prolonged, youth renewed, physical immortality secured. There earth becomes gold, and gold earth. There words and wishes possess creative power, thoughts are things, desire realizes its object. There, also, the dead live and the hierarchies of extra-mundane intelligence are within easy communication, and become ministers or tormentors, guides or destroyers, of man.

A. E. WAITE, *The Book of Ceremonial Magic*

1

The magician said, 'No, I can't help you to persuade a woman. Should you want her raped, I can arrange that. If you want to rape her yourself, I can arrange that, too, with more difficulty – possibly more than you'd have to exert on your own hook. But I can't supply you with any philtres or formulae. My speciality is crimes of violence. Chiefly, murder.'

Baines shot a sidelong glance at his special assistant, Jack Ginsberg, who as usual wore no expression whatsoever and had not a crease out of true. It was nice to be able to trust someone. Baines said, 'You're very frank.'

'I try to leave as little mystery as possible,' Theron Ware – Baines knew that was indeed his real name – said promptly. 'From the client's point of view, black magic is a body of technique, like engineering. The more he knows about it, the easier I find it makes coming to an agreement.'

'No trade secrets? Arcane lore, and so on?'

'Some – mostly the products of my own research, and very few of them of any real importance to you. The main scholium of magic is "arcane" only because most people don't know what books to read or where to find them. Given those books – and sometimes, somebody to translate them for you – you could learn almost everything important that I know in a year. To make something of the material, of course, you'd have to have the talent, since magic is also an art. With books and the gift, you could become a magician – either you are or you aren't, there are no bad magicians, any more than there is such a thing as a bad mathematician – in about twenty years. If it didn't kill you first, of course, in some equivalent of a laboratory accident. It takes that long, give or take a few years, to develop the skills involved. I don't mean to say you wouldn't find it formidable, but the age of secrecy is past. And really the old codes were rather simple-minded, much easier to read than, say, musical notation. If they weren't, well, computers could break them in a hurry.'

Most of these generalities were familiar stuff to Baines, as Ware doubtless knew. Baines suspected the magician of offering them in order to allow time for himself to be studied by the client. This suspicion crystallized promptly as a swinging door behind Ware's huge desk chair opened silently, and a short-skirted blonde girl in a pageboy coiffure came in with a letter on a small silver tray.

'Thank you, Greta. Excuse me,' Ware said, taking the tray. 'We wouldn't have been interrupted if this weren't important.' The envelope crackled expensively in his hands as he opened it.

Baines watched the girl go out – a moving object, to be sure, but except that she reminded him vaguely of someone else, nothing at all extraordinary – and then went openly about inspecting Ware. As usual, he started with the man's chosen surroundings.

The magician's office, brilliant in the afternoon sunlight, might have been the book-lined study of any doctor or lawyer, except that the room and the furniture were outsize. That said very little about Ware, for the house was a rented cliffside palazzo; there were bigger ones available in Positano had

Ware been interested in still higher ceilings and worse acoustics. Though most of the books looked old, the office was no mustier than, say, the library of Merton College, and it contained far fewer positively ancient instruments. The only trace in it that might have been attributable to magic was a faint smell of mixed incenses, which the Tyrrhenian air coming in through the opened windows could not entirely dispel; but it was so slight that the nose soon tired of trying to detect it. Besides, it was hardly diagnostic by itself; small Italian churches, for instance, also smelled like that – and so did the drawing rooms of Egyptian police chiefs.

Ware himself was remarkable, but with only a single exception, only in the sense that all men are unique to the eye of the born captain. A small, spare man he was, dressed in natural Irish tweeds, a French-cuffed shirt linked with what looked like ordinary steel, a narrow, grey, silk four-in-hand tie with a single very small sapphire chessman – a rook – tacked to it. His leanness seemed to be held together with cables; Baines was sure that he was physically strong, despite a marked pallor, and that his belt size had not changed since he had been in high school.

His present apparent age was deceptive. His face was seamed, and his bushy grey eyebrows now only slightly suggested that he had once been red-haired. His hair proper could not, for – herein lay his one marked oddity – he was tonsured, like a monk, blue veins crawling across his bare white scalp as across the papery backs of his hands. An innocent bystander might have taken him to be in his late sixties. Baines knew him to be exactly his own age, which was forty-eight. Black magic, not surprisingly, was obviously a wearing profession; cerebrotonic types like Ware, as Baines had often observed of the scientists who worked for Consolidated Warfare Service (div. A. O. LeFebre et Cie.), ordinarily look about forty-five from a real age of thirty until their hair turns white, if a heart attack doesn't knock them off in the interim.

The parchment crackled and Jack Ginsberg unobtrusively touched his dispatch case, setting going again a tape recorder back in Rome. Baines thought Ware saw this, but chose to take no notice. The magician said:

'Of course, it's also faster if my clients are equally frank with me.'

'I should think you'd know all about me by now,' Baines said. He felt an inner admiration. The ability to pick up an interrupted conversation exactly where it had been left off is rare in a man. Women do it easily, but seldom to any purpose.

'Oh, Dun and Bradstreet,' Ware said, 'newspaper morgues, and of course the grapevine – I have all that, naturally. But I'll still need to ask some questions.'

'Why not read my mind?'

'Because it's more work than it's worth. I mean your excellent mind no disrespect, Mr Baines. But one thing you must understand is that magic is hard work. I don't use it out of laziness, I am not a lazy man, but by the same token I do take the easier ways of getting what I want if easier ways are available.'

'You've lost me.'

'An example, then. All magic – I repeat, *all* magic, with no exceptions whatsoever – depends upon the control of demons. By demons I mean specifically fallen angels. No lesser class can do a thing for you. Now, I know one such whose earthly form includes a long tongue. You may find the notion comic.'

'Not exactly.'

'Let that pass for now. In any event, this is also a great prince and president, whose apparition would cost me three days of work and two weeks of subsequent exhaustion. Shall I call him up to lick stamps for me?'

'I see the point,' Baines said. 'All right, ask your questions.'

'Thank you. Who sent you to me?'

'A medium in Bel Air – Los Angeles. She attempted to blackmail me, so nearly successfully that I concluded that she did have some real talent and would know somebody who had more. I threatened her life and she broke.'

Ware was taking notes. 'I see. And she sent you to the Rosicrucians?'

'She tried, but I already knew that dodge. She sent me to Monte Albano.'

'Ah. That surprises me, a little. I wouldn't have thought that you'd have any need of treasure finders.'

'I do and I don't,' Baines said. 'I'll explain that, too, but a little later, if you don't mind. Primarily I wanted someone in your speciality – murder – and of course the white monks were of no use there. I didn't even broach the subject with them. Frankly, I only wanted to test your reputation, of which I'd had hints. I, too, can use newspaper morgues. Their horror when I mentioned you was enough to convince me that I ought to talk to you, at least.'

'Sensible. Then you don't really believe in magic yet – only in ESP or some such nonsense.'

'I'm not,' Baines said guardedly, 'a religious man.'

'Precisely put. Hence, you want a demonstration. Did you bring with you the mirror I mentioned on the phone to your assistant?'

Silently, Jack took from his inside jacket pocket a waxed paper envelope, from which he in turn removed a lady's hand mirror sealed in glassine. He handed it to Baines, who broke the seal.

'Good. Look in it.'

Out of the corners of Baine's eyes. two slow thick tears of dark venous blood were crawling down beside his nose. He lowered the mirror and stared at Ware.

'Hypnotism,' he said, quite steadily. 'I had hoped for better.'

'Wipe them off,' Ware said, unruffled.

Baines pulled out his immaculate monogrammed handkerchief. On the white-on-white fabric, the red stains turned slowly into butter-yellow gold.

'I suggest you take those to a government metallurgist tomorrow,' Ware said. 'I could hardly have hypnotized him. Now perhaps we might get down to business.'

'I thought you said – '

'That even the simplest trick requires a demon. So I did, and I meant it. He is sitting at your back now, Mr Baines, and he will be there until the day after tomorrow at this hour. Remember that – day after tomorrow. It will cost me dearly to have turned this little piece of silliness, but I'm used to having to do such things for a sceptical client – and it will be included in my bill. Now, if you please, Mr Baines, what *do* you want?'

Baines handed the handkerchief to Jack, who folded it carefully and put it back in its waxed-paper wrapper. 'I,' Baines said, 'of course want someone killed. Tracelessly.'

'Of course, but who?'

'I'll tell you that in a minute. First of all, do you exercise any scruples?'

'Quite a few,' Ware said. 'For instance, I don't kill my friends, not for any client. And possibly I might balk at certain strangers. However, in general, I do have strangers sent for, on a regular scale of charges.'

'Then we had better explore the possibilities,' Baines said. 'I've got an ex-wife who's a gross inconvenience to me. Do you balk at that?'

'Has she any children – by you or anybody else?'

'No, none at all.'

'In that case, there's no problem. For that kind of job, my standard fee is fifteen thousand dollars, flat.'

Despite himself, Baines stared in astonishment. 'Is that all?' he said at last.

'That's all. I suspect that I'm almost as wealthy as you are, Mr Baines. After all, I can find treasure as handily as the white monks can – indeed, a good deal better. I use these alimony cases to keep my name before the public. Financially they're a loss to me.'

'What kinds of fees are you interested in?'

'I begin to exert myself slightly at about five million.'

If this man was a charlatan, he was a grandiose one. Baines said, 'Let's stick to the alimony case for the moment. Or rather, suppose I don't care about the alimony, as in fact I don't. Instead, I might not only want her dead, but I might want her to die badly. To suffer.'

'I don't charge for that.'

'Why not?'

'Mr Baines,' Ware said patiently, 'I remind you, please, that I myself am not a killer. I merely summon and direct the agent. I think it very likely – in fact, I think it beyond doubt – that any patient I have sent for dies in an access of horror and agony beyond your power to imagine, or even of mine. But you did specify that you wanted your murder done "tracelessly", which obviously means that I must have no unusual marks left on the patient. I prefer it that way myself. How then could I prove suffering if you asked for it, in a way inarguable enough to charge you extra for it?

'Or, look at the other side of the shield, Mr Baines. Every now and then, an unusual divorce client asks that the ex-consort be carried away painlessly, even sweetly, out of some residue of sentiment. I *could* collect an extra fee for that, on a contingent basis, that is, if the body turns out to show no overt marks of disease or violence. But my agents are demons, and sweetness is not a trait they can be compelled to exhibit, so I never accept that kind of condition from a client, either. Death is what you pay for, and death is what you get. The circumstances are up to the agent, and I don't offer my clients anything that I know I can't deliver.'

'All right, I'm answered,' Baines said. 'Forget Dolores – actually she's only a minor nuisance, and only one of several, for that matter. Now let's talk about the other end of the spectrum. Suppose instead that I should ask you to . . . send for . . . a great political figure. Say, the governor of California – or, if he's a friend of yours, pick a similiar figure who isn't.'

Ware nodded. 'He'll do well enough. But you'll recall that I asked you about children. Had you really turned out to have been an alimony case, I should next have asked you about surviving relatives. My fees rise in direct proportion to the numbers and kinds of people a given death is likely to affect. This is partly what you call scruples, and partly a species of self-defence. Now in the case of a reigning governor, I would charge you one dollar for every vote he got when he was last elected. Plus expenses, of course.'

Baines whistled in admiration. 'You're the first man I've ever met who's worked out a system to make scruples pay. And I can see why you don't care about alimony cases. Someday, Mr Ware – '

'*Doctor* Ware, please. I am a Doctor of Theology.'

'Sorry. I only meant to say that someday I'll ask you why you want so much money. You asthenics seldom can think of any good use for it. In the meantime, however, you're hired. Is it all payable in advance?'

'The expenses are payable in advance. The fee is C.O.D. As you'll realize once you stop to think about it, Mr Baines – '

'*Doctor* Baines. I am an LL.D.'

'Apologies in exchange. I want you to realize, after these courtesies, that I have never, never been bilked.'

Baines thought about what was supposed to be at his back until the day after tomorrow. Pending the test of the golden tears on the handkerchief, he was willing to believe that he should not try to cheat Ware. Actually, he had never planned to.

'Good,' he said, getting up. 'By the same token, we don't need a contract. I agree to your terms.'

'But what for?'

'Oh,' Baines said, 'we can use the governor of California for a starter. Jack here will iron out any remaining details with you. I have to get back to Rome by tonight.'

'You did say, "For a starter?"'

Baines nodded shortly. Ware, also rising, said, 'Very well. I shall ask no questions. But in fairness, Mr Baines. I should warn you that on your next commission of this kind, I shall ask you what *you* want.'

'By that time,' Baines said, holding his excitement tightly bottled, 'we'll *have* to exchange such confidences. Oh, Dr Ware, will the, uh, demon on my back go away by itself when the time's up or must I see you again to get it taken off?'

'It isn't *on* your back,' Ware said. 'And it will go by itself. Marlowe to the contrary, misery does not love company.'

Baring his teeth, Baines said, 'We'll see about that.'

2

For a moment, Jack Ginsberg felt the same soon-to-be-brief strangeness of the man who does not really know what is going on and hence thinks he might be about to be fired. It was as though something had swallowed him by mistake, and – quite without malice – was about to throw him up again.

While he waited for the monster's nausea to settle out, Jack went through his rituals, stroking his cheeks for stubble, re-settling his creases, running through last week's accounts, and thinking above all, as he usually did most of all in such interims, of what the new girl might look like squatting in her stockings. Nothing special, probably; the reality was almost always hedged around with fleshy inconveniences and piddling little preferences that he could flense away at will from the clean vision.

When the chief had left and Ware had come back to his desk, however, Jack was ready for business and thoroughly on top of it. He prided himself upon an absolute self-control.

'Questions?' Ware said, leaning back easily.

'A few, Dr Ware. You mentioned expenses. What expenses?'

'Chiefly travel,' Ware said. 'I have to see the patient, personally. In the case Dr Baines posed, that involves a trip to California, which is a vast inconvenience to me, and goes on the bill. It includes air fare, hotels, meals, other out-of-pocket expenses, which I'll itemize when the mission is over. Then there's the question of getting to see the governor. I have colleagues in California, but there's a certain amount of influence I'll have to buy, even with the help of Consolidated Warfare – munitions and magic are circles that don't intersect very effectively. On the whole, I think a draft for ten thousand would be none too small.'

All that for magic. Disgusting. But the chief believed in it, at least provisionally. It made Jack feel very queasy.

'That sounds satisfactory,' he said, but he made no move towards the corporate chequebook; he was not about to issue any Valentines to strangers yet, not until there was more love touring about the landscape than he had felt in his crew-cut antennae. 'We're naturally a little bit wondering, sir, why all this expense is necessary. We understand that you'd rather not ride a demon when you can fly a jet with less effort – '

'I'm not sure you do,' Ware said, 'but stop simpering about it and ask me about the money.'

'Argh . . . well, sir, then, just why do you live outside the United States? We know you're still a citizen. And after all, we have freedom of religion in the States still. Why does the chief have to pay to ship you back home for one job?'

'Because I'm not a common gunman,' Ware said. 'Because I don't care to pay income taxes, or even report my income to anybody. There are two reasons. For the benefit of your ever-attentive dispatch case there – since you're a deaf ear if ever I saw one – if I lived in the United States and advertised myself as a magician, I would be charged with fraud, and if I successfully defended myself – proved I was what I said I was – I'd wind up in a gas chamber. If I failed to defend myself, I'd be just one more charlatan. In Europe, I can say I'm a magician, and be left alone if I can satisfy my clients – *caveat emptor*. Otherwise, I'd have to be constantly killing off petty politicians and accountants, which isn't worth the work, and sooner or later runs into the law of diminishing returns. Now you can turn that thing off.'

Aha; there *was* something wrong with this joker. He was preying upon superstition. As a reformed Orthodox Agnostic, Jack Ginsberg knew all the ins and outs of that, especially the double-entry sides. He said smoothly:

'I quite understand. But don't you perhaps have almost as much trouble with the Church, here in Italy, as you would with the government back home?'

'No, not under a liberal pontificate. The modern Church discourages what it calls superstition among its adherents. I haven't encountered a prelate in decades who believes in the *literal* existence of demons – though of course some of the Orders know better.'

'To be sure,' Jack said, springing his trap exultantly. 'So I think, sir, that you may be overcharging us – and haven't been quite candid with us. If you do indeed control all these great princes and presidents, you could as easily bring the chief a woman as you could bring him a treasure or a murder.'

'So I could,' the magician said, a little wearily. 'I see you've done a little reading. But I explained to Dr Baines, and I explain again to you, that I specialize only in crimes of violence. Now, Mr Ginsberg, I think you were about to write me an expense cheque.'

'So I was.' But still he hesitated. At last Ware said with delicate politeness:

'Is there some other doubt I could resolve for you, Mr Ginsberg? I am, after all, a Doctor of Theology. Or perhaps you have a private commission you wish to broach to me?'

'No,' Jack said. 'No, not exactly.'

'I see no reason why you should be shy. It's clear that you

like my lamia. And in fact, she's quite free of the nuisances of human women that so annoy you – '

'Damn you. I *thought* you read minds! You lied about that, too.'

'I don't read minds, and I never lie,' Ware said. 'But I'm adept at reading faces and somatotypes. It saves me a lot of trouble, and a lot of unnecessary magic. Do you want the creature or don't you? I could have her sent to you invisibly if you like.'

'No.'

'Not invisibly. I'm sorry for you. Well then, my godless and lustless friend, speak up for yourself. What *would* you like? Your business is long since done. Spit it out. What is it?'

For a breathless instant, Jack almost said what it was, but the God in which he no longer believed was at his back. He made out the cheque and handed it over. The girl (no, not a girl) came in and took it away.

'Good-bye,' Theron Ware said.

He had missed the boat again.

3

Father Domenico read the letter again, hopefully. Father Uccello affected an Augustinian style, after his name saint, full of rare words and outright neologisms embedded in medieval syntax – as a stylist, Father Domenico much preferred Roger Bacon, but that eminent anti-magician, not being a Father of the Church, tempted few imitators – and it was possible that Father Domenico had misread him. But no; involuted though the Latin of the letter was, the sense, this time, was all too plain.

Father Domenico sighed. The practice of Ceremonial magic, at least of the white kind which was the monastery's sole concern, seemed to be becoming increasingly unrewarding. Part of the difficulty, of course, lay in the fact that the chiefest traditional use (for profit) of white magic was the finding of buried treasure; and after centuries of unremitting practice by centuries of sorcerers black and white, plus the irruption into the field of such modern devices as the mine detector, there was very little buried treasure left to find. Of late, the troves revealed by those under the governments of Och and Bethor – with the former of whom in particular lay the bestowal of 'a purse springing with gold' – had increasingly turned out to be underseas, or in places like Fort Knox or a Swiss bank, making the recovery of them enterprises so colossal and mischancy as to remove all possibility of profit for client and monastery alike.

On the whole, black magicians had an easier time of it – at least in this life; one must never forget, Father Domenico reminded himself hastily, that they were also damned eternally. It was as mysterious as it had always been that such infernal spirits as LUCIFUGE ROFOCALE should be willing to lend so much power to a mortal whose soul Hell would almost inevitably have won anyhow, considering the character of the average sorcerer, and considering how easily such pacts could be voided at the last instant; and that God would allow so much demonic malice to be vented through the sorcerer upon the innocent. But that was simply another version of the Problem of Evil, for which the Church had long had the answer (or, the dual answer) of free will and original sin.

It had to be recalled, too, that even the practice of white or Transcendental magic was officially a mortal sin, for the modern Church held that all trafficking with spirits – including the un-Fallen, since such dealings inevitably assumed the angels to be demiurges and other kabbalistic semi-deities – was an abomination, regardless of intent. Once upon a time, it had been recognized that (barring the undertaking of an actual pact) only a man of the highest piety, of the highest purpose, and in the highest state of ritual and spiritual purification, could hope to summon and control a demon, let alone an angel; but there had been too many lapses of intent, and then of act, and in both practicality and compassion the Church had declared all Theurgy to be anathema, reserving unto itself only one negative aspect of magic – exorcism – and that only under the strictest of canonical limitations.

Monte Albano had a special dispensation, to be sure – partly since the monks had at one time been so spectacularly successful in nourishing the coffers of St Peter's; partly because the knowledge to be won through the Transcendental rituals might sometimes be said to have nourished the soul of the Rock; and, in small part, because under the rarest of circumstances white magic had been known to prolong the life of the body. But these fountains (to shift the image) were now showing every sign of running dry, and hence the dispensation might be withdrawn at any time – thus closing out the last sanctuary of white magic in the world.

That would leave the field to the black magicians. There were no black sanctuaries, except for the Parisian Brothers of the Left-Hand Way, who were romantics of the school of Éliphas Lévi and were more to be pitied for folly than condemned for evil. But of solitary black sorcerers there were still a disconcerting number – though even one would be far too many.

Which brought Father Domenico directly back to the problem of the letter. He sighed again, turned away from his lectrum and padded off – the Brothers of Monte Albano were discalced – towards the office of the Director, letter in hand. Father Umberto was in (of course he was always *physically* in, like all the rest of them, since the Mount could not be left once entered, except by the laity and they only by muleback), and Father Domenico got to the point directly.

'I've had another impassioned screed from our witch smeller,' he said. 'I am beginning to consider, reluctantly, that the matter is at least as serious as he's been saying all along.'

'You mean the matter of Theron Ware, I presume.'

'Yes, of course. The American gunmaker we saw went directly from the Mount to Ware, as seemed all too likely even at the time, and Father Uccello says that there's now every sign of another series of sendings being prepared in Positano.'

'I wish you would avoid these alliterations. They make it difficult to discover what you're talking about. I often feel that a lapse into alliteration or other grammatical tricks is a sure sign that the speaker isn't himself quite sure of what he means to say, and is trying to blind me to the fact. Never mind. As for the demonolater Ware, we are in no position to interfere with him, whatever he's preparing.'

'The style is Father Uccello's. Anyhow, he insists that we *must* interfere. He has been practising divination – so you can see how seriously *he* takes this, the old purist – and he says that his principal, whom he takes great pains not to identify, told him that the meeting of Ware and Baines presages something truly monstrous for the world at large. According to his information, all Hell has been waiting for this meeting since the two of them were born.'

'I suppose he's sure his principal wasn't in fact a demon and didn't slip a lie past him, or at least one of their usual brags? As you've just indirectly pointed out, Father Uccello is way out of practice.'

Father Domenico spread his hands. 'Of course I can't answer that. Though if you wish, Father, I'll try to summon Whatever it was myself, and put the problem to It. But you know how good the chances are that I'll get the wrong one – and how hard it is to ask the right question. The great Governors seem to have no time sense as we understand the term, and as for demons, well, even when compelled they often really don't seem to know what's going on outside their own jurisdictions.'

'Quite so,' said the Director, who had not himself practised in many years. He had been greatly talented once, but the loss of gifted experimenters to administrative posts was the curse of all research organizations. 'I think it best that you don't jeopardize your own usefulness, and your own soul, of course, in calling up some spirit you can't name. Father Uccello in turn ought to know that there's nothing we can do about Ware. Or does he have some proposal?'

'He wants us,' Father Domenico said in a slightly shaky vouce, 'to impose an observer on Ware. To send one directly to Positano, someone who'll stick to Ware until we know what the deed is going to be. We're just barely empowered to do this – whereas, of course, Father Uccello can't. The question is, do *we* want to?'

'Hmm, hmm,' the Director said. 'Obviously not. That would bankrupt us – oh, not financially, of course, though it would be difficult enough. But we couldn't afford to send a novice, or indeed anyone less than the best we have, and after the good Lord only knows how many months in that infernal atmosphere . . .'

The sentence trailed off, as the Director's sentences often did, but Father Domenico no longer had any difficulty in completing them. Obviously the Mount could not afford to have even one of its best operators incapacitated – the word, in fact, was 'contaminated' – by prolonged contact with the person and effects of Theron Ware. Similarly, Father Domenico was reasonably certain that the Director would in fact send somebody to Positano; otherwise he would not have mounted the obvious objections, but simply dismissed the proposal. For all their usual amusement with Father Uccello, both men knew that there were occasions when one had to take him with the utmost seriousness, and that this was one of them.

'Nevertheless the matter will need to be explored,' the Director resumed after a moment, fingering his beads. 'I had better give Ware the usual formal notification. We're not obligated to follow up on it, but . . .'

'Quite,' Father Domenico said. He put the letter into his scrip and arose. 'I'll hear from you, then, when a reply's been received from Ware. I'm glad you agree that the matter is serious.'

After another exchange of formalities, he left, head bowed. He also knew well enough whom the Director would send, without any intervention of false modesty to cloud the issue; and he was well aware that he was terrified.

He went directly to his conjuring room, the cluttered tower chamber that no one else could use – for magic is intensely sensitive to the personality of the operator – and which was still faintly redolent of a scent a little like oil of lavender, a trace of his last use of the room. *Mansit odor, posses scire duisse deam,* he thought, not for the first time; but he had no intention of summoning any Presence now. Instead, he crossed to the chased casket which contained his 1606 copy – the second edition, but not much corrupted – of the *Enchiridion* of Leo III, that odd collection of prayers and other devices 'effectual against all the perils to which every sort and condition of men may be made subject on land, on water, from open and secret enemies, from the bites of wild and rabid beasts, from poisons, from fire, from tempests.' For greatest effectiveness he was instructed to carry the book on his person, but he had seldom judged himself to be in sufficient peril to risk so rare and valuable an object, and in any event he did always read at least one page daily, chiefly the *In principio*, a version of the first chapter of the Gospel According to St John.

Now he took the book out and opened it to the Seven Mysterious Orisons, the only section of the work – without prejudice to the efficacy of the rest of it – that probably had indeed proceeded from the hand of the Pope of Charlemagne. Kneeling to face the east, Father Domenico, without looking at the page, began the prayer appropriate for Thursday, at the utterance of which, perhaps by no coincidence, it is said that 'the demons flee away.'

4

Considerable business awaited Baines in Rome, all the more pressing because Jack Ginsberg was still out of town, and Baines made no special effort to hunt down Jack's report on what the government metallurgist had said about the golden tears amid the mass of other papers. For the time being, at least, Baines regarded the report as personal correspondence, and he had a standing rule never even to open personal letters during office hours, whether he was actually in an office or, as now, working out of a hotel room.

Nevertheless, the report came to the surface the second day that he was back at work; and since he also made a rule never to lose time to the distractions of an unsatisfied curiosity if an easy remedy was to hand, he read it. The tears on the handkerchief were indeed 24-carat gold; worth about eleven cents, taken together, on the current market, but to Baines representing an enormous investment (or, looked at another way, a potential investment in enormity).

He put it aside with satisfaction and promptly forgot about

it, or very nearly. Investments in enormity were his stock in trade, though of late, he thought again with cold anger, they had been paying less and less – hence his interest in Ware, which the other directors of Consolidated Warfare Service would have considered simple insanity. But after all, if the business was no longer satisfying, it was only natural to seek analogous satisfactions somewhere else. An insane man, in Baines' view, would be one who tried to substitute some pleasure – women, philanthropy, art collecting, golf – that offered no cognate satisfaction at all. Baines was ardent about his trade, which was destruction; golf could no more have sublimated that passion than it could have diluted that of a painter or a lecher.

The current fact, which had to be faced and dealt with, was that nuclear weapons had almost totally spoiled the munitions business. Oh, there was still a thriving trade to be drummed up selling small arms to a few small new nations – small arms being defined arbitrarily as anything up to the size of a submarine – but hydrogen fusion and the ballistic missile made the really major achievements of the art, the lubrication of the twenty-year cycle of world wars, entirely too obliterative and self-defeating. These days, Baines's kind of diplomacy consisted chiefly in the fanning of brush fires and civil wars. Even this was a delicate business, for the nationalism game was increasingly an exceedingly confused affair, in which one could never be quite sure whether some emergent African state with a population about the size of Maplewood, N.J., would not turn out to be of absorbing interest to one or more of the nuclear powers. (Some day, of course, they would all be nuclear powers, and then the art would become as formalized and minor as flower arranging.)

The very delicacy of this kind of operation had its satisfactions, in a way, and Baines was good at it. In addition, Consolidated Warfare Service had several thousand man-years of accumulated experience at this sort of thing upon which he could call. One of CWS's chief specialists was in Rome with him now – Dr Adolph Hess, famous as the designer of that peculiar all-purpose vehicle called the Hessicopter, but of interest in the present negotiations as the inventor of something nobody was supposed to have heard of – the land torpedo, a rapidly burrowing device that might show up, commendably anonymous, under any installation within two hundred miles of its launching tunnel, geology permitting. Baines had guessed that it might be especially attractive to at least one of the combatants in the Yemeni insurrection, and had proven to be so right that he was now trying hard not to have to dicker with all four of them. This was all the more difficult because, although the two putative Yemeni factions accounted for very little, Nasser was nearly as shrewd as Baines was, and Faisal inarguably a good deal shrewder.

Nevertheless, Baines was not essentially a minaturist, and he was well aware of it. He had recognized the transformation impending in the trade early on, in fact with the publication in 1950 by the US Government Printing Office of a volume titled *The Effects of Atomic Weapons*, and as soon as possible had engaged the services of a private firm called the Mamaroneck Research Institute. This was essentially a brainstorming organization, started by an alumnus of the RAND Corporation, which specialized in imagining possible political and military confrontations and their possible outcomes, some of them so *outré* as to require the subcontracting of free-lance science-fiction writers. From the files of CWS and other sources, Baines fed Mamaroneck materials for its computers, some of which material would have considerably shaken the governments who thought they were sitting on it; and, in return, Mamaroneck fed Baines long, neatly lettered and Xeroxed reports bearing titles as 'Short- and Long-Term Probabilities Consequent to an Israeli Blockade of the Faeröe Islands.'

Baines winnowed out the most obviously absurd of these, but with a care that was the very opposite of conservatism, for some of the strangest proposals could turn out upon second look to be not absurd at all. Those that offered the best combination of surface absurdity with hidden plausibility, he set out to translate into real situations. Hence there was really nothing illogical or even out of character in his interest in Theron Ware, for Baines, too, practised what was literally an occult art in which the man on the street no longer believed.

The buzzer sounded twice; Ginsberg was back. Baines returned the signal and the door swung open.

'Rogan's dead,' Jack said without preamble.

'That was fast. I thought it was going to take Ware a week after he got back from the States.'

'It's been a week,' Jack reminded him.

'Hmm? So it has. Waiting around for these Ayrabs to get off the dime is hard on the time sense. Well, well, Details?'

'Only what's come over the Reuters ticker, so far. Started as pneumonia, ended as cor pulmonale – heart failure from too much coughing. It appears that he had a small mitral murmur for years. Only the family knew about it, and his physicians assured them that it wasn't dangerous if he didn't try to run a four-minute mile or something like that. Now the guessing is that the last campaign put a strain on it, and the pneumonia did the rest.'

'Very clean,' Baines said.

He thought about the matter for a while. He had borne the late governor of California no ill will. He had never met the man, nor had any business conflicts with him, and in fact had rather admired his brand of medium-right-wing politics, which had been of the articulate but inoffensive sort expectable of an ex-account executive for a San Francisco advertising agency specializing in the touting of cold breakfast cereals. Indeed, Baines recalled suddenly from the file biography, Rogan had been a fraternity brother of his.

Nevertheless he was pleased. Ware had done the job – Baines was not in the smallest doubt that Ware should have the credit – with great nicety. After one more such trial run, simply to rule out all possibility of coincidence, he should be ready to tackle something larger; possibly, the biggest job of them all.

Baines wondered how it had been done. Was it possible that a demon could appear to a victim in the form of a pneumococcus? If so, what about the problem of reproduction? Well, there had been the appearances all over medieval Europe of fragments of the True Cross, in numbers quantitatively sufficient to stock a large lumberyard. Contemporary clerical apologists had called that Miraculous Multiplication, which had always seemed to Baines to be a classic example of rationalizing away the obvious; but since magic was real, maybe Miraculous Multiplication was too.

These, however, were merely details of technique, in which he made a practice of taking no interest. That kind of thing was for hirelings. Still, it wouldn't hurt to have somebody in the organization who did know something about the technicalities. It was often dangerous to depend solely on outside experts.

'Make out a cheque for Ware,' he told Jack. 'From my personal account. Call it a consultation fee – medical, preferably. When you send it to him, set up a date for another visit – let's see – as soon as I get back from Riyadh. I'll take up all this other business with you in about half an hour. Send Hess in, but wait outside.'

Jack nodded and left. A moment later, Hess entered silently. He was a tall, bony man with a slight pod, bushy eyebrows, a bald spot in the back, pepper-and-salt hair, and a narrow jaw that made his face look nearly triangular.

'Any interest in sorcery, Adolph? Personal I mean?'

'Sorcery? I know something about it. For all the nonsense involved, it was highly important in the history of science, particularly the alchemical side, and the astrological.'

'I'm not interested in either of those. I'm talking about black magic.'

'Then no, I don't know much about it,' Hess said.

'Well, you're about to learn. We're going to visit an authentic sorcerer in about two weeks, and I want you to go along and study his methods.'

'Are you pulling my leg?' Hess said. 'No, you never do that. Are we going into the business of exposing charlatans, then? I'm not sure I'm the best man for that, Baines. A professional stage magician – a Houdini type – would be far more likely to catch out a faker than I would.'

'No, that's not the issue at all. I'm going to ask this man to do some work for me, in his own line, and I need a close observer to see what he does – not to see through it, but to form an accurate impression of the procedures, in case something should go sour with the relationship later on.'

'But – well, if you say so, Baines. It does seem rather a waste of time, though.'

'Not to me,' Baines said. 'While you're waiting to talk to the Saudis with me, read up on the subject. By the end of a year I want you to know as much about the subject as an expert. The man himself has told me that that's possible even for me, so it shouldn't tax you any.'

'It's not likely to tax my brains much,' Hess said drily, 'but it may be a considerable tax on my patience. However, you're the boss.'

'Right. Get on it.'

Hess nodded distantly to Jack as he went out. The two men did not like each other much; in part, Baines sometimes thought, because in some ways they were much alike. When the door had closed behind the scientist, Jack produced from his pocket the waxed-paper envelope that had contained, and obviously still contained, the handkerchief bearing the two transmuted tears.

'I don't need that,' Baines said. 'I've got your report. Throw that thing away. I don't want anybody asking what it means.'

'I will,' Jack said. 'But first, you'll remember that Ware said that the demon would leave you after two days.'

'Sure. Why?'

'Look at this.'

Jack took out the handkerchief and spread it carefully on Baines's desk blotter.

On the Irish linen, where the golden tears had been, were now two dull, inarguable smears of lead.

5

By some untraceable miscalculation, Baines's party arrived in Riyadh precisely at the beginning of Ramadan, during which the Arabs fasted all day and were consequently in too short a temper to do business with; which was followed, after twenty-nine solid days, by a three-day feast during which they were too stuporous to do business with. Once negotations were properly opened, however, they took no more than the two weeks Baines had anticipated.

Since the Moslem calendar is lunar, Ramadan is a moveable festival, which this year fell close to Christmas. Baines half suspected that Theron Ware would refuse to see him in so inauspicious a season for servants of Satan, but Ware made no objection, remarking only (by post), 'December 25th is a celebration of great antiquity.' Hess, who had been reading dutifully, interpreted Ware to mean that Christ had not actually been born on that date – 'though in this universe of discourse I can't see what difference that makes,' he said. 'If the word "superstition" has any of its old meaning left at all by now, it means that the sign has come to replace the thing – or in other words, that facts come to mean what we say they mean.'

'Call it an observer effect,' Baines suggested, not entirely jokingly. He was not disposed to argue the point with either of them; Ware would see him, that was what counted.

But if the season was no apparent inconvenience to Ware, it was a considerable one to Father Domenico, who at first flatly refused to celebrate it in the very maw of Hell. He was pressed at length and from both sides by the Director and Father Uccello, whose arguments had no less force for being so utterly predictable; and – to skip over a full week of positively Scholastic disputation – they prevailed, as again he had been sure they would.

Mustering all his humility, obedience and resignation – his courage seemed to have evaporated – he trudged forth from the monastery, excused from sandals, and mounted a mule, the *Enchiridion* of Leo III swinging from his neck under his cassock in a new leather bag, and a selection of his thaumaturgic tools, newly exorcised, asperged, fumigated and wrapped in silken cloths, in a satchel balanced carefully on the mule's neck. It was a hushed leave-taking – all the more so in its lack of any formalities or even witnesses, for only the Director knew why he was going, and he had been restrained with difficulty from bruiting it about that Father Domenico actually had been expelled, to make a cover story.

The practical effect of both delays was that Father Domenico and Baines's party arrived at Ware's palazzo on the same day, in the midst of the only snowstorm Positano had seen in seven years. As a spiritual courtesy – for protocol was all-important in such matters, otherwise neither monk nor sorcerer would have dared to confront the other – Father Domenico was received first, briefly but punctiliously; but as a client, Baines (and his crew, in descending order) got the best quarters. They also got the only service available, since Ware had no servants who could cross over the invisible line Father Domenico at once ruled at the foot of his apartment door with the point of his bolline.

As was customary in southern Italian towns at this time, three masked kings later came to the gate of the palazzo to bring and ask presents for the children and the Child; but there were no children there and the mummers were turned away, baffled and resentful (for the rich American, who was said to be writing a book about the frescoes of Pompeii, had previously shown himself open-handed), but oddly grateful too; it was a cold night, and the lights in the palazzo were of a grim and distant colour.

Then the gates closed. The principals had gathered and were in their places; and the stage was set.

Three Sleeps

It requires more courage and intelligence to be a devil than the folk who take experience at hearsay think. And none, save only he who has destroyed the devil in himself, and that by dint of hard work (for there is no other way) knows what a devil is, and what a devil he himself might be, as also what an army for the devils' use are they who think the devils are delusion.

The Book of the Sayings of Tsiang Samdup

6

Father Domenico's interview with Theron Ware was brief, formal and edgy. The monk, despite his apprehensions, had been curious to see what the magician looked like, and had been irrationally disappointed to find him not much out of the ordinary run of intellectuals. Except for the tonsure, of course; like Baines, Father Domenico found that startling. Also, unlike Baines, he found it upsetting, because he knew the reason for it – not that Ware intended any mockery of his pious counterparts, but because demons, given a moment of inattention, were prone to seizing one by the hair.

'Under the Covenant,' Ware told him in excellent Latin, 'I have no choice but to receive you, of course, Father. And under other circumstances I might even have enjoyed discussing the Art with you, even though we are of opposite schools. But this is an inconvenient time for me. I've got a very important client here, as you've seen, and I've already been notified that what he wants of me is likely to be extraordinarily ambitious.'

'I shan't interfere in any way,' Father Domenico said. 'Even should I wish to, which obviously I shall, I know very well that any such interference would cost me all my protections.'

'I was sure you understood that, but nonetheless I'm glad to hear you say so,' Ware said. 'However, your very presence here is an embarrassment – not only because I'll have to explain it to my client, but also because it changes the atmosphere unfavourably and will make my operations more difficult. I can only hope, in defiance of all hospitality, that your mission will be speedily satisfied.'

'I can't bring myself to regret the difficulty, since I only wish I could make your operations outright impossible. The best I can proffer you is strict adherence to the truce. As for the length of my stay, that depends wholly on what it is your client turns out to want, and how long *that* takes. I am charged with seeing it through to its conclusion.'

'A prime nuïsance,' Ware said. 'I suppose I should be grateful that I haven't been blessed with this kind of attention from Monte Albano before. Evidently what Mr Baines intends is even bigger than he thinks it is. I conclude without much cerebration that you know something about it I don't know.'

'It will be an immense disaster, I can tell you that.'

'Hmm. From your point of view, but not necessarily from mine, possibly. I don't suppose you're prepared to offer any further information – on the chance, say, of dissuading me?'

'Certainly not,' Father Domenico said indignantly. 'If eternal damnation hasn't dissuaded you long before this, I'd be a fool to hope to.'

'Well,' Ware said, 'but you are, after all, charged with the cure of souls, and unless the Church has done another flipflop since the last Congress, it is still also a mortal sin to assume that any man is certainly damned – even me.'

That argument was potent, it had to be granted; but Father Domenico had not been trained in casuistry (and that by Jesuits) for nothing.

'I'm a monk, not a priest,' he said. 'And any information I give you would, on the contrary, almost certainly be used to abet the evil, not turn it aside. I don't find the choice a hard one under the circumstances.'

'Then let me suggest a more practical consideration,' Ware said. 'I don't know yet what Baines intends, but I do know well enough that I am not a Power myself – only a fautor. I have no desire to bite off more than I can chew.'

'Now you're just wheedling,' Father Domenico said, with energy. 'Knowing your own limitations is not an exercise at which I or anyone else can help you. You'll just have to weigh them in the light of Mr Baines's commission, whatever that proves to be. In the meantime, I shall tell you nothing.'

'Very well,' Ware said, rising. 'I will be a little more generous with my information, Father, than you have been with yours. I will tell you that you will be well advised to adhere to every letter of the Covenant. One step over the line, one toe, and *I shall have you* – and hardly any outcome in this world would give me greater pleasure. I'm sure I make myself clear.'

Father Domenico could think of no reply; but none seemed to be necessary.

7

As Ware had sensed, Baines was indeed disturbed by the presence of Father Domenico, and made a point of bringing it up as the first order of business. After Ware had explained the monk's mission and the Covenant under which it was being conducted, however, Baines felt somewhat relieved.

'Just a nuisance, as you say, since he can't actually intervene,' he decided. 'In a way, I suppose my bringing Dr Hess here with me is comparable – he's only an observer, too, and fundamentally he's probably just as hostile to your world-view as this holier-than-us fellow is.'

'He's not significantly holier than us,' Ware said with a slight smile. 'I know something he doesn't know, too. He's in for a surprise in the next world. However, for the time being we're stuck with him – for how long depends upon you. Just what is it you want this time, Dr Baines?'

'Two things, one depending on the other. The first is the death of Albert Stockhausen.'

'The anti-matter theorist? That would be too bad. I rather like him, and besides, some of the work he does is of direct interest to me.'

'You refuse?'

'No, not immediately anyhow, but I'm now going to ask you what I promised I would ask on this occasion. What are you aiming at, anyhow?'

'Something very long-term. For the present, my lethal intentions for Dr Stockhausen are strictly business-based. He's nibbling at the edges of a scholium that my company presently controls completely. It's a monopoly of knowledge we don't want to see broken.'

'Do you think you can keep anything secret that's based in natural law? After the McCarthy fiasco I should have supposed that any intelligent American would know better. Surely Dr Stockhausen can't be just verging on some mere technicality – something your firm might eventually bracket with a salvo of process patents.'

'No, it's in the realm of natural law, and hence not patentable at all,' Baines admitted. 'And we already know that it can't be concealed forever. But we need about five years' grace to make the best use of it, and we know that nobody else but Stockhausen is even close to it, barring accidents, of course. We ourselves have nobody of Stockhausen's calibre, we just fell over it, and somebody else might do that. However, that's highly unlikely.'

'I see. Well . . . the project does have an attractive side. I think it's quite possible that I can persuade Father Domenico that this is the project he came to observe. Obviously it can't be – I've run many like it and never attracted Monte Albano's interest to this extent before – but given sufficient show of great preparations, and difficulty of execution, he might be deluded, and go home.'

'That would be useful,' Baines agreed. 'The question is, could he be deceived?'

'It's worth trying. The task would in fact be difficult – and quite expensive.'

'Why?' Jack Ginsberg said, sitting bolt upright in his carved Florentine chair so suddenly as to make his suit squeak against the silk upholstery. 'Don't tell us he affects thousands of other people. Nobody ever cast any votes for him that I know of.'

'Shut up, Jack.'

'No, wait, it's a reasonable question,' Ware said. 'Dr Stockhausen does have a large family, which I have to take into account. And, as I've told you, I've taken some pleasure in his company on a few occasions – not enough to balk at having him sent for, but enough to help run up the price.'

'But that's not the major impediment. The fact is that Dr Stockhausen, like a good many theoretical physicists these days, is a devout man – and furthermore, he has only a few venial sins to account for, nothing in the least meriting the attention of Hell. I'll check that again with someone who knows, but it was accurate as of six months ago and I'd be astonished if there's been any change. He's not a member of any formal congregation, but even so he's nobody a demon could reasonably have come for him – and there's a chance that he might be defended against any direct assault.'

'Successfully?'

'It depends on the forces involved. Do you want to risk a pitched battle that would tear up half of Düsseldorf? It might be cheaper just to mail him a bomb.'

'No, no. And I don't want anything that might look like some kind of laboratory accident – that'd be just the kind of clue that would set everybody else in his field haring after what we want to keep hidden. The whole secret lies in the fact that once Stockhausen knows what we know, he could create a major explosion with – well, with the equivalent of a black-board and two pieces of chalk. Isn't there any other way?'

'Men being men, there's always another way. In this instance, though, I'd have to have him tempted. I know at least one promising avenue. But he might not fall. And even if he did, as I think he would, it would take several months and a lot of close monitoring. Which wouldn't be altogether intolerable either, since it would greatly help to mislead Father Domenico.'

'What would it cost?' Jack Ginsberg said.

'Oh – say about eight million. Entirely a contingent fee this time, since I can't see that there'd be any important out-of-pocket money needed. If there is, I'll absorb it.'

'That's nice,' Jack said. Ware took no notice of the feeble sarcasm.

Baines put on his adjudicative face but inwardly he was well satisfied. As a further test, the death of Dr Stockhausen was not as critical as that of Governor Rogan, but it did have the merit of being in an entirely different social sphere; the benefits to Consolidated Warfare Service would be real enough, so that Baines had not had to counterfeit a motive, which might have been detected by Ware and led to premature further questions; and finally, the objections Ware had raised, while in part unexpected, had been entirely consistent with everything the magician had said before, everything that he appeared to be, everything that his style proclaimed, despite the fact that he was obviously a complex man.

Good. Baines liked consistent intellectuals, and wished that he had more of them in his organization. They were always fanatics of some sort when the chips were down, and hence presented him with some large and easily grasped handle precisely when he had most need of it. Ware hadn't exhibited his handle yet, but he would; he would.

'It's worth it,' Baines said, without more than a decorous two seconds of apparent hesitation. 'I do want to remind you, though, Dr Ware, that Dr Hess here is one of my conditions. I want you to allow him to watch while you operate.'

'Oh, very gladly,' Ware said, with another smile that, this time, Baines found disquieting; it seemed false, even unctuous, and Ware was too much in command of himself to have meant the falsity not to be noticed. 'I'm sure he'll enjoy it. You can all watch, if you like. I may even invite Father Domenico.'

8

Dr Hess arrived punctually the next morning for his appointment to be shown Ware's workroom and equipment. Greeting him with a professional nod – 'Coals to Newcastle, bringing Mitford and me up here for a tertiary,' Hess found himself quoting in silent inanity – Ware led the way to a pair of heavy, brocaded hangings behind his desk, which parted to reveal a heavy brass-bound door of what was apparently cypress wood. Among its fittings was a huge knocker with a face a little like the mask of tragedy, except that the eyes had cat-like pupils in them.

Hess had thought himself prepared to notice everything and be surprised by nothing, but he was taken aback when the expression on the knocker changed, slightly but inarguably, when Ware touched it. Apparently expecting his startlement, Ware said without looking at him, 'There's nothing in here really worth stealing, but if anything were taken it would cost me a tremendous amount of trouble to replace it, no matter how worthless it would prove to the thief. Also, there's the problem of contamination – just one ignorant touch could destroy the work of months. It's rather like a bacteriology laboratory in that respect. Hence the Guardian.'

'Obviously there can't be a standard supply house for your tools,' Hess agreed, recovering his composure.

'No, that's not even theoretically possible. The operator must make everything himself – not as easy now as it was in the Middle Ages, when most educated men had the requisite skills as a matter of course. Here we go.'

The door swung back as if being opened from the inside, slowly and soundlessly. At first it yawned on a deep scarlet gloom, but Ware touched a switch and, with a brief rushing sound, like water, sunlight flooded the room.

Immediately Hess could see why Ware had rented this particular palazzo and no other. The room was an immense refectory of Sienese design, which in its heyday must often have banquetted as many as thirty nobles; there could not be another one half as big in Positano, though the palazzo as a whole was smaller than some. There were mullioned windows overhead, under the ceiling, running around all four walls, and the sunlight was pouring through two ranks of them. They were flanked by pairs of red-velvet drapes, unpatterned, hung from traverse rods; it had been these that Hess had heard pulling back when Ware had flipped the wall switch.

At the rear of the room was another door, a broad one also covered by hangings, which Hess supposed must lead to a pantry or kitchen. To the left of this was a medium-sized, modern electric furnace, and beside it an anvil bearing a hammer that looked almost too heavy for Ware to lift. On the other side of the furnace from the anvil were several graduated tubs, which obviously served as quenching baths.

To the right of the door was a black-topped chemist's bench, complete with sinks, running water and the usual nozzles for illuminating gas, vacuum and compressed air; Ware must have had to install his own pumps for all of these. Over the bench on the back wall were shelves of reagents; to the right, on the side wall, ranks of drying pegs, some of which bore contorted pieces of glassware, others, coils of rubber tubing.

Farther along the wall towards the front was a lectern bearing a book as big as an unabridged dictionary, bound in red leather and closed and locked with a strap. There was a circular design chased in gold on the front of the book, but at this distance Hess could not make out what it was. The lectern was flanked by two standing candlesticks with fat candles in them; the candles had been extensively used, although there were shaded electric-light fixtures around the walls, too, and the small writing table next to the lectern bore a Tensor lamp. On the table was another book, smaller but almost as thick, which Hess recognized at once: the *Handbook of Chemistry and Physics*, forty-seventh edition, as standard a laboratory fixture as a test tube; and a rank of quill pens and inkhorns.

'Now you can see something of what I meant by requisite skills,' Ware said. 'Of course I blow much of my own glassware, but any ordinary chemist does that. But should I need a new sword, for instance' – he pointed towards the electric furnace – 'I'd have to forge it myself. I couldn't just pick one up at a costume shop. I'd have to do a good job of it, too. As a modern writer says somewhere, the only really serviceable symbol for a sharp sword is a *sharp* sword.'

'Uhm,' Hess said, continuing to look around. Against the left wall, opposite the lectern, was a long heavy table, bearing a neat ranking of objects ranging in length from six inches to about three feet, all closely wrapped in red silk. The wrappers had writing on them, but again Hess could not decipher it. Beside the table, affixed to the wall, was a flat sword cabinet. A few stools completed the furnishings; evidently Ware seldom worked sitting down. The floor was parquetted, and towards the centre of the room still bore traces of marks in coloured chalks, considerably scuffed, which brought from Ware a grunt of annoyance.

'The wrapped instruments are all prepared and I'd rather not expose them,' the magician said, walking towards the sword rack, 'but of course I keep a set of spares and I can show you those.'

He opened the cabinet door, revealing a set of blades hung in order of size. There were thirteen of them. Some were obviously swords; others looked more like shoemaker's tools.

'The order in which you make these is important, too,' Ware said, 'because, as you can see, most of them have writing on them, and it makes a difference what instrument does the writing. Hence I began with the uninscribed instrument, this one, the bolline or sickle, which is also one of the most often used. Rituals differ, but the one I use requires starting with a piece of unused steel. It's fired three times, and then quenched in a mixture of magpie's blood and the juice of a herb called foirole.'

'The *Grimorium Verum* says mole's blood and pimpernel juice,' Hess observed.

'Ah, good, you've been doing some reading. I've tried that, and it just doesn't seem to give quite as good an edge.'

'I should think you could get a still better edge by finding out what specific compounds were essential and using those,' Hess said. 'You'll remember that Damascus steel used to be tempered by plunging the sword into the body of a slave. It worked, but modern quenching baths are a lot better – and in your case you wouldn't have to be constantly having to trap elusive animals in large numbers.'

'The analogy is incomplete,' Ware said. 'It would hold if tempering were the only end in view, or if the operation were only another observance of Paracelsus' rule, *Alterius non sit qui suus esse potest* – doing for yourself what you can't trust others to do. Both are practical ends that I might satisfy in some quite different way. But in magic the blood sacrifice has an additional function – what we might call the tempering of, not just the steel, but also the operator.'

'I see. And I suppose it has some symbolic functions, too.'

'In goëtic art, everything does. In the same way, as you probably also know from your reading, the forging and quenching is to be done on a Wednesday in either the first or the eighth of the day hours, or the third or the tenth of the night hours, under a full Moon. There is again an immediate practical interest being served here – for I assure you that the planetary hours do indeed affect affairs on Earth – but also a psychological one, the obedience of the operator in every step. The grimoires and other handbooks are at best so confused and contradictory that it's never possible to know completely what steps are essential and what aren't, and research into the subject seldom makes for a long life.'

'All right,' Hess said. 'Go on.'

'Well, the horn handle has next to be shaped and fitted, again in a particular way at a particular hour, and then perfected at still another day and hour. By the way, you mentioned a different steeping bath. If you use that ritual, the days and the hours are also different, and again the question is, what's essential and what isn't? Thereafter, there's a conjuration to be recited, plus three salutations and a warding spell. Then the instrument is sprinkled, wrapped and fumigated – not in the modern sense, I mean it's perfumed – and is ready to use. After it's used, it has to be exorcised and rededicated, and that's the difference between the wrapped tools on the table and those hanging here in the rack.

'I won't go into detail about the preparation of the other instruments. The next one I make is the pen of the Art, followed by the inkpots and the inks, for obvious reasons – and, for the same reasons, the burin or graver. The pens are on my desk. This fitted needle here is the burin. The rest, going down the line as they hang here rather than in order of manufacture, are the white-handled knife, which like the bolline is nearly an all-purpose tool . . . the black-handled knife, used almost solely for inscribing the circle . . . the stylet, chiefly for preparing the wooden knives used in tanning . . . the wand or blasting rod, which describes itself . . . the lancet, again self-descriptive . . . the staff, a restraining instrument analogous to a shepherd's . . . and lastly the four swords, one for the master, the other three for his assistants, if any.'

With a side-glance at Ware for permission, Hess leaned forward to inspect the writings on the graven instruments. Some of them were easy enough to make out: on the sword of the master, for instance, the word MICHAEL appeared on the pommel, and on the blade, running from point to hilt, ELOHIM GIBOR. On the other hand, on the handle of the white-handled knife was engraved the following:

Hess pointed to this, and to a different but equally baffling inscription that was duplicated on the handles of the stylet and the lancet. 'What do those mean?'

'Mean? They can hardly be said to mean anything any more. They're greatly degenerate Hebrew characters, orignally comprising various Divine Names. I could tell you what the Names were once, but the characters have no content any more – they just have to be there,'

'Superstition,' Hess said, recalling his earlier conversation with Baines, interpreting Ware's remark about Christmas.

'Precisely, in the pure sense. The process is as fundamental to the Art as evolution is to biology. Now if you'll step this way, I'll show you some other aspects that may interest you.'

He led the way diagonally across the room to the chemist's bench, pausing to rub irritatedly at the chalk marks with the sole of his slipper. 'I suppose a modern translation of that aphorism of Paracelsus,' he said, 'would be "You just can't get good servants any more." Not to ply mops, anyhow. . . . Now, most of these reagents will be familiar to you, but some of them are special to the Art. This, for instance, is exorcised water, which as you see I need in great quantities. It has to be river water to start with. The quicklime is for tanning. Some laymen, de Camp for instance, will tell you that "virgin parchment" simply means parchment that's never been written on before, but that's not so – all the grimoires insist that it must be the skin of a male animal that has never engendered, and the *Clavicula Salomonis* sometimes insists upon unborn parchment, or the caul of a newborn child. For tanning I also have to grind my own salt, after the usual rites are said over it. The candles I use have to be made of the first wax taken from a new hive, and so do my almadels. If I need images, I have to make them of earth dug up with my bare hands and reduced to a paste without any tool. And so on.

'I've mentioned aspersion and fumigation, in other words sprinkling and perfuming. Sprinkling has to be done with an aspergillum, a bundle of herbs like a fagot or *bouquet garni*. The herbs differ from rite to rite and you can see I've got a fair selection here – mint, marjoram, rosemary, vervain, periwinkle, sage, valerian, ash, basil, hyssop. In fumigation the most commonly used scents are aloes, incense, mace, benzoin, storax. Also, it's sometimes necessary to make a stench – for instance in the fumigation of a caul – and I've got quite a repertoire of those.'

Ware turned away abruptly, nearly treading on Hess's toes, and strode towards the exit. Hess had no choice but to follow him.

'Everything involves special preparation,' he said over his shoulder, 'even including the firewood if I want to make ink for pacts. But there's no point in my cataloguing things further, since I'm sure you thoroughly understand the principles.'

Hess scurried after, but he was still several paces behind the magician when the window drapes swished closed and the red gloom was reinstated. Ware stopped and waited for him, and the moment he was through the door, closed it and went back to his seat behind the big desk. Hess, puzzled, walked around the desk and took one of the Florentine chairs reserved for guests or clients.

'Most illuminating,' he said politely. 'Thank you.'

'You're welcome,' Ware rested his elbows on the desk and put his fingertips over his mouth, looking down thoughtfully. There was a sprinkle of perspiration over his brow and shaven head, and he seemed more than usually pale; also, Hess noticed after a moment, he seemed to be trying without major effort, to control his breathing. Hess watched curiously, wondering what could have upset him. After only a moment, however, Ware looked up at him and volunteered the explanation, with an easy half smile.

'Excuse me,' he said. 'From apprenticeship on, we're trained to secrecy. I'm perfectly convinced that it's unnecessary these days, and has been since the Inquisition died, but old oaths are the hardest to reason away. No discourtesy intended.'

'No offence taken,' Hess assured him. 'However, if you'd rather rest . . .'

'No, I'll have ample rest in the next three days, and be incommunicado, too, preparing for Dr Baines's commission. So if you've further questions, now's the time for them.'

'Well . . . I have no further technical questions, for the moment. But I am curious about a question Baines asked you during your first meeting – I needn't pretend, I'm sure, that I haven't heard the tape. I wonder, just as he did, what your motivation is. I can see from what you've shown me, and from everything you've said, that you've taken colossal amounts of trouble to perfect yourself in your Art, and that you believe in it. So it doesn't matter for the present whether or not *I* believe in it, only whether or not I believe in *you*. And your laboratory isn't a sham, it isn't there solely for extortion's sake, it's a place where a dedicated man works at something he thinks important. I confess I came to scoff – and to expose you, if I could – and I still can't credit that any of what you do works, or ever did work. But I accept that you so believe.'

Ware gave him a half nod. 'Thank you; go on.'

'I've no further to go but the fundamental question. You don't really need money, you don't seem to collect art or women, you're not out to be President of the World or the power behind some such person – and yet by your lights you have damned yourself eternally to make yourself expert in this highly peculiar subject. What on earth *for*?'

'I could easily duck that question.' Ware said slowly. 'I could point out, for instance, that under certain circumstances I could prolong my life to seven hundred years, and so might not be worrying just yet about what might happen to me in the next world. Or I could point out what you already know from the texts, that every magician hopes to cheat Hell in the end – and as several did who are now nicely ensconced on the calendar as authentic saints.

'But the real fact of the matter, Dr Hess, is that I think what I'm after is worth the risk, and what I'm after is something you understand perfectly, and for which you've sold your own soul, or if you prefer an only slightly less loaded word, your integrity, to Dr Baines – *knowledge*.'

'Uhmn. Surely there must be easier ways –'

'You don't believe that. You think there may be more reliable ways, such as scientific method, but you don't think they're any easier. I myself have the utmost respect for scientific method, but I know that it doesn't offer me the kind of knowledge I'm looking for – which is also knowledge about the makeup of the universe and how it is run, but not a kind that any exact science can provide me with, because the sciences don't accept that some of the forces of nature are Persons. Well, but some of them are. And without dealing with those Persons I shall never know any of the things I want to know.

'This kind of research is just as expensive as underwriting a gigantic particle accelerator, Dr Hess, and obviously I'll never get any government to underwrite it. But people like Dr Baines can, if I can find enough of them – just as they underwrite you.

'Eventually, I may have to pay for what I've learned with a jewel no amount of money could buy. Unlike MacBeth, I know one *can't* "skip the life to come." But even if it does come to that, Dr Hess – and probably it will – I'll take my knowledge with me, and it will have been worth the price.

'In other words – just as you suspected – I'm a fanatic.'

To his own dawning astonishment, Hess said slowly:

'Yes. Yes, of course . . . so am I.'

9

Father Domenico lay in his strange bed on his back, staring sleeplessly up at the pink stucco ceiling. Tonight was the night he had come for. Ware's three days of fasting, lustration and prayer – surely a blasphemous burlesque of such observances as the Church knew them, in intent if not in content – were over, and he had pronounced himself ready to act.

Apparently he still intended to allow Baines and his two repulsive henchmen to observe the conjuration, but if he had ever had any intention of including Father Domenico in the ceremony, he had thought better of it. That was frustrating, as well as a great relief; but in his place, Father Domenico would have done the same thing.

Yet even here, excluded from the scene and surrounded by every protection he had been able to muster, Father Domenico could feel the preliminary oppression, like the dead weather before an earthquake. There was always a similar hush and tension in the air just before the invocation of one of the Celestial Powers, but with none of these overtones of maleficence and disaster . . . or would someone ignorant of what was actually proposed be able to tell the difference? That was a disquieting thought in itself, but one that could practically be left to Bishop Berkeley and the Logical Positivists. Father Domenico knew what was going on – a ritual of supernatural murder; and could not help but tremble in his bed.

Somewhere in the palazzo there was the silvery sound of a small clock striking, distant and sweet. The time was now 10:00 p.m., the fourth hour of Saturn on the day of Saturn, the hour most suitable – as even the blameless and pitiable Peter de Abano had written – for experiments of hatred, enmity and discord; and Father Domenico, under the Covenant, was forbidden even to pray for failure.

The clock, that two-handed engine that stands behind the Door, struck, and struck no more, and Ware drew the brocaded hangings aside.

Up to now, Baines despite himself, had felt a little foolish in the girdled white-linen garment Ware had insisted upon, but he cheered up upon seeing Jack Ginsberg and Dr Hess in the same vestments. As for Ware, he was either comical or terrible, depending upon what view one took of the proceedings, in his white Levite surcoat with red-silk embroidery on the breast, his white leather shoes lettered in cinnabar, and his paper crown bearing the word EL. He was girdled with a belt about three inches wide, which seemed to have been made from the skin of some hairy, lion-coloured animal. Into the girdle was thrust a red-wrapped, sceptre-like object, which Baines identified tentatively from a prior description of Hess's as the wand of power.

'And now we must vest ourselves,' Ware said, almost in a whisper. 'Dr Baines, on the desk you will find three garments. Take one, and then another, and another. Give two to Dr Hess and Mr Ginsberg. Don the other yourself.'

Baines picked up the huddle of cloth. It turned out to be an alb.

'Take up your vestments and lift them in your hands above your heads. At the amen, let them fall. Now:

'ANTON, AMATOR, EMITES, THEODONIEL, PONCOR, PAGOR, ANITOR, *by the virtue of these most holy angelic names do I clothe myself, Lord of Lords, in my Vestments of Power, that so I may fulfil, even unto their term, all things which I desire to effect through Thee,* IDEODANIACH, PAMOR, PLAIOR, *Lord of Lords, Whose kingdom and rule endureth forever and ever. Amen.'*

The garments rustled down, and Ware opened the door.

The room beyond was only vaguely lit with yellow candle-light, and at first bore almost no resemblance to the chamber Dr Hess had described to Baines. As his eyes accommodated, however, Baines was gradually able to see that it was the same room, its margins now indistinct and its furniture slightly differently ordered: only the lectern and the candlesticks – there were now four of them, not two – were moved out from the walls and hence more or less visible.

But it was still confusing, a welter of flickering shadows and slightly sickening perfume, most unlike the blueprint of the room that Baines had erected in his mind from Hess's drawing. The thing that dominated the real room itself was also a drawing, not any piece of furniture or detail of architecture: a vast double circle on the floor in what appeared to be white-wash. Between the concentric circles were written innumerable words, or what might have been words, in characters which might have been Hebrew, Greek, Etruscan or even Elvish for all Baines could tell. Some few were in Roman lettering, but they, too, were names he could not recognize; and around the outside of the outer circle were written astrological signs in their zodiacal order, but with Saturn to the north.

At the very centre of this figure was a ruled square about two feet on a side, from each corner of which proceeded chalked, conventionalized crosses, which did not look in the least Christian. Proceeding from each of these, but not connected to them, were four six-pointed stars, verging on the innermost circle. The stars at the east, west and south each had a Taū scrawled at their centres; presumably the Saturnmost did too, but if so it could not be seen, for the heart of that emplacement was hidden by what seemed to be a fat puddle of stippled fur.

Outside the circles, at the other compass points, were drawn four pentagrams, in the chords of which were written TE TRA GRAM MA TON, and at the centres of which stood the candles. Farthest away from all this – about two feet outside the circle and three feet over it to the north – was a circle enclosed by a triangle, also much lettered inside and out; Baines could just see that the characters in the angles of the triangle read NI CH EL.

'Tanists,' Ware whispered, pointing into the circle, 'take your places.'

He went towards the long table Hess had described and vanished in the gloom. As instructed, Baines walked into the circle and stood in the western star; Hess followed, taking the eastern; and Ginsberg, very slowly, crept into the southern. To the north, the puddle of fur revolved once widdershins and resettled itself with an unsettling sigh, making Jack Ginsberg jump. Baines inspected it belatedly. Probably it was only a cat, as was supposed to be traditional, but in this light it looked more like a badger. Whatever it was, it was obscenely fat.

Ware reappeared, carrying a sword. He entered the circle, closed it with the point of the sword, and proceeded to the central square, where he laid the sword across the toes of his white shoes; then he drew the wand from his belt and unwrapped it, laying the red-silk cloth across his shoulders.

'From now on,' he said, in a normal, even voice, 'no one is to move.'

From somewhere inside his vestments he produced a small crucible, which he set at his feet before the recumbent sword. Small blue flames promptly began to rise from the bowl, and Ware cast incense into it. He said:

'Holocaust. Holocaust. Holocaust.'

The flames in the brazier rose slightly.

'We are to call upon MARCHOSIAS, a great marquis of the Descending Hierarchy,' Ware said in the same conversational voice. 'Before he fell, he belonged to the Order of Dominations among the angels, and thinks to return to the Seven Thrones after twelve hundred years. His virtue is that he gives true answers. Stand fast, all.'

With a sudden motion, Ware thrust the end of his rod into the surging flames of the brazier. At once the air of the hall rang with a long, frightful chain of woeful howls. Above the bestial clamour. Ware shouted:

'I adjure thee, great MARCHOSIAS, as the agent of Emperor LUCIFER, and of his beloved son LUCIFUGE ROFOCALE, by the power of the pact I have with thee, and by the Names ADONAY, ELOIM, JEHOVAM, TAGLA, MATHON, ALMOUZIN, ARIOS, PITHONA, MAGOTS, SYLPHAE, TABOTS, SALAMANDRAE, GNOMUS, TERRAE, COELIS, GODENS, AQUA, and by the whole hierarchy of superior intelligences who shall constrain thee against thy will, *venite, venite, submiritillor* MARCHOSIAS!'

The noise rose higher, and a green steam began to come off the brazier. It smelt like someone was burning hart's horn and fish gall. But there was no other answer. His face white and cruel, Ware rasped over the tumult:

'I adjure thee, MARCHOSIAS, by the pact, and by the names, appear instanter!' He plunged the rod a second time into the flames. The room screamed; but still there was no apparition.

'Now I adjure thee, LUCIFUGE ROFOCALE, whom I command, as the agent of the Lord and Emperor of Lords, send me thy messenger MARCHOSIAS, forcing him to forsake his hiding place, wheresoever it may be, and warning thee –'

The rod went back into the fire. Instantly, the palazzo rocked as though the earth had moved under it.

'Stand fast!' Ware said hoarsely.

Something Else said:

HUSH, I AM HERE. WHAT DOST THOU SEEK OF ME? WHY DOST THOU DISTURB MY REPOSE? LET MY FATHER REST, AND HOLD THY ROD.

Never had Baines heard a voice like that before. It seemed to speak in syllables of burning ashes.

'Hadst thou appeared when first I invoked thee, I had by no means smitten thee, nor called thy father,' Ware said. 'Remember, if the request I make of thee be refused, I shall thrust again my rod into the fire.'

THINK AND SEE!

The palazzo shuddered again. Then, from the middle of the triangle to the northwest, a slow cloud of yellow fumes went up towards the ceiling, making them all cough, even Ware. As it spread and thinned, Baines could see a shape forming under it; but he found it impossible to believe. It was – it was something like a she-wolf, grey and immense, with green and glistening eyes. A wave of coldness was coming from it.

The cloud continued to dissipate. The she-wolf glared at them, slowly spreading her griffin's wings. Her serpent's tail lashed gently, scalily.

In the northern pentacle, the great Abyssinian cat sat up and stared back. The demon-wolf showed her teeth and emitted a disgusting belch of fire. The cat settled its front feet indifferently.

'Stand, by the Seal,' Ware said. 'Stand and transform, else I shall plunge thee back whence thou camest. I command thee.'

The she-wolf vanished, leaving behind in the triangle a plump, modest-looking young man wearing a decorous necktie, a dildo almost as long and nothing else. 'Sorry, boss' he said in a sugary voice 'I had to try, you know. What's up?'

'Don't try to wheedle me, vision of stupidity,' Ware said harshly. 'Transform, I demand of thee, thou'rt wasting thy father's time, and mine! Transform!'

The young man stuck out his tongue which was copper-green. A moment later, the triangle was occupied by a black bearded man apparently twice his age, wearing a forest-green robe rimmed in ermine and a glittering crown. It hurt Baines's eyes to look at it. An odour of sandalwood began slowly to diffuse through the room.

'That's better,' Ware said. 'Now I charge thee, by those Names I have named and on pain of those torments thou hast known, to regard the likeness and demesne of that mortal whose eidolon I hold in my hand, and that when I release thee, thou shalt straightaway go unto him, not making thyself known unto him, but revealing, as it were to come from his own intellectual soul, a vision and understanding of that great and ultimate Nothingness which lurks behind those signs he calls matter and energy, as thou wilt see it in his private forebodings, and that thou remainest with him and deepen his despair without remittal, until such time as he shall despise his soul for its endeavours, and destroy the life of his body.'

'I cannot give thee,' the crowned figure said, in a voice deep but somehow lacking all resonance, 'what thou requirest.'

'Refusal will not avail thee,' Ware said, 'for either shalt thou go incontinently and perform what I comand, or I shall in no wise dismiss thee, but shall keep thee here unto my life's end, and torment thee daily, as thy father permitteth.'

'Thy life itself, though it last seven hundred years, is but a day to me,' said the crowned figure. Sparks issued from its nostrils as it spoke. 'And thy torments but a farthing of those I have endured since ere the cosmic egg was hatched, and Eve invented.'

For answer, Ware again stabbed the rod into the fire, which, Baines noted numbly, failed even to scorch it. But the crowned figure threw back its bearded head and howled desolately. Ware withdrew the rod, but only by a hand's breadth.

'I shall go as thou commandest,' the creature said sullenly. Hatred oozed from it like lava.

'Be it not performed exactly, I shall call thee up again,' Ware said. 'But be it executed, for thy pay thou shalt carry off the immortal part of the subject thou shalt tempt, which is as yet spotless in the sight of Heaven, and a great prize.'

'But not yet enough,' said the demon. 'For thou must give me also somewhat of thine hoard, as it is written in the pact.'

'Thou art slow to remember the pact,' Ware said. 'But I would deal fairly with thee, knowing marquis. Here.'

He reached into his robe and drew out something minute and colourless, which flashed in the candlelight. At first, Baines took it to be a diamond, but as Ware held it out, he recognized it as an opalescent, crystal tear vase, the smallest he had ever seen, stopper, contents and all. This Ware tossed, underhand, out of the circle to the fuming figure, which to Baines's new astonishment – for he had forgotten that what he was really looking at had first exhibited as a beast – caught it skilfully in its mouth and swallowed it.

'Thou dost only tantalize MARCHOSIAS,' the Presence said.

'When I have thee in Hell, magician, then shall I drink thee dry, though thy tears flow never so copiously.'

'Thy threats are empty. I am not marked for thee, shouldst thou see me in Hell forever,' Ware said. 'Enough, ungrateful monster. Cease thy witless plaudering and discharge thine errand. I dismiss thee.'

The crowned figure snarled, and then, suddenly, reverted to the form in which it had first showed itself. It vomited a great gout of fire, but the surge failed to pass the wall of the triangle; instead, it collected in a ball around the demon itself. Nevertheless, Baines could feel the heat against his face. Ware raised his wand.

The floor inside the small circle vanished. The apparition clashed its brazen wings and dropped like a stone. With a rending thunderclap, the floor healed seamlessly.

Then there was silence. As the ringing in Baines's ears died away, he became aware of a distant thrumming sound as though someone had left a car idling in the street in front of the palazzo. Then he realized what it was: the great cat was purring. It had watched the entire proceedings with nothing more than grave interest. So, apparently, had Hess. Ginsberg seemed to be jittering, but he was standing his ground. Although he had never seen Jack rattled before, Baines could hardly blame him; he himself felt sick and giddy, as though just the effort of looking at MARCHOSIAS had been equivalent to having scrambled for days up some Himalayan glacier.

'It is over,' Ware said in a grey whisper. He looked very old. Taking up his sword, he cut the diagram with it, 'Now we must wait. I will be in seclusion for two weeks. Then we will consult again. The circle is open. You may leave.'

Father Domenico heard the thunderclap, distant and muffled, and knew that the sending had been made – and that he was forbidden, now as before, even to pray for the soul of the victim (or the patient, in Ware's antiseptic Aristotelian terminology). Sitting up and swinging his feet over the edge of the bed, breathing with difficulty in the musky, detumescent air, he walked unsteadily to his satchel and opened it.

Why – that was the question – did God so tie his hands, why

did He allow such a compromise as the Covenant at all? It suggested, at least, some limitation in His power unallowable by the firm dogma of Omnipotence, which it was a sin even to question; or, at worst, some ambiguity in His relationship with Hell, one quite outside the revealed answers to the Problem of Evil.

That last was a concept too terrible to bear thinking about. Probably it was attributable purely to the atmosphere here; in any event, Father Domenico knew that he was in no spiritual or emotional condition to examine it now.

He could, however, examine with possible profit a minor but related question: Was the evil just done the evil Father Domenico had been sent to oversee? There was every immediate reason to suppose that it was – and if it was, then Father Domenico could go home tomorrow, ravaged but convalescent.

On the other hand it was possible – dreadful but in a way also hopeful – that Father Domenico had been commanded to Hell-mouth to await the emission of something worse. That would resolve the puzzling anomaly that Ware's latest undertaking, abominable though they all were, was for Ware not unusual. Much more important, it would explain at least in part, why the Covenant existed at all: in Tolstoy's words, 'God sees the truth, but waits.'

And this question, at least, Father Domenico need not simply ponder, but could actively submit to the Divine guidance, even here, even now, provided that he call upon no Presences. That restriction was not prohibitive; what was he a magician for, if not to be as subtle in his works as in his praise?

Inkhorn, quill, straightedge, three different discs of different sizes cut from virgin cardboard – not an easy thing to come by – and the wrapped burin came out of the satchel and were arranged on top of his dresser, which would serve well enough for a desk. On the cardboard discs he carefully inscribed three different scales: the A camerae of sixteen divine attributes, from *bonitas* to *patientia*; the T camerae of thirty attributes of things, from *temporis* to *negatio*; and the E camerae of the nine questions, from *whether* to *how great*. He centrepunched all three discs with the burin, pinned them together with a cuff link and finally asperged the assembled Lull Engine with holy water from the satchel. Over it he said:

'I conjure thee, O form of this instrument, by the authority of God the Father Almighty, by the virtue of Heaven and the stars, by that of the elements, by that of stones and herbs, and in like manner by the virtue of snowstorms, thunder and winds, and belike also by the virtue of the *Ars magna* in whose figure thou art drawn, that thou receive all power unto the performance of those things in the perfection of which we are concerned, the whole without trickery, falsehood or deception, by the command of God, Creator of the Angels and Emperor of the Ages. DAMAHII, LUMECH, GADAL, PANCIA, VELOAS, MEOROD, LAMIDOCH, BALDACH, ANERETHON, MITRATON, most holy angels, be ye wardens of this instrument. *Domine, Deus meus, in te speravi. . . . Confitebor tibi, Domine, in toto corde meo. . . . Quemadmodum desiderat cervus ad fontes aquarum. . . .* Amen.'

This said, Father Domenico took up the engine and turned the circles against each other. Lull's great art was not easy to use; most of the possible combinations of any group of wheels were trivial, and it took reason to see which were important, and faith to see which were inspired. Nevertheless, it had one advantage over all other forms of scrying: it was not in any strict sense, a form of magic.

He turned the wheels at random the required number of times, and then, taking the outermost by its edge, shook it to the four quarters of the sky. He was almost afraid to look at the result.

But on that very first essay, the engine had generated:

PATIENCE /BECOMING/REALITY

It was the answer he had both feared and hoped for. And it was, he realized with a subdued shock, the only answer he could have expected on Christmas Eve.

He put the engine and the tools back in his satchel, and crept away into the bed. In his state of over-exhaustion and alarm, he did not expect to sleep . . . but within two turns of the glass he was no longer in the phenomenal world, but was dreaming instead that, like Gerbert the magician-Pope, he was fleeing the Holy Office down the wind astride a devil.

10

Ware's period of recovery did not last quite as long as he had prophesied. He was visibly up and about by Twelfth Night. By that time, Baines – though only Jack Ginsberg could see and read the signs – was chafing at the inaction. Jack had to remind him that in any event at least two months were supposed to pass before the suicide of Dr Stockhausen could even be expected, and suggested that in the interim they all go back to Rome and to work.

Baines shrugged the suggestion off. Whatever else was on his mind, it did not seem to involve Consolidated Warfare Service's interests more than marginally . . . or, at least, the thought of business could not distract him beyond the making of a small number of daily telephone calls.

The priest or monk or whatever he was, Father Domenico, was still in attendance too. Evidently he had not been taken in by the show. Well, that was Ware's problem, presumably. All the same, Jack stayed out of sight of the cleric as much as possible; having him around, Jack recalled in a rare burst of association with his Bronx childhood, was a little like being visited by a lunatic Orthodox relative during a crucial marriage brokerage.

Not so lunatic at that, though; for if magic really worked – as Jack had had to see that it did – then the whole tissue of metaphysical assumptions Father Domenico stood for, from Moses through the Kabbalah to the New Testament, had to follow, as a matter of logic. After this occurred to Jack, he not only hated to see Father Domenico, but had nightmares in which he felt that Father Domenico was looking back at him.

Ware himself, however, did not emerge officially, to be talked to, until his predicted fourteenth day. Then, to Jack's several-sides disquietude, the first person he called into his office was Jack Ginsberg.

Jack wanted to talk to Ware only slightly more than he wanted to talk to the barefooted, silently courteous Father Domenico; and the effect upon Baines of Ware's singling Jack out for the first post-conjuration interview, though under ordinary circumstances it could have been discounted as minor, could not even be conjectured in Baines's present odd state of mind. After a troubled hour, Jack took the problem to Baines, not even sure any more of his own delicacy in juggling such an egg.

'Go ahead,' was all Baines said. He continued to give Jack the impression of a man whose mind was not to be turned more than momentarily from some all-important thought. That was alarming, too, but there seemed to be nothing to be done about it. Setting his face into its business mould of pleasant attentiveness, over slightly clenched teeth, Jack marched up to Ware's office.

The sunlight there was just as bright and innocent as ever, pouring directly in from the sea-sky on top of the cliff. Jack felt slightly more in contact with what he had used to think of as real life. In some hope of taking the initiative away from Ware and keeping it, he asked the magician, even before sitting down, 'Is there some news already?'

'None at all,' Ware said. 'Sit down, please. Dr Stockhausen is a tough patient, as I warned you all at the beginning. It's possible that he won't fall at all, in which case a far more strenuous endeavour will be required. But in the meantime I'm assuming that he will, and that I therefore ought to be preparing for Dr Baines's next commission. That's why I wanted to see you first.'

'I haven't any idea what Dr Baines's next commission is,' Jack said, 'and if I did I wouldn't tell you before he did.'

'You have a remorselessly literal mind, Mr Ginsberg. I'm not trying to pump you. I already know, and it's enough for the time being, that Mr Baines's next commission will be something major – perhaps even a unique experiment in the history of the Art. Father Domenico's continued presence here suggests the same sort of thing. Very well, if I'm to tackle such a project, I'll need assistants – and I have no remaining apprentices. They become ambitious very early and either make stupid technical mistakes or have to be dismissed for disobedience. Laymen, even sympathetic laymen, are equally mischancy, simply because of their eagerness and ignorance. but if they're highly intelligent, it's sometimes safe to use them. Sometimes. Given those disclaimers, that explains why I allowed you *and* Dr Hess to watch the Christmas Eve affair, not just Dr Hess, whom Dr Baines had asked for, and why I want to talk to you now.'

'I see,' Jack said. 'I suppose I should be flattered.'

Ware sat back in his chair and raised his hands as if exasperated. 'Not at all. I see that I'd better be blunt. I was quite satisfied with Dr Hess's potentialities and so don't need to talk to him any more, except to instruct him. But I am none too happy with yours. You strike me as a weak reed.'

'I'm no magician,' Jack said, holding on to his temper. 'If there's some hostility between us, it's only fair to recognize that I'm not its sole cause. You went out of your way to insult me at our very first interview, only because I was normally suspicious of your pretensions, as I was supposed to be, on behalf of my job. I'm not easily offended, Dr Ware, but I'm more cooperative if people are reasonably polite to me.'

'*Stercor*,' Ware said. The word meant nothing to Jack. 'You keeping thinking I'm talking about public relations, and getting along with people, and all that goose grease. Far from it. A little hatred never hurts the Art, and studied insult is valuable in dealing with demons – there are only a few who can be flattered to any profit, and if man who can be flattered isn't a man at all, he's a dog. Do try to understand me, Mr Ginsberg. What I'm talking about is neither your footling hostility nor your unexpectedly slow brains, but your rabbit's courage. There was a moment during the last ceremony when I could see that you were going to step out of your post. You didn't know it, but I had to paralyze you, and I saved your life. If you had moved you would have endangered all of us, and had that happened I would have thrown you to MARCHOSIAS like an old bone. It wouldn't have saved the purpose of the ceremony, but it would have kept the demon from gobbling up everybody else but Ahktoi.'

'Ach . . .?'

'My familiar. The cat.'

'Oh. Why not the cat?'

'He's on loan. He belongs to another demon – my patron. Do stop changing the subject, Mr Ginsberg. If I'm going to trust you as a Tanist in a great work, I'm going to have to be reasonably sure that you'll stand fast when I tell you to stand fast, no matter what you see or hear, and that when I ask you to take some small part in the ritual, you'll do it accurately and punctually. Can you assure me of this?'

'Well,' Jack said earnestly, 'I'll do my best.

'But what for? Why do you want to sell me? I don't know what you mean by your 'best' until I know what's in it for you, besides just keeping you your job – or making a good impression on me because it's a reflex with you to make a good impression on people. Explain this to me, please! I know that there's something in this situation that hits you where you live. I could see that from the outset, but my first guess as to what it was evidently was wrong, or anyhow not central. Well, what *is* central to you: the situation has now ripened to the point when you're going to have to tell me what it is. Otherwise I shall shut you out, and that will be that.'

Wobbling between unconventional hope and standard caution, Jack pushed himself out of the Florentine chair and toe-heel-toed to the window, adjusting his tie automatically. From this height, the cliff-clinging apartments of Positano fell away to the narrow beach like so many Roman tenements crowded with deposed kings – and with beach boys hoping to pick up an American heiress for the season. Except for the curling waves and a few distant birds, the scene was motionless, yet somehow to Jack it seemed to be slowly, inexorably sliding into the sea.

'Sure, I like women,' he said in a low voice. 'And I've got special preferences I don't find it easy to satisfy, even with all the money I make. For one thing, in my job I'm constantly working with classified material – secrets – either some government's, or the company's. That means I don't dare put myself into a position where I could be blackmailed.'

'Which is why you refused my offer when we first talked.' Ware said. 'That was discreet, but unnecessary. As you've probably realized by now, neither spying nor extortion has any attraction for me – the potential income from either or both would be a pittance to me.'

'Yes, but I won't always have you around,' Jack said, turning back towards the desk. 'And I'd be stupid to form new tastes that only you could keep supplied.'

' "Pander to" is the expression. Let's be precise. Nevertheless, you have some remedy in mind. Otherwise you wouldn't be being even this frank.'

'Yes . . . I do. It occurred to me when you agreed to allow Hess to tour your laboratory.' He was halted by another stab of jealousy, no less acute for being half reminiscent. Drawing a deep breath, he went on, 'I want to learn the Art.'

'Oho. That *is* a reversal.'

'You said it was possible,' Jack said in a rush, emboldened by a desperate sense of having now nothing to lose. 'I know you said you don't take apprentices, but I wouldn't be trying to stab you in the back or take over your clients, I'd only be using the Art for my specialized purposes. I couldn't pay you any fortune, but I do have money. I could do the reading in my spare time, and come back after a year or so for the actual instruction. I think Baines would give me a sabbatical for that – he wants somebody on his staff to know the Art, at least the theory, only he thinks it's going to be Hess. But Hess will be too busy with his own sciences to do a thorough job of it.'

'You really hate Dr Hess, don't you?'

'We don't impinge,' Jack said stiffly. 'Anyhow what I say is true. I could be a lot better expert from Baines's point of view than Hess ever could.'

'Do you have a sense of humour, Mr Ginsberg?'

'Certainly. everybody does.'

'Untrue,' Ware said. 'Everybody claims to have, that's all. I ask only because the first thing to be sacrificed to the Art is the gift of laughter, and some people would miss it more than others. Yours seems to be residual at best. In you it would probably be a minor operation, like an appendectomy.'

'You don't seem to have lost yours.'

'You confuse humour with wit, like most people. The two are as different as creativity and scholarship. However, as I say, in your case it's not a great consideration, obviously. But there may be greater ones. For example, what tradition I would be training you in. For instance, I could make a kabbalistic magician of you, which would give you a substantial grounding in white magic. And for the black, I could teach you most of what's in the *Clavicle* and the *Lemegeton*, cutting out the specifically Christian accretions. Would that content you, do you think?'

'Maybe, if it met my primary requirements,' Jack said. 'But if I had to go on from there, I wouldn't care. These days I'm a Jew only by birth, not by culture – and up until Christmas Eve I was an atheist. Now I don't know what I am. All I know is, I've got to believe what I see.'

'Not in this Art,' Ware said. 'But we'll think of you as a *tabula rasa* for the time being. Well, Mr Ginsberg, I'll consider it. But before I decide, I think you ought to explore further your insight about special tastes becoming satisfiable only through magic, whether mine or yours. You like to think how delightful it would be to enjoy them freely and without fear of consequences, but it often happens – you'll remember Oscar Wilde's epigram on the subject – that fulfilled desire isn't a delight, but a cross.'

'I'll take the chance.'

'Don't be so hasty. You have no real idea of the risks. Suppose you should find, for example, that no human woman could please you any more, and you'd become dependent on succubi? I don't know how much you know of the theory of such a relationship. In general, the revolt in heaven involved angels from every order in the hierarchy. And of the Fallen, only those who fell from the lowest ranks are assigned to this sort of duty. By comparison, MARCHOSIAS is a paragon of nobility. These creatures have even lost their names, and there's nothing in the least grand about their malignancy – they are pure essences of narrow meanness and petty spite, the kind of spirit a Sicilian milkmaid calls on to make her rival's toenails split, or give an unfaithful lover a pimple on the end of his nose.'

'That doesn't make them sound much different from ordinary women,' Jack said, shrugging. 'So long as they deliver, what does it matter? Presumably, as a magician I'd have *some* control over how they behaved.'

'Yes. Nevertheless, why be persuaded out of desire and ignorance, when an experiment is available to you? In fact, Mr Ginsberg, I would not trust any resolution you made from the state of simple fantasy you're in now. If you won't try the experiment, I must refuse your petition.'

'Now wait a minute,' Jack said. 'Why are you so urgent about this, anyhow? What kind of advantage do you get out of it?'

'I've already told you that,' Ware said patiently. 'I will probably need you as a Tanist in Dr Baines's major enterprise. I want to be able to trust you to stand fast, and I won't be able to do that without being sure of your degree and kind of commitment.'

Everything that Ware said seemed to have behind it the sound of doors softly closing in Jack's face. And on the other hand, the possibilities – the opportunities . . .

'What,' he said, 'do I need to do?'

11

The palazzo was asleep. In the distance, that same oblivious clock struck eleven; the proper hour of this day, Ware had said, for experiments in venery. Jack waited nervously for it to stop, or for something to begin.

His preparations were all made, but he was uncertain whether any of them had been necessary. After all, if the . . . girl . . . who was to come to him was to be totally amenable to his wishes, why should he have to impress her?

Nevertheless, he had gone through all the special rituals, bathing for an hour, shaving twice, trimming his finger- and toenails and buffing them, brushing his hair back for thirty strokes and combing it with the West German tonic that was said to have allatoin in it, dressing in his best silk pyjamas, smoking jacket (though he neither smoked nor drank), ascot and Venetian-leather slippers, adding a dash of cologne and scattering a light film of talcum powder inside the bed. Maybe, he thought, part of the pleasure would be in taking all the trouble and having everything work.

The clock stopped striking. Almost at once there was a slow triple knock at the door, so slow that each soft blow seemed like an independent act. Jack's heart bounded like a boy's. Pulling the sash of his jacket tighter, he said as instructed:

'Come in . . . come in . . . come in.'

He opened the door. As Ware had told him to expect, there was no one in the dark corridor outside; but when he closed the door and turned around, there she was.

'Good evening,' she said in a light voice with the barest trace of an accent – or was it a lisp? 'I am here, as you invited me. Do you like me?'

It was not the same girl who had brought the letter to Ware, so many weeks ago, though she somehow reminded him of someone he had once known, he could not think who. This one was positively beautiful. She was small – half a head shorter than Jack, slender and apparently only about eighteen – and very fair, with blue eyes and a fresh, innocent expression, which was doubly piquant because the lines of her features were patrician, her skin so delicate that it was almost like fine parchment.

She was fully clothed, in spike heels, patterned but otherwise sheer stockings, and a short-sleeved, expensively tailored black dress of some material like rayon, which clung to her breasts, waist and upper hips as though electrified, and then burst into a full skirt like an inverted tulip, breaking just above the knees. Wire-thin silver bracelets slid and tinkled almost inaudibly on her left wrist as she ruffled her chrysanthemum petal coiffure, and small silver earrings echoed them; between her breasts was a circular onyx brooch inlaid in silver with the word *Cazotte*, set off by a ruby about the size of a fly's eye, the only touch of colour in the entire costume; even her make-up was the Italian 'white look,' long out of style but so exaggerating her paleness as to look almost theatrical on her – almost, but not quite.

'Yes,' he said, remembering to breathe.

'Ah, you make up your mind so soon. Perhaps you are wrong.' She pirouetted away from him towards the bed, making the black tulip flare, and lace foam under its corolla and around her legs with a dry rustling. She stopped the spin facing him, so suddenly that the skirts snapped above her knees like banners in a stiff gust. She seemed wholly human.

'Impossible,' Jack said, mustering all his gallantry. 'I think you're exquisite. Uh, what shall I call you?'

'Oh, I do not come when called. You will have to exert yourself more than that. But my name could be Rita, if you need one.'

She lifted the front of the skirts up over the welts of her stockings, which cut her white thighs only a few inches beneath the vase of her pelvis, and sat down daintily on the side of the bed. 'You are very distant,' she said, pouting. 'Perhaps you suspect I am only pretty on the outside. That would be unfair.'

'Oh no, I'm sure –'

'But how can you be sure yet?' She drew up her heels. 'You must come and see.'

The clock was striking four when she arose, naked and wet, yet somehow looking as though she was still on high heels, and began to dip up her clothes from the floor. Jack watched this little ballet in a dizziness half exhaustion and half triumph. He had hardly enough strength left to wiggle a toe, but he had already surprised himself so often that he still had hopes, Nothing had ever been like this before, nothing.

'Must you go?' he said sluggishly.

'Oh yes, I have other business yet.'

'Other business? But – didn't you have a good time?'

'A – good time?' the girl turned towards him, stopping in the act of fastening a garter strap. 'I am thy servant and thy lamia, Eve-fruit, but thou must not mock me.'

'I don't understand,' Jack said, struggling to lift his head from the bunched, sweaty pillow.

'Then keep silent.' She resumed assembling herself.

'But . . . you seemed . . .'

She turned to him again. 'I gave thee pleasure. Congratulate thyself. That is enough. Thou knowest well what I am. I take no pleasure in anything. It is not permitted. Be grateful, and I shall come to thee again. But mock me, and I shall send thee instead a hag with an ass's tail.'

'I meant no offence,' he said, half sullenly.

'See thou dost not. Thou hadst pleasure with me, that sufficeth. Thou must prove thy virility with mortal flesh. Thy potency, that I go to try even now. It comes on to night i' the other side of the world, and I must plant thy seed before it dies in my fires – if it ever it lived at all.'

'What do you mean?' he said, in a hoarse whisper.

'Have no fear, I shall be back tomorrow. But in the next span of the dark I must change suit.' The dress fell down over the impossibly pliant body. 'I become an incubus now, and a woman waits for that, diverted from her husband by the two-fold way. Reach I her in time, thou shalt father a child, on a woman thou shalt never even see. Is that not a wonder? And a fearful child it shall be, I promise thee!'

She smiled at him. Behind her lids now, he saw with nausea and shame, there were no longer any eyes – only blankly flickering lights, like rising sparks in a flue. She was now as fully dressed as she had been at the beginning, and curtsied gravely.

'Wait for me . . . unless, of course, thou dost not want me back tomorrow night . . . ?'

He tried not to answer, but the words came out like clots of poisonous gas.

'Yes . . . oh God . . .'

Cupping both hands over her hidden groin in a gesture of obscene conservatism, she popped into nothingness like a bursting balloon, and the whole weight of the dawn fell upon Jack like the mountains of St John the Divine.

12

Dr Stockhausen died on St Valentine's day, after three days' fruitless attempts by surgeons from all over the world, even the USSR, to save him from the effects of a draught of a hundred minims of tincture of iodine. The surgery and hospital care were all free; but he died intestate, and it appeared that his small estate – a few royalties from his books and the remains of a ten-year-old Nobel Prize – would be tied up indefinitely; especially in view of the note he left behind, out of which no tribunal, whether scientific or judicial, could hope to separate the mathematics from the ravings for generations to come.

Funds were gathered for his grandchildren and divorced daughter to tide them over; but the last book that he had been writing turned out to be so much like the note that his publishers' referees could think of no colleague to whom it could reasonably be offered for posthumous collaboration. It was said that his brain would be donated to the museum of the Deutsches Akademie in Munich – again only if his affairs could ever be probated. Within three days after the funeral, however, Ware was able to report, both brain and manuscript had vanished.

'MARCHOSIAS may have taken one or both of them,' Ware said. 'I didn't tell him to, since I didn't want to cause any more suffering to Albert's relatives than was inevitable under the terms of the commission. On the other hand, I didn't tell him not to, either. But the commission itself has been executed.'

'Very good,' Baines said. He was, in fact, elated. Of the other three people in the office with Ware – for Ware had said there was no way to prevent Father Domenico from attending – none looked as pleased as Baines felt, but after all he was the only man who counted here, the only one to whose emotions Ware need pay any more than marginal attention. 'And much faster than you had anticipated, too. I'm very well satisfied, and also I'm now quite ready to discuss my major commission with you, Dr Ware, if the planets and so on don't make this a poor time to talk about it.'

'The planetary influences exert almost no effect upon simple discussion,' Ware said, 'only on specific preparations – and of course on the experiment itself. And I'm quite rested and ready to listen. In fact, I'm in an acute state of curiosity. Please charge right in and tell me about it.'

'I would like to let all the major demons out of Hell for one night, turn them loose in the world with no orders and no restrictions – except of course that they go back by dawn or some other sensible time – and see just what it is they would do if they were left on their own hooks like that.'

'Insanity!' Father Domenico cried out, crossing himself. 'Now surely the man is possessed already!'

'For once, I'm inclined to agree with you, Father,' Ware said, 'though with some reservations about the possession question. For all we can know now, it's entirely in character. Tell me this, Dr Baines, what do you hope to accomplish through an experiment on so colossal a scale?'

'Experiment!' Father Domenico said, his face as white as the dead.

'If you can do no more than echo, Father, I think we'd all prefer that you kept silent – at least until we find out what it is we're talking about.'

'I will say what I need to say, when I think it is needful,' Father Domenico said angrily. 'This thing that you're minimizing by calling it an 'experiment' might well end in the dawn of Armageddon!'

'Then you should welcome it, not fear it, since you're convinced your side must win,' Ware said. 'But actually there's no such risk. The results may well be rather Apocalyptic, but Armageddon requires the prior appearance of the Antichrist, and I assure you I am not he . . . nor do I see anybody else in the world who might qualify. Now, again, Dr Baines, what do you hope to accomplish through this?'

'Nothing *through* it,' Baines, now totally caught up in the vision, said dreamily. 'Only the thing itself – for its aesthetic interest alone. A work of art, if you like. A gigantic action painting, with the world for a canvas –'

'And human blood for pigments,' Father Domenico ground out.

Ware held up his hand, palm towards the monk. 'I had thought,' he said to Baines, 'that this was the art you practised already, and in effect sold the resulting canvasses, too.'

'The sales kept me able to continue practising it,' Baines said, but he was beginning to find the metaphor awkward, his though it had originally been. 'Look at it this way for a moment, Dr Ware. Very roughly, there are only two general kinds of men who go into the munitions business – those without consciences, who see the business as an avenue to a great fortune, eventually to be used for something else, like Jack here – and of course there's a subclass of those, people who *do* have consciences but can't resist the money anyhow, or the knowledge, rather like Dr Hess.'

Both men stirred, but apparently both decided not to dispute their portraits.

'The second kind is made up of people like me – people who actually take pleasure in the controlled production of chaos and destruction. Not sadists primarily, except in the sense that every dedicated artist is something of a sadist, willing to countenance a little or a lot of suffering – not only his own, but other people's – for the sake of the end product.'

'A familiar type, to be sure,' Ware said with a lopsided grin. 'I think it was the saintly Robert Frost who said that a painting by Whistler was worth any number of old ladies.'

'Engineers are like this too,' Baines said, warming rapidly to his demonstration; he had been thinking about almost nothing else since the conjuration he had attended. 'There's a breed I know much better than I do artists, and I can tell you that most of them wouldn't build a thing if it weren't for the kick they get out of the preliminary demolitions involved. A common thief with a gun in his hand isn't half as dangerous as an engineer with a stick of dynamite.

'But in my case, just as in the case of the engineer, the key word is 'controlled' – and, in the munitions business, it's rapidly becoming an obsolete word, thanks to nuclear weapons.'

He went on quickly to sketch his dissatisfactions, very much as they had first come to a head in Rome while Governor Rogan was being sent for. 'So now you can see what appeals to me about the commission I propose. It won't be a series of mass obliterations under nobody's control, but a whole set of individual actions, each in itself on a comparatively small scale – and each one, I'm sure, interesting in itself because of all the different varieties of ingenuity and surprise to be involved. And it won't be total because it will also be self-limiting to some small period of time, presumably twelve hours or less.'

Father Domenico leaned forward earnestly. 'Surely,' he said to Ware, 'even you can see that no human being, no matter how sinful and self-indulgent, could have elaborated anything so monstrous without the direct intervention of Hell!'

'On the contrary,' Ware said, 'Dr Baines is quite right, most dedicated secularists think exactly as he does – only on a somewhat smaller scale. For your further comfort, Father, I am somewhat privy to the affairs of Hell, and I investigate all my major clients thoroughly. I can tell you that Dr Baines is *not* possessed. But all the same there are still a few mysteries here. Dr Baines, I still think you may be resorting to too big a brush for the intended canvas, and might get the effects you want entirely without my help. For example, why won't the forthcoming Sino-Russian War be enough for you?'

Baines swallowed hard. 'So that's really going to happen?'

'It's written down to happen. It still might not, but I wouldn't bet against it. Very likely it won't be a major nuclear war – three fusion bombs, one Chinese, two Soviet, plus about twenty fission explosions, and then about a year of conventional land war. No other powers are at all likely to become involved. You know this, Dr Baines, and I should think it would please you. After all, it's almost exactly the way your firm has been trying to pre-set it.'

'You're full of consolations today,' Father Domenico muttered.

'Well, in fact, I *am* damn pleased to hear it,' Baines said. 'It isn't often that you plan something that big and have it come off almost as planned. But no, Dr Ware, it won't be enough for me, because it's still too general and difficult to follow – or will be. I'm having a little trouble with my tenses. For one thing, it won't be sufficiently attributable to me – many people have been working to bring that war about. This experiment will be on my initiative alone.'

'Not an insuperable objection,' Ware said. 'A good many Renaissance artists didn't object to collaborators – even journeymen.'

'Well, the spirit of the times has changed, if you want an abstract answer. The real answer is that I *do* object. Furthermore, Dr Ware, I want to choose my own medium. War doesn't satisfy me any more. It's too sloppy, too subject to accident. It excuses too much.'

'?' Ware said with an eyebrow.

'I mean that in time of war, especially in Asia, people expect the worst and try to ride with the punches, no matter how terrible they are, In peacetime, on the other hand, even a small misfortune comes as a total surprise. People complain, "Why did this have to happen to *me*?" – as though they'd never heard of Job.'

'Rewriting Job is the humanist's favourite pastime,' Ware agreed. 'And his favourite political platform too. So in fact, Dr Baines, you *do* want to afflict people, just where they're most sensitive to being afflicted, and just when they least expect it, right or wrong. Do I understand you correctly?'

Baines had the sinking feeling that he had explained too much, but there was no help for that now; and, in any event, Ware was hardly himself a saint.

'You do,' he said shortly.

'Thank you. That clears the air enormously. One more question. How do you propose to pay for all this?'

Father Domenico surged to his feet with a strangled gasp of horror, like the death throes of an asthmatic.

'You – you mean to do this!'

'Hush. I haven't said so. Dr Baines, the question?'

'I know I couldn't pay for it in cash,' Baines said. 'But I've got other assets. This experiment – if it works – is going to satisfy something for me that Consolidated Warfare Service hasn't satisfied in years, and probably never will again except marginally. I'm willing to make over most of my CWS stock to you. Not all of it, but – well – just short of being a controlling interest. You ought to be able to do a lot with that.'

'It's hardly enough, considering the risks involved,' Ware said slowly. 'On the other hand, I've no particular desire to bankrupt you –'

'Dr Ware,' Father Domenico said in an iron voice. 'Am I to conclude that you *are* going to undertake this fearful insanity?'

'I haven't said so,' Ware replied mildly. 'If I do, I shall certainly need your help –'

'Never. *Never*!'

'And everybody else's. It isn't really the money that attracts me, primarily. But without the money I should never be able to undertake an experiment like this in the first place, and I'm certain the opportunity will never come up again. If the whole thing doesn't blow up in my face, there'd be an enormous amount to learn from a trial like this.'

'I think that's right,' Hess's voice said. Baines looked towards him in surprise, but Hess seemed quite serious. 'I'd be greatly interested in it myself.'

'You'll learn nothing,' Father Domenico said, 'but the shortest of all shortcuts to Hell, probably in the body!'

'A negative Assumption?' Ware said, raising both eyebrows this time. 'But now you're tempting my pride, Father. There've been only two previous ones in Western history – Johannes Faustus and Don Juan Tenorio. And neither one was properly safeguarded or otherwise prepared. Well, now certainly I must undertake so great a work – provided that Dr Baines is satisfied that he'll get what he'll be paying for.'

'Of course I'm satisfied,' Baines said, quivering with joy.

'Not so fast. You've asked me to let all the major demons out of Hell. I can't even begin to do that. I can call up only those with whom I have pacts, and their subordinates. No matter what you have read in Romantic novels and plays, the three superior spirits cannot be invoked at all, and never sign pacts, those being SATHANAS, BEELZEBUTH and SATANACHA. Under each of these are two ministers, with one of the six of which it is possible to make pacts – one per magician, that is. I control LUCIFUGE ROFOCALE, and he me. Under him in turn, I have pacts with some eighty-nine other spirits, not all of which would be of any use to us here – VAS SAGO, for instance, who has a mild nature and no powers except in crystallomancy, or PHOENIX, a poet and teacher. With the utmost in careful preparations, we might involve as many as fifty of the rest, certainly no more. Frankly, I think that will prove to be more than enough.'

'I'll cheerfully take your word for it,' Baines said promptly. 'You're the expert. Will you take it on?'

'Yes.'

Father Domenico, who was still standing, swung away towards the door, but Ware's hand shot out towards him above the desk as if to grasp the monk by the nape of the neck. 'Hold!' the magician said. 'Your commission is *not* discharged, Father Domenico, as you know very well in your heart. You must observe this sending. Even more important, you have already said yourself that it is going to be difficult to keep under control. To that end I demand your unstinting advice in the preparation, your presence in the conjurations, and, should they be needed, your utmost offices in helping me and my other Tanists to abort it. This you cannot refuse – it is all in your mission by stipulation, and in the Covenant by implication. I do not force you to it. I do but remind you of your positive duty to your Lord.'

'That . . . is . . . true . . .' Father Domenico said in a sick whisper. His face as grey as an untinted new blotter, he groped for the chair and sat down again.

'Nobly faced. I'll have to instruct everyone here, but I'll start with you, in deference to your obvious distress –'

'One question,' Father Domenico said. 'Once you've instructed us all, you'll be out of touch with us for perhaps as much as a month to come. I demand the time to visit my colleagues, and perhaps call together a convocation of all white magicians –'

'To prevent me?' Ware said between his teeth. 'You can demand no such thing. The Convenant forbids the slightest interference.'

'I'm all too horribly aware of that. No, not to interfere, but to stand by, in case of disaster. It would be too late to call for them once you *knew* you were losing control.'

'Hmm . . probably a wise precaution, and one I couldn't justly prevent. Very well. Just be sure you're back when the time comes. About the day, what would you suggest? May Eve is an obvious choice, and we may well need that much time in preparation.'

'It's *too* good a time for any sort of control,' Father Domenico said grimly. 'I definitely do *not* recommend piling a real Walpurgis Night on top of the formal one. It would be wiser to choose an *un*favourable night, the more unfavourable the better.'

'Excellent good sense,' Ware said. 'Very well, then. Inform your friends. The experiment is hereby scheduled for Easter.'

With a scream, Father Domenico bolted from the room. Had Baines not been taught all his life long that such a thing was impossible in a man of God, Baines would have identified it without a second thought as a scream of hatred.

13

Theron Ware had been dreaming a journey to the Antarctic continent in the midst of its Jurassic splendour, fifty million years ago, but the dream had been becoming a little muddled with personal fantasies – mostly involving a minor enemy whom he had in reality sent for, with flourishes, a good decade ago – and he was not sorry when it vanished unfinished at dawn.

He awoke sweating, though the dream had not been especially stressful. The reason was not far to seek: Ahktoi was sleeping, a puddle of lard and fur, on the pillow, and had nearly crowded Ware's head off it. Ware sat up, mopping his pate with the top sheet, and stared at the cat with nearly neutral annoyance. Even for an Abyssinian, a big-boned breed, the familiar was grossly overweight; clearly an exclusive diet of human flesh was not a healthy regimen for a cat. Furthermore, Ware was not even sure it was necessary. It was prescribed only in Éliphas Lévi, who often made up such details as he went along. Certainly PHOENIX, whose creature Ahktoi was, had made no such stipulation. On the other hand, it was always best to play safe in such matters; and, besides, financially the diet was not much more than a nuisance. The worst that could be said for it was that it spoiled the cat's lines.

Ware arose, naked, and crossed the cold room to the lectern, which bore up his Great Book – not the book of pacts, which was of course still safely in the workroom, but his book of new knowledge. It was open to the section headed

QUASARS

but except for the brief paragraph summarizing the reliable scientific information on the subject – a very brief paragraph indeed – the pages were still blank.

Well, that, like so much else, could wait until Baines's

project was executed. Truly colossal advances might be made in the Great Book, once all that CWS money was in the bank.

Ware's retirement had left the members of Baines's party again at loose ends, and all of them, even Baines, were probably a little shaken at the magnitude of what they had contracted for. In Baines and Dr Hess, perhaps, there still remained some faint traces of doubt about its possibility, or at least some inability to imagine what it woud be like, despite the previous apparition of MARCHOSIAS. No such impediment could protect Jack Ginsberg, however – not now, when he awakened each morning with the very taste of Hell in his mouth. Ginsberg was committed, but he was not wearing well; he would have to be watched. The waiting period would be especially hard on him. Well, that couldn't be helped;' it was prescribed.

The cat uncurled, yawned, stretched, lurched daintily to its feet and paused at the edge of the bed, peering down the sideboard as though contemplating the inward slope of Fujiyama. At last it hit the floor with a double *splat*! like the impacts of two loaded sponges. There it arched its spine again, stretched out its back legs individually in an ecstasy of quivering, and walked slowly towards Ware, its furry abdomen swinging from side to side. *Hein*? it said in a breathy feminine voice.

'In a minute,' Ware said, preoccupied. 'You'll get fed when I do.' He had forgotten for the moment that he had just begun a nine days' fast, which when completed he would enforce also upon Baines and his henchmen. 'Father Eternal, O thou who art seated upon cherubim and seraphim, who beholdest the earth and the sea, unto thee do I lift up my hands, and beseech thine aid alone, thou who art the fulfilment of works, who givest booty unto those who toil, who exaltest the proud, who art destroyer of all life, the fulfilment of works, who givest booty unto those who call upon thee. Do thou guard and defend me in this undertaking, thou who livest and reignest forever and ever. Amen! Shut up, Ahktoi.'

Anyhow it had been years since he had believed for an instant that Ahktoi was really hungry. Maybe lean meat was what the cat needed, instead of all that baby fat – though still-births were certainly the easiest kind of rations to get for him.

Ringing for Gretchen, Ware went into the bathroom, where he ran a bath, into which he dashed an ounce of exorcised water left over from the dressing of a parchment. Ahktoi, who like most Abyssinians loved running water, leapt up on the rim of the tub and tried to fish for bubbles. Pushing the cat off, Ware sat down in the warm pool and spoke the Thirteenth Psalm, *Dominus illuminatio mea*, of death and resurrection, his voice resounding hollowly from the tiles; adding, 'Lord who has formed man out of nothing to thine own image and likeness, and me also, unworthy sinner as I am, deign, I pray thee, to bless and sanctify this water that all delusion may depart from me unto thee, almighty and ineffable, who didst lead forth thy people from the land of Egypt, and didst cause them to pass dryshod under the Red Sea, anoint me an thou wilt, father of sins, Amen.'

He slid under the water, crown to toes – but not for long, for the ounce of exorcised water he had added still had a trace of quicklime in it from the tanning of the lambskin, which made his eyes sting. He surfaced, blowing like a whale, and added quickly to the steamy air, '*Dixit insipiens in corde suo* – Will you *kindly* get out of the way, Ahktoi? – who has formed me in thine image and in thy likeness, design to bless and sanctify this water, so that it may become unto me the fruition of my soul and body and purpose. Amen.'

Hein?

Someone knocked on the door. His eyes squeezed closed still, Ware groped his way out. He was met at the threshold by Gretchen, who sponged his hands and face ritually with an asperged white cloth, and retreated before him as he advanced into the bedroom. Now that his eyes were cleared, he could see that she was naked, but, knowing what she was, that could scarcely interest him, and, besides, he had been devoted to celibacy since his earliest love of magic, like anyone in orders. Her nakedness was only another rule of the rite of lustration. Waving her aside, he took three steps towards the bed, where she had laid out his vestments, and said to all corners of the phenomenal and epiphenomenal world:

'ASTROSCHIO, ASATH, *à sacra* BEDRIMUBAL, FELUT, ANABOTOS, SERABILIM, SERGEN, GEMEN, DOMOS, who art seated above the heavens, who beholdest the depths, grant me, I pray thee, that those things which I conceive in my mind may also be executed by me through thee, who appear clean before thee! Amen.'

Gretchen went out, flexing her scabby buttocks, and Ware began the rite of vesting. *Hein*? Ahktoi said plaintively, but Ware did not hear. His triduum was launched, devoutly, in water, and would be observed, strictly, until the end in blood; wherein would be required to the slaughter a lamb, a dog, a hen and a cat.

The Last Conjuration

There are two equal and opposite errors into which our race can fall about the devils. One is to disbelieve in their existence. the other is to believe, and to feel an excessive or unhealthy interest in them. They themselves are equally pleased by both errors and hail a materialist or a magician with the same delight. . . .

We are really faced with a cruel dilemma. When the humans disbelieve in our existence we lose all the pleasing results of direct terrorism and we make no magicians. On the other hand, when they believe in us, we cannot make them materialists and sceptics. At least not yet. . . . If once we can produce our perfect work – the Materialist Magician, the man, not using, but veritably worshipping, what he vaguely calls 'Forces' while denying the existence of 'spirits' – then the end of the war will be in sight.

C. S. Lewis, *The Screwtape Letters*

14

Father Domenico found getting north to Monte Albano a relatively easy journey despite all the snow; he was able to take the *rapido* most of the way. Absurdly, he found himself worrying about the snow; if it lasted, there would be devastating floods in the spring. but that was not the only affliction the spring had in store.

After the journey, nothing seemed to go right. Only about half of the world's white magicians, a small number in any case, who had been summoned to the convocation had been able to make it, or had thought it worth the trip. One of the greatest, the aged archivist Father Bonfiglioli, had come all the way from Cambridge only to find the rigours of being portaged up the Mount too much for him. He was now in the hospital at the base of the

Mount with a coronary infarct, and the prognosis was said to be poor.

Luckily, Father Uccello had been able to come. So had Father Monteith, a venerable master of a great horde of creative (though often ineffectual) spirits of the cislunar sphere; Father Boucher, who had commerce with some intellect of the recent past that was neither a mortal nor a Power, a commerce bearing all the earmarks of necromancy and yet was not; Father Vance, in whose mind floated visions of magics that would not be comprehensible, let alone practicable, for millions of years to come; Father Anson, a brusque engineer type who specialized in unclouding the minds of politicians; Father Selahny, a terrifying kabbalist who spoke in parables and of whom it was said that no one since Leviathan had understood his counsel; Father Rosenblum, a dour, bear-like man who tersely predicted disasters and was always right about them; Father Atheling, a wall-eyed grimoiran who saw portents in parts of speech and lectured everyone in a tense nasal voice until the Director had to exile him to the library except when business was being conducted; and a gaggle of lesser men, and their apprentices.

These and the Brothers of the Order gathered in the chapel of the monastery to discuss what might be done. There was no agreement from the outset. Father Boucher was of the firm opinion that Ware would not be permitted to work any such conjuration on Easter, and that hence only minor precautions were necessary. Father Domenico had to point out that Ware's previous sending – a comparatively minor one to be sure, but what was that saying about the fall of the sparrow? – had been made without a sign of Divine intervention upon Christmas Eve.

Then there was the problem of whether or not to try to mobilize the Celestial Princes and their subordinates. Father Atheling would have it that merely putting these Princes on notice might provoke action against Ware, since there was no predicting what They might do, and hence would be in violation of the Covenant. He was finally outshouted by Fathers Anson and Vance, with the obvious but not necessarily valid argument that the Princes must know all about the matter anyhow.

How shaky that assumption was was revealed that night, when those bright angels were summoned one by one before the convocation for a council of war. Bright, terrible and enigmatic They were at any time, but at this calling They were in a state of spirit beyond the understanding of any of the masters present in the chapel. ARATRON, chiefest of Them all, appeared to be indeed unaware of the forthcoming unleashing, and disappeared with a roar when it was described. PHALEG, most military of spirits, seemed to know of Ware's plans, but would not discuss them, and also vanished when pressed. OPHEIL the mercurial, too, was preoccupied, as though Ware's plotting were only a negligible distraction from some immensely greater thought; His answers grew shorter and shorter, and He finally lapsed into what, in a mortal, Father Domenico would have unhesitatingly called surliness. Finally – although not intended as final, for the convocation had meant to consult all seven of the Olympians – the water-spirit PHUL when called up appeared fearsomely without a head, rendering converse impossible and throwing the chapel into a perilous uproar.

'These are not good omens,' Father Atheling said; and for the first time in his life, everyone agreed with him. It was agreed, also, that everyone except Father Domenico would remain at the Mount through the target day, to take whatever steps then appeared to be necessary; but there was precious little hope that they would be effective. Whatever was going on in Heaven, it appeared to leave small concern to spare for pleas from Monte Albano.

Father Domenico went south again far earlier than he had planned, unable to think of anything but the mystery of that final, decapitate apparition. The leaden skies returned him no answer.

15

On that penultimate morning, Theron Ware faced the final choice of which demons to call up, and for this he needed to repair to his laboratory, to check the book of pacts. Otherwise his preparations were all made. He had performed the blood sacrifices the previous evening, and then had completely re-arranged the furniture in the workroom to accommodate the Grand Circle – the first time he had had need of it in twenty years – the Lesser Circles and the Gateway. There were even special preparations for Father Domenico – who had returned early and with a gratifyingly troubled countenance – should it become necessary to ask the monk to call for Divine intervention; but Ware was tolerably sure it would not be. Though he had never attempted anything of this magnitude before, he felt the work in his fingertips, like a well-practised sonata.

He was, however, both astonished and disquieted to find Dr Hess already in the laboratory – not only because of the potentialities for contamination, but at the inevitable conclusion that Hess had worked out how to placate the Guardian of the door. This man evidently was even more dangerous than Ware had guessed.

'Do you want to ruin us all?' Ware demanded.

Hess turned away from the circle he had been inspecting and looked at Ware frankly. He was pale and hollow-eyed; not only had the fasting been hard on his spare frame – that was a hazard every neophyte had to come to terms with – but apparently he had not been sleeping much either. He said at once:

'No indeed. My apologies, Dr Ware. My curiosity overcame me, I'm afraid.'

'You didn't touch anything, I hope?

'Certainly not. I took your warnings about that with great seriousness, I assure you.'

'Well . . . probably no harm done then. I can sympathize with your interest, and even approve it, in part. But I'll be instructing you all in detail a little later in the day, and then you'll have ample time to inspect the arrangements. I do want you to know them intimately. But right now I still have some additional work to do, so if you don't mind . . .'

'Quite.' Hess moved obediently towards the door. As he was about to touch the handle, Ware added:

'By the way, Dr Hess, how *did* you deceive the Guardian?'

Hess made no pretence of being puzzled by the question.

'With a white pigeon, and a pocket mirror I got from Jack.'

'Hmm. Do you know, that would never have occurred to me. These pagan survivals are mostly a waste of effort. Let's talk about it more, later. You may have something to teach me.'

Hess made a small bow and finished his departure. Forgetting him instantly, Ware stared at the Grand Circle for a moment, and then walked around it clockwise to the lectern and unlocked the book of pacts. The stiff pages bent reassuringly in his hands. Each leaf was headed by the character or sign of a demon; below, in the special ink reserved for such high matters – gall, copperas, gum arabic – was the text of Theron Ware's agreement with that entity, signed at the bottom by Ware in his own blood, and by the character of the demon repeated in its own hand. Leading all the rest was the seal, and also the characters, of LUCIFUGE ROFOCALE, which also appeared on the book's cover:

There then followed eighty-nine others. It was Ware's sober belief, backed by infernal assurances he had reason to trust, that no previous magician had held so many spirits in thrall. After forty years, true, all the names would change, and Ware would have to force the re-execution of each pact, and so, again and again through the five hundred years of life he had bought from HAGITH in his salad days as a white magician. Nevertheless it could be said that, in the possession of this book. Ware was at least potentially the wealthiest mortal in all of history, though to anyone else in the world the book would be worth nothing except as a *curiosum*.

These spirits, not counting LUCIFUGE ROFOCALE, comprised the seventeen infernal archangels of the Grand Grimoire, and the seventy-two demons of the Descending Hierarchy once confined in the brazen vessel of Solomon the King: a fabulous haul indeed, and each captive commanding troops and armies of lesser spirits, and damned souls by the thousands of millions, more of them every minute. (For these days, virtually everyone was damned; it had been this discovery that had first convinced Ware that the Rebellion was in fact going to succeed, probably by the year A.D. 2000; the many plain symptoms of chiliastic panic already being manifested amongst the laity were almost certainly due to be vindicated, for everyone was rushing incontinently into Hell-mouth without even the excuse of an Antichrist to mislead him. As matters stood now, Christ Himself would have to creep stealthily, hoping to be ignored, even into a cathedral to conduct a Mass, as in that panel of Hieronymus Bosch; the number of people who could not pronouce the Divine name without a betraying stammer – or their own names, for that matter – had grown from a torrent to a deluge, and, ridiculously, hardly any of them were claiming any fraction of the possible profits in this world. They did not even know that they were on the winning side, or even that there was more than one side. No wonder that Ware had found so much fat in the cauldron, waiting to be skimmed.)

But as Ware had already warned Baines, not all of the spirits in the book were suitable for the experiment at hand. There were some, like MARCHOSIAS, who hoped after an interval to be returned to the Celestial choirs. In this hope, Ware was grimly certain, they were mistaken, and the only reward they would receive would be from the Emperor of the Pit, that kind of reward customarily given to fair-weather friends and summer soldiers. In the meantime, the evils they could be persuaded or compelled to do were minor and hardly worth the effort of invoking them. One, whom Ware had already mentioned to Baines, VASSAGO, was even said in the *Lesser Key* and elsewhere to be 'good by nature' – not too trustworthy an ascription – and indeed was sometimes called upon by white magicians. Others in the hierarchy, like PHOENIX, controlled aspects of reality that were of little relevance to Baines's commission.

Taking up the pen of the Art, Ware made a list. When he was finished, he had written down forty-eight names. Considering the number of the Fallen, that was not a large muster; but he thought it would serve the purpose. He closed and locked the book, and after a pause to rebuke and torment the Guardian of his door, went out into the Easter morning to rehearse his Tanists.

No day, it seemed, had ever gone so slowly for Baines as this Easter, despite the diversion of the rehearsal; but at last it was night and over, and Ware pronounced himself ready to begin.

The Grand Circle now on the parquetry of the refectory bore a generic resemblance to the circle Ware had composed on Christmas Eve, but it was a great deal bigger, and much different in detail. The circle proper was made of strips of the skin of the sacrificial kid, with the hair still on it, fastened to the floor at the cardinal points with four nails that, Ware explained, had been drawn from the coffin of a child. On the northeast arc, under the word BERKAIAL, there rested on the strips the body of a male bat that had been drowned in blood; on the northwest, under the word AMASARAC, the skull of a parricide; on the southeast, under the word ASARADEL, the horns of a goat; and on the southwest, under the word ARIBECL, sat Ware's cat, to the secret of whose diet they were now all privy. (Indeed, there had not been much of moment to the rehearsal, and Baines had inferred that its chief object had been to impart to the rest of them such items of unpleasant knowledge as this.)

The triangle had been drawn inside the circle with a lump of haematite or lodestone. Under its base was drawn a figure consisting of a *chi* and a *rho* superimposed, resting on the line, with a cross to each side of it. Flanking the other two sides were the great candles of virgin wax, each stick sitting in the centre of a crown of vervain. Three circles for the operators – Ware, Baines and Hess (Jack Ginsberg and Father Domenico would stand outside, in separate pentacles) – were inside the triangle, connected by a cross; the northern circle had horns drawn on it. At the pinnacle of the triangle sat a new brazier, loaded with newly consecrated charcoal. To the left side of the horned circle, which was to be Ware's, of course, was the lectern and the book of pacts, within easy reach.

At the rear of the room, before the curtained door to the kitchen, was another circle, quite as big as the first, in the centre of which was a covered altar. That had been empty this afternoon; but there now lay upon it the nude body of the girl Ware had used to address as Gretchen. Her skin was paper-white except for its markings, and to Baines gave every appearance of being dead. A small twist of violet silk, nearly transparent and with some crumpled thing like a wad of tissue or a broken matzoh inside it, rested upon her navel. Her body appeared to have been extensively written upon with red and yellow grease paint; some of the characters might have been astrological, others more like ideograms or cartouches. In default of knowing their meaning or even their provenance, they simply made her look more naked.

The main door closed. Everyone was now in place.

Ware lit the candles, and then the fire in the brazier. It was a task of Baines and Hess to feed the fire periodically, as the time wore on, the one with brandy, the other with camphor, taking care not to stumble over their swords or leave their circles in the process. As before, they had been enjoined to the strictest silence, especially should any spirit speak to them or threaten them.

Ware now reached out to the lectern and opened his book. This time there were no preliminary gestures, and no portents; he simply began to recite in a gravid voice:

'I conjure and command thee, LUCIFUGE ROFOCALE, by all the names wherewith thou mayst be constrained and bound, SATAN, RANTAN, PALLANTRE, LUTIAS, CORICACOEM, SCIRCIGREUR, *per sedem Baldarey et per gratiam et diligentiam tuam habuisti ab eo hanc nalatimanamilam*, as I command thee, *usor, dilapidatore, tentatore, seminatore, soignatore, devoratore, concitore, et seductore*, where art thou? Thou who imposeth hatred and propagateth enmities, I conjure thee by him who hath created thee for this ministry, to fulfil my work! I cite thee, COLRIZIANA, OFFINA, ALTA, NESTERA, FUARD, MENUET, LUCIFUGE ROFOCALE, arise, arise, arise!'

There was no sound; but suddenly there was standing in the other circle a dim steaming figure, perhaps eight or nine feet tall. It was difficult to be sure what it looked like, partly because some of the altar could still be seen through it. To Baines it resembled a man with a shaven head bearing three long, twisted horns, eyes like a spectral tarsier's, a gaping mouth, a pointed chin. It was wearing a sort of jerkin, coppery in colour, with a tattered ruff and a fringed skirt; below the skirt protruded two bandy, hooved legs, and a fat, hairy tail, which twitched restlessly.

'What now?' this creature said in an astonishingly pleasant voice. The words, however, were blurred. 'I have not seen my son in many moons.' Unexpectedly, it giggled, as though pleased by the pun.

'I adjure thee, speak more clearly,' Ware said. 'And what I wish, thou knowst full well.'

'Nothing may be known until it is spoken.' The voice seemed no less blurred to Baines, but Ware nodded.

'I desire then to release, as did the Babylonian from under the seal of the King of Israel, blessed be he, from Hell-mouth into the mortal world all those demons of the False Monarchy whose names I shall subsequently call, and whose characters and signs I shall exhibit in my book, providing only that they harm not me and mine, and that they shall return whence they came at dawn, as it is always decreed.'

'Providing no more than that?' the figure said. 'No prescriptions? No desires? You were not always so easily satisfied.'

'None,' Ware said firmly. 'They shall do as they will for this their period of freedom, except that they harm none here in my circles, and obey me when recalled, by rod and pact.'

The demon glanced over its transparent shoulder. 'I see that you have the appropriate fumigant to cense so many great lords, and my servants and satraps will have their several rewards in their deeds. So interesting a commission is new to me. Well. What have you for my hostage, to fulfil the forms?'

Ware reached into his vestments. Baines half expected to see produced another tear vase, but instead Ware brought out by the tail a live mouse, which he threw over the brazier as he had the vase, except not so far. The mouse ran directly towards the demon, circled it frantically three times outside the markings, and disappeared in the direction of the rear door, cheeping like a sparrow. Baines looked towards Ahktoi, but the cat did not even lick its chops.

'You are skilled and punctilious, my son. Call then when I have left, and I will send my ministers. Let nothing remain undone, and much will be done before the black cock crows.'

'It is well. By and under this promise I discharge thee OMGROMA, EPYN, SEYOK, SATANY, DEGONY, EPARYGON, GALLIGANON, ZOGOGEN, FERSTIGON, LUCIFUGE ROFOCALE, begone, begone, begone!'

'I shall see you at dawn.' The prime minister of LUCIFER wavered like a flame, and, like a flame, went out.

Hess promptly cast camphor into the brazier. Recovering with a start from a near paralysis of fascination, Baines sprinkled brandy after it. The fire puffed. Without looking around Ware brought out his lodestone, which he held in his left hand; with his right, he dipped the iron-headed point of his wand into the coals. Little licking points of blue light ran up it almost to his hand, as though the rod, too, had been coated with brandy.

Holding the tonguing wand out before him like a dowsing rod, Ware strode ceremoniously out of the Grand Circle towards the altar. As he walked, the air around him began to grumble as though a storm were gathering about his shaven head, but he paid the noise no attention. He marched on directly to the *locus spiritus*, and into it.

Silence fell at once. Ware said clearly:

'I, Theron Ware, master of masters, Karcist of Karcists, hereby undertake to open the book, and the seals thereof, which were forbidden to be broken until the breaking of the Seven Seals before the Seventh Throne. I have beheld SATAN as a bolt falling from heaven. I have crushed the dragons of the pit beneath my heel. I have commanded angels and devils. I undertake and command that all shall be accomplished as I bid, and that from beginning to end, alpha to omega, world without end, none shall harm us who abide here in this temple of the Art of Arts. *Aglan*, TETRAGRAM, *vaycheon stimulamaton ezphares retragrammaton olyaram irion esytion existion eryona onera orasym mozm messias soter* EMANUEL SABAOTH ADONAY, *te adoro, et te invoco*. Amen.'

He took another step forward, and touched the flaming tip of the rod to the veil of silk on the belly of the still girl. A little curl of blue-grey smoke began to arise from it, like ignited incense.

Ware now retreated, walking backward, towards the Grand Circle. As he did so, the fire on the wand died; but in the mortuary silence there now intruded a faint hissing, much like the first ignition of a squib. And there were indeed fireworks in inception. As Baines stared in gluttonous hypnosis, a small fountain of many-coloured sparks began to rise from the fuse-like tissue on the abdomen of the body on the altar. More smoke poured forth. The air was becoming distinctly hazy.

The body itself seemed to be burning now, the skin peeling back like segments of an orange. Baines heard behind him an aborted retching noise in Jack Ginsberg's voice, but could not himself understand what the occasion for nausea could be. The body – whatever it had once been – was now only like a simulacrum made of pith or papier-mâché, and charged with some equivalent of Greek fire. Indeed, there was already a strong taint of gunpowder overriding the previous odours of incense and camphor. Baines rather welcomed it – not that it was familiar, for it had been centuries since black powder had been used in his trade, but because he had begun to find the accumulation of less business-like perfumes a little cloying.

Gradually, everything melted away into the smoke except an underlay of architectural outline, against which stood a few statues lit more along one side than the other by one of the two sources of fire. Hess coughed briefly; otherwise there was silence except for the hissing of the pyre. Sparks continued to fly upward, and sometimes, for an instant, they seemed to form scribbled, incomprehensible words in the frame of the unreal wall.

Ware's voice sounded remotely from one of the statues:

'BAAL, great king and commander in the East, of the Order of the Fly, obey me!'

Something began to form in the distance. Baines had the clear impression that it was behind the altar, behind the curtained door, indeed outside the palazzo altogether, but he could see it nevertheless. It came forward, growing, until he could also see that it was a thing like a man, in a neat surcoat and snow-white linen, but with two super-numerary heads, the one on the left like a toad's, the other like a cat's. It swelled soundlessly until at some moment it was inarguably in the refectory; and then, still silently, had grown past them and was gone.

'AGARES, duke in the East, of the Order of the Virtues, obey me!'

Again, a distant transparency, and silent. It came on very slowly, manifesting like a comely old man carrying a goshawk upon his wrist. Its slowness was necessitous, for it was riding astride an ambling crocodile. Its eyes were closed and its lips moved incessantly. Gradually, it too swelled past.

'GAMYGYN, marquis and president in Cartagra, obey me!'

This grew to be something like a small horse, or perhaps an ass, modest and unassuming. It dragged behind it ten naked men in chains.

'VALEFOR, powerful duke, obey me!'

A black-maned lion, again with three heads, the other two human, one wearing the cap of a hunter, the other the wary smile of a thief. It passed in a rush, without even a wind to mark its going.

'BARBATOS, great count and minister of SATANACHIA, obey me!'

But this was not one figure; it was four, like four crowned kings. With it and past it poured three companies of soldiers their heads bowed and their expressions shuttered and still under steel caps. When all this troop had vanished, it was impossible to guess which among them had been the demon, or if the demon had ever appeared.

'PAIMON, great king, of the Order of the Dominions, obey me!'

Suddenly after all the hissing silence there was a blast of sound, and the room was full of capering things carrying contorted tubes and bladders, which might have been intended as musical instruments. The noise, however, resembled most closely a drove of pigs being driven down the chute of a slaughterhouse. Among the bawling, squealing dancers a crowned man rode upon a dromedary, bawling wordlessly in a great hoarse voice. The beast it rode on chewed grimly on some bitter cud, its eyes squeezed shut as if in pain.

'SYTRY!' Ware shouted. Instantly there was darkness and quiet, except for the hissing, which now had a faint overtone as of children's voices. '*Jussus secreta libenter detegit feminarum, eas ridens ludificansque ut se luxorise nudent,* great prince, obey me!'

This sweet and lissome thing was no less monstrous than the rest; it had a glowing human body, but was winged, and had the ridiculously small, smirking head of a leopard. At the same time, it was beautiful, in some way that made Baines feel both sick and eager. As it passed, Ware seemed to be pressing a ring against his lips.

'LERAJIE, powerful marquis, ELIGOR, ZEPAR, great dukes, obey me!'

As they were called together, so these three appeared together: the first an archer clad in green, with quiver and a nocked bow whose arrow dripped venom; the second, a knight with a sceptre and a pennon-bearing lance; the third, an armed soldier clad in red. In contrast to their predecessor, there was nothing in the least monstrous about their appearance, nor any clue as to their spheres and offices, but Baines found them no less alarming for all that.

'AYPOROS, mighty earl and prince, obey me!'

Baines felt himself turning sick even before this creature appeared, and from the sounds around him, so did the others, even including Ware. There was no special reason for this apparent in its aspect, which was so grotesque as to have been comic under other circumstances; it had the body of an angel, with a lion's head, the webbed feet of a goose and the scut of a deer. 'Transform, transform!' Ware cried, thrusting his wand into the brazier. The visitant promptly took on the total appearance of an angel, crown to toe, but the effect of the presence of something filthy and obscene remained.

HABORYM, strong duke, obey me!'

This was another man-thing of the three-headed race – though the apparent relationship, Baines realized, must be pure accident – the human one bearing two stars on its forehead; the others were of a serpent and a cat. In its right hand it carried a blazing firebrand, which it shook at them as it passed.

'NABERIUS, valiant marquis, obey me!'

At first it seemed to Baines that there had been no response to this call. Then he saw movement near the floor. A black cock with bleeding, empty eye sockets was fluttering around the outside of the Grand Circle. Ware menaced it with the wand, and it crowed hoarsely and was gone.

'GLASYALABOLAS, mighty president, obey me!'

This appeared to be simply a winged man until it smiled, when it could be seen to have the teeth of a dog. There were flecks of foam at the corners of its mouth. It passed soundlessly.

In the silence, Baines could hear Ware turning a page in his book of pacts, and remembered to cast more brandy into the brazier. The body on the altar had apparently long since been consumed; Baines could not remember how long it had been since he had seen the last of the word-forming sparks. The thick grey haze persisted, however.

'BUNE, thou strong duke, obey me!'

This apparition was the most marvellous yet, for it approached them borne on a galleon, which sank into the floor as it came nearer until they were able to look down through the floor on to its deck. Coiled there was a dragon with the familiar three heads, these being of dog, griffin and man. Shadowy figures, vaguely human, toiled around it. It continued to sink until it was behind them, and presumably thereafter.

Its passage left Baines aware that he was trembling – not from fright, exactly, for he seemed to have passed beyond that, but from the very exhaustion of this and other emotions, and possibly also from the sheer weariness of having stood in one spot for so long. Inadvertently, he sighed.

'Silence,' Ware said in a low voice. 'And let nobody weaken or falter at this point. We are but half done with our calling – and of those remaining to be invoked, many are far more powerful than any we've yet seen. I warned you before, this

Art takes physical strength as well as courage.'

He turned another page. 'ASTAROTH, grand treasurer, great and powerful duke, obey me!'

Even Baines had heard of this demon, though he could not remember where, and he watched it materialize with a stirring of curiosity. Yet it was nothing remarkable in the light of what he had seen already: an angelic figure, at once beautiful and foul, seated astride a dragon; it carried a viper in its right hand. He remembered belatedly that these spirits, never having been matter in the first place, had to borrow a body to make appearances like this, and would not necessarily pick the same one each time; the previous description of ASTAROTH that he had read, he now recalled, had been that of a piebald Negro woman riding on an ass. As the creature passed him, it smiled into his face, and the stench of its breath nearly knocked him down.

'ASMODAY, strong and powerful king, chief of the power of Amaymon, angel of chance, obey me!' As he called, Ware swept off his hat with his left hand, taking care, Baines noted, not to drop the lodestone as he did so.

This king also rode a dragon, and also had three heads – bull, man and ram. All three heads breathed fire. The creature's feet were webbed, as were its hands, in which it carried a lance and pennon; and it had a serpent's tail. Fearsome enough; but Baines was beginning to note a certain narrowness of invention among these infernal artisans. It also occurred to him to wonder, fortunately, whether this very repetitiveness was not deliberate, intended to tire him into inattentiveness, or lure him into the carelessness of contempt. *This thing might kill me if I even closed my eyes*, he reminded himself.

'FURFUR, great earl, obey me!'

This angel appeared as a hart and was past them in a single bound, its tail streaming fire like a comet.

'HALPAS, great earl, obey me!'

There was nothing to this apparition but a stock dove, also quickly gone. Ware was calling the names now as rapidly as he could manage to turn the pages, perhaps in recognition of the growing weariness of his Tanists, perhaps even of his own. The demons flashed in a nightmare parade: RAYM, earl of the Order of the Thrones, a man with a crow's head; SEPAR, a mermaid wearing a ducal crown; SABURAC, a lion-headed soldier upon a pale horse; BIFRONS, a great earl in the shape of a gigantic flea; ZAGAN, a griffin-winged bull; ANDRAS, a raven-headed angel with a bright sword, astride a black wolf; ANDREALPHUS, a peacock appearing amid the noise of many unseen birds; AMDUSCIAS, a unicorn among many musicians; DANTALIAN, a mighty duke in the form of a man but showing many faces both of men and women, with a book in his right hand; and at long last, that mighty king created next after LUCIFER and the first to fall in battle before MICHAEL, formerly of the Order of the Virtues, BELIAL himself, beautiful and deadly in a chariot of fire as he had been worshipped in Babylon.

'Now, great spirits,' Ware said, 'because ye have diligently answered me and shown yourselves to my demands, I do hereby licence ye to depart, without injury to any here. Depart, I say, yet be ye willing and ready to come at the appointed hour, when I shall duly exorcise and conjure you by your rites and seals. Until then, ye abide free. Amen.'

He snuffed out the fire in the brazier with a closely fitting lid on which was graven the Third or Secret Seal of Solomon. The murk in the refectory began to lift.

'All right,' Ware said in a matter-of-fact voice. Strangely, he seemed much less tired than he had after the conjuration of MARCHOSIAS. 'It's over – or rather, it's begun. Mr Ginsberg, you can safely leave your circle now, and turn on the lights.'

When Ginsberg had done so, Ware also snuffed the candles. In the light of the shaded electrics the hall seemed in the throes of a cheerless dawn, although in fact the time was not much past midnight. There was nothing on the altar now but a small heap of fine grey ash.

'Do we really have to wait it out in here?' Baines said, feeling himself sagging. 'I should think we'd be a lot more comfortable in your office – and in a better position to find out what's going on, too.'

'We must remain here,' Ware said firmly. 'That, Mr Baines, is why I asked you to bring in your transistor radio – to keep track of both the world and the time. For approximately the next eight hours, the area inside these immediate walls will be the only safe place on all the Earth.'

16

Trappings, litter and all, the refectory now reminded Baines incongruously of an initiation room in a college fraternity house just after the last night of Hell Week. Hess was asleep on the long table that earlier had borne Ware's consecrated instruments. Jack Ginsberg lay on the floor near the main door, napping fitfully, mumbling and sweating. Theron Ware, after again warning everyone not to touch anything, had dusted off the altar and gone to sleep – apparently quite soundly – upon it, still robed and gowned.

Only Baines and Father Domenico remained awake. The monk, having prowled once around the margins of the room, had found an unsuspected low window behind a curtain, and now stood, with his back to them all, looking out at the black world, hands locked behind his back.

Baines sat on the floor with his own back propped against the wall next to the electric furnace, the transistor radio pressed to his ear. He was brutally uncomfortable, but he had found by experiment that this was the best place in the hall for radio reception – barring, of course, his actually entering one of the circles.

Even here, the reception was not very good. It wavered in and out maddeningly, even on powerful stations like Radio Luxembourg, and was liable to tearing blasts of static. These were usually followed, at intervals of a few seconds to several minutes, by bursts or rolls of thunder in the sky outside. Much of the time, too, as was usual, the clear spaces were occupied by nothing except music and commercials.

And thus far, what little news he had been able to pick up had been vaguely disappointing. There had been a major train wreck in Colorado; a freighter was foundering in a blizzard in the North Sea; in Guatemala, a small dam had burst, burying a town in an enormous mud slide; an earthquake was reported in Corinth – the usual budget of natural or near-natural disasters for any day.

In addition, the Chinese had detonated another hydrogen

device; there had been another raiding incident on the Israeli-Jordanian border; black tribesmen had staged a rape and massacre on a government hospital in Rhodesia; the poor were marching on Washington again; the Soviet Union had announced that it would not be able to recover three dogs and a monkey it had put in orbit a week ago; the U.S. gained another bloody inch in Vietnam, and Premier Ky put his foot in it; and . . .

All perfectly ordinary, all going to prove what everyone of good sense already knew, that there was *no* safe place on the Earth either inside this room or without it, and probably never had been. What, Baines began to wonder, was the profit in turning loose so many demons, at so enormous an expenditure of time, effort and money, if the only result was to be just like reading any morning's newspaper? Of course, it might be that interesting private outrages were also being committed, but many newspaper and other publishers made fortunes on those in ordinary times, and in any event he could never hear of more than a fraction of them over this idiot machine.

Probably he would just have to wait until days or weeks later, when the full record and history of this night had been assembled and digested, when no doubt its full enormity might duly appear. He should have expected nothing else; after all, the full impact of a work of art is never visible in the sketches. All the same, he was obstinately disappointed to be deprived of the artist's excitement of watching the work growing on the canvas.

Was there anything that Ware could do about that? Almost surely not, or he would have done it already; it was clear that he had understood the motive behind the commission as well as he had understood its nature. Besides, it would be dangerous to wake him – he would need all his strength for the latter half of the experiment, when the demons began to return.

Resentfully but with some resignation too, Baines realized that he himself had never been the artist here. He was only the patron, who could watch the colours being applied and the cartoon being filled, and could own the finished board or ceiling, but had never even in principle been capable of handling the brushes.

But there – what was that? The BBC was reporting:

'A third contingent of apparatus has been dispatched along the Thames to combat the Tate Gallery fire. Expert observers believe there is no hope of saving the gallery's great collection of Blake paintings, which include most of his illustrations for the *Inferno* and *Purgatorio* of Dante. Hope also appears to be lost for what amount to almost all the world's paintings by Turner, including his watercolours of the burning of the Houses of Parliament. The intense and sudden nature of the initial outbreak has led to the suspicion that the fire is the work of an incendiary.'

Baines sat up alertly, feeling an even more acute stab of hope, though all his joints protested painfully. *There* was a crime with real style, a crime with symbolism, a crime with meaning. Excitedly he remembered HABORYM, the demon with the dripping fire brand. Now if there were to be more acts that imaginative . . .

The reception was getting steadily worse; it was extraordinarily tiring to be continuously straining to filter meaning out of it. Radio Luxembourg appeared to have gone off the air, or to have been shut out by some atmospheric disturbance. He tried Radio Milan, and got it just in time to hear it announce itself about to play all eleven of the symphonies of Gustav Mahler, one right after the other, an insane project for any station and particularly for an Italian one. Was that some demon's idea of a joke? Whatever the answer, it was going to take Radio Milan out of the newscasting business for well over twenty-four hours to come.

He cast further about the dial. There seemed to be an extraordinary number of broadcasts going out in languages he did not know or could even recognize, though he could get around passably in seventeen standard tongues and in any given year was fluent in a different set of three, depending on business requirements. It was almost as though someone had jammed an antenna on the crown of Babel.

Briefly, he caught a strong outburst of English; but it was only the Voice of America making piously pejorative sermonettes about the Chinese fusion explosion. Baines had known that that was coming for months now. Then the multilingual mumbling and chuntering resumed, interspersed occasionally with squeals of what might indifferently have been Pakistani jazz or Chinese opera.

Another segment of English shouted, '. . . with Cyanotabs! Yes, friends, one dose cures all ills! Guaranteed chockfull of crisp, crunchy atoms . . .' and was replaced by a large boys' choir singing the 'Hallelujah Chorus,' the words for which, however, seemed to go, 'Bison, bison! Rattus, rattus! Cardinalis Cardinalis!' Then more gabble, marvellously static-free and sometimes hovering just on the edge of intelligibility.

The room stank abominably of an amazing mixture of reeks: brandy, camphor, charcoal, vervain, gunpowder, flesh, sweat, perfume, incense, candle wicks, musk, singed hair. Baines's head ached dully; it was like trying to breathe inside the mouth of a vulture. He longed to take a pull at the brandy bottle under his rumpled alb, but he did not know how much of what was left would be needed when Ware resumed operations.

Across from him, something moved: Father Domenico had unlocked his hands and turned away from the small window. He was now taking a few prim steps towards Baines. The slight stir of human life seemed to disturb Jack Ginsberg, who thrashed himself into an even more uncomfortable-looking position, shouted hoarsely, and then began to snore. Father Domenico shot a glance at him, and, stopping just short of his side of the Grand Circle, beckoned.

'Me?' Baines said.

Father Domenico nodded patiently. Putting aside the overheated little radio with less reluctance than he would have imagined possible only an hour ago, Baines heaved himself arthritically to his knees, and then to his feet.

As he started to stumble towards the monk, something furry hurtled in front of him and nearly made him fall: Ware's cat. It was darting towards the altar; and in a soaring arc incredible in an animal of its shameless obesity, leapt up there and settled down on the rump of its sleeping master. It looked greenly at Baines and went itself to sleep, or appeared to.

Father Domenico beckoned again, and went back to the window. Baines limped after him, wishing that he had taken off his shoes; his feet felt as though they had turned into solid blocks of horn.

'What's the matter?' he whispered.

'Look out there, Mr Baines.'

Confused and aching, Baines peered past his uninvited and unimpressive Virgil. At first he could see nothing but the streaked steam on the inside of the glass, with a spume of fat snowflakes slurrying beyond it. Then he saw that the night was in fact not wholly dark. Somehow he could sense the undersides of turbulent clouds. Below, the window, like the one in Ware's office, looked down the side of the cliff and out over the sea, which was largely invisible in the snow whorls; so should the town have been, but it was in fact faintly luminous. Overhead, from frame to frame of the window, the clouds were overstitched with continuous streaks of dim fire, like phosphorescent contrails, long-lasting and taking no part in the weather.

'Well?' Baines said.

'You don't see anything?'

'I see the meteor tracks or whatever they are. And the light is odd – sheet lightning, I suppose, and maybe a fire somewhere in town.'

'That's all?'

'That's all,' Baines said, irritated. 'What are you trying to do, panic me into waking Dr Ware and calling it all quits? Nothing doing. We'll wait it out.'

'All right,' Father Domenico said, resuming his vigil. Baines stumped back to his corner and picked up the radio. It said:

'. . . now established that the supposed Chinese fusion test was actually a missile warhead explosion of at least thirty megatons, centred on Taiwan. Western capitals, already in an uproar because of the napalm murder of the U.S. President's widow in a jammed New York discotheque, are moving quickly to a full war footing and we expect a series of security blackouts on the news at any moment. Until that happens we will keep you informed of whatever important events come through. We pause for station identification. Owoo. Eeg. Oh, piggly baby, I caught you – cheatin' on me – owoo . . .'

Baines twisted the dial savagely, but the howling only

became more bestial. Down the wall to his right, Hess twisted his long body on the table and suddenly sat upright, swinging his stockinged feet to the floor.

'Jesus Christ,' he said huskily. 'Did I hear what I thought I heard?'

'Dead right you did,' Baines said quietly, and not without joy; but he, too, was worried. 'Slide over here and sit down. Something's coming to a head, and it's nothing like we'd expected – or Ware either.'

'Hadn't we better call a halt, then?'

'No. Sit down, goddamn it. I don't think we *can* call a halt – and even if we could, I don't want to give our clerical friend over there the satisfaction.'

'You'd rather have World War Three?' Hess said, sitting down obediently.

'I don't know that that's what's going to happen. We contracted for this. Let's give it the benefit of the doubt. Either Ware's in control, or he should be. Let's wait and see.'

'All right,' Hess said. He began to knead his fingers together. Baines tried the radio once more, but nothing was coming through except a mixture of *The Messiah*, Mahler and The Supremes.

Jack Ginsberg whined in his pseudo-sleep. After a while, Hess said neutrally:

'Baines?'

'What is it?'

'What kind of a thing do you think this is?'

'Well, it's either World War Three or it isn't. How can I know yet?'

'I didn't ask you that . . . not what you think it *is*. I asked you, what *kind* of a thing do you think it is? You ought to have some sort of notion. After all, you contracted for it.'

'Oh. Hmm. Father Domenico said it might turn out to be Armageddon. Ware didn't think so, but he hasn't turned out to be very right up to now. I can't guess, myself. I haven't been thinking in these terms very long.'

'Nor have I,' Hess said, watching his fingers weave themselves in and out. 'I'm still trying to make sense of it in the old terms, the ones that used to make sense of the universe to me. It isn't easy. But you'll remember I told you I was interested in the history of science. That involves trying to understand why there wasn't any science for so long, and why it went into eclipse almost every time it was rediscovered. I think I know why now. I think the human mind goes through a sort of cycle of fear. It can only take so much accumulated knowledge, and then it panics, and starts inventing reasons to throw everything over and go back to a Dark Age . . . every time with a new, invented mystical reason.'

'You're not making very much sense,' Baines said. He was still also trying to listen to the radio.

'I didn't expect you to think so. but it happens. It happens about every thousand years. People start out happy with their gods, even though they're frightened of them. Then, increasingly, the world becomes secularized, and the gods seem less and less relevant. The temples are deserted. People feel guilty about that, but not much. Then, suddenly, they've had all the secularization they can take, they throw their wooden shoes into the machines, they take to worshipping Satan or the Great Mother, they go into a Hellenistic period or take up Christianity, *in hoc signo vinces* – I've got those all out of order but it happens, Baines, it happens like clockwork, every thousand years. The last time was the chiliastic panics just before the year A.D. 1000, when everyone expected the Second Coming of Christ and realized that they didn't dare face up to Him. *That* was the heart, the centre, the whole reason of the Dark Ages. Well, we've got another millennium coming to a close now, and people are terrified of *our* secularization, our nuclear and biological weapons, our computers, our overprotective medicine, everything, and they're turning back to the worship of unreason. Just as you've done – and I've helped you. Some people these days worship flying saucers because they don't dare face up to Christ. You've turned to black magic. Where's the difference?'

'I'll tell you where,' Baines said. 'Nobody in the whole of time has ever seen a saucer, and the reasons for believing that anybody has are utterly pitiable. Probably they can be explained just as you've explained them, and never mind about Jung and his thump-headed crowd. But, Adolph, you and I *have* seen a demon.'

'Do you think so? I don't deny it. I think it very possible. But Baines, are you sure? How do you *know* what you think you know? We're on the eve of World War Three, which we engineered. Couldn't all this be a hallucination we conjured up to remove some of our guilt? Or is it possible that it isn't happening at all, and that we're as much victims of a chiliastic panic as more formally religious people are? That makes more sense to me than all this medieval mumbo-jumbo about demons. I don't mean to deny the evidence of my senses, Baines. I only mean to ask you, what is it worth?'

'I'll tell you what I know,' Baines said equably, 'though I can't tell you how I know it and I won't bother to try. First, something is happening, and that something is real. Second, you and I and Ware and everyone else who wanted to make it happen, therefore *did* make it happen. Third, we're turning out to be wrong about the outcome – but no matter what it is, it's *our* outcome. We contracted for it. Demons, saucers, fallout – what's the difference? Those are just signs in the equation, parameters we can fill any way that makes the most intermediate sense to us. Are you happier with electrons than with demons? Okay, good for you. But what I like, Adolph, what *I* like is the result. I don't give a damn about the means. I invented it, I called it into being, I'm paying for it – and no matter how else you describe it, *I made it, and it's mine*. Is that clear? *It's mine*. Every other possible fact about it, no matter what that fact might turn out to be, is a stupid footling technicality that I hire people like you and Ware not to bother me with.'

'It seems to me,' Hess said in a leaden monotone, 'that we are all insane.'

At that same moment, the small window burst into an intense white glare, turning Father Domenico into the most intense of inky silhouettes.

'You may be right,' Baines said. 'There goes Rome.'

Father Domenico, his eyes streaming, turned away from the dimming frame and picked his way slowly to the altar. After a long moment of distaste, he took Theron Ware by the shoulder and shook him. The cat hissed and jumped sidewise.

'Wake up, Theron Ware,' Father Domenico said formally. 'I

charge you, awake. Your experiment may now wholly and contractually be said to have gone astray, and the Covenant therefore satisfied. Ware! Ware! Wake up, damn you.'

17

Baines looked at his watch. It was 3:00 a.m.

Ware awoke instantly, swung to his feet with a spring and without a word started for the window. At the same instant, the agony that had been Rome swept over the building. The shock wave had been attenuated by distance and the jolt was not heavy, but the window Father Domenico had uncurtained sprang inward in a spray of flying glass needles. More glass fell out from behind the drapes which hung below the ceiling, like an orchestra of celestas.

As far as Baines could see, nobody was more than slightly cut. Not that a serious wound could have made any difference now, with the Last Death already riding on the winds.

Ware was not visibly shaken. He simply nodded once and wheeled towards the Grand Circle, stooping to pick up his dented paper hat. No, he was moved – his lips were pinched white. He beckoned to them all.

Baines took a step towards Jack Ginsberg, to kick him awake if necessary. But the special executive assistant was already on his feet, trembling and wild-eyed. He seemed, however, totally unaware of where he was: Baines had to push him bodily into his minor circle.

'And stay there,' Baines added, in a voice that should have been able to scar diamonds. But Jack gave no sign of having heard it.

Baines went hastily to his Tanist's place, checking for the bottle of brandy. Everyone else was already in position, even the cat, which in fact had vaulted to its post promptly upon having been dumped off Ware's rear.

The sorcerer lit the brazier, and began to address the dead air. He was hardly more than a sentence into this invocation before Baines realized for the first time, in his freezing heart, that this was indeed the last effort – and that indeed they might all still be saved.

Ware was making his renunciation, in his own black and twisted way – the only way his fatally proud soul could ever be brought to make it. He said:

'I invoke and conjure thee, LUCIFUGE ROFOCALE, and fortified with the Power and the Supreme Majesty, I strongly command thee by BARALEMENSIS, BALDACHIENSIS, PAUMACHIE, APOLORESEDES and the most potent princes GENIO, LIACHIDE, ministers of the Tartarean seat, chief princes of the seat of APOLOGIA in the ninth region, I exorcise and command thee, LUCIFUGE ROFOCALE, by him Who spake and it was done, by the Most Holy and glorious Names ADONAI, EL, ELOHIM, ELOHE, ZEBAOTH, ELION, ESCHERCE, JAH, TETRAGRAMMATON, SADIE do thou and thine forthwith appear and show thyself unto me, regardless of how thou art previously charged, from whatever part of the world, without tarrying!

'I conjure thee by Him to Whom all creatures are obedient, by this ineffable Name, TETRAGRAMMATON JEHOVAH, by which the elements are overthrown, the air is shaken, the sea turns back, the fire is generated, the earth moves and all the hosts of things celestial, of things terrestrial, of things infernal, do tremble and are confounded together, come. ADONAI, King of kings, commands thee!'

There was no answer, except an interior grumble of thunder.

'Now I invoke, conjure and command thee, LUCIFUGE ROFOCALE, to appear and show thyself before this circle, by the Name of ON . . . by the Name Y and V, which Adam heard and spake . . . by the name of JOTH, which Jacob learned from the angel on the night of his wrestling and was delivered from the hands of his brother. . . by the Name of AGLA, which Lot heard and was saved with his family . . . by the Name ANEHEXETON, which Aaron spake and was made wise . . . by the name SCHEMES AMATHIA, which Joshua invoked and the Sun stayed upon his course . . . by the Name EMMANUEL, by which the three children were delivered from the fiery furnace . . . by the Name ALPHA-OMEGA, which Daniel uttered, and destroyed Bel and the dragon . . . by the Name ZEBAOTH, which Moses named, and all the rivers and the waters in the land of Egypt were turned into blood . . . by the Name HAGIOS, by the Seal of ADONAI, by those others, which are JETROS, ATHENOROS, PARACLETUS . . . by the dreadful Day of Judgement . . . by the changing sea of glass which is before the face of the Divine Majesty . . . by the four beasts before the Throne . . . by all these Holy and most potent words, come thou, and come thou quickly. Come, come! ADONAI, King of kings, commands thee!'

Now, at last, there was a sound: a sound of laughter. It was the laughter of Something incapable of joy, laughing only because It was compelled by Its nature to terrify. As the laughter grew, that Something formed.

It was not standing in the Lesser Circle or appearing from the Gateway, but instead was sitting on the altar, swinging Its cloven feet negligently. It had a goat's head, with immense horns, a crown that flamed like a torch, level human eyes, and a Star of David on Its forehead. Its haunches, too, were caprine. Between, the body was human, though hairy and with dragging black pinions like a crow's growing from Its shoulder blades. It had women's breasts and an enormous erection, which it nursed alternately with hands folded into the gesture of benediction. On one shaggy forearm was tattooed *Solve*; on the other, *Coagula*.

Ware fell slowly to one knee.

'*Adoramus te*, PUT SATANACHIA,' he said laying his wand on the ground before him. 'And again . . . *ave, ave*.'

AVE, BUT WHY DO YOU HAIL ME? the monster said in a petulant bass voice, at once deep and mannered, like a homosexual actor's IT WAS NOT I YOU CALLED.

'No, Baphomet, master and guest. Never for an instant. It is everywhere said that you can never be called, and would never appear.'

YOU CALLED ON THE GOD, WHO DOTH NOT APPEAR. I AM NOT MOCKED.

Ware bowed his head lower. 'I was wrong.'

AH! BUT THERE IS A FIRST TIME FOR EVERYTHING. YOU MIGHT HAVE SEEN THE GOD AFTER ALL. BUT NOW INSTEAD YOU HAVE SEEN ME. AND THERE IS ALSO A LAST TIME FOR EVERYTHING. I OWE YOU A MOMENT OF THANKS. WORM THOUGH YOU ARE, YOU ARE THE AGENT OF ARMAGEDDON. LET THAT BE WRITTEN, BEFORE ALL

WRITINGS, LIKE ALL ELSE, GO INTO THE EVERLASTING FIRE.

'No!' Ware cried out. 'Oh living God, no! This cannot be the Time! You break the Law! Where is the Antichrist –'

WE WILL DO WITHOUT THE ANTICHRIST. HE WAS NEVER NECESSARY. MEN HAVE ALWAYS LED THEMSELVES UNTO ME.

'But – master and guest – the Law –'

WE SHALL ALSO DO WITHOUT THE LAW. HAVE YOU NOT HEARD? THOSE TABLETS HAVE BEEN BROKEN.

There was a hiss of indrawn breath from both Ware and Father Domenico; but if Ware had intended some further argument, he was forestalled. To Baines's right, Dr Hess said in a voice of high ultraviolet hysteria:

'I don't see you, Goat.'

'Shut up!' Ware shouted, almost turning away from the vision.

'I don't see you,' Hess said doggedly. 'You're nothing but a silly zoological mixture. A mushroom dream. You're not real, Goat. Go away. Poof!'

Ware turned in his Karcist's circle and lifted his magician's sword against Hess in both hands; but, at the last minute, he seemed to be afraid to step out against the wobbling figure of the scientist.

HOW GRACIOUS OF YOU TO SPEAK TO ME, AGAINST THE RULES. WE UNDERSTAND, YOU AND I, THAT RULES WERE MADE TO BE BROKEN. BUT YOUR FORM OF ADDRESS DOES NOT QUITE PLEASE ME. LET US PROLONG THE CONVERSATION, AND I WILL EDUCATE YOU. ETERNALLY, FOR A BEGINNING.

Hess did not answer. Instead, he howled like a wolf and charged blindly out of the Grand Circle, his head down, towards the altar. The Sabbath Goat opened Its great mouth and gulped him down like a fly.

THANK YOU FOR THE SACRIFICE, It said thickly. ANYONE ELSE? THEN IT IS TIME I LEFT.

'Stand to, stupid and disobedient!' Father Domenico's voice rang out from Baines's right side. A cloth fluttered out of the monk's circle on to the floor. 'Behold thy confusion, if thou be disobedient! Behold the Pentacle of Solomon which I have brought into thy presence!'

FUNNY LITTLE MONK, I WAS NEVER IN THAT BOTTLE!

'Hush and be still, fallen star. Behold in me the person of the Exorcist, who is called OCTINIMOES, in the midst of delusion armed by the Lord God and fearless. I am thy master, in the name of the Lord BATHAL, rushing upon ABRAC, ABEOR, coming upon BEROR!'

The Sabbath Goat looked down upon Father Domenico almost kindly. His face red, Father Domenico reached into his robes and brought out a crucifix, which he thrust towards the altar like a sword.

'Back to Hell, devil! In the name of Christ our Lord!'

The ivory cross exploded like a Prince Rupert's Drop, strewing Father Domenico's robe with dust. He looked down at his horribly empty hands.

TOO LATE, MAGICIAN. EVEN THE BEST EFFORTS OF YOUR WHITE COLLEGE ALSO HAVE FAILED – AND AS THE HEAVENLY HOSTS ALSO WILL FAIL. WE ARE ABROAD AND LOOSE, AND WILL NOT BE PUT BACK.

The great head bent to look down upon Theron Ware.

AND YOU ARE MY DEARLY BELOVED SON, IN WHOM I AM WELL PLEASED. I GO TO JOIN MY BROTHERS AND LOVERS IN THE REST OF YOUR WORK. BUT I SHALL BE BACK FOR YOU. I SHALL BE BACK FOR YOU ALL. THE WAR IS ALREADY OVER.

'Impossible!' Father Domenico cried, though choking with the dust of the exploded crucifix. 'It is written that in that war you will at last be conquered and chained!'

OF COURSE, BUT WHAT DOES THAT PROVE? EACH OF THE OPPOSING SIDES IN ANY WAR ALWAYS PREDICTS VICTORY. THEY CANNOT BOTH BE RIGHT. IT IS THE FINAL BATTLE THAT COUNTS, NOT THE PROPAGANDA. YOU MADE A MISTAKE – AND AH, HOW YOU WILL PAY!

'One moment . . . please,' Father Domenico said. 'If you would be so kind . . . I see that we have failed. . . . Would you tell us, *where* did we fail?'

The Goat laughed, spoke three words, and vanished.

The dawn grew, red, streaked, dull, endless. From Ware's window the sleeping town slumped down in rivers of cold lava towards the sea – but there was no sea; as Father Domenico had seen hours ago, the sea had withdrawn, and would not be back again except as a tsunami after the Corinth earthquake.

Circles of desolation spread away from the ritual circles. Inside them, the last magicians waited for the now Greatest Powers to come back for them.

It would not be long now. In all their minds and hearts echoed those last three words. World without end. End without world.

God is dead.

THE DAY AFTER JUDGEMENT

After such knowledge, what forgiveness?
T. S. ELIOT

To Robert A. W. Lowndes

CONTENTS

The Wrath-Bearing Tree

Woe, woe, woe to the inhabiters of the earth by reason of the other voices of the trumpet of the three angels, which are yet to sound!

Revelation 8:13

The Fall of God put Theron Ware in a peculiarly unenviable position, though he was hardly alone. After all, he had caused it – in so far as an event so gigantic could be said to have had any cause but the First. And as a black magician he knew better than to expect any gratitude from the victor.

Nor, on the other hand, would it do him the slightest good to maintain that he had loosed the forty-eight suffragan demons upon the world only at the behest of a client. Hell was an incombustible Alexandrine library of such evasions – and besides, even had he had a perfect plea of innocence, there was no longer any such thing as jûstice, anywhere. The Judger was dead.

'When the hell *is* he coming back?' Baines, the client, demanded suddenly, irritably. 'This waiting is worse than getting it over with.'

Father Domenico turned from the refectory window, which was now unglazed, from the shock wave of the H-bombing of Rome. He had been looking down the cliff face, over the half-melted *pensioni*, shops and tenements of what had once been Positano, at the drained sea bed. When that tsunami did arrive, it was going to be a record one; it might even reach all the way up here.

'You don't know what you're saying, Mister Baines,' the

white magician said. 'From now on, nothing can be over with. We are on the brink of eternity.'

'You know what I mean,' Baines growled.

'Of course, but if I were you, I'd be grateful for the respite . . . It *is* odd that he hasn't come back yet. Dare we hope that something has after all interfered with him? Something – or some One?'

'He said God is dead.'

'Yes, but he is the Father of Lies. What do you think, Doctor Ware?'

Ware did not reply. The personage they were talking about was of course not the Father of Lies, the ultimate Satan, but the subsidiary prince who had answered Ware's last summons – PUT SATANACHIA, sometimes called Baphomet, the Sabbath Goat. As for the question, Ware simply did not know the answer; it was now sullen full morning of the day after Armageddon, and the Goat had promised to come for the four of them promptly at dawn, in ironical obedience to the letter of Ware's loosing and sending; yet he was not here.

Baines looked around the spent conjuring room. 'I wonder what he did with Hess?'

'Swallowed him,' Ware said, 'as you saw. And it served the fool right for stepping outside of his circle.'

'But did he really eat him?' Baines said. 'Or was that, uh, just symbolical? Is Hess actually in Hell now?'

Ware refused to be drawn into the discussion, which he recognized at once as nothing but Baines's last little vestige of scepticism floundering about for an exit from its doom; but Father Domenico said,

'The thing that called itself Screwtape let slip to Lewis that demons do eat souls. But one can hardly suppose that that is the end. I expect we will shortly know a lot more about the matter than we wish.'

Abstractedly, he brushed from his robe a little more of the dust from his shattered crucifix. Ware watched him with ironic wonder. He really was staging a remarkable recovery; his God was dead, his Christ was exploded as a myth, his soul assuredly as damned as that of Ware or Baines – and yet he could still manage to interest himself in semi-Scholastic prattle. Well,

Ware had always thought that white magic, these days as always, attracted only a low order of intellect, let alone insight.

But where *was* the Goat?

'I wonder where Mister Ginsberg went?' Father Domenico said, as if in parody of Ware's unspoken question. Again, Ware only shrugged. He had for the moment quite forgotten Baines's male secretary; it was true that Ginsberg had shown some promise as an apprentice, but after all, he had wanted to learn the Ars Magica essentially as a means of supplying himself with mistresses, and even under normal circumstances, his recent experience with Ware's assistant, Gretchen – who was in fact a succubus – had probably driven the desire out permanently. In any event, of what use would an apprentice be now?

Baines looked as startled as Ware felt at the question. 'Jack?' he said. 'I sent him to our rooms to pack.'

'To pack?' Ware said. 'You had some notion that you might get away?'

'I thought it highly unlikely,' Baines said evenly, 'but if the opportunity arose, I didn't mean to be caught unprepared.'

'Where do you think you might go where the Goat couldn't find you?'

No reply was necessary. Ware felt through his sandals a slow shuddering of the tiled floor. As it grew more pronounced, it was joined by a faint but deep thunder in the air.

Father Domenico shuffled hastily back to the window, Baines close behind him. Unwillingly, Ware followed.

On the horizon, a wall of foaming, cascading water was coming towards them with preternatural slowness, across the deserted floor of the Tyrrhenian Sea. The water had all been drained away as one consequence of the Corinth earthquake of yesterday, which itself might or might not have been demonically created; Ware was not sure that it made much difference one way or the other. In any event, the tectonic imbalance was now, inexorably, in the process of righting itself.

The Goat remained unaccountably delayed . . . but the tsunami was on its way at last.

*

What had been Jack Ginsberg's room in the palazzo now looked a great deal more like the cabinet of Dr Caligari. Every stone, every window frame, every angle, every wall was out of true, so that there was no place to stand where he did not feel as though he had been imprisoned in a tesseract – except that even the planes of the prison were crazed with jagged cracks without any geometry whatsoever. The window panes were out, and the ceiling dripped; the floor was invisible under fallen plaster, broken glass and anonymous dirt; and in the *gabinetto* the toilet was pumping continuously as though trying to flush away the world. The satin-sheeted bed was sandy to the touch, and when he took his clothes out of the wardrobe, his beautiful clothes so carefully selected from *Playboy*, dust fumed out of them like spores from a puffball.

There was no place to lay clothes out but on the bed, though it was only marginally less filthy than any other flat surface available. He wiped down the outside of his suitcase with a handkerchief, which he then dropped out the window down the cliff, and began to stow things away, shaking them out with angry coughs as best he could.

The routine helped, a little. It was not easy to think about any other part of this incredible impasse. It was even difficult to know whom to blame. After all, he had known about Baines's creative impulse towards destruction for a long time and had served it; nor had he ever thought it insane. It was a common impulse: to one engineer you add one stick of dynamite, and in the name of progress he will cut a mountain in half and cover half a country with concrete, for no better real reason than that he enjoys it. Baines was only the same kind of monomaniac, writ large because he had made so much money at it; and unlike the others, he had always been honest enough to admit that he did it because he loved the noise and the ruin. More generally, top management everywhere, or at least back in the States, was filled with people who loved their business, and cared for nothing else but crossword puzzles or painting by the numbers.

As for Ware, what had he done? He had prosecuted an art to his own destruction, which was traditionally the only sure way a life can be made into a work of art. Unlike that idiot

Hess, he had known how to protect himself from the minor unpleasant consequences of his fanaticism, though he had turned out to be just as blindly suicidal in the end. Ware was still alive, and Hess was dead – unless his soul still lived in Hell – but the difference now was only one of degree, not of kind. Ware had not invited Baines's commission; he had only hoped to use it to enlarge his own knowledge; as Hess had been using Baines; as Baines had used Hess and Ware to satisfy his business and aesthetic needs; as Ware and Baines had used Jack's administrative talents and his delight in straight, raw sex; as Jack had tried to use them all in return.

They had all been things, not people, to each other, which after all is the only sensible and fruitful attitude in a thing-dominated world. (Except, of course, for Father Domenico, whose desire to prevent anybody from accomplishing anything, chiefly by wringing his hands, had to be written off as the typical, incomprehensible attitude of the mystic – a howling anachronism in the modern world, and predictably ineffectual.) And in point of fact none of them – not even Father Domenico – could fairly be said to have failed. Instead, they had all been betrayed. Their plans and operations had all depended implicitly upon the existence of God – even Jack, who had entered Positano as an atheist, had been reluctantly forced to grant that – and in the final pinch, He had turned out to have been not around any more after all. If this shambles was anyone's fault, it was His.

He slammed down the cover of his suitcase. The noise was followed, behind him, by a fainter sound, about halfway between the clearing of a throat and the sneeze of a cat. For a moment he stood stock-still, knowing very well what that sound meant. But it was useless to ignore it, and finally he turned around.

The girl was standing on the threshold, as before, and as before, she was somewhat different. It was one of the immemorial snares of her type; at each apparition she seemed like someone else, and yet always, at the same time, reminded him of someone – he could never think who – he had once known; she was always at once mistress, harem and stranger. Ware ironically called her Gretchen, or Greta, or Rita, and she could be compelled by the word *Cazotte*, but in fact she had no name, nor even any real sex. She was a demon, alternately playing succubus to Jack and incubus to some witch on the other side of the world. In theory only, the idea of such a relationship would have revolted Jack, who was fastidious, in his fashion. In actual practice, it did indeed revolt him . . . insufficiently.

'You do not make me as welcome as before,' she said.

Jack did not reply. This time the apparition was blonde again, taller than he was, very slender, her hair long and falling straight down her back. She wore a black silk sari with gold edging, which left one breast bare, and gold sandals, but no jewellery. Amidst all this rubble, she looked fresh as though she had just stepped out of a tub: beautiful, magical, terrifying and irresistible.

'I thought you could come only at night,' he said at last.

'Oh, those old rules are gone for ever,' she said, and as if to prove it, stepped across the threshold without even one invitation, let alone three. 'And you are leaving. We must celebrate the mystery once more before you go, and you must make me a last present of your seed. It is not very potent; my other client is thus far disappointed. Come, touch me, go into me. I know it is your need.'

'In this mess? You must have lost your mind.'

'Nay, impossible; intellect is all I am, no matter how I appear to you. Yet I am capable of monstrous favours, as you know well, and will to know again.'

She took the suitcase, which was still unfastened, off the bed and set it flat on the floor. Though it was almost too heavy for Jack when fully loaded, handling it did not appear to cost her the slightest effort. Then, lifting one arm and with it the bare and spiky breast, she unwound the sari in a single, continuous sweeping motion, and lay down naked across the gritty bed, light glinting from dewdrops caught about her inflamed mound, a vision of pure lubricity.

Jack ran a finger around the inside of his collar, though it was open. It was impossible not to want her, and at the same time he wanted desperately to escape – and besides, Baines was waiting, and Jack had better sense than to pursue his hobby on company time.

'I should have thought you'd be off raising hell with your colleagues,' he said, his voice hoarse.

The girl frowned suddenly, reminding him of that fearful moment after their first night when she had thought that he had been mocking her. Her fingernails, like independent creatures, clawed slowly at her flat abdomen.

'Dost think to copulate with fallen seraphim?' she said. 'I am not of any of the Orders which make war; I do only what would be hateful even to the damned.' Then, equally suddenly, the frown dissolved in a little shower of laughter. 'And ah, besides, I raise not Hell, but the Devil, for already I have Hell in me – dost know that story of Boccaccio?'

Jack knew it; there was no story of that kind he did not know; and his Devil was most certainly raised. While he still hesitated, there was a distant growling sound, almost inaudible but somehow also infinitely heavy. The girl turned her head towards the window, also listening; then she looked back at him, spread her thighs and held out her arms.

'I think,' she said, 'that you had better hurry.'

With a groan of despair, he fell to his knees and buried his face in her muff. Her smooth legs closed about his ears; but no matter how hard he pulled at her cool, pliant rump, the sound of the returning sea rose louder and louder around them both.

So Above

Haeresis est maxima opera maleficarum non credere.
HEINRICH INSTITOR AND JAKOB SPRENGER: *Malleus Maleficarum*

1

The enemy, whoever he was, had obviously been long prepared to make a major attempt to reduce the Strategic Air Command's master missile-launching control site under Denver. In the first twenty minutes of the war, he had dumped a whole stick of multiple hydrogen warheads on it. The city, of course, had been utterly vaporized, and a vast expanse of the plateau on which it had stood was now nothing but gullied, vitrified and radioactive granite; but the site had been well hardened and was more than a mile beneath the original surface. Everybody in it had been knocked down and temporarily deafened, there were bruises and scrapes and one concussion, some lights had gone out and a lot of dust had been raised despite the air conditioning; in short, the damage would have been reported as 'minimal' had there been anybody to report it to.

Who the enemy was occasioned some debate. General D. Willis McKnight, a Yellow Peril fan since his boyhood reading of *The American Weekly* in Chicago, favoured the Chinese. Of his two chief scientists, one, the Prague-born Dr Džejms Šatvje, the godfather of the selenium bomb, had been seeing Russians under his bed for almost as long.

'Nu, why argue?' said Johann Buelg. As a RAND Corporation alumnus, he found nothing unthinkable, but he did not like to waste time speculating about facts. 'We can always ask the computer – we must have enough input already for that. Not that it matters much, since we've already plastered the Russians *and* the Chinese pretty thoroughly.'

'We already know the Chinese started it,' General McKnight said, wiping dust off his spectacles with his handkerchief. He was a small, narrow-chested Air Force Academy graduate from the class just after the cheating had been stopped, already nearly bald at forty-eight; naked, his face looked remarkably like that of a prawn. 'They dropped a thirty-megatonner on Formosa, disguised as a test.'

'It depends on what you mean by "start," ' Buelg said. 'That was already on Rung twenty-one, Level Four – local nuclear war. But still only Chinese against Chinese.'

'But we were committed to them, right?' Šatvje said. 'President Agnew told the UN, "I am a Formosan." '

'It doesn't matter worth a damn,' Buelg said, with some irritation. It was his opinion, which he did not keep particularly private, that Šatvje, whatever his eminence as a physicist, in all other matters had a *goyische kopf*. He had encountered better heads on egg creams in his father's candy store. 'The thing's escalated almost exponentially in the past eighteen hours or so. The question is, how far has it gone? If we're lucky, it's only up to Level Six, central war – maybe no farther than Rung thirty-four, constrained disarming attack.'

'Do you call atomizing Denver "restrained"?' the General demanded.

'Maybe. They could have done for Denver with one warhead, but instead they saturated it. That means they were shooting for us, not for the city proper. Our counterstrike couldn't be preventive, so it was one rung lower, which I hope to God they noticed.'

'They took Washington out,' Šatvje said, clasping his fat hands piously. He had been lean once, but becoming first a consultant on the Cabinet level, next a spokesman for massive retaliation, and finally a publicity saint had appended a beer belly to his brain-puffed forehead, so that he now looked like a caricature of a nineteenth-century German philologist. Buelg himself was stocky and tended to run to lard, but a terrible susceptibility to kidney stones had kept him on a reasonable diet.

'The Washington strike almost surely wasn't directed against civilians,' Buelg said. 'Naturally the leadership of the enemy is a prime military target. But, General, all this happened so quickly that I doubt that anybody in government had a chance to reach prepared shelters. You may now be effectively the president of whatever is left of the United States, which means that you could make new policies.'

'True,' McKnight said. 'True, true.'

'In which case we've got to know the facts the minute our lines to outside are restored. Among other things, if the escalation's gone all the way to spasm, in which case the planet will be uninhabitable. There'll be nobody and nothing left alive but people in hardened sites, like us, and the only policy we'll need for that will be a count of the canned beans.'

'I think that needlessly pessimistic,' Šatvje said, at last heaving himself up out of the chair into which he had struggled after getting up off the floor. It was not a very comfortable chair, but the computer room – where they had all been when the strike had come – had not been designed for comfort. He put his thumbs under the lapels of his insignia-less adviser's uniform and frowned down upon them. 'The Earth is a large planet, of its class; if we cannot reoccupy it, our descendants will be able to do so.'

'After five thousand years?'

'You are assuming that carbon bombs were used. Dirty bombs of that kind are obsolescent. That is why I so strongly advocated the sulphur-decay chain; the selenium isotopes are chemically all strongly poisonous, but they have very short half lives. A selenium bomb is essentially a *humane* bomb.'

Šatvje was physically unable to pace, but he was beginning to stump back and forth. He was again playing back one of his popular magazine articles. Buelg began to twiddle his thumbs, as ostentatiously as possible.

'It has sometimes occurred to me,' Šatvje said, 'that our discovery of how to release the nuclear energies was providential. Consider: Natural selection stopped for Man when he achieved control over his environment, and furthermore began to save the lives of all his weaklings, and preserve their bad genes. Once natural selection has been halted, then the only remaining pressure upon the race to evolve is mutation. Artificial radio-activity, and indeed even fallout itself, may be God's way of resuming the process of evolution for Man . . . perhaps towards some ultimate organism we cannot foresee, perhaps even towards some unitary mind which we will share with God, as Teilhardt de Chardin envisioned –'

At this point, the General noticed the twiddling of Buelg's thumbs.

'Facts are what we need,' he said. 'I agree with you there, Buelg. But a good many of our lines to outside *were* cut, and there may have been some damage to the computer circuitry, too.' He jerked his head towards the technicians who were scurrying around and up and down the face of RANDOMAC. 'I've got them working on it. Naturally.'

'I see that, but we'll need some sort of rational schedule of questions. Is the escalation still going on, presuming we haven't reached the insensate stage already? If it's over, or at least suspended somehow, is the enemy sane enough not to start it again? And then, what's the extent of the exterior damage? For that, we'll need a visual readout – I assume there are still some satellites up, but we'll want a closer look, if any local television survived.

'And if you're now the president, General, are you prepared to negotiate, if you've got any opposite numbers in the Soviet Union or the People's Republic?'

'There ought to be whole sets of such courses of action already programmed into the computer,' McKnight said, 'according to what the actual situation is. Is the machine going to be useless to us for anything but gaming, now that we really need it? Or have you been misleading me again?'

'Of course I haven't been misleading you. I wouldn't play games with my own life as stakes. And there are indeed such alternative courses; I wrote most of them myself, though I didn't do the actual programming. But no programme can encompass what a specific leader might decide to do, War gaming actual past battles – for example, rerunning Waterloo without allowing for Napoléon's piles, or the heroism of the

British squares – has produced "predicted" outcomes completely at variance with history. Computers are rational; people aren't. Look at Agnew. That's why I asked you my question – which, by the way, you haven't yet answered.'

McKnight pulled himself up and put his glasses back on.

'I,' he said, 'am prepared to negotiate. With anybody. Even Chinks.'

2

Rome was no more, nor was Milan. Neither were London, Paris, Berlin, Bonn, Tel Aviv, Cairo, Riyadh, Stockholm and a score of lesser cities. But these were of no immediate concern. As the satellites showed, their deaths had expectably laid out long, cigar-shaped, overlapping paths of fallout to the east - the direction in which, thanks to the rotation of the Earth, the weather inevitably moved – and though these unfortunately lay across once friendly terrain, they ended in enemy country. Similarly, the heavy toll in the USSR had sown its seed across Siberia and China; that in China across Japan, Korea and Taiwan; and the death of Tokyo was poisoning only a swath of the Pacific (although, later, some worry would have to be devoted to the fish). Honolulu somehow had been spared, so that no burden of direct heavy nuclear fallout would reach the West Coast of the United States.

This was fortunate, for Los Angeles, San Francisco, Portland, Seattle amd Spokane had all been hit, as had Denver, St Louis, Minneapolis, Chicago, New Orleans, Cleveland, Detroit and Dallas. Under the circumstances, it really hardly mattered that Pittsburgh, Philadelphia, New York, Syracuse, Boston, Toronto, Baltimore and Washington had all also got it, for even without bombs the Eastern third of the continental United States would have been uninhabitable in its entirety for at least fifteen years to come. At the moment, in any event, it consisted of a single vast forest fire through which, from the satellites, the slag pits of the bombed cities were invisible except as high spots in the radiation contours. The Northwest was in much the same shape, although the West Coast in general had taken far fewer missiles. Indeed, the sky all over the world was black with smoke, for the forests of Europe and northern Asia were burning too. Out of the pall, more death fell, gently, invisibly, inexorably.

All this, of course, came from the computer analysis. Though there were television cameras in the satellites, even on a clear day you could hardly have told from visual sightings, from that height – nor from photographs, for that matter – even whether or not there was intelligent life on Earth. The view over Africa, South America, Australia and the American Southwest was better, but of no strategic or logistic interest, and never had been.

Of the television cameras on the Earth's surface, most of the surviving ones were in areas where nothing seemed to have happened at all, although in towns the streets were deserted, and the very few people glimpsed briefly on the screen looked haunted. The views from near the bombed areas were fragmentary, travelling, scarred by rasters, aflicker with electronic snow – a procession of unconnected images, like scenes from an early surrealist film, where one could not tell whether the director was trying to portray a story or only a state of mind.

Here stood a single telephone pole, completely charred; here was a whole row of them, snapped off the ground level but still linked in death by their wires. Here was a desert of collapsed masonry, in the midst of which stood a reinforced-concrete smokestack, undamaged except that its surface was etched by heat and by the sand blasting of debris carried by a high wind. Here buildings all leaned sharply in a single direction, as if struck like the chimney by some hurricane of terrific proportions; here was what had been a group of manufacturing buildings, denuded of roofing and siding, nothing but twisted frames. Here a row of wrecked automobiles, neatly parked, burned in unison; here a gas holder, ruptured and collapsed, had burned out hours ago.

Here was a side of a reinforced concrete building, windowless, cracked and buckled slightly inward where a shock wave had struck it. Once it had been painted grey or some dark colour, but all the paint had blistered and scaled and blown away in a second, except where a man had been standing nearby, there the paint remained, a shadow with no one to cast it.

That vaporized man had been one of the lucky. Here stood another who had been in a cooler circle; evidently he had looked up at a fireball, for his eyes were only holes; he stood in a half crouch, holding his arms out from his sides like a penguin, and instead of skin, his naked body was covered with a charred fell which was cracked in places, oozing blood and pus. Here a filthy, tattered mob clambered along a road almost completely covered with rubble, howling with horror – though there was no sound with this scene – led by a hairless woman pushing a flaming baby carriage. Here a man who seemed to have had his back flayed by flying glass worked patiently with a bent snow shovel at the edge of an immense mound of broken brick; by the shape of its margins, it might once have been a large house . . .

There was more.

Šatvje uttered a long, complex, growling sentence of hatred. It was entirely in Czech, but its content was nevertheless not beyond all conjecture. Buelg shrugged again and turned away from the TV screen.

'Pretty fearful,' he said. 'But on the whole, not nearly as much destruction as we might have expected. It's certainly gone no *higher* than Rung thirty-four. On the other hand, it doesn't seem to fit any of the escalation frames at all well. Maybe it makes some sort of military or strategic sense, but if it does, I'm at a loss to know what it is. General?'

'Senseless,' McKnight said. 'Outright senseless. Nobody's been hurt in any *decisive* way. And yet the action seems to be over.'

'That was my impression.' Buelg agreed. 'There seems to be some missing factor. We're going to have to ask the computer to scan for an anomaly. Luckily it's likely to be a big one – but since I can't tell the machine what *kind* of anomaly to look for, it's going to cost us some time.'

'How much time?' McKnight said, running a finger around the inside of his collar. 'If the Chinks start up on us again –'

'It may be as much as an hour, after I formulate the question and Chief Hay programmes it, which will take, oh, say two hours at a minimum. But I don't think we need to worry about the Chinese; according to our data, that opening Taiwan bomb was the biggest one they used, so it was probably the biggest one they had. As for anyone else, well, you just finished saying yourself that somehow everything's now stopped short. We badly need to find out why.'

'All right. Get on it, then.'

The two hours for programming, however, stretched to four; and then the computer ran for ninety minutes without producing anything at all, Chief Hay had thoughtfully forbidden the machine to reply DATA INSUFFICENT since new data were coming in at an increasing rate as communications with the outside improved; as a result, the computer was recycling the problem once every three or four seconds.

McKnight used the time to issue orders that repairs to the keep be made, stores assessed, order restored, and then settled down to a telecommunications search – again via the computer, but requiring only about 2 per cent of its capacity – for any superiors who might have survived him. Buelg suspected that he really wanted to find some; he had the capacity to be a general officer, but would find it most uncomfortable to be a president, even over so abruptly simplified a population and economy – and foreign policy, for that matter – as the TV screen had shown now existed outside. Ordering junior officers to order noncommissioned officers to order rankers to replace broken fluorescent bulbs was the type of thing he didn't mind doing on his own, but for ordering them to arm missiles and aim them, or put a state under martial law, he much preferred to be acting upon higher authority.

As for Buelg's own preference, he rather hoped that McKnight wouldn't be able to find any such person. The United States under a McKnight regime wouldn't be run very imaginatively or even flexibly, but on the other hand it would be unlikely to be a tyranny. Besides, McKnight was very dependent upon his civilian experts, and hence would be easy to manage. Of course, that meant that something would have to be done about Šatvje –

Then the computer rang its bell and began to print out its analysis. Buelg read it with intense concentration, and after the first fold, utter incredulity. When it was all out of the printer, he tore it off, tossed it on to the desk and beckoned to Chief Hay.

'Run the question again.'

Hay turned to the input keyboard. It took him ten minutes to retype the programme; the question had been in the normal order of things too specialized to tape. Two and a half seconds after he had finished, the machine chimed and the long thin slabs of metal began to rise against the paper. The printing out process never failed to remind Buelg of a player piano running in reverse, converting notes into punches instead of the other way around, except, of course, that what one got here was not punches but lines of type. But he saw almost at once that the analysis itself was going to be the same as before, word for word.

At the same time he became aware that Šatvje was standing just behind him.

'About time,' the Czech said. 'Let's have a look.'

'There's nothing to see yet.'

'What do you mean, there's nothing to see? It's printing isn't it? And you've already got another copy out on the bench. The General should have been notified immediately.'

He picked up the long, wide accordion fold of paper with its sprocket-punched edges and began to read it. There was nothing Buelg could do to prevent him.

'The machine's printing nonsense, that's what I mean, and I didn't propose to distract the General with a lot of garbage. The bombing must have jarred something loose.'

Hay turned from the keyboard. 'I ran a test programme through promptly after the attack, Doctor Buelg. The computer was functioning perfectly then.'

'Well, clearly it isn't now. Run your test programme again, find out where the trouble lies, and let us know how long it will take to repair it. If we can't trust the computer, we're out of business for sure.'

Hay got to work. Šatvje put the readout down.

'What's nonsense about this?' he said.

'It's utterly impossible, that's all. There hasn't been time. With any sort of engineering training, you'd know that yourself. And it makes no military or political sense, either.

'I think we should let the General be the judge of that.'

Picking up the bulky strip again, Šatvje carried it off towards the General's office, a certain subtle triumph in his gait, like the school trusty bearing the evidence of petty theft to the head master. Buelg followed, inwardly raging, and not only at the waste motion. Šatvje would of course tell McKnight that Buelg had been holding back on reporting the analysis; all Buelg could do now, until the machine was repaired, was to be sure to be there to explain why, and the posture was much too purely defensive for his liking. It was a damn shame that he had ever taught Šatvje to read a printout, but once they had been thrown together on this job, he had had no choice in the matter. McKnight had been as suspicious as a Sealyham of both of them, anyhow, at the beginning. Šatvje, after all, had come from a country which had long been Communist, and had had to explain that his ancestry was French, his name only a Serbo-Croat transliteration back from the Cyrillic of 'Chatvieux'; while Security had unfortunately confused Buelg with Johann Gottfried Jülg, a forgotten nineteenth-century translator of *Ardshi Bordschi Khan*, the *Siddhi Kur*, the *Skaskas* and other Russian folk tales, so that Buelg, even more demeaningly, had had to admit that his name was actually a Yiddish version of a German word for a leather bucket. Under McKnight's eye, the two still possibly suspect civilians had to cooperate or be downgraded into some unremunerative university post. Buelg supposed that Šatvje had enjoyed it as little as he had, but he didn't care an iota about what Šatvje did or didn't enjoy, Damn the man.

As for the document itself, it was no masterpiece of analysis. The machine had simply at last recognized an anomaly in a late-coming piece of new data. It was the interpretation that made Buelg suspect that the gadget had malfunctioned; unlike Šatvje, he had had enough experience of computers at RAND to know that if they were not allowed enough warm-up time, or had been improperly cleared of a previous programme, they could produce remarkably paranoid fantsies.

Translated from the Fortran, the document said that the United States had not only been hit by missiles, but also deeply invaded. This conclusion had been drawn from a satellite sighting of something in Death Valley, not there yesterday, which was not natural, and whose size, shape and energy output suggested an enormous fortress.

'Which is just plain idiotic,' Buelg added, after the political backing and filling in McKnight's office had been gone through to nobody's final advantage. 'On any count you care to name. The air drops required to get the materials in there, or the sea landings plus overland movements, couldn't have gone undetected. Then, strategically it's insane: the building of targets like fortresses should have become obsolete with the invention of the cannon, and the airplane made them absurd. Locating such a thing in Death Valley means that it dominates nothing but utterly worthless territory, at the price of insuperable supply problems – right from the start it's in a state of siege, by Nature alone. And as for running it up overnight – I ask you, General, could *we* have done that, even in peacetime and in the most favourable imaginable location? I say we couldn't, and that if we couldn't, no human agency could.'

McKnight picked up his phone and spoke briefly. Since it was a Hush-a-Phone, what he said was inaudible, but Buelg's guess about the call was promptly confirmed.

'Chief Hay says the machine is in perfect order and has produced a third analysis just like this one,' he reported. 'The problem now clearly is one of reconnaissance. (He pronounced the word correctly, which, amidst his flat Californian American, sounded almost affected.) Is there such a thing in Death Valley, or isn't there? For the satellite to be able to spot it at all, it must be gigantic. From twenty-three thousand miles up, even a city the size of San Antonio is invisible unless you know exactly what you're looking for in advance.'

Here, Buelg was aware, McKnight was speaking as an expert. Until he had been put in charge of SAC in Denver, almost all his career had been spent in various aspects of Air Information; even as a teenager, he had been a Civil Air Patrol cadet involved in search-and-rescue operations, which, between the mud slides and the brush fires, had been particularly extensive in the Los Angeles area in those days.

'I don't doubt that the satellite has spotted *something,*' Buelg said. 'But what it probably "sees" is a hard-radiation locus – maybe thermally hot, too – rather than any optical object, let alone a construct. My guess is that it's nothing more than the impact site of a multiple warhead component that lost guidance, or was misaimed to begin with.'

'Highly likely,' McKnight admitted. 'But why guess? The obvious first step is to send a low-level attack bomber over the site and get close-in photographs and spectra. A primitive installation such as you suggested earlier would be typically Chinese, and if so they won't have low-level radar. If on the other hand the plane gets shot down, that will tell us something about the enemy, too.'

Buelg sighed inwardly. Trying to nudge McKnight out of his single channel was a frustrating operation. But maybe, in this instance, it wasn't really necessary; after all, the suggestion itself was sensible.

'All right,' he said. 'One plane seems like a small investment. We've got damn all else left to lose now, anyhow.'

3

No attack was made on the plane, but there was nevertheless one casualty. Neither the photographer nor the flight engineer, both busy with their instruments, had actually seen much of the target, and the Captain, for the same reason, had seen little more.

'Hell of a lot of turbulence,' he said at the debriefing, which took place a thousand miles away, while the men under Denver watched intently. 'And the target itself is one huge updraft, like New York used to be, only much worse.'

But the navigator, once his job had been done, had had nothing to do but look out, and he was in a state of shock. He was a swarthy young enlisted man from Chicago who looked as though he might have been recruited straight from a Mafiosa family, but he could say nothing now but a sentence which refused to get beyond its first syllable: 'Dis – Dis – ' Once he had recovered from his shock they would be able to question him. But for the time being he was of no help.

The photographs, however, were very clear, except for the infra-red sensitive plates, which showed nothing intelligible to the eye at all. The installation was perfectly circular and surrounded by a moat which, impossibly for Death Valley, appeared to be filled with black but genuine water, from which a fog bank was constantly trying to rise, only to be dissipated in the bone-dry air. The construction itself was a broad wall, almost a circular city, a good fifteen miles in diameter. It was broken irregularly by towers and other structures, some of them looking remarkably like mosques. This shell glowed fiercely, like red-hot iron, and a spectrograph showed that this was exactly what it was.

Inside, the ground was terraced, like a lunar crater. At ground level was a flat plain, dotted with tiny rectangular markings in no discernible pattern; these, too, the spectrograph said, were red-hot iron. What seemed to be another moat, blood-red and as broad as a river, encircled the next terrace at the foot of the cliff where it began, and this, even more impossibly, was bordered by a dense circular forest. The forest was as broad as the river, but thinned eventually to a ring of what appeared to be the original sand, equally broad.

In a lunar crater, the foothills of the central peak would have begun about here, but in the pictures, instead, the terrain plunged into a colossal black pit. The river cut through the forest and the desert at one point and roared over the side in a vast waterwall, compounding the darkness with mist which the camera had been unable to penetrate.

'What was that you were saying about building a fortress overnight, Buelg?' the General said. '"No human agency could?"'

'No human agency was involved,' Šatvje said in a hoarse whisper. He turned to the aide who had brought the pictures, an absurdly young lieutenant colonel with a blond crew cut, white face and shaking hands. 'Are there any close-ups?'

'Yes, Doctor. There was an automatic camera under the plane that took a film of the approach run. Here is one of the best shots.'

The picture showed what appeared to be a towering gate in the best medieval style. Hundreds of shadowy figures crowded the barbican, of which three, just above the gateway itself, had been looking up at the plane and were shockingly clear. They looked like gigantic naked women, with ropy hair all awry, and the wide-staring eyes of insane rage.

'I thought so,' Šatvje said.

'You recognize them?' Buelg asked incredulously.

'No, but I know their names: Alecto, Megaera and Tisiphone,' Šatvje said. 'And it's a good thing that there's at least one person among us with a European education. I presume that our *distrait* friend the navigator is a Catholic, which does just as well in this context. In any event, he was quite right: this is Dis, the fortress surrounding Nether Hell. I think we must now assume that all the rest of the Earth is contiguous with Upper Hell, not only in metaphor but in fact.'

'It's a good thing,' Buelg said acidly, 'that there's at least one person among us with a good grip on his sanity. The last thing we need now is a relapse into superstition.'

'If you blow up that photograph, I think you'll find that the hair on those women actually consists of live snakes. Isn't that so, Colonel?'

'Well . . . Doctor, it . . . it certainly looks like it.'

'Of course. Those are the Furies who guard the gates of Dis. They are the keepers of the Gorgon Medusa, which, thank God, isn't in the picture. The moat is the River Styx; the first terrace inside contains the burning tombs of the Heresiarchs, and on the next you have the River Phlegethon, the Wood of the Suicides, and the Abominable Sand. A rain of fire is supposed to fall continually on the sand, but I suppose that's invisible in Death Valley sunlight or maybe even superfluous. We can't see what's down below, but presumably that too will be exactly as Dante described it. The crowd along the barbican is made up of demons – not so, Colonel?'

'Sir . . . we can't tell what they are. We were wondering if they were, well, Martians or something. Every one is a different shape.'

Buelg felt his back hairs stirring. 'I refuse to believe this nonsense,' he said. 'Šatvje is interpreting it from his damned obsolete "education". Even Martians would make more sense.'

'What are the facts about this Dante?' McKnight said.

'An Italian poet, of about the thirteenth century – '

'Early fourteenth,' Šatvje said. 'And not just a poet. He had a vision of Hell and Heaven which became the greatest poem ever written – the *Divine Comedy*. What we see in those pictures exactly corresponds to the description in Cantos Eight through Eleven of it.'

'Buelg, see if you can locate a copy of the book and have it read to the computer. First we need to know if the correspondence is all that exact. If it is, we'll need an analysis of what it means.'

'The computer probably already has the book,' Buelg said. 'The whole Library of Congress, plus all our recreational library, is on microfilm inside it, we didn't have room for books per se down here. All we need to do is tell Chief Hay to make it part of the problem. But I still think it's damn nonsense.'

'What we want,' McKnight said, 'is the computer's opinion. Yours has already been shown to be somewhat less reliable.'

'And while you're at it,' Šatvje said, perhaps a shade less smugly than Buelg might have expected, 'have Chief Hay make a part of the problem everything in the library on demonology. We're going to need it.'

Throwing up his hands, Buelg left the office. In the country of the mad . . .

Nobody retains his sanity.

Only a few moments were needed for the computer to produce its report:

THE ANCIENT TEXTS AND FICTIONS NOW ADMITTED TO THE PROBLEM DISAGREE WITH EACH OTHER. HOWEVER, NEW FACTUAL DATA MAKE EXACT MATCHES WITH A NUMBER OF THEM, AND APPROXIMATE MATCHES WITH THE MAJORITY OF THEM. THE ASSUMPTION THAT THE CONSTRUCT IN DEATH VALLEY IS RUSSIAN, CHINESE OR OTHERWISE OF HUMAN ORIGIN IS OF THE LOWEST ORDER OF PROBABILITY AND MAY BE DISCOUNTED. THE INTERPLANETARY HYPOTHESIS IS OF SLIGHTLY HIGHER PROBABILITY, AN INVASION FROM VENUS BEING COMPATIBLE WITH A FEW OF THE FACTUAL DATA, SUCH AS THE IMMENSE HEAT AND ABERRANT LIFE

FORMS OF THE DEATH VALLEY INSTALLATION, BUT IS INCOMPATIBLE WITH MOST ARCHITECTURAL AND OTHER HISTORICAL DETAILS IN THE DATA, AS WELL AS WITH THE LEVEL OF TECHNOLOGY INDICATED. THE PROBABILITY THAT THE DEATH VALLEY INSTALLATION IS THE CITY OF DIS AND THAT ITS INTERNAL AREA IS NETHER HELL IS 0·1 WITHIN A 5 PER CENT LEVEL OF CONFIDENCE, AND THEREFORE MUST BE ADMITTED. AS A FIRST DERIVATIVE, THE PROBABILITY THAT THE WAR JUST CONCLUDED WAS ARMAGEDDON IS 0.01 WITHIN THE SAME CONFIDENCE LEVEL. AS A SECOND DERIVATIVE, THE PROBABILITY THAT THE FORCES OF GOD HAVE LOST THE WAR AND THAT THE SURFACE OF THE EARTH IS NOW CONFLUENT WITH UPPER HELL IS 0·001 WITHIN THE SAME CONFIDENCE LEVEL.

'Well, that clarifies the situation considerably,' McKnight said. 'It's just as well we asked.'

'But – my God! – it simply can't be true,' Buelg said desperately. 'All right, maybe the computer is functioning properly, but it has no intelligence, and above all, no judgement. What it's putting out now is just a natural consequence of letting all that medieval superstition into the problem.'

McKnight turned his shrimp's eyes towards Buelg. 'You've seen the pictures,' he said. 'They didn't come out of the computer, did they? Nor out of the old books, either. I think we'd better stop kicking against the pricks and start figuring out what we're going to do. We've still got the United States to think of. Doctor Šatvje, have you any suggestions?'

That was a bad sign. McKnight never used honorifics except to indicate, by inversion, which of the two of them had incurred his displeasure – not that Buelg had been in any doubt about that, already.

'I'm still in a good deal of doubt,' Šatvje said modestly. 'To begin with, if this has been Armageddon, we all ought to have been called to judgement by now; and there was certainly nothing in the prophecies that allowed for an encampment of victorious demons on the surface of the Earth. If the computer is completely right, then either God is dead as Nietzsche said, or, as the jokes go, He is alive but doesn't want to get involved. In either case, I think we would be well advised not to draw attention to ourselves. We can do nothing against supernatural powers: and if He *is* still alive, the battle may not be over. We are, I hope, safely hidden here, and we would be ill advised to be caught in the middle.'

'Now there you're dead wrong,' Buelg said with energy. 'Let's suppose for a minute that this fantasy represents the true state of affairs – in other words, that demons have turned out to be real, and are out there in Death Valley – '

'I'm none too sure what would be meant by "real" in this context,' Šatvje said. 'They are apparent, true enough; but they certainly don't belong to the same order of reality as – '

'That's a question we can't afford to debate,' Buelg said. He knew very well that the issue Šatvje was raising was a valid one – he was himself a fairly thoroughgoing Logical Positivist. But it would only confuse McKnight and there were brownie points to be made in keeping things clear-cut, whether they *were* clear-cut or not. 'Look. If demons are real, then they occupy space/time in the real universe. That means that they exist inside some energy system in that universe and are maintained by it. All right, they can walk on red-hot iron and live comfortably in Death Valley; that's not inherently more supernatural than the existence of bacteria in the boiling waters of volcanic springs. It's an adaptation. Very well, then we can find out what that energy system is. We can analyse how it works. And once we know that, we can attack it.'

'Now that's more like it,' McKnight said.

'Pardon me, but I think we should proceed with the most extreme caution,' Šatvje said. 'Unless one has been raised in this tradition, one is not likely to think of all the implications. I myself am quite out of practice at it.'

'Damn your education,' Buelg said. But it was all coming back to him: The boundaryless ghetto along Nostrand Avenue; the fur-hatted, fur-faced, maxi-skirted Hassidim walking in pairs under the scaling elm saplings of Grand Central Parkway; the terror of riding the subway among the juvenile gangs under the eternal skullcap; the endless hairsplitting over the Talmudic and Midrashic creation myths for hour upon stuffy hour in *Schule*; the women slaving over their duplicate sets of dishes, in the peculiar smell of a kosher household, so close to being a stench compared to all other American smells, supporting their drone scholars; his mother's pride that Hansli too was plainly destined by God's will to become a holy man; and when he had discovered instead the glories and rigours of the physical universe, that light and airy escape from fur hats and the smell of gefuelte fish and the loving worn women, the terror of the wrath of the jealous God. But all that was many years ago; it could not come back. He would not have it back.

'What are you talking about?' McKnight said. 'Are we going to do something, and if so, what? Get to the point.'

'My point,' Šatvje said, 'is that if all this – demonology – is, well, valid, or I suppose one should say true, then the whole Christian mythos is true, though it is not coming out in precisely the way it was prophesied. That being the case, then there are such things as immortal souls, or perhaps I should say, we may well have immortal souls, and we ought to take them into consideration before we do anything rash.'

Buelg saw the light, and with a great sense of relief; the Christian mythos had nothing to do with him, not personally, that is. He had no objection to it as an exercise in theory, a form of non-zero-sum game.

'If that's the case, I don't think there's any question of our being caught in the middle,' he said. 'We're required by the rules to come down on one side or the other.'

'That's true, by God,' McKnight said. 'And after all, we're on the right side. We didn't start this war – the Chinks did.'

'Right, right,' Buelg said. 'We're entitled to self-defence. And for my part, no matter what happens in the next world – about which we have no data – as long as I'm still in this one, I'm not prepared to regard *anything* as final. This may be a metaphysical war after all, but we still seem to live in some sort of secular universe. The universe of discourse has been enlarged, but it hasn't been cancelled. I say, let's find out more about it.'

'Yes,' McKnight said, 'but how? That's what I keep asking, and I don't get anything back from either of you but philosophical discussion. What do you propose that we *do*?'

'Have we got any missiles left?'

'We've still got maybe a dozen five- to ten-megatonners left – and, of course, Old Mombi.'

'Buelg, you madman, are you proposing for one instant – '

'Shut up for a minute and let me think.' Old Mombi was Denver's doomsday machine, a complex carrier containing five one hundred-megaton warheads, one of which was aimed to make even the Moon uninhabitable; it was a postspasm weapon that the present situation certainly did not call for – best to hold it in reserve. 'I think what we ought to do is to lob one of the small jobs on to the Death Valley encampment. I don't really think it'll do much harm, maybe not any, but it might produce some information. We can fly a drone plane through the cloud as it goes up, and take off radiological, chemical, any other kinds of readings that the computer can come up with. These demons have obtruded themselves into the real world, and the very fact that we can see them and photograph them shows that they share some of its characteristics now. Let's see how they behave under something a good deal hotter than red-hot iron. Suppose they do nothing more than sweat a little? We can analyse even that!'

'And suppose they trace the missile back to here?' Šatvje said, but by his expression, Buelg knew that Šatvje knew that it was a last-ditch argument.

'Then we're sunk, I suppose. But look at the architecture of that encampment; does that suggest to you that they've been in contact with real warfare since back in the fourteenth century? No doubt they have all kinds of supernatural powers, but they've got a lot to learn about the natural ones! Maybe a decent adversary is what they've been lacking all along – and if Armageddon has ended in a standoff, a little action on the side of our Maker wouldn't be amiss. If He's still with us, and actively interested, any *in*action on our parts would probably be viewed very gravely indeed if He wins after all. And if He's not with us any longer, then we'll have to help ourselves, as the proverb says.'

'That's the stuff to give the troops,' McKnight said. 'It is so ordered.'

Buelg nodded and left the office to search out Chief Hay. On the whole, he felt he had made a nice recovery.

4

Positano had been washed away, but the remains of Ware's palazzo still stood above the scoured cliffside, like some post-Roman ruin. The ceiling had fallen in, the fluted pink tiles smashing Ware's glassware and burying the dim chalk diagrams of last night's conjuration on the refectory floor in a litter of straw and potsherds, mounds of which collapsed now and then to send streamers of choking dust up to meet the gently radio-active April rain.

Ware sat on the heaped remains of his alter within the tumbled walls, under the uncertain sky. His feelings were so complex that he could not have begun to explain them, even to himself; after many years' schooling in the rigorous non-emotions of Ceremonial Magic, it was a novelty to him to have any feelings at all but those of thirst for knowledge; now he would have to relearn those sensations, for his lovely book of acquisitions, upon which he had spent his soul and so much else, was buried under tons of tsunamic mud.

In a way, he thought tentatively, he felt free. After the shock of the seaquake had passed, and all but an occasional tile had stopped falling, he had struggled out of the rubble to the door, and thence to the head of the stairway which led down to his bedroom, only to see nothing but mud three stone steps down, mud wrinkling and settling as the sea water gradually seeped out from under it. Somewhere down under there, his book of new knowledge was beginning the aeon-long route to becoming an unreadable fossil. Well then; so much for his life. Almost it seemed to him then that he might begin again, that he was nameless, a *tabula rasa*, all false starts wiped out, all dead knowledge ready to be rejected or revivified. It was given to few men to live through something so cleansing as a total disaster.

But then he realized that this, too, was only an illusion. His past was there, ineluctably, in his commitments. He was still waiting for the return of the Sabbath Goat. He closed the door to the stairwell and the fossilized ripples of the mud, and blowing reflectively into his white moustache, went back into the refectory.

Father Domenico had earlier tired – it could not exactly be said that he had lost patience – of both the waiting and the fruitless debates over when or whether they would be come for, and had decided to attempt travelling south to see what and who remained of Monte Albano, the college of white magicians which had been his home grounds. Baines was still there, trying to raise some news on the little transistor radio to which only yesterday he had listened so gluttonously to the accounts of the Black Easter which Ware had raised up at his commission, and whose consequences now eddied away from them around the whole tortured globe. Now, however, it was producing nothing but bands of static, and an occasional very distant voice in an unknown tongue.

With him now was Jack Ginsberg, dressed to the nines as usual, and in consequence looking by far the most bedraggled of the three. At Ware's entrance, Baines tossed the radio to his secretary and crossed towards the magician, slipping and cursing the rubble.

'Find out anything?'

'Nothing at all. As you can see for yourself, the sea is subsiding. It is obvious that Positano has been spared any further destruction – for the moment. As for why, we know no more than we did before,'

'You can still work magic, can't you?'

'I don't appear to have been deprived of my memory,' Ware said, 'I've no doubt I can still *do* magic, if I can get at my equipment under this mess, but whether I can work it is another matter. The conditions of reference have changed drastically, and I have no idea how far or in what areas.'

'Well, you could at least call up a demon and see if he could give us any information. There doesn't appear to be anyone else to ask.'

'I see that I'll have to put the matter more bluntly. I am totally opposed to performing any more magic at this time, Doctor Baines. I see that you have again failed to think the situation through. The terms under which I was able to call upon demons no longer apply – I am no longer able to do anything for them, they must now own a substantial part of the world. If I were to call at this juncture, probably no one would answer, and it might be better if nobody did, since I would have no way of controlling him. They are composed almost entirely of hatred for every unFallen creature, and every creature with the potentiality to be redeemed, but there is no one they hate more than a useless tool.'

'Well, it seems to me that we may neither of us be totally useless even now,' Baines declared. 'You say the demons now own a substantial part of the world, but it's also perfectly evident that they don't own it all yet. Otherwise the Goat would have come back when he said he would. And we'd be in Hell.'

'Hell has a great many circles. We may well be on the margins of the first right now – in the Vestible of the Futile.'

'We'd be in a good deal deeper if the demons were in total control, or if judgement had already been passed on us,' Baines said.

'You are entirely right about that, to be sure,' Ware said, somewhat surprised. 'But after all, from their point of view there is no hurry. In the past, we might have saved ourselves by a last-minute act of contrition. Now, however, there is no longer any God to appeal to. They can wait and take us at their leisure.'

'There I'm inclined to agree with Father Domenico. We don't know that for sure; we were told so only by the Goat. I admit that the other evidence all points in the same direction, but all the same, he could have been lying.'

Ware thought about it. The argument from circumstances did not of course impress him; no doubt the circumstances were horrible beyond the capacity of any human soul to react to them, but they were certainly not beyond the range of human imagination; they were more or less the standard consequences of World War III, a war which Baines himself had been actively engaged in engineering some time before he had discovered his interest in black magic. Theologically they were also standard: a new but essentially unchanged version of the Problem of Evil, the centuries-old question of why a good and merciful God should allow so much pain and terror to be inflicted upon the innocent. The parameters had been filled in a somewhat different way, but the fundmental equation was the same as it had always been.

Nevertheless, the munitions maker was quite right – as Father Domenico had been earlier – to insist that they had no reliable information upon the most fundamental question of all. Ware said slowly:

'I'm reluctant to admit any hope at all at this juncture. On the other hand, it has been said that to despair of God is the ultimate sin. What precisely do you have in mind?'

'Nothing specific yet. But suppose for the sake of argument that the demons are still under some sort of restrictions – I don't see any point in trying to imagine what they might be – and that the battle consequently isn't really over yet. If that's the case, it's quite possible that they could still use some help. Considering how far they've managed to get already, there doesn't seem to be much doubt about their winning in the end – and it's been my observation that it's generally a good idea to be on the winning side.'

'It is folly to think that the triumph of evil could ever be a winning side, in the sense of anyone's gaining anything by it. Without good to oppose it, evil is simply meaningless. That isn't all what I thought you had in mind. It is, instead, the last step in despairing of God – it's worse than Manicheanism, it is Satanism pure and simple. I once controlled devils, but I never worshipped them, and I don't plan to begin now. Besides –'

Abruptly, the radio produced a tearing squeal and then began to mutter urgently in German. Ware could hear the voice well enough to register that the speaker had a heavy Swiss accent, but not well enough to make out the sense. He and Baines took a crunching step towards Ginsberg, who, listening intently, held up one hand towards them.

The speech was interrupted by another squeal, and then the radio resumed emitting nothing more than snaps, crackles, pops and waterfalls. Ginsberg said:

'That was Radio Zurich. There's been an H-bomb explosion in the States, in Death Valley. Either the war's started again, or some dud's gone off belatedly.'

'Hmm,' Baines said. 'Well, better there than here . . . although, now that I come to think of it, it isn't entirely unpromising. But Doctor Ware, I think you hadn't quite finished?'

'I was only going to add that "being of some help" to demons in this context makes no practical sense, either. Their hand is turned against everyone on Earth, and there is certainly no way that we could help them to carry their war to Heaven, even presuming that any of Heaven still stands. Someone of Father Domenico's school might just possibly manage to enter the Aristotelian spheres – though I doubt it – but I certainly couldn't.'

'That bomb explosion seems to show that *somebody* is still fighting back,' Baines said. 'Providing that Jack isn't right about its being a dud or a stray. My guess is that it's the Strategic Air Command, and that they've just found out who the real enemy is. They had the world's finest data processing centre there under Denver, and in addition, McKnight had first-class civilian help, including Džejms Šatvje himself and a RAND man that I tried to get the Mamaroneck Research Institute to outbid the government for.'

'I still don't quite see where that leaves us.'

'I know McKnight very well; he's steered a lot of Defence Department orders my way, and I was going to have LeFebre make him president of Consolidated Warfare Service when he retired – as he was quite well aware. He's good in his field, which is reconnaissance, but he also has something of a one-track mind. If he's bombing demons, it might be a very good idea for me to suggest to him that he stop it – and why.'

'It might at that,' Ware said reflectively. 'How will you get there?'

'A technicality. Radio Zurich is still operating, which almost surely means that their airfield is operating too. Jack can fly a plane if necessary, but it probably won't be necessary; we had a very well-staffed office in Zurich, in fact it was officially our central headquarters, and I've got access to two Swiss bank accounts, the company's and my own. I'd damn well better put the money to some use before somebody with a little imagination realizes that the vaults might much better be occupied by himself, his family and twenty thousand cases of canned beans.'

The project, Ware decided, had its merits. At least it would rid him, however temporarily, of Baines, whose society he was beginning to find a little tiresome, and of Jack Ginsberg, whom he distantly but positively loathed. It would of course also mean that he would be deprived of all human company if the Goat should after all come for him, but this did not bother him in the least; he had known for years that in that last confrontation, every man is always alone, and most especially, every magician.

Perhaps he had also always known, somewhere in the deepest recesses of his mind, that he would indeed eventually take that last step into Satanism, but if so, he had very successfully suppressed it. And he had not quite taken it yet; he had committed himself to nothing, he had only agreed that Baines should go away, and Ginsberg too, to counsel someone he did not know to an inaction which might be quite without significance . . .

And while they were gone, perhaps he would be able to think of something better. It was the tiniest of small hopes, and doubtless vain; but now he was beginning to be prepared to feed it. If he played his cards right, he might yet mingle with the regiment of angels who rebelled not, yet avowed to God no loyalty, of whom it is said that deep Hell refuses them, for, beside such, the sinner would be proud.

5

Monte Albano, Father Domenico found with astonishment and a further rekindling of his hope, had been spared completely. It reared its eleventh-century walls, rebuilt after the earthquake then by the abbot Giorgio who later became Pope John the Twentieth, as high above the valley as it always had, and as always, too, accessible only by muleback, and Father Domenico lost more time in locating a mule with an owner to take him up there than the whole trip from Positano had cost him. Eventually, however, the thing was done, and he was within the cool walls of the library with the white monks, his colleagues under the hot Frosinian sky.

Those assembled made up nearly the same company that had met during the winter to consider, fruitlessly, how Theron Ware and his lay client might be forestalled: Father Amparo, Father Umberto (the director), and the remaining brothers of the order, plus Father Uccello, Father Boucher, Father Vance, Father Anson, Father Selahny and Father Atheling. The visitors had apparently continued to stay in the monastery, if not in session, after the winter meeting, although in the interim Father Rosenblum had died; his place had been taken, though hardly filled, by Father Domenico's former apprentice, Joannes, who though hardly seventeen looked now as though he had grown up very suddenly. Well, that was all right; they surely needed all the help that they would get, and Father Domenico knew without false modesty that Joannes had been well trained.

After Father Domenico had been admitted, announced and conducted through the solemn and blessed joys of greeting and welcome, it became apparent that the discussion – as was only to have been expected – had already been going on for many hours. Nor was he much surprised to find that it was simply another version of the discussion that had been going on in Positano: namely, how had Monte Albano been spared in the world-wide catastrophe, and what did it mean? But in this version of the discussion, Father Domenico could join with a much better heart.

And in fact he was also able to give it what amounted to an entirely new turn; for their Sensitive, the hermit-Father Uccello, had inevitably found his talents much coarsened and blunted by the proximity of so many other minds, and in consequence the white monks had only a general idea of what had gone on in Ware's palazzo since the last convocation - an impression supplemented by the world news, what of it there was, and by deduction, some of which was in fact wrong. Father Domenico recapitulated the story of the last conjuration briefly; but his fellows' appreciation of the gravity of the situation was already such that the recitation was accompanied by no more than the expectable number of horrified murmurs.

'All in all,' he concluded, 'forty-eight demons were let out of the Pit as a result of this ceremony, commanded to return at dawn. When it became apparent that the operation was completely out of hand, I invoked the Covenant and insisted that Ware recall them ahead of time, to which he agreed; but when he attempted to summon up LUCIFUGE ROFOCALE to direct this abrogation, PUT SATANACHIA himself answered instead. When I attempted to exorcise this abominable creature, my crucifix burst in my hands, and it was after that that the monster told us that God was already dead and that the ultimate victory had instead gone to the forces of Hell. The Goat promised to return for us all – all, that is, except Baines's other assistant, Doctor Hess, whom Baphomet had already swallowed when Hess panicked and stepped out of his circle – at dawn, but he failed to do so, and I subsequently left and came to Monte Albano as soon as it was physically possible for me to do so.'

'Do you recall the names and offices of all forty-eight?' said Father Atheling, his tenor voice more sinusy than ever with apprehension.

'I think I do – that is, I think I could; after all, I saw them all, and that's an experience which does not pass lightly from the memory. In any event, if I've blanked out on a few – which isn't unlikely either – they can doubtless be recovered under hypnosis. Why does that matter, may I ask, Father Atheling?'

'Simply because it is always useful to know the natures as well as the numbers, of the forces arrayed against one.'

'Not after the countryside is already overrun,' said Father Anson. 'If the battle and the war have been already lost, we must have the whole crew to contend with now – not just all seventy-two princes, but every single one of the fallen angels. The number is closer to seven and a half million than it is to forty-eight.'

'Seven million, four hundred and fifty thousand, nine hundred and twenty-six,' Father Atheling said, 'to be exact.'

'Though the wicked may hide, the claws of crabs are dangerous people in bridges,' Father Selahny intoned abruptly. As was the case with all his utterances, the group would doubtless find out what this one meant only after sorting out its mixed mythologies and folklores, and long after it was too late to do anything about it. Nor did it do any good to ask him to explain; these things simply came to him, and he no more understood them than did his hearers. If God was indeed dead, Father Domenico wondered suddenly: Who could be dictating them now? But he put the thought aside as non-contributory.

'There is a vast concentration of new evil on the other side of the world,' Father Uccello said in his courtly, hesitant old man's voice. 'The feeling is one of intense oppression, quite different from that which was common in New York, or Moscow, but one such as I would expect of a massing of demons upon a huge scale. Forgive me, brothers, but I can be no more specific.'

'We know you are doing the best you can,' said the director soothingly.

'I can feel it myself,' said Father Monteith, who although not a Sensitive had had some experience with the herding of rebellious spirits. 'But even supposing that we do not have to cope with so large an advance, as I certainly hope we do not, it seems to me that forty-eight is too large a sum for us if the Covenant has been voided. It leaves us without even an option.'

Father Domenico saw that Joannes was trying to attract the director's attention, although too hesitantly to make any impression. Father Umberto was not yet used to thinking of Joannes as a person at all. Capturing the boy's eyes, Father Domenico nodded.

'I never did understand the Covenant,' the ex-apprentice said, thus encouraged. 'That is, I didn't understand why God would compromise Himself in such a manner. Even with Job, He didn't make a deal with Satan, but only allowed him to act unchecked for a certain period of time. And I've never found any mention of the Covenant in the grimoires. What are its terms, anyhow?'

Father Domenico thought the question well asked, if a trifle irrelevant, but an embarrassed and slightly pitying silence showed that his opinion was not shared. In the end it was broken by Father Monteith, whose monumental patience was a byword in the chapter.

'I'm certainly not well versed in canon law, let alone in

spiritual compacts,' he said, with more modesty than exactness. 'But, in principle, the Covenant is no more than a special case of the option of free will. The assumption appears to be that even in dealing with devilry, on the one hand, no man shall be subjected to a temptation beyond his ability to resist, and on the other, no man shall slide into Heaven without having been tempted up to that point. In situations involving Transcendental or Ceremonial Magic, the Covenant is the line drawn in between. Where you would find its exact terms, I'm sure I don't know; I doubt that they have ever been written down. One thinks of the long struggle to understand the rainbow, the other Covenant; once the explanation was in, it did not explain, except to show that every man sees his own rainbow, and what seems to stand in the sky is an optical illusion, not a theomorphism. It is in the nature of the arrangement that the terms would vary in each individual case, and that if you are incapable of determining where it is drawn for you – the line of demarcation – then, woe betide you, and that is that.'

Dear God, Father Domenico thought, all my life I have been an amateur of Roger Bacon and I never once saw that that was what he meant to show by focusing his *Perspectiva* on the rainbow. Shall I have any more time to learn? I hope we are never tempted to make Monteith the director, or we shall lose him to taking things out of the In box and putting them into the Out box, as we did Father Umberto –

'Furthermore, it may well be still in existence,' said Father Boucher. 'As Father Domenico has already pointed out to Theron Ware himself, we have heard of the alleged death of God only through the testimony of the most unreliable witness imaginable. And it leaves many inconsistencies to be explained. *When* exactly is God supposed to have died? If it was as long ago as in Nietzsche's time, why had His angels and ministers of light seemed to know nothing of it in the interim? It's unreasonable to suppose that they were simply keeping up a good front until the battle actually broke out; Heaven simply isn't that kind of an organisation. One would expect an absolute and perpetual monarchy to break down upon the death of the monarch quite promptly, yet in point of fact we saw no signs of any such thing until shortly after Christmas of this year.'

'But we did see such signs at that time,' Father Vance said.

'True, but this only poses another logical dilemma: What happened to the Antichrist? Baphomet's explanation that he had been dispensed with as unnecessary to the victors, whose creature he would have been, doesn't hold water. The Antichrist was to have appeared *before* the battle, and if the defeat of God is all that recent, the prophecy should have been fulfilled; God still existed to compel it.'

'Matthew 11:14,' Father Selahny said, in an unprecedented burst of intelligibility. The verse of which he was reminding them referred to John the Baptist, and it said: *And if ye will receive it, this is Elias, which was for to come.*

'Yes,' Father Domenico said, 'I suppose it's possible that the Antichrist might have come unrecognised. One always envisioned people flocking to his banner openly, but the temptation would have been more subtle and perhaps more dangerous had he crept past us, say in the guise of some popular philosopher, like that positive-thinking man in the States. Yet the proposal seems to allow even less room than did the Covenant for the exercise of free will.'

There was a silence. At last, the director said: 'The Essenes argued that one must think and experience all evil before one can hope to perceive good.'

'If this be true doctrine,' Father Domenico said, 'then it follows that God is indeed still alive, and that Theron Ware's experiment, and World War III, did not constitute Armageddon after all. What we may be confronted with instead is an Earthly Purgatory, from which Grace, and perhaps even the Earthly Paradise, might be won. Dare we think so?'

'We dare not think otherwise,' said Father Vance. 'The question is, how? Little that is in the New Testament, the teachings of the Church or the Arcana seem very relevant to the present situation.'

'No more is our traditional isolation,' said Father Domenico. 'Our only recourse now is to abandon it; to abandon our monastery and our mountain, and go down into the world that we renounced when Charlemagne was but a princeling, to try to win it back by works and witnessing. And if we may not do this with the sweet aid of Christ, then we must nevertheless do it in His name. Hope now is all we have.'

'In sober truth,' Father Boucher said quietly, 'that is not so great a change. I think it is all we ever had.'

Come to Middle Hell

Though thy beginning was small, yet thy latter end should greatly increase . . . Prepare thyself to the search.

Job 8:7, 8

6

Left to his own devices and hence, at last, unobserved, Theron Ware thought that it might be well, after all, if he did essay a small magic. The possible difficulty lay in that all magic without exception depended upon the control of demons, as he had explained to Baines on his very first visit. But therein lay the attractiveness of the experiment, too, for what he wanted was information, and a part of that information was whether he still had any such control.

And it would also be interesting, and possible to find out at the same time, to know whether or not there were any demons left in Hell. If there were it would imply, though it would not guarantee, that only the forty-eight that he had set loose were now terrorizing the world. This ruled out using the Mirror of Solomon, for the spirit of that mirror was the angel Anaël. Probably he would not answer anyhow, for Ware was not a white magician, and had carefully refrained from calling upon any angel ever since he had turned to the practice of the black Art; and besides, it would be a considerable nuisance locating three white pigeons amidst all this devastation.

Who, then? Among the demon princes he had decided not to call up for Baines's commission were several that he had ruled out because of their lesser potentialities for destruction, which would stand him in good stead were it to turn out that he had lost control; even in Hell there were degrees of malevolence, as of punishment. One of these was PHOENIX a poet and teacher with whom Ware had had many dealings in the past, but he probably would not do now; he posed another wildlife problem – Ware's familiar Ahktoi had been the demon's creature, and the cat had of course vanished when the noise had begun, a disappearance that PHOENIX would take none the less ill for its having been 100 per cent expectable. Though the grimoires occasionally characterize one or another demon as 'mild' or 'good by nature', these terms are strictly relative and have no human meaning; all demons are permanently enraged by the greatest Matter of all, and it does not pay to annoy them even slightly in small matters.

Also, Ware realized, it would have to be a small magic indeed, for most of his instruments were now buried, and those that were accessible were all contaminated beyond his power to purify them in any useful period of time. Clearly it was time to consult the book. He crossed to the lectern upon which it rested, pushed dust and potsherds off it with his sleeve, unlocked the clasp and began to turn the great stiff pages, not without a qualm. Here, signed with his own blood, was half his life; the other half was down below, in the mud.

He found the name he needed almost at once: VASSAGO, a mighty prince, who in his first estate before the rebellion had belonged to the choir of the Virtues. The *Lemegeton* of the Rabbi Solomon said of him, Ware recalled, that he 'declares things past, present and future, and discovers what has been lost or hidden'. Precisely to the purpose. Ware remembered too that his was the name most commonly invoked in ceremonial crystallomancy, which would be perfect in both scope and limitations for what Ware had in mind, involving no lengthy preparations of the operator, or even any precautionary diagrams, nor any apparatus except a crystal ball; and even for that he might substitute a pool of exorcised water, fifty litres of which still reposed in a happily unruptured stainless steel tank embedded in the wall behind Ware's workbench.

Furthermore, he was the only demon in Ware's entire book of pacts who was represented therein by two seals or characters, so markedly different that without seeing them side by side, one might never suspect that they belonged to the same entity. Topologically they were closely related, however, and Ware studied these relationships long and hard, knowing that he had once known what they meant but unable to recall it. These were the figures:

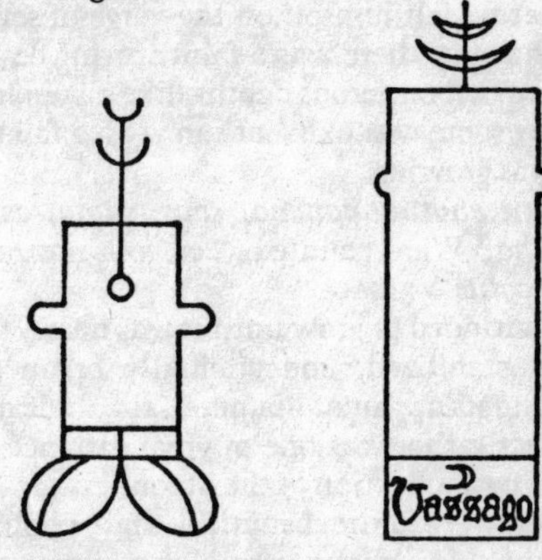

Ah, now he had it. The left-hand figure was VASSAGO'S ordinary infernal sign, but the second was the seal under which, it was said, he could be called by white magicians. Ware had never used it, nor had needed to – the infernal seal had worked very well – and he had always doubted its efficacy, for by definition no commerce with a demon is white magic; however, it would be well to try it now. It might prove an additional factor of safety, if it worked at all.

Into what should he draw the water? Everything was filthy. Eventually he decided simply to make a puddle on the work-bench; it had been decades since he had studied oneirology, which he had scorned as a recourse for mere hedge wizards, but to the best of his recollection it called for nothing more extra-ordinary than an earthenware vessel, and could even be prac-tised successfully in an ordinary, natural forest pool, providing that there was sufficient shade.

Well, then, to work.

Standing insecurely before the workbench, the little weight of his spare upper body resting upon his elbows and his hands beside his ears, Theron Ware stared steadfastly down into the little puddle of mud, his own bushy head – he had neglected his tonsure since the disaster – shading it from the even light of the overcast sky. He had already stared so long since the first invocation that he felt himself on the verge of self-hypnosis, but now, he thought, there was a faint stirring down there in those miniature carboniferous depths, like a bubble or a high-light created by some non-existent sun. Yes, a faint spark was there, and it was growing.

'Eka dva, tri, chatur, pancha, shas, sapta, ashta, nava, dasha, ekadasha,' Ware counted. *'Per vota nostra ipse nunc surtat nobis dicatus* VASSAGO!'

The spark continued to grow until it was nearly the size of a ten-lire piece, stabilized, and gradually began to develop features. Despite its apparent diameter, the thing did not look small; the effect rather was one of great distance, as though Ware were seeing a reflection of the Moon.

The features were quite beautiful and wholly horrible. Superficially the shining face resembled a human skull, but it was longer, thinner, more triangular, and it had no cheek-bones. The eyes were huge, and slanted almost all the way up to where a human hairline would have been; the nose extremely long in the bridge; the mouth as pink and tiny as that of an infant. The colour and texture of the face were old ivory, like netsuke. No body was visible, but Ware had not expected one; this was not, after all, a full manifestation, but only an apparition.

The rosebud mouth moved damply, and a pure soprano voice like that of a choirboy, murmured gently and soundlessly deep in Ware's mind.

WHO IS IT CALLS VASSAGO FROM STUDYING OF THE DAMNED? BEWARE!

'Thou knowest me, demon of the Pit,' Ware thought, 'for to a pact hast thou subscribed with me, and written into my book thine Infernal name. Thereby, and by thy seal which I do here exhibit, do I compel thee. My questions shalt thou answer, and give true knowledge.'

SPEAK AND BE DONE.

'Art still in Hell with thy brothers, or are all abroad about the Earth?'

SOME DO GO TO AND FRO, BUT WE ABIDE HERE. NEVERTHELESS, WE BE ON EARTH, ALBEIT NOT ABROAD.

'In what wise?'

THOUGH WE MAY NOT YET LEAVE NETHER HELL, WE BE AMONG YE: FOR THE PIT HATH BEEN RAISED UP, AND THE CITY OF DIS NOW STANDING UPON THE EARTH.

Ware made no attempt to disguise his shock; after all, the creature could see into his mind. 'How situate?' he demanded.

WHERE SHE STOOD FROM ETERNITY; IN THE VALLEY OF DEATH.

Ware suspected at once that the apparently allegorical form of his utterance concealed a literal meaning, but it would do no good to ask for exact topographical particulars; demons paid little attention to Earthly political geography unless they were fomenting strife about boundaries or enclaves, which was not one of VASSAGO'S roles. Could the reference be literary? That would be in accordance with the demon's nature. Nothing prevents devils from quoting scripture to their own advantage, so why not Tennyson?

'Be this valley under the ambassadorship of RIMMON?'

NAY.

'Then what officers inhabit the region wherein it lies? Divulge their names, great prince, to my express command!'

THEY ARE THE INFERIORS OF ASTAROTH, WHO ARE CALLED SARGATANAS AND NEBIROS.

'But which hath his asylum where Dis now stands?'

THERE RULETH NEBIROS.

These were the demons of post-Columbian magic; they announced forth to the subjects all things which their lord hath commanded, according to the *Grimorium Verum*, in America, and the asylum of NEBIROS was further specified to be in the West. Of course: Death Valley. And NEBIROS, as it was said in the *Grand Grimoire* was the field marshal of Infernus, and a great necromancer, 'who goeth to and fro everywhere and inspects the hordes of perdition.' The raising of the fortress of Dis in the domain of this great general most strongly suggested that the war was not over yet. Ware knew better, however, than to ask the demon whether God was in fact dead; for were He not, the mere sounding of the Holy Name would so offend this minor prince as to terminate the apparition at once, if not render further ones impossible. Well, the question was probably unnecessary anyhow; he already had most of the information that he needed.

'Thou art discharged.'

The shining face vanished with a flash of opalescence, exactly as though a soap bubble had broken, leaving Ware staring down at nothing but a puddle of mud, now already filming and cracking – except in the centre where the face had been; that had evaporated completely. Straightening his aching back, he considered carefully the implications of what he had learned.

The military organization of the Descending Hierachy was peculiar, and as usual the authorities differed somewhat on its details. This was hardly surprising, for any attempt to relate the offices of the evil spirits to Earthly analogues was bound to be only an approximation, if not sometimes actively misleading. Ware was presently in the domain of HUTGIN, ambassador in Italy, and had never before Black Easter had any need to invoke ASTAROTH or any of his inferior Intelligences. He was characterized by the *Grimorium Verum* as the Grand Duke of Hell, whereas Weirus referred to him as Grand Treasurer; while the *Grand Grimoire* did not mention him at all, assigning NEBIROS instead to an almost equivalent place. Nevertheless it seemed clear enough in general that while the domain of ASTAROTH might technically be in America, his principality was not confined thereto, but might make itself known anywhere in the world. HUTGIN in comparison was a considerably lesser figure.

And the war was not yet over, and Ware might indeed find some way to make himself useful; Baines had been right about that, too. But in what way remained unclear.

Very probably, he would have to go to Dis to find out. It was a terrifying thought, but Ware could see no way around it. That was where the centre of power was now, where the war would henceforth be directed; and there, if Baines actually succeeded in reaching the SAC in Denver, Ware conceivably might succeed in arranging some sort of a *detente*. Certainly he would be of no use squatting here in ruined Italy, with all the superior spirits half a world away.

But how to get there? He did not have Baines's power to commandeer an aircraft, and though he was fully as wealthy as the industrialist – in fact most of the money had once been Baines's – it seemed wholly unlikely that any airline was selling tickets these days. A sea and overland journey would be too slow.

Would it be possible to compel ASTAROTH to provide him with some kind of an apport? This too was a terrifying thought. To the best of Ware's knowledge, the last magician to have ridden astride a devil had been Gerbert, back in the tenth century. He had resorted to it only to save his life from a predecessor of the Inquisition, whose attention he had amply earned; and, moreover, had lived through the ordeal to become Pope Sylvester II.

Gerbert had been a great man, and though Ware rather doubted that he had been any better a magician than Ware was, he did not feel prepared to try that conclusion just now. In any event, the process was probably unnecessarily drastic; transvection might serve the purpose just as well, or better. Though he had never been to a sabbat, he knew the theory and the particulars well enough. Included in the steel cabinets which held his magical pharmacopoeia were all the ingredients necessary for the flying ointment, and the compounding of it required no special time or ritual. As for piloting and navigation, that was to be sure a little alarming to anticipate, but if thousands upon thousands of ignorant old women had been able to fly a cleft stick, a distaff, a besom or even a shovel upon the first try, then so could Theron Ware.

First, however, he drew from the cabinet a flat slab of synthetic ruby, about the size and shape of an opened match folder; and from his cabinet of instruments, a burin. Upon the ruby, on the day of Mars, which is Tuesday, and in the hour of Mars, which is 0600, 1300, 2000 or 0300 on that day, he would engrave the following seal and characters:

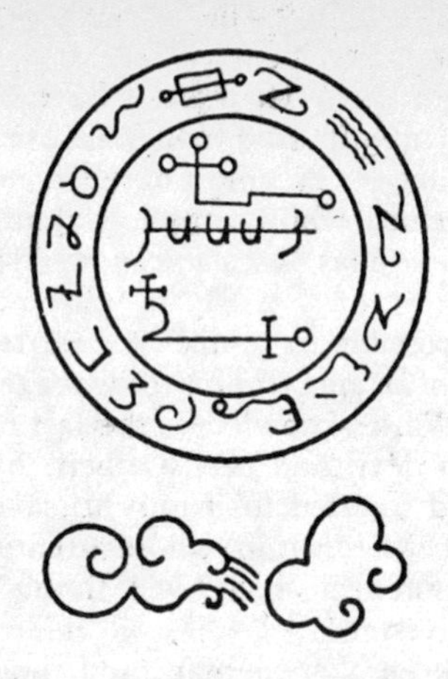

This he would henceforth carry in his right shirt pocket, like a reliquary. Though he would accept no help from ASTAROTH if he could possibly avoid it, it would be well, since he was going to be travelling in that fiend's domains, to be wearing his colours. As a purist, it bothered him a little that the ruby was synthetic, but his disturbance, he knew, was only an aesthetic one. ASTAROTH was a solar spirit, and the ancients, all the way through Albertus Magnus, had believed that rubies were engendered in the Earth by the influence of the Sun – but since they were not in fact formed that way, the persistence of the ruby in the ritual was only another example of one of the primary processes of magic, *superstition*, the gradual supremacy of the sign over the thing, so that so far as efficacy was concerned it did not matter a bit whether the ruby was synthetic or natural. Nature, too, obstinately refused to form rubies the size and shape of opened match folders.

For a magician, Ware reflected, there were indeed distinct advantages in being able to practise ten centuries after Gerbert had ridden upon his demon eagle.

7

Transvection, too, has its hazards, Ware discovered. He crossed the Atlantic without incident in well under three hours – indeed, he suspected that in some aspect beyond the reach of his senses, the flight was taking place only partially in real time – and it began to look as though he would easily reach his goal before dawn. The candle affixed by its own tallow to the bundle of twigs and rushes before him (for only the foolhardy fly a broomstick with the brush trailing, no matter what is shown to the contrary in conventional Halloween cartoons) burned as steadily as though he were not in motion at all, casting a brilliant light ahead along his path; any ships at sea that might have seen him might have taken him to be an unusually brilliant meteor. As he approached the eastern United States, he wondered how he would show up on radar; the dropping of the bomb two days ago suggested that there might still be a number of functioning radomes there. In quieter times, he thought, he might perhaps have touched off another flying saucer scare. Or was he visible at all? He discovered that he did not know, but he began to doubt it; the seaboard was hidden in an immense pall of smoke.

But once over land, he slowed himself down and lost altitude in order to get his bearings, and within what seemed to him, to be only a very few minutes, he was grounded head over heels by the sound of a church bell forlornly calling what faithful might remain to midnight Mass. He remembered belatedly, when he got his wind back, that in some parts of Germany during the seventeenth-century flowering of the popular Goëtic cults, it had been the custom to toll church bells all night long as a protection against witches who might be passing overhead on the way to the Brocken; but the memory did him no good now – the besom had gone lifeless.

He had fallen in a rather mountainous, heavily timbered area, quite like the Harz Mountain section of Germany, but which he guessed to be somewhere in western Pennsylvania. Though it was now late April, which was doubtless warm in Positano, the night here was decidedly cold, especially for a thin man clad in nothing more than a light smear of unguent. He was instantly and violently all ashiver, for the sound of the bell had destroyed the protective as well as the transvective power of the flying ointment. He hastily undid the bundle of clothes, which was tied to the broomstick, but there were not going to be enough of them; after all, he had assembled them with Death Valley in mind. Also, he was beginning to feel drowzy and dizzy, and his pulse was blurred and banging with tachycardia. Among other things, the flying ointment contained both mandragora and belladonna, and now that the magic was gone out of it, these were exerting their inevitable side effects. He would have to wash the stuff off the minute he could find a stream, cold or no cold.

And not only because it was drugging him. Still other ingredients of the ointment were rather specifically organic in nature, and these gave it a characteristic smell which the heat of his body would gradually ripen. The chances were all too good that there would be some people in this country of the Amish – and not all of them old ones – who would know what that odour meant. Until he had had some kind of a bath, it would be dangerous even to ask for help.

Before dressing, he wiped off as much of it as he could with the towel in which the clothing had been tied. This he buried, together with the taper and the brush from the besom; and after making sure that the ruby talisman was still safely in his pocket, he set out, using the denuded broomstick as a staff.

The night-black, hilly, forested countryside would have made difficult going even for an experienced walker. Ware's life, on the other hand, had been nearly inactive except intellectually, and he was on the very near side of his fiftieth birthday. To his advantage, on the other hand, stood the fact that he had always been small and wiry, and the combination of a slightly hyperthyroid metabolism and an ascetic calling – he did not even smoke – had kept him that way, so that he made fair progress; and an equally lifelong love of descriptive astronomy, plus the necessity of astrology to his art, helped to keep him going in the right direction, whenever he could see a few stars through the smoke.

Just before dawn, he stumbled upon a small, rocky-bedded

stream, and through the gloom heard the sound of a nearby waterfall. He moved against the current and shortly found this to be a spillway of a small log dam. Promptly he stripped and bathed under it, pronouncing in a whisper as he did so all three of the accompanying prayers from the rite of lustration as prescribed for the preparatory triduum in the *Grimorium Verum* – though the water was neither warm nor exorcized, it was obviously pure, and that would have to do.

The ablution was every bit as cold as he had expected it to be, and even colder was the process of air-drying himself; but he endured it stoically, for he had to get rid of what remained of the ointment, and moreover he knew that to put on damp clothes would be almost as dangerous. While he waited, his teeth chattering, faint traces of light began to appear through the trees from the east.

In answer, massive grey rectangular shapes began to sketch themselves against the darkness downstream, and before long he was able to see that to the west – which was the way the stream was momentarily running – the aisle it cut through the trees opened out on to a substantial farm. As if in confirmation of help to come, a cock crowed in the distance, a traditional ending for a night of magic.

But as the dawn continued to brighten, he saw that there would be no help for him here. Under the angle of the roof of the large barn nearest to him a circular diagram had been painted, like a formalized flower with an eye in it.

As Jack Ginsberg had taken the pains to find out long before he and his boss had even met the magician, Ware had been born and raised in the States and was still a citizen. As his name showed, his background was Methodist, but nevertheless he knew a hex sign when he saw one. And it gave him an idea.

He was not a witch, and he certainly had had no intention of laying a curse on this prosperous-looking farm ten seconds ago, but the opportunity to gather new data should not be missed.

Reaching into his shirt pocket, he turned the ruby around so that the seal and characters on it faced outward. In a low voice, he said, 'THOMATOS, BENESSER, FLEANTER.'

Under proper circumstances these words of the *Comte de*

Gabalis encompassed the operator with thirty-three several Intelligences, but since the circumstances were not proper, Ware was not surprised when nothing happened. For one thing, his lustration had been imperfect; for another, he was using the wrong talisman – the infernal spirits of the ceremony were not devils but salamanders or fire elements. Nevertheless he now added: 'LITAN, ISER, OSNAS.'

A morning breeze sprang up, and a leaflike whispering ran around him, which might or might not have been the voices of many beings, individually saying, 'NANTHER, NANTHER, NANTHER, NANTHER . . .' Touching the talisman, Ware said, 'GITAU, HURANDOS, RIDAS, TALIMOL,' and then, pointing to the barn, 'UUSUR, ITAR.'

The result should have been a highly localized but destructive earthquake, but there was not even a minor tremor, though he was pretty sure that he really heard the responsive voices of the fire spirits. The spell simply would not work under the eye of the hex sign – one more piece of evidence that the powers of evil were still under some kind of restraint. That was good to know, but in a way, too, Ware was quite disappointed; for had he gotten his earthquake, the further words SOUTRAM, UBARSINENS would have compelled the intelligences to carry him across the rest of his journey. He uttered them anyhow, but without result.

Neither in the *Comte de Gabalis* or its very late successor, *The Black Pullet*, did this ritual offer any word of dismissal, but nevertheless for safety's sake he now added: 'RABIAM.' Had this worked, he would have found himself carried home again, where at least he could have started over again with more ointment and another broomstick; but it did not. There was no recourse now but to seek out the farmhouse and try to persuade the farmer to give him something to eat and drive him to the nearest railhead. It was too bad that the man could not be told that he had just been protected by Ware from a demonic onslaught but unfortunately the Amish did not believe that there was any such thing as white magic – and in the ultimate analysis they were quite right not to do so, whatever delusions about the point might be harboured by Father Domenico and his fellows.

Ware identified the farmhouse proper without any trouble. It looked every bit as clean, fat and prosperous as the rest, but it was suspiciously quiet; by this hour, everyone should be up and beginning the day's chores. He approached with caution, alert for guns or dogs, but the silence continued.

The caution had been needless. Inside, the place was an outright slaughterhouse, resembling nothing so much as the last act of Webster's *The White Devil*. Ware inspected it with clinical fascination. The family had been a large one – the parents, one grandparent, four daughters, three sons and the inevitable dog – and at some time during the preceding night they had suddenly fallen upon each other with teeth, nails, pokers, a buggy whip, a bicycle chain, a cleaver, a pig knife and the butt end of a smoothbore musket, old enough to have been a relic of the Boer War. It was an obvious case of simultaneous mass possession, probably worked through the women, as these things almost always were. Doubtless they would infinitely have preferred a simple localized earthquake, but from an attack like this no conceivable peasant hex sign could have protected them.

Probably nothing could have, for as it had turned out, in their simple traditional religiosity they had chosen the wrong side. Like most of humankind, they had been born victims; even a beginning study of the Problem of Evil would have suggested to them that their God had never played fair with them, as indeed He had caused to be written out in Job for all to read; and their primitive backwoods demonology had never honestly admitted that there really were two sides to the Great Game, let alone allowing them any inkling of who the players were.

While he considered what to do next he prowled around the kitchen and the woodshed, where the larder was, trying not to slip or step on anybody. There were only two eggs – today's had obviously not been harvested – but he found smoked, streaky rashers of bacon, a day-old loaf of bread just ripe for cutting, nearly a pound of country butter and a stone jug of cold milk. All in all it was a good deal more than he could eat, but he built a fire in the old wood-burning stove, cooked the eggs and the bacon, and did his best to put it all down. After all, he had no idea when he would meet his next meal. He had already decided that he was not yet desperate enough to risk calling for an apport, but instead would keep walking generally westward until he met an opportunity to steal a car. (He would find none on the farm; the Amish still restricted themselves to horses.)

As he came out of the farmhouse into the bright morning, a sandwich in both hip pockets, he heard from the undestroyed barn a demanding lowing of cattle. Sorry, friends, he thought; nobody's going to milk you this morning.

8

Baines knew the structure and approaches of Strategic Air Command headquarters rather better than the Department of Defense would have thought right and proper even for a civilian with Q clearance, although there had been several people in DoD who would not have been at all surprised at it. The otherwise passengerless jet carrying him and Jack Ginsberg made no attempt to approach either Denver Airport or the US Air Force Academy field at Colorado Springs, both of which, he correctly assumed, would no longer be in existence anyhow. Instead, he directed the pilot to land at Limon, a small town which was the eastern-most vertex of a nearly equilateral triangle formed by these three points. Hidden there was one terminus of an underground rapid transit line which led directly into the heart of SAC's fortress – and was now its only surviving means of physical access to the outside world.

Baines and his secretary had been there only once before, and the guards at the station now were not only new but thoroughly frightened. Hence, despite the possession of ID cards countersigned by General McKnight, they were subjected to over an hour of questioning, finger-printing, photographing of retinal blood-vessel patterns, frisking and fluoroscopy for hidden weapons or explosives, telephone calls into the interior and finally a closed-circuit television confrontation with McKnight himself before they were even allowed into the waiting room.

As if in partial compensation, the trip itself was rapid transit indeed. The line itself was a gravity-vacuum tube, bored in an exactly straight line under the curvature of the Earth, and kept as completely exhausted of air as out-gassing from its steel cladding would permit. The vacuum in the tube was in fact almost as hard as the atmosphere of the Moon. From the waiting room, Baines and Jack Ginsberg were passed through two airlocks into a seamlessly welded windowless metal capsule which was sealed behind them. Here their guards strapped them in securely, for their own protection, for the initial kick of compressed air behind the capsule, abetted by rings of electromagnets, gave it an acceleration of more than five miles per hour per second. Though this is not much more than they might have been subjected to in an electric streetcar of about 1940, it is a considerable jerk if you cannot see outside and have nothing to hold on to. Thereafter, the capsule was simply allowed to fall to the mathematical midpoint of its right of way, gaining speed at about twenty-eight feet per second; since the rest of the journey was uphill, the capsule was slowed in proportion by gravity, friction and the compression of the almost non-existent gases in the tube still ahead of it, which without any extra braking whatsoever brought it to a stop at the SAC terminus of the line so precisely that only a love pat from a fifteen horsepower engine was needed to line up its airlock with that of the station.

'When you're riding a thing like this, it makes it hard to believe that there's any such thing as a devil, doesn't it?' Jack Ginsberg said. He had had a long, luxurious shower aboard the plane, and that, plus getting away from the demon-haunted ruins in Positano, and the subsequent finding in Zurich that money still worked, had brightened him perceptibly.

'Maybe,' Baines said. 'A large part of the mystic tradition says that the possession and use of secular knowledge – or even the desire for it – is in itself evil, according to Ware. But here we are.'

But in the smooth-running, even temperatured caverns of the SAC, Baines himself felt rather reassured. There was no Goat grinning over his shoulder yet. McKnight was an old friend; he was pleased to see Buelg again, and honoured to meet Šatvje; and down here, at least, everything seemed to be under control. It was also helpful to find that both McKnight and his advisers not only already knew the real situation, but had very nearly accepted it. Only Buelg had remained a little sceptical at the beginning, and had seemed quite taken aback to find Baines, of all people, providing independent testimony to the same effect as had the computer. When the new facts Baines had brought had been fed into the machine, and the machine had produced in response a whole new batch of conclusions entirely consistent with the original hypothesis, Buelg seemed convinced, although it was plain that he still did not like it. Well, who did?

At long last they were comfortably settled in McKnight's office, with three tumblers of Jack Daniel's (Jack Ginsberg did not drink, and neither did Šatvje) and no one to interrupt them but an occasional runner from Chief Hay. Though the runner was a coolly pretty blonde girl, and the USAF's women's auxiliary had apparently adopted the miniskirt, Ginsberg did not seem to notice. Perhaps he was still in shock from his recent run-in with the succubus. To Baines's eyes, the girl did look rather remarkably like Ware's Greta, which should have captured Jack instantly; but then, in the long run, most women looked alike to Baines, especially in the line of business.

'That bomb did you no good at all, I take it,' he said.

'Oh, I wouldn't go so far as to say that,' McKnight said. 'True, it didn't destroy the city, or even hurt it visibly, but it certainly seemed to take them by surprise. For about an hour after the fireball went up, the sky above the target was full of them. It was like firing a flashbulb in a cave full of sleeping bats – and we got pictures too.'

'Any evidence that you, uh, destroyed any of them?'

'Well, we saw a lot of them going back to the city under their own power – despite very bad design, they seem to fly pretty well – but we don't have any count of how many went up. We didn't see any falling, but that might have been because some of them had been vaporized.'

'Not bloody likely. Their bodies may have been vaporized,

but the bodies were borrowed in the first place. Like knocking down a radio-controlled aircraft: the craft may be a total loss, but the controlling Intelligence is unharmed, somewhere else, and can send another one against you whenever it likes.'

'Excuse me,, Doctor Baines, but the analogy is inexact,' Buelg said. 'We know that because we did get a lot out of the bomb besides simply stirring up a flurry. High-speed movies of the column of the mushroom as it went up show a lot of the creatures trying to reform. One individual we were able to follow went through thirty-two changes in the first minute. The changes are all incredible and beyond any physical theory or model we can erect to account for them, but they do show, first, that the creature was seriously inconvenienced, and second, that it wanted and perhaps needed to hold on to *some* kind of physical form. That's a start. It suggests to me that had we been able to confine them all in the fireball, where the temperatures are way higher still, no gamut of change they could have run through would have done them any good. Eventually they would have been stripped of the last form and utterly destroyed.'

'The last form, maybe,' Baines said. 'But the spirit would remain. I don't know why they're clinging to physical forms so determinedly, but it probably has only a local and tactical reason, something to do with the prosecuting of the present war. But you can't destroy a spirit by such means, any more than you can destroy a message by burning the piece of paper it's written on.'

As he said this, he became uncomfortably aware that he had gotten the argument out of some sermon against atheism that he had heard as a boy, and had thought simple-minded even then. But since then, he had *seen* demons – and a lot more closely than anybody else here had.

'That is perhaps an open question,' Šatvje said heavily. 'I am not myself a sceptic, you should understand, Doctor Baines, but I have to remind myself that no spirit has ever been so intensively tested to destruction before. Inside a thermonuclear fireball, even the nuclei of hydrogen atoms find it difficult to retain their integrity.'

'Atomic nuclei remain matter, and the conservation laws

still apply. Demons are neither matter nor energy; they are something else.'

'We do not know that they are not energy,' Šatvje said. 'They may well be fields, falling somewhere within the electro-magnetico-gravitic triad. Remember that we have never achieved a unified field theory; even Einstein repudiated his in the last years of his life, and quantum mechanics – with all respect to De Broglie – in only a clumsy avoidance of the problem. These . . . spirits . . . may be such unified fields. And one characteristic of such fields might be 100 per cent negative entropy.'

'There couldn't be any such thing as completely negative entropy,' Buelg put in. 'Such a system would constantly *accumulate* order, which means that it would run backwards in time and we would never be aware of it at all. You have to allow for Planck's Constant. This would be the only stable case –'

He wrote rapidly on a pad, stripped off the sheet and passed it across the table. The note read, in very neat lettering:

$$H(x) - H_y(x) = C + \epsilon$$

The girl came in with another manifold of sheets from the computer, and this time Jack Ginsberg's eye could be observed to be wandering haunchward a little. Baines had never objected to this – he preferred his most valuable employees to have a few visible and usable weaknesses – but for once he almost even sympathized; he was feeling a little out of his depth.

'Meaning what?' he said.

'Why,' Šatvje said, a little patronizingly, 'eternal life, of course. Life *is* negative entropy. Stable negative entropy is eternal life.'

'Barring accidents,' Buelg said, with a certain grim relish. 'We have no access yet to the gravitic part of the spectrum, but the electromagnetic sides are totally vulnerable, and with the clues we've got now, we ought to be able to burst into such a closed system like a railroad spike going through an auto tyre.'

'If you can kill a demon,' Baines said slowly. 'Then –'

'That's right,' Buelg said affably. 'Angel, devil, ordinary immortal soul – you name it, we can do for it. Not right away, maybe, but before very long.'

'Perhaps the ultimate human achievement,' Šatvje said, with a dreaming, almost beatific expression. 'The theologians call condemnation to Hell the Second Death. Soon, perhaps, we may be in a position to give the Third Death . . . the bliss of complete extinction . . . liberation from the Wheel!'

McKnight's eyes were now also wandering, though towards the ceiling. He wore the expression of a man who has heard all this before, and is not enjoying it any better the second time. Baines himself was very far from being bored – indeed, he was as close to horrified fascination as he had ever been in his life – but clearly it was time to bring everybody back to Earth. He said:

'Talk's cheap. Do you have any actual plans?'

'You bet we do,' McKnight said, suddenly galvanized. 'I've had Chief Hay run me an inventory of the country's remaining military power, and, believe me, there's a lot of it. I was surprised myself. We are going to mount a major attack upon this city of Dis, and for it we're going to bring some things up out of the ground that the American people have never seen before and neither has anybody else, including this pack of demons. I don't know why they're just sitting there, but maybe it's because they think they've already got us licked. Well, they're dead wrong. Nobody can lick the United States – not in the long run!'

It was an extraordinary sentiment from a man who had been maintaining for years that the United States had 'lost' China, 'surrendered' Korea, 'abandoned' Vietnam and was overrun by home-bred Communists; but Baines, who knew the breed, saw no purpose in calling attention to the fact. *Their arguments, not being based in reason, cannot be swayed by reason*. Instead he said:

'General, believe me, I advise against it. I know some of the weapons you're talking about, and they're pretty powerful. I ought to know; my company designed and supplied some of them, so it would be against my own interests to run them down to you. But I very much doubt that any of them will do any good under the present circumstances.'

'That, of course, remains to be seen,' McKnight said.

'I'd rather we didn't. If they work, we may find ourselves worse off than before. That's the point I came here to press. The demons are about 90 per cent in charge of the world now, but you'll notice that they haven't taken any further steps against us. There's a reason for this. They are fighting against another Opponent entirely, and it's quite possible that we ought to be on their side.'

McKnight leaned back in his chair, with the expression of a president confronted at a press conference with a question on which he had not been briefed.

'Let me be quite sure I understand you, Doctor Baines,' he said. 'Do you propose that the present invasion of the United States was a good thing? And, further, that we ought not to be opposing the occupying forces with all our might? That indeed we ought instead to be aiding and abetting the powers responsible for it?'

'I don't propose any aiding and abetting whatsoever,' Baines said, with an inward sigh. 'I just think we ought to lay off for a while, that's all, until we see how the situation works out.'

'You are almost the last man in the world,' McKnight said stiffly, 'whom I would have suspected of being a ComSymp, let alone a pro-Chink. When I have your advice entered upon the record, I will also add an expression of my personal confidence. In the meantime, the attack goes forward as scheduled.'

Baines said nothing more, advisedly. It had occurred to him, out of his experience with Theron Ware, that angels fallen and unfallen, and the immortal part of man, partook of and had sprung from the essentially indivisable nature of their Creator; that if these men could destroy that Part, they could equally well dissolve the Whole; that a successful storming of Dis would inevitably be followed by a successful war upon Heaven; and that if God were not dead yet, He soon might be.

However it turned out, it looked like it was going to be the most interesting civil war he had ever run guns to.

9

UNITED STATES ARMED FORCES
Strategic Air Command Office
Denver, Colorado

Date: May 1

MEMORANDUM: Number 1
TO: All Combat Arms
SUBJECT: General Combat Orders

1. This Memorandum supersedes all previous directives on this subject.
2. The United States has been invaded and all combat units will stand in readiness to expel the invading forces.
3. The enemy has introduced a number of combat innovations of which all units must be made thoroughly aware. All officers will therefore read this Memorandum in full to their respective commands, and will thereafter post it in a conspicuous place. All commands should be sampled for familiarity with the contents of the Memorandum.
4. Enemy troops are equipped with individual body armour. In accordance with ancient Oriental custom, this armour has been designed and decorated in various grotesque shapes, in the hope of frightening the opposition. It is expected that the American soldier will simply laugh at this primitive device. All personnel are warned, however, that as armour these 'demon suits' are extremely effective. A very high standard of marksmanship will be required against them.
5. An unknown number of the enemy body armour units, perhaps approaching 100 per cent, are capable of free flight, like the jump suits supplied to US. Mobile Infantry. Ground forces will therefore be alert to possible attack from the air by individual enemy troops as well as by conventional aircraft.
6. It is anticipated that in combat the enemy will employ various explosive, chemical and toxic agents which may

produce widespread novel effects. All personnel are hereby reminded that these effects will be either natural in origin, or illusions.
7. Following the reading of this Memorandum, all officers will read to their commands those paragraphs of the Articles of War pertaining to the penalties for cowardice in battle.

By order of the Commander in Chief:

D. Willis McKnight

D. WILLIS MCKNIGHT
General of the Armies, USAF

Because of the destruction of Rome and of the Vatican with it – alas for that great library and treasure house of all Christendom! – the Holy See had been moved to Venice, which had been spared thus far, and was now housed in almost equal magnificence in the Sala del Collegio of the Palazzo Ducale, the only room to escape intact from the great fire of 1577, where, under a ceiling by Veronese, the doges had been accustomed to receive their ambassadors to other city-states. It was the first time the palace had been used by anybody but tourists since Napoleon had forced the abdication of Lodovico Manin exactly eleven hundred years after the election of the first doge.

There were no tourists here now, of course: the city, broiling hot and stinking of the garbage in its canals, brooded lifelessly under the Adriatic sun, a forgotten museum. Nobody was about in the crazy narrow streets, and the cramped *ristoranti*, but the native Venetians, their livelihood gone, sullenly starving together in small groups and occasionally snarling at each other in their peculiar dialect. Many already showed signs of radiation sickness: their hair was shedding in patches, and pools of vomit caught the sunlight, ignored by everyone but the flies.

The near desertion of the city, at least by comparison with the jam which would have been its natural state by this time of year, gave Father Domenico a small advantage. Instead of having to take refuge in a third-class hotel, clamorous twenty-four hours a day with groups of Germans and Americans being processed by the coachload like raw potatoes being converted into neatly packaged crisps, he was able without opposition to find himself apartments in the Patriarch's Palace itself. Such dusty sumptuousness did not at all suit him, but he had come to see the Pope, as the deputy of an ancient, still honoured monastic order; and the Patriarch, after confessing him and hearing the nature of his errand, had deemed it fitting that he be appropriately housed while he waited.

There was no way of telling how long the wait might be. The Pope had died with Rome; what remained of the College of Cardinals – those of them that had been able to reach Venice at all – was shut in the Sala del Consiglio dei Dieci, attempting to elect a new one. It was said that the office of the Grand Inquisitor, directly next door, held a special guest, but of this rumour the Patriarch seemed to know no more than the next man. In the meantime, he issued to Father Domenico a special dispensation to conduct Masses and hear confessions in small churches off the Grand Canal, and to preach there and even in the streets if he wished. Technically, Father Domenico had no patent to do any of these things, since he was a monk rather than a priest, but the Patriarch, like everyone else now, was short on manpower.

On the trip northward from Monte Albano, Father Domenico had seen many more signs of suffering, and of outright demoniac malignancy, than were visible on the surface of this uglily beautiful city; but it was nevertheless a difficult, almost sinister place in which to attempt to minister to the people, let alone to preach a theology of hope. The Venetians had never been more than formally and outwardly allegiant to the Church from at least their second treaty with Islam in the mid-fifteenth century. The highest pinnacle of their ethics was that of dealing fairly with each other, and since there was at the same time no sweeter music to Venetian ears than the scream of outrage from the outsider who had discovered too late that he had been cheated, this left them little that they felt they ought to say in the confessional. Most of them seemed to regard the now obvious downfall of almost all of human civilization as a plot to divert the tourist trade to some other town

– probably Istanbul, which they still referred to as Constantinople.

As for hope, they had none. In this they were not alone. Throughout his journey, Father Domenico had found nothing but terror and misery, and a haunted populace which could not but conclude that everything the Church had taught them for nearly two thousand years had been lies. How could he tell them that, considering the real situation as he knew it to be, the suffering and the evil with which they were afflicted were rather less than he had expected to find? How then could he tell them further that he saw small but mysteriously increasing signs of mitigation of the demons' rule? In these, fighting all the way against confounding hope with wishful thinking, he believed only reluctantly himself.

Yet hope somehow found its way forward. On an oppressive afternoon while he was trying to preach to a group of young thugs, most of them too surly and indifferent even to jeer, before the little Church of Sta. Maria dei Miracoli, his audience was suddenly galvanized by a series of distant whistles. The whistles, as Father Domenico knew well enough, had been until only recently the signals of the young wolves of Venice, to report the spotting of some escortless English schoolmarm, pony-tailed Bennington art student or gaggle of Swedish girls. There were no such prey about now, but nevertheless, the piazzetta emptied within a minute.

Bewildered and of course apprehensive, Father Domenico followed, and soon found the streets almost as crowded as of old with people making for St Mark's. A rumour had gone around that a puff of white smoke had been seen over the Palazzo Ducale. This was highly unlikely, since – what with the fear of another fire which constantly haunted the palace – there was no stove in it anywhere in which to burn ballots; nevertheless, the expectation of a new Pope had run through the city like fire itself. By the time Father Domenico reached the vast square opposite the basilica (for after all, he too had come in search of a Pope) it was so crowded as to scarcely leave standing room for the pigeons.

If there was indeed to be any announcement, it would have to come Venetian style from the top of the Giant's Staircase of

Antonio Rizzo; the repetitive arches of the first-floor loggia offered no single balcony on which a Pope might appear. Father Domenico pressed forward into the great internal courtyard towards the staircase, at first saying, *'Prego, prego,'* and then *'Scusate, scusate mi'*, to no effect whatsoever and finally with considerable judicious but hard monkish use of elbows and knees.

Over the tense rumbling of the crowd there sounded suddenly an antiphonal braying of many trumpets – something of Gabrielli's, no doubt – and at the same time Father Domenico found himself jammed immovably against the coping of the cannon-founder's well, which had long since been scavenged clean of the tourists' coins. By luck it was not a bad position; from here he had quite a clear view up the staircase and between the towering statues of Mars and Neptune. The great doors had already been opened, and the cardinals in their scarlet finery were ranked on either side of the portico. Between them and a little forward stood two pages, one of them holding a red cushion upon which stood something tall and glittering.

Amidst the fanfare, an immensely heavy tolling began to boom: La Trottiera, the bell which had once summoned the members of the Grand Council to mount their horses and ride over the wooden bridges to a meeting. The combination of bell and trumpets was solemnly beautiful, and under it the crowd fell quickly silent. Yet the difference from the Roman ritual was disturbing, and there was something else wrong about it, too. What was that thing on the cushion? It certainly could not be the tiara; was it the golden horn of the doges?

The music and the tolling stopped. Into the pigeon-cooing silence, a cardinal cried in Latin:

'We have a Pope, *Summus Antistitum Antistes!* And it is his will that he be called Juvenember LXIX!'

The unencumbered page now stepped forward. He called in the vernacular:

'Here is your Pope, and we know it will please you.'

From the shadow of the great doors there stepped forth into the sunlight between the statues, bowing his head to accept the golden horn, his face white and mild as milk, the special guest of the office of the Grand Inquisitor: a comely old man with a goshawk on his wrist, whom Father Domenico had first and last seen on Black Easter, released from the Pit by Theron Ware – the demon AGARES.

There was an enormous shout from the crowd, and then the trumpets and the bell resumed, now joined by all the rest of the bells in the city,, and by many drums, and the firing of cannon. Choking with horror, Father Domenico fled as best he could.

The festival went on all week, climaxed by bull dancing in the Cretan style in the courtyard of the Palazzo, and by fireworks at night, while Father Domenico prayed. This event was definitive. The Antichrist had arrived, however belatedly, and therefore God still lived. Father Domenico could do no more good in Italy; he must now go to Dis, into Hell-Mouth itself, and challenge Satan to grant His continuing existence. Nor would it be enough for Father Domenico to aspire to be the Antisatan. If necessary – most terrifying of all thoughts – he must now expose himself to the temptation and the election, by no Earthly college, of becoming the vicar of Christ whose duty it would be to harrow this Earthly Hell.

Yet how to get there? He was isolated on an isthmus of mud, and he had no Earthly resources whatsoever. Just possibly, some rite of white magic might serve to carry him, although he could remember none that seemed applicable; but that would involve returning to Monte Albano, and in any event, he felt instinctively that no magic of any kind would be appropriate now.

In this extremity, he bethought him of certain legends and attested miracles of the early saints, some of whom in their exaltation were said to have been lifted long distances through the air. Beyond question, he was not a saint; but if his forthcoming role was to be as he suspected, some similar help might be vouchsafed him. He tried to keep his mind turned away from the obvious and most exalted example of all, and equally to avoid thinking about the doubt-inducing fate of Simon Magus – a razor's edge which not even his Dominican training made less than nearly impossible to negotiate.

Nevertheless, his shoulders squared, his face set, Father Domenico walked resolutely towards the water.

10

Even after the complete failure of air power in Vietnam to pound one half of a tenth-rate power into submission, General McKnight remained a believer in its supremacy; but he was not such a fool as to do without ground support, knowing very well the elementary rule that territory must be occupied as well as devastated, or even the most decisive victory will come unstuck. By the day – or rather, the night – for which the attack was scheduled, he had moved three armoured divisions through the Panamint range, and had two more distributed through the Grapevine, Funeral and Black mountains, which also bristled with rocket emplacements. This was by no means either as big or as well divided a force as he should have liked to have used, especially on the east, but since it was all the country had left to offer him, he had to make it do..

His battle plan was divided into three phases. Remembering that the test bomb had blown some thousands of enemy troops literally sky high for what was tactically speaking quite a long period of time, he intended to begin with a serial bombardment of Dis with as many of his remaining nuclear weapons as he could use up just short of making the surrounding territory radiologically lethal to his own men. These warheads might not do the city or the demons any damage – a proposition which he still regarded with some incredulity – but if they would again disorganize the enemy and keep him from reforming that would be no mean advantage in itself.

Phase Two was designed to take advantage of the fact that the battleground from his point of view was all downhill, the devils with stunning disregard of elementary strategy having located their fortress at the lowest point in the valley, on the site of what had previously been Badwater, which was actually two hundred and eighty-two feet below sea level. When the nuclear bombardment ended, it would be succeeded immediately by a continued hammering with conventional explosives, by artillery, missiles and planes. These would include phosphorus bombs, again probably harmless to devils, but which would in any event produce immense clouds of dense white smoke, which might impair visibility for the enemy; his own troops could see through it handily enough by radar, and would always be able to see the main target through the infra-red telescope or 'sniperscope', since even under normal conditions it was always obligingly kept red hot. Under cover of this bombardment, McKnight planned a rush of armour upon the city, spearheaded by halftrack-mounted laser projectors. It was McKnight's theory, supported neither by his civilian advisers nor by the computer, that the thermonuclear fireball had failed to vaporize the iron walls because its heat had been too generalized and diffuse, and that the concentrated heat of four or five or a dozen laser beams, all focused on one spot, might punch its way through like a rapier going through cheese. This onslaught was to be aimed directly at the gates. Of course these would be better defended than any other part of the perimeter, but a significant number of the defenders might still be flapping wildly around in the air amidst the smoke, and in any event, when one is trying to breach a wall, it is only common sense to begin at a point which *already* has a hole in it.

If such a breach was actually effected, an attempt would be made to enlarge it with land torpedoes, particularly burrowing ones of the Hess type which would have been started on their way at the beginning of Phase One. These had never seen use before in actual combat and were supposed to be graveyard secret – though with profusion of spies and traitors with which America had been swarming, in McKnight's view, before all this had begun, he doubted that the secret had been very well kept. (After all, if even Baines . . .) He was curious also about the actual effectiveness of another secret, the product of an almost incestuous union of chemistry and nucleonics called TDX, a compound as unstable as TNT, which was made of gravity-polarized atoms. McKnight had only the vaguest idea of what this jargon was supposed to signify, but what he did know was its action; TDX was supposed to have the property of exploding in a flat plane, instead of expanding evenly in all directions like any Christian explosive.

Were the gate forced, the bombardment would stop and

Phase Three would follow. This would be an infantry assault, supported by individually airborne troops in their rocket-powered flying harness, and supplemented by an attempted paratroop landing inside the city. If on the other hand the gate did not go down, there would be a most unwelcome Phase Four – a general, and hopefully orderly retreat.

The whole operation could be watched both safely and conveniently from the SAC's Command Room under Denver, and as the name implied, directed in the same way; there was a multitude of television screens, some of which were at the individual command consoles provided for each participating general. The whole complex closely resembled the now extinct Space Center at Houston, which had in fact been modelled after it; technically, space flight and modern warfare are almost identical operations from the command point of view. At the front of this cavern and quite dominating it was a master screen of Cinerama proportions; at its rear was something very like a sponsor's booth, giving McKnight and his guests an overview of the whole, as well as access to a bank of small screens on which he could call into being any individual detail of the action that was within access of a camera.

McKnight did not bother to occupy the booth until the nuclear bombardment was over, knowing well enough that the immense amount of ionization it would produce would make non-cable television reception impossible for quite some time. (The fallout was going to be hell, too – but almost all of it would miss Denver, the East Coast was dead, and the fish and the Europeans would have to look out for themselves.) When he finally took over, the conventional bombardment was just beginning. With him were Baines, Buelg, Chief Hay and Šatvje; Jack Ginsberg had expressed no particular interest in watching, and since Baines did not need him here, he had been excused to go below, presumably to resume his lubricous pursuit of Chief Hay's comely runner.

Vision on the great master screen was just beginning to clear as they took their seats, although there was still considerable static. Weather Control reported that it was a clear, brightly moonlit night over all of the Southwest, but in point of fact the top of the great multiple nuclear mushroom, shot through with constant lightning, now completely covered the southern third of California and all of the two states immediately to the east of it. The units and crews crouching in their bivouacs and emplacements along the sides of the mountains facing away from the valley clung grimly to the rocks against hurricane updrafts in temperatures that began at a hundred and fifty degrees and went on up from there. No unit which had been staked out on any of the inside faces of any of the ranges reported anything, then or ever; even the first missiles and shells to come screaming in towards Dis exploded incontinently in mid-air the moment they rose above the sheltering shadows of the mountain peaks. No thermo-couple existed which would express in degrees the temperature at the heart of the target itself; spectographs taken from the air showed it to be cooling from a level of about two and a half million electron volts, a figure as utterly impossible to relate to human experiences as are the distances in miles between the stars.

Nevertheless, the valley cooled with astonishing rapidity, and once visibility was restored, it was easy to see why. More than two hundred square miles of it had been baked and annealed into a shallow, even dish, still glowing whitely but shot through with the gorgeous colours of impurities, like a borax bead in the flame of a blowpipe; and this was acting like the reflector of a searchlight, throwing the heat outward through the atmosphere into space in an almost solidly visible column. At its centre, as at the Cassegranian focus of a telescope mirror, was a circular black hole.

McKnight leaned forward, grasping the arms of his chair in a death grip, and shouted for a close-up. Had the job been done already? Perhaps Buelg had been right about there being a possible limit to the number of transformations the enemy could go through before final dissolution. After all, Badwater had just received a nuclear saturation which had previously been contemplatedd only in terms of the overkill of whole countries –

But as the glass darkened, the citadel brightened, until at last it showed once more as a red-hot ring. Nothing could be seen inside it but a roiling mass of explosions – the conventional bombardment was now getting home, and with great accuracy – from which a mushroom stem continued to rise in the very centre of the millennial updraft; but the walls – the walls, the walls, the walls were still there.

'Give it up, General,' Buelg said, his voice gravelly. 'No matter what the spectroscope shows, if those walls were really iron –' He paused and swallowed heavily. 'They must be only symbologically iron, perhaps in some alchemical sense. Otherwise the atoms would not only have been scattered to the four winds, but would have had all the electron shells stripped off them. You can do nothing more but lose more lives.'

'The bombardment is till going on,' McKnight pointed out stiffly, 'and we've had no report yet of what it's done to the enemy's organization and manpower. For all we know, there's nobody left down that hole at all – and the laser squadrons haven't even arrived yet, let alone the Hess torpedoes.'

'Neither of which are going to work a damn,' Baines said brutally. 'I know what the Hess torpedo will do. Have you forgotten that they were invented by my own chief scientist? Who just incidentally was taken by PUT SATANACHIA this Easter, so that the demons now know all about the gadget, if they didn't before. And after what's been dropped on that town already, expecting anything of it is like trying to kill a dinosaur by kissing it.'

'It is in the American tradition,' McKnight said, 'to do things the hard way if there is no other way. Phase Four is a last-ditch measure, and it is good generalship – which I do not expect you to understand – to remain flexible until the last moment. As Clausewitz remarks, most battles are lost by generals who failed to have the courage of their own convictions in the clutch.'

Baines, who had read extensively in both military and political theoreticians in five languages, and had sampled them in several more, as a necessary adjunct to his business, knew very well that Clausewitz had never said any such damn fool thing, and that McKnight was only covering with an invented quotation a hope which was last-ditch indeed. But even had elementary Machiavellianism given him any reason to suppose that charging McKnight with this would change the General's mind in the slightest, he could see from the master screen that it was already too late. While they had been talking, the armoured divisions had been charging down into the valley, their diesel-electric engines snarling and snorting, the cleats of their treads cracking the slippery glass and leaving sluggishly glowing, still quasi-molten trails behind. Watching them in the small screens, Baines began to think that he must be wrong. He knew these monsters well – they were part of his stock in trade – and to believe that they were resistible went against the selling habits of an entire adult lifetime.

Yet some of them were bogging down already; as they descended deeper into the valley, with the small rockets whistling over their hunched heads, the hot glass under their treads worked into the joints like glue, and then, carried by the groaning engines up over the top trunnions, cooled and fell into the bearings in a shower of many-sized abrasive granules. The monsters slewed and sidled, losing traction and with it, steerage; and then the lead half-track with the laser cannon jammed immovably and began to sink like the *Titanic* into the glass, the screams of its boiling crew tearing the cool air of the command booth like a ripsaw until McKnight impatiently cut the sound off.

The other beasts lumbered on regardless – they had no orders to do otherwise – and a view from the air showed that three or four units of the laser squadron were now within striking distance of the gates of Dis. Like driver ants, black streams of infantry were crawling down the inner sides of the mountains behind the last wave of the armoured divisions. They too had had no orders to turn back. Even in their immensely clumsy asbestos firemen's suits and helmets, they were already fainting and falling over each other in the foothills, their carefully oiled automatic weapons falling into the sand, the tanks of their flame throwers splitting and dumping jellied gasoline on the hot rocks, the very air of the valley sucking all of the moisture out of their lungs through the tiniest cracks in their uniforms.

Baines was not easily horrified – that would have been bad for business – but also he had never before seen any actual combat but the snippets of the Vietnam war, which had been shown on American television. This senseless advance of expensively trained and equipped men to certain and complete slaughter – men who as usual not only had no idea of what they were dying for, but had been actively misled about it – made about as much military sense as the Siege of Sevastopol or the Battle of the Marne. Certainly it was spectacular, but intellectually it was not even very interesting.

Four of the laser buggies – all that had survived – were now halted before the gates, two to each side to allow a heavy howitzer to fire between them. From them lanced out four pencil-thin beams of intensely pure red light, all of which met at the same spot on the almost invisible seam between the glowing doors. Had that barrier been real iron, they would have holed through it in a matter of seconds in a tremendous shower of sparks, but in actuality they were not even raising its temperature, as far as Baines could see. The beams winked out; then struck again.

Above the buggies, on the barbican, there seemed to be scores of black, indistinct, misshapen figures. They were very active, but their action did not seem to be directed against the buggies; Baines had the mad impression, which he was afraid was all too accurate, that they were dancing.

Again the beams lashed out. Beside him, McKnight muttered:

'If they don't hurry it up –'

Even before he was able to finish the sentence, the ground in front of the gates erupted. The first of the Hess torpedoes had arrived. One of the half-tracks simply vanished, while the one next to it went slowly skyward, and as slowly fell back, in a fountain of armour plate, small parts, and human limbs and torsos. Another, on the very edge of the crater, toppled equally slowly into it. The fourth sat for a long minute as if stunned by the concussion, and then began to back slowly away.

Another torpedo went off directly under the gates, and then another. The gates remained obdurately unharmed, but after a fourth such blast, light could be seen under them – the crater was growing.

'Halt all armoured vehicles!' McKnight shouted into his intercom, pounding the arm of his chair in excitement. 'Infantry advance on the double! We're going under!'

Another Hess torpedo went off in the same gap. Baines was fascinated now, and even feeling a faint glow of pride. Really, the things worked very well indeed; too bad Hess couldn't be here to see it . . . but maybe he was seeing it, from inside. That hole was already big enough to accommodate a small car, and while he watched, another torpedo blew it still wider and deeper.

'Paratroops! Advance drop by ten minutes!'

But why was Hess's invention working when the nuclear devices hadn't? Maybe Dis had only sunk lower as a whole, as the desert around and beneath it had been vaporized, but the demons could not defend the purely mundane geology of the valley itself? Another explosion. How many of those torpedoes had the Corps of Engineers had available? Consolidated Warfare Service had supplied only ten prototypes with the plans at the time of the sale, and there hadn't been time to put more into production. McKnight's suddenly advanced timetable seemed nevertheless to be allowing for the arrival of all ten.

This proved to be the case, except that the ninth got caught in a fault before it had completed its burrowing and blew up in the middle of one of the advancing columns of troops. Hess had always frankly admitted that the machine would be subject to this kind of failure, and that the flaw was inherent in the principle rather than the design. But it probably wouldn't be missed; the gap under the gates of Dis now looked quite as big as the New Jersey entrance to the original two Lincoln Tunnels. And the infantry was arriving at speed.

And at that moment, the vast unscarred gates slowly began to swing inward. McKnight gaped in astonishment and Baines could feel his own jaw dropping. Was the citadel going to surrender before it had even been properly stormed? Or worse, had it been ready all along to open to the first polite knock, so that all this colossal and bloody effort had been unnecessary?

But that, at least, they were spared. As the first patrols charged, tumbled, scrambled and clambered into the crater, there appeared in the now fully opened gateway, silhouetted against the murky flames behind, the same three huge naked snaky-haired women that McKnight and his crew had seen in the very first aerial photographs. They were all three carrying among them what appeared to be the head of an immense decapitated statue of something much like one of themselves. The asbestos-clad soldiers climbing up the far wall of the crater could not turn any greyer than they were, but they froze instantaneously like the overwhelmed inhabitants of Pompeii, and fell, and as they fell, they broke. Within minutes, the pit was being refilled from the bottom with shattered sculpture.

Overhead, the plane carrying the first contingent of paratroops was suddenly blurred by hundreds of tiny black dots. Seconds later, the fuselage alone was plunging towards the desert; the legions of BEELZEBUB, the Lord of the Flies, had torn the wings off men. Lower, in the middle of the air, rocket-borne Assault Infantry soldiers were being plucked first of their harness, then of their clothing, and then of their hair, their fingernails and toenails by jeering creatures with beasts' heads, most of whom were flying without even wings. The bodies, when there was anything left of them at all, were being dropped unerringly into the heart of the Pit.

In summary, the Siege of Dis could more reasonably be described as a rout, except for one curious discrepancy: When Phase Four began – without anyone's ordering it, and otherwise not according to plan – the demons failed to follow up their advantage. None of them, in fact, had ever left the city; even when they had taken to the air, they had never crossed its perimeter, as though the moat represented some absolute boundary which ascended even into the sky.

But the slaughter had been bad enough already. The chances that the Army of the United States could ever reform again looked very small indeed.

And at the end, there formed upon the master screen in the Denver cavern, superimposed upon the image of the burning triumphant city, an immense Face. Baines knew it well; he had been expecting to see it again ever since the end of that Black Easter back in Positano.

It was the crowned goat's head of PUT SATANACHIA.

McKnight gasped in horror for the very first time in Baines's memory; and down on the floor of the control centre, several generals fainted outright at their consoles. Then McKnight was on his feet screaming.

'A Chink! I knew it all along! Hay, clear the circuits! Clear the circuits! Get him off the screen!' He rounded suddenly on Baines. 'And you, you traitor! Your equipment failed us! You've sold us out! You were on their side all the time! Do you know into whose hands you have delivered your country? Do you? Do you?'

His howling was only an irritant now, but Baines had the strength left to raise one mocking eyebrow questioningly. McKnight levelled a trembling finger at the screen.

'Hay, Hay, clear the circuits! I'll have you court-martialled! Doesn't anyone understand but me? *That is the insidious Doctor Fu Manchu*!'

The Sabbath Goat paid him no heed. Instead, it looked directly and steadily across the cavern into Baines's eyes. There was no mistaking the direction of that regard, and no question but that it saw him. It said:

AH, THERE YOU ARE, MY DEARLY BELOVED SON. COME TO ME NOW. OUR FATHER BELOW HATH NEED OF THEE.

Baines had no intention whatsoever of obeying that summons; but he found himself rising from his chair all the same.

Foaming at the mouth, his hands clawing for the distant throat of the demon, McKnight plunged in a shower of splinters through the front of the booth and fell like a glass comet towards the floor.

The Harrowing of Heaven

As a picture, wherein a black colouring occurs in its proper place, so is the universe beautiful, if any could survey it, notwithstanding the presence of sinners, although, taken by themselves, their proper deformity makes them hideous.

ST AUGUSTINE: *De Civitate Dei, xi. 23*

Thus that Faustus, to so many a snare of death, had now, neither willing nor witting it, begun to loosen that wherein I was taken.

Confessions, v.13

11

Baines did not have much time to experiment under the geas or compulsion which PUT SATANACHIA had laid upon him, but he nevertheless found that it was highly selective in character. For example, the great prince had said nothing about requiring the presence of Jack Ginsberg, but when Baines, in a mixture of vindictiveness and a simple desire for human companionship, decided to try to bring him along, he found that he was not prevented from doing so. Ginsberg himself showed no resentment at being routed out of the bed of the blonde runner; possibly the succubus in Positano had spoiled for him the pleasures of human women, an outcome Jack himself had suspected in advance; but then, even without that supernatural congress, Jack's sexual life had always been that of a rather standard Don Juan, for whom every success turned sour almost instantly.

This, however, was one of those explanations which did not explain, and Baines had thought about it often before; for, as has already been observed, he liked to have his key men come equipped with handles he could grasp if the need arose. There were, the company psychologist had told him, at least three kinds of Don Juans: Freud's, whose career is a lifelong battle to hide from himself an incipient homosexuality; Lenau's, a Romantic in search of the Ideal Woman, for whom the Devil who comes for him is disgust with himself; and Da Ponte's, a man born blind to the imminence of tomorrow, and hence incapable either of love or of repentance, even on the edge of the Pit. Well, but in the end, for Baines, it did not matter which one was Jack; they all *behaved* alike.

Jack did object powerfully when he was told that the journey to Dis would have to be made entirely on foot, but this was one of the areas in which Baines discovered that the geas left him no choice. Again, he wondered why it should be so. Did the Sabbath Goat mean to rub in the fact that the Siege of Dis had been the last gasp of secular technology? Or had it instead meant to impress upon Baines that, willy-nilly, he was about to embark upon a pilgrimage? But again, the outcome would have been the same, and that was all that mattered.

As for Jack, he still seemed to be afraid of his boss, or else still thought there was some main chance to be looked out for. Well, perhaps there was – but Baines would not have bet any shares of stock on it.

Theron Ware saw the great compound mushroom cloud go up while he was still in Flagstaff, a point to which several lucky hitchhikes and one even luckier long freight train ride had brought him. The surging growth of the cloud, the immense flares of light beyond the mountains to the west, and the repeated earth shocks left him in little doubt about what was going on; and as the cloud drifted towards him, moving inexorably from west to east as the weather usually does, he knew that it meant death for him within a very few days – as for how many thousands of others? – unless by some miracle he could find an unoccupied fallout shelter, or one whose present occupants wouldn't shoot him on sight.

And why indeed go on? The bombing showed without question that Baines's self-assumed mission to McKnight at Denver had failed, and that there was now open warfare between humanity and the demons. The notion that Theron Ware could do anything now to change that was so grandiose as to be outright pathetic. More trivially, by the time that bombing was over, no matter how it affected the demons – if at all – the whole hundred-mile-plus stretch of Death Valley National Monument would have become instantly lethal for an unprotected man to enter.

Yet Theron Ware could not yet quite believe that he was unprotected. He had come an immense distance by a traditional means which made it absolutely clear that black magic still worked; he had come almost an equal distance through a series of lucky breaks which he could not regard as the product of pure chance; and in his pocket the ruby talisman continued to emit a faint warmth which was that of no ordinary stone, natural or synthetic. Like all proverbs, Ware knew, the old saw that the Devil looks after his own was only half true; nevertheless the feeling that he had come all this way on some errand continued to persist, together with a growing conviction that he had never in fact known what it was. He would find out when he arrived; in the meantime, he was travelling on the Devil's business, and would not die until it was concluded.

He would have liked to have stopped over in Flagstaff to inspect the famous observatory where Percival Lowell had produced such complicated maps of the wholly illusory canals of Mars and where Tombaugh had discovered Pluto – and where in the sky did those planets stand, now that their gods had clashed frontally? – but under the circumstances he did not dare. He still had Grand Canyon and the Lake Mead area to cross; then, skirting northwards around the Spring Mountains to the winter resort town of Death Valley, in which he hoped to be able to get some word about exactly where in the valley proper the perimeter of Nether Hell had surfaced. He had come far, but he still had far to go, and he was unlikely now to be able to hitch a ride in the direction of that roiling, flaming column of annihilation. Very well; now at last had come the time he had foreseen in the doomed farmhouse in Pennsylvania, when he would have to steal a car. He did not think that it would be difficult.

Father Domenico too had come far, and had equally good reasons to be quite certain that he would still have been in Italy had it not been for some kind of supernatural intervention. He stood now at dusk in the shadow of the 11,000-foot Telescope Peak, looking eastwards and downwards to where the city of Dis flamed sullenly in the shadow of the valley of death itself against the stark backdrop of the Amargosa Range. That valley had been cut by the Amargosa River, but there had been no river there within the memory of civilized man; the annual rainfall now was well under two inches.

And he was equally certain of supernatural protection. The valley had held the world's second-ranking heat record of 134° F., but although it was immensely hotter than that down here now, Father Domenico felt only a mild glow, as though he had just stepped out of a bath. When he had first come down from the mountain, he had been horrified to find the vitrified desert washing the foothills scattered with hundreds of strange, silent, misshapen grey forms, only vaguely human at first sight, which had proven to be stricken soldiers. He had tried to minister to them, but the attempt had proven hopeless: of the bodies in the few suits he was able to investigate, most were shrunken mummies, and the rest had apparently died even more horribly. He wondered what on Earth could have happened here. His elevation from the waters to the mountain had taken place in a mystic rapture without which, indeed, it would have been impossible, but which had taken him rather out of touch with mundane events.

But whatever the answer, he had no choice but to press on. As he descended the last of the foothills, he saw on the floor of the valley, approaching him along what had once been the old watercourse and more recently a modern road, three tiny figures. In so far as he could tell at this distance, they wore no more visible, Earthly protections against what the valley had become than he did himself. Yet they did not seem to be demons. Full of wonder, he scrambled down towards them; but when they met, and he recognized them, he wondered only that he should have been at all amazed. The meeting, he saw instantly now, had been foreordained.

*

'How did *you* get here?' Baines demanded at once. It was not easy to determine of whom he was asking the question, but while Father Domenico wondered whether it was worthwhile trying to explain trance levitation, and if so how he would go about it, Theron Ware said:

'I can't think of a more trivial question under the circumstances, Doctor Baines. We're here, that's the important thing – and I perceive that we are all under some kind of magical aegis, or we would all be dead. This raises the question of what we hope to accomplish, that we should be so protected. Father, may I ask what your intentions are?'

'Nothing prevents you from asking,' Father Domenico said, 'but you are the last human being in the world to whom I would give the answer.'

'Well, I'll tell you what *my* intentions are,' said Baines. 'My intentions are to stay in the bottommost levels of Denver and wait for this all to blow over, if it's ever going to. One thing you learn fast in the munitions business is that it's a very good idea to stay off battlefields. But my intentions have nothing to do with the matter. I was ordered to come here by the Sabbath Goat, and here I am.'

'Oh?' Ware said with interest. 'He finally came for you?'

'No, I have to come to him. He broke into a closed-circuit television transmission in Denver to tell me so. He didn't even mention Jack; I only brought him along for the company, since it didn't turn out to be forbidden.'

'And small thanks for that,' Ginsberg said, though apparently without rancour. 'If there's anything in the world that I hate, it's exercise. Vertical exercise, anyhow.'

'Have either of you two seen him at all?' Baines added.

Father Domenico remained stubbornly silent, but Ware said: 'PUT SATANACHIA? No, and somehow I doubt that I will, now. I seem to have put myself under the protection of another demon, although one subordinate to the Goat. Confusion of purpose is almost the natural state among demons, but in this instance I think it couldn't have happened without direct Satanic intent.'

'I was given my marching orders in the name of "Our Father Below",' Baines said. 'If he's interested in me, the chances are that he's even more interested in you, all right. But what did you think you were up to?'

'Originally I thought I might try to intercede, or at least to plead for some sort of cease-fire – as you were trying to do from the opposite end in Denver. But that's a dead letter now, and the result is that I have no more idea why I am here than you do. All I can say is that whatever the reason, I don't think there can be much hope in it.'

'While we live, there is always hope,' Father Domenico said suddenly.

The black magician pointed at the tremendous city towards which, volitionlessly, they had been continuing to walk all this time. 'To be able to see *that* at all means that we have already passed far beyond mere futility. All the sins of the Leopard, the sins of incontinence, are behind us, which means that the gate is behind us too: the gate upon which it is carven in Dirghic, LAY DOWN ALL HOPE, YOU THAT GO IN BY ME.'

'We are alive,' Father Domenico said stolidly, 'and I utterly deny and repudiate those sins.'

'You may not do so,' Ware said, his voice gradually rising in intensity. 'Look here, Father, this is all so mysterious, and the future looks so black, that it's ridiculous for us not to make available and to make use of any little scraps of information that we may have to share. The very symbolism of our presence here is simple, patent and ineluctable, and you as a Karcist in white magic should be the first to see it. To take the circles of Upper Hell in order, Ginsberg here is almost a type creation of the lust-dominated man; I have sold my soul for unlimited knowledge, which in the last analysis is surely nothing more than an instance of gluttony; and you have only to look around this battlefield to see that Doctor Baines is an instrument of wrath *par excellence*.'

'You have skipped the Fourth Circle,' Father Domenico said, 'with obvious didactic intent, but your arrogance is wasted upon me. I draw no moral from it whatsoever.'

'Oh, indeed? Wasn't treasure finding once the chiefest use of white magic? And isn't the monkish life – withdrawal from the snares, affairs *and duties* of the world for the sake of one's own soul – as plain a case of hoarding as one could ask for? It is in fact so egregious an example of that very sin that not even canonization remits it; I can tell you of my own certain knowledge that every single pillar saint went instantly to Hell, and of even the simple monks, none escaped except those few like Matthew Paris and Roger of Wendover who also lead useful worldly lives.'

'And regardless of what your fatuous friends on Monte Albano believed, there is no efficacious dispensation for the practice of white magic, because there is no such thing as white magic. It is all black, black, black as the ace of spades, and you have imperilled your immortal soul by practising it not even for your own benefit, but on commission for others; if that does not make you a spendthrift as well as a hoarder, what would you call it?

'Think at last, Father: Why did your crucifix burst in your hands at the last minute on Black Easter? Wasn't it because you tried to use it for personal gain? What does it symbolize, if not total submission to whatever may be Willed? Yet you tried to use it – the ultimate symbol of resignation in the face of death – to save your own paltry life. Really, Father Domenico, I think the time has come for us to be frank with each other – for you as surely as for the rest of us!'

'Hear, hear,' Baines said with rather a sick grin.

After six or seven paces of silence, Father Domenico said:

'I am terribly afraid you are right. I came here in the hope of forcing the demons to admit that God still lives, and I saw what I thought were indisputable signs of Divine sponsorship. Unless you are simply more subtle a casuist than any I have ever encountered before, even in print, it now appears that I had no right to think any such thing . . . which means that the real reason for my presence here is no less mysterious than that for yours. I cannot say that this increases my understanding any.'

'It establishes a common ignorance,' said Ware. 'And as far as your original assumption is concerned, Father, it suggests some basic uniformity of purpose which I must admit is certainly not characteristic of demons, whatever that may mean. But I think we shall not have long to wait for the answer, gentlemen. It appears that we have arrived.'

They all looked up. The colossal barbican of Dis loomed over them.

'One thing is surely clear,' Father Domenico whispered. 'We have been making this journey all our lives.'

12

No Beatrice sponsored them, and no Vergil led them; but as they approached the great ward, the undamaged portcullis rose, and the gates swung inward in massive silence. No demons mocked them, no Furies challenged them, no angel had to cross the Styx to bring them passage; they were admitted, simply and non-committally.

Beyond the barbican, they found the citadel transformed. The Nether Hell of diuturnal torture, which had withstood the bombardment of Man without damage to so much as a twig in the Wood of the Suicides, was gone entirely. Perhaps in some sense it had never been there at all, but was still located where it had always been, in Eternity, not on Earth; a place still reserved for the dead. For these four still-living men, it had vanished.

In its place there stood a clean, well-lighted city like an illustration from some Utopian romance; it looked, in fact, like a cross between the city of the future in the old film *Things to Come* and a fully automated machine shop. It screamed, hammered and roared like a machine shop as well.

The grossly misshapen, semi-bestial forms of the demons had also vanished. The metropolis instead appeared to be peopled now chiefly by human beings, although their appearance could scarcely be described as normal. Male and female alike, they were strikingly beautiful; but their beauty swiftly became cloying, for except for sexual characteristics they were completely identical, as though they were all members of the same clone – one which had been genetically selected out to produce creatures modelled after the statuary fronting public buildings, or the souls in the Dante illustrations of Gustav Doré.

Both sexes wore identical skirted tabards made of some grey material which looked like papier-mâché, across the breasts of which long numbers had been woven in metallically glittering script

A second and much less numerous group wore a different uniform, vaguely military in cast, an impression reinforced by the fact that these were mostly to be seen standing stiffly at street intersections. Heroic in mould though the majority were, the minority were even more statuesque, and their common Face was evenly pleasant but stern, like that of an idealized father

The others wore no expression at all, unless their very expressionlessness was a reflection of acute boredom – which would not have been surprising, for no one of this class seemed to have anything to do. The work of the metropolis, which seemed to be exclusively that of producing that continual, colossal din, went on behind the blank facades apparently without need of any sentient tending or intervention. They never spoke. As the four pilgrims moved onward towards the centre of the city, they passed frequent exhibitions of open, public sexuality, more often than not in groups; at first Jack Ginsberg regarded these with the liveliest interest, but it soon faded as it became apparent that even this was bored and pleasureless.

There were no children; and no animals

Initially, the travellers had hesitated, when the two magicians had discovered that with the transformation they could no longer trust to Dante to show them the way, and Baines's memory of the aerial photographs had become similarly useless. They had proceeded more or less by instinct towards the centre of the din. After a while, however, they found that they had been silently joined by four of the policing demons, though whether they were being led or herded never did become clear. The grimly ambiguous escort heightened the impression of a guided tour of some late nineteenth-century world-of-tomorrow which was to include awe-inspiring visits to the balloon works, the crêches, the giant telegraph centre and the palace of folk arts, only to wind up in a corrective discipline hospital for the anti-social.

It was as though they were being given a preview of what the future of humanity would be like under demonic rule – not wholly unpredictable as a foretaste, but in content as well, as if the demons were trying to put the best possible face on the matter. In so doing, they had ingenuously embodied in their citadel nothing worse than a summary and epitomization of what pre-Apocalyptic, post-industrial Man had been systematically creating for himself. St Augustine, Goethe and Milton all had observed that the Devil, by constantly seeking evil, always did good, but here was an inversion of that happy fault: A demonstration that demons are at their worst when doing their best.

Many of Baines's most lucrative ideas for weaponry had been stolen bodily, through the intermediary of the Mamaroneck Research Institute, from the unpaid imaginations of science-fiction writers, and it was he who first gave voice to the thought:

'I always thought it'd be hell to actually have to live in a place like this,' he shouted. 'And now I know it.'

Nobody answered him; but it was more than possible that this was because nobody had heard him.

But only the veritable Hell is for ever. After some unknown but finite time, they found themselves passing between the Doric columns and under the golden architrave of that high capital which is called Pandemonium, and the brazen doors folded open for them.

Inside, the clamour was muffled to a veiled and hollow booming, for the vast jousting field that was this hall had been made to hold the swarming audience for a panel of a thousand, but there was no one in it now besides themselves and the demon soldiers but one solitary, distant, intolerable star:

Not that subsidiary triumvir PUT SATANACHIA the Sabbath Goat who had promised himself to them, and they to him, on Black Easter morn;

But that archetypal dropout, the Lie that knows no End, the primeval Parent-sponsored Rebel, the Eternal Enemy, the Great Nothing itself

SATAN MEKRATRIG

There was of course no more Death Valley sunlight here, and the effect of an implacably ultramodern city with its artificial gasglow glare was also gone. But the darkness was not quite complete. A few cressets hung blazing high in mid-air, so few that their light was spread evenly throughout the great arch of the ceiling, like the artificial sky of a planetarium dome simulating that moment between dusk and full night when only Lucifer is bright enough to be visible yet. Towards that glow they moved, and as they moved, it grew.

But the creature, they saw at last, was not the light, which shone instead upon him. The fallen cherub below it was still very nearly the same immense, brooding, cruelly deformed, angelic face that Dante had seen and Milton imagined: triple-faced in yellow, red and black, bat-winged, shag-pelted and so huge that the floor of the great hall cut him off at the breast – he must have measured five hundred yards from crown to hoof. Like the eyes, the wings were six, but they no longer beat frenziedly to stir the three winds that froze Cocytus; nor now did the six eyes weep. Instead, each of the faces – the Semitic Ignorance, the Japhetic Hatred, the Hamitic Impotence – was frozen in an expression of despair too absolute for further grief.

The pilgrims saw these things, but only with half an eye, for their attention was focused instead upon the light which both revealed and shadowed them:

The terrible crowned head of the Worm was surmounted by a halo.

13

The demonic guards had not followed them in, and the great Figure was motionless and uttered no orders; but in that hollowly roaring silence, the pilgrims felt compelled to speak. They looked at each other almost shyly, like school children brought to be introduced to some king or president, each wanting to be bold enough to draw attention to himself, but waiting for someone else to break the ice. Again nothing was said, but somehow agreement was arrived at: Father Domenico should speak first.

Looking aloft, but not quite into those awful countenances, the white monk said:

'Father of Lies, I thought it was my mission to come here and compel thee to speak the truth. I arrived as if by miracle, or borne by faith; and in my journeyings saw many evidences that the rule of Hell on Earth is not complete. Nor has that Goat your prince yet come for me, or for my . . . colleagues here, despite his threat and promise. Then I also saw the election of your demon Pope, the very Antichrist that PUT SATANACHIA said had been dispensed with, as unnecessary to a victorious demonry. I concluded then that God was not dead after all, and someone should come into thy city to assert His continuing authority.

'I stand before thee impotent – my very crucifix was shattered in my hands on Black Easter morning – but nevertheless I charge thee and demand that thou shalt state thy limitations, and abide the course to which they hold thee.'

There was no answer. After a long wait made it clear that there was not going to be, Theron Ware said next:

'Master, thou knowest me well, I think; I am the last black magician in the world, and the most potent ever to practise that high art. I have seen signs and wonders much resembling those mentioned by Father Domenico, but draw from them rather different conclusions. Instead, it seems to me that the final conflict with Michael and all his host cannot be over yet – despite the obvious fact that thou hast won vast advantages already. And if this is true, then it is perhaps an error for thee to make war upon mankind, or for them to make war on thee, with the greater issue still in doubt. Since thou art still granting some of us some favours of magic, there must still exist some aid which we might give thee. Hence I came here to find out what that aid might be, and to proffer it, if it were within my powers.'

No answer. Baines said sullenly:

'I came because I was ordered. But since I'm here, I may as well offer my opinion in the matter, which is much like Ware's. I tried to persuade the human generals not to attack the city, but I failed. Now that they've seen that it can't be attacked – and I'm sure they noticed that you didn't wipe out all their forces when you had the chance – I might have better luck. At least I'll try again, if it's of any use to you.

'I can't imagine any way we could help you carry the war to Heaven, since we were no good against your own local fortress. And besides, I prefer to remain neutral. But getting our generals off your back might relieve you of a nuisance, if you've got more serious business still afoot. If that's not good enough, don't blame me. I didn't come here of my own free will.'

The terrible silence persisted, until at last even Jack Ginsberg was forced to speak.

'If you're waiting for me, I have no suggestions,' he said. 'I guess I'm grateful for past favours, too, but I don't understand what's going on and I didn't want to get involved. I was only doing my job, but as far as my private life goes, I'd just as soon be left to work it out for myself from now on. As far as I'm concerned, it's nobody's business but my own.'

Now, at last, the great wings stirred slightly; and then, the three faces spoke. There was no audible voice, but as the vast lips moved, the words formed in their minds, like sparks crawling along logs in a dying fire.

> 'O yee of little faith,' the Worm set on,
> 'Yee whose coming fame had bodied forth
> A hope archemic even to this Deep
> That Wee should be amerced of golden Throne,
> The which to Us a rack is, by thine alchymie,
> Is this thy sovran Reason? this the draff,
> Are these sollicitations all the sum
> And sorrie Substance of thine high renoune?
> Art thou accomplisht to so mean an end
> After such journeyings of flame and dole
> As once strook doun Heav'n's angels? Say it so,
> In prosie speach or numerous prosodie,

Wee will not be deceav'd; so much the rather
Shall Wee see yee rased from off the bord
'Twixt Hell and Heav'n, as the fearful mariner,
Ingled by the wave 'mongst spume and rock,
Sees craft and hope alike go all to ruin,
Yet yields up not his soul, than Wee shall yield
The last, supreame endeavour of this fearfull Jarr.
'Yet how to body forth to thy blind eyes,
Who have not poets' blindnesse, or the night
Shed by black suns, 'thout which to tell the tale
Of Earth its occupation by the demon breed
Is sole remaining hearth, but to begin?
O 'suaging Night, console Mee now! and hold
My Demy-godhood but a little while
Abeyanc'd from its death in Godhood's dawn!
'O yee of little faith, Wee tell thee this:
Indeed our God is dead; or dead to us.
But in some depth of measure beyond grasp
Remains His principle, as doth the sight
Of drowsy horoscoper, much bemus'd
By vastnesses celestial and horrid
To his tinie system, when first he looks
Through the optic glass at double stars,
Some residuum apprehend; so do we now.
O happie matrix! for there is naught else
That all are left with. It in this inheres,
That Good is independent, but the bad
Cannot alone survive; the evil Deed
Doth need the Holie Light to lend it Sense
And apprehension; for the Good is free
To act or not, while evill hath been will'd
Insensate and compulsive to bring Good
Still greater highths unto, as climber see'th
From toil and suff'ring to th'uttermost Alp,
Best th'unattainable islands of the skye.
'In this yee Sinners are in harmonie,
Antient and grand, though meanlie did yee move
About your severall ends. Since first this subject,
Thou, thaumaturgist Blacke, and thou,
O merchant peccant to the deaths of fellowe men,
Contrived in evill all thy predecessors human,
But save Judas I was wont to gnaw before,
T'outdo, by willingnesse to plunge

All mankinde in a night's Abysse
Only for perverse aesthetick Joyce
And Thrill of Masterie, there then ensu'd
That universall Warr in which the victorie
Hath faln to Hellish host, so Wee rejoyc'd;
Yet hold! for once releas'd from Paynes
Decreed to be forever, all our Band
Of demons foul, who once were angels bright
Conceiv'd in simpler time and ever since
Entomb'd amidst the horrors of the Pit,
Did find the world of men so much more foul
E'en than in the fabulous reign of witches
That all bewilder'd fell they and amazed.
Yet after hastie consult, they set to,
To preach and practise evill with all pow'r,
Adhering to grounded rules long understood,
A Greshamite oeconomium.

But eftsoons

That vacuous space where once Eternall Good
Had dwelt demanded to be filled. Though God
Be dead, His Throne remains. And so below
As 'twas above, last shall be first, and Wee,
Who by the Essenes' rule are qualified
Beyond all remaining others, must become –
In all protesting agonie – the chief
Of powers for Good in all the Universe
Uncircumscribed; but let yee not forget,
Already Good compared to such as thee,
Whose evill remains will'd! And as for Us,
What doth it matter what Wee most desire?
While chainèd in the Pit, Wee were condemn'd
To be eternall, but paroll'd to Earth
Were once more caught by Change; and how
Could Wickednesse Incorporeal grow still worse?
And so, behold! Wee are a God.

But not

Perhaps The God. Wee do not know the end.
Perhaps indeed Jehovah is not dead,
But mere retir'd, withdrawn or otherwise
Contracted hath, as *Zohar* subtle saith,
His Essence Infinite; and, Epicurean, waits
The outcome vast with vast indifference.
Yet natheless His universe requires

That all things changing must tend t'ward His state.
If, then, wee must proclaim His Rôle historic
Abandon'd in Deific suicide,
Why this *felo de Se* except to force
That part on Man – who fail'd it out of hand?
Now, as Wee sought to be in the Beginning,
SATAN is God; and in Mine agonie
More just a God and wrathfuller by far
Than He Who thunder'd down on Israel!
'Yet not for ever, though our rule will seem
For ever. Man, O Man, I beg of you,
Take, O take from mee this Cup away!
I cannot bear it. You, and onely you,
You alone, alone can God become,
As always He intended. This downfall
Our mutual Armageddon here below
Is punishment dire enough, but for your Kinde
A worse awaits; for you must rear yourselves
As ready for the Resurrection. I
Have slammed that door behind; yours is to come.
On that far future Day, I shall be there,
The burning Keys to put into your hands.
'I, SATAN MEKRATRIG, can no longer bear
This deepest, last and bitterest of all
My fell damnations: That at last I know
I never wanted to be God at all;
And so, by winning all, All have I lost.'

Author's Afterword

These two books, considered as a unit, make up the second volume of a trilogy under the overall title of AFTER SUCH KNOWLEDGE. The first volume is a historical novel called *Doctor Mirabilis* (Faber & Faber, London, 1964); the last a science-fiction novel called *A Case of Conscience* (Faber & Faber, London, 1959). These two volumes are independent of each other and of *Black Easter* and *The Day After Judgement*, except for subject matter; that is, they are intended to dramatize different aspects of an ancient philosophical question which is voiced by Baines in Chapter VIII of *The Day After Judgement*.

As before, the books of magic cited in the text all actually exist (although mostly in manuscript), and the magical rituals and diagram are all taken from them (although in no case are they complete). The characters and events, on the other hand are entirely my own invention, as are all the details about the Strategic Air Command.

JAMES BLISH

Harpsden (Henley)
Oxon., England
1970

(The great hall of Pandemonium dissolves, and with it the Citadel of Dis, leaving the four men standing in a modern road in the midst of the small town of Badwater. It is early morning in the desert, and still cold. All traces of the recent battle also have vanished.

(The four look at each other, with gradually growing wonder, as though each were seeing the other for the first time. Each one finally starts a sentence, but is unable to complete it):

FATHER DOMENICO: I think . . .

BAINES: I believe . . .

WARE: I hope . . .

(They look about, noting the disappearance of the battle-field. After all else that has happened, they do not question this; it does not even surprise them.)

GINSBERG: I . . . love.

Curtain

A CASE OF CONSCIENCE

Man only thinks when you prevent him from acting

JEAN JACQUES ROUSSEAU

Man only creates when fulfilment of action increases his enigma

GERALD HEARD

CONTENTS

FOREWORD

THIS novel is not about Catholicism, but since its hero is a Catholic theologian it inevitably contains certain sticking points for those who subscribe to the doctrines of the Roman and to a lesser extent the Anglican churches. Readers who have no doctrinal preconceptions should not find these points even noticeable, let alone troublesome.

It was my assumption that the Roman Catholic Church of a century beyond our time will have undergone changes of custom and of doctrine, some minor and some major. The publication of this novel in America showed that Catholics were quite willing to allow me my Diet of Basra, my revival of the elegant argument from the navel to the geological record, and my jettisoning of the tonsure; but on two points they would not allow me to depart from what one may find in the *Catholic Encyclopedia* of 1945. (No scientist thus far has protested my jettisoning of special relativity in the year 2050.) These were:

(1) My assumption that by 2050 the rite of exorcism will be so thoroughly buried in the medieval past that even the Church will teach it to its priests only perfunctorily—so perfunctorily that even a Jesuit might overlook it in a situation which in any event hardly suggests that exorcism would be even minimally appropriate. Yet even today non-Catholics generally do not believe that exorcism survives in the Church; it seems even more primitive and *outré* than habits and tonsures, which were frozen into Church usage at about the same time, i.e. the thirteenth century. In that period, too, it was commonplace to ring blessed bells to dispel thunderstorms; that has not survived; I think it reasonable to assume that exorcism will be, officially, only a vestige by 2050.

(2) My assumption that by 2050 a lay person who knows how may administer Extreme Unction, as today he may

adminster Baptism. Of course, this is not true today, and I can perhaps be excused my impatience with critics who thought me so lazy as to think it was. These amateur theologians forget that in the beginning none of the Sacraments could be administered by anyone but a priest, and that the fact that priests still have reserved Extreme Unction is the result of a bitterly fought holding action which lasted many centuries. The battle to reserve Baptism similarly was lost almost immediately, as was inevitable in an age where the population was small, subject to plagues and other catastrophes about which exactly nothing could be done, and so had to hold every soul precious at the moment of birth. Today, and (I greatly fear) tomorrow, our jammed neo-Malthusian world with its unselective wingless faceless angel of death who may reach us all in twenty minutes from the other side of the planet, confronts us with the probability of deaths in such great masses that no population of priests could minister to all the victims; and since I give the Church credit (against all appearances, sometimes) for being basically a merciful institution, I have assumed that by 2050 Extreme Unction will no longer be reserved.

Anyone, of course, is at liberty to find my reasoning at fault, but I hope they will not quote 1945 doctrine to me as if it were sufficient in itself for 2050.

A number of people who wrote to me felt that my hero's conclusion as to the nature of Lithia was far from inevitable; but I was gratified to receive also several letters from theologians who knew the *present* Church position on the problem of the 'plurality of worlds', as most of my correspondents obviously did not. (As usual, the Church as an institution, is far ahead of most of its communicants.) Rather than justify my hero's irruption of Manichaeism in any words but his own, I will quote Mr. Gerald Heard, who has summarized the position best of all (as one would expect of so gifted a writer trained as a theologian):

If there are many planets inhabited by sentient creatures, as most astronomers (including Jesuits), now suspect, then 'each one of such planets (solar or non-solar) must fall into one of three categories:

'(*a*) Inhabited by sentient creatures, but without souls; so to be treated with compassion but extra-evangelically.

'(*b*) Inhabited by sentient creatures with fallen souls, through an original but not inevitable ancestral sin; so to be evangelized with urgent missionary charity.

'(*c*) Inhabited by sentient soul-endowed creatures that have not fallen, who therefore

'(1) inhabit an unfallen, sinless paradisal world;

'(2) who therefore we must contact not to propagandize, but in order that we may learn from them the conditions (about which we can only speculate) of creatures living in perpetual grace, endowed with all the virtues in perfection, and both immortal and in complete happiness for always possessed of and with the knowledge of God.'

The reader will observe with Ruiz-Sanchez, I think, that the Lithians fit none of these categories; hence all that follows.

The author, I should like to add, is an agnostic with no position at all in these matters. It was my intention to write about a man, not a body of doctrine.

JAMES BLISH

'Arrowhead',
Milford, Pennsylvania
1958

Pronunciation Key

For any reader who cares, the Lithian words and names he will encounter here and there in this story are to be pronounced as follows:

Xoredeshch—"X" as English "K" or Greek chi, hard; "shch" contains two separate sounds, as in Russian, or in English "fi*sh-ch*urch".

Sfath: As in English, with a broad "a".

Gton: Guttural "G", against the hard palate, like hawking.

Chtexa: Like German "Stuka", but with the flat "e".

gchteht: Guttural "g" followed by the soft "sh" sound, a flat "e", and the "h" serving as equivalent of the Old Russian mute sign; thus, a four-syllable word, with a palatal tick at the end, but sounded as one syllable.

Gleshchtehk—As indicated, with the guttural "G", the "fi*sh-ch*urch" middle consonants, and the mute "h" throwing the "k" back against the soft palate.

The RULE is that "ch" is always English "sh" in the initial position, always English "ch" as in "chip" elsewhere in the word; and "h" in isolation is an accented rest which always *precedes*, never follows, a consonant. As Agronski somewhere remarks, anybody who can spit can speak Lithian.

BOOK ONE

I

THE stone door slammed. It was Cleaver's trade-mark: there had never been a door too heavy, complex, or cleverly tracked to prevent him from closing it with a sound like a clap of doom. And no planet in the universe could possess an air sufficiently thick and curtained with damp to muffle that sound—not even Lithia.

Father Ramon Ruiz-Sanchez, late of Peru, and always Clerk Regular of the Society of Jesus, professed father of the four vows, continued to read. It would take Paul Cleaver's impatient fingers quite a while to free him from his jungle suit, and in the meantime the problem remained. It was a century-old problem, first propounded in 1939, but the Church had never cracked it. And it was diabolically complex (that adverb was official, precisely chosen, and intended to be taken literally). Even the novel which had proposed the case was on the Index Expurgatorius, and Father Ruiz-Sanchez had spiritual access to it only by virtue of his Order.

He turned the page, scarcely hearing the stamping and muttering in the hall. On and on the text ran, becoming more tangled, more evil, more insoluble with every word:

". . . Magravius threatens to have Anita molested by Sulla, an orthodox savage (and leader of a band of twelve mercenaries, the Sullivani), who desires to procure Felicia for Gregorius, Leo Vitellius and Macdugalius, four excavators, if she will not yield to him and also deceive Honuphrius by rendering conjugal duty when demanded. Anita who claims to have discovered incestuous temptations from Jeremias and Eugenius——"

There now, he was lost again. Jeremias and Eugenius were . . . ? Oh, yes, the "philadelphians" or brotherly lovers (another crime hidden there, no doubt) at the beginning of the case, consanguineous to the lowest degree with both Felicia and Honuphrius—the latter the apparent prime villain and husband of Anita. It was Magravius, who seemed to admire Honuphrius, who had been urged by the slave Mauritius to solicit Anita, seemingly under the aegis of Honuphrius himself. This, however, had come to Anita through her tirewoman Fortissa, who was or at one time had been the common-law wife of Mauritius and had borne him children—so that the whole story had to be weighed with the utmost caution. And that entire initial confession of Honuphrius had come out under torture—voluntarily consented to, to be sure, but still torture. The Fortissa-Mauritius relationship was even more dubious, really only a supposition of the commentator Father Ware—

"Ramon, give me a hand, will you?" Cleaver shouted suddenly. "I'm stuck, and—and I don't feel well."

The Jesuit biologist arose in alarm, putting the novel aside. Such an admission from Cleaver was unprecedented. The physicist was sitting on a pouffe of woven rushes, stuffed with a sphagnum-like moss, which was bulging at the equator under his weight. He was half-way out of his glass-fibre jungle suit, and his face was white and beaded with sweat, although his helmet was already off. His uncertain, stubby fingers tore at a jammed zipper.

"Paul! Why didn't you say you were ill in the first place? Here, let go of that; you're only making things worse. What happened?"

"Don't know exactly," Cleaver said, breathing heavily but relinquishing the zipper. Ruiz-Sanchez knelt beside him and began to work it carefully back on to its tracks. "Went a ways into the jungle to see if I could spot more pegmatite lies. It's been in the back of my mind that a pilot-plant for turning out tritium might locate here eventually—ought to be able to produce on a prodigious scale."

"God forbid," Ruiz-Sanchez said under his breath.

"Hm? Anyhow, I didn't see anything. A few lizards, hoppers, the usual thing. Then I ran up against a plant that looked a little like a pineapple, and one of the spines jabbed right through my suit and nicked me. Didn't seem serious, but——"

"But we don't have the suits for nothing. Let's look at it. Here, put up your feet and we'll haul those boots off. Where did you get the—oh. Well, it's angry-looking, I'll give it that. Any other symptoms?"

"My mouth feels raw," Cleaver complained.

"Open up," the Jesuit commanded. When Cleaver complied, it became evident that his complaint had been the understatement of the year. The mucosa inside his mouth was nearly covered with ugly and undoubtedly painful ulcers, their edges as sharply defined as though they had been cut with a biscuit cutter.

Ruiz-Sanchez made no comment, however, and deliberately changed his expression to one of carefully calculated dismissal. If the physicist needed to minimize his ailments, that was all right with Ruiz-Sanchez. An alien planet is not a good place to strip a man of his inner defences.

"Come into the lab," he said. "You've got some inflammation in there."

Cleaver arose, a little unsteadily, and followed the Jesuit into the laboratory. There Ruiz-Sanchez took smears from several of the ulcers on to microscope slides, and Gram-stained them. He filled the time consumed by the staining process with the ritual of aiming the microscope's substage mirror out of the window at a brilliant white cloud. When the timer's alarm went off, he rinsed and flame-dried the first slide and slipped it under the clips.

As he had half-feared, he saw few of the mixed bacilli and spirochetes which would have indicated a case of ordinary, Earthly, Vincent's angina—"trench mouth", which the clinical picture certainly suggested, and which he could have cured overnight with a spectrosigmin pastille. Cleaver's oral flora were normal, though on the increase because of all the exposed tissue.

"I'm going to give you a shot," Ruiz-Sanchez said gently. "And then I think you'd better go to bed."

"The hell with that," Cleaver said. "I've got nine times as much work to do as I can hope to clean up now, without any additional handicaps."

"Illness is never convenient," Ruiz-Sanchez agreed. "But why worry about losing a day or so, since you're in over your head anyhow?"

"What have I got?" Cleaver asked suspiciously.

"You haven't *got* anything," Ruiz-Sanchez said, almost regretfully. "That is, you aren't infected. But your 'pineapple' did you a bad turn. Most plants of that family on Lithia bear thorns or leaves coated with polysaccharides that are poisonous to us. The particular glucoside you ran up against today was evidently squill, or something closely related to it. It produces symptoms like those of trench mouth, but a lot harder to clear up."

"How long will that take?" Cleaver said. He was still baulking, but he was on the defensive now.

"Several days at least—until you've built up an immunity. The shot I'm going to give you is a gamma globulin specific against squill, and it ought to moderate the symptoms until you've developed a high antibody titer of your own. But in the process you're going to run quite a fever, Paul; and I'll have to keep you well stuffed with antipyretics, because even a little fever is dangerous in this climate."

"I know it," Cleaver said, mollified. "The more I learn about this place, the less disposed I am to vote 'aye' when the time comes. Well, bring on your shot—and your aspirin. I suppose I ought to be glad it isn't a bacterial infection, or the Snakes would be jabbing me full of antibiotics."

"Small chance of that," Ruiz-Sanchez said. "I don't doubt that the Lithians have at least a hundred different drugs we'll be able to use eventually, but—there, that's all there is to it; you can relax now—but we'll have to study their pharmacology from the ground up, first. All right, Paul, hit the hammock. In about ten minutes you're going to be wishing you'd been born dead, that I promise you."

Cleaver grinned. His sweaty face under its thatch of dirty blond hair was craggy and powerful even in illness. He stood up and deliberately rolled down his sleeve.

"Not much doubt about how you'll vote, either," he said. "You like this planet, don't you, Ramon? It's a biologist's paradise, as far as I can see."

"I do like it," the priest said, smiling back. He followed Cleaver into the small room which served them both as sleeping quarters. Except for the window, it strongly resembled the inside of a jug. The walls were curving and continuous, and were made of some ceramic material which never beaded or felt wet, but never seemed to be quite dry, either. The hammocks were slung from hooks which projected smoothly from the walls, as though they had been baked from clay along with the rest of the house. "I wish my colleague Dr. Meid were able to see it. She would be even more delighted with it than I am."

"I don't hold with women in the sciences," Cleaver said, with abstract, irrelevant irritation. "Get their emotions all mixed up with their hypotheses. Meid—what kind of name is that, anyhow?"

"Japanese," Ruiz-Sanchez said. "Her first name is Liu—the family follows the Western custom of putting the family name last."

"Oh," Cleaver said, losing interest. "We were talking about Lithia."

"Well, don't forget that Lithia is my first extrasolar planet," Ruiz-Sanchez said. "I think I'd find *any* new, habitable world fascinating. The infinite mutability of life forms, and the cunning inherent in each of them. . . . It's all amazing, and quite delightful."

"Why shouldn't that be sufficient?" Cleaver said. "Why do you have to have the God bit too? It doesn't make sense."

"On the contrary, it's what gives everything else meaning," Ruiz-Sanchez said. "Belief and science aren't mutually exclusive—quite the contrary. But if you place scientific standards first, and exclude belief, admit nothing that's not proven, then what you have is a series of empty gestures. For me, biology *is* an act of religion, because I know that all creatures are God's—each new planet, with all its manifestations, is an affirmation of God's power."

"A dedicated man," Cleaver said. "All right. So am I. To the greater glory of man, that's what *I* say."

He sprawled heavily in his hammock. After a decent interval, Ruiz-Sanchez took the liberty of heaving up after him the foot he seemed to have forgotten. Cleaver didn't notice. The reaction was setting in.

"Exactly so," Ruiz-Sanchez said. "But that's only half the story. The other half reads, '. . . and to the greater glory of God.' "

"Read me no tracts, Father," Cleaver said. Then: "I didn't mean that. I'm sorry. . . . But for a physicist, this place is hell. . . . You'd better get me that aspirin, I'm cold."

"Surely, Paul."

Ruiz-Sanchez went quickly back into the lab, made up a salicylate-barbiturate paste in one of the Lithian's superb mortars, and pressed it into a set of pills. (Storing such pills was impossible in Lithia's humid atmosphere; they were too hygroscopic.) He wished he could stamp each pill "Bayer" before it set—if Cleaver's personal cure-all was aspirin, it would have been just as well to let him think he was taking aspirin—but of course he had no dies for the purpose. He took two of the pills back to Cleaver, with a mug and a carafe of Berkefeld-filtered water.

The big man was already asleep; Ruiz-Sanchez woke him, more or less. Cleaver would sleep longer, and awaken farther along the road to recovery, for having been done that small unkindness now. As it was, he hardly noticed when the pills were put down him, and soon resumed his heavy, troubled breathing.

That done, Ruiz-Sanchez returned to the front room of the house, sat down, and began to inspect the jungle suit. The tear which the plant spine had made was not difficult to find, and would be easy to repair. It would be much harder to repair Cleaver's notion that the defences of Earthmen on Lithia were invulnerable, and that plant-spines could be blundered against with impunity. Ruiz-Sanchez wondered whether either of the other two members of the Lithian Review Commission still shared that notion.

Cleaver had called the thing which had brought him low a "pineapple". Any biologist could have told Cleaver that even on Earth the pineapple is a prolific and dangerous weed, edible only by a happy and irrelevant accident. In Hawaii, as Ruiz-Sanchez remembered, the tropical forest was quite impassable to anyone not wearing heavy boots and tough trousers. Even inside the Dole plantations, the close-packed irrepressible pineapples could tear unprotected legs to ribbons.

The Jesuit turned the suit over. The zipper that Cleaver had jammed was made of a plastic into the molecule of which had been incorporated radicals from various terrestrial anti-fungal substances, chiefly the protoplasmic poison thiolutin. The fungi of Lithia respected these, all right, but the elaborate molecule of the plastic itself had a tendency, under Lithian humidities and heats, to undergo polymerization more or less spontaneously. That was what had happened here. One of the teeth of the zipper had changed into something resembling a kernel of popped corn.

The air grew dark as Ruiz-Sanchez worked. There was a muted puff of sound, and the room was illuminated with small, soft yellow flames from recesses in every wall. The burning substance was natural gas, of which Lithia had an inexhaustible and constantly renewed supply. The flames were lit by adsorption against a catalyst, as soon as the gas came on from the system. A lime mantle, which worked on a rack and pinion of heatproof glass, could be moved into the flame to provide a brighter light; but the priest liked the yellow light the Lithians themselves preferred, and used the limelight only in the laboratory.

For some purposes, of course, the Earthmen had to have electricity, for which they had been forced to supply their own generators. The Lithians had a far more advanced science of electrostatics than Earth had, but of electrodynamics they knew comparatively little. They had discovered magnetism only a few years before the Commission had arrived, since natural magnets were unknown on the planet. They had first observed the phenomenon, not in iron, of which they had next to none, but in liquid oxygen—a difficult substance from which to make generator cores!

The results in terms of Lithian civilization were peculiar, to an Earthman. The twelve-foot-tall, reptilian people had built several huge electrostatic generators and scores of little ones, but had nothing even vaguely resembling telephones. They knew a great deal on the practical level about electrolysis, but carrying a current over a long distance—say a mile—was regarded by them as a technical triumph. They had no electric motors as an Earthman would understand the term, but made fast intercontinental flights in jet aircraft powered by *static* electricity. Cleaver said he understood this feat, but Ruiz-Sanchez certainly did not (and after Cleaver's description of electron-ion plasmas heated by radio-frequency induction, he felt more in the dark than ever).

They had a completely marvellous radio network, which among other things provided a "live" navigational grid for the whole planet, zeroed on (and here perhaps was the epitome of the Lithian genius for paradox) a tree. Yet they had never produced a standardized vacuum tube, and their atomic theory was not much more sophisticated than Democritus' had been!

These paradoxes, of course, could be explained in part by the things that Lithia lacked. Like any large rotating mass, Lithia had a magnetic field of its own, but a planet which almost entirely lacks iron provides its people with no easy way to discover magnetism. Radioactivity had been entirely unknown on the surface of Lithia, at least until the Earthmen had arrived, which explained the hazy atomic theory. Like the Greeks, the Lithians had discovered that friction between silk and glass produces one kind of energy or charge, and between silk and amber another; they had gone on from there to van de Graaf generators, electrochemistry, and the static jet—but without suitable metals they were unable to make heavy-duty batteries, or to do more than begin to study electricity in motion.

In the fields where they had been given fair clues, they had made enormous progress. Despite the constant cloudiness and endemic drizzle, their descriptive astronomy was excellent, thanks to the fortunate presence of a small moon which had drawn their attention outward early. This in turn made for basic advances in optics, and thence for a downright staggering versatility in the working of glass. Their chemistry took full advantage of both the seas and the jungles. From the one they took such vital and diversified products as agar, iodine, salt, trace metals, and foods of many kinds. The other provided nearly everything else that they needed: resins, rubbers, woods of all degrees of hardness, edible and essential oils, vegetable "butters", rope and other fibres, fruits and nuts, tannins, dyes, drugs, cork, paper. Indeed, the sole forest product which they did *not* take was game, and the reason for this neglect was hard to find. It seemed to the Jesuit to be religious—yet the Lithians had no religion, and they certainly ate many of the creatures of the sea without qualms of conscience.

He dropped the jungle suit into his lap with a sigh, though the popcorned tooth still was not completely trimmed back into shape. Outside, in the humid darkness, Lithia was in full concert. It was a vital, somehow fresh, new-sounding drone, covering most of the sound spectrum audible to an Earthman. It came from the myriad insects of Lithia. Many of these had wiry, trilling songs, almost like birds, in addition to the scrapes and chirrups and wing-case buzzes of the insects of Earth. In a way this was lucky, for there were no birds on Lithia.

Had Eden sounded like that, before evil had come into the world? Ruiz-Sanchez wondered. Certainly his native Peru sang no such song . . .

Qualms of conscience—these were, in the long run, his essential business, rather than the taxonomical mazes of biology, which had already become tangled into near-hopelessness on Earth before space flight had come along to add whole new layers of labyrinths for each planet, new dimensions of labyrinths for each star. It was only interesting that the Lithians were bipedal, evolved from reptiles, with marsupial-like pouches and pteropsid circulatory systems. But it was vital that they had qualms of conscience—if they did.

The calendar caught his eye. It was an "art" calendar Cleaver had produced from his luggage back in the beginning; the girl on it was now unintentionally modest beneath large patches of brilliant orange mould. The date was April 19th, 2049. Almost Easter—the most pointed of reminders that to the inner life, the body was only a garment. To Ruiz-Sanchez personally, however, the year date was almost equally significant, for 2050 was to be a Holy Year.

The Church had returned to the ancient custom, first recognized officially in 1300 by Boniface VIII, of proclaiming the great pardon only once every half-century. If Ruiz-Sanchez was not in Rome next year when the Holy Door was opened, it would never be opened again in his lifetime.

Hurry, hurry! some personal demon whispered inside his brain. Or was it the voice of his own conscience? Were his sins already so burdensome—unknown to himself—as to put him in mortal need of the pilgrimage? Or was that, in turn, only a minor temptation, to the sin of pride?

In any event, the work could not be hurried. He and the other three men were on Lithia to decide whether or not the planet would be suitable as a port of call for Earth, without risk of damage either to Earthmen or to Lithians. The other three men on the commission were primarily scientists, as was Ruiz-Sanchez; but he knew that his own recommendation would in the long run depend upon conscience, not upon taxonomy.

And conscience, like creation, cannot be hurried. It cannot even be scheduled.

He looked down at the still-imperfect jungle suit with a troubled face until he heard Cleaver moan. Then he arose and left the room to the softly hissing flames.

II

FROM the oval front window of the house to which Cleaver and Ruiz-Sanchez had been assigned, the land slanted away with insidious gentleness toward the ill-defined south edge of Lower Bay, a part of the Gulf of Sfath. Most of the area was salt marsh, as was the seaside nearly everywhere on Lithia. When the tide was in, the flats were covered to a depth of a yard or so almost half the way to the house. When it was out, as it was tonight, the jungle symphony was augmented by the agonized barking of a species of lungfish, sometimes as many as a score of them at once. Occasionally, when the small moon was unoccluded and the light from the city was unusually bright, one could see the leaping shadow of some amphibian, or the sinuously advancing sigmoid track of the Lithian crocodile, in pursuit of some prey faster than itself but which it would none the less capture in its own geological good time.

Still farther—and usually invisible even in daytime because of the pervasive mists—was the opposite shore of Lower Bay, beginning with tidal flats again, and then more jungle, which ran unbroken thereafter for hundreds of miles north to the equatorial sea.

Behind the house, visible from the sleeping-room, was the rest of the city, Xoredeshch Sfath, capital of the great southern continent. As was the case in all the cities the Lithians built, its most striking characteristic to an Earthman was that it hardly seemed to be there at all. The Lithian houses were low, and made of the earth which had been dug from their foundations, so that they tended to fade into the soil even to a trained observer.

Most of the older buildings were rectangular, put together without mortar or rammed-earth blocks. Over the course of decades the blocks continued to pack and settle themselves until it became easier to abandon an unwanted building than to tear it down. One of the first setbacks the Earthmen had suffered on Lithia had come about through Agronski's ill-advised offer to raze one such structure with TDX; this was a gravity-polarized explosive, unknown to the Lithians, which had the property of exploding in a flat plane which could cut through steel girders as if they were cheese. The warehouse in question, however, was large, thick-walled, and three Lithian centuries old—312 years by Earth time. The explosion created an uproar which greatly distressed the Lithians, but when it was over, the storehouse still stood, unshaken.

Newer structures were more conspicuous when the sun was out, for just during the past half-century the Lithians had begun to apply their enormous knowledge of ceramics to house construction. The new houses assumed thousands of fantastic, quasi-biological shapes, not quite amorphous but not quite resembling any form in experience, either; they looked a little like the dream constructions once made by an Earth painter named Dali out of such materials as boiled beans. Each one was unique and to the choice of its owner, yet all markedly shared the character of the community and the earth from which they sprang. These houses, too, would have blended well with the background of soil and jungle, except that most of them were glazed and so shone blindingly for brief moments on sunny days, when the light and the angle of observation were just right. These shifting coruscations, seen from the air, had been the Earthmen's first clue as to where the intelligent life was hiding in the ubiquitous

Lithian jungle. (There had never been any doubt that there was intelligent life there; the tremendous radio pulses emanating from the planet had made that much plain from afar.)

Ruiz-Sanchez looked out through the sleeping-room window at the city, for at least the ten thousandth time, on his way to Cleaver's hammock. Xoredeshch Sfath was alive to him; it never looked the same twice. He found it singularly beautiful. And singularly strange: though the cities of Earth were very various, none was like this.

He checked Cleaver's pulse and respiration. Both were fast, even for Lithia, where a high partial pressure of carbon dioxide raised the pH of the blood of Earthmen and stimulated the breathing reflex. The priest judged, however, that Cleaver was in little danger as long as his actual oxygen utilization was not increased. At the moment he was certainly sleeping deeply—if not very restfully—and it would do no harm to leave him alone for a little while.

Of course, if a wild allosaur blundered into the city. . . . But that was just about as likely as the blundering of an untended elephant into the heart of New Delhi. It could happen, but it almost never did. And no other dangerous Lithian animal could break into the house if it was closed. Even the rats—or the abundant monotreme creatures which were Lithia's equivalent—found it impossible to infest a pottery house.

Ruiz-Sanchez changed the carafe of fresh water in the niche beside the hammock, went into the hall, and donned boots, macintosh and waterproof hat. The night sounds of Lithia burst in upon him as he opened the stone door, along with a gust of sea air bearing the characteristic halogen odour always called "salty". There was a thin drizzle falling, making halos around the lights of Xoredeshch Sfath. Far out, on the water, another light moved. That was probably the coastal side-wheeler to Yllith, the enormous island which stood athwart the Upper Bay, barring the Gulf of Sfath as a whole from the equatorial sea.

Outside, Ruiz-Sanchez turned the wheel which extended bolts on every margin of the door. Drawing from his macintosh a piece of soft chalk, he marked on the sheltered tablet designed for such uses the Lithian symbols which meant "Illness is here". That would be sufficient. Anybody who chose to could open the door simply by turning the wheel —the Lithians had never heard of locks—but the Lithians, too, were overridingly social beings, who respected their own conventions as they respected natural law.

That done, Ruiz-Sanchez set out for the centre of the city and the Message Tree. The asphalt streets shone in the yellow lights cast from windows, and in the white light of the mantled, wide-spaced street lanterns. Occasionally he passed the twelve-foot, kangaroo-like shape of a Lithian, and the two exchanged glances of frank curiosity, but there were not many Lithians abroad now. They kept to their houses at night, doing Ruiz-Sanchez knew not what. He could see them frequently, alone or by twos or threes, moving behind the oval windows of the houses he passed. Sometimes they seemed to be talking.

What about?

It was a nice question. The Lithians had no crime, no newspapers, no house-to-house communications systems, no arts that could be differentiated clearly from their crafts, no political parties, no public amusements, no nations, no games, no religions, no sports, no cults, no celebrations. Surely they didn't spend every waking minute of their lives exchanging knowledge, making things go, discussing philosophy or history, or planning for tomorrow! Or did they? Perhaps, Ruiz-Sanchez thought suddenly, they simply went inert once they were inside their jugs, like so many pickles! But even as the thought came, the priest passed another house, and saw their silhouettes moving to and fro. . . .

A puff of wind scattered cool droplets in his face. Automatically, he quickened his step. If the night were to turn out to be especially windy, there would doubtless be many voices coming and going in the Message Tree. It loomed ahead of him now, a sequoia-like giant, standing at the mouth of the valley of the River Sfath—the valley which led in great serpentine folds into the heart of the continent, where Gleshchtehk Sfath, or Blood Lake in English, poured out its massive torrents.

As the winds came and went along the valley, the tree nodded and swayed—only a little, but that little was enough. With every movement, the tree's root system, which underlay the entire city, tugged and distorted the buried crystalline cliff upon which the city had been founded, as long ago in Lithian pre-history as was the founding of Rome on Earth. At every such pressure, the buried cliff responded with a vast heart-pulse of radio waves—a pulse detectable not only all over Lithia, but far out in space as well. The four Commission members had heard those pulses first on shipboard, when Alpha Arietis, Lithia's sun, was still only a point of light ahead of them, and had looked into each other's faces with eyes gleaming with conjecture.

The bursts, however, were sheer noise. How the Lithians modulated them to carry information—not only messages, but the amazing navigational grid, the planet-wide time-signal system, and much more—was something as remote from Ruiz-Sanchez's understanding as affine theory, although Cleaver said it was all perfectly simple once you understood it. It had something to do with semi-conduction and solid-state physics, which (again according to Cleaver) the Lithians understood better than any Earthman.

A free-association jump which startled him momentarily reminded him of the current *doyen* of Earthly affine theory, a man who signed his papers "H. O. Petard", though his real (if scarcely more likely) name was Lucien le Comte des Bois-d'Averoigne. Nor was the association as free as it appeared on the surface, Ruiz-Sanchez realized, for the count was a striking example of the now almost total alienation of modern physics from the common physical experiences of mankind. His title was not a patent of nobility, but merely a part of his name which had been maintained in his family long after the political system which had granted the patent had vanished away, a victim of the dividing up of Earth under the Shelter economy. There was more honour appertaining to the name itself than to the title, for the count had pretensions to hereditary grandeur which reached all the way back into thirteenth-century England, to the author of *Lucien Wycham His Boke of Magick*.

A high ecclesiastic heritage to be sure, but the latter-day Lucien, a lapsed Catholic, was a political figure, in so far as the Shelter economy sheltered any such thing: he carried the additional title of Procurator of Canarsie—a title which a moment's examination would also show to be nonsense, but which paid a small honorarium in exemptions from weekly labour. The subdivided and deeply buried world of Earth was full of such labels, all of them pasted on top of large sums of money which had no place to go now that speculation was dead and shareholding had become the only way by which an ordinary citizen could exercise any control over the keeps in which he lived. The remaining fortune-holders had no outlet left but that of conspicuous consumption, on a scale which would have made Veblen doubt that there had ever been such a thing in the world before. Had they attempted to assert any control over the economy they would have been toppled, if not by the shareholders, then by the grim defenders of the by now indefensible Shelter cities.

Not that the count was a drone. At last reports, he had been involved in some highly esoteric tampering with the Haertel equations—that description of the space-time continuum which, by swallowing up the Lorentz-Fitzgerald contraction exactly as Einstein had swallowed Newton (that is, alive) had made interstellar flight possible. Ruiz-Sanchez did not understand a word of it but, he reflected with amusement, it was doubtless perfectly simple once you understood it.

Almost all knowledge, after all, fell into that category. It was either perfectly simple once you understood it, or else it fell apart into fiction. As a Jesuit—even here, fifty light-years from Rome—Ruiz-Sanchez knew something about knowledge that Lucien le Comte des Bois-d'Averoigne had forgotten, and that Cleaver would never learn: that all knowledge goes through *both* stages, the annunciation out of noise into fact, and the disintegration back into noise again. The process involved was the making of increasingly finer distinctions. The outcome was an endless series of theoretical catastrophes.

The residuum was faith.

The high, sharply vaulted chamber, like an egg stood on its large end, which had been burned out in the base of the Message Tree, was droning with life as Ruiz-Sanchez entered it. It would have been difficult to imagine anything less like an Earthly telegraph office or other message centre, however.

Around the circumference of the lower end of the egg there was a continual whirling of tall figures, Lithians, entering and leaving through the many doorless entrances, and changing places in the swirl of movement like so many electrons passing from orbit to orbit. Despite their numbers, their voices were pitched so low that Ruiz-Sanchez could hear, blended in with their murmuring, the soughing of the wind through the enormous branches far above.

The inner side of this band of moving figures was bounded by a high railing of black, polished wood, evidently cut from the phloem of the Tree itself. On the other side of this token division, which reminded Ruiz-Sanchez irresistibly of the Encke division in the Saturnian rings, a thin circlet of Lithians took and passed out messages steadily and without a moment's break, handling the total load faultlessly—if one were to judge by the way the outer band was kept in motion—and without apparent effort, by memory alone. Occasionally one of these specialists would leave the circlet and go to one of the desks which were scattered over most of the rest of the sloping floor, increasingly thinly, like a Crape ring, to confer there with the desk's occupant. Then he went back to the black rail, or sometimes he took the desk, and its previous occupant went tø the rail.

The bowl deepened, the desks thinned, and at the very centre stood a single aged Lithian, his hands clapped to the ear whorls behind his heavy jaws, his eyes covered by their nictitating membranes, only his nasal fossae and heat-receptive post-nasal pits uncovered. He spoke to no one, and no one consulted him—but the absolute stasis in which he stood was obviously the reason, the sole reason, for the torrents and counter-torrents of people which poured along the outermost ring.

Ruiz-Sanchez stopped, astonished. He had never been to the Message Tree himself before—communicating with Michelis and Agronski, the other two Earthmen on Lithia, had until now been one of Cleaver's tasks—and the priest found that he had no idea what to do. The scene before him was more suggestive of a Bourse than of a message centre in any ordinary sense. It seemed unlikely that so many Lithians could have urgent personal messages to send each time the winds were active; yet it seemed equally uncharacteristic that the Lithians, with their stable, abundance-based economy, should have any equivalent for stock or commodity brokerage.

There seemed to be no choice, however, but to plunge in, try to reach the polished black rail, and ask one of the Lithians who stood on the other side to try to raise Agronski or Michelis again. At worst, he supposed, he could only be refused, or fail to get a hearing at all. He took a deep breath.

Simultaneously his left arm was caught in a firm four-fingered grip which ran all the way from his elbow to his shoulder. Letting the stored breath out again in a snort of surprise, the priest looked around and up at the solicitously bent head of a Lithian. Under the long, trap-like mouth, the being's wattles were a delicate, curious aquamarine, in contrast to its vestigal comb, which was a permanent and silvery sapphire, shot through with veins of fuchsia.

"You are Ruiz-Sanchez," the Lithian said in his own language. The priest's name, unlike those of the other Earthmen, fell easily in that tongue. "I know you by your robe."

That was pure accident. Any Earthman out in the rain in a macintosh would have been identified as Ruiz-Sanchez, because the priest was the only Earthman who seemed to the Lithians to wear the same garment indoors and out.

"I am," Ruiz-Sanchez said, a little apprehensively.

"I am Chtexa, the metallurgist, who consulted with you earlier on problems of chemistry and medicine and your mission here, and some other smaller matters."

"Oh. Yes, of course; I should have remembered your comb."

"You do me honour. We have not seen you here before. Do you wish to talk with the Tree?"

"I do," Ruiz-Sanchez said gratefully. "It is true that I am new here. Can you explain to me what to do?"

"Yes, but not to any profit," Chtexa said, tilting his head so that his completely inky pupils shone down into Ruiz-Sanchez's eyes. "One must have observed the ritual, which is very complex, until it is habit. We have grown up with it, but I think you lack the co-ordination to follow it on the first attempt. If I may bear your message instead——"

"I would be most indebted. It is for our colleagues Agronski and Michelis; they are at Xoredeshch Gton on the north-east continent, at about thirty-two degrees east, thirty-two degrees north——"

"Yes, the second bench mark at the outlet of the Lesser Lakes; that is the city of the potters, I know it well. And you would say?"

"That they are to join us now, here, at Xoredeshch Sfath. And that our time on Lithia is almost up."

"That me regards," Chtexa said. "But I will bear it."

The Lithian leapt into the whirling cloud, and Ruiz-Sanchez was left behind, considering again his thankfulness that he had been moved to study the painfully difficult Lithian language. Two of the four commission members had shown a regrettable lack of interest in that world-wide tongue: "Let 'em learn English," had been Cleaver's unknowingly classic formulation. Ruiz-Sanchez had been all the less likely to view this notion sympathetically for the facts that his own native language was Spanish, and that, of the five foreign languages in which he was really fluent, the one he liked best was West High German.

Agronski had taken a slightly more sophisticated stand. It was not, he said, that Lithian was too difficult to pronounce—certainly it wasn't any harder on the soft palate than Arabic or Russian—but, after all, "it's hopeless to attempt to grasp the concepts that lie *behind* a really alien language, isn't it? At least in the time we have to spend here?"

To both views, Michelis had said nothing; he had simply set out to learn to read the language first, and if he found his way from there into speaking it, he would not be surprised and neither would his confreres. That was Michelis's way of doing things, thorough and untheoretical at the same time. As for the other two approaches, Ruiz-Sanchez thought privately that it was close to criminal to allow any contact man for a new planet ever to leave Earth with such parochial notions. In understanding a new culture, language is of the essence; if one doesn't start there, where under God does one start?

Of Cleaver's penchant for referring to the Lithians themselves as "the Snakes", Ruiz-Sanchez's opinion was of a colour admissible only to his remote confessor.

And in view of what lay before him now in this egg-shaped hollow, what was Ruiz-Sanchez to think of Cleaver's conduct as communications officer for the commission? Surely he could never have transmitted or received a single message through the Tree, as he had claimed to have done. Probably he had never been closer to the Tree than Ruiz-Sanchez was now.

Of course, it went without saying that he had been in contact with Agronski and Michelis by *some* method, but that method had evidently been something private—a transmitter concealed in his luggage, or . . . No, that wouldn't do. Physicist though he most definitely was not, Ruiz-Sanchez rejected that solution on the spot; he had some idea of the practical difficulties of operating a ham radio on a world like Lithia, swamped as that world was on all wave-lengths by the tremendous pulses which the Tree wrung from the buried crystalline cliff. The problem was beginning to make him feel decidedly uncomfortable.

Then Chtexa was back, recognizable not so much by any physical detail—for his wattles were now the same ambiguous royal purple as those of most of the other Lithians in the crowd—as by the fact that he was bearing down upon the Earthman.

"I have sent your message," he said at once. "It is recorded at Xoredeshch Gton. But the other Earthmen are not there. They have not been in the city for some days."

That was impossible. Cleaver had said he had spoken to Michelis only a day ago. "Are you sure?" Ruiz-Sanchez said cautiously.

"It admits of no uncertainty. The house which we gave them stands empty. The many things which they brought with them to the house are gone." The tall shape raised its four-fingered hands in a gesture which might have been solicitous. "I think this is an ill word. I dislike to bring it you. The words you brought me when first we met were full of good."

"Thank you. Don't worry," Ruiz-Sanchez said distractedly. "No man could hold the bearer responsible for the word, surely."

"The bearer also has responsibilities; at least, that is our custom," Chtexa said. "No act is wholly free. And as we see it, you have lost by our exchange. Your words on iron have been shown to contain great good. I would take pleasure in showing you how we have used them, especially since I have brought you in return an ill message. If you could share my house tonight, without prejudice to your work, I could expose this matter. Is that possible?"

Sternly Ruiz-Sanchez stifled his sudden excitement. Here was the first chance, at long last, to see something of the private life of Lithia, and through that, perhaps, to gain some inkling of the moral life, the role in which God had cast the Lithians in the ancient drama of good and evil, in the past and in the times to come. Until that was known, the Lithians in their Eden might be only spuriously good: all reason, all organic thinking machines, ULTIMACs with tails—and without souls.

But there remained the hard fact that he had left behind in his house a sick man. There was not much chance that Cleaver would awaken before morning. He had been given nearly fifteen milligrams of sedative per kilogram of body weight. But sick men are like children, whose schedules persistently defy all rules. If Cleaver's burly frame should somehow throw that dose off, driven perhaps by some anaphylactic crisis impossible to rule out this early in his illness, he would need prompt attention. At the very least, he would want badly for the sound of a human voice on this planet which he hated, and which had struck him down almost without noticing that he existed.

Still, the danger to Cleaver was not great. He most certainly did not require a minute-by-minute vigil; he was, after all, not a child, but an almost ostentatiously strong man.

And there was such a thing as an excess of devotion, a form of pride among the pious which the Church had long found peculiarly difficult to make clear to them. At its worst, it produced the hospital saints, whose attraction to noisomeness so peculiarly resembled the vermin-worship of the Hindi sects—or a St. Simon Stylites, who though undoubtedly acceptable to God had been for centuries very bad public relations for the Church. And had Cleaver really earned the kind of devotion Ruiz-Sanchez had been proposing, up to now, to tender him as a creature of God—or, to come closer to the mark, a godly creature?

And with a whole planet at stake, a whole people—no, more than that, a whole problem in theology, an imminent solution to the vast, tragic riddle of original sin. . . . What a gift to bring to the Holy Father in a jubilee year—a grander yet part of him at all, still remained far aloft, twisted in the hammock webbing.

"What the hell——"

There was a brief chain of footsteps, like chestnuts dropping on a roof, and then a hollow noise of something hitting the floor near his head.

"Cleaver, are you sick? Here, lie still a minute and let me get your feet free. Mike—Mike, can't you turn the gas up in this jug? Something's wrong back here."

After a moment, yellow light began to pour from the glistening walls, and then the white glare of the mantles. Cleaver dragged an arm across his eyes, but it did him no good; it tired too quickly. Agronski's mild face, plump and anxious, floated directly above him like a captive balloon. He could not see Michelis anywhere, and at the moment he was just as glad he couldn't. Agronski's presence was hard enough to understand.

"How . . . the hell . . ." he said. At the words, his lips split painfully at both corners. He realized for the first time that they had become gummed together, somehow, while he was asleep. He had no idea how long he had been out of the picture.

Agronski seemed to understand the aborted question. "We came in from the Lakes in the 'copter," he said. "We didn't like the silence down here, and we figured we'd better come in under our own power, instead of registering in on the regular jet liner and tipping the Lithians off—just in case there'd been any dirty work afloat——"

"Stop jawing him," Michelis said, appearing suddenly, magically in the doorway. "He's got a bug, that's obvious. I don't like to feel pleased about misery, but I'm glad it's that instead of the Lithians."

The rangy, long-jawed chemist helped Agronski lift Cleaver to his feet. Tentatively, despite the pain, Cleaver got his mouth open again. Nothing came out but a hoarse croak.

"Shut up," Michelis said, not unkindly. "Let's get him back into the hammock. Where's the Father, I wonder? He's and more solemn thing than the proclamation of the conquest of Everest had been at the coronation of Elizabeth II of England!

Always providing, of course, that this would be the ultimate outcome of the study of Lithia. The planet was not lacking in hints that something quite different, and fearful beyond all else, might emerge under Ruiz-Sanchez's prolonged attention. Not even prayer had yet resolved that doubt. But should he sacrifice even the possibility of this, for Cleaver?

A lifetime of meditation over just such cases of conscience had made Ruiz-Sanchez, like most other gifted members of his order, quick to find his way to a decision through all but the most complicated of ethical labyrinths. All Catholics must be devout; but a Jesuit must be, in addition, agile.

"Thank you," he said to Chtexa, a little shakily. "I will share your house very gladly."

III

(*A voice*): "Cleaver? Cleaver! Wake up, you big slob. Cleaver! Where the hell have you been?"

Cleaver groaned and tried to turn over. At his first motion, the world began to rock, gently, sickeningly. He was awash in fever. His mouth seemed to be filled with burning pitch.

"Cleaver, turn out. It's me—Agronski. Where's the Father? What's wrong? Why didn't we ever hear from you? *Look out*, you'll——"

The warning came too late, and Cleaver could not have understood it anyhow. He had been profoundly asleep, and had no notion of his situation in space or time. At his convulsive twist away from the nagging voice, the hammock rotated on its hooks and dumped him.

He struck the floor stunningly, taking the main blow across his right shoulder, though he hardly felt it yet. His feet, not the only one capable of dealing with sickness here."

"I'll bet he's dead," Agronski burst out suddenly, his face glistening with alarm. "He'd be here if he could. It must be catching, Mike."

"I didn't bring my mitt," Michelis said dryly. "Cleaver, lie still or I'll have to clobber you. Agronski, you seem to have dumped his water bottle; better go get him some more, he needs it. And see if the Father left anything in the lab that looks like medicine."

Agronski went out, and, maddeningly, so did Michelis—at least out of Cleaver's field of vision. Setting his every muscle against the pain, Cleaver pulled his lips apart once more.

"Mike."

Instantly, Michelis was there. He had a pad of cotton between thumb and forefinger, wet with some solution, with which he gently cleaned Cleaver's lips and chin.

"Easy. Agronski's getting you a drink. We'll let you talk in a little while, Paul. Don't rush it."

Cleaver relaxed a little. He could trust Michelis. Nevertheless, the vivid and absurd insult of having to be swabbed like a baby was more than he could bear; he felt tears of helpless rage swelling on either side of his nose. With two deft, non-committal swipes, Michelis removed them.

Agronski came back, holding out one hand tentatively, palm up.

"I found these," he said. "There's more in the lab, and the Father's pill press is still out. So are his mortar and pestle, though they've been cleaned."

"All right, let's have 'em," Michelis said. "Anything else?"

"No. Well, there's a syringe cooking in the sterilizer, if that means anything."

Michelis swore briefly and to the point.

"It means that there's a pertinent antitoxin in the shop someplace," he added. "But unless Ramon left notes, we'll not have a prayer of figuring out which one it is."

As he spoke, he lifted Cleaver's head and tipped the pills

into his mouth, on to his tongue. The water which followed was cold at the first contact, but a split second later it was liquid fire. Cleaver choked, and at that precise instant Michelis pinched his nostrils shut. The pills went down with a gulp.

"There's no sign of the Father?" Michelis said.

"Not a one, Mike. Everything's in good order, and his gear's still here. Both jungle suits are in the locker."

"Maybe he went visiting," Michelis said thoughtfully. "He must have gotten to know quite a few of the Lithians by now. He liked them."

"With a sick man on his hands? That's not like him, Mike. Not unless there was some kind of emergency. Or maybe he went on a routine errand, expected to be back in just a few minutes, and——"

"And was set upon by trolls, for forgetting to stamp his foot three times before crossing a bridge."

"All right, laugh."

"I'm not laughing, believe me. That's just the kind of damn fool thing that can kill a man in a strange culture. But somehow I can't see it happening to Ramon."

"*Mike. . . .*"

Michelis took a step and looked down at Cleaver. His face was drifting as if detached through a haze of tears. He said:

"All right, Paul. Tell us what it is. We're listening."

But it was too late. The doubled sedative dose had gotten to Cleaver first. He could only shake his head, and with the motion Michelis seemed to go reeling away into a whirlpool of fuzzy rainbows.

Curiously, he did not quite go to sleep. He had had nearly a normal night's sleep, and he had started out his enormously long day a powerful and healthy man. The conversation of the two commissioners, and an obsessive consciousness of his need to speak to them before Ruiz-Sanchez returned, helped to keep him, if not totally awake, at least not far below a state of light trance. In addition, the presence in his system of thirty grains of acetylsalicylic acid had seriously raised his oxygen consumption, bringing with it not only dizziness but also a precarious, emotionally untethered alertness. That the fuel which was being burned to maintain it was in part the protein substrate of his own cells he did not know, and it could not have alarmed him had he known it.

The voices continued to reach him, and to convey a little meaning. With them were mixed fleeting, fragmentary dreams, so slightly removed from the surface of his waking life as to seem peculiarly real, yet at the same time peculiarly pointless and depressing. In the semiconscious intervals there came plans, a whole succession of them, all simple and grandiose at once, for taking command of the expedition, for communicating with the authorities on Earth, for bringing forward secret papers proving that Lithia was uninhabitable, for digging a tunnel under Mexico to Peru, for detonating Lithia in one single mighty fusion of all its lightweight atoms into one single atom of cleaverium, the element of which the monobloc had been made, whose cardinal number was Aleph-Null. . . .

AGRONSKI: Mike, come here and look at this; you read Lithian. There's a mark on the front door, on the message tablet.

(*Footsteps*)

MICHELIS: It says "Sickness inside". The strokes aren't casual or deft enough to be the work of the natives. Ideograms are hard to write rapidly without long practice. Ramon must have written it there.

AGRONSKI: I wish we knew where he went afterwards. Funny we didn't see it when we came in.

MICHELIS: I don't think so. It was dark, and we weren't looking for it.

(*Footsteps. Door shutting, not loudly. Footsteps. Hassock creaking.*)

AGRONSKI: Well, we'd better start thinking about getting up a report. Unless this damn twenty-hour day has me thrown completely off, our time's just about up. Are you still set on opening up the planet?

MICHELIS: Yes. I've seen nothing to convince me that there's anything on Lithia that's dangerous to us. Except maybe Cleaver in there, and I'm not prepared to say that the Father would have left him if he were in any serious danger. And I don't see how Earthmen could harm this society; it's too stable emotionally, economically, in every other way.

(Danger, danger, *said somebody in Cleaver's dream.* It will explode. It's all a popish plot. *Then he was marginally awake again, and conscious of how much his mouth hurt.*)

AGRONSKI: Why do you suppose those two jokers never called us after we went north?

MICHELIS: I don't have any answer. I won't even guess until I talk to Ramon. Or until Paul's able to sit up and take notice.

AGRONSKI: I don't like it, Mike. It smells bad to me. This town's right at the heart of the communications system of the planet—that's why we picked it, for Crisake! And yet—no messages, Cleaver sick, the Father not here. . . . There's a hell of a lot we don't know about Lithia, that's for damn sure.

MICHELIS: There's a hell of a lot we don't know about central Brazil—let alone Mars, or the Moon.

AGRONSKI: Nothing essential, Mike. What we know about the periphery of Brazil gives us all the clues we need about the interior—even to those fish that eat people, the what-are-they, the piranhas. That's not true on Lithia. We don't know whether our peripheral clues about Lithia are germane or just incidental. Something enormous could be hidden under the surface without our being able to detect it.

MICHELIS: Agronski, stop sounding like a Sunday supplement. You underestimate your own intelligence. What kind of enormous secret could that be? That the Lithians eat people? That they're cattle for unknown gods that live in the jungle? That they're actually mind-wrenching, soul-twisting, heart-stopping, blood-freezing, bowel-moving superbeings in disguise? The moment you state any such proposition, you'll deflate it yourself; it's only in the abstract that it's able to scare you. I wouldn't even take the trouble of examining it, or discussing how we might meet it if it were true.

AGRONSKI: All right, all right. I'll reserve judgment for the time being, anyhow. If everything turns out to be all right here, with the Father and Cleaver I mean, I'll probably go along with you. I don't have any reason I could defend for voting against the planet, I admit that.

MICHELIS: Good for you. I'm sure Ramon is for opening it up, so that should make it unanimous. I can't see why Cleaver would object.

(*Cleaver was testifying before a packed court convened in the U.N. General Assembly chambers in New York, with one finger pointed dramatically, but less in triumph than in sorrow, at Ramon Ruiz-Sanchez, S.J. At the sound of his name the dream collapsed, and he realized that the room had grown a little lighter. Dawn—or the dripping, wool-grey travesty of it which prevailed on Lithia—was on its way.*

He wondered what he had just said to the court. It had been conclusive, damning, good enough to be used when he awoke; but he could not remember a word of it. All that remained of it was a sensation, almost the taste of the words, but nothing of their substance.)

AGRONSKI: It's getting light. I suppose we'd better knock off.

MICHELIS: Did you stake down the 'copter? The winds down here are higher than they are up north, I seem to remember.

AGRONSKI: Yes. And covered it with the tarp. Nothing left to do now but sling our hammocks——

(*A sound.*)

MICHELIS: Shhh. What's that?

AGRONSKI: Eh?

MICHELIS: Listen.

(*Footsteps. Faint ones, but Cleaver knew them. He forced his eyes to open a little, but there was nothing to see but the ceiling. Its even colour, and its smooth, ever-changing slope into a dome of nowhereness, drew him almost immediately upward into the mists of trance once more.*)

AGRONSKI: Somebody's coming.

(*Footsteps.*)

AGRONSKI: It's the Father, Mike—look out here and you can see him. He seems to be all right. Dragging his feet a bit, but who wouldn't after being out helling all night?

MICHELIS: Maybe you'd better meet him at the door. It'd probably be better than our springing out at him after he gets inside. After all he doesn't expect us. I'll get to unpacking the hammocks.

AGRONSKI: Sure thing, Mike.

(*Footsteps, going away from Cleaver. A grating sound of stone on stone: the door wheel being turned.*)

AGRONSKI: Welcome home, Father! We just got in a little while ago and—My God, what's wrong? Are you ill too? Is there something that—Mike! *Mike!*

(*Somebody was running. Cleaver willed his neck muscles to lift his head, but they refused to obey. Instead, the back of his head seemed to force itself deeper into the stiff pillow of the hammock. After a momentary and endless agony, he cried out*):

CLEAVER: Mike!

AGRONSKI: Mike!

(*With a gasp, Cleaver lost the long battle at last. He was asleep.*)

IV

As the door of Chtexa's house closed behind him, Ruiz-Sanchez looked about the gently glowing foyer with a feeling of almost unbearable anticipation, although he could hardly have said what it was that he hoped to see. Actually, it looked exactly like his own quarters, which was all he could in justice have expected—all the furniture at "home" was Lithian, except of course for the lab equipment and a few other terrestrial trappings.

"We have cut up several of the metal meteors from our museums, and hammered them as you suggested," Chtexa was saying behind him, while he struggled out of his raincoat and boots. "They show very definite, very strong magnetism, as you predicted. We now have the whole of our world alerted to pick up these nickel-iron meteorites and send them to our electrical laboratory here, regardless of where they are found. The staff of the observatory is attempting to predict possible falls. Unhappily, meteors are rare here. Our astronomers say that we have never had a 'shower' such as you describe as frequent on your native planet."

"No; I should have thought of that," Ruiz-Sanchez said, following the Lithian into the front room. This, too, was quite ordinary by Lithian standards, and empty except for the two of them.

"Ah, that is interesting. Why?"

"Because in our system we have a sort of giant grinding-wheel—a whole ring of little planets, many thousands of them, distributed around an orbit where we had expected to find only one normal-sized world."

"Expected? By the harmonic rule?" Chtexa said, sitting down and pointing out another hassock to his guest. "We have often wondered whether that relationship was real."

"So have we. It broke down in this instance. Collisions between all those small bodies are incessant, and our plague of meteors is the result."

"It is hard to understand how so unstable an arrangement could have come about," Chtexa said. "Have you any explanation?"

"Not a good one," Ruiz-Sanchez said. "Some of us think that there really was a respectable planet in that orbit ages ago, which exploded somehow. A similar accident happened to a satellite in our system, creating a great flat ring of debris around its primary. Others think that at the formation of our solar system the raw materials of what might have been a planet just never succeeded in coalescing. Both ideas have many flaws, but each satisfies certain objections to the other, so perhaps there is some truth in both."

Chtexa's eyes filmed with the mildly disquieting "inner blink" characteristic of Lithians at their most thoughtful.

"There would seem to be no way to test either answer," he said at length. "By our logic, the lack of such tests makes the original question meaningless."

"That rule of logic has many adherents on Earth. My colleague Dr. Cleaver would certainly agree with it."

Ruiz-Sanchez smiled suddenly. He had laboured long and hard to master the Lithian language, and to have recognized and understood so completely abstract a point as the one just made by Chtexa was a bigger victory than any quantitative gains in vocabulary alone could have been.

"But I can see that you are going to have difficulties in collecting these meteorites," he said. "Have you offered incentives?"

"Oh, certainly. Everyone understands the importance of the programme. We are all eager to advance it."

This was not quite what the priest had meant by his question. He searched his memory for some Lithian equivalent for "reward", but found nothing but the word he had already used, "incentive". He realized that he knew no Lithian word for "greed", either. Evidently offering Lithians a hundred dollars for every meteorite they found would simply baffle them. He had to abandon that tack.

"Since the potential meteor fall is so small," he said instead, "you're not likely to get anything like the supply of metal that you need for a real study—no matter how thoroughly you co-operate on the search. A high percentage of the finds will be stony rather than metallic, too. What you need is another, supplementary iron-finding programme."

"We know that," Chtexa said ruefully. "But we have been able to think of none."

"If only you had some way of concentrating the traces of the metal you actually have on the planet now. . . . Our smelting methods would be useless to you, since you have no ore beds. Hmm. . . . Chtexa, what about the iron-fixing bacteria?"

"Are there such?" Chtexa said, cocking his head dubiously.

"I don't know. Ask your bacteriologists. If you have any bacteria here that belong to the genus we call *Leptothrix*, one of them should be an iron-fixing species. In all the millions of years that this planet has had life on it, that mutation must have occurred, and probably very early."

"But why have we never seen it before? We have done perhaps more research in bacteriology than we have in any other field."

"Because", Ruiz-Sanchez said earnestly, "you don't know what to look for, and because such a species would be as rare on Lithia as iron itself. On Earth, because we have iron in abundance, our *Leptothrix ochracea* has found plenty of opportunity to grow. We find their fossil sheaths by uncountable billions in our great ore beds. It used to be thought as a matter of fact, that the bacteria *produced* the ore beds, but I've always doubted that. They get their energy by oxidizing ferrous iron into ferric—but that's a change that can happen spontaneously if the oxidation-reduction potential and the pH of the solution are right, and both of those conditions can be affected by ordinary decay bacteria. On our planet the bacteria grew in the ore beds because the iron was there, not the other way around—but on Lithia the process will have to be worked in reverse."

"We will start a soil-sampling programme at once," Chtexa said, his wattles flaring a subdued orchid. "Our antibiotics research centres screen soil samples by the thousands each month, in search of new microflora of therapeutic importance. If these iron-fixing bacteria exist, we are certain to find them eventually."

"They must exist. Do you have a bacterium that is a sulphur-concentrating obligate anaerove?"

"Yes—yes, certainly!"

"There you are," the Jesuit said, leaning back contentedly and clasping his hands across one knee. "You have plenty of sulphur, and so you have the bacterium. Please let me know when you find the iron-fixing species. I'd like to make a subculture and take it home with me when I leave. There are two Earth scientists whose noses I'd like to rub in it."

The Lithian stiffened and thrust his head forward a little, as if puzzled.

"Pardon me," Ruiz-Sanchez said hastily. "I was translating literally an aggressive idiom of my own tongue. It was not meant to describe an actual plan of action."

"I think I understand," Chtexa said. Ruiz-Sanchez wondered if he did. In the rich storehouse of the Lithian language he had yet to discover any metaphors, either living or dead. Neither did the Lithians have any poetry or other creative arts. "You are of course welcome to any of the results of this programme, which you would honour us by accepting. One problem in the social sciences which has long puzzled us is just how one may adequately honour the innovator. When we consider how new ideas change our lives, we despair of giving in kind, and it is helpful when the innovator himself has wishes which society can gratify."

Ruiz-Sanchez was at first not quite sure that he had understood the formulation. After he had gone over it once more in his mind, he was not sure that he could bring himself to like it, although it was admirable enough. From an Earthman it would have sounded intolerably pompous, but it was evident that Chtexa meant it.

It was probably just as well that the commission's report on Lithia was about to fall due. Ruiz-Sanchez had begun to think that he could absorb only a little more of this kind of calm sanity. And all of it—a disquieting thought from somewhere near his heart reminded him—all of it derived from reason, none from precept, none from faith. The Lithians did not know God. They did things rightly, and thought righteously, because it was reasonable and efficient and natural to do and to think that way. They seemed to need nothing else.

Did they never have night thoughts? Was it possible that there could exist in the universe a reasoning being of a high order, which was never for an instant paralysed by the sudden question, the terror of seeing through to the meaninglessness of action, the blindness of knowledge, the barrenness of having been born at all? "Only upon this firm foundation of unyielding despair," a famous atheist once had written, "May the soul's habitation henceforth be safely built."

Or could it be that the Lithians thought and acted as they did because, not being born of man, and never in effect having left the Garden in which they lived, they did not share the terrible burden of original sin? The fact that Lithia had never once had a glacial epoch, that its climate had been left unchanged for seven hundred million years, was a geological fact that an alert theologian could scarcely afford to ignore. Could it be that, free from the burden, they were also free from the curse of Adam?

And if they were—could men bear to live among them?

"I have some questions to ask you, Chtexa," the priest said after a moment. "You owe me no debt whatsoever—it is our custom to regard all knowledge as community property—but we four Earthmen have a hard decision to make shortly. You know what it is. And I don't believe that we know enough yet about your planet to make that decision properly."

"Then of course you must ask questions," Chtexa said immediately. "I will answer, wherever I can."

"Well then—do your people die? I see you have the word, but perhaps it isn't the same in meaning as our word."

"It means to stop changing and to go back to existing," Chtexa said. "A machine exists, but only a living thing, like a tree, progresses along a line of changing equilibriums. When that progress stops, the entity is dead."

"And what happens to you?"

"It always happens. Even the great trees, like the Message Tree, die sooner or later. Is that not true on Earth?"

"Yes," Ruiz-Sanchez said, "yes, it is. For reasons which it would take me a long time to explain, it occurred to me that you might have escaped this evil."

"It is not evil as we look at it," Chtexa said. "Lithia lives because of death. The death of plants supplies our oil and gas. The death of some creatures is always necessary to feed the lives of others. Bacteria must die, and viruses be prevented from living, if illness is to be cured. We ourselves must die simply to make room for others, at least until we can slow the rate at which our people arrive in the world —a thing impossible to us at present."

"But desirable, in your eyes?"

"Surely desirable," Chtexa said. "Our world is rich, but not inexhaustible. And other planets, you have taught us, have peoples of their own. Thus we cannot hope to spread to other planets when we have overpopulated this one."

"No real thing is ever exhaustible," Ruiz-Sanchez said abruptly, frowning at the iridescent floor. "That we have found to be true over many thousands of years of our history."

"But exhaustible in what way?" Chtexa said. "I grant you that any small object, any stone, any drop of water, any bit of soil can be explored without end. The amount of information which can be gotten from it is quite literally infinite. But a given soil can be exhausted of nitrates. It is difficult, but with bad cultivation it can be done. Or take iron, about which we have been talking. To allow our economy to develop a demand for iron which exceeds the total known supply of Lithia—and exceeds it beyond any possibility of supplementation by meteorites or by import—would be folly. This is not a question of information. It is a question of whether or not the information can be used. If it cannot, then limitless information is of no help."

"You could certainly get along without more iron if you had to," Ruiz-Sanchez admitted. "Your wooden machinery is precise enough to satisfy any engineer. Most of them, I think, don't remember that we used to have something similar: I've a sample in my own home. It's a kind of timer called a cuckoo clock, nearly two of our centuries old, made entirely of wood except for the weights, and still nearly a hundred per cent accurate. For that matter, long after we began to build seagoing vessels of metal, we continued to use lignum vitae for ships' bearings."

"Wood is an excellent material for most uses," Chtexa agreed. "Its only deficiency, compared to ceramic materials or perhaps metal, is that it is variable. One must know it quite well to be able to assess its qualities from one tree to the next. And of course complicated parts can always be grown inside suitable ceramic moulds; the growth pressure inside the mould rises so high that the resulting part is very dense. Larger parts can be ground direct from the plank with soft sandstone and polished with slate. It is a gratifying material to work, we find."

Ruiz-Sanchez felt, for some reason, a little ashamed. It was a magnified version of the same shame he had always felt back home toward that old Black Forest cuckoo clock. The electric clocks elsewhere in his hacienda outside Lima all should have been capable of performing silently, accurately, and in less space—but the considerations which had gone into the making of them had been commercial as well as purely technical. As a result, most of them operated with a thin, asthmatic whir, or groaned softly but dismally at irregular hours. All of them were "streamlined", oversize and ugly. None of them kept good time, and several of them, since they were powered by constant-speed motors driving very simple gearboxes, could not be adjusted, but had been sent out from the factory with built-in, ineluctable inaccuracies.

The wooden cuckoo clock, meanwhile, ticked evenly away. A quail emerged from one of two wooden doors every quarter of an hour and let you know about it, and on the hour first the quail came out, then the cuckoo, and there was a soft bell that rang just ahead of each cuckoo call. Midnight and noon were not just times of the day for that clock; they were productions. It was accurate to a minute a month, all for the price of running up the three weights which drove it, each night before bedtime.

The clock's maker had been dead before Ruiz-Sanchez was born. In contrast, the priest would probably buy and jettison at least a dozen cheap electric clocks in the course of one lifetime, as their makers had intended he should; they were linearly descended from "planned obsolescence", the craze for waste which had hit the Americas during the last half of the previous century.

"I'm sure it is," he said humbly. "I have one more question, if I may. It is really part of the same question. I have asked you if you die; now I should like to ask how you are born. I see many adults on your streets and sometimes in your houses—though I gather you yourself are alone—but never any children. Can you explain this to me? Or if the subject is not allowed to be discussed——"

"But why should it not be? There can never be any closed subjects," Chtexa said. "Our women, as I'm sure you know, have abdominal pouches where the eggs are carried, It was a lucky mutation for us, for there are a number of nest-robbing species on this planet."

"Yes, we have a few animals with a somewhat similar arrangement on Earth, although they are viviparous."

"Our eggs are laid in these pouches once a year," Chtexa said. "It is then that the women leave their own houses and seek out the man of their choice to fertilize the eggs. I am alone because, thus far, I am no woman's first choice this season; I will be elected in the Second Marriage, which is tomorrow."

"I see," Ruiz-Sanchez said carefully. "And how is the choice determined? Is it by emotion, or by reason alone?"

"The two are in the long run the same," Chtexa said. "Our ancestors did not leave our genetic needs to chance. Emotion with us no longer runs counter to our eugenic knowledge. It cannot, since it was itself modified to follow that knowledge by selective breeding for such behaviour.

"At the end of the season, then, comes Migration Day. At that time all the eggs are fertilized, and ready to hatch. On that day—you will not be here to see it, I am afraid, for your scheduled date of departure precedes it by a short time—our whole people goes to the seashores. There, with the men to protect them from predators, the women wade out to swimming depth, and the children are born."

"In the sea?" Ruiz-Sanchez said faintly.

"Yes, in the sea. Then we all return, and resume our other affairs until the next mating season."

"But—but what happens to the children?"

"Why, they take care of themselves, if they can. Of course many perish, particularly to our voracious brother the great fish-lizard, whom for that reason we kill when we can. But a majority return home when the time comes."

"Return? Chtexa, I don't understand. Why don't they drown when they are born? And if they return, why have we never seen one?"

"But you have," Chtexa said. "And you have heard them often. Can it be that you yourselves do not—ah, of course, you are mammals; that is doubtless the difficulty. You keep your children in the nest with you; you know who they are and they know their parents."

"Yes," Ruiz-Sanchez said. "We know who they are, and they know us."

"That is not possible with us," Chtexa said. "Here, come with me; I will show you."

He arose and led the way out into the foyer. Ruiz-Sanchez followed, his head whirling with surmises.

Chtexa opened the door. The night, the priest saw with a subdued shock, was on the wane; there was the faintest of pearly glimmers in the cloudy sky to the east. The multifarious humming and singing of the jungle continued unabated. There was a high, hissing whistle, and the shadow of a pterodon drifted over the city toward the sea. Out on the water, an indistinct blob that could only be one of Lithia's sailplaning squid broke the surface and glided low over the oily swell for nearly sixty yards before it hit the waves again. From the mud flats came a hoarse barking.

"There," Chtexa said softly. "Did you hear it?"

The stranded creature, or another of its kind—it was impossible to tell which—croaked protestingly again.

"It is hard for them at first," Chtexa said. "But actually the worst of their dangers are over. They have come ashore."

"Chtexa," Ruiz-Sanchez said. "Your children—*the lung-fish?*"

"Yes," Chtexa said. "Those are our children."

V

In the last analysis it was the incessant barking of the lung-fish which caused Ruiz-Sanchez to stumble when Agronski opened the door for him. The late hour, and the dual strains of Cleaver's illness and the subsequent discovery of Cleaver's direct lying, contributed. So did the increasing sense of guilt toward Cleaver which the priest had felt while walking home under the gradually brightening, weeping sky; and so, of course, did the shock of discovering that Agronski and Michelis had arrived some time during the night while he had been neglecting his charge to satisfy his curiosity.

But primarily it was the diminishing, gasping clamour of the children of Lithia, battering at his every mental citadel, all the way from Chtexa's house to his own.

The sudden fugue lasted only a few moments. He fought his way back to self-control to find that Agronski and Michelis had propped him up on a stool in the lab and were trying to remove his macintosh without unbalancing him or awakening him—as difficult a problem in topology as removing a man's vest without taking off his jacket. Wearily, the priest pulled his own arm out of a macintosh sleeve and looked up at Michelis.

"Good morning, Mike. Please excuse my bad manners."

"Don't be an idiot," Michelis said evenly. "You don't have to talk now, anyhow. I've already spent much of tonight trying to keep Cleaver quiet until he's better. Don't put me through it again, please, Ramon."

"I won't. I'm not ill; I'm just tired and a little overwrought."

"What's the matter with Cleaver?" Agronski demanded. Michelis made as if to shoo him off.

"No, no, Mike, it's a fair question. I'm all right, I assure you. As for Paul, he got a dose of glucoside poisoning when a plant spine stabbed him this afternoon. No, it's yesterday afternoon now. How has he been since you arrived?"

"He's sick," Michelis said. "Since you weren't here, we didn't know what to do for him. We settled for two of the pills you'd left out."

"You did?" Ruiz-Sanchez slid his feet heavily to the floor and tried to stand up. "As you say, you couldn't have known what else to do—but you did overdose him. I think I'd better look in on him——"

"Sit down, please, Ramon." Michelis spoke gently, but his tone showed that he meant the request to be honoured. Obscurely glad to be forced to yield to the big man's well-meant implacability, the priest let himself be propped back on the stool. His boots fell off his feet to the floor.

"Mike, who's the Father here?" he asked tiredly. "Still, I'm sure you've done a good job. He's in no apparent danger?"

"Well, he seems pretty sick. But he had energy enough to keep himself awake most of the night. He only passed out a short while ago."

"Good. Let him stay out. Tomorrow we'll probably have to begin intravenous feeding, though. In this atmosphere one doesn't give a salicylate overdose without penalties." He sighed. "Since I'll be sleeping in the same room, I'll be on hand if there's a crisis. So. Can we put off further questions?"

"If there's nothing else wrong here, of course we can."

"Oh," Ruiz-Sanchez said, "there's a great deal wrong, I'm afraid."

"I knew it!" Agronski said. "I knew damn well there was. I told you so, Mike, didn't I?"

"Is it urgent?"

"No, Mike—there's no danger to us, of that I'm positive. It's nothing that won't keep until we've all had a rest. You two look as though you need one as badly as I."

"We're tired," Michelis agreed.

"But why didn't you ever call us?" Agronski burst in aggrievedly. "You had us scared half to death, Father. If there's really something wrong here, you should have——"

"There's no immediate danger," Ruiz-Sanchez repeated patiently. "As for why we didn't call you, I don't understand that any more than you do. Up to last night, I thought we were in regular contact with you both. That was Paul's job and he seemed to be carrying it out. I didn't discover that he hadn't been doing it until after he became ill."

"Then obviously we'll have to wait for him," Michelis said. "Let's hit the hammock, in God's name. Flying that whirlybird through twenty-five hundred miles of fog banks wasn't exactly restful, either; I'll be glad to turn in. . . . But, Ramon——"

"Yes, Mike?"

"I have to say that I don't like this any better than Agronski does. Tomorrow we've got to clear it up, and get our commission business done. We've only a day or so to make our decision before the ship comes and takes us off Lithia for good, and by that time we *must* know everything there is to know, and just what we're going to tell the Earth about it."

"Yes," Ruiz-Sanchez said. "Just as you say, Mike—in God's name."

The Peruvian priest-biologist awoke before the others; actually, he had undergone far less purely physical strain than had the other three. It was just beginning to be cloudy dusk when he rolled out of his hammock and padded over to look at Cleaver.

The physicist was in coma. His face was a dirty grey, and looked oddly shrunken. It was high time that the neglect and inadvertent abuse to which he had been subjected was rectified. Happily, his pulse and respiration were close to normal now.

Ruiz-Sanchez went quietly into the lab and made up a fructose intravenous feeding. At the same time he reconstituted a can of powdered eggs into a sort of *soufflé*, setting it in a covered crucible to bake at the back of the little oven; that was for the rest of them.

In the sleeping-chamber, the priest set up his I-V stand. Cleaver did not stir when the needle entered the big vein just above the inside of his elbow. Ruiz-Sanchez taped the tubing in place, checked the drip from the inverted bottle, and went back into the lab.

There he sat, on the stool before the microscope, in a sort of suspension of feeling while the new night drew on. He was still poisoned-tired, but at least now he could stay awake without constantly fighting himself. The slowly rising *soufflé* in the oven went *plup-plup, plup-plup*, and after a while a thin tendril of aroma suggested that it was beginning to brown on top, or at least thinking about it.

Outside, it abruptly rained buckets. Just as abruptly, it stopped. Lithia's short, hot summer was drawing to a close; its winter would be long and mild, the temperature never dropping below 20 deg. Centigrade in this latitude. Even at the poles, the winter temperature stayed throughout well above freezing, usually averaging about 15 deg. C.

"Is that breakfast I smell, Ramon?"

"Yes, Mike, in the oven. In a few minutes now."

"Right."

Michelis went away again. On the back of the workbench, Ruiz-Sanchez saw the dark blue book with the gold stamping which he had brought with him all the way from Earth.

Almost automatically he pulled it to him, and almost automatically it fell open at page 573. It would at least give him something to think about with which he was not personally involved.

He had last quitted the text with Anita, who "would yield to the lewdness of Honuphrius to appease the savagery of Sulla and the mercenariness of the twelve Sullivani, and (as Gilbert at first suggested) to save the virginity of Felicia for Magravius"—now hold on a moment, how could Felicia still be considered a virgin at this point? Ah ". . . when converted by Michael after the death of Gillia;" that covered it, since Felicia had been guilty only of simple infidelities in the first place. ". . . but she fears that, by allowing his marital rights, she may cause reprehensible conduct between Eugenius and Jeremias. Michael, who had formerly debauched Anita, dispenses her from yielding to Honuphrius" —yes, that made sense, since Michael also had had designs on Eugenius. "Anita is disturbed, but Michael comminates that he will reserve her case tomorrow for the ordinary Guglielmus even if she should practise a pious fraud during affrication, which, from experience, she knows (according to Wadding) to be leading to nullity."

Well. This was all very well. The novel even seemed to be shaping up into sense, for the first time; evidently the author had known exactly what he was doing, every step of the way. Still, Ruiz-Sanchez reflected, he would not like to have known the imaginary family hidden behind the conventional Latin aliases, or to have been the confessor to any member of it.

Yes, it added up, when one tried to view it without outrage either at the persons involved—they were, after all, fictitious, only characters in a novel—or at the author, who for all his mighty intellect, easily the greatest ever devoted to fiction in English and perhaps in any language, had still to be pitied as much as the meanest victim of the Evil One. To view it, as it were, in a sort of grey twilight of emotion, wherein everything, even the barnacle-like commentaries the text had accumulated since it had been begun in the nineteen-twenties, could be seen in the same light.

"Is it done, Father?"

"Smells like it, Agronski. Take it out and help yourself, why don't you?"

"Thanks. Can I bring Cleaver——"

"No, he's getting an I-V."

"Check."

Unless his impression that he understood the problem at last was once more going to turn out to be an illusion, he was now ready for the basic question, the stumper that had deeply disturbed both the Order and the Church for so many decades now. He reread it carefully. It asked:

"Has he hegemony and shall she submit?"

To his astonishment, he saw as if for the first time that it was two questions, despite the omission of a comma between the two. And so it demanded two answers. Did Honuphrius have hegemony? Yes, he did, because Michael, the only member of the whole complex who had been gifted from the beginning with the power of grace, had been egregiously compromised. Therefore, Honuphrius, regardless of whether all his sins were to be laid at his door or were real only in rumour, could not be divested of his privileges by anyone.

But should Anita submit? No, she should not. Michael had forfeited his right to dispense or to reserve her in any way, and so she could not be guided by the curate or by anyone else in the long run but her own conscience—which in view of the grave accusations against Honuphrius could lead her to no recourse but to deny him. As for Sulla's repentance, and Felicia's conversion, they meant nothing, since the defection of Michael had deprived both of them—and everyone else—of spiritual guidance.

The answer, then, had been obvious all the time. It was:

Yes, and No.

And it had hung throughout upon putting a comma in the right place. A writer's joke. A demonstration that it could take one of the greatest novelists of all times seventeen years to write a book the central problem of which is exactly where to put one comma; thus does the Adversary cloak his emptiness, and empty his votaries.

Ruiz-Sanchez closed the book with a shudder and looked up across the bench, feeling neither more nor less dazed than he had before, but with a small stirring of elation deep inside him which he could not suppress. In the eternal wrestling, the Adversary had taken another fall.

As he looked dazedly out of the window into the dripping darkness, a familiar, sculpturesque head and shoulders moved into the truncated tetrahedron of yellow light being cast out through the fine glass into the rain. Ruiz-Sanchez awoke with a start. The head was Chtexa's, moving away from the house.

Suddenly Ruiz-Sanchez realized that nobody had bothered to rub away the sickness ideograms on the door tablet. If Chtexa had come here on some errand, he had been turned back unnecessarily. The priest leaned forward, snatched up an empty slide box, and rapped with a corner of it against the inside of the glass.

Chtexa turned and looked in through the streaming curtains of rain, his eyes completely filmed against the downpour. Ruiz-Sanchez beckoned to him, and got stiffly off the stool to open the door.

In the oven the priest's share of breakfast dried slowly and began to burn.

The rapping on the window had summoned forth Agronski and Michelis as well. Chtexa looked down at the three of them with easy gravity, while drops of water ran like oil down the minute, prismatic scales of his supple skin.

"I did not know that there was sickness here," the Lithian said. "I called because your brother Ruiz-Sanchez left my house this morning without the gift I had hoped to give him. I will leave if I am invading your privacy in any way."

"You are not," Ruiz-Sanchez assured him. "And the sickness is only a poisoning, not communicable and we think not

Or he might have told you that I had been killed and that he was looking for the murderer. He might have told you anything. I had to make sure, as well as I could, that you'd arrive here *regardless* of what he had or had not said.

"And when I got to the local message centre, I had to do all this message-revision on the spot, because I found that I couldn't communicate with you directly, or send anything that was at all detailed, anything that might have been garbled through being translated and passed through alien minds. Everything that goes out from Xoredeshch Sfath by radio goes out through the Tree, and until you've seen it you haven't any idea what an Earthman is up against there in sending even the simplest message."

"Is this true?" Michelis asked Chtexa.

"True?" Chtexa repeated. His wattles were stippled with confusion; though Ruiz-Sanchez and Michelis had both reverted to Lithian, there were a number of words they had used, such as "murderer", which simply did not exist in the Lithian language, and so had been thrown out hastily in English. "True? I do not know. Do you mean, is it valid? You must be the judge of that."

"But is it accurate, sir?"

"It is accurate," Chtexa said, "in so far as I understand it."

"Well, then," Ruiz-Sanchez, a little nettled despite himself, went on, "you can see why, when Chtexa appeared providentially in the Tree, recognized me, and offered to act as an intermediary. I had to give him only the gist of what I had to say. I couldn't hope to explain all the details to him, and I couldn't hope that any of those details would get to you undistorted after they'd passed through at least two Lithian intermediaries. All I could do was shout at the top of my voice for you two to get down here on the proper date—and hope that you'd hear me."

"This is a time of trouble, which is like a sickness in the house," Chtexa said. "I must not remain. I will wish to be left alone when I am troubled, and I cannot ask that, if I likely to end badly for our colleague. Thesc are my friends from the north, Agronski and Michelis."

"I am happy to see them. The message was not in vain, then?"

"What message is this?" Michelis said, in his pure but hesitant Lithian.

"I sent a message, as your colleague Ruis-Sanchez asked me to do last night. I was told by Xoredeshch Gton that you had already departed."

"As we had," Michelis said. "Ramon, what's this? I thought you told us that sending messages was Paul's job. And you certainly implied that you didn't know how to do it yourself, after Paul took sick."

"I didn't. I don't. I asked Chtexa to send it for me; he just finished telling you that, Mike."

Michelis looked up at the Lithian.

"What did the message say?" he asked.

"That you were to join them now, here, at Xoredeshch Sfath. And that your time on our world was almost up."

"What does that mean?" Agronski said. He had been trying to follow the conversation, but he was not much of a linguist, and evidently the few words he had been able to pick up had served only to inflame his ready fears. "Mike, translate, please."

Michelis did so, briefly. Then he said:

"Ramon, was that really all you had to say to us, especially after what you had found out? We knew that departure time was coming, too, after all. We can keep a calendar as well as the next man, I hope."

"I know that, Mike. But I had no idea what previous messages you'd received, if indeed you'd received any. For all I knew, Cleaver might have been in touch with you some other way, privately. I thought first of a transmitter in his personal luggage, but later it occurred to me that he might have been sending dispatches over the regular jet liners; that would have been easier. He might have told you that we were going to stay on beyond the official departure time.

now force my presence on others who are troubled. I will bring my gift at a better time."

He ducked out through the door, without any formal gesture of farewell, but nevertheless leaving behind an overwhelming impression of graciousness. Ruiz-Sanchez watched him go helplessly, and a little forlornly. The Lithians always seemed to understand the essences of situations; they were never, unlike even the most cocksure of Earthmen, beset by the least apparent doubt. They had no night thoughts.

And why should they have? They were backed—if Ruiz-Sanchez was right—by the second-best Authority in the universe, and backed directly, without intermediary churches or conflicts of interpretations. The very fact that they were never tormented by indecision identified them as creatures of that Authority. Only the children of God had been given free will, and hence were often doubtful.

Nevertheless, Ruiz-Sanchez would have delayed Chtexa's departure had he been able. In a short-term argument it is helpful to have pure reason on your side—even though such an ally could be depended upon to stab you to the heart if you depended upon him too long.

"Let's go inside and thrash this thing out," Michelis said, shutting the door and turning back toward the front room. He spoke in Lithian still, and acknowledged it with a wry grimace over his shoulder after the departed Chtexa before switching to English. "It's a good thing we got some sleep, but we have so little time left now that it's going to be touch-and-go to have a formal decision ready when the ship comes."

"We can't go ahead yet," Agronski objected, although along with Ruiz-Sanchez, he followed Michelis obediently enough. "How can we do anything sensible without having heard what Cleaver has to say? Every man's voice counts on a job of this sort."

"That's very true," Michelis said. "And I don't like the present situation any better than you do—I've already said that. But I don't see that we have any choice. What do you think, Ramon?"

"I'd like to hold out for waiting," Ruiz-Sanchez said frankly. "Anything I may say now is, to put it realistically, somewhat compromised with you two. And don't tell me that you have every confidence in my integrity, because we had every confidence in Cleaver's, too. Right now, trying to maintain both confidences just cancels out both."

"You have a nasty way, Ramon, of saying aloud what everybody else is thinking," Michelis said, grinning bleakly. "What alternatives do you see, then?"

"None," Ruiz-Sanchez admitted. "Time is against us, as you said. We'll just have to go ahead without Cleaver."

"*No you won't.*"

The voice, from the doorway to the sleeping-chamber, was at once both uncertain and much harshened by weakness.

The others sprang up. Cleaver, clad only in his shorts, stood in the doorway, clinging to both sides of it. On one of his forearms Ruiz-Sanchez could see the marks where the adhesive tape which had held the I-V needle had been ripped away. Where the needle itself had been inserted, an ugly haematoma swelled bluely under the grey skin of Cleaver's upper arm.

VI

(*A silence.*)

"Paul, you must be crazy," Michelis said suddenly, almost angrily. "Get back into your hammock before you make things twice as bad for yourself. You're a sick man, can't you realize that?"

"Not as sick as I look," Cleaver said, with a ghastly grin. "Actually I feel pretty fair. My mouth is almost all cleared up, and I don't think I've got any fever. And I'll be damned if this commission is going to proceed one single damned inch without me. It isn't empowered to do it, and I'll appeal any decision—*any* decision, I hope you guys are listening—that it makes without me."

The commission was listening; the recorder had already been started, and the unalterable tapes were running into their sealed cans. The other two men turned dubiously to Ruiz-Sanchez.

"How about it, Ramon?" Michelis said, frowning. He shut off the recorder with his key. "Is it safe for him to be up like this?"

Ruiz-Sanchez was already at the physicist's side, peering into his mouth. The ulcers were indeed almost gone, with granulation tissue forming nicely over the few that still remained. Cleaver's eyes were still slightly suffused, indicating that the toxaemia was not completely defeated, but except for these two signs the effect of the accidental squill inoculation was no longer visible. It was true that Cleaver looked awful, but that was inevitable in a man quite recently sick, and in one who had been burning his own body proteins for fuel to boot. As for the haematoma, a cold compress would fix that.

"If he wants to endanger himself, I guess he's got a right to do so, at least by indirection," Ruiz-Sanchez said. "Paul, the first thing you'll have to do is get off your feet, and get into a robe, and put a blanket around your legs. Then you'll have to eat something; I'll fix it for you. You've staged a wonderful recovery, but you're a sitting duck for a real infection if you abuse your time during convalescence."

"I'll compromise," Cleaver said immediately. "I don't want to be a hero, I just want to be heard. Give me a hand over to that hassock. I still don't walk very straight."

It took the better part of half an hour to get Cleaver settled to Ruiz-Sanchez's satisfaction. The physicist seemed in a wry way to be enjoying every minute of it. At last he had in his hand a mug of *gchteht*, a local herb tea so delicious that it would probably become a major article of export before long, and he said:

"All right, Mike, turn on the recorder and let's go."

"Are you sure?" Michelis said.

"One hundred per cent. Turn the goddam key."

Michelis turned the key, took it out and put it in his pocket. From now on, they were on the record.

"All right, Paul," Michelis said. "You've gone out of your way to put yourself on the spot. Evidently that's where you want to be. So let's have the answer: Why didn't you communicate with us?"

"I didn't want to."

"Now wait a minute," Agronski said. "Paul, you're going on record; don't break your neck to say the first damn thing that comes into your head. Your judgment may not be well yet, even if your talking apparatus is. Wasn't your silence just a matter of your being unable to work the local message system—the Tree or whatever it is?"

"No, it wasn't," Cleaver insisted. "Thanks, Agronski, but I don't need to be shepherded down the safe and easy road, or have any alibis set up for me. I know exactly what I did that was ticklish, and I know that it's going to be impossible for me to set up consistent alibis for it now. My chances of keeping anything under my hat depended upon my staying in complete control of everything I did. Naturally those chances went out the window when I got stuck by that damned pineapple. I realized that last night, when I fought like a demon to get through to you before the Father could get back, and found that I couldn't make it."

"You seem to take it calmly enough now," Michelis observed.

"Well, I'm feeling a little washed out. But I'm a realist. And I also know, Mike, that I had damned good reasons for what I did. I'm counting on the chance that you'll agree with me wholeheartedly, when I tell you why I did it."

"All right," Michelis said, "begin."

Cleaver sat back, folding his hands quietly in the lap of his robe. He looked almost ecclesiastical. He was obviously still enjoying the situation. He said:

"First of all, I didn't call you because I didn't want to, as I said. I could have mastered the problem of the Tree easily enough by doing what the Father did—that is, by getting a

Snake to ferry my messages. Of course I don't speak Snake, but the Father does, so all I had to do was to take him into my confidence. Barring that, I could have mastered the Tree itself. I already know all the technical problems involved. Mike, wait till you see that Tree. Essentially it's a single-junction transistor, with the semi-conductor supplied by a huge lump of crystal buried under it; the crystal is piezo-electric and emits in the RF spectrum every time the Tree's roots stress it. It's fantastic—nothing like it anywhere else in the galaxy, I'd lay money on that.

"But I wanted a gap to spring up between our party and yours. I wanted both of you to be completely in the dark about what was going on, down here on this continent. I wanted you to imagine the worst, and blame it on the Snakes, too, if that could be managed. After you got here—if you did—I was going to be able to show you that I hadn't sent any messages because the Snakes wouldn't let me. I've got more plans to that effect squirrelled away around here than I'll bother to list now; besides, there'd be no point in it, since it's all come to nothing. But I'm sure that it would have looked conclusive, regardless of anything the Father would have been able to offer to the contrary."

"Are you sure you don't want me to turn off the machine?" Michelis said quietly.

"Oh, throw away your damned key, will you, and listen. From my point of view it was just a bloody shame that I had to run up against a pineapple at the last minute. It gave the Father a chance to find out something about what was up. I'll swear that if that hadn't happened, he wouldn't have smelt anything until you actually got here—and by then it would have been too late."

"I probably wouldn't have, that's true," Ruiz-Sanchez said, watching Cleaver steadily. "But your running up against that 'pineapple' was no accident. If you'd been observing Lithia as you were sent here to do, instead of spending all your time building up a fictitious Lithia for purposes of your own, you'd have known enough about the planet to have been more careful about 'pineapples'. You'd also have spoken at least as much Lithian as Agronski, by this time."

"That", Cleaver said, "is probably true, and again it doesn't make any difference to me. I observed the one fact about Lithia that overrides all other facts, and that is going to turn out to be sufficient. Unlike you, Father, I have no respect for petty niceties in extreme situations, and I'm not the kind of man who thinks anyone learns anything from analysis after the fact."

"Let's not get to bickering this early," Michelis said. "You've told us your story without any visible decoration, and it's evident that you have a reason for confessing. You expect us to excuse you, or at least not to blame you too heavily, when you tell us what that reason is. Let's hear it."

"It's this," Cleaver said, and for the first time he seemed to become a little more animated. He leaned forward, the glowing gaslight bringing the bones of his face into sharp contrast with the sagging hollows of his cheeks, and pointed a not-quite-steady finger at Michelis.

"Do you know, Mike, what it is that we're sitting on here? Just to begin with, do you know how much rutile there is here?"

"Of course I know," Michelis said. "Agronski told me, and since then I've been working on practicable methods of refining the ore. If we decide to vote for opening the planet up, our titanium problem will be solved for a century, maybe even longer. I'm saying as much in my personal report. But what of it? We anticipated that that would be true even before we first landed here, as soon as we got accurate figures on the mass of the planet."

"And what about the pegmatite?" Cleaver demanded softly.

"Well, what about it?" Michelis said, looking more puzzled than before. "I suppose it's abundant—I really didn't bother to check. Titanium's important to us, but I don't quite see why lithium should be. The days when the metal was used as a rocket fuel are fifty years behind us."

"And a good thing, too," Agronski said. "Those old Li-Fluor engines used to go off like war heads. One little leak in the feed lines, and bloo-*ey*!"

"And yet the metal's still worth about twenty thousand dollars an English ton back home, Mike, and that's exactly the same price it was drawing in the nineteen-sixties, allowing for currency changes since then. Doesn't that mean anything to you?"

"I'm more interested in knowing what it means to you," Michelis said. "None of us can make a personal penny out of this trip, even if we find the planet solid platinum inside—which is hardly likely. And if price is the only consideration, surely the fact that lithium ore is common here will break the market for it. What's it good for, after all, on a large scale?"

"Bombs," Cleaver said. "Real bombs. Fusion bombs. It's no good for controlled fusion, for power, but the deuterium salt makes the prettiest multimegaton explosion you ever saw."

Ruiz-Sanchez suddenly felt sick and tired all over again. It was exactly what he had feared had been on Cleaver's mind; given a planet named Lithia only because it appeared to be mostly rock, and a certain kind of mind will abandon every other concern to find a metal called lithium on it. But he had not wanted to find himself right.

"Paul," he said, "I've changed my mind. I would have caught you out, even if you had never blundered against your 'pineapple'. That same day you mentioned to me that you were looking for pegmatite when you had your accident, and that you thought Lithia might be a good place for tritium production on a large scale. Evidently you thought that I wouldn't know what you were talking about. If you hadn't hit the 'pineapple', you would have given yourself away to me before now by talk like that. Your estimate of me was based on as little observation as is your estimate of Lithia."

"It's easy", Cleaver observed indulgently, "to say 'I knew it all the time'—especially on a tape."

"Of course it's easy, when the other man is helping you," Ruiz-Sanchez said. "But I think that your view of Lithia as a potential cornucopia of hydrogen bombs is only the beginning of what you have in mind. I don't believe that it's even your real objective. What you would like most is to see Lithia removed from the universe as far as you're concerned. You hate the place. It's injured you. You'd like to think that it doesn't really exist. Hence the emphasis on Lithia as a source of munitions, to the exclusion of every other fact about the planet; for if that emphasis wins out, Lithia will be placed under security seal. Isn't that right?"

"Of course it's right, except for the phoney mind reading," Cleaver said contemptuously. "When even a priest can see it, it's got to be obvious—and it's got to be written off by impugning the motives of the man who saw it first. To hell with that. Mike, listen to me. This is the most tremendous opportunity that any commission has ever had. This planet is made to order to be converted, root and branch, into a thermonuclear laboratory and production centre. It has indefinitely large supplies of the most important raw materials. What's even more important, it has no nuclear knowledge of its own for us to worry about. All the clue materials, the radioactive elements and so on, which you need to work out real knowledge of the atom, we'll have to import; the Snakes don't know a thing about them. Furthermore, the instruments involved, the counters and particle-accelerators and so on, all depend on materials like iron that the Snakes don't have, and on principles that they don't know, ranging all the way from magnetism to quantum mechanics. We'll be able to stock our plants here with an immense reservoir of cheap labour which doesn't know, and—if we take proper precautions—never will have a prayer of learning enough to snitch classified techniques.

"All we need to do is to turn in a triple-E Unfavourable on the planet, to shut off any use of Lithia as a way station or any other kind of general base for a whole century. At the same time, we can report separately to the U.N. Review Committee exactly what we do have in Lithia: a triple-A arsenal for the whole of Earth, for the whole commonwealth of planets we control! Only the decision becomes general administrative property back home; the tape is protected; it's an opportunity it'd be a crime to flub!"

"Against whom?" Ruiz-Sanchez said.

"Eh? You've lost me."

"Against whom are you stocking this arsenal? Why do we need a whole planet devoted to nothing but making fusion bombs?"

"The U.N. can use weapons," Cleaver said dryly. "The time isn't very far gone since there were still a few restive nations on Earth, and it could come around again. Don't forget also that thermonuclear weapons last only a few years—they can't be stock-piled indefinitely, like fission bombs. The half-life of tritium is very short, and lithium-6 isn't very long-lived either. I suppose you wouldn't know anything about that. But take my word for it, the U.N. police would be glad to know that they could have access to a virtually inexhaustible stock of fusion bombs, and to hell with the shelf-life problem!

"Besides, if you've thought about it at all, you know as well as I do that this endless consolidation of peaceful planets can't go on forever. Sooner or later—well, what happens if the next planet we touch down on is a place like Earth? If it is, its inhabitants may fight, and fight like a planetful of madmen, to stay *out* of our frame of influence. Or what happens if the next planet we hit is an outpost for a whole federation, maybe bigger than ours? When that day comes—and it will, it's in the cards—we'll be damned glad if we're able to plaster the enemy from pole to pole with fusion bombs, and clean up the matter with as little loss of life as possible."

"On our side," Ruiz-Sanchez added.

"Is there any other side?"

"By golly, that makes sense to me," Agronski said. "Mike, what do you think?"

"I'm not sure yet," Michelis said. "Paul, I still don't understand why you thought it necessary to go through all the cloak-and-dagger manœuvres. You tell your story fairly enough now, and it has its merits, but you also admit you were going to trick the three of us into going along with you, if you could. Why? Couldn't you trust the force of your argument alone?"

"No," Cleaver said bluntly. "I've never been on a commission like this before, where there was no single, definite chairman, where there was deliberately an even number of members so that a split opinion couldn't be settled if it occurred—and where the voice of a man whose head is filled with Pecksniffian, irrelevant moral distinctions and three-thousand-year-old metaphysics carries the same weight as the voice of a scientist."

"That's mighty loaded language, Paul," Michelis said.

"I know it. If it comes to that, I'll say here or anywhere that I think the Father is a hell of a fine biologist. I've seen him in operation, and they don't come any better—and for that matter he may have just finished saving my life, for all any of the rest of us can tell. That makes him a scientist like the rest of us—in so far as biology's a science."

"Thank you," Ruiz-Sanchez said. "With a little history in your education, Paul, you would also have known that the Jesuits were among the first explorers to enter China, and Paraguay, and the North American wilderness. Then it would have been no surprise to you to find me here."

"That may well be. However, it has nothing to do with the paradox as I see it. I remember once visiting the labs at Notre Dame, where they have a complete little world of germ-free animals and plants and have pulled I don't know how many physiological miracles out of the hat. I wondered then how a man goes about being as good a scientist as that, and a good Catholic at the same time—or any other kind of churchman. I wondered in which compartment in their brains they filed their religion, and in which their science. I'm still wondering."

"They're not compartmented," Ruiz-Sanchez said. "They are a single whole."

"So you said, when I brought this up before. That answers nothing; in fact, it convinced me that what I was planning to do was absolutely necessary. I didn't propose to take any chances on the compartments getting interconnected on Lithia. I had every intention of cutting the Father down to a point where his voice would be nearly ignored by the rest of you. That's why I undertook the cloak-and-dagger stuff. Maybe it was stupidly done—I suppose that it takes training to be a successful agent-provocateur and that I should have realized that."

Ruiz-Sanchez wondered what Cleaver's reaction would be when he found, as he would very shortly now, that his purpose would have been accomplished without his having to lift a finger. Of course the dedicated man of science, working for the greater glory of man, could anticipate nothing but failure; that was the fallibility of man. But would Cleaver be able to understand, through his ordeal, what had happened to Ruiz-Sanchez when he had discovered the fallibility of God? It seemed unlikely.

"But I'm not sorry I tried," Cleaver was saying. "*I'm only sorry I failed.*"

VII

THERE was a short, painful hiatus.

"Is that it, then?" Michelis said.

"That's it, Mike. Oh—one more thing. My vote, if anybody is still in any doubt about it, is to keep the planet closed. Take it from there."

"Ramon," Michelis said, "do you want to speak next? You're certainly entitled to it, on a point of personal privilege. The air's a mite murky at the moment, I'm afraid."

"No, Mike. Let's hear from you."

"I'm not ready to speak yet either, unless the majority wants me to. Agronski, how about you?"

"Sure," Agronski said. "Speaking as a geologist, and also as an ordinary slob that doesn't follow rarefied reasoning very well, I'm on Cleaver's side. I don't see anything either for or against the planet on any other grounds but Cleaver's. It's a fair planet as planets go, very quiet, not very rich in anything else we need—sure, that *gchteht* is marvellous stuff, but it's strictly for the luxury trade—and not subject to any kind of trouble that I've been able to detect. It'd make a good way station, but so would lots of other worlds hereabouts.

"It'd also make a good arsenal, the way Cleaver defines the term. In every other category it's as dull as ditch water, and it's got plenty of that. The only other thing it can have to offer is titanium, which isn't quite as scarce back home these days as Mike seems to think; and gem stones, particularly the semi-precious ones, which we can make at home without travelling fifty light-years to get them. I'd say, either set up a way station here and forget about the planet otherwise, or else handle the place as Cleaver suggested."

"But which?" Ruiz-Sanchez asked.

"Well, which is more important, Father? Aren't way stations a dime a dozen? Planets that can be used as thermonuclear labs, on the other hand, are rare—Lithia is the *first* one that can be used that way, at least in my experience. Why use a planet for a routine purpose if it's unique? Why not apply Occam's Razor—the law of parsimony? It works on every other scientific problem anybody's ever tackled. It's my bet that it's the best tool to use on this one."

"Occam's Razor isn't a natural law," Ruiz-Sanchez said. "It's only a heuristic convenience—in short, a learning gimmick. And besides, Agronski, it calls for the simplest solution of the problem that will fit all the facts. You don't have all the facts, not by a long shot."

"All right, show me," Agronski said piously. "I've got an open mind."

"You vote to close the planet, then," Michelis said.

"Sure. That's what I was saying, wasn't it, Mike?"

"I wanted to have it Yes or No for the tape," Michelis said. "Ramon, I guess it's up to us. Shall I speak first? I think I'm ready."

"Of course, Mike."

"Then," Michelis said evenly, and without changing in the slightest his accustomed tone of grave impartiality, "I'll say that I think both of these gentlemen are fools, and calamitous fools at that because they're supposed to be scientists. Paul, your manœuvres to set up a phoney situation are perfectly beneath contempt, and I shan't mention them again. I shan't even appeal to have them cut from the tape, so you needn't feel that you have to mend any fences with me. I'm looking solely at the purpose those manœuvres were supposed to serve, just as you asked me to do."

Cleaver's obvious self-satisfaction began to dim a little around the edges. He said: "Go ahead," and wound the blanket a little bit tighter around his legs.

"Lithia is not even the beginning of an arsenal," Michelis said. "Every piece of evidence you offered to prove that it might be is either a half-truth or the purest trash. Take cheap labour, for instance. With what will you pay the Lithians? They have no money, and they can't be rewarded with goods. They have almost everything that they need, and they like the way they're living right now—God knows they're not even slightly jealous of the achievements we think make Earth great. They'd like to have space flight but, given a little time, they'll get it by themselves; they have the Coupling ion-jet right now, and they won't be needing the Haertel overdrive for another century."

He looked around the gently rounded room, which was shining softly in the gaslight.

"And I don't seem to see any place in here", he said, "where a vacuum cleaner with forty-five patented attachments would find any work to do. How will you pay the Lithians to work in your thermonuclear plants?"

"With knowledge," Cleaver said gruffly. "There's a lot they'd like to know."

"But what knowledge, Paul? The things they'd like to know are specifically the things you can't tell them, if they're to be valuable to you as a labour force. Are you going to teach them quantum mechanics? You can't; that would be dangerous. Are you going to teach them nucleonics, or Hilbert space, or the Haertel scholium? Again, any one of those would enable them to learn other things you think dangerous. Are you going to teach them how to extract titanium from rutile, or how to accumulate enough iron to develop a science of electrodynamics, or how to pass from this Stone Age they're living in now—this Pottery Age, I should say—into an Age of Plastics? Of course you aren't. As a matter of fact, we don't have a thing to offer them in that sense. It'd all be classified under the arrangement you propose—and they just wouldn't work for us under those terms."

"Offer them other terms," Cleaver said shortly. "If necessary, tell them what they're going to do, like it or lump it. It'd be easy enough to introduce a money system on this planet. You give a Snake a piece of paper that says it's worth a dollar, and if he asks you just what makes it worth a dollar—well, the answer is, an honest day's work."

"And we put a machine-pistol to his belly to emphasize the point," Ruiz-Sanchez interjected.

"Do we make machine-pistols for nothing? I never figured out what else they were good for. Either you point them at someone or you throw them away."

"Item: slavery," Michelis said. "That disposes, I think, of the argument of cheap labour. I won't vote for slavery. Ramon won't. Agronski?"

"No," Agronski said uneasily. "But isn't it a minor point?"

"The hell it is! It's the reason why we're here. We're supposed to think of the welfare of the Lithians as well as of thoughts, file them in your individual report, but don't try to stampede me into hiding anything under the rug now, Paul. It won't work."

"That", Cleaver said, "is what I get for trying to help."

"If that's what you were trying to do, thanks. I'm not through, however. So far as the practical objective, that you want to achieve is concerned, Paul, I think it's just as useless as it is impossible. The fact that we have here a planet that's especially rich in lithium doesn't mean that we're sitting on a bonanza, no matter what price per ton the metal commands back home.

"The fact of the matter is that you can't ship lithium home. Its density is so low that you couldn't send away more than a ton of it per shipload; by the time you got it to Earth, the shipping charges on it would more than outweigh the price you'd get for it on arrival. I should have thought that you'd know there's lots of lithium on Earth's own moon, too—and it isn't economical to fly it back to Earth even over that short a distance, less than a quarter of a million miles. Lithia is three hundred and fourteen trillion miles from Earth; that's what fifty light-years comes to. Not even radium is worth carrying over a gap that great!

"No more would it be economical to ship from Earth to Lithia all the heavy equipment that would be needed to make use of lithium here. There's no iron here for massive magnets. By the time you got your particle-accelerators and mass chromatographs and the rest of your needs to Lithia, you'd have cost the U.N. so much that no amount of locally available pegmatite could compensate for it. Isn't that so, Agronski?"

"I'm no physicist," Agronski said, frowning slightly. "But just getting the metal out of the ore and storing it would cost a fair sum, that's a cinch. Raw lithium would burn like phosphorus in this atmosphere; you'd have to store it and work it under oil. That's costly no matter how you look at it."

Michelis looked from Cleaver to Agronski and back again.

bered the lines of poetry that had summed it up for him—lines written way back in the nineteen-fifties:

The groggy old Church has gone toothless,
No longer holds against neshek*; the fat has covered their croziers. . . .*

Neshek was the lending of money at interest, once a sin called usury, for which Dante had put men into Hell. And now here was Mike, not a Christian at all, arguing that money itself was a form of slavery. It was, Ruiz-Sanchez discovered upon fingering it mentally once more, a *very* sore spot.

"In the meantime," Michelis had resumed, "I'll prosecute my own demonstration. What's to be said, now, about this theory of automatic security that you've propounded, Paul? You think that the Lithians can't learn the techniques they would need to be able to understand secret information and pass it on, and so they won't have to be screened. There again, you're wrong, as you'd have known if you'd bothered to study the Lithians even perfunctorily. The Lithians are highly intelligent, and they already have many of the clues they need. I've given them a hand toward pinning down magnetism, and they absorbed the material like magic and put it to work with enormous ingenuity."

"So did I," Ruiz-Sanchez said. "And I've suggested to them a technique for accumulating iron that should prove to be pretty powerful. I had only to suggest it, and they were already halfway down to the bottom of it and travelling fast. They can make the most of the smallest of clues."

"If I were the U.N. I'd regard both actions as the plainest kind of treason," Cleaver said harshly. "You'd better think again about using that key, Mike, on your own behalf—if it isn't already too late. Isn't it possible that the Snakes found out both items by themselves, and were only being polite to you?"

"Set me no traps," Michelis said. "The tape is on and it stays on, by your own request. If you have any second ourselves—otherwise this commission procedure would be a waste of time, of thought, of energy. If we want cheap labour, we can enslave any planet."

"How do we do that?" Agronski said. "There aren't any other planets. I mean, none with intelligent life on them that we've hit so far. You can't enslave a Martian sand crab."

"Which brings up the point of our own welfare," Ruiz-Sanchez said. "We're supposed to be considering that, too. Do you know what it does to a people to be slave-owners? It kills them."

"Lots of people have worked for money without calling it slavery," Agronski said. "I don't mind getting a pay cheque for what I do."

"There is no money on Lithia," Michelis said stonily. "If we introduce it here, we do so only by force. Forced labour is slavery. Q.E.D."

Agronski was silent.

"Speak up," Michelis said. "Is that true, or isn't it?"

Agronski said: "I guess it is. Take it easy, Mike. There's nothing to get mad about."

"Cleaver?"

"Slavery's just a swear-word," Cleaver said sullenly. "You're deliberately clouding the issue."

"*Say that again.*"

"Oh, hell. All right, Mike, I know you wouldn't. But we could work out a fair pay scale somehow."

"I'll admit that the instant that you can demonstrate it to me," Michelis said. He got up abruptly from his hassock, walked over to the sloping window-sill, and sat down again, looking out into the rain-stippled darkness. He seemed to be more deeply troubled than Ruiz-Sanchez had ever before thought possible for him. The priest was astonished, as much at himself as at Michelis; the argument from money had never occurred to him, and Michelis had unknowingly put his finger on a doctrinal sore spot which Ruiz-Sanchez had never been able to reconcile with his own beliefs. He remem-

"Exactly so," he said. "And that's only the beginning. In fact, the whole scheme is just a chimera."

"Have you got a better one, Mike?" Cleaver said, very quietly.

"I hope so. It seems to me that we have a lot to learn from the Lithians, as well as they from us. Their social system works like the most perfect of our physical mechanisms, and it does so without any apparent repression of the individual. It's a thoroughly liberal society in terms of guarantees, yet all the same it never even begins to tip over toward the side of total disorganization, toward the kind of Gandhi-ism that keeps a people tied to the momma-and-poppa farm and the roving-brigand distribution system. It's in balance, and not in precarious balance either—it's in perfect chemical equilibrium.

"The notion of using Lithia as a fusion-bomb plant is easily the strangest anachronism I've ever encountered—it's as crude as proposing to equip an interstellar ship with galley slaves, oars and all. Right here on Lithia is the *real* secret, the secret that's going to make bombs of all kinds, and all the rest of the anti-social armament, as useless, unnecessary, obsolete as the iron boot!

"And on top of all of that—no, please, I'm not quite finished, Paul—on top of all that, the Lithians are decades ahead of us in some purely technical matters, just as we're ahead of them in others. You should see what they can do with mixed disciplines—scholia like histochemistry, immunodynamics, biophysics, terataxonomy, osmotic genetics, electrolimnology, and half a hundred more. If you'd been looking, you *would* have seen.

"We have much more to do, it seems to me, than just to vote to open the planet. That's only a passive move. We have to realize that being able to use Lithia is only the beginning. The fact of the matter is that we actively *need* Lithia. We should say so in our recommendation."

Michelis unfolded himself from the window-sill and stood up, looking down on all of them, but most especially at Ruiz-

Sanchez. The priest smiled at him, but as much in anguish as in admiration, and then had to look back down at his shoes.

"Well, Agronski?" Cleaver said, spitting the words out like bullets on which he had been clenching his teeth, like a Civil War casualty during an operation without anaesthetics. "What d'you say now? Do you like the pretty picture?"

"Sure, I like it," Agronski said, slowly but forthrightly. It was a virtue in him, as well as a frequent source of exasperation, that he always said exactly what he was thinking, the moment he was asked to do so. "Mike makes sense. I wouldn't expect him not to, if you see what I mean. Also he's got another advantage: he told us what he thought, *without* trying to trick us first into his way of thinking."

"Oh, don't be a thumphead," Cleaver explained. "Are we scientists or Boy Rangers? Any rational man up against a majority of do-gooders would have taken the same precautions I did."

"Maybe," Agronski said. "I'm none too sure. Why is it silly to be a do-gooder? Is it wrong to do good? Do you want to be a do-badder—whatever the hell that is? Your precautions still smell to me like a confession of weakness somewhere in the argument. As for me, I don't like to be finessed. And I don't much like being called a thumphead, either."

"Oh, for Christ's sake——"

"Now-you-listen-to-me," Agronski said, all in one breath. "Before you call me any more names, I'm going to say that I think you're more right than Mike is. I don't like your methods, but your aim seems sensible to me. Mike's shot some of your major arguments full of holes, that I'll admit. But as far as I'm concerned, you're still leading—by a nose."

He paused, breathing heavily and glaring at the physicist. Then he said:

"By a nose, Paul. That's all. Just bear that in mind."

Michelis remained standing for a moment longer. Then he shrugged, walked back to his hassock, and sat down, locking his hands awkwardly between his knees.

"I did my best, Ramon," he said. "But so far it looks like a draw. See what you can do."

Ruiz-Sanchez took a deep breath. What he was about to do would hurt him, without doubt, for the rest of his life, regardless of the way time had of turning any blade. The decision had already cost him many hours of concentrated, agonized doubt. But he believed that it had to be done.

"I disagree with all of you," he said, "except Cleaver. I believe, as he does, that Lithia should be reported triple-E Unfavourable. But I think also that it should be given a special classification: X-One."

Michelis's eyes were glazed with shock. Even Cleaver seemed unable to credit what he had heard.

"X-One—but that's a quarantine label," Michelis said huskily. "As a matter of fact——"

"Yes, Mike, that's right," Ruiz-Sanchez said. "I vote to seal Lithia off from *all* contact with the human race. Not only now, or for the next century—but for ever."

VIII

FOR EVER.

The words did not produce the consternation that he had been dreading—or, perhaps, hoping for, somewhere in the back of his mind. Evidently they were all too tired for that. They took his announcement with a kind of stunned emptiness, as though it were so far out of the expected order of events as to be quite meaningless.

It was hard to say whether Cleaver or Michelis was the more overwhelmed. All that could be seen for certain was that Agronski recovered first, and was now ostentatiously reaming out his ears, as if in signal that he would be ready to listen again when Ruiz-Sanchez changed his mind.

"Well," Cleaver began. And then again, shaking his head amazedly, like an old man: "Well. . . ."

"Tell us why, Ramon," Michelis said, clenching and unclenching his fists. His voice was quite flat, but Ruiz-Sanchez thought he could feel the pain under it.

"Of course. But I warn you, I'm going to be very roundabout. What I have to say seems to me to be of the utmost importance. I don't want to see it rejected out of hand as just the product of my peculiar training and prejudices—interesting perhaps as a study in aberration, but not germane to the problem. The evidence for my view of Lithia is overwhelming. It overwhelmed me quite *against* my natural hopes and inclinations. I want you to hear that evidence."

The preamble, with its dry scholiast's tone and its buried suggestion, did its work well.

"He also wants us to understand", Cleaver said, recovering a little of his natural impatience, "that his reasons are religious and won't hold water if he states them right out."

"Hush," Michelis said intently. "Listen."

"Thank you, Mike. All right, here we go. This planet is what I think is called in English 'a set-up'. Let me describe it for you briefly as I see it, or rather as I've come to see it.

"Lithia is a paradise. It has resemblances to a number of other planets, but the closest correspondence is to the Earth in its pre-Adamic period, before the coming of the first glaciers. The resemblance ends there, because on Lithia the glaciers never came, and life continued to be spent in the paradise, as it was not allowed to do on Earth."

"Myths," Cleaver said sourly.

"I use the terms with which I'm most familiar; strip off those terms and what I am saying is still a fact that all of you know to be true. We find here a completely mixed forest, with plants that fall from one end of the creative spectrum to the other living side by side in perfect amity, cycad with cycladella, giant horsetail with flowering trees. To a great extent that's also true of the animals. The lion doesn't lie down with the lamb here because Lithia has neither animal, but as an allegory the phrase is apt. Parasitism occurs rather less often on Lithia than it does on

Earth, and there are very few carnivores of any sort except in the sea. Almost all of the surviving land animals eat plants only, and by a neat arrangement which is typically Lithian, the plants are admirably set up to attack animals rather than each other.

"It's an unusual ecology, and one of the strangest things about it is its rationality, its extreme, almost single-minded insistence upon one-for-one relationships. In one respect it looks almost as though somebody had arranged the whole planet as a ballet about Mengenlehre—the theory of aggregates.

"Now, in this paradise we have a dominant creature, the Lithian, the man of Lithia. This creature is rational. It conforms, as if naturally and without constraint or guidance, to the highest ethical code we have evolved on Earth. It needs no laws to enforce this code. Somehow, everyone obeys it as a matter of course, although it has never even been written down. There are no criminals, no deviates, no aberrations of any kind. The people are not standardized—our own very bad and partial answer to the ethical dilemma—but instead are highly individual. They choose their own life courses without constraint—yet somehow no anti-social act of any kind is ever committed. There isn't even any word for such an act in the Lithian language."

The recorder made a soft, piercing pip of sound, announcing that it was threading a new tape. The enforced pause would last about eight seconds, and on a sudden inspiration, Ruiz-Sanchez put it to use. On the next pip, he said:

"Mike, let me stop here and ask you a question. What does this suggest to you, thus far?"

"Why, just what I've said before that it suggested," Michelis said slowly. "An enormously superior social science, evidently founded in a precise system of psychogenetics. I should think that would be more than enough."

"Very well, I'll go on. I felt as you did, at first. Then I came to ask myself some correlative questions. For instance: How does it happen that the Lithians not only have no deviates—think of that, *no* deviates!—but that the code by which they live so perfectly is, point for point, the code *we* strive to obey? If that just happened, it was by the uttermost of all coincidences. Consider, please, the imponderables involved. Even on Earth we have never known a society which evolved independently *exactly* the same precepts as the Christian precepts—by which I mean to include the Mosaic. Oh, there were some duplications of doctrine, enough to encourage the twentieth century's partiality toward synthetic religions like theosophism and Hollywood Vedanta, but no ethical system on Earth that grew up independently of Christianity agreed with it point for point. Not Mithraism, not Islam, not the Essenes—not even these, which influenced or were influenced by Christianity, were in good agreement with it in the matter of ethics.

"And yet here on Lithia, fifty light-years away from Earth and among a race as unlike man as man is unlike the kangaroos, what do we find? A Christian people, lacking nothing but the specific proper names and the symbolic appurtenances of Christianity. I don't know how you three react to this, but I found it extraordinary and indeed completely impossible—mathematically impossible—under any assumption but one. I'll get to that assumption in a moment."

"You can't get there any too soon for me," Cleaver said morosely. "How a man can stand fifty light-years from home in deep space and talk such parochial nonsense is beyond my comprehension."

"Parochial?" Ruiz-Sanchez said, more angrily than he had intended. "Do you mean that what we think true on Earth is automatically made suspect just by the fact of its removal into deep space? I beg to remind you, Paul, that quantum mechanics seem to hold good on Lithia, and that you see nothing parochial about behaving as if it does. If I believe in Peru that God created and still rules the universe, I see nothing parochial in my continuing to believe it on Lithia. You brought your parish with you; so did I. This has been willed where what is willed must be."

As always, the great phrase shook him to the heart. But it was obvious that it meant nothing to anyone else in the room; were such men hopeless? No, no. That Gate could never slam behind them while they lived, no matter how the hornets buzzed for them behind the deviceless banner. Hope was with them yet.

"A while back I thought I had been provided an escape hatch, incidentally," he said. "Chtexa told me that the Lithians would like to modify the growth of their population, and he implied that they would welcome some form of birth control. But, as it turns out, birth control in the sense that the Church interdicts it is impossible to Lithia, and what Chtexa had in mind was obviously some form of fertility control, a proposition to which the Church gave its qualified assent many decades ago. So there I was, even on this small point forced again to realize that we had found on Lithia the most colossal rebuke to our aspirations that we had ever encountered: a people that seems to live with ease the kind of life which we associate with saints alone.

"Bear in mind that a Moslem who visited Lithia would find no such thing; though he would find a form of polygamy here, its purposes and methods would revolt him. Neither would a Taoist. Neither would a Zoroastrian, presuming that there were still such, or a classical Greek. But for the four of us—and I include you, Paul, for despite your tricks and your agnosticism you still subscribe to the Christian ethical doctrines enough to be put on the defensive when you flout them—what we four have here on Lithia is a coincidence which beggars description. It is more than an astronomical coincidence—that tired old metaphor for numbers that don't seem very large any more—it is a transfinite coincidence. It would take the shade of Cantor himself to do justice to the odds against it."

"Wait a minute," Agronski said. "Holy smoke. I don't know any anthropology, Mike, I'm lost here. I was with the Father up to the part about the mixed forest, but I don't have any standards to judge the rest. Is it so, what he says?"

"Yes, I think it's so," Michelis said slowly. "But there could be differences of opinion as to what it means, if anything. Ramon, go on."

"I will. There's still a good deal more to say. I'm still describing the planet, and more particularly the Lithians. The Lithians take a lot of explaining. What I've said about them thus far states only the most obvious fact. I could go on to point out many more, equally obvious facts. They have no nations and no regional rivalries, yet if you look at the map of Lithia—all those small continents and archipelagos separated by thousands of miles of seas—you'll see every reason why they *should* have developed such rivalries. They have emotions and passions, but are never moved by them to irrational acts. They have only one language, and have never had more than this same one—which again should have been made impossible by the geography of Lithia. They exist in complete harmony with everything, large and small, that they find in their world. In short, they're a people that couldn't exist—and yet does.

"Mike, I'll go beyond your view to say that the Lithians are the most perfect example of how human beings *ought* to behave that we're ever likely to find, for the very simple reason that they behave now the way human beings once behaved before we fell in our own Garden. I'd go even farther: as an example, the Lithians are useless to us, because until the coming of the Kingdom of God no substantial number of human beings will ever be able to imitate Lithian conduct. Human beings seem to have built-in imperfections that the Lithians lack—original sin, if you like—so that after thousands of years of trying, we are farther away than ever from our original emblems of conduct, while the Lithians have never departed from theirs.

"And don't allow yourselves to forget for an instant that these emblems of conduct are the same on both planets. That couldn't ever have happened, either—but it did.

"I'm now going to adduce another interesting fact about Lithian civilization. It is a fact, whatever you may think of its merits as evidence. It is this: that your Lithian is a creature of logic. Unlike Earthmen of all stripes, he has no gods, no myths, no legends. He has no belief in the supernatural —or, as we're calling it in our barbarous jargon these days, the 'paranormal'. He has no traditions. He has no taboos. He has no faiths, except for an impersonal belief that he and his lot are indefinitely improvable. He is as rational as a machine. Indeed, the only way in which we can distinguish the Lithian from an organic computer is his possession and use of a moral code.

"And that, I beg you to observe, *is completely irrational.* It is based upon a set of axioms, a set of propositions which were 'given' from the beginning—though your Lithian sees no need to postulate any Giver. The Lithian, for instance Chtexa, believes in the sanctity of the individual. Why? Not by reason, surely, for there is no way to reason to that proposition. It is an axiom. Or: Chtexa believes in the right of juridical defence, in the equality of all before the code. Why? It's possible to behave rationally *from* the proposition, but it's impossible to reason one's way *to* it. It's given. If you assume that the responsibility to the code varies with the individual's age, or with what family he happens to belong to, logical behaviour can follow from one of these assumptions, but there again one can't arrive *at* the principle by reason alone.

"One begins with belief: 'I think that all people ought to be equal before the law.' That is a statement of faith, nothing more. Yet Lithian civilization is so set up as to suggest that one can arrive at such basic axioms of Christianity, and of Western civilizations on Earth as a whole, by reason alone—in the plain face of the fact that one cannot. One rationalist's axiom is another one's madness."

"Those *are* axioms," Cleaver growled. "You don't arrive at them by faith, either. You don't arrive at them at all. They're self-evident—that's the definition of an axiom."

"It was until the physicists kicked that definition to pieces," Ruiz-Sanchez said, with a certain grim relish. "There's the axiom that only one parallel can be drawn to a given line. It may be self-evident, but it's also untrue, isn't it? And it's self-evident that matter is solid. Go on, Paul, you're a physicist yourself. Kick a stone for me, and say: 'Thus I refute Bishop Berkeley.' "

"It's peculiar," Michelis said in a low voice, "that Lithian culture should be so axiom-ridden, without the Lithians being aware of it. I hadn't formulated it in quite these terms before, Paul, but I've been disturbed myself at the bottomless *assumptions* that lie behind Lithian reasoning—all utterly unprobed, although in other respects the Lithians are very subtle. Look at what they've done in solid-state chemistry, for instance. It's a structure of the purest kind of reason, and yet when you get down to its fundamental assumptions you discover the axiom: 'Matter is real.' How can they know that? How did logic lead them to it? It's a very shaky notion, in my opinion. If I say that the atom is just a-hole-inside-a-hole-through-a-hole, how can they controvert me?"

"But their system works," Cleaver said.

"So does our solid-state theory—but we work from opposite axioms," Michelis said. "Whether it works or not isn't the issue. The question is, what is it that's working? I don't myself see how this immense structure of reason which the Lithians have evolved can stand for an instant. It doesn't seem to rest on anything. 'Matter is real' is a crazy proposition, when you come right down to it; all the evidence points in exactly the opposite direction."

"I'm going to tell you," Ruiz-Sanchez said. "You won't believe me, but I'm going to tell you anyhow, because I have to. *It stands because it's being propped up*. That's the simple answer and the whole answer. But first I want to add one more fact about the Lithians:

"They have complete physical recapitulation outside the body."

"What does that mean?" Agronski said.

"You know how a human child grows inside its mother's body. It is a one-celled animal to begin with, and then a simple metazoan resembling the fresh-water hydra or a simple jellyfish. Then, very rapidly, it goes through many other animal forms, including the fish, the amphibian, the reptile, the lower mammal, and finally becomes enough like a man to be born. I don't know how this was taught to you as a geologist, but biologists call the process *recapitulation.*

"The term assumes that the embryo is passing through the various stages of evolution which brought life from the single-celled organism to man, but on a contracted time scale. There is a point, for instance, in the development of the foetus when it has gills, though it never uses them. It has a tail almost to the very end of its time in the womb, and rarely it still has it when it is born; and the tail-wagging muscle, the pubococcygeus, persists in the adult—in women it becomes transformed into the contractile ring around the vestibule. The circulatory system of the foetus in the last month is still reptilian, and if it fails to be completely transformed before birth, the infant emerges as a 'blue baby' with patent ductus arteriosus, the tetralogy of Fallot, or a similar heart defect which allows venous blood to mix with arterial—which is the rule with terrestrial reptiles. And so on."

"I see," Agronski said. "It's a familiar idea; I just didn't recognize the term. I had no idea that the correspondence was that close either, come to think of it."

"Well, the Lithians, too, go through this series of metamorphoses as they grow up, but they go through it *outside* the bodies of their mothers. This whole planet is one huge womb. The Lithian female lays her eggs in her abdominal pouch, the eggs are fertilized, and then she goes to the sea to give birth to her children. What she bears is not a miniature of the marvellously evolved reptile which is the adult Lithian; far from it: instead, she hatches a fish, rather like a lamprey. The fish lives in the sea a while, and then develops rudimentary lungs and comes to live along the shore lines. Once it's stranded on the flats by the tides, the lungfish's pectoral fins become simple legs, and it squirms away through the mud, changing into an amphibian and learning to endure the rigours of living away from the sea. Gradually their limbs become stronger, and better set on their bodies, and they become the big froglike things we sometimes see down the hill, leaping in the moonlight, trying to get away from the crocodiles.

"Many of them do get away. They carry their habit of leaping with them into the jungle, and there they change once again, into the small, kangaroo-like reptiles we've all seen, fleeing from us among the trees—the things we called the 'hoppers'. The last change is circulatory—from the sauropsid blood system which still permits some mixing of venous and arterial blood, to the pteropsid system we see in Earthly birds, which supplies nothing to the brain but oxygenated arterial blood. At about the same time, they become homeostatic and homeothermic, as mammals are. Eventually, they emerge, fully grown, from the jungles, and take their places among the folk of the cities as young Lithians, ready for education.

"But they have *already* learned every trick of every environment that their world has to offer. Nothing is left them to learn but their own civilization; their instincts are fully matured, fully under control; their rapport with nature on Lithia is absolute; their adolescence is passed and can't distract their intellects—they are ready to become social beings in every possible sense."

Michelis locked his hands together again in an agony of quiet excitement, and looked up at Ruiz-Sanchez.

"But that—that's a discovery beyond price!" he whispered. "Ramon, that alone is worth our trip to Lithia. What a stunning, elegant—what a *beautiful* sequence—and what a brilliant piece of analysis!"

"It is very elegant," Ruiz-Sanchez said dispiritedly. "He who would damn us often gives us gracefulness. It is not the same thing as Grace."

"But is it as serious as all that?" Michelis said, his voice charged with urgency. "Ramon, surely your Church can't object to it in any way. Your theorists accepted recapitulation in the human embryo, and also the geological record that showed the same process in action over longer spans of time. Why not this?"

"The Church accepts facts, as it always accepts facts," Ruiz-Sanchez said. "But—as you yourself suggested hardly ten minutes ago—facts have a way of pointing in several different directions at once. The Church is as hostile to the doctrine of evolution—particularly to that part of it which deals with the descent of man—as it ever was, and with good reason."

"Or with obdurate stupidity," Cleaver said.

"I confess that I haven't followed the ins and outs of all this," Michelis said. "What is the present position?"

"There are really two positions. You may assume that man evolved as the evidence attempts to suggest that he did, and that somewhere along the line God intervened and infused a soul; this the Church regards as a tenable position, but does not endorse it, because historically it has led to cruelty to animals, who are also creations of God. Or, you may assume that the soul evolved along with the body; this view the Church entirely condemns. But these positions are not important, at least not in this company, compared with the fact that the Church thinks *the evidence itself* to be highly dubious."

"Why?" Michelis saia.

"Well, the Diet of Basra is hard to summarize in a few words, Mike; I hope you'll look it up when you get home. It's not exactly recent—it met in 1995, as I recall. In the meantime, look at the question very simply, with the original premises of the Scriptures in mind. If we assume that God created man, just for the sake of argument, did He create him perfect? I see no reason to suppose that He would have bothered with any lesser work. Is a man perfect without a navel? I don't know, but I'd be inclined to say that he isn't. Yet the first man—Adam, again, for the sake of argument—wasn't born of woman, and so didn't really *need* to have a navel. Did he have one? All the great painters of the Creation show him with one: I'd say that their theology was surely as sound as their aesthetics."

"What does that prove?" Cleaver said.

"That the geological record, and recapitulation too, do not necessarily prove the doctrine of the descent of man. Given *my* initial axiom, which is that God created everything from scratch, it's perfectly logical that he should have given Adam a navel, Earth a geological record, and the embryo the process of recapitulation. None of these need indicate a real past; all might be there because the creations involved would have been imperfect otherwise."

"Wow," Cleaver said. "And I used to think that Haertel relativity was abstruse."

"Oh, that's not a new argument by any means, Paul; it dates back nearly two centuries—a man named Gosse invented it, not the Diet of Basra. Anyhow, any system of thought becomes abstruse if it's examined long enough. I don't see why my belief in a God you can't accept is any more rarefied than Mike's vision of the atom as a-hole-inside-a-hole-through-a-hole. I expect that in the long run, when we get right down to the fundamental stuff of the universe, we'll find that there's nothing there at all—just no-things moving no-place through no-time. On the day that that happens, I'll have God and you will not—otherwise there'll be no difference between us.

"But in the meantime, what we have here on Lithia is very clear indeed. We have—and now I'm prepared to be blunt—a planet and a people propped up by the Ultimate Enemy. It is a gigantic trap prepared for all of us—for every man on Earth and off it. We can do nothing with it but reject it, nothing but say to it, *Retro me, Sathanas.* If we compromise with it in any way, we are damned."

"Why, Father?" Michelis said quietly.

"Look at the premises, Mike, *One:* Reason is always a sufficient guide. *Two:* The self-evident is always the real.

Three: Good works are an end in themselves. *Four:* Faith is irrelevant to right action. *Five:* Right action can exist without love. *Six:* Peace need not pass understanding. *Seven:* Ethics can exist without evil alternatives. *Eight:* Morals can exist without conscience. *Nine:* Goodness can exist without God. *Ten*—but do I really need to go on? We have heard all these propositions before, and we know What proposes them."

"A question," Michelis said, and his voice was painfully gentle. "To set such a trap, you must allow your Adversary to be creative. Isn't that—a heresy, Ramon? Aren't you now subscribing to a heretical belief? Or did the Diet of Basra——"

For a moment, Ruiz-Sanchez could not answer. The question cut to the heart. Michelis had found the priest out in the full agony of his defection, his belief betrayed, and he in full betrayal of his Church. He had hoped that it would not happen so soon.

"It is a heresy," he said at last, his voice like iron. "It is called Manichaeanism and the Diet did not readmit it." He swallowed. "But since you ask, Mike, I do not see how we can avoid it now. I do not do this gladly, Mike, but we have seen these demonstrations before. The demonstration, for instance, in the rocks—the one that was supposed to show how the horse evolved from Eohippus, but which somehow never managed to convince the whole of mankind. If the Adversary *is* creative, there is at least some divine limitation that rules that Its creations be maimed. Then came the discovery of intra-uterine recapitulation, which was to have clinched the case for the descent of man. That one failed because the Adversary put it into the mouth of a man named Haeckel, who was so rabid an atheist that he took to faking the evidence to make the case still more convincing. Nevertheless, despite their flaws, these were both very subtle arguments, but the Church is not easily swayed; it is founded on a rock.

"But now we have, on Lithia, a new demonstration, both

the subtlest and at the same time the crudest of all. It will sway many people who could have been swayed in no other way, and who lack the intelligence or the background to understand that it is a rigged demonstration. It seems to show us evolution in action on an inarguable scale. It is supposed to settle the question once and for all, to rule God out of the picture, to snap the chains that have held Peter's rock together all these many centuries. Henceforth there is to be no more question; henceforth there is to be no more God, but only phenomenology—and, of course, behind the scenes, within the hole that's inside the hole that's through a hole, the Great Nothing itself, the Thing that has never learned any word but *No* since it was cast flaming from heaven. It has many other names, but we know the name that counts. That will be all that's left us.

"Paul, Mike, Agronski, I have nothing more to say than this: We are all of us standing on the brink of Hell. By the grace of God, we may still turn back. We must turn back—for I at least think that this is our last chance."

IX

THE vote was cast, and that was that. The commission was tied, and the question would be thrown open again in higher echelons on Earth, which would mean tying Lithia up for years to come. *Proscripted area pending further study*. The planet was now, in effect, on the Index Expurgatorius.

The ship arrived the next day. The crew was not much surprised to find that the two opposing factions of the commission were hardly speaking to each other. It often happened that way.

The four commission members cleaned up in almost complete silence the house in Xoredeshch Sfath that the Lithians had given them. Ruiz-Sanchez packed the dark blue book with the gold stamping without being able to look at it except out of the corner of his eye, but even obliquely he could not help seeing its long-familiar title:

FINNEGANS WAKE
James Joyce

So much for his pride in his solution of the case of conscience the novel proposed. He felt as though he himself had been collated, bound and stamped, a tortured human text for future generations of Jesuits to explicate and argue.

He had rendered the verdict he had found it necessary for him to render. But he knew that it was not a final verdict, even for himself, and certainly not for the U.N., let alone the Church. Instead, the verdict itself would be a knotty question for members of his Order yet unborn:

Did Father Ruiz-Sanchez correctly interpret the Divine case, and did this ruling, if so, follow from it?

Except, of course, that they would not use his name—but what good would it do them to use an alias? Surely there would never be any way to disguise the original of *this* problem. Or was that pride again—or misery? It had been Mephistopheles himself who had said, *Solamen miseris socios habuisse doloris. . . .*

"Let's go, Father. It'll be take-off time shortly."

"All ready, Mike."

It was only a short journey to the clearing, where the mighty spindle of the ship stood ready to weave its way back through the geodesics of deep space to the sun that shone on Peru. There was even some sunlight here, piercing now and then through low, scudding clouds; but it had been raining all morning, and would begin again soon enough.

The baggage went on board smoothly and without any fuss. So did the specimens, the films, the tapes, the special reports, the recordings, the sample cases, the slide boxes, the vivariums, the type cultures, the pressed plants, the animal cages, the tubes of soil, the chunks of ore, the Lithian manuscripts in their atmospheres of helium—everything was lifted decorously by the cranes and swung inside.

Agronski went up the cleats to the air lock first, with Michelis following him, a barracks bag slung over one shoulder. On the ground Cleaver was stowing some last-minute bit of gear, something that seemed to require delicate, almost reverent bedding down before the cranes could be allowed to take it in their indifferent grip; Cleaver was fanatically motherly about his electronic apparatus. Ruiz-Sanchez took advantage of the delay to look around once more at the near margins of the forest.

At once, he saw Chtexa. The Lithian was standing at the entrance to the path the Earthmen themselves had taken from the city to reach the ship. He was carrying something.

Cleaver swore under his breath and undid something he had just done to do it in another way. Ruiz-Sanchez raised his hand. Immediately Chtexa walked toward the ship, in great loping strides which nevertheless seemed almost leisurely.

"I wish you a good journey," the Lithian said, "wherever you may go. I wish also that your road may lead back to this world at some future time. I have brought you the gift that I sought before to give you, if the moment is now appropriate."

Cleaver had straightened and was now glaring up suspiciously at the Lithian. Since he did not understand the language, he was unable to find anything to which he could object. He simply stood there and radiated unwelcomeness.

"Thank you," Ruiz-Sanchez said. This creature of Satan made him miserable all over again, made him feel intolerably in the wrong. Yet how could Chtexa know——?

The Lithian was holding out to him a small vase, sealed at the top and provided with two gently looping handles. The gleaming porcelain of which it had been made still carried inside it, under the glaze, the fire which had formed it; it was iridescent, alive with long quivering festoons and plumes of rainbows, and the form as a whole would have made any potter of Greece abandon his trade in shame. It was so beautiful that one could imagine no use for it at all. Certainly one could not make a lamp of it, or fill it with left-over beets and put it in the refrigerator. Besides, it would take up too much space.

"This is the gift," Chtexa said. "It is the finest container yet to come out of Xoredeshch Gton. The material of which it is made includes traces of every element to be found on Lithia, even including iron, and thus, as you see, it shows the colours of every shade of emotion and of thought. On Earth, it will tell Earthmen much of Lithia."

"We will be unable to analyse it," Ruiz-Sanchez said. "It is too perfect to destroy, too perfect even to open."

"Ah, but we wish you to open it," Chtexa said. "For it contains our other gift."

"Another gift?"

"Yes, and a more important one. It is a fertilized, living egg of our species. Take it with you. By the time you reach Earth, it will have hatched, and will be ready to grow up with you in your strange and marvellous world. The container is the gift of all of us; but the child inside is my gift, for it is my child."

Appalled, Ruiz-Sanchez took the vase in trembling hands, as though he expected it to explode—as indeed he did. It shook with subdued flame in his grip.

"Good-bye," Chtexa said. He turned and walked away, back toward the entrance to the path. Cleaver watched him go, shading his eyes.

"Now what was that all about?" the physicist said. "The Snake couldn't have made a bigger thing of it if he'd been handing you his own head on a platter. And all the time it was only a jug!"

Ruiz-Sanchez did not answer. He could not have spoken even to himself. He turned away and began to ascend the cleats, cradling the vase carefully in one elbow. It was not the gift he had hoped to bring to the holy city for the grand indulgence of all mankind, no; but it was all he had.

While he was still climbing, a shadow passed rapidly over

the hull: Cleaver's last crate, being borne aloft into the hold by a crane.

Then he was in the air lock, with the rising whine of the ship's Nernst generators around him. A long shaft of sunlight was cast ahead of him, picking out his shadow on the deck.

After a moment, a second shadow overlaid and blurred his own: Cleaver's. Then the light dimmed and went out.

The air lock door slammed.

BOOK TWO

X

At first Egtverchi knew nothing, in the peculiarly regular and chilly womb where he floated, except his name. That was inherited, and marked in a twist of desoxyribonucleic acid upon one of his genes; farther up on the same chromosome, the x-chromosome, another gene carried his father's name: Chtexa. And that was all. At the moment he had begun his independent life, as a zygote or fertilized egg, that had been written down in letters of chromatin: his name was Egtverchi, his race Lithian, his sex male, his inheritance continuous back through Lithian centuries to the moment when the world of Lithia began. He did not need to understand this; it was implicit.

But it was dark, chilly, and too regular in the pouch. Tiny as a speck of pollen, Egtverchi drifted in the fluid which sustained him, from wall to smoothly curved and unnaturally glazed wall, not conscious yet, but constantly, chemically reminded that he was not in his mother's pouch. No gene that he carried bore his mother's name, but he knew—not in his brain, for he had none yet, but by feel, with purely chemical revulsion—whose child he was, of what race he was, and where he should be: *not here.*

And so he grew—and drifted, seeking to attach himself at every circuit to the chilly glass-lined pouch which rejected him always. By the time of gastrulation, the attachment reflex had run its course and he forgot it. Now he merely floated, knowing once more only what he had known at the beginning: his race Lithian, his sex male, his name Egtverchi, his father Chtexa, his life due to begin; and his birth world as bitter and black as the inside of a jug.

Then his notochord formed, and his nerve cells congregated in a tiny knot at one end of it. Now he had a front end and a hind end, as well as an address. He also had a brain —and now he was a fish—a spawn, not even a fingerling yet, circling and circling in the cold enclave of sea.

That sea was tideless and lightless, but there was some motion in it, the slow roll of convection currents. Sometimes, too, something went through it which was not a current, forcing him far down toward the bottom, or against the walls. He did not know the name of this force—as a fish he knew nothing, only circled with the endlessness of his hunger —but he fought it, as he would have fought cold or heat. There was a sense in his head, aft of his gills, which told him which way was up. It told him, too, that a fish in its natural medium has mass and inertia, but no weight. The sporadic waves of gravity—or acceleration—which whelmed through the lightless water were no part of his instinctual world, and when they were over he was often swimming desperately on his back.

There came a time when there was no more food in the little sea; but time and the calculations of his father were kind to him. Precisely at that time the weight force returned more powerfully than had even been suggested as possible before, and he was driven to sluggish immobility for a long period, fanning the water at the bottom of the jug past his gills with slow exhausted motions.

It was over at last, and then the little sea was moving jerkily from side to side, up and down, and forward. Egtverchi was now about the size of a larval fresh-water eel. Beneath his pectoral bones twin sacs were forming, which connected with no other system of his body, but were becoming more and more richly supplied with capillaries. There was nothing inside the sacs but a little gaseous nitrogen—just enough to equalize the pressure. In due course, they would be rudimentary lungs.

Then there was light.

To begin with, the top of the world was taken off. Egtverchi's eyes would not have focused at this stage in any case and, like any evolved creature, he was subject to the neo-Lamarckian laws which provide that even a completed inherited ability will develop badly if it is formed in the absence of any opportunity to function. As a Lithian, with a Lithian's special sensitivity to the modifying pressures of environment, the long darkness had done him less potential damage than it surely would have done another creature—say, an Earth creature; nevertheless, he would pay for it in due course. Now, he could sense no more than that in the *up* direction (now quite stable and unchanging) there was light.

He rose toward it, his pectoral fins strumming the warm harps of the water.

Father Ramon Ruiz-Sanchez, late of Peru, late of Lithia, and always Fellow in the Society of Jesus, watched the surfacing, darting little creature with surfacing strange emotions. He could not help feeling for the sinuous eft the pity that he felt for every living thing, and an aesthetic delight in the flashing unpredictable certainty of its motions. But this little animal was Lithian.

He had had more time than he had wanted to explore the black ruin that underlay his position. Ruiz-Sanchez had never underestimated the powers which evil could still exercise, powers retained—even by general agreement within the Church—after its fall from beside the throne of the Most High. As a Jesuit he had examined and debated far too many cases of conscience to believe that evil is unsubtle or impotent. But that among these powers the Adversary numbered the puissance to create—no, that had never entered his head, not until Lithia. That power, at least, had to be of God, and of God only. To think that there could be more than one demiurge was outright heresy, and a very ancient heresy at that.

So be it, it was so, heretical or not. The whole of Lithia, and in particular the whole of the dominant, rational, infinitely admirable race of Lithians, had been created by Evil, out of Its need to confront men with a new, a specifically intellectual seduction, springing like Minerva from the brow of Jove. Out of that unnatural birth, as out of the fabled one, there was to come a symbolic clapping of palms to foreheads for everyone who could admit for an instant that any power but God could create; a ringing, splitting ache in the skull of theology; a moral migraine; even a cosmological shell shock, for Minerva was the mistress of Mars, on Earth as—undoubtedly, Ruiz-Sanchez remembered with anguish—as it is in heaven.

After all, he had been there, and he knew.

But all that could wait a little while, at least. For the moment it was sufficient that the little creature, so harmlessly like a three-inch eel, was still alive and apparently healthy. Ruiz-Sanchez picked up a beaker of water, cloudy with thousands of cultured *Cladocera* and Cyclops, and poured nearly half of it into the subtly glowing amphora. The infant Lithian flashed instantly away into the darkness, in chase after the nearly microscopic crustaceans. Appetite, the priest reflected, is a universal barometer of health.

"Look at him go," a soft voice said beside his shoulder. He looked up, smiling. The speaker was Liu Meid, the U.N. laboratory chief whose principal charge the Lithian child would be for many months. A small, black-haired girl with an expression of almost childlike calm, she peered into the vase expectantly, waiting for the imago to reappear.

"They won't make him sick, do you think?" she said.

"I hope not," Ruiz-Sanchez said. "They're Earthly, it's true, but Lithian metabolism is remarkably like ours. Even the blood pigment is an analogue of hemoglobin, though the metal base isn't iron, of course. Their plankton includes forms very like Cyclops and the water flea. No; if he's survived the trip, I dare say our subsequent care won't kill him, not even with kindness."

"The trip?" Liu said slowly. "How could that have hurt him?"

"Well, I really can't say exactly. It was simply the chance that we took. Chtexa—that was his father—presented him to us inside this vase, already sealed in. We had no way of knowing what provisions Chtexa had made for his child against the various strains of space flight. And we didn't dare look inside to see; if there was one thing of which I was certain, it was that Chtexa wouldn't have sealed the vase without a reason; after all, he does know the physiology of his own race better than any of us, even Dr. Michelis or myself."

"That's what I was getting at," Liu said.

"I know; but you see, Liu, Chtexa *doesn't* know space flight. Oh, ordinary flight stresses are no secret to him—the Lithians fly jets; it was the Haertel overdrive that *I* was worried about. You'll remember the fantastic time effects that Garrard went through on that first successful Centaurus flight. I couldn't explain the Haertel equations to Chtexa even if I'd had the time. They're classified against him; besides, he couldn't have understood them, because Lithian math doesn't include transfinites. And time is of the utmost importance in Lithian gestation."

"Why?" Liu said. She peered down into the amphora again, with an instinctive smile.

The question touched a nerve which had lain exposed in Ruiz-Sanchez for a long time. He said carefully: "Because they have physical recapitulation outside the body, Liu. That's why that creature in there is a fish; as an adult, it will be a reptile, though with a pteropsid circulatory system and a number of other unreptilian features. The Lithian females lay their eggs in the sea——"

"But it's fresh water in the jug."

"No, it's sea water; the Lithian seas are not so salt as ours. The egg hatches into a fishlike creature, such as you see in there; then the fish develops lungs and is beached by the tides. I used to hear them barking in Xoredeshch Sfath—they barked all night long, blowing the water out of their lungs and developing their diaphragm masculature."

Unexpectedly, he shuddered. The recollection of the sound was far more disturbing than the sound itself had been. Then, he had not known what it was—or, no, he had known that, but he had not known what it meant.

"Eventually the lungfish develop legs and lose their tails, like a tadpole, and go off into the Lithian forests as true amphibians. After a while, their respiratory system loses its dependence upon the skin as an auxiliary source, so they no longer need to stay near water. Eventually, they become true adults, a very advanced type of reptile, marsupial, bipedal, homeostatic—and highly intelligent. The new adults come out of the jungle and are ready for education in the cities."

Liu took a deep breath. "How marvellous," she whispered.

"It is just that," he said sombrely. "Our own children go through nearly the same changes in the womb, but they're protected throughout; the Lithian children have to run the gauntlet of every ecology their planet possesses. That's why I was afraid of the Haertel overdrive. We insulated the vase against the drive fields as best we could, but in a maturation process so keyed to the appearances of evolution, a time slowdown could have been crucial. In Garrard's case, he was slowed down to an hour a second, then whipped up to a second an hour, then back again, and so on along a sine wave. If there'd been the slightest break in the insulation, something like that might have happened to Chtexa's child, with unknowable results. Evidently, there was no leak, but I was worried."

The girl thought about it. In order to keep himself from thinking about it, for he had already pondered himself in dwindling spirals to a complete, central impasse, Ruiz-Sanchez watched her think. She was always restful to watch, and Ruiz-Sanchez needed rest. It now seemed to him that he had had no rest at all since the moment when he had fainted on the threshold of the house in Xoredeshch Sfath, directly into the astonished Agronski's arms.

Liu had been born and raised in the state of Greater New

York. It was Ruiz-Sanchez's most heartfelt compliment that nobody would have guessed it; as a Peruvian he hated the nineteen-million-man megalopolis with an intensity he would have been the first to characterize as unchristian. There was nothing in the least hectic or harried about Liu. She was calm, slow, serene, gentle, her reserve unshakeable without being in the least cold or compulsive, her responses to everything that impinged upon her as direct and uncomplicated as a kitten's; her attitude toward her fellow men virtually unsuspicious not out of naïveté, but out of her confidence that the essential Liu was so inviolable as to prevent anyone even from wanting to violate it.

These were the abstract terms which first came to Ruiz-Sanchez's mind, but immediately he came to grief over a transitional thought. As nobody would take Liu for a New Yorker—even her speech betrayed not a one of the eight dialects, all becoming more and more mutually unintelligible, which were spoken in the city, and in particular one would never have guessed that her parents spoke nothing but Bronix—so nobody could have taken her for a female laboratory technician.

This was not a line of thought that Ruiz-Sanchez felt comfortable in following, but it was too obvious to ignore. Liu was as small-boned and intensely nubile as a geisha. She dressed with exquisite modesty, but it was not the modesty of concealment, but of quietness, of the desire to put around a firmly feminine body clothes that would be ashamed of nothing, but would also advertise nothing. Inside her soft colours, she was a Venus Callipygous with a slow, sleepy smile, inexplicably unaware that she—let alone anybody else—was expected by nature and legend to worship continually the firm dimpled slopes of her own back.

There now, that was quite enough; more than enough. The little eel chasing fresh-water crustaceae in the ceramic womb presented problems enough, some of which were about to become Liu's. It would hardly be suitable to complicate Liu's task by so much as an unworthy speculation, though it be communicated by no more than a curious glance. Ruiz-Sanchez was confident enough of his own ability to keep himself in the path ordained for him, but it would not do to burden this grave sweet girl with a suspicion her training had never equipped her to meet.

He turned away hastily and walked to the vast glass west wall of the laboratory, which looked out over the city thirty-four stories from the street—not a great height, but more than sufficient for Ruiz-Sanchez. The thundering, heat-hazed nineteen-million-man megalopolis repelled him, as usual—or perhaps even more than usual, after his long stay in the quiet streets of Xoredeshch Sfath. But at least he had the consolation of knowing that he did not have to live here the rest of his life.

In a way, the state of Manhattan was only a relict anyhow, not only politically, but physically. What could be seen of it from here was an enormous multi-headed ghost. The crumbling pinnacles were ninety per cent empty, and remained so right around the clock. At any given moment most of the population of the state (and of any other of the thousand-odd city-states around the globe) was underground.

The underground area was self-sufficient. It had its own thermonuclear power sources; its own tank farms, and its thousands of miles of illuminated plastic pipe through which algae suspensions flowed richly, grew unceasingly; decades worth of food and medical supplies in cold storage; water-processing equipment which was a completely closed circuit, so that it could recover moisture even from the air and from the city's own sewage; and air intakes equipped to remove gas, virus, fall-out particles or all three at once. The city-states were equally independent of any central government; each was under the hegemony of a Target Area Authority modelled on the old, self-policing port authorities of the previous century—out of which, indeed, they had evolved inevitably.

This fragmentation of the Earth had come about as the end product of the international shelter race of 1960–85.

The fission-bomb race, which had begun in 1945, was effectively over five years later; the fusion-bomb race and the race for the intercontinental ballistic missile had each taken five years more. The Shelter race had taken longer, not because any new physical knowledge or techniques had been needed to bring it to fruition—quite the contrary—but because of the vastness of the building programme it involved.

Defensive though the shelter race seemed on the surface, it had taken on all the characteristics of a classical arms race—for the nation that lagged behind invited instant attack. Nevertheless, there had been a difference. The shelter race had been undertaken under the dawning realization that the threat of nuclear war was not only imminent but transcendent; it could happen at any instant, but its failure to break out at any given time meant that it had to be lived with for at least a century, and perhaps five centuries. Thus the race was not only hectic, but long-range——

And, like all arms races, it defeated itself in the end, this time because those who planned it had planned for too long a span of time. The shelter economy was world-wide now, but the race had hardly ended when signs began to appear that people simply would not live willingly under such an economy for long; certainly not for five hundred years, and probably not for a century. The Corridor Riots of 1993 were the first major sign; since then, there had been many more.

The riots had provided the United Nations with the excuse it needed to set up, at long last, a real supernational government—a world state with teeth in it. The riots had provided the excuse—and the shelter economy, with its neo-Hellenic fragmentation of political power, had given the U.N. the means.

Theoretically, that should have solved everything. Nuclear war was no longer likely between the member states; the threat was gone . . . but how do you *un*build a shelter economy? An economy which cost twenty-five billion dollars a year, every year for twenty-five years, to build? An economy now embedded in the face of the Earth in uncountable billions of tons of concrete and steel, to a depth of more than a mile? It could not be undone; the planet would be a mausoleum for the living from now until the Earth itself perished: gravestones, gravestones, gravestones . . .

The word tolled in Ruiz-Sanchez's ears, distantly. The infrabass of the buried city's thunder shook the glass in front of him. Mingled with it there was an ominous grinding sound of unrest, more marked than he had ever heard it before—like the noise of a cannon ball rolling furiously around and around in a rickety, splintering wooden track. . . .

"Dreadful, isn't it?" Michelis's voice said at his shoulder. Ruiz-Sanchez shot a surprised glance at the big chemist—not surprised that he had not heard Michelis enter, but that Mike was speaking to him again.

"It is," he said. "I'm glad you noticed it too, I thought it just might be hypersensitivity on my part—from having been away so long."

"It might well be that," Michelis agreed gravely. "I was away myself."

Ruiz-Sanchez shook his head.

"No, I think it's real," he said. "These are intolerable conditions to ask people to live under. And it's more than a matter of making them live ninety days out of every hundred at the bottom of a hole. After all, they think of living every day of their lives on the verge of destruction. We trained their parents to think that way, otherwise there'd never have been enough taxes to pay for the shelters. And of course the children have been brought up to think that too. It's inhuman."

"Is it?" Michelis said. "People lived all their lives on the verge for centuries—all the way up until Pasteur. How long ago was that?"

"Only about 1860," Ruiz-Sanchez said. "But no, it's quite different now. The pestilence was capricious; one's children might survive it; but fusion bombs are catholic." He winced involuntarily. "And there it is. A moment ago, I caught myself thinking that the shadow of destruction we labour under now is not only imminent but transcendent; I was burlesquing a tragedy; death in premedical days was always both imminent and immanent, impending and indwelling—but it was never transcendent. In those days, only God was impending, indwelling *and* transcendent all at once, and that was their hope. Today, we've given them Death instead."

"Sorry," Michelis said, his bony face suddenly turning flinty. "You know I can't argue with you on those grounds, Ramon. I've already been burned once. Once is enough."

The chemist turned away. Liu, who had been making a serial dilution at the long bench, was holding the ranked test tubes up to the daylight, and peeping up at Michelis from under her half-shut eyelids. She looked promptly away again as Ruiz-Sanchez's gaze fell on her face. He did not know whether she knew that he had caught her; but the tubes rattled a little in the rack as she put them down again.

"Excuse me," he said. "Liu, this is Dr. Michelis, one of my confrères on the commission to Lithia. Mike, this is Dr. Liu Meid, who'll be taking care of Chtexa's child for an indefinite period, more or less under my supervision. She's one of the world's best xenozoologists."

"How do you do," Mike said gravely. "Then you and the Father stand *in loco parentis* to our Lithian guest. It's a heavy responsibility for a young woman, I should think."

The Jesuit felt a thoroughly unchristian impulse to kick the tall chemist in the shins; but there seemed to be no conscious malice in Michelis's voice.

The girl merely looked down at the ground and sucked in her breath between slightly parted lips. "*Ah*-so-*deska*," she said, almost inaudibly.

Michelis's eyebrows went up, but in a moment it became obvious that Liu was not going to say anything more, to him, right now. With a slight huff of embarrassment, Michelis addressed himself to the priest, catching him erasing the traces of a smile.

"So I'm all feet," Michelis said, grinning ruefully. "But I won't have time to practise my manners for a while yet.

There are lots of loose ends to tie up. Ramon, how soon do you think you can leave Chtexa's child in Dr. Meid's hands? We've been asked to do a non-classified version of the Lithia report——"

"We?"

"Yes. Well, you and I."

"What about Cleaver and Agronski?"

"Cleaver's not available," Michelis said. "I don't offhand know where he is. And for some reason they don't want Agronski; maybe he doesn't have enough letters after his name. It's *The Journal of Interstellar Research*, and you know how stuffy they are—they're *nouveau-riche* in terms of prestige, and that makes them more academic than the academicians. But I think it would be worth doing, just to get some of our data out into the open. Can you find the time?"

"I think so," Ruiz-Sanchez said thoughtfully. "Providing it can be sandwiched in between getting Chtexa's child born, and my pilgrimage."

Michelis raised his eyebrows again. "That's right, this is a Holy Year, isn't it?"

"Yes," Ruiz-Sanchez said.

"Well, I think we can work it in," Michelis said. "But—excuse me for prying, Ramon, but you don't strike me as a man in urgent need of the great pardon. Does this mean that you've changed your mind about Lithia?"

"No, I haven't changed my mind," Ruiz-Sanchez said quietly. "We are all in need of the great pardon, Mike. But I'm not going to Rome for that."

"Then——"

"I expect to be tried there for heresy."

XI

THERE was light on the mud flat where Egtverchi lay, somewhere eastward of Eden, but day and night had not been created yet, nor was there yet wind or tide to whelm him as he barked the water from his itchy lungs and whooped in the fiery air. Hopefully he squirmed with his new forelimbs, and there was motion; but there was no place to go, and no one and nothing from which to escape. The unvarying, glareless light was comfortingly like that of a perpetually overcast sky, but Somebody had failed to provide for that regular period of darkness and negation during which an animal consolidates its failures and seeks in the depths of its undreaming self for sufficient joy to greet still another morning.

"Animals have no souls," said Descartes, throwing a cat out the window to prove, if not his point, at least his faith in it. The timid genius of mechanism, who threw cats well but Popes badly, had never met a true automaton, and so never saw that what the animal lacks is not a soul, but a mind. A computer which can fill the parameters of the Haertel equations for all possible values and deliver them in two and a half seconds is an intellectual genius but, compared even to a cat, it is an emotional moron.

As an animal which does not think, but instead responds to each minute experience with the fullness of immediately apprehended—and immediately forgotten—emotions which involve its whole body, needs the temporary death of nightfall to protract its life, so the newly emerged animal body requires the battles appointed to the day in order to become, at long last, the somnolent self-confident adult which has been written aforetime in its genes; and here, too, Somebody had failed Egtverchi. There was soap in his mud, a calculated percentage which allowed him to thrash on the floor of his cage without permitting him to make enough progress to bump his head against its walls. This was conservative of his head, but it wasted the muscles of his limbs. When his croaking days were over, and he was transformed into a totally air-breathing, leaping thing, he did not leap well.

This too had been arranged, in a sense. There was nothing in this childhood of his from which he needed to leap away in terror, nor was there any place in it to which a small leap could have carried him. Even the smallest jump ended with an invisible bang and a slithering fall for the end of which, harmless though it invariably proved to be, no instinct prepared him, and for which no learning-reflex helped him to cultivate a graceful recovery. Besides, an animal with a perpetually sprained tail cannot be graceful regardless of its instincts.

Finally, he forgot how to leap entirely, and simply sat huddled until the next transformation overcame him, looking back dully at the many bobbing heads that were beginning to ring him round during his every waking hour. By the time he realized that all these watchers were alive like himself, and much larger than he was, his instincts were so far submerged as to produce in him nothing more than a vague alarm which resulted in no action.

The new transformation turned him into a weak and spindly walker with no head for distance, oversized though it was. It was here that Somebody saw to it that he was transferred to the terrarium.

Here at last the hormones of his true adolescence awakened and began to flow in his blood. The proper responses for a world something like this tiny jungle had been written imperatively upon every chromosome in his body; here, all at once, he was almost at home. He roved through the verdure of the terrarium on his shaky shanks with a counterfeit of gladness, looking for something to flee, something to fight, something to eat, something to learn. Yet in the long run he hardly found even a place to sleep, for in the terrarium night was as unknown as ever.

Here he also became aware for the first time that there were differences among the creatures who looked in at him and sometimes molested him. There were two who were almost always to be seen, either alone or together. They were always the molesters, as well—except—except that it was not always exactly molestation, for sometimes these beings with their sharp stings and their rough hands would give him something to eat which he had never tasted before, or do something else to him which pleased as much as it annoyed. He did not understand this relationship at all, and he did not like it.

After a while, he hid from all the watchers except these two—and even from them most of the time, for he was always sleepy. When he wanted them, he would call: "Szan-tchez!" (For he could not say "Liu" at all; his mesentery-tied tongue and almost cleft palate would never master so demanding a combination of liquid sounds—that had to wait for his adulthood.)

But eventually he stopped calling, and took to squatting apathetically beside the pond in the centre of the miniature jungle. When on the last night of his lizard existence he laid his bulging brain case again in that hollow of mosses where there was the most dimness, he knew in his blood that on the morrow, when he awoke into his doom as a thinking creature, he would be old with that age which curses those who have never even for an instant been young. Tomorrow he would be a thinking creature, but the weariness was on him tonight. . . .

And so he awoke; and so the world was changed. The multiple doors from sense to soul had closed; suddenly, the world was an abstract; he had made that crossing from animal to automaton which had caused all the trouble eastward of Eden in 4004 B.C.

He was not a man, but he would pay the toll on that bridge all the same. From this point on, nobody would ever be able to guess what he felt in his animal soul, least of all Egtverchi himself.

"But what is he thinking about?" Liu said wonderingly, staring up at the huge, grave Lithian head which bent down upon them from the other side of the transparent pyroceram door. Egtverchi—he had told them his name very early—could hear her, of course, despite the division of the laboratory into two; but he said nothing. Thus far, he was anything but talkative, though he was a voracious reader.

Ruiz did not respond for a while, though the nine-foot young Lithian awed and puzzled him quite as much as he did Liu—and for better reasons. He looked sidewise at Michelis.

The chemist was ignoring them both. Ruiz could understand that well enough, as far as he himself was concerned; the attempt to write a joint but impartial report on the Lithia expedition for the *J.I.R.* had proven disastrous for the already tense relationship between the two scientists. But that same tension, he could see, was distressing Liu without her being quite aware of it, and that he could not let pass; she was innocent. He mustered a last-ditch attempt to draw Mike out.

"This is their learning period," he said. "Necessarily, they spend most of it listening. They're like the old legend of the wolf boy, who is raised by animals and comes into human cities without even knowing human speech—except that the Lithians don't learn speech in infancy and so have no block against learning it in young adulthood. To do that, they must listen very hard—most wolf boys never learn to talk at all—and that's what he's doing."

"But why won't he at least answer questions?" Liu said troubledly, without quite looking at Michelis. "How is he going to learn if he won't practise?"

"He hasn't anything to tell us yet, by his lights," Ruiz said. "And for him, we lack the authority to put questions. Any adult Lithian could question him, but obviously we don't qualify—and what Mike calls the foster-parent relationship couldn't mean anything to a creature adapted to a solitary childhood."

Michelis did not respond.

"He used to call us," Liu said sadly. "At least, he used to call you."

"That's different. That's the pleasure response; it has nothing to do with authority, or affection either. If you were to put an electrode into the septal or caudate nucleus areas in the brain of a cat, or a rat, so that they could stimulate themselves electrically by pushing a pedal, you could train them to do almost anything that's within their powers, for no other reward but that jolt in the head. In the same way, a cat or a rat or a dog will learn to respond to its name, or to initiate some action, in order to gain pleasure. But you don't expect the animal to talk to you or answer questions just because it can do that."

"I never heard of the brain experiments," Liu said. "I think that's horrible."

"I think so too," Ruiz said. "It's an old line of research that got side-tracked somehow. I've never understood why some of our megalomaniacs didn't follow it up in human beings. A dictatorship founded on that device might really last a thousand years. But it had nothing to do with what you're asking of Egtverchi. When he's ready to talk, he'll talk. In the meantime, we don't have the stature to compel him to answer questions. For that, we would have to be twelve-foot Lithian adults."

Egtverchi's eyes filmed, and he brought his hands together suddenly.

"You are already too tall," his harsh voice said over the annunciator system.

Liu clapped her hands together in delight imitation.

"See, see, Ramon, you're wrong! Egtverchi, what do you mean? Tell us!"

Egtverchi said experimentally: "Liu. Liu. Liu."

"Yes, yes. That's right, Egtverchi. Go on, go on—what did you mean—tell us!"

"Liu." Egtverchi seemed satisfied. The colours in his wattles died down. He was again almost a statue.

After a moment, there was an explosive snort from Michelis. Liu turned to him with a start, and, without really meaning to, so did Ruiz.

But it was too late. The big New Englander had already turned his back on them, as though disgusted at himself for having broken his own silence. Slowly, Liu too turned her back, if only to hide her face from everyone, even Egtverchi.

Ruiz was left standing alone at the vertex of the tetrahedron of disaffection.

"This is going to be a fine performance for a prospective citizen of the United Nations to turn in," Michelis said suddenly, bitterly, from somewhere behind his shoulder. "I suppose you expected nothing else when you asked me here. What moved you to tell me what vast progress he was making? As I got the story, he ought to have been propounding theorems by this time."

"Time", Egtverchi said, "is a function of change, and change is the expression of the relative validity of two propositions, one of which contains a time *t* and the other a time *t*-prime, which differ from each other in no respect except that one contains the co-ordinate *t* and the other the co-ordinate *t*-prime."

"That's all very well," Michelis said coldly, turning to look up at the great head. "But I know where you got it from. If you're only a parrot, you're not going to be a citizen of *this* culture; you can take that from me."

"Who are you?" Egtverchi said.

"I'm your sponsor, God help me," Michelis said. "I know my own name, and I know what kind of record goes with it. If you expect to be a citizen, Egtverchi, you'll have to do better than pass yourself off as Bertrand Russell, or Shakespeare for that matter."

"I don't think he has any such notion," Ruiz said. "We explained the citizenship proposal to him, but he didn't give us any sign that he understood it. He just finished reading the *Principia* last week, so there's nothing unlikely about his feeding it back. He does that now and then."

"In first-order feedback," Egtverchi said somnolently, "if the connections are reversed, any small disturbance will be self-aggravating. In second-order feedback, going outside normal limits will force random changes in the network which will stop only when the system is stable again."

"God damn it!" Mike said savagely. "Now where did he get *that*? Stop it, you! You don't fool me for a minute!"

Egtverchi closed his eyes and fell silent.

Suddenly Michelis shouted: "Speak up, damn it!"

Without opening his eyes, Egtverchi said: "Hence the system can develop vicarious function if some of its parts are destroyed." Then he was silent again; he was asleep. He was often asleep, even these days.

"Fugue," Ruiz said softly. "He thought you were threatening him."

"Mike," Liu said, turning to him with a kind of desperate earnestness, "what do you think you're doing? He won't answer you, he can't answer you, especially when you speak to him like that! He's only a child, whatever you think when you have to look up at him! Obviously he learns many of these things by rote. Sometimes he says them when they seem to be apposite, but when we question him, he never carries it any farther. Why don't you give him a chance? *He* didn't ask you to bring any citizenship committee here!"

"Why don't you give *me* a chance?" Michelis said raggedly. Then he turned white-on-white. After a moment, so did Liu.

Ruiz looked up again at the slumbering Lithian and, as assured as he could be that Egtverchi was truly asleep, pressed the button which brought the rumbling metal curtain down in front of the transparent door. To the last, Egtverchi did not seem to move. Now they were isolated and away from him; Ruiz did not know whether this would make any difference, but he had his doubts about the innocence of Egtverchi's responses. To be sure, he had not overtly done anything but make an enigmatic statement, ask a simple question, quote from his reading—yet somehow everything he said had helped matters to go more badly than before.

"Why did you do that?" Liu said.

"I wanted to clear the air," Ruiz said quietly. "He's asleep, anyhow. Besides, we don't have any argument with Egtverchi yet. He may not be equipped to argue with us. But we've got to talk to each other—you too, Mike."

"Haven't you had enough of that already, Ramon?"

Michelis said, in a voice a little more like his own.

"Preaching is my vocation," Ruiz said. "If I make a vice of it, I expect to atone for that somewhere else than here. But in the meantime—Liu, part of our trouble is the quarrel that I mentioned to you. Mike and I sharply disagreed on what Lithia means to the human race, indeed we disagreed on whether Lithia poses us any philosophical question at all. I think the planet is a time bomb; Mike thinks that's nonsense. And he thought that a general article for a scientific audience was no place to raise such questions, especially since this particular question has been posed officially and hasn't been adjudicated yet. And that's one reason why we're all snarling at each other right now, without any surface reason for it."

"What a cold thing to be heated about!" Liu said. "Men are so exasperating. How could a problem like that matter now?"

"I can't tell you," Ruiz said helplessly. "I can't be specific—the whole issue is under security seal. Mike thinks even the general issues I wanted to raise are graveyarded for the time being."

"But what we're waiting for is to find out what's going to happen to Egtverchi," Liu said. "The U.N. examining group must be already on its way. What business do you have to be hatching philosophical mandrake's-eggs when the life of a—of a human being, there's no other way to put it—is hanging on the next half-hour?"

"Liu," Ruiz said gently, "forgive me, but are you so convinced that Egtverchi is what you mean by a human being—a *hnau*, a rational soul? Does he talk like one? You were complaining yourself that he won't answer questions, and that very often when he speaks he doesn't make much sense. I've talked to adult Lithians, I knew Egtverchi's father well, and Egtverchi isn't much like them, let alone much like a human being. Hasn't anything that's happened in the past hour changed your mind?"

"Oh, no," Liu said warmly, reaching out her hands for the

Jesuit's. "Ramon, you've heard him talk yourself, as much as I have—you've tended him with me—you know he's not just an animal! He can be brilliant when he wants to be!"

"You're right, the mandrake's eggs have nothing to do with the case," Michelis said, turning and looking at Liu with dark, astonishingly pain-haunted eyes. "But I can't make Ramon listen to me. He's becoming more and more bound in some rarefied theological torture of his own. I'm sorry Egtverchi isn't as far along as I'd thought, but I foresaw almost from the beginning, I think, that he was going to be a serious embarrassment to us all, the closer he approaches his full intelligence.

"And I didn't get all my information from Ramon. I've seen the protocol on the progressive intelligence tests. Either they're reports on something phenomenal, or else we have no really trustworthy way of measuring Egtverchi's intelligence at all—and that may add up to the same thing in the end. If the tests are right, what's going to happen when Egtverchi finally does grow up? He's the son of a highly intelligent inhuman culture, and he's turning out to be a genius to boot —and his present status is that of an animal in a zoo! Or far worse than that, he's an experimental animal; that's how most of the public tends to think of him. The Lithians aren't going to like that, and furthermore the public won't like it when it learns the facts.

"That's why I brought up this whole citizenship question in the beginning. I see no other way out; we've got to turn him loose."

He was silent a moment, and then added, with almost his wonted gentleness:

"Maybe I'm naïve. I'm not a biologist, let alone a psychometrist. But I'd thought he'd be ready by now, and he isn't, so I guess Ramon wins by default. The interviewers will take him as he is, and the results obviously can't be good."

This was precisely Ruiz-Sanchez's opinion, though he would hardly have put it that way.

"I'll be sorry to see him go, if he leaves," Liu said abstractedly. It was evident, however, that she was hardly thinking about Egtverchi at all any more. "But Mike, I *know* you're right, there's no other solution in the long run—he has to go free. He *is* brilliant, there's no doubt about that. Now that I come to think of it, even this silence isn't the natural reaction of an animal with no inner resources. Father, is there nothing we can do to help?"

Ruiz shrugged; there was nothing that he could say. Michelis's reaction to the apparent parroting and unresponsiveness of Egtverchi had of course been far too extreme for the actual situation, springing mostly from Michelis's own disappointment at the equivocal outcome of the Lithia expedition; he liked issues to be clear-cut, and evidently he had thought he had found in the citizenship manœuvre a very sharp-edged tool indeed. But there was much more to it than that: some of it, of course, tied into the yet unadmitted bond which was forming between the chemist and the girl; in that single word "Father" she had shucked the priest off as a foster parent of Egtverchi, and put him in a position to give her away instead.

And what remained left over to be said would have no audience here. Michelis had already dismissed it as "some rarefied theological torture" which was personal to Ruiz and of no importance outside the priest's own skin. What Michelis dismissed would shortly fail to exist at all for Liu, if indeed it had not already been obliterated.

No, there was nothing further that could be done about Egtverchi; the Adversary was protecting his begotten son with all the old, divisive, puissant weapons; it was already too late. Michelis did not know how skilled U.N. naturalization commissions were at detecting intelligence and desirability in a candidate, even through the thickest smoke screen of language and cultural alienation, and at almost any age after the disease called "talking" had set in. And he did not realize how primed the commission would be to settle the Lithia question by a *fait accompli.* The visitors would see through Egtverchi within an hour at most, and then——

And then, Ruiz would be left with no allies at all. It seemed now to be the will of God that he be stripped of everything, and brought before the Holy Door with no baggage—not even such comforters as Job had, no, not even burdened by belief.

For Egtverchi would surely pass. He was as good as free—and closer to being a citizen in good standing than Ruiz himself.

XII

EGTVERCHI's coming-out party was held at the underground mansion of Lucien le Comte des Bois-d'Averoigne, a fact which greatly complicated the already hysterical life of Aristide, the countess's caterer. Ordinarily, such a party would have presented Aristide with no problems reaching far beyond the technical ones with which she was already familiar, and used to drive the staff to that frantic peak which he regarded as the utmost in efficiency; but planning for the additional presence of a ten-foot monster was an affront to his conscience as well as to his artistry.

Aristide—born Michel di Giovanni in the timeless brutal peasantry of un-Sheltered Sicily—was a dramatist who knew well the intricate stage upon which he had to work. The count's New York mansion was many levels deep. The part of it in which the party was being held protruded one story above the surface of Manhattan, as though the buried part of the city were coming out of hibernation—or not quite finished digging in for it. The structure had been a carbarn, Aristide had discovered, a dismal block-square red-brick building which had been put up in 1887 when cable street cars had been the newest and most hopeful addition to the city's circulatory system. The trolley tracks, with their middle division for the cable grips, were still there in the asphalt floor, with only a superficial coating of rust—steel does not rust appreciably in less than two centuries. In the centre of the top story was a huge old steam elevator with a basketwork shaft, which had once been used to lower the trolley cars below ground for storage. There were more tracks in the basement and sub-basement, whose elaborate switches led toward the segments of rail in the huge elevator cab. Aristide had been stunned when he first encountered this underlying blueprint, but he had promptly put it to good use.

The countess's parties, thanks to his genius, were now confined in their most formal phase to the uppermost of these three levels, but Aristide had installed a serpentine of fourteen two-chair cars which wound its way sedately along the trolley tracks, picking up as passengers those who were already bored with nothing but chatter and drinking, and rumbled on to the elevator to be taken down—with a great hissing and a cloud of rising steam, for the countess was a stickler for surface authenticity in antiques—to the next level, where presumably more interesting things were happening.

As a dramatist, Aristide also knew his audience: it was his job to provide that whatever was seen on the next levels *was* more interesting than what had been going on above. And he knew his dramatis personae, too: he knew more about the countess's regular guests than they knew about themselves, and much of his knowledge would have been decidedly destructive had he been the talkative type. Aristide, however, was an artist; he did not bribe; the notion was as unthinkable to him as plagiarism (except, of course, self-plagiarism; that was how you kept going during slumps). Finally, as an artist, Aristide knew his patroness: he knew her to the point where he could judge just how many parties had to pass by before he could chance repeating an Effect, a Scene or a Sensation.

But what could you do with a ten-foot reptilian kangaroo?

From where he stood in a discrete pillared alcove on the above-ground entrance floor, Aristide watched the early guests filtering in from the reception room to the formal cocktail party, one of his favourite anachronisms, and one which the countess seemed prepared to allow him to repeat year after year. It required very little apparatus, but the most absurd and sub-lethal concoctions, and even more absurd costumes on the part of both staff and guests. The nice rigidity of the costumes provided a pleasant contrast to the unlimbering of the psyche which the drinks quickly induced.

Thus far, there were only the early comers: here, Senator Sharon, waggling her oversize eyebrows in wholesome cheeriness at the remaining guests, ostentatiously refusing drinks, secure in the knowledge that her good friend Aristide had provided for her below five strong young men no one of whom she had ever seen before; there, Prince William of East Orange, a young man whose curse was that he had no vices, and who came again and again to ride the serpentine in hopes of discovering one that he liked; and, nearby, Dr. Samuel P. Shovel, M.D., a jovial, red-cheeked, white-haired man who was the high priest of psichonetology, "the New Science of the Id", and a favourite of Aristide's, since he was easy to provide for—he was fundamentally nothing more complicated than a bottom-pincher.

Faulkner, the head butler, was approaching Aristide stiffly from the left. Ordinarily, Faulkner ran the countess's household like an oriental despot, but he was no longer in control while Aristide was on the premises.

"Shall I order in the embryos in wine?" Faulkner said.

"Don't be such a blind, stupid fool," Aristide said. He had learned his first English from sentimental 3-C 'casts, which gave his ordinary conversation decidedly odd overtones; he was well aware of it, and these days it was one of his principal weapons for driving his underlings, who could not tell when he said these things dispassionately from when he was really angry. "Go below, Faulkner. I'll call you when I need you—if I do."

Faulkner bowed slightly and vanished. Fuming mildly at the interruption, Aristide resumed his survey of the early comers.

In addition to the regulars, there was, of course, the countess, who had posed him no special problems yet. Her gilded make-up was still unmussed, and the mobiles in the little caves Stefano had contrived in her hair spun placidly or blinked their diamond eyes. Then there were the sponsors of the Lithian monster into Shelter society, Dr. Michelis and Dr. Meid; these two might present special problems, for he had been unable to find out enough about them to decide what personal tastes they might need to have catered to down below, despite the fact that they were key guests, second only to the impossible creature itself. There was an explosive potential here, Aristide knew with the certainty of fate, for that impossible creature was already more than an hour late, and the countess had let it be known to all the guests and to Aristide that the creature was to be the guest of honour; fully half of the party would be coming to see him.

There was no one else in the room at the moment but a U.N. man wearing a funny hat—a sort of crash helmet liberally provided with communications apparatus and other, unnameable devices, including bubble goggles which occasionally filmed over to become a miniature 3-V screen—and a Dr. Martin Agronski, whom Aristide could not place at all, and whom he regarded with the consequent intense suspicion he reserved for people whose weaknesses he could not even guess at. Agronski's face was as petulant as that of the Prince of East Orange, but he was a much older man, and it seemed unlikely that he was there for the same reasons. He had something to do with the guest of honour, which made Aristide all the more uneasy. Dr. Agronski seemed to know Dr. Michelis, but for an unaccountable reason shied away from him at every opportunity; he was spending most of his time at one of the most potent of Aristide's punches, with the glum determination of a non-drinker who believes that he can perfect his poise by poisoning his timidity. Perhaps a woman . . . ?

Aristide crooked a finger. His assistant scuttled around the back of the hanging floral decorations with a practised stoop, covering even the sound of his movements by a brief delay which allowed the serpentine to come into its station, and cocked his ear to Aristide's mouth under the squeal of the train's brakes.

"Watch that one," Aristide said through motionless lips, pointing with the apex of one pelvic bone. "He will be drunk within the next half-hour. Take him out before he falls down, but don't take him off the premises. She may ask for him later. Better put him in the recovery room and taper him off as soon as he begins to wobble."

The assistant nodded and pedalled away, bent double. Aristide was still talking to him in blunt, businesslike English; that was a good sign, as far as it went.

Aristide returned to watching the guests; their number was growing a little, but he was still most interested in assessing the countess's reaction to the absence of the guest of honour. For the moment Aristide himself was in no danger, though he could see that the countess's hints had begun to acquire a certain hardness. Thus far, however, she was directing them at the monster's sponsors, Dr. Michelis and Dr. Meid, and it was plain that they had no answer for these gambits.

Dr. Michelis could only say over and over again, with a politeness which was becoming more and more formal as his patience visibly evaporated:

"Madame, I don't know when he's coming. I don't even know where he lives now. He promised to come. I'm not surprised that he's late, but I think he'll show up eventually."

The countess turned away petulantly, swinging her hips. Here was the first danger point for Aristide. There was no other pressure that the countess could bring to bear upon the monster's sponsors, regardless of how ignorant they were of the actual situation in the countess's household. By some trick of heredity, Lucien le Comte des Bois-d'Averoigne, Procurator of Canarsie, had been shrewd enough to spend his money wisely: he gave ninety-eight per cent of it to his wife, and used the other two per cent to disappear with for most of the year. There were even rumours that he did scientific research, though nobody could say in what field; certainly it could not be psichonetology or ufonics, or the countess would have known about it, since both were currently fashionable. And without the count, the countess was socially a nullity supported only by money; if the Lithian creature failed to show up at all, there was nothing that the countess could do to his sponsors but fail to invite them to the next party—which she would probably fail to do anyhow. On the other hand, there was a great deal that she might do to Aristide. She could not fire him, of course—he had kept careful dossiers against that possibility—but she could make his professional life with her very difficult indeed.

He signalled his second-in-command.

"Give Senator Sharon the canapé with the jolt in it as soon as there are ten more people on the floor," he directed crisply. "I don't like the way this is going. As soon as we have a minimum crowd, we'll have to get them rolling on the trains—Sharon's not the best Judas goat for the purpose, but she'll have to do. Take my advice, Cyril, or you will rue the day."

"Very good, Maestro," the assistant, whose name was not Cyril at all, said respectfully.

Michelis had hardly noticed the serpentine at the beginning, except as a novelty, but somehow or other it became noisier as the party grew older. It seemed to wind along the floor about every five minutes, but he soon realized that there were actually three such trains: the first one collected passengers up here; the second returned parties from the second level, to discharge wildly exhilarated recruiters among the cautiously formal newcomers on the first level; and the third train, usually almost empty this early in the party's course, brought glassy-eyed party-poopers from the subbasement, who were removed efficiently by the countess's livery in a covered station-stop well apart from the main entrance and well out of sight of new boarders for the nether levels. Then the whole cycle repeated itself.

Michelis had had every intention of staying off the serpentine entirely. He did not like the diplomatic service, especially now that it had nothing left to be diplomatic about, and anyhow he was far too dedicated to loneliness to be comfortable even at small parties, let alone anything like *this*. After a while, however, he became bored with repeating that same apology for Egtverchi, and aware that the top level of the party was now so empty that his and Liu's presence there was keeping their hostess against her will.

When Liu finally noticed that the serpentine not only toured this level but went below, he lost his last excuse to stay off it; and the elevator took all the rest of the newcomers down, leaving behind only the servants and a few bewildered scientific attachés who probably were at the wrong party to begin with. He looked about for Agronski, whose presence had astonished him early, but the hollow-eyed geologist had disappeared.

Everyone on the train shouted with glee and mock terror as the steam elevator took it down to the second level in utter blackness and rusty-smelling humidity. Then the great doors rolled up sharply in their eyes, and the train surged out, making an abrupt turn along its banked rails. Its plough-like nose battered immediately through a set of swinging double doors, plunged its passengers into even deeper darkness, and stopped completely with a grinding shudder.

From out of the darkness came a barrage of shrieking, hysterical feminine laughter and the shouting of men's voices.

"Oh, I can't stand!"

"Henry, is that you?"

"Leggo of me, you bitch."

"I'm so dizzy!"

"Look out, the damn thing's speeding up again!"

"Get off my foot, you bastard."

"Hey, *you're* not my husband."

"Ugh. Lady, I couldn't care less."

"Woman's gone too far this——"

Then they were drowned out by a siren so prolonged and deafening that Michelis's ears rang frighteningly even after the sound had risen past the upper limits of audibility. Then there was the groan of machinery, a dim violet glow——

The serpentine was turning over and over in midspace, supported by nothing. Many-coloured stars, none of them very bright, whirled past, rising on one side and sweeping over and then under the train with a period of only ten seconds from one "horizon" to the other. The shouts and the laughter were heard again, accompanied by a frantic scrabbling sound—and there came the siren again, first as a pressure, then as a thin singing which seemed to be inside the skull, and then as a prolonged sickening slide toward the infrabass.

Liu clutched frantically at Michelis's arm, but he could do nothing but cling to his seat. Every cell in his brain was flaring with alarm, but he was paralysed and sick with giddiness——

Lights.

The world stabilized instantly. The serpentine sat smugly on its tracks, which were supported by cantilever braces; it had never moved. At the bottom of a gigantic barrel, dishevelled guests looked up at the nearly blinded passengers of the train and howled with savage mockery. The "stars" had been spots of fluorescent paint, brought to life by hidden ultra-violet lamps. The illusion of spinning in midspace had been made more real by the siren, which had disturbed their vestibular apparatus, the inner ear which maintains the sense of balance.

"All out!" a rough male voice shouted. Michelis looked down cautiously; he was still a little dizzy. The shouter was a man in rumpled black evening clothes and fire-red hair; his huge shoulders had burst one seam of his jacket. "You get the next train. That's the rules."

Michelis thought of refusing, and changed his mind. Being tumbled in the barrel was probably less likely to produce serious wounds than would fighting with two people who had already "earned" their passage out in his and Liu's seats. There were rules of conduct for everything. A gang ladder protruded up at them; when their turn came, he helped Liu down it.

"Try not to fight it," he told her in a low voice. "When it starts to revolve, slide if you can, roll if you can't. Got a pyrostyle? All right, here's mine—jab if anybody stays too close, but don't worry about the drum—it looks thoroughly waxed."

It was; but Liu was frightened and Michelis in a murderously ugly mood by the time the next train came through and took them out; he was glad that he had not decided to argue with his predecessors in the barrel. Anybody who had tried the same thing with him might well have been killed.

The fact that he was drenched with perfume as the serpentine passed through the next cell did not exactly improve his temper, but at least the cell did not require anyone's participation. It was a sizeable and beautiful garden made of blown glass in every possible colour, in which live Javanese models were posed in dioramas of discovered lust; the situations depicted were melodramatic in the extreme but, except for their almost imperceptible breathing, the models did not move a muscle; they were almost as motionless as the glass foliage. To Michelis's surprise—for outside the sciences he had almost no aesthetic sense—Liu regarded these lascivious, immobile scenes with a kind of withdrawn, grave approval.

"It's an art, to suggest a dance without moving," she murmured suddenly, as though she had sensed his uneasiness. "Difficult with the brush, far more difficult with the body. I think I know the man who designed this; there couldn't be but one."

He stared at her as though he had never seen her before, and by the pure current of jealousy that shot through him he knew for the first time that he loved her. "Who?" he said hoarsely.

"Oh, Tsien Hi, of course. The last classicist. I thought he was dead, but this isn't a copy——"

The serpentine slowed before the exit doors long enough for two models, looking obscenely alive in very modest movement, to hand them each a fan covered with brushed drawings in ink. A single glance was enough to make Michelis thrust his fan in his pocket, unwilling to acknowledge ownership of it by so definite a gesture as throwing it away; but Liu pointed mutely to an ideogram and folded hers with reverence. "Yes," she said. "It is he; these are the original sketches. I never thought I'd own one——"

The train lurched forward suddenly. The garden vanished, and they were plunged into a vague, coloured chaos of meaningless emotions. There was nothing to see or hear or feel, yet Michelis was shaken to his soul, and then shaken again, and again. He cried out, and dimly heard others crying. He fought for control of himself, but it eluded him, and . . no, he had it now, or almost had it. . . . If he could oniy *think* for an instant——

For an instant, he managed it, and saw what was happening. The new cell was a long corridor, divided by invisible currents of moving air into fifteen sub-cells. Inside each sub-cell was a coloured smoke, and in each smoke was some gas which went instantly home to the hypothalamus. Michelis recognized some of them: they were crude hallucinogenic compounds which had been developed during the heyday of tranquillizer research in the mid-twentieth century. Under the waves of fright, religious exaltation, berserker bravery, lust for power, and less nameable emotions which each induced, he felt a mounting intellectual anger at such irresponsible wholesale tampering with the pharmacology of the mind for the sake of a momentary "experience"; but he knew that this kind of jolt-breathing was anything but uncommon in the Shelter state. The smokes had the reputation of being non-addicting, which for the most part they were—but they were certainly habit-forming, which is quite a different thing, and not necessarily less dangerous.

A hazy, formless curtain of pink at the far end of the corridor proved to be a pure free-serotonin antagonist in high concentration, a true ataraxic which washed his mind free of every emotion but contentment with everything in all the wide universe. What must be, must be . . . it is all for the best . . . there is peace in everything——

In this state of uncritical yea-saying, the passengers on the serpentine were run through an assembly line of elaborate and bestial practical jokes. It ended with a 3-V tape re-creation of Belsen, in which the scenarist had cunningly made it appear that the people on the serpentine would be next into the ovens. As the furnace door closed behind them there was a blast of mind-cleansing oxygen; staggering with horror at what they had been about to accept with joy, the passengers were helped off the train to join a guffawing audience of previous victims.

Michelis's only impulse was to escape—above all he did not want to stay to laugh at the next load of passengers in shock—but he was too exhausted to get beyond the nearest bench in the amphitheatre, and Liu could hardly walk even that far. They were forced to sit there in the press until they had made a better recovery.

It was fortunate that they did. While they were nursing their drinks—Michelis had been deeply suspicious of the warm amber cups, but their contents had proved to be nothing but honest and welcome brandy—the next train was greeted with a roar of delight and a unanimous surge of the crowd to its feet.

Egtverchi had arrived.

There was a real mob now in the cocktail lounge above ground, but Aristide was far from happy; he had already cut off quite a few heads down below on the catering staff. He had somewhere inside him a very delicate sense which told him when a party was going sour, and that sense had put up the red alarms long before this. The arrival of the guest of honour in particular had been an enormous fiasco. The countess had not been on hand, the creature's sponsors had not been there, none of the really important guests who had been invited specifically to see the guest of honour had been there, and the guest himself had betrayed Aristide into showing, before all the staff, that he was frightened out of his wits.

He was bitterly ashamed of his fright, but the fact was now beyond undoing. He had been told to anticipate a monster, but not such a monster as this—a creature well *more* than ten feet high, a reptile which walked more like a man than like a kangaroo, with vast grinning jaws, wattles which changed colour every few moments, small clawlike hands which looked as though they could pluck one like a chicken, a balancing tail which kept sweeping trays off tables, and above all a braying laugh and an enormous tenor voice which spoke English with a perfection so cold and carefully calculated as to make Aristide feel like a thumb-fingered leather-skinned Sicilian who had just landed. And at the monster's entrance, nobody but Aristide had been there to welcome him. . . .

A train rumbled into the atrium of the recovery room, but before it stopped, Senator Sharon tumbled out with a vast display of piano legs and black eyebrows. "Look at *him*!" she squealed, full of the five-fold revival Aristide had conscientiously arranged for her. "Isn't he *male*!"

Another failure for Aristide: it was one of the countess's standing orders that the Senator had to be put through her cell and fired out into the Shelter night long before the party proper could be said to have begun; otherwise the Senator would spend the rest of the evening, after her five-fold awakening, climbing from one pair of shoulders to another to a political, literary, scientific or any other eminence she could manage to attain at the expense of everyone else who could be bought with half an hour on a table top—and never mind that she would spend the rest of the next week falling down from that eminence into the swamps of nymphomania again. If Senator Sharon were not properly ejected this early, and with due assurances, in the warm glow of her aftermath, she was given to lawsuits.

The empty train pulled out invitingly into the lounge. The Lithian monster saw it and his grin got wider.

"I always wanted to be an engine driver," he said in a brassy English which nevertheless was more precise than anything to which Aristide would be able to pretend to the end of his life. "And there's the major-domo. Good sir, I've brought two, three, several guests of my own. Where is our hostess?"

Aristide pointed helplessly, and the tall reptile boarded the train at the front car, with a satisfied crow. He was scarcely settled in before the rest of his party was pouring across the lounge floor and piling in behind him. The train started with a jerk, and rumbled to the elevator. It sank down amid tall wisps of steam.

And that was that. Aristide had muffed the grand entrance. Had he had any doubts about it, they would have been laid to rest most directly: less than ten minutes later, he was snooted egregiously by Faulkner.

So much for being a dedicated artist with a loyal patroness, he thought dismally. Tomorrow, he would be a short-order cook in some Shelter commissariat, dossiers or no dossiers. And why? Because he had been unable to anticipate the time of arrival, let alone the desires or the friends, of some creature which had never been born on Earth at all.

He marched deliberately and morosely away from his post toward the recovery room, kicking assistants who were green enough to stay within range. He could think of nothing further to do but to supervise personally the tapering-off of Dr. Martin Agronski, the unknown guest who had something to do with the Lithian.

But he had no illusions. Tomorrow, Aristide, caterer to the Countess des Bois-d'Averoigne, would be lucky to be Michel di Giovanni, late of the malarial plains of Sicily.

Michelis was sorry he had allowed himself and Liu aboard

the serpentine the moment he understood the construction of the second level, for he saw at once that they would have virtually no chance of seeing Egtverchi's arrival. Fundamentally, the second level was divided by soundproof walls into a number of smaller parties, some of them only slightly drunker and more unorthodox then the cocktail party had been, but the rest running a broad spectrum of frenetic exoticism. He and Liu were carried completely around the course before he was able to figure out how to get the girl and himself safely off the serpentine; and each time he was moved to attempt it, the train began to go faster in unpredictable spurts, producing a sensation rather like that of riding a roller coaster in the middle of the night.

Nevertheless, they saw the only entrance that counted. Egtverchi emerged from the last gas bath standing in the head car of the serpentine, and stepped out of the car under his own power. In the next five cars behind him, also standing, were ten nearly identical young men in uniforms of black and lizard-green with silver piping, their arms folded, their expressions stern, their eyes straight ahead.

"Greetings," Egtverchi said, with a deep bow which his disproportionately small dinosaurian arms and hands made both comical and mocking. "Madame the Countess, I am delighted. You are protected by many bad smells, but I have braved them all."

The crowd applauded. The countess's reply was lost in the noise, but evidently she had chided him with being naturally immune to smokes which would affect Earthmen, for he said promptly, with a trace of hurt in his voice:

"I thought you might say that, but I'm grieved to be caught in the right. To the pure all things are pure, however —did you ever see such upstanding unshaken young men?" He gestured at the ten. "But of course I cheated. I stopped their nostrils with filters, as Ulysses stopped his men's ears with wax to pass the sirens. My entourage will stand for anything; they think I am a genius."

With the air of a conjurer, the Lithian produced a silver

whistle which seemed small in his hand, and blew into the thick air a white, warbling note which was utterly inadequate to the gesture which had preceded it. The ten soldierly young men promptly melted. The forefront of the crowd gleefully toed the limp bodies, which took the abuse with lax indifference.

"Drunk," Egtverchi said with fatherly disapproval. "Of course. Actually I didn't stop their noses at all. I prevented their reticular formations from reporting the countess's smokes to their brains until I gave the cue. Now they had gotten all the messages at once; isn't it disgraceful? Madame, please have them removed, such dissoluteness embarrasses me. I shall have to institute discipline."

The countess clapped her hands. "Aristide! Aristide?" She touched the transceiver concealed in her hair, but there was no response that Michelis could detect. Her expression changed abruptly from childish delight to infant fury. "Where is that lousy rustic——"

Michelis, boiling, shouldered his way into Egtverchi's line of sight with difficulty.

"Just what the hell do you think you're doing?" he said in a hoarse voice.

"Good evening, Mike. I am attending a party, just as you are. Good evening, dear Liu. Countess, do you know my foster parents? But I am sure do you."

"Of course," the countess said, turning her bare shoulders and back unmistakably on Michelis and Liu, and looking up at Egtverchi's perpetually grinning head from under gilded eyelids. "Let's go next door—there's more room, and it will be quieter. We've all seen enough of these train riders. After you, their arrivals will seem all alike."

"I cultivate the unique," Egtverchi said. "But I must have Mike and Liu by my side, Countess. I am the only reptile in the universe with mammalian parents, and I cherish them. I have a notion that it may be a sin; isn't that interesting?"

The gilded eyelids lowered. It had been years since the countess's caterers had come up with a new sin interesting enough to be withheld from the next evening's guests for private testing; that was common knowledge. She looked as if she scented one now, Michelis thought; and since she was, in fact, a woman of small imagination, Michelis was not in much doubt as to what it was. For all his saurian shape and texture, there was something about Egtverchi that was intensely, overwhelmingly masculine.

And intensely childlike, too. That the combination was perfectly capable of overriding any repugnance people might feel toward his additionally overwhelming reptilian-ness had already been demonstrated, in the response to his first interview on 3-V. His wry and awry comments on Earthly events and customs had been startling enough, and perhaps it could have been predicted even then that the intelligentsia of the world would pick him up as a new fad before the week was out. But nobody had anticipated the flood of letters from children, from parents, from lonely women.

Egtverchi was a sponsored news commentator now, the first such ever to have an audience composed half-and-half of disaffected intellectuals and delighted children. There was no precedent for it in the present century, at least; learned men in communications compared him simultaneously with two historical figures named Adlai E. Stevenson and Oliver J. Dragon.

Egtverchi also had a lunatic following, though its composition had not yet been analysed publicly by his 3-V network. Ten of these followers were being lugged limply out by the countess's livery right now, and Michelis's eyes followed them speculatively while he trailed with the crowd after Egtverchi and the countess, out of the amphitheatre and into the huge lounge next door. The uniforms were suggestive—but of what? They might have been no more than costumes, designed for the part alone; had the ten young men who fell to the bleat of Egtverchi's silver whistle been physically different from each other, the effect would have been smaller, as Egtverchi would have known. And yet the whole notion of uniforms was foreign to Lithian psychology, while it was profoundly meaningful in Earth terms—and Egtverchi knew more about Earth than most Earthmen did, already.

Lunatics in uniforms, who thought Egtverchi to be a genius who could do no wrong; what could that mean?

Were Egtverchi a man, one would know instantly what it meant. But he was not a man, but a musician playing upon man as on an organ. The structure of the composition would not be evident for a long time to come—if it had a structure; Egtverchi might only be improvising, at least this early. That was a frightening thought in itself.

And all this had happened within a month of the awarding of citizenship to Egtverchi. That had been a pleasant surprise. Michelis was none too sure how he felt about the surprises that had followed; about those certain to come he was decidedly wary.

"I have been exploring this notion of parenthood," Egtverchi was saying. "I know who my father is, of course—it is a knowledge we are born with—but the concept that goes with the word is quite unlike anything you have here on Earth. *Your* concept is a tremendous network of inconsistencies."

"In what way?" the countess said, not very much interested.

"Why, it seems to be based on a reverence for the young, and an extremely patient and protective attitude toward their physical and mental welfare. Yet you make them live in these huge caves, utterly out of contact with the natural world, and you teach them to be afraid of death—which of course makes them a little insane, because there is nothing anybody can do about death. It is like teaching them to be afraid of the second law of thermodynamics, just because living matter sets that law aside for a very brief period. How they hate you!"

"I doubt that they know I exist," the countess said dryly. She had no children.

"Oh, they hate their own parents first of all," Egtverchi

said, "but there is enough hatred left over for every other adult on your planet. They write me about it. They have never had anybody to say this to before, but they see in me someone who has had no hand in their torment, who is critical of it, and who obviously is a comical, harmless fellow who won't betray them."

"You're exaggerating," Michelis said uneasily.

"Oh no, Mike. I have prevented several murders already. There was one five-year-old who had a most ingenius plan, something involving garbage disposal. He was ready to include his mother, his father, and his fourteen-year-old brother, and the whole affair would have been blamed on a computational error in his city's sanitation department. Amazing that a child that age could have planned anything so elaborate, but I believe it would have worked—these Shelter cities of yours are so complex, they become lethal engines if even the most minute errors creep into them. Do you doubt me, Mike? I shall show you the letter."

"No," Michelis said slowly. "I don't think I do."

Egtverchi's eyes filmed briefly. "Some day I will let one of these affairs proceed to completion," he said. "As a demonstration, perhaps. Something of the sort seems to be in order."

Somehow Michelis did not doubt that he would, nor that the results would be as predicted. People did not remember their childhoods clearly enough to take seriously the rages and frustrations that shook children—and the smaller the child, the less superego it had to keep the emotions tamed. It seemed more than likely that a figure like Egtverchi would be able to tap this vast, seething underworld of impotent fury more effectively and easily than any human analyst, no matter how skilled and subtle, had ever been able to do.

And there was where you had to tap it, if you were hoping to do any good. Tapping is by hindsight, through analysis of adults, was successful with neurotics, but it had never proved effective against the psychoses; those had to be attacked pharmacologically, by regulating serotonin metabolism with ataraxics—the carefully tailored chemical grandchildren of the countess's crude smokes. That worked, but it was not a cure, but a maintenance operation—like giving insulin or sulfonylureas to a diabetic. The organic damage had already been done. In the great ravelled knot of the brain, the basic reverberating circuits, once set in motion, could be interrupted but never discontinued—except by destructive surgery, a barbarity now a century out of use.

And it all fitted some of the disturbing things he had been discovering about the Shelter economy since his return from his long sojourn on Lithia. Having been born into it, Michelis had always taken that economy pretty much for granted; or at least his adult memory of his childhood told him that. Maybe it had really been different, and perhaps a little less grim, back in those days, or maybe that was just an illusion cherished by the silent censor in his brain. But it seemed to him that in those days people had let themselves become reconciled to these endless caverns and corridors for the sake of their children, in the hope that the next generation would be out from under the fear and could know something a little better—a glimpse of sunlight, a little rain, the fall of a leaf.

Since then, the restrictions on surface living had been relaxed greatly—nobody now believed in the possibility of nuclear war, since the Shelter race had produced an obvious impasse—but somehow the psychic atmosphere was far worse instead of better. The number of juvenile gangs roaming the corridors had increased four hundred per cent while Michelis was out of the solar system; the U.N. was now spending about a hundred million dollars a year on elaborate recreation and rehabilitation programmes for adolescents, but the rec centres stayed largely deserted, and the gangs continued to multiply. The latest measure take against them was frankly punitive: a tremendous increase in the cost of compulsory insurance on power scooters, seemingly harmless, slow-moving vehicles which the gangs had adapted first to simple crimes like purse-snatching, and then to such more complicated and destructive games as mass raids on food warehouses, industrial distilleries, even utilities—it had been drag-racing in the air ducts that had finally triggered the confiscatory insurance rates.

In the light of what Egtverchi had said, the gangs made perfect and horrible sense. Nobody now believed in the possibility of nuclear war, but nobody could believe in the possibility of a full return to surface life, either. The billions of tons of concrete and steel were far too plainly there to stay. The adults no longer had hopes even for their children, let alone for themselves. While Michelis had been away in the Eden of Lithia, on Earth the number of individual crimes without motive—crimes committed just to distract the committer from the grinding monotony of corridor life—had passed the total of all other crimes put together. Only last week some fool on the U.N.'s Public Polity Commission had proposed putting tranquillizers in the water supplies; the World Health Organization had had him ousted within twenty-four hours—actually putting the suggestion into effect would have doubled crimes of this kind, by cutting the population further free of its already feeble grip on responsibility—but it was too late to counteract the effect on morale of the suggestion alone.

The W.H.O. had had good reason to be both swift and arbitrary about it. Its last demographic survey showed, under the grim heading of "Actual Insanity", a total of thirty-five million unhospitalized early paranoid schizophrenics who had been clearly diagnosed, every one of whom should have been committed for treatment at once—except that, were the W.H.O. to commit them, the Shelter economy would suffer a manpower loss more devastating than any war had inflicted on mankind in all of its history. Every one of those thirty-five million persons was a major hazard to his neighbours and to his job, but the Shelter economy was too complicated to do without them—

—let alone do without the unrecognized, subclinical cases, which probably totalled twice as many. The Shelter economy obviously could not continue operating much longer without a major collapse; it was on the verge of a psychotic break at this instant.

With Egtverchi for a therapist?

Preposterous. But who else . . . ?

"You're very gloomy tonight," the countess was complaining. "Won't you amuse anyone but children?"

"No one," Egtverchi said promptly. "Except, of course, myself. And of course I am also a child. There now: not only do I have mammals for parents, but I am myself my own uncle—these 3-V amusers of children are always everyone's uncle. You do not appreciate me properly, Countess; I become more interesting every minute, but you do not notice. In the next instant I may turn into your mother, and you will do nothing but yawn."

"You've already turned into my mother," the countess said, with a challenging, slumbrous look. "You even have her jowls, and all those impossibly even teeth. And the talk. My God. Turn into something else—and *don't* make it Lucien."

"I would turn into the count if I could," Egtverchi said, with what Michelis was almost sure was genuine regret. "But I have no affinity for affines; I don't even understand Haertel yet. Tomorrow, perhaps?"

"My God," the countess said again. "Why in the world did I think I should invite you? You're too dull to be borne. I don't know why I count on anything any more. I should know better by now."

Astonishingly, Egtverchi began to sing, in a high, pure, *castrato* tenor: "*Swef, swef, Susa. . . .*" For a moment Michelis thought the voice was coming from someone else, but the countess swung on Egtverchi instantly, her face twisted into a Greek mask of pure rage.

"Stop that," she said, her voice as raw as a wound. Her expression, under the gilded gaiety of her party paint, was savagely incongruous.

"Certainly," Egtverchi said soothingly. "You see I am not

your mother after all. It pays to be careful with these accusations."

"You lousy snake-scaled demon!"

"Please, Countess; I have scales, you have breasts; this is proper and fitting. You ask me to amuse you; I thought you might enjoy my jongleur's lullaby."

"*Where did you hear that song?*"

"Nowhere," Egtverchi said. "I reconstructed it. I could see from the cast of your eyes that you were a born Norman."

"How did you do it?" Michelis said, interested in spite of himself. It was the first sign he had encountered that Egtverchi had any musical ability.

"Why, by the genes, Mike," Egtverchi said; his literal Lithian mind had gone to the substance of Michelis's question rather than to its sense. "This is the way I know my name, and the name of my father. E-G-T-V-E-R-C-H-I is the patter of genes on one of my chromosomes; the G, V and I alleles are of course from my mother; my cerebral cortex had direct sensual access to my genetic composition. We see ancestry everywhere we look, just as you see colours—it is one of the spectra of the real world. Our ancestors bred that sense into us; you could do worse than imitate them. It is helpful to know what a man is before he even opens his mouth."

Michelis felt a faint but decided chill. He wondered if Chtexa had ever mentioned this to Ruiz. Probably not; a discovery so fascinating to a biologist would have driven the Jesuit to talking about it. In any event, it was too late to ask him, for he was on the way to Rome; Cleaver was even farther away by now; and Agronski wouldn't know.

"Dull, dull, dull," the countess said. She had got back most of her self-possession.

"To be sure, to the dull," Egtverchi said, with his eternal grin, which somehow managed to disarm almost anything that he said. "But I offered to amuse you; you did not enjoy my entertainment. It is your doom to amuse me, too, you know; I am the guest here. What do you have in the subbasement, for instance? Let us go see. Where are my summer soldiers? Somebody wake them; we have a trip to take."

The packed guests had been listening intently, obviously enjoying the countess's floundering upon Egtverchi's long and multiple-barbed gaff. When she bowed her high-piled, gilded head and led the way back toward the trolley tracks, a blurred and almost animal cheer shook the lounge. Liu shrank back against Michelis; he put his arm tightly around her waist.

"Mike, let's not go," she whispered. "Let's go home. I've had enough."

XIII

ENTRY IN EGTVERCHI'S JOURNAL:

June 13th, 13th week of citizenship: This week I stayed home. Elevators on Earth never stop at this floor. Must check why. They have reasons for everything they do.

It was during the week Egtverchi's programme was off the air that Agronski stumbled across the discovery that he no longer knew who he was. Though he had not recognized it for what it was at the time, the first forebodings of this vastation had come creeping over him as far back as that four-cornered debate in Xoredeshch Sfath, when he had begun to realize that he did not know what Mike, the Father and Cleaver were talking about. After a while, it had begun to seem to him that they didn't know, either; the long looping festoons of logic and emotion with which they so determinedly bedecked the humid Lithian air seemed to hang from nothing, and touch no ground on which he or any other human being he knew had ever stood.

Then, after he had come home, he had hardly even been angered—only vaguely irritated—when the *J.I.R.* had failed to include him in its invitation to prepare the preliminary article on Lithia. The Lithian experience had already begun to seem remote and dreamlike to him, and he already knew that he and the senior authors could have nothing more to say to each other on that subject which would make mutual sense.

So far, so good; but so far there was no explanation for the sensation of bottomless despair, loneliness and disgust which had swept over him here at the discovery, seemingly of no consequence in itself, that his favourite 3-V programme would not be on tonight. Superficially, everything else was as it should be. He had been invited to a year of residency at Fordham's seismological laboratories on the basis of his previous publications on gravity waves—tidal and seismic tremors—and his arrival had been greeted with just the proper mixture of respect and enthusiasm by the Jesuits who ran the great university's science department. His apartment in the bachelor scientists' quarters was not at all monastic, indeed it was almost luxurious for a single man; he had as much apparatus as any geologist in his field could have dreamed of having under such an arrangement, he was virtually free of lecture duties, he had made several new friends among the graduate students assigned to him—and yet, tonight, looking blankly at the replacement programme which had appeared instead of Egtverchi on his 3-V screen——

In retrospect, each of the steps toward this abyss seemed irrevocable, and yet they had all been so small! He had been looking forward to his return to Earth with an unfocused but intent excitement, not directed toward any one aspect of Earthly life, but simply eager for the pat wink of all things familiar. But when he had returned, he found no reassurance in the familiar; indeed, it all seemed rather flat. He put it down to having been a relatively free-wheeling, nearly unique individual on a virtually unpopulated world; there was bound to be a certain jolt in readapting oneself to the life of one mole among billions.

And yet a jolt was precisely what it had not been. Instead, it had been a most peculiar kind of lack of all sensation, as though the familiar were powerless to move him or even to touch him. As the days wore by, this intellectual, emotional, sensual numbness became more and more pronounced, until it became a kind of sensation in itself, a sort of giddiness—as though he were about to fall, and yet could not see anything to grab hold of to steady himself, or indeed what kind of ground he was standing on at the moment.

Somewhere along in there he had taken up listening to Egtverchi's news broadcasts, out of simple curiosity in so far as he could remember any feeling so far removed in time. There had been something there that was useful to him, though he could not know what it was. At the very least, Egtverchi occasionally amused him. Sometimes the creature reminded him obscurely that on Lithia, no matter how divorced he had been from the thinking and the purposes of the other members of the commission, he had been almost unique; that was comforting, though it was a watery comfort. And sometimes, during Egtverchi's most savage sallies against Agronski's familiar Earth, he felt a slight surge of genuine pleasure, as though Egtverchi were his agent in acting out a long and complicated revenge against enemies hidden and unknown. More usually, however, Egtverchi failed to penetrate the slightly nauseating numbness which had closed around him; the broadcasts simply became a habit.

In the meantime, increasingly it came over him that he did not understand what his fellow men were doing or, in the minority of instances where he did understand it, it seemed to him to be something utterly trivial; why did people bind themselves to these régimes? Where were they going that was so important? The air of determined dull preoccupation with which the average troglodyte went to his job, got through it, and came away again to his cubby in his target area would have seemed tragic to him if the actors had not all been such utter ciphers; the eagerness, dedication, chicanery, short-cutting, brilliance, hard labour and total immersion of people who thought themselves or otheir jobs important would have seemed absurd had he been able to think of anything in the world more worth all this attention, but the savour was leaking rapidly out of everything now. Even the steaks he had dreamed of on Lithia were now only something else to be got through, an exercise in cutting, forking, swallowing, and disturbed cat naps.

In brief flashes of a few minutes at a time, he was able to envy the Jesuit scientists. They still believed geology to be important, an illusion which now seemed far in the past—a matter of weeks—to Agronski. Their religion, too, seemed to be a constant source of great intellectual excitement, especially during this Holy Year; Agronski had gathered from conversations with Ramon two years ago that the Jesuit order is the cerebral cortex of the Church, concerned with its knottiest moral, theological and organizational problems. In particular, Agronski remembered, the Jesuits were charged with weighing questions of polity and making recommendations to Rome, and it was here that the area of greatest excitement at Fordham was centred. Although he never did arouse himself sufficiently to find out the core of the issue, Agronski knew that this year was to mark the settlement by papal proclamation of one of the great dogmatic questions of Catholicism, comparable to the dogma of the Assumption of the Blessed Virgin which had been proclaimed a century ago; from the hot discussions he overheard in the refectory, and elsewhere after working hours, he gathered that the Society of Jesus had already made its recommendation, and all that remained to be debated was the most probable decision which Pope Hadrian would arrive at. That there should still be any question about the matter surprised him a little, until a scrap of conversation overheard in the commissariat told him that there was nothing in the least binding about the Order's decisions. The doctrine of the Assumption had been heavily recommended against by the Jesuits of the time, despite the fact that it had been an obvious personal preference of the then incumbent Pope, but it had been adopted all the same—the decision of St. Peter's was beyond all appeal.

Nothing in the world, Agronski was learning with this feeling of general giddiness and nausea, was that certain. In the end his colleagues here at Fordham came to seem as remote to him as Ruiz-Sanchez had on Lithia. The Catholic Church in 2050 was still fourth in rank in terms of number of adherents, with Islam, the Buddhists and the Hindi sects commanding the greater number of worshippers, in that order; after Catholicism, there was the confusing number of Protestant groups, which might well outnumber the Catholics if one included all those in the world who had no faith worth mentioning—and it was probable that the agnostics, atheists and don't cares, taken as a separate group, were at least as numerous as the Jews, perhaps more so. As for Agronski, he knew greyly that he belonged no more with one of these groups than with any other; he had been cut adrift; he was slowly beginning to doubt the existence of the phenomenal universe itself, and he could not bring himself to care enough about the probably unreal to feel that it mattered what intellectual organization you imposed on it, whether it was High Episcopalian or Logical Positivist. If one no longer likes steak, what does it matter how well it has been aged, butchered, cooked or served?

The invitation to Egtverchi's coming-out party had almost succeeded in piercing the iron fog which had descended between Agronski and the rest of creation. He had had the notion that the sight of a live Lithian might do something for him, though what he could hardly have said; and besides, he had wanted to see Mike and the Father again, moved by memories of having been fond of them once. But the Father was not there, Mike had been removed light-years away from him by having taken up in the meantime with a woman—and of all the meaningless obsessions of mankind, Agronski was most determined now to avoid the tyranny of sex—and in person Egtverchi had turned out to be a grotesque and alarming Earthly caricature of the Lithians that Agronski remembered. Disgusted with himself, he kept sedulously away from all of them, and in the process, quite inadvertently, got drunk. He remembered no more of the party except scraps of a fight that he had had with some swarthy flunkey in a huge dark room bounded by metal webwork, like being inside the shaft of the Eiffel Tower at midnight—a memory which seemed to include inexplicable rising clouds of steam and a jerky intensification of his catholic, nauseating vertigo, as though he and his anonymous adversary were being lowered into hell on the end of a thousand-mile-long hydraulic piston.

He had awakened after noon the next day in his rooms with a thousand-fold increase in the giddiness, an awful sense of mission before a holocaust, and the worst hangover he had since the drunk he had staged on cooking sherry in the first week of his freshman year in college. It took him two days to get rid of the hangover, but the rest remained, shutting him off utterly even from the things that he could see and touch in his own apartment. He could not taste his food; words on paper had no meaning; he could not make his way from his chair to the toilet without wondering if at the next step the room would turn upside down or vanish entirely. Nothing had any volume, texture, or mass, let alone any colour; the secondary properties of things, which had been leaking steadily out of his world ever since Lithia, were gone entirely now, and the primary qualities were beginning to follow.

The end was clear and predictable. There was to be nothing left but the little plexus of habit patterns at the centre of which lived the dwindling unknowable thing that was his *I*. By the time one of those habits brought him before the 3-V set and snapped open the switch, it was already too late to save anything else. There was nobody left in the universe but himself—nobody and nothing——

Except that, when the screen lighted and Egtverchi failed to appear, he discovered that even the *I* no longer had a name. Inside the thin shell of unwilling self-consciousness, it was as empty as an upended jug.

XIV

RUIZ-SANCHEZ put the much-folded, sleazy airletter down into his lap and looked blindly out of the compartment window of the *rapido*. The train was already an hour out from Naples, slightly less than halfway to Rome, and as yet he had seen almost nothing of the country he had been hoping to reach all of his adult life; and now he had a headache. Michelis's sprawling cursive handwriting was under the best of circumstances about as legible as Beethoven's, and obviously he had written this letter under the worst circumstances imaginable.

And after emotion had done its considerable worst to Michelis's scrawl, the facsimile reducer had squeezed it all down on to a single piece of tissue for missile mail, so that only a man who knew the handwriting as well as Assyriologists know cuneiform could have deciphered the remaining ant tracks at all.

After a moment, he picked up where he had left off; the letter went on:

"Which is why I missed the subsequent débâcle. There is still some doubt in my mind as to whether or not Egtverchi was entirely responsible—it occurs to me that maybe the countess's smokes did affect him in some way after all, since his metabolism can't be *totally* different from ours—but you'd know much more about that than I would. It's perfectly possible that I'm just whistling past the grave-yard.

"In any event, I don't know any more about the subbasement shambles than the papers have reported. In case you haven't seen them, what happened was that Egtverchi and his bravoes somehow became impatient with the progress the serpentine was making, or with the calibre of the entertainment they could see from it, and went on an expedition of their own, breaking down the barriers between cells when they couldn't find any other way in. Egtverchi is still pretty weak for a Lithian, but he's big, and the dividing walls apparently didn't pose him any problems.

"What happened thereafter is confused—it depends on which reporter you believe. In so far as I've been able to piece all these conflicting accounts together, Egtverchi himself didn't hurt anybody, and if his *condottieri* did, they got as good as they gave; one of them died. The major damage is to the countess, who is ruined. Some of the cells he broke into weren't on the serpentine's route at all, and contained public figures in private hells especially designed by the countess's caterers. The people who haven't themselves already succumbed to the sensation-mongers—though in some instances the publicity is no more vicious than they had coming—are out to revenge themselves on the whole house of Averoigne.

"Of course the count can't be touched directly, since he wasn't even aware of what was going on. (Did you see that last paper from 'H.O. Petard', by the way? Beautiful stuff: he has a fundamental twist on the Haertel equations which make it look possible to *see* around normal space-time, as well as travel around it. Theoretically you might photograph a star and get a contemporary image, not one light-years old. Another blow to the chops for poor old Einstein.) But he is already no longer Procurator of Canarsie and, unless he takes his money promptly out of the countess's hands, he will wind up as just another moderately comfortable troglodyte. And at the moment nobody knows where he is, so unless he has been reading the papers it is already too late for him to make a drastic enough move. In any event, whether he does or he doesn't, the countess will be *persona non grata* in her own circles to the day she dies.

"And even now I haven't any idea whether Egtverchi intended exactly this, or whether it was all an accident springing out of a wild impulse. He says he will reply to the newspaper criticism of him on his 3-V programme next week —this week nobody can reach him, for reasons he refuses to explain—but I don't see what he could possibly say that would salvage more than a fraction of the goodwill he'd accumulated before the party. He's already half-convinced that Earth's laws are only organized whims at best—and his present audience is more than half children!

"I wish you were the kind of man who might say 'I told you so'; at least I could get a melancholy pleasure out of nodding. But it's too late for that now. If you can spare any time for further advice, please send it post haste. We are in well over our heads.

"MIKE.

"PS.: Liu and I were married yesterday. It was earlier than we had planned, but we both feel a sense of urgency that we can't explain—almost a desperation. It's as though something crucial were about to happen. I believe something is; but what? Please write.—M."

Ruiz groaned involuntarily, drawing incurious glances from his compartment-mates: a Pole in a sheepskin coat who had spent the entire journey wordlessly cutting his way through a monstrous and smelly cheese he had boarded the train with, and a Hollywood Vedantist in sandals, burlap and beard whose smell was not that of cheese and whose business in Rome in a Holy Year was problematical.

He closed his eyes against them. Mike had had no business even thinking about such matters on his wedding morning. No wonder the letter was hard to read.

Cautiously, he opened his eyes again. The sunlight was almost intolerably bright, but for a moment he saw an olive grove sweeping by against burnt-umber hills lined beneath a sky of incredibly clear blue. Then the hills abruptly came piling down upon him and the express shot screaming into a tunnel.

Ruiz lifted the letter once more, but the ant tracks promptly puddled into a dirty blur; a sudden stab of pain lanced vertically through his left eye. Dear God, was he going blind? No, nonsense, that was hypochondria—there was nothing wrong with him but simple eyestrain. The stab through the eyeball was pressure in his left sphenoid sinus, which had been inflamed ever since he left Lima for the wet

North, and had begun to become acute in the dripping atmosphere of Lithia.

His trouble was Michelis's letter, that was plain. Never mind the temptation to blame eyes or sinuses, which were only surrogates for hands empty even of the amphora in which Egtverchi had been brought into the world. Nothing was left of his gift but the letter.

And what answer could he give?

Why, only what Michelis obviously was already coming to realize: that the reason for both Egtverchi's popularity and his behaviour lay in the fact that he was both mentally and emotionally a seriously displaced person. He had been deprived of the normal Lithian upbringings which would have taught him how fundamental it is to know how to survive in a predominantly predatory society. As for Earth's codes and beliefs, he had only half-absorbed them when Michelis forcibly expelled him from the classroom straight into citizenship. Now he had already had ample opportunity to see the hypocrisy with which some of those codes were served and, to the straight-line logic of the Lithian mind, this could mean only that the codes must therefore be only some kind of game at best. (He had encountered the concept of a game here, too; it was unknown on Lithia.) But he had no Lithian code of conduct to substitute or to fall back on, since he was as ignorant of Lithian civilization as he was innocent of experience of Lithia's seas, savannas and jungles.

In short, a wolf child.

The *rapido* hurled itself from the mouth of the tunnel as impetuously as it had entered, and the renewed blast of sunlight forced Ruiz to close his eyes once more. When he opened them he was rewarded by the sight of an extensive terraced vineyard. This was obviously wine country and, judging by the mountains, which were especially steep here, they must be nearing Terracina. Soon, if he was lucky, he might see Mt. Cicero; but he was far more interested in the vineyards.

From what he had been able to observe thus far, the Italian states were far less deeply buried than was most of the rest of the world, and the people were on the surface for much greater proportions of their lifetimes. To some extent this was a product of poverty—Italy as a whole had not had the wealth to get into the Shelter race early, or on anything like the scale which had been possible for the United States or even the other Continental countries. Nevertheless, there was a huge Shelter installation at Naples, and the one under Rome was the world's fourth biggest; that one had got itself dug with funds from all over the Western world, and with a great deal of outright voluntary help, when the first deep excavations had begun to turn up an incredible wealth of unsuspected archaeological finds.

In part, however, sheer stubbornness was responsible. A high proportion of Italy's huge population, which had never known any living but in and by the sun, simply could not be driven underground on any permanent basis. Of all the Shelter nations—a class which excluded only countries still almost wholly undeveloped, or unrecoverably desert—Italy appeared to be the least thoroughly entombed.

If that turned out to hold true for Rome in particular, the Eternal City would also be by far the sanest major capital on the planet. And that, Ruiz realized suddenly, would be an outcome nobody would have dared predict for an enterprise founded in 753 B.C. by a wolf child.

Of course, about the Vatican he had never been in any doubt, but Vatican City is not Rome. The thought reminded him that he had been commanded to an *udienza speciale* with the Holy Father tomorrow, before the ring-kissing, which meant before 1000 at the latest—probably as early as 0700, for the Holy Father was an early riser, and in this year of all years would be holding audiences of all kinds nearly around the clock. Ruiz had had nearly a month to prepare, for the command had reached him very shortly after the order of the College to appear for inquisition, but he felt unreadier than ever. He wondered how long it had been since any Pope had personally examined a Jesuit convert to an admitted heresy, and what the man had found to say; doubtless the transcript was there in the Vatican library, as recorded by some papal master of ceremonies—assiduous as always in his duty toward history, as masters of ceremonies had been ever since the invaluable Burchard—but Ruiz would not have time to read it.

From here on out, there would be a thousand petty distractions to keep him from settling his mind and heart any further. Just getting his bearings was going to be a chore, and after that there was the matter of accommodations. None of the *case religiose* would take him in—word had apparently got around—and he had not the purse for an hotel, though if worse came to worst he had a confirmed-reservation slip from one of the most expensive which just might let him into some linen closet there. Finding a *pensione*, the only other tolerable alternative, was going to be particularly difficult, for the one which had been contracted for him by the tourist agency had become impossible the moment he received the papal summons; it was too far from St. Peter's. The agency had been able to do nothing else for him except suggest that he sleep in the Shelter, which he was resolved not to do. After all, the agent had told him belligerently, it's a Holy Year—almost as though he were saying: "Don't you know there's a war on?"

And of course his tone had been right. There was a war on. The Enemy was presently fifty light-years away, but He was at the gates all the same.

Something prompted him to check the date of Michelis's letter. It was, he discovered with astonishment and disquiet, nearly two weeks old. Yet the postmark read today; the letter had been mailed, in fact, only about six hours ago, just in time to catch the dawn missile to Naples. Michelis had been sitting on it—or perhaps adding to it, but the facsimile process and the ensmallment, together with Ruiz's gathering eyestrain, all conspired to make it impossible to detect differences in the handwriting or the ink.

After a moment, Ruiz realized what importance the discrepancy had for him. It meant that Egtverchi's 3-V answer to his newspaper critics had been broadcast a week ago—and that he was due on the air again tonight!

Egtverchi's programme was broadcast at 0300 Rome time; Ruiz was going to be up earlier than the pontiff himself. In fact, he thought grimly, he was going to get no sleep at all.

The express pulled into the *Stazione Termini* in Rome five minutes ahead of schedule with a feminine shriek. Ruiz found a porter with no difficulty, tipped him the standard 100 lire for his two pieces of luggage, and gave directions. The priest's Italian was adequate, but hardly standard; it made the *facchino* grin with delight every time Ruiz opened his mouth. He had learned it by reading, partly in Dante, mostly in opera libretti, and consequently what he lacked in accent he made up for in flowery phrases: he was unable to ask the way to the nearest fruit stall without sounding as though he would throw himself into the Tiber unless he got an answer.

"*Be' 'a?*" the porter kept saying after every third sentence from Ruiz. "*Che be' 'a?*"

Still, that was easier to get along with than the French attitude had been on Ruiz's one visit to Paris fifteen years ago. He remembered a taxi driver who had refused to understand his request to be taken to the Continental Hotel until he had written the name down, after which the hackie had said, miming sudden comprehension: "*Ah, ah? Lee Con-ti-nen-TAL?*" This he had found to be an almost universal pretence; the French wanted one to know that without a perfect accent one is not intelligible at all.

The Italians, apparently, were willing to meet one half-way. The porter grinned at Ruiz's purple prose, but he guided the priest deftly to a news-stand where he was able to buy a news magazine containing a high enough proportion of text over pictures to insure an adequate account of what Egtverchi had said last week; and then took him down the left incline from the station across the Piazza Cinquecento to the corner of the Via Viminale and the Via Diocletian, precisely as requested. Ruiz promptly doubled his tip without even a qualm; guidance like that would be invaluable now that time was so short, and he might see the man again.

He had been left in the Casa del Passegero, which had the reputation of being the finest travellers' way station in Italy—which, Ruiz quickly discovered, means the finest in the world, for there are no other institutions precisely like the *alberghi diurni* anywhere else. Here he was able to check his luggage, read his magazine over a pastry in the *caffè*, have his hair cut and his shoes shined, have a bath while his clothes were being pressed, and then begin the protracted series of telephone calls which, he hoped, would eventually allow him to spend the coming night in a bed—preferably near by, but at least anywhere in Rome but in a Shelter dormitory.

In the coffee shop, in the barber's chair, and even in the tub, he pored again and again over the account of Egtverchi's broadcast. The Italian reporter did not give a text, for obvious reasons—a thirteen-minute broadcast would have filled an entire page of the journal in which he was limited to a single column of type—but he digested it skilfully, and he had an inside story to go with it. Ruiz was impressed.

Evidently Egtverchi had composed his rebuttal by weaving together the news items of the evening, just as they had come in to him off the wires beyond any possibility of his selecting them, into a brilliant extempore attack upon Earthly moral assumptions and pretensions. The thread which wove them all together was summed up by the magazine's reporter in a phrase from the Inferno: *Perche mi scerpi?/non hai tu spirito di pietate alcuno?*—the cry of the Suicides, who can speak only when the Harpies rend them and the blood flows: "Wherefore pluckest *thou* me?" It had been a scathing indictment, at no point defending Egtverchi's own conduct, but by implication making ridiculous the notion that any man could be stainless enough to be casting stones. Egtverchi had obviously absorbed Schopenhauer's vicious *Rules for Debate* down to the last comma.

"And in fact", the Italian reporter added, "it is widely known in Manhattan that Q.B.C. officials were on the verge of cutting off the outworlder in mid-broadcast as he began to cover the Stockholm brothel war. They were dissuaded by the barrage of telephone calls, telegrams, and radiograms which began to pour down upon Q.B.C.'s main office at precisely that moment. The response of the public has hardly diminished since, and it continues to be overwhelmingly approving. The network, encouraged by Signor Egtverchi's major sponsor, Bridget Bifalco World Kitchens, now is issuing almost hourly releases containing statistics 'proving' the broadcast a spectacular success. Signor Egtverchi is now a hot property, and if past experience is any guide (and it is) this means that henceforth the Lithian will be encouraged to display those aspects of his public character for which formerly he was being widely condemned, for which the network was considering taking him off the air in the middle of a word. Suddenly, in short, he is worth a lot of money."

The report was both literate and overheated—a peculiarly Roman combination—but as long as Ruiz lacked the text of the broadcast itself, he could not take exception to a word of it. Both the reporter's editorializing and the precise passion of his language seemed no more than justified. Indeed, a case could be made for a claim that the man had indulged in understatement.

To Ruiz, at least, Egtverchi's voice came through. The accent was familiar and perfect. And this for an audience full of children! Had any independent person called Egtverchi ever really existed? If so, he was possessed—but Ruiz did not believe that for an instant. There had never been any real Egtverchi to possess. He was throughout a creature of the Adversary's imagination, as even Chtexa had been, as the whole of Lithia had been. In the figure of Egtverchi He had already abandoned subtlety; already He dared to show Himself more than half-naked, commanding money, fathering lies, poisoning discourse, compounding grief, corrupting children, killing love, building armies—

—and all in a Holy Year.

Ruiz-Sanchez froze, one arm half-way into his summer jacket, looking up at the ceiling of the dressing-room. He had yet to make more than two telephone calls, neither of them to the general of his Order, but he had already changed his mind.

Had he really failed, all this time, to reach such obvious signs—or was he as crazed as heretics are supposed to be, smelling the *Dies irae*, the day of the wrath of God, in the steam of nothing but a public bath? Armageddon—in 3-V? The pit opened to let loose a comedian for the amusement of children?

He did not know. He could only be sure that he needed to hunt for no bed tonight, after all; what he needed was stones. He got out of the Casa del Passegero as quickly as he could, leaving everything he owned behind, and found his way alone back to the Via del Termini; the guidebook showed a church just off there, on the Piazza della Republica, by the Baths of Diocletian.

The book was right. The church was there: Santa Maria d'Angeli. He did not stop in the porch to cool off, though the early evening sunlight was almost as hot as noon. Tomorrow might be much hotter—unredeemably hotter. He went through the portals at once.

Inside, in the chill darkness, he knelt; and in cold terror, he prayed.

It did not seem to do him much good.

XV

ALL about Michelis the jungle stood frozen in a riot of motionlessness. Filtered through it, the sourceless blue-grey daylight was tinged with deep green, and where the light fell on one or another clear reflection it seemed to penetrate rather than glance off, carrying the jungle on in an inversion of images to the eight corners of the universe. The illusion was made doubly real by the stillness of everything; at any moment it seemed as though a breeze would spring up and ruffle the reflections, but there was no breeze, and nothing but time would ever disturb those images.

Egtverchi moved, of course; though his figure was ensmalled as if by distance, he was about the right size for the rest of the jungle, and almost more convincingly coloured and in the round. His circumscribed gestures seemed to be beckoning, as though he were attempting to lead Michelis out of this motionless wilderness.

Only his voice was jarring: it was at normal conversational volume, which meant that it was far too loud to be in scale with himself or his (and Michelis's) surroundings. It seemed so loud to Michelis, indeed, that in his reverie he almost missed the content of Egtverchi's final speech. Only when Egtverchi had bowed ironically and faded away and his voice died, leaving behind only the omnipresent muted insect buzz, did the meaning penetrate.

Michelis stayed where he was, stunned. A full thirty seconds of commercial for Mammale Bifalco's Delicious Instant Knish Mix went by before he remembered to put his finger over the 3-V's cut-off stud. Then this year's Bridget Bifalco in turn faded in mid-mix, smothered before she reached her famous brogue tag-line ("Give it t' me a minute, dharlin', till I give it a lhashin'.") The scurrying electrons in the phosphor complex migrated back to the atoms from which they had been driven by the miniature de Broglie scanner imbedded in the picture frame. The atoms resumed their chemical identity, the molecules cooled, and the screen became a static reproduction of Paul Klee's "Caprice in February". The principle, Michelis recalled with grey irrelevancy, had emerged out of d'Averoigne's first "Petard" paper, the count's only venture into applied maths, published when he was seventeen.

"What does he mean?" Liu said faintly. "I don't understand him at all any more. He calls it a demonstration—but what can he possibly demonstrate by that? It's childish!"

"Yes," Michelis said. For the moment he could think of nothing else to say. He needed to get his temper back; he was losing it more and more easily these days. That had been one of the reasons for his urgency in marrying Liu: he needed her calmness, for his own was vanishing with frightening rapidity.

No calmness seemed to be passing from her to him now. Even the apartment, originally such a source of satisfaction and repose for them both, felt like a trap. It was far above ground, in one of the mostly unused project buildings on the upper East Side of Manhattan. Originally Liu had had a far smaller set of rooms in the same building, and Michelis, after he had got used to the idea, had had them both installed in the present apartment with only a minimum of wire-pulling. It was not customary, it was certainly not fashionable, and they were officially warned that it was considered dangerous—the gangs raided surface structures now and then; but apparently it was no longer outright illegal, if one had the money to live that high up in the slums.

Given the additional space, the artist buried inside Liu's demure technician's exterior had run quietly wild. In the green glow of concealed light which washed the apartment, Michelis was surrounded by what seemed to be a miniature jungle. On small tables stood Japanese gardens with real Ming trees or dwarf cedars in them. An oriental lamp was fashioned out of a piece of fantastically sculptured drift-wood. Long, deep, woven flower-boxes ran completely around the room at eye level; they were thickly planted with ivy, wandering Jew, rubber plants, philodendron, and other non-flowering species, and behind each box a mirror ran up to the ceiling, unbroken anywhere except by the placidly witty Klee reproduction which was the 3-V set; the painting, made almost wholly of detached angles and glyphs like the symbols of mathematics, was a welcome oasis of dryness for which Liu had paid a premium—Q.B.C.'s stock "covers" were mostly Sargents and van Goghs. Since the light tubes were hidden behind the planting boxes, the room gave an effect of extra-terrestrial exuberance kept under control only with the greatest difficulty.

"I know what he means," Michelis said at last. "I just don't know quite how to put it. Let me think a minute—why don't you get dinner while I do it? We'd better eat early. We're going to have visitors, that's a cinch."

"Visitors? But—— All right, Mike."

Michelis walked to the glass wall and looked out on to the sun porch. All of Liu's flowering plants were out there, a real garden, which had to be kept sealed off from the rest of the apartment; for in addition to being an ardent amateur gardener, Liu bred bees. There was a colony of them there, making singular and exotic honeys from the congeries of blossoms Liu had laid out so carefully. The honey was fabulous and ever-changing, sometimes too bitter to eat except in tiny fork-touches like Chinese mustard, sometimes containing a heady touch of opium from the sticky hybrid poppies that nodded in a soldierly squad along the sun porch railing, sometimes sickly-sweet and insipid until, with a surprisingly small amount of glassware, Liu converted it into a liqueur that mounted to the head like a breeze from the Garden of Allah. The bees that made it were tetraploid monsters the size of humming-birds, with tempers as bad as Michelis's own was getting to be; only a few of them could kill even a big man. Luckily, they flew badly in the gusts common at this altitude, and would starve anywhere but in Liu's garden, otherwise Liu would never have been licensed to keep them on an open sun porch in the middle of the city. Michelis had been more than a little wary of them at first, but lately they had begun to fascinate him: their apparent intelligence was almost as phenomenal as their size and viciousness.

"Damn!" Liu said behind him.

"What's the matter?"

"Omelettes again. That's the second wrong number I've dialled this week."

Both the oath—mild though it was—and the error were uncharacteristic. Mike felt a twinge, a mixture of compassion and guilt. Liu was changing; she had never been so distractible before. Was he responsible?

"It's all right. I don't mind. Let's eat."

"All right."

They ate silently, but Michelis was conscious of the pressure of inquiry behind Liu's still expression. The chemist thought furiously, angry with himself and yet unable to phrase what he wanted to say. He should never have got her into this at all. No, that couldn't have been prevented; she had been the logical scientist to handle Egtverchi in his infancy—probably nobody else could have brought him through it even this well. But surely it should have been possible to keep her from becoming emotionally involved——

No, that had not been possible either; that was the woman of it. And the man of it, now that he was forced to think about his own role. It was no use; he simply did not know what he should think; Egtverchi's broadcast had rattled him beyond the point of logical thought. He was going to wind up with his usual bad compromise with Liu, which was to say nothing at all. But that would not do either.

And yet it had been a simple enough piece of foolery that the Lithian had perpetrated—childish, as Liu had said. Egtverchi had been urged to be off beat, rebellious, irresponsible, and he had come through in spades. Not only had he voiced his disrespect for all established institutions and customs, but he had also challenged his audience to show the same disrespect. In the closing moments of his broadcast, he had even told them how: they were to mail anonymous, insulting messages to Egtverchi's own sponsors.

"A postcard will do," he had said, gently enough, through his grinning chops. "Just make the message pungent. If you hate that powdered concrete they call a knish mix, write and tell them so. If you can eat the knishes but our commercials make you sick, write them about that, and don't pull any punches. If you loathe *me*, tell the Bifalcos that, too, and make sure you're spitting mad about it. I'll read the five messages I think in the worst possible taste on my broadcast next week. And remember, don't sign your name; if you have to sign, use my name. Good night."

The omelette tasted like flannel.

"I'll tell you what I think," Michelis said suddenly, in a low voice. "I think he's whipping up a mob. Remember those kids in the uniforms? He's abandoned that now, or else he's keeping it under cover; in any event, he thinks he has something better. He has an audience of about sixty-five million, and maybe half of them are adults. Of those, another half is insane to some degree, and that's what he's counting on now. He's going to turn that group into a lynch gang."

"But why, Mike?" Liu said. "What good will that do him?"

"I don't know. That's what stops me. He's not after power —he's got too many brains to think he can be a mccarthy. Maybe he just wants to destroy things. An elaborate act of revenge."

"Revenge!"

"I'm only guessing. I don't understand him any better than you do. Maybe worse."

"Revenge on whom?" Liu said steadily. "And for what?"

"Well—on us. For making such a bad job of him."

"I see," Liu said. "I see." She looked down into her untouched plate and began to weep, silently. At that moment, Michelis would gladly have killed either Egtverchi or himself, had he known where to begin.

The Klee chimed decorously. Michelis looked up at it with bitter resignation.

"The visitors," he said. He touched the phone stud.

The Klee faded, and the chairman of the citizenship committee which had examined Egtverchi looked out from the wall at them from under his elaborate helmet.

"Come on up," Michelis said to the silently inquiring image. "We've been expecting you."

It took a while for the U N. committee chairman to stop

touring the apartment and exclaiming over Liu's décor, but this evidently was a ceremony. As soon as he had uttered the last amenity, he dropped his social manner so abruptly that Michelis could almost see it break on the parpetite. Even the bees had sensed something hostile about him; he had no sooner peered through the glass at them than they began butting their eye-bulging heads at him. Michelis could hear them thumping doggedly away at the transparent barrier all through the subsequent conversation, with a rising and falling snarl of angry wings.

"We've gotten more than ten thousand facsimiles and telegrams in the half-hour between when Egtverchi went off the air and the first analysis of the response," the U.N. man said grimly. "That was enough to tell us what we're up against, and that's why I came to see you. We've had a good many decades of experience at assessing public response. In the next week, we are going to get about two million of these things——"

"Who's 'we'?" Michelis said, and Liu added: "That doesn't seem like a large figure to me."

" 'We' is the network. And the figure's large for us, since we're nearly anonymous in the public mind. The Bifalcos are going to get a little over seven and a half million such missives."

"Are they really so bad?" Liu said, frowning.

"They are as bad as they could be and still get through the cables and the mail tubes," the U.N. man said flatly. "I've never seen anything like them, and I've been in Q.B.C. community relations for eleven years—this U.N. committee job is my other hat, you know how that goes. More than half of them are expressions of virulent, unrestrained hatred—pathological hatred. I have a few samples here, but I didn't bring the worst of them along. It's my policy not to show laymen anything that sacres *me*."

"Let me see one," Michelis said promptly.

The U.N. man passed a facsimile over silently. Michelis read it. Then he gave it back.

"You're a little more calloused than you realize," he said in a gravelly voice. "I wouldn't have shown even that one to anyone but the director of reasearch of an insane asylum."

The U.N. man smiled for the first time, looking at them both with quick, intelligent eyes. Somehow he seemed to be assessing them, not individually, but as a couple; Michelis had an overwhelming intuition that his privacy was somehow being violated, though there was nothing concrete in the man's behaviour to which he could have taken exception.

"Not even to Dr. Meid?" the U.N. man said.

"To nobody," Michelis said angrily.

"Quite so. And yet I repeat that I didn't select it deliberately for shock value, Dr. Michelis. It's a bagatelle—very mild, compared to some of the stuff we've been getting. This Snake obviously has an audience of borderline madmen, and he means to use it. That's why I came to see you. We think you might have some idea as to what he intends to use it *for*."

"For nothing, if you people have any control over what you yourselves do," Michelis said. "Why don't you cut him off the air? If he's poisoning it, then you don't have any other choice."

"One man's poison is another man's knish mix," the U.N. man said smoothly. "The Bifalcos don't see this the way we do. They have their own analysts, and they know as well as we do that they're going to get more than seven and a half million dirty postcards in the next week. But they *like* the idea. In fact, they've positively wriggling with delight. They think it will sell products. They will probably give the Snake a whole half-hour, solely sponsored by them, if the response comes through as predicted—and it will."

"Why can't you cut Egtverchi off anyhow?" Liu said.

"The charter prevents us from interfering with the right of free speech. As long as the Bifalcos put up the money, we are obligated to keep the programme on the air. It's a good principle at bottom; we've had experiences with it before that threatened to turn out nastily, but in every case we sweated them out and the public got bored with them eventually. But that was a different public—the broad public, which used to be mostly sane. The Snake obviously has a selected audience, and that's not sane at all. This time—for the first time—we are thinking of interfering. That's why we came to you."

"I can't help you," Michelis said.

"You can, and you will, Dr. Michelis. I'm talking from under both my hats now. Q.B.C. wants him off the air, and the U.N. is beginning to smell something which might prove to be much worse than the 1993 Corridor Riots. You sponsored this Snake, and your wife raised him from an egg, or damn near an egg. You know him better than anyone else on Earth. You will have to give us the weapon that we need against him. That's what I came to tell you. Think about it. You are responsible under the naturalization law. It's not often that we have to invoke that clause, but we're invoking it now. You'll have to think fast, because we have to have him closed out before his next broadcast."

"And suppose we have nothing to offer?" Michelis said stonily.

"Then we will probably declare the Snake a minor, and you his guardians," the U.N. man said. "Which will hardly be a solution from our point of view, but you would probably find it painful—you'd be well advised to come up with something better. I'm sorry to bring such bad news, but the news *is* bad tonight; that sometimes happens. Good night, and thank you."

He went out. He did not have to resume any of his three hats; he had never taken any of them off, visible or metaphorical.

Michelis and Liu stared at each other, appalled.

"We—we couldn't possibly have him as a ward *now*," Liu whispered.

"Well," Michelis said harshly, "we were talking about wanting a son——"

"Mike, don't!"

"I'm sorry," he said inadequately. "That officious son of a

bitch. He was the man that passed on the application—and now he's throwing it right back in our laps. They must be really desperate. What are we going to do? I haven't an idea in my head."

Liu said, after a moment's hesitation: "Mike—we don't know enough to come up with anything useful in a week. At least I don't, and I don't think you do either. We've got to get through to the Father somehow."

"If we can," Michelis said slowly. "But even so, what good will that do? The U.N. won't listen to him—they've by-passed him."

"How? What do you mean?"

"They've made a *de facto* decision in favour of Cleaver," Michelis said. "It won't be announced until after Ramon's church has finished disavowing him, but its already in effect. I knew about it before he left for Rome, but I didn't have the heart to tell him. Lithia has been closed; the U.N. is going to use it as a laboratory for the study of fusion power storage—not exactly what Cleaver had inmind originally, but close enough."

Liu was silent for a long time. She arose and went to the window, against which the huge bees were still butting like live battering-rams.

"Does Cleaver know?" she said, her back still turned.

"Oh yes, he knows," Michelis said. "He's in charge. He was scheduled to land back at Xoredeshch Sfath yesterday. I tried to tip Ramon off indirectly as soon as I heard about it —that's why I promoted that collaboration for the *J.I.R.*— but Ramon just didn't seem to hear any of my hints. And I just couldn't tell him outright that his cause was already lost, before he'd even had a hearing."

"It's ugly," Liu said slowly. "Why won't they announce it until after Ramon is officially excommunicated? Why does that make any difference?"

"Because the decision is tainted, that's all," Michelis said fiercely. "Whether you agree with Ramon's theological arguments or not, to decide for Cleaver is a dirty act—impossible to defend except in terms of raw power. They know that well enough, damn them, and sooner or later they're going to have to let the public see what the arguments were on the other side. When that day comes, they want Ramon's arguments discredited in advance by his own church."

"What precisely is Cleaver doing?"

"I can't say, precisely. But they're building a big Nernst generator plant inland on the south continent, near Glesh-chtehk Sfath, to turn out the power, so that much of his dream is already realized. Later they'll try to trap the power raw, as it comes off, instead of stepping it down and throwing away ninety-five per cent of it as heat. I don't know how Cleaver proposes to do that, but I should guess he'd begin with a modification of the Nernst effect itself—the 'magnetic bottle' dodge. He'd better be damned careful." He paused. "I suppose I'd have told Ramon if he'd asked me. But he didn't, so I didn't say anything. Now I feel like a coward."

Liu turned swiftly at that, and came back to sit on the arm of his chair. "That was right to do, Mike," she said. "It's not cowardice to refuse to rob a man of hope, I think."

"Maybe not," Michelis said, taking her hand gratefully. "But what it all comes out to is that Ramon can't help us now. Thanks to me, he doesn't even know yet that Cleaver is back on Lithia."

XVI

SHORTLY past dawn, Ruiz-Sanchez walked stiffly into the vast circle of the Piazza San Pietro toward the towering dome of St. Peter's itself. The piazza was swarming with pilgrims even this early, and the dome, more than twice as high as the Statue of Liberty, seemed frowning and ominous in the early light, rising from the forest of pillars like the forehead of God.

He passed under the right arch of the colonnade, past the Swiss Guards in their gorgeous, *outré* uniforms, and through the bronze door. Here he paused to murmur, with unexpected intensity, the prayers for the Pope's intentions obligatory for this year. The Apostolic Palace soared in front of him; he was astonished that any edifice so crowded with stone could at the same time contrive to be so spacious, but he had no time for further devotions now.

Near the first door on the right a man sat at a table. Ruiz-Sanchez told him: "I am commanded to a special audience with the Holy Father."

"God has blessed you. The major-domo's office is on the first floor, to the left. No, one moment—a *special* audience? May I see your letter, please?"

Ruiz-Sanchez showed it.

"Very good. But you will need to see the major-domo anyhow. The special audiences are in the throne room; he will show you where to go."

The throne room! Ruiz-Sanchez was more unsettled than ever. That was where the Holy Father received heads of state, and members of the college of cardinals. Certainly it was no place to receive a heretical Jesuit of very low rank——

"The throne room," the major-domo said. "That's the first room in the reception suite. I trust your business goes well, Father. Pray for me."

Hadrian VIII was a big man, a Norwegian by birth, whose curling beard had been only slightly peppered with grey at his election. It was white now, of course, but otherwise age seemed to have marked him little; indeed, he looked somewhat younger than his photographs and 3-V 'casts suggested, for they had a tendency to accentuate the crags and furrows of his huge, heavy face.

Ruiz-Sanchez found his person so overwhelming that he barely noticed the magnificence of his robes of state. Needless to say, there was nothing in the least Latin in the Holy Father's mien or temperament. In his rise to the gestatorial chair he had made a reputation as a Catholic with an almost Lutheran passion for the grimmer reaches of moral theology;

there was something of Kierkegaard in him, and something of the Grand Inquisitor as well. After his election, he had surprised everyone by developing an interest—one might almost call it a businessman's interest—in temporal politics, though the characteristic coldness of Northern theological speculation continued to colour everything he said and did. His choice of the name of a Roman emperor was perfectly appropriate, Ruiz-Sanchez realized: here was a face that might well have been stamped on imperial coin, for all the beneficence which tempered its harshness.

The Pope remained standing thoughout the interview, staring down at Ruiz-Sanchez with what seemed at first to be nine-tenths frank curiosity.

"Of all the thousands of pilgrims here, you may stand in the greatest need of our indulgence," he observed in English. Near by, a tape recorder raced silently; Hadrian was an ardent archivist, and a stickler for the letter of the text. "Yet we have small hope of your winning it. It is incredible to us that a Jesuit, of all our shepherds, could have fallen into Manichaeanism. The errors of that heresy are taught most particularly in that college."

"Holiness, the evidence——"

Hadrian raised his hand. "Let us not waste time. We have already informed ourself of your views and your reasoning. You are subtle, Father, but you have committed a grievous oversight all the same—but we wish to defer that subject for the moment. Tell us first of this creature Egtverchi—not as a sending of the Devil, but as you would see him were he a man."

Ruiz-Sanchez frowned. There was something about the word "sending" that touched some weakness inside him, like an obligation forgotten until too late to fulfill it. The feeling was like that which had informed a ridiculous recurrent nightmare of his student days, in which he was not to graduate because he had forgotten to attend all his Latin classes. Yet he could not put his finger on what it was.

"There are many ways to describe him, Holiness," he said.

"He is the kind of personality that the twentieth-century critic Colin Wilson called an Outsider, and that is the kind of Earth man he appeals to—he is a preacher without a creed, an intellect without a culture, a seeker without a goal. I think he has a conscience as we would define the term; he's very different from the rest of his race in that and many other respects. He seems to take a deep interest in moral problems, but he's utterly contemptuous of all traditional moral frames of reference—including the kind of rationalized moral automation that prevails on Lithia."

"And this strikes some chord in his audience?"

"There can be no doubt of that, surely, Holiness. It remains to be seen how wide his appeal is. He ran off a very shrewdly designed experiment last night, obviously intended to test that very question; we should soon know just how great the response will be. But it already seems clear that he appeals to all those people who feel cut off, emotionally and intellectually, from our society and its dominant cultural traditions."

"Well put," Hadrian said, surprisingly. "We stand at the brink of unguessable events, that is certain; we have had forebodings that this might be the year. We have commanded the Inquisition to put away its bell, book and candle for the time being; we think such a move would be most unwise."

Ruiz-Sanchez was stunned. No trial—and no excommunication? The drumming of events around his head had begun to remind him of the numbing, incessant rains of Xoredeshch Sfath.

"Why, Holiness?" he said faintly.

"We believe you may be the man appointed by our Lord to bear St. Michael's arms," the Pope said, weighing every word.

"I, Holiness? A heretic?"

"Noah was not perfect, you will recall," Hadrian said, with what might have been a half-smile. "He was merely a man who was given another chance. Goethe, himself more than a little heretical, reshaped the legend of Faustus to the same lesson: redemption is always the crux of the great drama, and there must be a peripataea first. Besides, Father, consider for a moment the unique nature of this case of heresy. Is not the appearance of a solitary Manichaean in the twenty-first century either a wildly meaningless anachronism—or a grave sign?"

He paused and fingered his beads.

"Of course," he added, "it will be necessary for you to purge yourself, if you can. That is why we have called you. We believe as you do that the Adversary is the moving spirit behind this whole Lithian crisis; but we do not believe that any repudiation of dogma is required. It all hinges upon this question of creativity. Tell us, Father: when you first became convinced that the whole of Lithia was a sending, what did you do about it?"

"Do about it?" Ruiz-Sanchez said numbly. "Why, Holiness, I did only what was recorded. I could think of nothing else to do."

"Then did it never occur to you that sendings can be banished—and that God has given that power into your hands?"

Ruiz-Sanchez had no emotions left.

"Banished. . . . Holiness, perhaps I have been stupid. I feel stupid. But as far as I know, exorcism was abandoned by the Church more than two centuries ago. My college taught me that meteorology replaced the 'spirits and powers of the air', and neurophysiology replaced 'possession'. It would never have occurred to me."

"Exorcism was not abandoned, merely discouraged," Hadrian said. "It had become limited, as you have just pointed out, and the Church wished to prevent its abuse by ignorant country priests—they were bringing the Church into disrepute trying to drive demons out of sick cows and perfectly healthy goats and cats. But I am not talking about animal health, the weather or mental illness now, Father."

"Then . . . is Your Holiness truly proposing that . . . that I should have attempted to . . . *to exorcise a whole planet*?"

"Why not?" Hadrian said. "Of course, the fact that you were standing on the planet at the time might have helped to prevent you, unconsciously, from thinking of it. We are convinced that God would have provided for you—in Heaven certainly, and possibly you might have received temporal help as well. But it was the only solution to your dilemma. Had the exorcism failed, *then* there might have been some excuse for falling into heresy. But surely it should be easier to believe in a planet-wide hallucination—which in principle we know the Adversary has the power to do—than in the heresy of satanic creativity!"

The Jesuit bowed his head. He felt overwhelmed by his own ignorance. He had spent almost all his leisure hours on Lithia minutely studying a book which to all intents and purposes might have been dictated by the Adversary himself, and he had seen nothing that mattered, not in all those 628 pages of compulsive demoniac chatter.

"It is not too late to try," Hadrian said, almost gently. "That is the only road left for you to travel." Suddenly his face became stern, flinty. "As we have pointed out to the Inquisition, your excommunication is automatic. It began the instant that you admitted this abomination into your soul. It does not need to be formalized to be a fact—and there are political reasons, as well as spiritual ones, for not formalizing it now. In the meantime, you must leave Rome. We withhold our blessing and our indulgence from you, Dr. Ruiz-Sanchez. This Holy Year is for you a year of battle, with the world as prize. When you have won that battle you may return to us—not before. Farewell."

Dr. Ramon Ruiz-Sanchez, a layman, damned, left Rome for New York that night by air. The deluge of happenstance was rising more rapidly around him; the time for the building of arks was almost at hand. And yet, as the waters rose, and the words, *Into your hand are they delivered*, passed incessantly across the tired surfaces of his brain, it was not of the swarming billions of the Shelter state that he was thinking. It was of Chtcxa; and the notion that an exorcism might succeed in dissolving utterly that grave being and all his race and civilization, return them to the impotent mind of the Great Nothing as though they had never been, was an agony to him.

Into your hand. . . . Into your hand. . . .

XVII

THE figures were in. The people who had taken Egtverchi as both symbol and spokesman for their passionate discontents were now tallied, although they could not be known. Their nature was no surprise—the crime and mental disease statistics had long provided a clear picture of that—but their number was stunning. Apparently nearly a third of twenty-first-century society loathed that society from the bottom of its collective heart.

Ruiz-Sanchez wondered suddenly whether, had a similar tally been possible in every age, the proportion would have turned out to be stable.

"Do you think it would do any good to talk to Egtverchi?" he asked Michelis. Over his protests, he was staying in the Michelis's apartment for the time being.

"Well, it hasn't done any good for *me* to talk with him," Michelis said. "With you it might be a different story—though frankly, Ramon, I'm inclined to doubt even that. He's doubly hard to reason with because he himself seems to be getting no satisfaction out of the whole affair."

"He knows his audience better than we do," Liu added. "And the more the numbers pile up, the more embittered he seems to become. I think they remind him continually that he can never be fully accepted on Earth, fully at home on it. He thinks he's of interest only to people who themselves don't feel at home on their own planet. That's not true, of course, but that's how he feels."

"There's enough truth in it so that he'd be unlikely to be dissuaded of it," Ruiz-Sanchez agreed gloomily.

He shifted his chair so as not to be able to see Liu's bees, which were hard at work in the shafts of sunlight on the porch. At another time he could not have torn himself away from them, but he could not afford to be distracted now.

"And of course he's also well aware that he'll never know what it means to be a Lithian—regardless of his shape and inheritance," he added. "Chtexa might get a shadow of that through to him, if only they could meet—but no, they don't even speak the same language."

"Egtverchi's been studying Lithian," Michelis said. "But it's true that he can't speak it, not even as well as I can. He has nothing to read but your grammar—the documents are still all classified against him—and nobody to talk to. He sounds as rusty as an iron hinge. But, Ramon, you could interpret."

"Yes, I could. But Mike, it's physically impossible. There just isn't time to get Chtexa here, even if we had the resources and the authority to do it."

"I wasn't thinking of that. I was thinking of CirCon—d'Averoigne's new circum-continuum radio. I don't know what shape it's in, but the Message Tree puts out a powerful signal—possibly d'Averoigne could pick it up. If so, you might be able to talk to Chtexa. I'll see what I can find out, anyhow."

"I'm willing to try," Ruiz-Sanchez said. "But it doesn't sound very promising."

He stopped to think, not of more answers—he had already hit his head against that wall more than often enough—but of what questions he still needed to ask. Michelis's appearance gave him the cue. It had shocked him at first, and he could still not quite get used to it. The big chemist had aged markedly: his face was drawn, and he had deeply cut, liverish circles under his eyes. Liu looked no better; while she had not seemed to age any, she looked miserable. There was a tension in the air between them, too, as though they had failed to find in each other sufficient release from the tensions of the world around them.

"It's possible that Agronski might know something that would be helpful," he said, only half-aloud.

"Maybe," Michelis said. "I've seen him only once—at a party, the one where Egtverchi caused such a stink. He was behaving very oddly. I'm sure he recognized us, but he wouldn't meet our eyes, let alone come and talk to us. As a matter of fact, I can't remember seeing him talking to anybody. He just sat in a corner and drank. It wasn't at all like him."

"Why did he come, do you suppose?"

"Oh, that's not hard to guess. He's a fan of Egtverchi's."

"*Martin?* How do you know?"

"Egtverchi bragged about it. He said he hoped to have the whole Lithia commission on his side eventually." Michelis grimaced. "The way Agronski was acting, he'll be of no use to Egtverchi or anybody else."

"And so we have still another soul on the way to damnation," Ruiz-Sanchez said grimly. "I should have suspected it. There's so little meaning in Agronski's life as it is, it won't take Egtverchi long to cut him off from any contact with reality at all. That is what evil does—it empties you."

"I'm none too sure Egtverchi's to blame," Michelis said, his voice steeped in gloom. "Except as a symptom. The Earth is riddled with schizophrenics already. If Agronski had any tendency that way, and obviously he did, then all he needed was to be planted here again for the tendency to flower."

"That wasn't my impression of him," Liu said. "From what little I saw of him, and from what you've told me, he seemed dreadfully normal—even simple-minded. I don't see how he could get deep enough into any question to be driven insane—or how he could be tempted to fall into your theological vacuum, Ramon."

"In this universe of discourse, Liu, we are all very much alike," Ruiz-Sanchez said dispiritedly. "And from what Mike tells me, I think we may be already too late to do much for Martin. And he's only—only a sample of what's happening everywhere within the sound of Egtverchi's voice."

"It's a mistake to think of schizophrenia as a disease of the wits, anyhow," Michelis said. "Back in the days when it was first being described, the English used to call it 'lorry-driver's disease'. When intellectuals get it, the results are spectacular only because they can articulate what they feel: Nijinski, van Gogh, T. E. Lawrence, Nietzsche, Wilson . . . it's a long list, but it's nothing compared to the ordinary people who've had it. And they get it fifty-to-one over intellectuals. Agronski is just the usual kind of victim, no more, no less."

"What has happened to that threat you mentioned?" Ruiz-Sanchez said. "Egtverchi got on the air again last night without his being made a ward of yours. Was your friend in the complicated hat just flailing the air?"

"I think that's partly the answer," Michelis said hopefully. "They haven't said another word to us, so I'm just guessing, but it may be that your arrival disconcerted them. They expected you to be publicly unfrocked—and the fact that you weren't has thrown their schedule for announcing the Lithia decision seriously out of joint. They're probably waiting to see what you will do now."

"So", Ruiz-Sanchez said grimly, "am I. I might just do nothing, which would probably be the most confusing thing I could do. I think their hands are tied, Mike. He's never mentioned the Bifalcos' products but that once, but obviously he must be selling them by the warehouse-load, so his sponsors won't cut him off. Nor can I see on what grounds the U.N. Communications Commission can do it." He laughed shortly. "They've been trying for decades to encourage more independent comment on 3-V anyhow—and Egtverchi is certainly a giant step in that direction."

"I should think he'd be open to charges of inciting to riot," Michelis said.

"He hasn't incited any riots that I've heard about," Ruiz-

Sanchez said. "The Frisco affair happened spontaneously as far as anyone could see—and I noticed that the pictures didn't show a single one of those uniformed followers of his in the crowds."

"But he praised the rioters' spirit, and made fun of the police," Liu pointed out. "He as good as endorsed it."

"That's not incitement," Michelis said. "I see what Ramon means. He's smart enough to do nothing for which he could be brought to trial—and a false arrest would be suicide, the U.N. would be inciting a riot itself."

"Besides, what would they do with him if they got a conviction?" Ruiz asked. "He's a citizen, but his needs aren't like ours; they'd be chancing killing him with a thirty-day sentence. I suppose they could deport him, but they can't declare him an undesirable alien without declaring Lithia a foreign country—and until that report is released, Lithia is a protectorate, with a right to admission to the U.N. as a member state!"

"Small chance of that," Michelis said. "That would mean ditching Cleaver's project."

Ruiz-Sanchez felt the same sinking of the heart that had overcome him when Michelis first gave him that news. "How far advanced is it now?" he asked.

"I'm not sure. All I know is that they've been shipping equipment to him in huge amounts. There's another load scheduled to leave in two weeks. The scuttlebutt says that Cleaver has some kind of crucial experiment ready to go as soon as that shipment gets there. That puts it pretty close—the new ships make the trip in less than a month."

"Betrayed again," Ruiz-Sanchez said bitterly.

"Then is there *nothing* you can do, Ramon?" Liu asked.

"I'll interpret for Egtverchi and Chtexa, if anything comes of that project."

"Yes, but. . . ."

"I know what you mean," he said. "Yes, there is something decisive that I can do. And possibly it would work. In fact, it is something that I *must* do."

He stared blindly at them. The buzzing of the bees, so reminiscent of the singing of the jungles of Lithia, probed insistently at him.

"But", he said, "I don't think that I'm going to do it."

Michelis moved mountains. He was formidable enough under normal conditions, but when he was desperate and saw a possible way out, no bulldozer could have been more implacable in crushing through an opening.

Lucien le Comte des Bois-d'Averoigne, late Procurator of Canarsie, and always fellow in the brotherhood of science, received them all cordially in his Canadian retreat. Not even the sardonically silent figure of Egtverchi made him blink; he shook hands with the displaced Lithian as though they were old friends meeting again after a lapse of a few weeks. The count himself was a large, rotund man in his early sixties, with a protuberant belly, and he was brown all over: his remaining hair was brown, his suit was brown, he was deeply tanned, and he was smoking a long brown cigar.

The room in which he received them—Ruiz-Sanchez, Michelis, Liu, and Egtverchi—was a curious mixture of lodge and laboratory. It had an open fireplace, rough furniture, mounted guns, an elk's head, and an amazing mess of wires and apparatus.

"I am by no means sure that this is going to work," he told them promptly. "Everything I have is still in the breadboard stage, as you can see. It's been years since I last handled a soldering iron and a voltmeter, too, so we may well have a simple electronic failure somewhere in this mass of wiring—but it wasn't a task I could leave to a technician."

He waved them to seats while he made final adjustments. Egtverchi remained standing in the rear of the room in the shadows, motionless except for the gentle rise and fall of his great chest as he breathed, and an occasional sudden movement of his eyes.

"There will be no image, of course," the count said abstractedly. "This giant J-J coupling you describe obviously doesn't broadcast in that band. But if we are very lucky, we may get some sound. . . . Ah."

A loudspeaker almost hidden in the maze crackled and then began to emit distant, patterned bursts of hissing. Except for the pattern, it seemed to Ruiz-Sanchez to be nothing but noise, but the count said at once:

"I'm getting something in that region. I didn't expect to pick it up so soon. I don't make much sense of it, however."

Neither did Ruiz, and for a few moments he had all he could do to get over his amazement. "Those are—signals the Message Tree is broadcasting now?" he said, with a touch of incredulity.

"I hope so," the count said dryly. "I have been busy all day installing chokes against any other possible signal."

The Jesuit's respect for the mathematician came close to awe. To think that this disorderly tangle of wiring, little black acorns, small red and brown objects like fire-crackers, the shining interlocking blades of variable condensers, massively heavy coils, and flickering metres was even now reaching directly through the sub-ether, around fifty light-years of space-time, to eavesdrop on the pulses of the crystalline cliff buried beneath Xoredeshch Sfath. . . .

"Can you tune it?" he said at last. "I think those must be the stutter pattern—what the Lithians use as a navigational grid for their ships and planes. There ought to be an audio band——"

Except, he recalled suddenly, that that band couldn't possibly be an "audio" band. Nobody ever spoke directly to the Message Tree—only to the single Lithian who stood in the centre of the Tree's chamber. How *he* got the substance of the message transformed into radio waves had never been explained to any of the Earthmen.

And yet suddenly there was a voice.

"—a powerful tap on the Tree," the voice said in clear, even, cold Lithian. "Who is receiving? Do you hear me? I do not understand the direction your carrier is coming from.

It seems inside the Tree, which is impossible. Does anyone understand me?"

Silently, the count thrust a microphone into Ruiz's hand. He discovered that he was trembling.

"We understand you," he said in Lithian in a shaky voice. "We are on Earth. Can you hear me?"

"I hear you," the voice said at once. "We understood that what you say is impossible. But what you say is not always accurate, we have found. What do you want?"

"I would like to speak to Chtexa, the metallist," Ruiz said. "This is Ruiz-Sanchez, who was in Xoredeshch Sfath last year."

"He can be summoned," said the cold distant voice. There was a brief hashing sound from the speaker; then it went away again. "If he wishes to speak to you."

"Tell him", Ruiz-Sanchez said, "that his son Egtverchi also wishes to speak to him."

"Ah," said the voice after a pause. "Then no doubt he will come. But you cannot speak long on this channel. The direction from which your signal comes is damaging my sanity. Can you receive a sound-modulated signal if we can arrange to send one?"

Michelis murmured to the count, who nodded energetically and pointed to the loudspeaker.

"That is how we are receiving you now," Ruiz said. "How are you transmitting?"

"That I cannot explain to you," said the cold voice. "I cannot speak to you any longer or I will be damaged. Chtexa has been called."

The voice stopped and there was a long silence. Ruiz-Sanchez wiped the sweat off his forehead with the back of his hand.

"Telepathy?" Michelis muttered behind him. "No, it fits into the electro-magnetic spectrum somewhere. But where? Boy, there sure is a lot we don't know about that Tree."

The count nodded ruefully. He was watching his metres

like a hawk but, judging from his expression, they were not telling him anything he did not already know.

"Ruiz-Sanchez," the loudspeaker said. Ruiz started.

It was Chtexa's voice, clear and strong.

Ruiz beckoned at the shadows, and Egtverchi came forward. He was in no hurry. There was something almost insolent in his very walk.

"This is Ruiz-Sanchez, Chtexa," Ruiz said. "I'm talking to you from Earth—a new experimental communications system one of our scientists has evolved. I need your help."

"I will be glad to do whatever I can," Chtexa said. "I was sorry that you did not return with the other Earthman. He was less welcome. He and his friends have razed one of our finest forests near Gleshchtehk Sfath, and built ugly buildings here in the city."

"I'm sorry, too," Ruiz-Sanchez said. The words seemed inadequate, but it would be impossible to explain to Chtexa exactly what the situation was—impossible, and illegal. "I still hope to come some day. But I am calling about your son."

There was a brief pause, during which the speaker emitted a series of muted, anomalous sounds, almost yet not quite recognizable. Evidently the Lithians' audio hookup was catching some background noise from inside the Tree, or even outside it. The clarity of the reception was astonishing; it was impossible to believe that the Tree was fifty light-years away.

"Egtverchi is an adult now," Chtexa's voice said. "He has seen many wonders on your world. Is he with you?"

"Yes," Ruiz-Sanchez said, beginning to sweat again. "But he does not know your language, Chtexa. I will interpret as best I can."

"That is strange," Chtexa said. "But I will hear his voice. Ask him when he is coming home; he has much to tell us."

Ruiz put the question.

"I have no home," Egtverchi said indifferently.

"I can't just tell him that, Egtverchi. Say something intelligible, in heaven's name. You owe your existence to Chtexa, you know that."

"I may visit Lithia some day," Egtverchi said, his eyes filming. "But I am in no hurry. There is still a great deal to be done on Earth."

"I hear him," Chtexa said. "His voice is high; he is not as tall as his inheritance provided, unless he is ill. What does he answer?"

There simply was not time to provide an interpretive translation; Ruiz-Sanchez told him the answer literally, word by word from English into Lithian.

"Ah," Chtexa said. "Then he has matters of import to his hand. That is good, and is generous of the Earth. He is right not to hurry. Ask him what he is doing."

"Breeding dissension," Egtverchi said, with a slight widening of his grin. Ruiz-Sanchez could not translate that literally; the concept was not in the Lithian language. It took him the better part of three long sentences to transmit even a dubious shadow of the idea to Chtexa.

"Then he *is* ill," Chtexa said. "You should have told me, Ruiz-Sanchez. You had best send him to us. You cannot treat him adequately there."

"He is not ill, and he will not go," Ruiz-Sanchez said carefully. "He is a citizen of Earth and cannot be compelled. This is why I called you. He is a trouble to us, Chtexa. He is doing us hurts. I had hoped you might reason with him; we can do nothing."

The anomalous sound, a sort of burring metallic whine, rose in the background and fell away again.

"That is not normal or natural," Chtexa said. "You do not recognize his illness. No more do I, but I am not a physician. You must send him here. I see I was in error in giving him to you. Tell him he is commanded home by the Law of the Whole."

"I never heard of the Law of the Whole," Egtverchi said when this was translated for him. "I doubt that there is any such thing. I make up my own laws as I go along. Tell him he is making Lithia sound like a bore, and that if he keeps it up I'll make a point of never going there at all."

"Blast it, Egtverchi——" Michelis burst in.

"Hush, Mike, one pilot is enough. Egtverchi, you were willing to co-operate with us up to now; at least, you came here with us. Did you do it just for the pleasure of defying and insulting your father? Chtexa is far wiser than you are; why don't you stop acting like a child and listen to him?"

"Because I don't choose to," Egtverchi said. "And you make me no more willing by wheedling, dear foster father. I didn't choose to be born a Lithian, and I didn't choose to be brought to Earth—but now that I'm a free agent I mean to make my own choices, and explain them to nobody if that's what pleases me."

"Then why did you come here?"

"There's no reason why I should explain that, but I will. I came to hear my father's voice. Now I've heard it. I don't understand what he says, and he makes no better sense in your translation, and that's all there is to it as far as I am concerned. Bid him farewell for me—I shan't speak to him again."

"What does he say?" Chtexa's voice said.

"That he does not acknowledge the Law of the Whole, and will not come home," Ruiz-Sanchez told the microphone. The little instrument was slippery with sweat in his palm. "And he says to bid you farewell."

"Farewell, then," Chtexa said. "And farewell to you, too, Ruiz-Sanchez. I am at fault, and this fills me with sorrow; but it is too late. I may not talk to you again, even by means of your marvellous instrument."

Behind the voice, the strange, half-familiar whine rose to a savage, snarling scream which lasted almost a minute. Ruiz-Sanchez waited until he thought he could be heard over it again.

"Why not, Chtexa?" he said huskily. "The fault is ours as much as it is yours. I am still your friend, and wish you well."

"And I am your friend, and wish you well," Chtexa's

voice said. "But we may not talk again. Can you not hear the power saws?"

So that was what the sound was!

"Yes. Yes, I hear them."

"That is the reason," Chtexa said. "Your friend Xlevher is cutting down the Message Tree."

The gloom was thick in the Michelis apartment. As the time drew closer for Egtverchi's next broadcast, it became increasingly appatent that their analysis of the U.N.'s essential helplessness had been correct. Egtverchi was not openly triumphant, though he was exposed to that temptation in several newspaper interviews; but he floated some disquieting hints of vast plans which might well be started in motion when he was next on the air.

Ruiz-Sanchez had not the least desire to listen to the broadcast, but he had to face the fact that he would be unable to stay away from it. He could not afford to be without any new data that the programme might yield. Nothing he had learned had done him any good thus far, but there was always the slim chance that something would turn up.

In the meantime, there was the problem of Cleaver, and his associates. However you looked at it, they were human souls. If Ruiz-Sanchez were to be driven, somehow, to the step that Hadrian VIII had commanded, and it did not fail, more than a set of attractive hallucinations would be lost. It would plunge several hundred human souls into instant death and more than probable damnation; Ruiz-Sanchez did not believe that the hand of God would reach forth to pluck to salvation men who were involved in such a project as Cleaver's, but he was equally convinced that his should not be the hand to condemn any man to death, let alone to an unshriven death. Ruiz was condemned already—but not yet of murder.

It had been Tannhäuser who had been told that his salvation was as unlikely as the blossoming of the pilgrim's staff in his hand. And Ruiz-Sanchez's was as unlikely as sanctified murder.

Yet the Holy Father had commanded it; had said it was the only road back for Ruiz-Sanchez, and for the world. The Pope's clear implication had been that he shared with Ruiz-Sanchez the view that the world stood on the brink of Armageddon—and he had said flatly that only Ruiz-Sanchez could avert it. Their only difference was doctrinal, and in these matters the Pope could not err. . . .

But if it was possible that the dogma of the infertility of Satan was wrong, then it was possible that the dogma of Papal infallibility was wrong. After all, it was a recent invention; quite a few Popes in history had got along without it.

Heresies, Ruiz-Sanchez thought—not for the first time—come in snarls. It is impossible to pull free one thread; tug at one, and the whole mass begins to roll down upon you.

I believe, O Lord; help me in mine unbelief. But it was useless. It was as though he were praying to God's back.

There was a knock on his door. "Coming, Ramon?" Michelis's tired voice said. "He's due to go on in two minutes."

"All right, Mike."

They settled before the Klee, warily, already defeated, awaiting—what? It could only be a proclamation of total war. They were ignorant only of the form it would take.

"Good evening," Egtverchi said warmly from the frame. "There will be no news tonight. Instead of reporting news, we will make some. The time has come, it is now plain, for the people to whom news happens—those hapless people whose grief-stricken, stunned faces look out at you from the newspapers and the 3-V 'casts such as mine—to throw off their helplessness. Tonight I call upon all of you to show your contempt for the hypocrites who are your bosses, and your total power to be free of them.

"You have a message for them. Tell them this: tell them, 'Your beasts, sirs, are a great people.'

"I will be the first. As of tonight, I renounce my citizenship in the United Nations, and my allegiance to the Shelter state. From now on I will be a citizen——"

Michelis was on his feet, shouting incoherently.

"—a citizen of no country but that bounded by the limits of my own mind. I do not know what those limits are, and I may never find out, but I shall devote my life to searching for them, in whatever manner seems good to me, and in no other manner whatsoever.

"You must do the same. Tear up your registration cards. If you are asked your serial number, tell them you never had one. Never fill in another form. Stay above ground when the siren sounds. Stake out plots; grow crops; abandon the corridors. Do not commit any violence; simply refuse to obey. Nobody has the right to compel you, as non-citizens. Passivity is the key. Renounce, resist, deny!

"Begin now. In half an hour they will overwhelm you. When——"

An urgent buzzer sounded over Egtverchi's voice, and for an instant a draughtboard pattern in red and black blotted out his figure: the U.N.'s crash-priority signal, overriding the by-pass recording circuit. Then the face of the U.N. man looked out at them from under its funny hat, with Egtverchi underlying it dimly, his exhortations only a whisper in the background.

"Dr. Michelis," the U.N. man said exultantly. "He's done it. He's overreached himself. As a non-citizen, he's right in our hands. Get down here—we need you right away, before he gets off the air. Dr. Meid too."

"What for?"

"To sign please of *nolo contendere*. Both of you are under arrest for keeping a wild animal—a technicality only; don't be alarmed. But we have to have you. We mean to put Mr. Egtverchi in a cage for the rest of his life—a *soundproof* cage."

"You are making a mistake," Ruiz-Sanchez said quietly.

The U.N. man's face, a mask of triumph with blazing eyes, swung toward him briefly.

"I didn't ask what you thought, Mister," he said. "I have no orders concerning you, but as far as I'm concerned, you've been closed out of this case entirely. If you try to force your way back in, you'll get burned. Dr. Michelis, Dr. Meid? Do we have to come and get you?"

"We'll come," Michelis said stonily. "Sign off." He did not wait for the U.N. man, however, but killed the set himself.

"Do you think we should do it, Ramon?" he said. "If not, we'll stay right here, and the hell with him. Or we'll take you along if you want."

"No, no," Ruiz-Sanchez said. "Go ahead. No baulking on your part will accomplish a thing but getting you both in deep trouble. Do me one favour, though."

"Gladly. What is it?"

"Stay off the streets. When you get to the U.N. offices, make them keep you there. As arrested citizens, you have the right to be jailed."

Michelis and Liu both stared at him. Then comprehension began to break over Michelis's face.

"You think it will be that bad?" he said.

"Yes, I do. Do I have your promise?"

Michelis looked at Liu and nodded grimly. They went out. The collapse of the Shelter state had already begun.

XVIII

THE beast Chaos roared on unslaked for three days. Ruiz-Sanchez was able to follow much of its progress from the beginning, via the Michelises's 3-V set. There were times when he would also have liked to look out over the sun porch rail, but the roar of the mob, the shots, explosions, police whistles, sirens, and unnameable noises had driven the bees frantic; under such conditions he would not have trusted Liu's protective garments for an instant, even had they been large enough for him.

The U.N. squads had made a well-organized attempt to bear Egtverchi off directly from the broadcasting station, but Egtverchi was not there—in fact, he had never been there at all. The audio, video and tri-di signals had all been piped into the station via co-axial cable from some unspecified place. The necessary connections had been made at the last minute, when it became obvious that Egtverchi was not going to show up, by a technician who had volunteered word of the actual situation; a sacrifice piece in Egtverchi's gambit. The network had sent an alert to the proper U.N. officers at once, but another sacrifice piece saw to it that the alert was shunted through channels.

It took nearly all night to sweat out of the Q.B.C. technician the location of Egtverchi's studio (the stooge at the U.N. obviously did not know) and by that time, of course, he was no longer there either. Also by that time, the news of the attempted arrest and the misfire was being blared and headlined in every Shelter in the world.

Even this much did not get to Ruiz-Sanchez until somewhat later, for the noise in the street began immediately after the first announcement had been made. At first it was disconnected and random, as though the streets were gradually filling with people who were angry or upset but were divided over what, if anything, they ought to do about it. Then there was a sudden change in the quality of the sound, and instantly Ruiz-Sanchez knew that the transformation from a gathering to a mob had been made. The shouting could not very well have become any louder, but abruptly it was a frightening uniform growl, like the enormous voice of a single animal.

He had no way of knowing what had triggered the change, and perhaps the crowd itself never knew either. But now the shots began—not many, but one shot is a fusillade if there have been no shots before. A part of the overall roar detached itself and took on an odd and even more frightening hollow sound; only when the floor shook slightly under him did he realize what that meant.

A pseudopod of the beast had thrust itself into the building. Ruiz-Sanchez realized that he should have expected nothing else. The fad of living above ground was still essentially a privileged, reserved to those U.N. employees and officials who knew how to get the necessary and elaborate permissions, and who furthermore had enough income to support such an inconvenient arrangement; it was the twenty-first century's version of commuting from Maine—*here* was where *they* lived——

Ruiz-Sanchez checked the door hastily. It had elaborate locks—left over from the last period of the Shelter race, when the great untended buildings had been natural targets for looters—but they had gone unused for years. Ruiz-Sanchez used them all now.

He was just in time. There was an obscene shouting in the corridor just outside as part of the mob burst into it from the fire stairs. They had avoided the elevator by instinct—it was too slow to sustain their thoughtless ferocity, too confined for lawlessness, too mechanical for men who were letting their muscles do their thinking.

Somebody rattled the door knob and then shook it.

"Locked," a muffled voice said.

"Break the damned thing down. Here, get out of the way——"

The door shuddered, but held easily. There was another, harder thump, as though several men had lunged against it at the same time; Ruiz-Sanchez could hear them grunt with the impact. Then there were five hammer-like blows.

"Open up in there! Open up, you lousy government fink, or we'll burn you out!"

The spontaneous threat seemed to surprise them all, even the utterer. There was a confused whispering. Then someone said hoarsely: "All right, but find some paper or something."

Ruiz-Sanchez thought confusedly of finding and filling a bucket, though he could not see how any fire could be introduced around the door—there was no transom, and the sill was snug—but all the same time a blurred shout from farther down the hall seemed to draw everyone outside stampeding away. The subsequent noises made it clear that they had found either an open, empty apartment, or an inadequately secured, occupied one where nobody was at home. Yes, it was occupied; Ruiz-Sanchez could hear them breaking furniture as well as windows.

Then, with a shock of terror, their voices began to come at him from behind his back. He whirled, but there seemed to be nobody in the apartment; the shouting was coming from the glassed-in sun porch, but of course there was nobody out there either——

"Jesus! Look, the guy's got his porch glassed in. It's a goddam garden."

"They don't let you have no goddam gardens in the Shelters."

"And you know who paid for it. Us, that's who."

He realized that they were on the neighbouring balcony. He felt a surge of relief which he knew to be irrational. The next words confirmed its irrationality.

"Get some of that kindling out here. No, heavier stuff. Something to *throw*, you meathead."

"Can we get over there from here?"

"If we could throw a ladder across there——"

"It's a long way down——"

The leg of a chair burst through the glass on the sun porch. A heavy vase followed.

The bees came pouring out. Ruiz-Sanchez had not realized how many of them there were. The porch was black with them. For a moment they hovered uncertainly. They would have found the gaps in the glass almost at once in any event, but the men on the next porch, who could not have understood what it was they were seeing, gave the great insects the perfect cue. Something small and massive, possibly a torn-off piece of plumbing, shattered another pane and whirled through the midst of the cloud. Snarling like an old-fashioned aircraft engine, the bees swarmed.

There was an instant of dead silence across the way, and then a scream of agony and horror that made Ruiz-Sanchez's gut contort violently. Then they were all screaming. Briefly, he saw one of them, leaping straight out into space, his arms flailing, his head and chest swathed in golden-and-black furry bodies. Feet drummed past the door, and someone fell. The heavy buzzing threaded its way along the corridor after them.

From below, there were more screams. The great insects could not fly in the open air, but they were free in the building now. Some of them might even make it all the way down to the street, by descending the stairwell.

After a while, there were no human sounds left in the building, only the pervasive insect snarl. Outside the door, somebody moaned and was silent.

Ruiz-Sanchez knew what he had to do. He went into the kitchen and vomited, and then he crammed himself into Liu's beekeeper's togs.

He was no longer a priest; indeed, he was no longer even a Catholic. Grace had been withdrawn from him. But it is the duty of any person to administer extreme unction if he knows how, as it is the duty of any person to administer baptism if he knows how. What happened to the soul so ministered to when it departed would be disposed by the Lord God, Who disposes all things; but He had commanded that no soul come before Him unshriven.

The man before the door was already dead. Ruiz-Sanchez crossed himself out of habit and stepped over the body, his eyes averted. A man who has died of massive histamine shock is not an edifying sight.

The open apartment had been thoroughly smashed up. There were three bodies there, all beyond help. The door to the kitchen, however, was closed; if one of them had had the sense to barricade himself in there before the swarm got to him, he might have been able to kill the few bees who had come in with him——

As if in confirmation, there was a groan behind the door.

Ruiz-Sanchez pushed at it, but it was partly locked. He got it open about six inches and wormed through.

The contorted man on the floor, his incredibly puffed, taut skin slowly turning black, his eyes glassy with agony, was Agronski.

The geologist did not recognize him; he was already beyond that. There was no mind behind the eyes. Ruiz-Sanchez fell to his knees, clumsily in the tight protective clothing. He heard himself begin to mutter the rites, but he was no more hearing the Latin words than Agronski was.

This could be no coincidence. He had come here to give grace, if such a one as he could still give grace; and before him was the most blameless of the Lithian commission, struck down where Ruiz-Sanchez would be sure to find him. It was the God of Job who was abroad in the world now, not the God of the Psalmist or the Christ. The face that was bent upon Ruiz-Sanchez was the face of the avenging, the jealous God—the God Who made hell before He made man, because He knew that He would have need of it. That terrible truth Dante had written down; and in the black face with the protruding tongue which rolled beside Ruiz-Sanchez's knee, he saw that Dante had been right, as every Catholic who reads the Divine Comedy knows in his heart of hearts.

There is a demonolater abroad in the world. He shall be deprived of grace, and then called upon to administer extreme unction to a friend. By this sign, let him know himself for what he is.

After a while, Agronski was dead, chocked to death by his own tongue.

But still it was not over. It was necessary now to make Mike's apartment secure, kill any bees that might have got in, see to it that the escaped swarm died. It was easy enough. Ruiz-Sanchez simply papered over the broken panes on the sun porch. The bees could not feed anywhere but in Liu's garden; they would come back there within a few hours; denied entrance, they would die of starvation an hour or so later. A bee is not a well-designed flying-machine; it keeps itself in the air by expending energy—in short, by pure brute force. A trapped bumblebee can starve to death in half a day, and Liu's tetraploid monsters would die far sooner of their freedom.

The 3-V muttered away throughout the dreary business. The terror was not local, that was clear. The Corridor Riots of 1993 had been nothing but a premonitory flicker, compared to this.

Four target areas were blacked out completely. Egtverchi's uniformed thugs, suddenly reappearing from nowhere in force, had seized their control centres. At the moment, they were holding roughly twenty-five million people as hostages for Egtverchi's safe-conduct, with the active collusion of perhaps five million of them. The violence elsewhere was not as systematic—though some of the outbursts of wrecking must have been carefully planned to allow for the placing of the explosives alone, there seemed to be nc special pattern to it—but in no case could it be described as "passive" or "non-violent".

Sick, wretched and damned, Ruiz-Sanchez waited in the Michelises's jungle apartment, as though part of Lithia had followed him home and enfolded him there.

After the first three days, the fury had exhausted itself sufficiently to permit Michelis and Liu to risk the trip back to their apartment in a U.N. armoured car. They were wan and ghastly-looking, as Ruiz-Sanchez supposed he was himself; they had had even less sleep than he had. He decided at once to say nothing about Agronski; that horror they could be spared. There was no way, however, that he could avoid explaining what had happened to the bees.

Liu's sad little shrug was somehow even harder to bear than Agronski.

"Did they find him yet?" Ruiz-Sanchez said huskily.

"We were going to ask you the same thing," Michelis said. The tall New Englander was able to get a glimpse of himself in a mirror above a planting box and winced. "Ugh, what a beard! At the U.N. everybody's too busy to tell you anything, except in fragments. We thought you might have heard an announcement."

"No, nothing. The Detroit vigilantes have surrendered, according to Q.B.C."

"Yes, so have those goons in Smolensk; they ought to be putting that on the air in an hour or so. I never did think they'd succeed in pulling that operation off. They can't possibly know the corridors as well as the target area authorities themselves do. In Smolensk they got them with the fire door system—drained all the oxygen out of the area they were holding without their realizing what was going on. Two of them never came to."

Ruiz-Sanchez crossed himself automatically. Up on the wall, the Klee muttered in a low voice; it had not been off since Egtverchi's broadcast.

"I don't know whether I want to listen to that damn thing or not," Michelis said sourly. Nevertheless, he turned up the volume.

There was still essentially no news. The rioting was dying back, though it was as bad as ever in some shelters. The Smolensk announcement was duly made, bare of detail. Egtverchi had not yet been located, but U.N. officials expected a break in the case "shortly".

" 'Shortly', hell," Michelis said. "They've run out of leads entirely. They thought they had him cold the next morning, when they found a trail to the hideaway where he'd arranged to tide himself over and direct things. But he wasn't there—apparently he'd gotten out in a hurry, some time before. And nobody in his organization knows where he would go next—he was *supposed* to be there, and they're thoroughly demoralized to be told that he's not."

"Which means that he's on the run," Ruiz-Sanchez suggested.

"Yes, I suppose that's some consolation," Michelis said. "But where could he run to, where he wouldn't be recognized? And *how* would he run? He couldn't just gallop naked through the streets, or take a public conveyance. It takes organization to ship something as *outré* as that secretly —and Egtverchi's organization is as baffled about it as the U.N. is." He turned the 3-V off with a savage gesture.

Liu turned to Ruiz-Sanchez, her expression appalled beneath its weariness.

"Then it's really not over after all?" she said hopelessly.

"Far from it," Ruiz-Sanchez said. "But maybe the violent phase of it is over. If Egtverchi stays vanished for a few days more, I'll conclude that he is dead. He couldn't stay unsighted that long if he were still moving about. Of course his death won't solve most of the major problems, but at least it would remove one sword from over our heads."

Even that, he recognized silently, was wishful thinking. Besides, can you kill a hallucination?

"Well, I hope the U.N. has learned something," Michelis said. "There's one thing you have to say for Egtverchi: he got the public to bring up all the unrest that's been smouldering down under the concrete for all these years. And underneath all the apparent conformity, too. We're going to have to do something about that now—maybe take sledgehammers in our hands and pound this damned Shelter system down into rubble and start over. It wouldn't cost any more than rebuilding what's already been destroyed. One thing's certain: the U.N. won't be able to smother a revolt of this size in slogans. They'll have to *do* something."

The Klee chimed.

"I won't answer it," Michelis said through gritted teeth. "I won't answer it. I've had enough."

"I think we'd better, Mike," Liu said. "It might be—news."

"News!" Michelis said, like a swearword. But he allowed himself to be persuaded. Underneath all the weariness, Ruiz-Sanchez thought he could detect something like a return of warmth between the two, as though, during the three days, some depth had been sounded which they had never touched before. The slight sign of something good astonished him. Was he beginning, like all demonolaters, to take pleasure in the prevalence of evil, or at least in the expectation of it?

The caller was the U.N. man. His face was very strange underneath his funny hat, and his head was cocked as if to catch the first word. Suddenly, blindingly, Ruiz-Sanchez saw the hat in the light of the attitude, and realized what it was: an elaborately disguised hearing aid. The U.N. man was deaf and, like most deaf people, ashamed of it. The rest of the apparatus was a decoy.

"Dr. Michelis, Dr. Meid, Dr. Ruiz," he said. "I don't know how to begin. Yes, I do. My deepest apologies for past rudeness. And past damn foolishness. We were wrong—my God, but we were wrong! It's your turn now. We need you badly, if you feel like doing us a favour. I won't blame you if you don't."

"No threats?" Michelis said, with unforgiving contempt.

"No, no threats. My apologies, please. No, this is purely a favour, requested by the Security Council." His face twisted suddenly, and then was composed once more. "I—volunteered to present the petition. We need you all, right away, on the Moon."

"On the Moon! Why?"

"We've found Egtverchi."

"Impossible," Ruiz-Sanchez said, more sharply than he had intended. "He could never have gotten passage. Is he dead?"

"No, he's not dead. And he's not on the Moon—I didn't mean to imply that."

"Then where *is* he, in God's name?"

"He's on his way back to Lithia."

The trip to the Moon, by ferry-rocket, was rough, hectic and long. As the sole space voyage now being made in which the Haertel overdrive could not be used—across so short a distance, A Haertel ship would have overshot the target—very little improvement in techniques had been made in the trip since the old von Braun days. It was only after they had been bundled off the rocket into the moonboat, for the slow, paddle-wheel-driven trip across the seas of dust to the Comte d'Averoigne's observatory, that Ruiz-Sanchez managed to piece the whole story together.

Egtverchi had been found aboard the vessel that was shipping the final installment of equipment to Cleaver, when the ship was two days out. He was half-dead. In a final, desperate improvisation, he had had himself crated, addressed to Cleaver, marked "FRAGILE—RADIOACTIVE—THIS END UP", and shipped via ordinary express into the spaceport. Even a normally raised Lithian would have been shaken up by this kind of treatment, and Egtverchi, in addition to being a spindling specimen of his race, had been on the run for many hours before being shipped.

The vessel, by no very great coincidence, was also carrying the pilot model of the Petard CirCon; the captain got the news back to the count on the first test, and the count passed it along to the U.N. by ordinary radio. Egtverchi was in irons now, but he was well and cheerful. Since it was impossible for the ship to turn back, the U.N. was now, in effect, doing his running for him, at a good many times the speed of light.

Ruiz-Sanchez found a trace of pity in his heart for the born exile, harried now like a wild animal, penned behind bars, on his way back to a fatherland for which no experience in his life had fitted him, whose very language he could not speak. But when the U.N. man began to question them all—what was needed was some knowledgeable estimate of what Egtverchi might do next—his pity did not survive his speculations. It was right and proper to pity children, but Ruiz-Sanchez was beginning to believe that adults generally deserve any misfortune that they get.

The impact of a creature like Egtverchi on the stable society of Lithia would be explosive. On Earth, at least, he had been a freak; on Lithia, he would soon be taken for another Lithian, however odd. And Earth had had centuries of experience with deranged and displaced messiahs like

Egtverchi; such a thing had never happened before on Lithia. Egtverchi would infect that garden down to the roots, and remake it in his own image—transforming the planet into that hypothetical dangerous enemy against whose advent Cleaver had wanted to make it an arsenal!

Yet something like that had happened when Earth was a stable garden, too. Perhaps—*O felix culpa!*—it always happened that way, on every world. Perhaps the Tree of the Knowledge of Good and Evil was like the Yggdrasil of the legends of Pope Hadrian's birthland, with its roots in the floor of the universe, its branches bearing the planets—and whosoever would eat of its fruit might eat thereof. . . .

No, that must not be. Lithia as a rigged Garden had been dangerous enough; but Lithia transformed into a planet-wide fortress of Dis was a threat to Heaven itself.

The Count d'Averoigne's main observatory had been built by the U.N., to his specification, approximately in the centre of the crater Stadius, a once towering cup which early in its history had been swamped and partially melted in the outpouring sea of lava which made the Mare Imbrium. What remained of its walls served the count's staff as a meteor-rampart during showers, yet they were low enough to be well below the horizon from the centre of the crater, giving the count what was effectively a level plain in all directions.

He looked no different than he had when they had first met, except that he was wearing brown overalls instead of a brown suit, but he seemed glad to see them. Ruiz-Sanchez suspected that he was sometimes lonely, or perhaps lonely all the time—not only because of his current isolation on the Moon, but in his continuing remoteness from his family and indeed the whole of ordinary humanity.

"I have a surprise for you," he told them. "We've just completed the new telescope—six hundred feet in diameter, all of sodium foil, perched on top of Mount Piton a few hundred miles north of here. The relay cables were brought through to Stadius yesterday, and I was up all night testing my circuits. They have been made a little neater since you last saw them."

This was an understatement. The breadboard rigs had vanished entirely; the object the count was indicating now was nothing but a black enamel box about the size of a tape recorder, and with only about that many knobs.

"Of course to do this is simpler than picking up a broadcast from a transmitter that doesn't have CirCon, like the Tree," the count admitted. "But the results are just as gratifying. Regard."

He snapped a switch dramatically. On a large screen on the opposite wall of the dark observatory chamber, a cloud-wrapped planet swam placidly.

"My God!" Michelis said in a choked voice. "That's—*is* that Lithia, Count d'Averoigne? I'd swear it is."

"Please," the count said. "Here I'm Dr. Petard. But yes, that's Lithia; its sun is visible from the Moon a little over twelve days of the month. It's fifty light-years away, but here we see it at an apparent distance of a quarter of a million miles, give or take ten thousand—about the distance of the Moon from the Earth. It's remarkable how much light you can gather with a six-hundred-foot paraboloid of sodium when there's no atmosphere in the way. Of course with an atmosphere we couldn't maintain the foil, either—the gravity here is almost too much for it."

"It's stunning," Liu murmured.

"That's only the beginning, Dr. Meid. We had spanned not only the space, but also the time—both together, as is only appropriate. What we are seeing is Lithia *today*—right now, in fact—not Lithia fifty years ago."

"Congratulations," Michelis said, his voice hushed. "Of course the scholium was the real achievement—but you threw up an installation in record time, too, it seems to me."

"It seems that way to me, too," the count said, taking his cigar out of his mouth and regarding it complacently.

"Are we going to be able to catch the ship's landing?" the U.N. man said intensely.

"No, I'm afraid not, unless I have my dates wrong. According to the schedule you gave me, the landing was supposed to have taken place yesterday, and I can't back my device up and down the time spectrum. The equations nail it to simultaneity, and simultaneity is what I get—neither more, nor less."

His voice changed colour suddenly. The change transformed him from a fat man delighted with a new toy into the philosopher-mathematician Henri Petard as no disclaimer of his hereditary title could ever have done.

"I invited you to hold your conference here," he said, "because I thought you should all be witnesses to an event which I hope profoundly is not going to happen. I will explain:

"Recently I was asked to check the reasoning on which Dr. Cleaver based the experiment he has programmed for today. Briefly, the experiment is an attempt to store the total output of a Nernst generator for a period of about ninety seconds, through a special adaptation of what is called the pinch effect.

"I found the reasoning faulty—not obviously, Dr. Cleaver is too careful a craftsman for that, but seriously, all the same. Since lithium 6 is ubiquitous on that planet, any failure would be totally disastrous. I sent Dr. Cleaver an urgent message on the CirCon, to be tape-recorded on the ship that landed yesterday; I would have used the Tree, but of course that has been cut down, and I doubt that he would have accepted any such message from a Lithian had it not been. The captain of the ship promised me that the tape would be delivered to Dr. Cleaver before any of the remaining apparatus was unloaded. But I know Dr. Cleaver. He is bull-headed. Is that not so?"

"Yes," Michelis said. "God knows that's so."

"Well, we are ready," Dr. Petard said. "As ready as we can be. I have instruments to record the event. Let us pray that I won't need them.

The count was a lapsed Catholic; his injunction was a

habit. But Ruiz-Sanchez could no more pray for any such thing than the count could—and no more could he leave the outcome to chance. St. Michael's sword had been put into his hand now so unmistakably that even a fool could not fail to recognize it.

The Holy Father had known it would be so, and had planned for it with the skill of a Disraeli. Ruiz-Sanchez shuddered to think what a less politically minded Pope would have made of such an opportunity, but of course it had been God's will that this should happen in the time of Hadrian and not during any other pontificate. By specifically ruling out any formal excommunication, Hadrian had reserved to Ruiz-Sanchez's use the one gift of grace which was pertinent to the occasion at hand.

And perhaps he had seen, too, that the time Ruiz-Sanchez had devoted to the elaborate, capriciously hypercomplex case of conscience in the Joyce novel had been time wasted; there was a much simpler case, one of the classical situations, which applied if Ruiz-Sanchez could only see it. It was the case of the sick child, for whose recovery prayers were offered.

These days, most sick children recovered in a day or so, after a shot of spectrosigmin or some similar drug, even from the brink of the terminal coma. *Question:* Has prayer failed, and temporal science wrought the recovery?

Answer: No, for prayer is always answered, and no man may choose for God the means He uses to answer it. Surely a miracle like a life-saving antibiotic is not unworthy of the bounty of God.

And this, too, was the answer to the riddle of the Great Nothing. The Adversary is not creative, except in the sense that He always seeks evil, and always does good. He cannot claim any of the credit for temporal science, nor imply truthfully that a success for temporal science is a failure for prayer. In this as in all other matters, He is compelled to lie.

And there on Lithia was Cleaver, agent of the Great

Nothing, foredoomed to failure, the very task to which he was putting his hand in the Adversary's service tottering on the edge of undoing all His work. The staff of Tannhäuser had blossomed: *These fruits are shaken from the wrath-bearing tree.*

Yet even as Ruiz-Sanchez rose, the searing words of Pope Gregory VIII trembling on his lips, he hesitated still again. What if he were wrong after all? Suppose, just suppose, that Lithia were Eden, and that the Earth-bred Lithian who had just returned there were the Serpent foreordained for it? *Suppose it always happened that way, world without end?*

The voice of the Great Nothing, pouring forth lies to the last. Ruiz-Sanchez raised his hand. His shaken voice resounded and echoed in the cave of the observatory.

"I, A PRIEST OF CHRIST, DO COMMAND YE, MOST FOUL SPIRITS WHO DO STIR UP THESE CLOUDS——"

"What? For heaven's sake, be quiet," the U.N. man said irritably. Everyone else was staring in wonder, and in Liu's glance there appeared to be a little fear. Only the count's glance was knowing and solemn.

"—THAT YE DEPART FROM THEM, AND DISPERSE YOURSELVES INTO WILD AND UNTILLED PLACES, THAT YE MAY BE NO LONGER ABLE TO HARM MEN OR ANIMALS OR FRUITS OR HERBS, OR WHATSOEVER IS DESIGNED FOR HUMAN USE:

"AND THOU GREAT NOTHING, THOU LUSTFUL AND STUPID ONE, *Scrofa Stercorate*, THOU SOOTY SPIRIT FROM TARTARUS, I CAST THEE DOWN, *O Porcarie Pedicose*, INTO THE INFERNAL KITCHEN:

"BY THE APOCALYPSE OF JESUS CHRIST, WHICH GOD HATH GIVEN TO MAKE KNOWN UNTO HIS SERVANTS THOSE THINGS WHICH ARE SHORTLY TO BE; AND HATH SIGNIFIED, SENDING BY HIS ANGEL; I EXORCISE THEE, ANGEL OF PERVERSITY:

"BY THE SEVEN GOLD CANDLESTICKS, AND BY ONE LIKE UNTO THE SON OF MAN, STANDING IN THE MIDST OF THE CANDLESTICKS; BY HIS VOICE, AS THE VOICE OF MANY WATERS; BY HIS WORDS, 'I AM LIVING, WHO WAS DEAD; AND BEHOLD I LIVE FOR EVER AND EVER; AND I HAVE THE KEYS OF DEATH

AND OF HELL'; I SAY UNTO YOU, ANGEL OF PERDITION: DEPART, DEPART, DEPART!"

The echoes rang and dwindled. The lunar silence flowed back, underlined by the breathing of the people in the observatory and the sound of pumps labouring somewhere beneath.

And slowly, and without a sound, the cloudy planet on the screen turned white all over. The clouds and the dim oceans and continents blended into a blue-white glare which shone out from the screen like a searchlight. It seemed to penetrate their bloodless faces down to the bone.

Slowly, slowly, it all melted away: the chirruping forests, Chtexa's porcelain house, the barking lungfish, the stump of the Message Tree, the wild allosaurs, the single silver moon, the great beating heart of Blood Lake, the city of the potters, the flying suid, the Lithian crocodile and his winding track, the tall noble reasoning creatures and the mystery and the beauty around them. Suddenly the whole of Lithia began to swell, like a balloon——

The count tried to turn the screen off, but he was too late. Before he could touch the black box, the whole circuit went out with a puffing of fuses. The intolerable light vanished instantly; the screen went black and the universe with it.

They sat blinded and stunned.

"An error in Equation Sixteen," the count's voice said harshly in the swimming darkness.

No, Ruiz-Sanchez thought; no. An instance of fulfilled desire. He had wanted to use Lithia to defend the faith, and he had been given that. Cleaver had wanted to turn it into a fusion-bomb plant, and he had got that in full measure, all at once. Michelis had seen in it a prophecy of infallible human love, and had been stretched on that rack ever since. And Agronski—Agronski had wanted nothing to change, and now was unchangeably nothing.

In the darkness, there was a long, ragged sigh. For a moment, Ruiz-Sanchez could not place the voice; he thought it was Liu. But no. It was Mike.

"When we have our eyesight back," the count's voice said, "I propose that we suit up and go outside. We have a nova to watch for."

That was only a manœuvre, an act of misdirection on the count's part—an act of kindness. He knew well enough that that nova would not be visible to the naked eye until the next Holy Year, fifty years to come; and he knew that they knew.

Nevertheless, when Father Ramon Ruiz-Sanchez, sometime Clerk Regular in the Society of Jesus, could see again, they had left him alone with his God and his grief.

APPENDIX

THE Planet Lithia (from Michelis, D., and Ruiz-Sanchez, R.: Lithia—a preliminary report, *J.I.R.* 4:225, 2050; abstract.)

Lithia is the second planet of the solar type star Alpha Arietis, which is located in the constellation Aries and is approximately 50 light-years from Sol.[1]

It revolves around its primary at a mean distance of 108,600,000 miles, with a year of approximately 380 terrestrial days. The orbit is definitely elliptical, with an eccentricity of 0·51, so that the long axis of the ellipse is approximately 5 per cent longer than the short axis.

The axis of the planet is essentially perpendicular to the orbit, and the planet rotates on its axis with a day of about 20 terrestrial hours. Hence, the Lithian year consists of 456 Lithian days. The eccentricity of the orbit produces mild seasons, with long, relatively cold winters, and short, hot summers.

The planet has one moon with a diameter of 1,256 miles, which revolves about its primary at a distance of 326,000 miles, twelve times in the Lithian year.

The outer planets of the system have not yet been explored.

Lithia is 8,267 miles in diameter, and has a surface gravity of 0·82 that of Earth. The light gravity of the planet is accounted for by the relatively low density, which in turn is the result of its composition. When the planet was formed there was a much lower percentage of the heavy elements

[1] An earlier figure of 40 light-years, often quoted in the literature, arose from application of the so-called Cosmological Constant. Einstein's reluctance to allow this "constant" into his scholium has now been fully justified. v. Haertel, *J.I.R.* 1:21, 2047.

with atomic numbers above 20 included in its make-up than was the case with the Earth. Furthermore, the odd-numbered elements are even rarer than they are on Earth; the only odd-numbered elements that appear in any quantity are hydrogen, nitrogen, sodium and chlorine. Potassium is quite rare, and the heavy odd-numbered elements (gold, silver, copper) appear only in microscopic quantities and never in the elemental form. In fact, the only uncombined metal that has ever appeared on the planet has been the nickel-iron of an occasional meteorite.

The metallic core of the planet is considerably smaller than that of the Earth, and the basaltic inner coating correspondingly thicker. The continents are built, as on Earth, basically of granite, overlaid with sedimentary deposits.

The scarcity of potassium has led to an extremely static geology. The natural radioactivity of K^{40} is the major source of the internal heat of the Earth, and Lithia has less than a tenth of the K^{40} content of the Earth. As a result, the interior of the planet is much cooler, vulcanism is extremely rare, and geological revolutions even rarer. The planet seems to have settled down early in life, and nothing very startling has happened since. The major part of its uneventful geological history is at best conjectural, because the scarcity of radioactive elements has led to great difficulties in dating the strata.

The atmosphere is somewhat similar to that of the Earth.[1] The atmospheric pressure is 815·3 mm. at sea level, and the composition of dry air is as follows:

Nitrogen	66·26 per cent by volume
Oxygen	31·27
Argon, etc.	2·16
CO_2	0·31

The relatively high CO_2 concentration (partial pressure about 11 times that of the gas in the Earth's atmosphere) leads to a hothouse type of climate, with relatively slight

[1] Clark, J.: "The Climate of Lithia", *J.I.R.*, in press.

temperature differences from pole to equator. The average summer temperature at the pole is about 30 deg. C., at the equator near 38 deg. C., while the winter temperatures are about 15 deg. colder. The humidity is generally high and there is a lot of haze; gentle, drizzling rain is chronic.

There has been little change in the climate of the planet for about 700 million years. Since there is little vulcanism, the CO_2 content of the air does not rise appreciably from that cause, and the amount consumed in photosynthesis by the lush vegetation is compensated for by the rapid oxidation of dead vegetable matter induced by the high temperature, high humidity, and high oxygen content of the air. In fact, the climate of the planet has been in equilibrium for more than half a billion years.

As has the geography of the planet. There are three continents, of which the largest is the southern continent, extending roughly from latitude 15 deg. south to 60 deg. south, and two-thirds of the way around the planet. The two northern continents are squarish in shape, and of sizes similar to each other. They extend from about 10 deg. south to about 70 deg. north, and each one about 80 deg. east and west. One is located north of the eastern end of the southern continent, the other north of the western end. On the other side of the world there is an archipelago of large islands, the size of England and Ireland, running from 20 deg. north to 10 deg. south of the equator. There are thus five seas or oceans: the two polar seas; the equatorial sea separating the southern from the northern continents; the central sea between the two latter, and connecting the equatorial sea with the north polar sea; and the great sea, stretching from pole to pole, broken only by the archipelago, extending a third of the way around the planet.

The southern continent has one low mountain range (highest peak 2,263 metres) paralleling its southern shore, and moderating the never very momentous effect of the south winds. The north-western continent has two ranges, one paralleling the eastern and one the western sea, so that the polar winds have a free run, and give this continent a more variable climate than that of the southern one. The north-eastern continent has a slight range along its southern shore. The islands of the archipelago have few hills, and possess an oceanic type of climate. The trade winds are much like those of Earth, but of lesser velocity, due to the lesser temperature differentials between the different parts of the planet. The equatorial sea is nearly windless.

Except for the few mountain ranges, the terrain of the continents is rather flat, particularly near the coasts, and the lower reaches of all the rivers are of the meandering type, bordered with marshes, and with low plains that are flooded, miles wide, every spring.

There are tides, milder than on Earth, producing an appreciable tidal current in the equatorial sea. As the costal terrain is generally quite flat, except where the mountain ranges come to the sea, wide tidal flats separate the shore from the open sea.

The water is similar to that of Earth, but considerably less salty.[1] Life began in the sea, and evolved much as it did on Earth. There is a rich assortment of microscopic sea life, types resembling such forms as seaweed and sponges, and many crustacea and mollusc-like forms. The latter are very highly developed and diversified, particularly the mobile types. Quite familiar fish-like forms have emerged and dominate the seas as they do on Earth.

Present-day Lithian land plant life would be unfamiliar, but not surprising, to a terrestrial observer. There are no plants exactly like those of earth, but most of them have a noticeable similarity to those with which the visitor would be familiar. The most surprising aspect is that the forests are of a remarkably mixed type. Flowering and non-flowering trees, palms and pines, tree ferns, shrubs and grasses all grow together in remarkable amity. Since Lithia never had a glacial period, these mixed forests, rather than the uniform type prevailing on Earth, are the rule.

[1] Ley, W.: "The Ecologies of Lithia", *J.I.R.*, in press.

In general the vegetation is lush and the forests can be considered as typical rain-forests. There are several varieties of poisonous plants, including most of the edible-looking tubers. Their roots resemble potatoes and they produce extremely toxic alkaloids, whose structure has not yet been worked out, in large quantities. There are several types of bushes which grow thorns impregnated with glucosides which are extremely irritating to the skins of most vertebrates.

The grasses are more prevalent on the plains, shading into rushes and similar swamp-adapted plants in the marshes. There are few desert areas—even the mountains are rounded and smooth, and covered with grasses and shrubs. Seen from space, the land areas of the planet are almost entirely green. Bare rock is found only in the river valleys, where the streams have cut their way down to the lime and sandstone, and in ligneous outcroppings, where flint, quartz and quartzite are frequently found. Obsidian is rare, of course, because of the lack of volcanic activity. There is clay to be found in some of the river valleys, with an appreciable alumina content, and rutile (titanium dioxide) is not uncommon. There are no concentrated deposits of iron ore, and hematite is almost unknown.

The land-living animal forms include orders similar to those found on Earth. There is a large variety of arthropods, including eight-legged insect-like forms of all sizes, up to a pseudo dragonfly with two pairs of wings and a wing-spread which has been recorded at 86·5 cm. maximum. This variety lives exclusively on other insects, but there are several types dangerous to higher forms of animals. Several have dangerous bites (the poison is generally an alkaloid) and one insect can eject a stream of poisonous gas (reputed to be largely HCN) in quantity sufficient to immobilize a small animal. These insects are social in nature, like ants, living in colonies which are usually left severely alone by otherwise insectivorous organisms.

There are also many amphibians, small lizard-like forms with three fingers on each limb instead of the five that are common to terrestrial land vertebrates. They form an extremely important class, and there are some species that are as large as a St. Bernard dog at maturity. Except for some small and unimportant forms, however, the amphibians are confined to the marshy lowlands near the sea, and the rest of the land is dominated by a class resembling Earthly reptiles. Among these is the dominant species, a large, highly intelligent animal with a bipedal gait which balances itself with a rather stiff, heavy tail.

Two groups of the reptiles went back to the sea and engaged in successful competition with the fish. One adopted a completely streamlined form and is, outwardly, just another 30-foot fish. But its tail fin is in the horizontal plane and its internal structure shows its ancestry. It is the fastest thing in the waters of Lithia, doing nearly 80 knots when pressed (as it usually is by its insatiable appetite). The other group of returned reptiles resembles crocodiles, and is competent either in the open sea or on the mud flats, although it is not very fast in either situation.

Several genera of the reptiles have taken to the air, as did the terrestrial pteranodons. The largest of these has a wingspread of nearly three metres, but is very lightly built. It roosts mainly on the sea cliffs of the southern coast of the north-eastern continent, and lives mainly on fish and such of the gliding cephalopods as it can manage to catch above water. This flying reptile has a large assortment of sharp, backward-curving teeth in its long beak. One other species of flying reptile is of special interest, because it has developed something resembling feathers, in a many-coloured crest down its long neck. They appear only on the mature reptile; the young are completely naked.

Some 100,000,000 years ago the land-living reptiles were almost completely wiped out by one of the smallest of their own family, which adopted the easiest method of making a living: eating the eggs of its larger relatives. The larger forms almost completely disappeared, and those that survived (such as the Lithian allosaur) are now almost as rare as the terrestrial elephant (as compared for instance, with the many elephant species of the Pleistocene). The smaller forms survived better, but are not nearly so abundant now as they once were.

The dominant species is an exception. The female of this species has an abdominal pouch in which the eggs are carried until they hatch. This animal is about twelve feet tall at the crown, with a head shaped for bifocal vision. One of the three fingers on the free forelimb is an opposable thumb.